MINNESOTA BRIDES

MINNESOTA BRIDES

THREE-IN-ONE COLLECTION

JANET SPAETH

BARBOUR
PUBLISHING

The Ice Carnival © 2010 by Janet Spaeth
Kind-Hearted Woman © 2009 by Janet Spaeth
Remembrance © 2009 by Janet Spaeth

ISBN 978-1-61626-123-8

All scripture quotations are taken from the King James Version of the Bible.

This book is a work of fiction. Names, characters, places, and incidents are either products of the author's imagination or used fictitiously. Any similarity to actual people, organizations, and/or events is purely coincidental.

Cover design: Kirk DouPonce, DogEared Design

Published by Barbour Publishing, Inc., P.O. Box 719, Uhrichsville, Ohio 44683, www.barbourbooks.com

Our mission is to publish and distribute inspirational products offering exceptional value and biblical encouragement to the masses.

ecpa Member of the
Evangelical Christian
Publishers Association

Printed in the United States of America.

Dear Readers,

There's something heartwarming about looking into the past, at our ancestors' stories, to see how little we've really changed. Collectively, we are a loving people. We want to love, and we want to be loved. It's the way God made us.

And what better place to set a collection of love stories than in beautiful Minnesota? Let's travel though this incredible state and its history with these stories.

The Ice Carnival is set in St. Paul, against the backdrop of the first Winter Carnival, which continues today. St. Paul has been my home-away-from-home for several years now, and it's been an honor to write this story about such a fantastic city.

The Great Depression is the time period of *Kind-Hearted Woman*, which is set in the lovely Minnesota River Valley. One of my favorite memories when my children were small was a family trip we took, tracing the river as it glimmered golden in the sunlight and flowed across the southern part of the state.

There is a line in northern Minnesota where the prairie ends and the pines begin. I watch for it every time I drive Highway 2—this place where I leave the flatlands and head into the forest. This astonishing area is the setting for *Remembrance*.

Welcome to Minnesota! Enjoy your stay!

Sincerely,
Janet Spaeth

THE ICE CARNIVAL

Dedication

To Higher Ground at Sharon Lutheran Church: His heart stopped, my heart broke, but your hearts were big enough for both of us. Thank you for being there when I needed you so much.

Chapter 1

St. Paul, Minnesota
October 1885

Colorful leaves blew around Christal Everett's feet in an autumn rainbow of russet and gold. A sudden gust of air shook the trees above her, and more leaves cascaded down over her head, a veritable storm of October-painted maple and oak.

This was her favorite time of year. The world seemed so alive, almost as if celebrating a last hurrah before the long, quiet sleep of a Minnesota winter laid its white blanket over the city.

The temperature had already dropped today. What had started as a nice, sunny fall day had turned colder, with a touch of winter-to-come in the wind that had begun to pick up.

She tightened her shawl around her. Silly of her to have left the house with such a light wrap, but the morning had been sun-kissed and warm.

The days were getting shorter, and she hurried her steps homeward as shadows darkened and stretched around her. Bit by bit the wonderful houses on Summit Avenue came alive with light from inside. Just around the corner was her home. She knew that by the time she got there, her mother would have a kettle of tea ready and welcoming words to warm her heart.

Christal turned at the milliner's shop and squinted through the gathering wind toward her home. She'd dallied long enough as it was at the library, and it was time to get to work preparing dinner. Her mother had undoubtedly already started the roast.

She hurried along, her feet stirring the multicolored leaves that swirled around her shoes on the pavement. Being late seemed to be unavoidable with her, but there were so many wonderful books in the library, each one inviting her to explore its contents.

As she opened the door of her house, her mother's cheerful voice called to her. "At the library again, I presume?"

"Guilty!" Christal draped her shawl over the peg in the entryway and rubbed her hands together as she followed the delicious aroma emanating from the kitchen. "Something smells wonderful in here. What can I do?"

Mother handed her a cutting board with a loaf of freshly baked bread on it. "Why don't you cut this into slices while I finish setting the table. Did you hear that Dr. Bering is joining us later this evening?"

"I didn't know, but I'm glad. Maybe he'll play the piano for us!"

Alfred Bering had lived next door to them since they'd come to St. Paul. He was a mountain of a man, both literally and figuratively. He stood over six feet tall, and his love of cakes and breads had contributed to his substantial girth.

Yet he was a gentle giant. Hands the size of dinner plates had soothed the sick and cradled the newborn, and people came to him from all around St. Paul. He turned no one away, citing the Lord's Prayer: "Forgive us our debts, as we forgive our debtors." Once he had explained to Christal that not all debts were monetary, that we all owed each other something. He often claimed that in some manner or another, everyone paid him back in the Lord's way.

The Everett family's friendship with him was born of an early need and solidified with deep gratitude. He had been the one to see Christal through a bout with scarlet fever when she was ten and the continuing despair of rheumatic fever that had weakened her heart and kept her indoors, away from others her age.

Visits to church on Sunday mornings had been her sole outings, and books had become her friends, replacing those childhood acquaintances who had moved or drifted from her when she was ill. Dr. Bering's encouragement of a walking routine to strengthen her heart had brought her back to health.

Her parents, especially her mother, still coddled her protectively. It wasn't necessary, but it was easy to let them take care of her every need.

The sound of her father at the door drove away the remainder of her musings. "Papa!"

"None other!" Her father entered the kitchen and kissed his wife and then his daughter. "How did my lovelies spend their day?"

Christal's parents smiled at each other. It was clear that even after all these years, the two were madly in love with each other. She could see it in the way they looked at each other, their gazes locking and holding just a moment longer than with other people.

That was the kind of love she wanted. Someday she would meet a man who would look at her the same way her father looked at her mother, but so far, aside from a few tentative looks from young men in the congregation, nothing had come her way.

She sighed. Today she'd read a new book at the library. It was a children's book, but she'd been drawn by the gilded illustrations. The collection of fairy tales had taken her away from Minnesota and transported her to the land of imagination, where she had spent her afternoon.

They were charming little stories, but the fact was she lived in St. Paul, Minnesota, and there weren't princes and castles, not here anyway.

"That bread isn't going to slice itself," her mother said, laughing as she took the cutting board from Christal, the loaf still intact. "Dreaming is good, but wait until after dinner, please!"

"I'm sorry," Christal began. "I was just thinking about—"

"Hello, my dearest ones!" The grand pronouncement from the door interrupted her apology. Aunt Ruth swept in, her cerise-colored velvet dress reflecting the vivid hues of the trees outside the dining room window. Her deep black hair was piled high in a mass of curls, and elaborate earrings of garnet and pearls swung from her earlobes.

Aunt Ruth had her own apartment in the rambling house. It had been designed as maid quarters originally, but the Everetts had no maid. When Christal had become so terribly ill with rheumatic fever, Aunt Ruth had joined the Everett household to help out. She stayed, and for several years now they'd enjoyed her often-quirky style.

Christal helped her mother set out the dinner as Aunt Ruth and Papa discussed the weather, some events in the news, and preparations for a church gathering. "Dr. Bering is paying us a visit after dinner," Mother said as she seated herself. "You'll stay?"

Aunt Ruth patted the back of her flawlessly coiffed head. "Why, yes, I believe I will."

Papa smiled. "That's good. You are looking especially lovely, by the way."

Aunt Ruth sat straighter in her chair. "I believe it's time for you to ask the blessing, Matthew. Shall we bow our heads?"

Dinner sped by, as it always did, and Christal had just finished washing the last dish when she heard the awaited knock on the door. She wiped the plate, put it in the cupboard, and ran to the hallway.

Dr. Bering entered, accompanied by some windblown leaves, and she took his coat. "You'll play the piano, I hope," she said.

He laughed, a big rolling sound that poured from his round stomach. "Give my hands a chance to warm up, dear Christal. It's getting quite brisk out there. Winter is definitely on its way."

She hung his coat on the large wooden coatrack. It smelled of the smoke from many fireplaces, a sure sign of the deepening of fall.

He put his arm around her in a friendly embrace. "You could learn to play the piano yourself," he said. "There are many qualified teachers in the area. I would volunteer, but I'm not sure how I do it, so I certainly couldn't teach someone else."

"I've tried. You know that. But I just can't seem to learn it."

"Girl, you don't give yourself a chance. You need to practice every day. You can't play the piano until, well, until you actually play the piano."

She nodded. What he said was true, but the fact was that she didn't want to learn it at all. She wanted to be able to play the piano, to put her hands on the keys and have the wonderfully complex melodies flow forth just as they did when he played. She had no patience with the process of learning how to do it.

"Ruth!" Dr. Bering stopped and took Aunt Ruth's hand, raising it but stopping just short of kissing it. *Ever the gentleman,* Christal thought.

They sat in the parlor, sipping cups of black tea. Even through the everyday chitchat that surrounded her, Christal could feel something momentous was about to occur. But from whom? And what would it be?

Finally Dr. Bering set his teacup aside. It looked like a child's toy in his beefy hands. He cleared his throat and laced his fingers together across his vest and announced, "I have heard the most amazing news. St. Paul is going to have an ice carnival."

"An ice carnival? Here?" her mother asked.

"Yes, indeed. It's being planned for the first day of the new year."

"Are they daft?" Aunt Ruth frowned. "That's the worst time possible! Everyone will freeze to death!"

Papa nodded thoughtfully. "So he's really going through with it, is he?"

"Who is?" Christal leaned forward, nearly toppling out of her chair in her excitement. *An ice carnival!*

"George Thompson."

Christal hadn't met the *St. Paul Dispatch's* publisher, but she had certainly heard his name.

Dr. Bering looked at them all over the top of his half-rimmed glasses. "It's not totally official yet. Thompson and others are organizing a committee that will meet soon—November second to be exact—and things will get started. He's got big plans for St. Paul."

Aunt Ruth tsked. "Why on earth, though? What would have possessed such a normally intelligent man to do such a thing?"

Dr. Bering chuckled. "Rumor has it that he was prompted by a certain cheeky New York journalist who declared St. Paul uninhabitable during the winter months."

Christal hugged herself happily. This was wonderful news! An ice carnival! What could it be? Her mind spun with the possibilities, all painted with the bright illustrations of the books she'd read.

"But there's more. My nephew is coming to live with me."

Only the sound of the grandfather clock penetrated the silence that followed his announcement. Then everyone spoke at once, flinging out question after question until Dr. Bering finally held up his hand.

"Wait! Here are the details. His name is Isaac. I'm importing him from Florida, to put some muscle on those arms and to thicken up that thin southern blood. By the time he's spent a winter up north, he'll be in fine shape. He'll live with me, at least until he gets situated."

"That's wonderful!" Mrs. Everett said.

"He's doing the last parts of his medical studies here," Dr. Bering continued. "When he's ready, he can join my practice."

"What's he like?" Christal asked. "Does he enjoy books?"

The corpulent physician laughed. "Right now he's spending his time poring over medical tomes, but yes, he likes to read. You'll get along well with him, Christal. He's a bit shy, so he'll benefit from your joyous approach to life."

"His faith?" her father asked. "Of course, I'm interested in that."

Dr. Bering nodded vigorously. "He loves the Lord. He was raised with that. You'll find him a stalwart member of the congregation, Matthew. Now, might I play the piano for you? How about Beethoven's 'Für Elise'?"

Christal closed her eyes as the melodic notes flowed from Dr. Bering's fingertips. Life was always good, but now it seemed to be getting even better. An ice carnival. A new friend. And Beethoven.

Isaac Bering stood on the platform of the St. Paul train station and gazed around him. The trees were in full array, and the ground was strewn with shed leaves of vivid crimsons and golds, a regal array for the earth. It was stunning.

He shivered as wind whirled around his ears and leaves scrabbled across his feet. His uncle had warned him about the weather, and Isaac was, indeed, wearing his thickest coat, but the autumn air had a chill in it that told him he'd need something much more—and soon.

What had he gotten himself into? Momentary panic overtook him. He could have—should have—stayed in the safety of Florida, where the winds were warm and leaves, for the most part, stayed on the trees. Except for his uncle, he knew no one here, and even at that, Uncle Alfred was somewhat of an unknown. They knew each other primarily through correspondence. He wasn't even sure he'd recognize him.

But when Uncle Alfred had offered his home, and even more, to bring Isaac into his practice, he'd jumped at the chance eagerly. He could adapt to Minnesota. Others lived here and prospered.

He'd spent most of his life in the South, in medical school in Tallahassee and growing up in Key West, but he was up to the challenge of trying life in the North. He'd give it the best chance possible.

He straightened his backbone and stood straighter, and promptly raised his collar as the chilly wind poked icy tendrils down his neck.

A good heavy coat, a pair of fleecy gloves, sturdy overshoes, a woolly hat and muffler, and he'd be set. He could deal with a little cold.

"Isaac!"

He recognized his uncle, who hadn't changed much in the years since they'd seen each other. Uncle Alfred wrapped him in a bear hug, burying Isaac's face in the front of his jacket, which smelled of leather and wood smoke.

"It's good to see you," his uncle boomed. "Let's get your trunks and take you to the house so we can start to get you settled. How was your trip?"

Isaac couldn't stop looking at his surroundings. Never had he thought that St. Paul would be this much of a city. It was tucked away in the frozen north, after all. But St. Paul was big—bigger actually than anything he'd seen, except Chicago.

People bustled around him in an unceasing stream of humanity, like ants in an oversized anthill. Everyone seemed so busy and so sure of where they were going. If only he had their confidence.

Uncle Alfred's steady stream of words flowed over him in a meaningless cascade. If he could have slept on the train, he might be able to make sense of this, but the back-and-forth sway and the constant *ricketa-ricketa* of the wheels on the track, which had lulled his fellow passengers to sleep, had only served to keep him awake. He'd had mere sporadic snatches of sleep for the entire trip.

And he was cold.

"Are you all right, son?" His uncle looked at him in concern. "You look downright blue. Are you warm enough?"

Isaac nodded, clutching his arms to his chest in a feeble attempt at sustaining what bodily warmth he had. "Most of these people," he said, motioning to the pedestrians beside them, "are wearing only the lightest jackets. How do they do it?"

Uncle Alfred smiled. "I'm not going to give you the usual Minnesota patter about how it builds character, although I suspect it might, but the fact is that we're used to it. For us, this is simply a late autumn day. It will snow soon, maybe even next week, but to be honest with you, we tend to draw out the last moments of the waning season."

"People keep their houses warm, though, don't they?"

His uncle laughed. "Absolutely. We'll get you back to the house and put a cup of hot tea in your hands, and you'll feel better. Let's get going."

Uncle Alfred had hired a man to drive them and help with Isaac's baggage. Although, as he mentioned to Isaac, he did have his own carriage at the house. Soon Isaac was in the back of the wagon with his uncle. As they drove through the city, his uncle pointed out buildings and streets and occasionally waved at people on the streets, but it was a blur to Isaac, a big frozen blur.

Again, doubt assailed him. Had he done the right thing?

He'd taken it as his personal crusade since starting medical school to build the strength he'd need to be a good doctor. He'd been studying his Bible nightly, drawing from the powerful words of the Lord. One verse from Philippians had become his personal motto, and he repeated it at bedtime and each morning: "I can do all things through Christ which strengtheneth me."

Soon they were seated in Uncle Alfred's home, and, true to his word, his uncle had placed a large cup of black tea in Isaac's hands. He sat down across from his nephew and smiled.

"Excuse me if I study you for just a moment. I've been waiting for this, you see. Ever since your father told me that you were doing well at your medical studies but that you needed some practical experience, I prayed for this to come to pass." His uncle's voice was gentle, and in that moment, Isaac understood why the doctor was so loved by his patients. "If you decide it's not right for you, please come to me. Let's talk about it."

"Thank you, Uncle." Isaac took a swallow of the tea and promptly choked as the hot liquid scalded his throat.

Uncle Alfred handed him his handkerchief and chuckled. "Our air is too cold and our tea is too hot."

Whatever doubts had been attacking him before vanished like rain clouds in the afternoon sun. His uncle's good humor would make this a pleasant time indeed.

A knock on the door interrupted them, and Dr. Bering ushered in a group of people. "Isaac, I'd like you to meet some good friends of mine, the Everetts."

He rose to his feet to greet them as Uncle Alfred began the introductions. The minister and his wife, his sister, and his daughter—when she looked at him, her lips curved into a contagious smile. Her deep blue eyes were lit with happiness as she shook his hand.

Christal. That was her name. It fit her, too. She sparkled like crystal.

He became aware that his uncle was talking to him.

"Christal will show you around St. Paul. She walks everywhere, so you may end up with some blistered feet at first, but no one knows the city the way she does. You two will become great friends, I am sure."

"I'm so glad you're here," she said. Her words were simple but rang with honesty. "I'm delighted that God brought you here safely."

He realized that he was still holding her hand, and he dropped it suddenly. He opened his mouth to speak, but only a croak came out. "Er, yes."

Mentally he chided himself. Why was he acting like such a buffoon? It wasn't as if he had never spoken to a woman before. He'd had a nice social life in Florida and attended many social functions with women.

15

But none of them had such intelligent and lively eyes, and none of them sported a little curl of light brown hair that had escaped a coil of braids and trailed along a slender neck.

Oh, this was not good. Not good at all.

He realized that his uncle watched him, a smile playing across his face. Maybe he was wrong.

Perhaps this was good? Very good?

Chapter 2

"Please join us in the parlor," Dr. Bering said as he took Aunt Ruth's shawl from her shoulders and draped it carefully over an arm of the wire coatrack. "I've got tea ready, of course, and some spice cookies—the kind you like, Christal."

"Oh, thank you so much! They are my favorite. Isaac, have you gotten to try them yet?" she said, trying not to stare at the newcomer. He was really quite attractive. His amber-colored hair gleamed in the subdued lighting, and she almost sighed. If only her hair would be that shiny! But she was stuck with plain brown hair that wasn't straight enough to be obedient nor curly enough to style into fashionable ringlets.

He shook his head. "No, I'm sorry to say that my uncle has been guarding them, saying something about them being reserved for a young woman who liked them very much."

Papa hung his wife's cape on the wire rack as he spoke. "You are in for a rare treat, Isaac. Among the good doctor's many talents is baking."

"I don't know how much talent I have in the area," Dr. Bering said, "but I do enjoy it." He chuckled and patted his stomach. "As if anyone couldn't determine that from this girth! I've sampled too many of my culinary experiments."

"We're all standing here in this drafty hall," Aunt Ruth interjected, "but I believe you have some chairs in your parlor near the fireplace if I'm not mistaken. Alfred?" She held out her hand in an obvious directive for him to move the group into the house.

Christal started to follow when Isaac put his hand on her arm.

"Would you like for me to take your wrap?" he asked.

She'd forgotten that she still had on her old plaid jacket. She'd put it on at Aunt Ruth's bidding. The older woman had insisted that the evening chill in the air would climb into Christal's bones and give her consumption.

There was no point in arguing with Aunt Ruth by reminding her that the two houses were next door to each other, and Christal certainly wasn't going to tell her that she often ran between the two houses in the dead of winter with no coat at all. She'd thrown on the first thing that she touched in the closet—a red and green woolen jacket that was missing more buttons than it had kept. It was a disreputable bit of clothing, and she should have thrown it away long ago. As it was, she wore it when clearing the steps of snow or helping her father clean the gutters on the roof in the fall.

And now, meeting Isaac for the first time, she was wearing it.

He must think she was the silliest goose on the planet. Or the most poorly dressed one.

Knowing she was blushing, she ducked her head and quickly attended to removing the jacket. Then she realized that bad could indeed get worse. She had misbuttoned the jacket, too, so that it was crooked and poked out at an odd angle right above her waist.

She mutely handed the offending piece of clothing to him, and as she raised her eyes, she saw laughter dancing in his taffy-colored eyes.

"I was in a bit of a hurry," she said under her breath, and he laughed.

"I see that." He hung the jacket on the coatrack with the other garments and turned to her. "Cookies await. Shall we?"

He offered her his arm, and she took it, grateful that the awkward moment had passed.

As they entered the parlor, arm in arm, conversation stopped. Her parents, sitting together on the blue velvet divan, simply smiled, as did Dr. Bering, who was in a wing chair by the side of the fireplace.

Aunt Ruth, perched on the edge of a straight-backed chair, looked like a crimson-garbed queen about to hold court. She looked pointedly at their linked arms, and her back stiffened.

She moved as if to speak, and Christal froze. Her aunt often said the most outrageous things. Isaac had just gotten here, and he didn't know how she truly spoke her mind. *Please, God, don't let her. Not here, not now.*

And then Aunt Ruth shut her mouth, leaving the words unspoken.

Christal breathed a quiet sigh of relief and said a silent prayer of thanks to God for tempering the woman's words.

She had no idea what her aunt had considered saying. The elderly woman had a strong sense of propriety, so it might have been that she thought the action inappropriate, but the truth was that Aunt Ruth was liable to say anything. However, as spontaneous as she might be, she was never intentionally mean.

"We saved your seat," Dr. Bering said in his booming voice, indicating the padded rocking chair beside the piano. "And if Matthew will pass the platter your way, you can indulge in some spice cookies."

She curled into the familiar shape of her favorite chair and took the plate of cookies her father handed over to her. The aroma was heavenly, soft cinnamon and sharp nutmeg mingled together. She took two and gave the rest to Isaac, who had taken a seat on the hassock near the rocking chair.

"Try these."

He took a bite and smiled. "They're tremendous. Uncle, will you teach me to make these while I'm here? My skills in the kitchen are limited to scrambled eggs and chops, neither of which I do well."

"Good luck. I've tried to get this recipe from him forever, and he refuses to share. You'll never get it from him, and neither will I."

Dr. Bering waved his finger chidingly at Christal. "My dear child, never say 'Never.' Remember that the prize worth winning must be won."

Isaac leaned back and nodded. "I like that. *The prize worth winning must be won.*"

"So someday you will give me the recipe?" she asked eagerly.

Aunt Ruth cleared her throat. "It might help, child," she said, "if you could learn to light the stove."

Christal laughed. "Perhaps." Her aunt's words were true—Christal always needed help with the stove—but they stung nevertheless, and she made a mental note to work on learning it once she got home. It couldn't be that difficult. Why hadn't she ever learned how to do it properly?

Her mother intervened smoothly. "Isaac, please tell us about your family. We know that Dr. Bering is your uncle, but do you have family still in Florida?"

"Yes, ma'am." Isaac clasped his hands together, his fingers lacing and unlacing, as if he was uncomfortable with the attention. "My parents and my two sisters live in Key West. My older brother has relocated to Tennessee. He is married and has one child, a boy."

"My brother Walter is Isaac's father," Dr. Bering added. He beamed proudly at the young man.

"What drew you to medicine, Isaac?" Papa asked. "Is your father a physician, too?"

Isaac shook his head. "My father is a pharmacist."

"Now there's an interesting career," her father commented. "All those powders and potions and pills."

Aunt Ruth nodded approvingly. "I have my own remedies that suit me just fine for the most part, although I do like a drop or two of camphor when needed."

"Camphor can be very helpful, I believe," Isaac said. "My father often supplies it for deep chest congestion. It's quite effective."

"It sounds like there's a tendency toward the medical field in your family," Mother said. "Dr. Bering, was your father also interested in that sort of thing?"

Dr. Bering shook his head. "Not at all. He was a farrier and for a while had a small stable business that specialized in workhorses that businesses could use in construction. He certainly knew how to care for a horse, though, so perhaps he simply directed his mind toward horses while we focused on people."

"Did you see to the horses, too?" Christal asked. She could picture this gentle giant tending a dray horse. His large hands could easily shoe their over-sized hooves.

"I did. Even young Isaac got the chance to try it. Do you remember, Isaac?"

Isaac nodded. "I do recall some of it. They were the biggest horses I had ever seen. Their hooves were the size of me, or so I thought, and I was terrified they'd step on me. And worse, they wouldn't know it. They'd just keep on walking."

His uncle laughed. "Well, they were big and you were small. That's the truth."

"Did you get over your fear of those horses?" Christal ate the last of the spice cookies she had in her hand. This was one of her favorite moments, when the stories were told.

"I don't know that I was afraid of them as much as I was respectful of their gigantic feet. They are beautiful animals."

"What happened to the horses, Dr. Bering?" she asked.

"When my father retired, he could have sold them, but each one was precious to him, so he moved them all to his farm and let them stay until, one by one, they passed on to the Lord's pasture."

She nodded. Every good story needed a good ending, and this was a good ending.

She had many more questions, but she saw Isaac stifling a yawn. Her mother must have seen it, too, for she put her teacup on the side table and said, "This has been wonderful, but we really need to go back home. Tomorrow is Sunday, and the Lord's Day is a working day for the pastor's family, you know."

As they stood and then gathered their things from the coatrack, Dr. Bering put two more spice cookies, wrapped in a linen napkin, into Christal's hand. "I won't give you more, because I want you to come back tomorrow and take Isaac for a tour of the area after church."

She looked over at Isaac, who had taken the wretched plaid coat from the rack and now held it for her to slip into. "I'd be delighted to."

"Wear your most comfortable shoes," her father advised Isaac. "She knows every nook and cranny in the neighborhood and will probably try to show you all of them."

"I'm looking forward to that." He smiled, but she could see the lines of exhaustion around his eyes. He must be quite tired from his travels.

Christal slipped the napkin-wrapped bundle into her jacket pocket. "We'll walk through this neighborhood tomorrow. Nothing too strenuous."

"Make sure you dress warmly," Aunt Ruth interjected. "Even if you are a doctor in training, you should be careful with your own health. Bundle up."

"Oh, I will," he promised. "I am still used to the warm Floridian weather."

Aunt Ruth's blackberry-dark eyes turned toward Christal. "You, too,

Christal. Just because you're a Minnesotan doesn't mean you can't catch a chill. Button that jacket."

And do it right, Christal added mentally as she took care to match the button to the buttonhole. One button hung only by a thread, and as soon as she slid it into the hole, it sprang free, clattered across the glossy wooden floor, and came to rest against Isaac's foot.

Isaac bent over and picked it up. "I believe this is yours," he said, smiling as he handed it to her.

"Thank you," she muttered, her head down. *Could this get any worse?*

Her mother moved toward the door. "Dr. Bering, it's been a lovely evening. Thank you so much for the cookies and tea. Isaac, I am delighted to meet you, and I'm looking forward to getting to know you better."

Mother took Aunt Ruth's elbow and guided her out of the house, murmuring something to the older woman as they walked through the door.

"All I said," Aunt Ruth continued as they left the house, "was that she needed a coat. Why, look at tonight. If I hadn't said something, she would have left the house without anything on her arms. It's a good thing that I—"

Her aunt's voice fading into the October night, Christal made a promise to herself. First item of business when she got home: to shove the jacket into the ash can.

Isaac hummed as he joined his uncle for breakfast. He felt like a new man, refreshed and revitalized.

"You certainly sound chipper today," Uncle Alfred boomed.

"It's amazing how much good a solid night's sleep can do," Isaac said. "No wonder so many doctors recommend it."

His uncle chuckled. "Traveling, even though one does it all by sitting down nowadays, is oddly wearing, isn't it?"

"It is." Isaac spread jam across his toast. "By the way, I'm sorry about falling asleep so quickly after our guests left last night. I wanted to help you with the dishes, but I didn't make it that far."

"You were more asleep than awake as you climbed the stairs. I don't think my china would have fared well in your hands. Bacon or sausage, or both?"

"Bacon, please."

"Eggs are ready, too. Coffee or tea?"

"Coffee, but let me get it myself. You need to sit down and eat, too." Isaac pushed back his chair and began to stand, but his uncle motioned him to sit again.

"I've already eaten. I should warn you that I'm up every day as soon as the sun comes up." He reached for the coffeepot from the top of the stove, and after wrapping the handle with a thick green cloth, he poured a cup and handed it to Isaac. "I've always been an early riser. My mother used to say that I was part rooster."

Isaac laughed.

"She, however, was like a cat," his uncle went on. "She loved to sleep, so we made a deal. I wouldn't crow when I woke up. What that meant was that I learned early on to make my own breakfast, and if there's one lesson that's served me well all these years, that's it. A man who can make breakfast on his own starts every day with an advantage."

"Why is that?" Isaac asked.

"The man who heads off into his work without food in his stomach is hobbled. Food is our fuel. You know what your books taught you. The alimentary canal is meant to have food in it to provide energy, just as a fireplace must have wood to provide heat." He patted his rounded stomach. "Perhaps it shouldn't have as much as I put in mine, however. I guess sometimes I take my own advice too much."

"It must be difficult," Isaac commented as he dug into the eggs his uncle handed him, "with food as delicious as this."

"I like to cook, as you can see. By the way, we'll walk to church this morning. It's a grand Sunday morning. The sun is shining, and the air is crisp and bright."

" 'Crisp and bright'?" Isaac repeated. "Is that Minnesotan for 'cold'?"

Uncle Alfred grinned. "You learn fast, son. You learn fast."

Isaac ate the rest of his meal quickly and dashed upstairs to finish his preparations for going to church. As he straightened his tie using the mirror over the bureau in his room, he sighed. Right on the crown of his head, a lock of hair was twisted straight up into the air.

"I look like I have a handle on top of my head," he said as he tried to comb it into place. It sprang right back up. He wet the wayward section. It didn't help.

"We need to leave," his uncle called up the stairs.

Isaac had no choice except to let his hair go its rebellious way. He hoped that by the time he got to church it would have softened, or perhaps in church it would repent and return to lying flat.

When he got to the bottom of the stairs, his uncle patted him on the back. "We need to get going. You have a real treat ahead of you. Rev. Everett is a splendid preacher, very learned and precise yet very moving. We've been lucky to have him here all this time."

Isaac reached for his overcoat, and Uncle Alfred shook his head. "It's not that cold. You don't need it."

Isaac returned the coat to the rack. Somehow he wasn't at all reassured by Uncle Alfred's words.

His uncle smiled. "You'll be fine, but you are simply going to have to develop warmer blood, Isaac. That," he said as he put on his hat and turned to look at his nephew, "and the ability not to sleep with your hair kinked under your head. Wait here."

The doctor walked quickly to his room and returned with a bottle. "This is just a little pomade, and I apologize for the smell."

Before Isaac could protest, his uncle opened the bottle, swiped his fingertips across the top of it, and ran the stuff through Isaac's hair.

The scent of lilacs and roses was immediate, almost overpowering in its intensity. Isaac coughed and waved his hand in front of his nose trying desperately to stop the odor.

"Don't worry," Uncle Alfred said cheerfully as he pulled Isaac out the door. "By the time we get to church, it should have worn off."

" 'Should'? You mean there's no guarantee?"

"You know there are no guarantees on anything except death."

"Which might come sooner than expected if I have to keep inhaling this."

His uncle was right. The day was sunny. But once outside he had to keep himself from going back inside for his outer coat, knowing that they were late as it was. Perhaps if he walked quickly enough, he could generate enough body heat to keep himself from freezing to death before they got to church, which would—which *should*, he corrected his own thoughts—be heated.

This was a fine way to start the day, heading to worship stinking of flowers and worrying that despite it all, the recalcitrant lock would break free and point upward like a spire atop his head, perhaps reminding the other congregants that their ultimate destination lay heavenward. Plus, the small fact that he was so cold he couldn't feel his fingertips didn't help a bit.

Christal is going to be there, too, a little voice reminded him silently.

Oh, he was well aware that she would be there. She'd probably smell him before he got there, and then he'd be standing in all his wild-hair glory, his nose as red as a radish—it was too dreadful to imagine.

"Are you all right?" his uncle called, and Isaac realized he'd lagged behind. For a man as corpulent as he was, Uncle Alfred could certainly trot along at a steady pace.

Good. He'd arrive at church unable to speak, too, because he'd be so out of breath he'd be gasping for air.

This was getting worse.

He hunched his shoulders up. Perhaps that would warm his ears. He jammed his hands into his pockets and tightened them into fists, trying to expose as little flesh as possible to the cold.

How on earth did people manage this?

His uncle strode ahead—no overcoat, no muffler, no gloves, just his suit and hat. These people were insane. And winter was coming, when it would be even colder?

"Right here," his uncle called as he waited for Isaac to catch up to him. "This is the church."

Redeemer Church was built of grayish white stone with a sharply pointed steeple that rose into the sky.

Isaac leaned against the wrought iron railing and panted as he tried to regain his breath. "I must be terribly out of shape, Uncle Alfred."

Uncle Alfred clapped him on the back. "It was all uphill. On the way back, it's all downhill. Good metaphor for a church, wouldn't you say? Come in heavy laden and leave burdenless."

"That's good, Uncle. Let's go inside. I need to defrost."

His uncle smiled and shook his head. "You'll be one of us sooner than you think, Isaac."

"Is that a promise. . .or a threat?"

Uncle Alfred laughed. "Perhaps both."

Rev. Everett met them at the sanctuary door. "Welcome to both of you! Dr. Bering, you're looking well this morning. Isaac, it's good to have you with us."

The church was nearly full, and as Isaac paused to look for a spot where they could sit, his uncle whispered, "Follow me," and led him to the very front of the church to the pew where the Everetts were sitting, Aunt Ruth on the far end, Mrs. Everett in the middle, and Christal near the aisle.

There was room for only one person at the aisle end of the pew—certainly there was not enough room for someone of Uncle Alfred's girth—and the doctor murmured in Isaac's ear, "Sit here. I'll go to the other side."

The first grand notes of the processional were beginning, and the congregation stood. He slipped into the empty place and smiled as Christal held out the hymnal.

The day had just gotten considerably better. He was standing in church, singing the familiar notes of "All Hail the Power of Jesus' Name" with someone he already liked very much. He enjoyed singing in church. His ability—or, perhaps his inability—to stay on key was buoyed by the stronger voices of others, and he liked being able to blend his shaky tenor with their harmonies. The sun beamed through the rose window, the circular stained-glass window behind the altar, its multicolored geometrical pattern casting rainbows of purple across the worshippers. Christal's hair was tinged violet with a section of gold in the stained light.

In the back of church, someone coughed. He didn't want to turn around to see who it was, but the sound was alarming. It had the edge of a chronic condition, and a dangerous one.

Rev. Everett began the service, and Isaac found himself listening to him with growing eagerness. The minister was engaging, just as Uncle Alfred had said.

The theme of the service was strength through the Lord. Isaac clung to every word, noting the scripture the pastor had chosen: Genesis 32:24–31. He knew the story of Jacob wrestling with God, but never before had the story come alive the way it did with Rev. Everett's sermon.

"We will close with the hymn, 'Come, O Thou Traveler Unknown,' which is based upon this story," the minister said. "As you sing the words, think of Jacob, and think of your own struggles. Whom are you struggling with? Is it yourself? With others? Or is it God Himself?"

Rev. Everett paused, letting his words sink in, and then added, "After the service, I'd like you all to meet a traveler who is *not* unknown, or at least he won't be within a few minutes." The congregation chuckled. "Isaac Bering is Alfred Bering's nephew, and he's come to continue his medical studies with his uncle. Please stop in the back of the church and greet Isaac and welcome him to St. Paul and to Redeemer."

Isaac felt himself grow warm. Having everyone in the church look at him at the same time was a very odd feeling. He managed what he hoped was a happy-to-be-here smile as he sang the words of the recessional with everyone else.

Then he saw the situation that he was facing. Sitting in the front row meant that he was the last one out, and the entire congregation seemed to be waiting for him at the end of the aisle and into the narthex.

Women in their Sunday best, men in black suits buttoned up stiffly, young girls with their hair neatly braided, and boys in miniature versions of their fathers' clothing—they all stood, anticipating something from him.

It's just this once, he told himself. *Get through this and you will not have to do it again. Think of the scripture today. Wrestle with it. Win.*

Bolstered by the morning's lesson, he cleared his throat and spoke. "I am looking forward to getting to know all of you. I'm especially grateful to have the chance to meet you first in God's house."

It must have been the right thing to say, because the women beamed in approval and the men nodded with affirmation. He shook hands and talked socially to people until at last he had met all of them, including the elderly man who continued to cough even as he welcomed Isaac.

At last, it was done. He had never done anything like that in his entire life. This was the stuff his nightmares were made of, being the center of attention and having to make conversation with this many people he didn't know.

But he had done it. And, perhaps most importantly, he had lived.

"Are we going to go for a walk this afternoon?" Christal asked as she draped her shawl over her arm.

"Christal Maria Everett!" Aunt Ruth called from across the room. "Put the shawl around your shoulders, not over your elbow."

Christal rolled her eyes but not in anger. "Aunt Ruth gets cold," she said, "so I have to put on a shawl. And a coat. And a scarf, a hat, mittens, and a muff. Overshoes. Wrap in a blanket. And then maybe I can go outside."

"I am not deaf," Aunt Ruth shot back.

"But you're chilly."

The two women looked at each other and laughed. This was a scene that the two of them clearly enjoyed, a family joke of the best kind.

"Why don't we walk home together?" Christal suggested to Isaac. "We'll go down to Summit Avenue and then back up. Is that the way you came to church?"

He hated to admit that he hadn't seen much of anything on his way to church, not while he stumbled along, hunkered over, his chin tucked into his chest and shivering the entire time.

But the sun was out, the day was warming, and Christal was good company. They told the others of their plan and left the church.

The air had indeed lost its frosty edge, and the scene was glorious. The trees were robed in their autumn finery, and only the faintest hint of an October chill touched the light breeze.

"I love this time of year," Christal said as they walked together. She swung her shawl in front of her, and he suppressed a smile as he thought of what Aunt Ruth would have to say about that. "It's so pretty, isn't it? The earth is getting ready for winter, so God paints it as vividly as possible before all the color goes away, into the season of white, of snow and ice. What's your favorite season, Isaac?"

"I have to say that really all I've experienced is summer. Remember, I'm from Florida. Southern Florida. No snow there, so this is all new for me."

"Speaking of ice and snow," she said, stopping suddenly, "did Dr. Bering tell you about the ice carnival?"

"Ice carnival," he repeated. He shouldn't have been surprised. The people here didn't seem to know that snow and ice were cold, and that human beings were meant to be warm. Body temperature, after all, was 98.6 degrees. That was hardly compatible with living in the North.

He couldn't imagine what an ice carnival would be like. Cold, for sure.

"I don't know the details," she went on. "Dr. Bering told us about it. The man who's the publisher of the newspaper, the *St. Paul Dispatch*, is proposing it."

"Why on earth would anyone have a carnival of ice?" He shook his head. It made no sense.

She grinned at him. "Because apparently some people think it's too cold up here, that nobody could live here. Some newspaper writer said that."

"Smart fellow," he muttered under his breath.

Christal shook her head. "Give us some time. Your blood will thicken up, and you, too, will be making Aunt Ruth insane by going around in January without your coat."

"Blood thickening? Medical impossibility. Going around in January without a coat? Personal impossibility." He laughed.

"You say that now, but in the future, you'll be a tough Minnesotan, immune to the cold like the rest of us."

"Unlikely."

"Just wait. You'll see. Soon you won't be able to imagine a year without snow. By the way, how long will you stay here? Do you know?"

She swooped down and picked up a ruby and gold maple leaf and stuck it behind her ear. She looked like the picture of autumn itself.

"To be honest," he said, "I think I might stay, cold or no cold. Uncle Alfred is bringing me into his practice with the thought that eventually I'll take it over and he can retire. But of course that won't happen until I have more training and we're both comfortable with my medical skill."

"I think that would scare me," Christal said, "having someone's life in my hands."

How could he respond? Should he tell her the truth, that he was absolutely terrified of making a mistake? There couldn't be a costlier error than to make a decision that would result in death. It was irretrievable.

Would she think less of him if he spoke honestly, if he told her of his fears? He sidestepped the issue with a noncommittal response. "That's something all physicians have to face. We try to heal, using the meager tools available to us, and sometimes, with the Lord's help, we succeed. Sometimes we don't. We do what we can, both as doctors and as human beings. The rest we commit to His power."

Christal nodded. "Your uncle is a wonderful man, as well as being an extraordinary doctor. I know he prays for his patients. He did it for me, and I really think that's what makes him so good."

"I agree. I intend to follow in his footsteps in that regard, too."

A scruffy terrier raced down the sidewalk and leaped in joyous circles around Christal, who leaned over and cooed, "Aren't you the handsome boy? Aren't you? Yes, you are. You are a handsome boy!" Finally the dog stopped and collapsed in front of her, its belly up, until she reached down and rubbed the dog's stomach.

The dog popped back up and licked her hand.

"This is Bob," she explained to Isaac. "He's a happy dog."

"I guess so," he answered, reaching down to pat the terrier's head and being rewarded with an affectionate slurp on his palm.

"Bob will walk with us for a while, and then he'll remember that there was

27

a squirrel he was going to chase in the tree, or he'll wonder if it's time for dinner, or maybe he'll even decide he should take a nap. But all of a sudden, he'll turn around and run back home as fast as he can."

"He sounds like quite an interesting creature." The dog leaned against Isaac's leg and gazed up at him with adoring eyes. "And very friendly."

"He is. No walk in this neighborhood would be complete without Bob. He does seem to have taken to you, though, which is quite a compliment."

"Really?" He felt oddly proud of this affirmation from the scraggly dog.

"Did you have dogs back in Florida?" she asked as they resumed their walk, Bob trotting between them.

Isaac laughed. "There are lots of dogs in Florida."

"Silly! I meant, did *you* have a dog?"

"When I was in school, in Tallahassee, I rented a room from a woman who wouldn't allow anything alive in the rooms—except, of course, the boarders."

"That's too bad," Christal said, as her fingertips trailed across the top of Bob's head.

"I suspect she had some pretty good reasons. I heard that too many times people had moved out and left their pets behind, and she grew tired of trying to find new homes for the animals."

"That's irresponsible—of the owners, not of her. I can understand her reasoning then. Did you have any pets when you grew up?" Christal asked.

"Any pets? Well, sure. Let's see. There were an assortment of cats and kittens that came in and out of the yard—and in and out of the house, too, much to my mother's dismay—and my father always made sure that we had a dog."

"What kind of dog?" She grinned. "Bob wants to know."

"Labrador retrievers. One of Father's favorite things is to go to the shore with his dog and throw a stick into the ocean and let the dog get it. He says there's little in life as beautiful as a soaking wet Lab proudly trotting back with the stick. He says the dog almost smiles." Isaac thought back to the blissful expression the dog had when running out of the water. "Maybe it does."

"Labrador retrievers like water," Christal said.

"You've had them, too?"

She shook her head. "No. The house belongs to the church, and as much as I'd like to have a pet of some kind, it's out of the question. When I was little, though, I would smuggle in whatever I could that would fit in my pocket. I had caterpillars and black beetles and fireflies, and once I found a toad, but I lost him somewhere in the pantry."

He burst out laughing. "The pantry! You lost a toad in the pantry? Your parents must have been quite put out with you."

"They would have—if I'd told them about it."

"You didn't tell them?"

She looked at him, her dark blue eyes wide open and guileless, and he had a flash vision of what she must have looked like as a child. "I didn't have to. My mother found it."

"What did she do?"

"She put it back outside and then sat me down and explained that not all animals are meant to be pets, that God had them born outside because that was where they were supposed to spend their lives, and that I wasn't being kind to them bringing them inside. She said it was like putting them in prison."

"And—?" he prompted.

"And I thought she was wrong, and I told her so."

He was fascinated. "How old were you?"

"Four or five."

"What did she say when you said she was wrong?"

Christal's eyes lit impishly. "She didn't say much, because I had irrefutable logic—or so I thought."

"And your logic was—?"

"I said that Jesus had been born in a stable, which wasn't a house for people, yet He got to come inside. Nobody made Him stay in the stable."

He shook his head. "How did she respond?"

"She told me that kings are comfortable anywhere, but toads aren't." Christal shrugged. "It made perfect sense to me."

He liked her family even more, just hearing her talk about them.

"How do you like St. Paul so far?" she asked. "We have toads here, just in case you want one now that I've told you my story, but they're pretty much hidden away until summer."

"Thank you, but I'll pass on the toads. Even next summer they can stay outside. I agree with your mother on that. I have to say that I have never had the faintest inclination to try to make a pet of a toad. St. Paul, though, is very beautiful. I do believe that I chose a splendid time of year to be introduced to the city. The trees are lovelier than I could ever have imagined."

"Autumn is my favorite season, or at least it is right now," she said. "Ask me in the winter or the spring or the summer, and I might have a different answer. That's one aspect of living here that I really like: All seasons are so beautiful that I can't imagine living elsewhere. What's Florida like?"

"Florida is warm. And very humid. There are some wild storms that come in. The winds from the ocean can create some real chaos there."

"Have you ever experienced a hurricane?"

He nodded. "It was terrifying, but we came through. The wind whipped the rain so hard that the water came down like knives, or maybe I should say it came across like knives. The wind is so fierce that the rain goes sideways. There was quite a bit of damage, but we were sheltered enough that we didn't have much cleaning up to do afterwards."

She shivered. "I've read about hurricanes. We don't have them here—obviously—but there is the danger of tornadoes and blizzards and floods. No matter where we go, there will be some challenge from nature."

"Speaking of blizzards, just how cold does it get here?"

Bob stopped suddenly, nearly tripping Christal. He licked each of their hands, turned, and charged off in the direction they'd come.

"I guess that's the end of his walk!" Isaac watched the dog head for home.

"And we're nearing the end of ours."

Christal turned down a side street, and within moments they were in front of his uncle's house.

"Thank you so much," Isaac said to her.

"We'll do more exploring later," she said to him. "I want to show you the library, for one thing. I go there every day."

"Every day? You must have all the books memorized!"

"Oh, there are so many stories in there. Some I read again and again. They're like old friends to me. There are others that are new to me, and I'm always excited to open a new book and start a tale I haven't heard before."

She stopped and looked at him.

"Like me?" he asked. "Am I a new story?"

She tilted her head and studied his face. "I suppose you are. I guess the question is: Are you an adventure story? A mystery? A saga?"

His heart tripped just a bit in his chest. "And you? Are you a new story to me?"

She didn't respond, and he thought he might have been a bit too bold for this minister's daughter.

But then her lips began to curve into a slow smile. "I guess we will both have to find out."

She touched his arm lightly and turned, and with quick, light steps, she ran to her front door, where she stopped and faced him, grinning conspiratorially. "If Aunt Ruth asks, I was wearing my shawl the whole time."

He thought he already knew what kind of book she was. She was poetry.

~

Sunday dinner over, Christal's mother and father left on their afternoon pastoral visits, and Aunt Ruth retired to her room with her knitting and her Bible. "That," she had told Christal's parents, "is the proper way to spend the Sabbath, not out on the byways of St. Paul, trotting here and there like a midwestern Sherpa."

Her parents had merely nodded, and her father said, with a slight twinkle in his eyes, that he thought Christal was acting in the Lord's service by befriending a newcomer and helping him acclimate to his neighborhood.

Aunt Ruth answered with a sniff, but as she left the room, Christal was sure she saw a smile on her aunt's face. "Wear your jacket," the older woman called over her shoulder. "It's not July, you know."

Christal compromised with her shawl again. If necessary, she could tie it around her waist. Her aunt—and truthfully, her mother, too—would be horrified to see her doing that, but it was simply so much easier than trying to keep it wrapped around her shoulders and over her forearms. Having it around her midsection left her hands free to pet friendly dogs or pick up colorful leaves.

Isaac was waiting in the entryway next door. From the parlor behind him came the stentorian sounds of Dr. Bering's snoring.

"Are you ready to go for a walk?" she asked.

He looked behind him and grinned. "I suppose Uncle Alfred doesn't have any plans for me this afternoon."

Christal nodded. "Dr. Bering believes in Sunday rest."

"He is putting that into practice, judging from what we're hearing." He motioned toward the parlor.

"He does like his Sunday nap. But he also encourages walking as a way to health. He's told me as much. Of course," she added, leaning toward him and speaking in a conspiratorial whisper, "that doesn't apply to him. He explained it all to me once."

"Oh, he did, did he?" Amusement lit his face.

Isaac really should smile more, she thought. When he did, the worry lines and the creases over his nose, where he'd frowned too often and too long, probably as he studied his texts, vanished.

"Your uncle told me that for older people, recuperative sleep was one of the rare pleasures in life, especially in the afternoon. But we're too young for Sunday naps, so let's go for a walk. I have more of the neighborhood to show you, and I suspect that your uncle will keep you busy for the rest of the week, so this is our only chance."

Isaac reached for his overcoat, and she almost spoke but stopped. He'd just arrived, after all.

"I know," he said, "you think it's not at all cold here. I happen to know better. It is freezing. Uncle Alfred has assured me that I'll get used to it, but I don't know if that's true."

"Well, if you're going to get used to it, now's a good time to start. It'll snow soon."

"I'll get accustomed to it in stages, if you don't mind." He put on his overcoat. "In deference to the natives, though, I'll skip the hat and muffler and gloves."

"Don't tell Aunt Ruth. She'll have your head. Then freezing to death would be the least of your concerns."

They headed out the door.

"First we'll go by the library," she announced. "I know you'll spend lots of time there. I do."

He shook his head. "I don't know, Christal. I'm here to learn and study. The reading I'll be doing may not qualify as enjoyable to you, but at the moment, it's my life."

She waved away his objection. "I can't imagine life without my stories, and the library is where they are."

He seemed unconvinced, and Christal's steps slowed. Could it be possible that her new friend didn't share her love of reading?

She realized uneasily that she was interpreting it as a character flaw on his part, and it bothered her. Certainly people were allowed to have interests other than reading. Just because she found it fascinating didn't mean he had to.

God gifted people with varying talents and gave them different pursuits to enjoy. "Are you a musician, like your uncle? He plays the piano so beautifully."

"No, I'm sorry to say that I didn't inherit the Bering musical talent. I got my mother's wooden pitch."

She tried again. "Art? Do you paint?"

"No."

"Athletics? There are some superb organizations—"

"Along with my mother's wooden pitch, I got her arms and legs. No athletics. I can't catch a ball, nor run, without tripping."

"Do you cook?" She thought of her own deficiency in that area.

"No."

"Garden?"

"No."

"Travel! You like to travel, don't you?"

He sighed. "Again, no. Christal, I am a very boring person. Boring Bering."

"You are not boring!"

"I am, I'm sorry to say. Medical students are traditionally among the worst. We have a terrible leaning to single vision. We make the worst dinner companions and often have to be stopped short of an invigorating discussion of nephritis over pound cake and coffee."

"Nephritis?"

"Kidney disease."

"Oh." She could only imagine the details of such a conversation.

"If I begin to ramble on about gout or infections of the sinus cavities or spasms in the esophagus, you'll please bring me back to the here and now?"

She laughed. "With pleasure!"

They were nearly to the corner where the library was. It was, of course, closed on a Sunday afternoon, so all she could do was point out the brick building that housed the library on the second floor.

Perhaps it seemed odd to him that she had brought him all the way there, just to show him the exterior of the library—not that he seemed even faintly interested in it.

"There are doctors' offices on the ground level." She added the last bit with hope. Maybe at the very least that would entice him to return.

He didn't respond.

"There are all kinds of wonderful stories in there," she said, "even, I'm sure, about the history of inflamed nostrils and the philosophy of sutures."

His roar of laughter filled the almost empty street, and the few pedestrians that were out on a Sunday stopped and smiled curiously at the sound.

He reached for her hand and held it in his. "I am so sorry. I'm afraid I've offended you."

She knew she was growing flushed, partially because he had done just that, even though she had fought her reaction to his indifference, and partially because he was holding on to her hand and it felt so good.

"Philosophy of sutures, indeed. Christal, I am having an absolutely wonderful time today. Why, I'm not even cold."

His nose was red, and the tips of his ears were bright crimson. The chest of his overcoat rose and fell rapidly. The poor fellow looked wretchedly uncomfortable.

"You are cold, and I've probably worn you out," she said, taking pity on her new friend. She touched his arm. "Let's go back. We'll walk more slowly, and the next time you can wear a hat and scarf and gloves. Truthfully, you'll probably need them by then."

"The next time," he repeated. "Until it warms up, that's as likely as my taking my own tonsils out."

Her heart sagged in disappointment, but she reminded herself again that God made all of His creatures blessed in diverse ways. He didn't *have* to like reading to be her friend, and he didn't *have* to like the cold weather as much as she did.

"You know, it could warm up again a bit," she said in what she hoped was an encouraging voice. "Indian summer usually comes earlier, like the end of September or the beginning of October, but there's nothing to say it couldn't happen now."

"Really?" he asked, his voice perked with renewed optimism.

"I think it could," she declared stoutly. "Why, even as I stand here, I can still smell the remnants of a garden, so they haven't all died."

He drew a deep breath, and his forehead puckered in confusion. "I can't smell it. Are you sure?"

"I am. Lilacs and roses. There's been a hint of them all day. So maybe summer still has one more hurrah in it."

Isaac cleared his throat and ran his hand over the top of his head. Why were his cheeks suddenly as florid as his ears and his nose? Was he really *that* cold?

Christal shrugged away the odd gesture. Southerners!

Christal closed her Bible and placed it on her bedside. When she had fallen ill nearly a decade ago with scarlet fever, she'd begun her own tradition of reading the twenty-third Psalm each night before going to sleep. Of course she had it memorized, but the comfort of holding the Bible that had been hers since she was an infant was part of the ritual.

The promise of the psalm that she would walk through the threat of death, *"the valley of the shadow of death,"* had been soothing. The days when she had hovered between life and death were tempered by the words *"I will fear no evil for thou art with me."* Even when she hadn't been able to talk, when she was lost in the dreams of a high fever, she had held the words close to her heart.

She could see a glow from the upstairs window of Dr. Bering's house next door. One of the men was awake, too, reading perhaps.

The night air was sweet with the smell of fireplaces, and she padded over to the window to open it an inch or two to let the aroma in and to chase the staleness of the closed room out.

From below her came the faint notes of Beethoven's "Moonlight Sonata." Dr. Bering must be playing the piano in his parlor.

There had never been such a beautiful piece of music. She sat beside the window and rested her chin on the windowsill and let the notes float over her. It was liquid.

She closed her eyes and let her mind drift as she revisited all of the wonderful things that had happened in the course of the day. This had been an absolutely perfect day, from worshipping with Isaac and getting to know him a bit, to this serene end with "Moonlight Sonata" and smoke-scented air.

Isaac. Her thoughts paused and lingered. Isaac.

There was something very special about him. How special, she didn't know yet. Only God knew that.

Christal opened her eyes and looked again at the house next to hers. Isaac Bering was going to be a good friend—that much she knew. One should never overlook the value of a good friend.

Especially, she thought with a grin, a good friend who was as handsome as Isaac.

The October night breeze had an edge to it, and she closed the window some more, leaving it open enough to freshen the air and allow the music in.

"Good night," she said softly to the house next door. "Good night, and God bless you."

Chapter 3

T here is a door between my office and my living quarters," Uncle Alfred explained as he led Isaac through the heavy oak door that separated the entryway and the waiting room of his medical suite.

"Just one door? Why is that?" Isaac asked.

"There are several reasons for that," his uncle responded, "but the major one is simply to keep myself from spending all of my evenings in here, reading and puttering. I guess you could say it's symbolic. A doctor must keep a part of his life separate from the practice of medicine."

The waiting room was situated on the front corner of the house so that windows opened two of the walls to daylight. An opulently upholstered sofa with golden oak arms polished to a silken sheen sat along one side of the room, while wing chairs covered in burgundy brocade were positioned next to the small fireplace.

A glass-fronted bookcase held three rows of leather-bound volumes, each with the title stamped in gold. Isaac wandered over to them. Many of them he recognized from his own early school studies, but the others weren't familiar.

On a small table three volumes were placed in an inviting display near a figurine of an angel holding a child. Isaac picked them up and read the authors aloud. "Charles Dickens. John Keats. Jules Verne. This is quite the assortment here, Uncle Alfred. Are you reading these, or are they for your patients as they wait?"

"I keep them here for anyone to read. If a patient or his family happens to start reading a book and wants to continue, he's more than welcome to take it."

"Aren't you worried about losing the book?" Isaac touched the thick binding of one of the volumes. It wasn't an inexpensive edition.

"I always get them back, but even if I didn't, I wouldn't care. Books are meant to be shared."

His uncle clearly shared Christal's love of reading. It baffled Isaac. These kinds of books, with things like poetry and tales, served no educational purpose that he could see. Why else would one read, unless one wanted to increase one's knowledge? "You've read these?"

"Indeed." Uncle Alfred opened the Jules Verne volume. "Ah, *Around the World in Eighty Days*. What an intriguing story! Have you read it, Isaac?"

"No, I'm sorry, I haven't. Schooling seems to occupy almost every waking minute of my time."

His uncle shook his shaggy head. "Don't let yourself fall into that trap, my boy. A good doctor reads novels, visits with people, goes to concerts, gets out and about. The more you know, the better you'll be as a physician. People rarely act like they're shown in the textbooks. The cases in there are artificial. It's important for you to know what's going on in the world, to find out what people are really like."

He shoved the book into Isaac's hands. "Read this."

Isaac stared at the novel. "But this is fiction."

"Yes." Uncle Alfred hooked his thumbs under his suspenders and watched Isaac with a slightly bemused expression. "You don't like fiction?"

"I do, I guess." Isaac was at a loss. He hadn't read a novel in years. "Shouldn't I be reading medical texts at this stage? After all, I'm here to learn."

"You will learn by reading novels, too, Isaac. Stretch your mind. Expand your knowledge. Learn expansively."

Jules Verne? He'd heard of Jules Verne and his novels of fantastic adventures that did not take place in the world Isaac knew. His uncle wanted him to read something by a Frenchman that was based upon a science that didn't exist? Science and fiction—now there were two terms that should never go together.

He started to put the book back onto the table, but his uncle stopped him. "I'm serious, Isaac. Read the book. Try something different."

Try something different? Wasn't he already trying something different, leaving his home in Florida and moving north, coming into a land of ice and snow that his body would take months, if not years, to get used to? He had left the rest of his family and his friends and committed himself to at least two years with an uncle he barely knew—an uncle he respected but with whom he'd spent little time.

He looked back at the books on the shelves. He was used to spending long hours poring over medical tomes filled with information that he would desperately need, and yet here he was being told to read a novel filled with crazy science.

His uncle led him through the rest of the office area, through the examination room with its assortment of tools and instruments that his uncle used in the course of the day, and on into the lab and surgery.

He took one look at the surgical bed and swallowed. This was the part he was not ready for. The dangers were so great.

Uncle Alfred must have understood his nephew's hesitation, for he rubbed Isaac's shoulder in sympathy. "I hope the day never comes, Isaac, when you walk in here and aren't overcome with the enormity of the responsibility you face. If you ever lose that and become complacent, your doctoring skills will have failed you."

Isaac leaned against the bed to steady himself. He had made a terrible mistake. He was not meant to be a doctor.

He looked at his hands, trembling and unsure. At some point, he would stand in the room and his fingers would grip a scalpel. He would be expected to cut into a patient's skin and open his body and heal him.

A mere mortal could not do that. *He* could not do that.

"You'll be fine," his uncle declared. "This self-doubt does serve a purpose, you know. It means that you will think before you act, which is imperative for a physician. You do, however, need to control it. You'll be no good if you're unconscious on the bed beside your patient. One of you has to hold the scalpel, and it really should be you."

He led Isaac out of the surgery area, through the examination room, and back to the waiting area. "My first patient will be here soon. I would like for you to join me in the evaluation of his symptoms."

Isaac put the Jules Verne volume on the table. "I promise," he said, before his uncle could object, "to take it with me when I'm through here."

"Good, because—well, hello, Mr. Lawrence." Uncle Alfred helped the patient off with his coat.

Isaac recognized the man from church the day before. His cough had punctuated the service, and yet he had stayed to meet Isaac afterward.

"So your throat is quite irritated?" Uncle Alfred led Mr. Lawrence into the examination room. "I'd better take a look at it. By the way, this is my nephew, Isaac Bering, who is going to continue in my footsteps. You might remember him from church yesterday."

"I do," the man replied, stopping for a moment as coughing wracked his body. Then he continued, "Isaac, I'm praying you enjoy your time here. Your uncle is a good man and a good doctor."

"Thank you, Mr. Lawrence. From what I've seen of the city, I'm impressed. It's beautiful. And I concur with your assessment of my uncle."

"You two will make this old doctor blush," Uncle Alfred said. "Mr. Lawrence, I hope you don't mind if Isaac joins us today."

And with those words, Isaac's journey into medicine took one step forward.

⁓

"And wear your jacket!"

Aunt Ruth's words followed Christal as she left the house. The morning air still retained a bit of the night's chill, but the sun blasted away, and soon the day would warm up considerably.

She had a jacket with her—not the dreaded plaid one, though. She reminded herself again that she needed to get that horrible garment into the fire as soon as possible. This one was a sedate black short coat, the one she usually wore to church. A bit fancy, perhaps, for her errand, but it was better than the plaid jacket.

The door opened at Dr. Bering's house, and she watched Isaac steadying John Lawrence on his way down the front walk. Mr. Lawrence was coughing badly, and she immediately prayed for his health. Over the past two or three months, the elderly man had developed a deep congestion that seemed to have grown worse every time she saw him.

"Hello, Mr. Lawrence!" she called, waving at him. "Hello, Isaac!"

Isaac raised his free hand in a salute. "I'm going to go with Mr. Lawrence here to see his bird, Aristotle."

She smiled. Aristotle was a mangy-looking and terribly ill-tempered bird "of some undetermined heritage, an avian vagabond," but she suspected that the bird was a common crow.

As far as she'd been able to tell, Aristotle's sole talent was that he was in love with the image he saw in the mirror that Mr. Lawrence had put behind his cage. *Just like some people I know,* Aunt Ruth had sniffed after a visit when Aristotle had been particularly rambunctious and bitten the feather off her new hat.

Christal had wondered if perhaps the bird realized the source of the feather—one of its distant and undoubtedly deceased relatives—and had attacked the feather as a way of punishing Aunt Ruth.

The bird's place in Mr. Lawrence's heart was well known, but Dr. Bering, she was sure, hadn't sent Isaac out just to see the bird.

"Would you like to come, too?" Mr. Lawrence asked, covering his mouth as the coughing rose again.

"I'd love to see Aristotle. Let me just pop back in and tell my mother that I'm going with you two first."

She turned and went back into the house. Her mother was headed up the stairs with an armful of folded linens and stopped. "I thought you were going to the library."

"I am, but first may I go with Isaac to see Mr. Lawrence's bird? They're going now, and Mr. Lawrence invited me."

Mother shifted the sheets and frowned slightly. "You know, I think that would be a good idea. He sounds so sick lately, and I'm worried about him. Christal, without being obvious about it, will you take a look at his home and see if he might need some help? I can't think that he's able to keep up with it, not as ill as he must be."

"I will." She kissed her mother lightly on the cheek. "I'll see you later."

She rejoined the two men and walked with them to Mr. Lawrence's house. It was less than two blocks away, but the elderly man walked so slowly that it took them almost half an hour.

His house was small and sunlit. As soon as they walked into the living room, loud squawking and chirping broke the morning calm.

Aristotle hopped from one foot to the other in a kind of wild dance. Up and down the rod that crossed his cage he went, screeching and shrieking until Mr. Lawrence hobbled over to see him.

"Aristotle, are you glad to see me? Say hello to your papa! Say hello!"

Isaac looked at Christal, and they smiled as the aged man fussed over his beloved bird. He opened the door and thrust his hand inside the cage. The bird popped onto it and immediately bit his knuckle.

"Here's my boy!" Mr. Lawrence announced as he held Aristotle out to Christal and Isaac.

She tried not to smile as Isaac nodded uneasily, as if not sure if he was expected to let the bird get on him or to pet it.

The question was resolved quickly when the bird flew to the top of the bookcase with a great shower of feathers that dropped off him and drifted onto every nearby surface.

"Should I get him?" Isaac asked. The expression on his face clearly showed that he hoped the answer was no.

"He'll be fine. I let him out to stretch his wings every once in a while." Mr. Lawrence stopped as a round of coughing took over.

"My uncle has given you a bottle of medicinal syrup for that," Isaac said, reaching into his pocket. "Let's get some in you before I leave."

"I'll get a spoon," Christal said. "I know where the kitchen is."

The dishes were piled on the counter, crusted with dried food. Mr. Lawrence had apparently made some effort to clean a few of them, judging from the ones that were drying on a towel near the sink.

Her mother's fears were right. The poor man was overwhelmed with housekeeping now that he was sick.

He hadn't always been like this. Usually the house was spotless. But now dust motes as thick as June stars danced in the sunlit living room, and the bright light through the window showed where he had missed cleaning up after his bird.

Christal blinked as tears burned into her eyes. Was Mr. Lawrence going to get better? He had to! She couldn't bear seeing him like this, failing so dramatically.

As she found a clean spoon, wiping it off just in case, she remembered when she had been younger and had come to his house to see the bird and to look at his flower garden. Now both he and the bird were old, and the flower garden had gone to weeds.

She ran her fingertips over her cheeks to dry off the last vestiges of tears and practiced a smile. There. She could go back in and see him.

"I've got it!" she sang out as she joined the two men. Isaac stood beside Mr.

Lawrence, comforting him as yet another set of coughs shook his frail body. The medicine was already in his hand. Even the cork was out.

"Here," he said, taking the spoon from her and pouring the syrup into it. "This will help control the spasms in your lungs, and it'll let you sleep."

Aristotle flapped his wings and shrieked from his perch on the bookcase.

"I wish I could get him back in his cage," she said to Isaac, "but I'm afraid he'd tear me apart."

"He's a good bird," Mr. Lawrence said from the chair, his voice growing slurred as the medication quickly took effect. The sedation in the syrup, combined with the effort of the walk to and from Dr. Bering's office and the wearying rounds of deep coughing had clearly exhausted him. "He'll go back in."

And with that, he put his head to one side and fell asleep.

"Well," Isaac said, "I guess that's that."

Christal took a throw from the divan and covered the older man. "I'll tell my mother. She'll come in and see to him."

They tiptoed out of the room as Aristotle made another loop around the room, coming to rest this time on the curtain rod.

Isaac shook his head. "I'm not going after that creature."

"Nor am I. We'll leave him. There's food in his cage, I noticed, so I'm sure he'll head back in there eventually."

Once they were out on the street, Isaac shook his head. "That poor man."

"He's sick, isn't he, Isaac?" She reached out and grasped the sleeve of his coat, making him stop. "Tell me, please."

"Yes, he's sick."

"Is he going to get better?" *Please say yes,* she added mentally.

He shrugged and looked away. "That's God's decision."

A sob tore at her throat. That was answer enough.

She dropped her hand from his arm and shoved it into her coat pocket. It wasn't fair. "People should live forever. They should never get sick."

He didn't speak at first. Then, "Well, of course we live forever. Not on earth, but in heaven." He smiled wryly. "Here I am, telling a pastor's daughter about eternal life."

"I do know that, and it is a comfort, but still, that's for the person dying. They get to go on to eternal life, while we who are left here have to wait for our turn. I don't like that part."

"I know," he said softly.

"I've been to a lot of funerals as a minister's daughter. Sometimes I barely even knew the person, sometimes not at all. But sometimes I did know them well, and it hurts so badly." She sighed. "I understand it all, but I don't like seeing people in pain."

"Nor do I, Christal, nor do I." They began to walk back toward the Bering house. "That is the reason I became a doctor, to try to ease pain wherever I could."

Neither one said anything until at last Christal said, "You know, Mr. Lawrence could have walked home by himself. He's weak and he proceeds slowly, but he walks everywhere he goes. I wonder why your uncle sent you with him."

Isaac stared thoughtfully at the road ahead. "Uncle Alfred cares about his patients as people. Each one is an individual human being, and their needs extend beyond what they might tell him in the consulting room. I suspect he wanted me to see Mr. Lawrence's home and to see his relationship with that silly bird."

She looked at him curiously. "Why?"

"Because that's all part of who John Lawrence is. He's a person. Right now he's a person who has a terrible cough." He shook his head. "I don't know. I don't know what to think, except that Uncle Alfred's success as a physician is due, in part, to his ability to treat the person, not the disease."

That made sense to her. Dr. Bering had an astonishing talent to understand his patients and their needs.

They were at the foot of the walk to her house. "I'm going to go in and talk to my mother about Mr. Lawrence. I'm sure she will make sure his house is put in order—and don't worry, she'll do it in a way that he probably won't even realize it."

"Not realize it?" Isaac asked. "Be realistic, Christal. You saw it. If she cleans even a little corner of the house, it'll be noticeable."

Christal smiled. "Many years of being a good minister's wife have given her plenty of experience in being tactful with those in the congregation who are in need but don't admit it. She'll find a way to take care of it so he won't be hurt. By the way, I'm going to the library in a while. That's where I was headed originally. Would you like to join me?"

She held her breath as she awaited his answer. It was silly, wanting him to join her there, but the fact was that if she could create a perfect friend for herself, it would be someone who would love the trips to the library as much as she did.

"I can't. My uncle has patients all day long, and I need to be back there, learning at his side."

Her disappointment must have shown on her face, for he touched her hand. "I will go another time, Christal. It's important to you, so it's important to me."

It was the perfect answer. He smiled at her, his golden brown eyes meeting hers directly. The sun had risen to its midmorning glory, and his hair caught the light.

She was so glad he was here.

At last she shook herself out of her reverie. It could only have lasted a second or two, but it seemed longer. "I'll see you another time then."

He reached out and touched her arm. "Yes, indeed."

As he walked over to his uncle's house, she headed up the walkway to her own front door and marveled at how much happier he made her. Even in the midst of pending sorrow, he brought something very special into her life.

Her mother met her in the entryway as Christal was taking off her jacket. "Christal, what did you see?"

"There are dishes that need to be washed, the furniture is dusty, and the bird is loose. That's all I saw, but it's quite a lot."

Mother reached for her coat. Her ragbag was at her feet, ready for service.

"I'm going over now, then. Can you please let Aunt Ruth know? She's in the parlor with her knitting."

"I'll go with you." The library could wait. This was more important. "Let me—"

"We'll all go." Aunt Ruth's tone brooked no discussion. Christal hadn't even heard her come into the hall. "The three of us should be able to put the house to rights quickly. We need to be careful not to disturb him while we're there, so the sooner we can get done, the better."

"I think he's asleep," Christal offered. "He must have been tired anyway, and then Isaac gave him some syrup that Dr. Bering had sent. There must be some powerful medicine in it. He fell asleep almost immediately."

Her mother and aunt looked at each other and nodded. "For the cough," Mother said. "He has to sleep in order to build up his strength to battle the cough."

"Put on your jackets, both of you," Aunt Ruth ordered as they were leaving. Christal and her mother grinned at each other—and put on their jackets.

The three women trekked the short distance to Mr. Lawrence's home, as Mother and Aunt Ruth mapped out a strategy for dealing with the situation there. Her mother listed the contents of her bag. "Rags, of course. A bar of good strong soap. That scrub brush we use on the stairs in the back. Vinegar. Ammonia."

They arrived at the Lawrence home. Mother knocked. When there was no response, she opened the door and called out softly, "John Lawrence? Mr. Lawrence? It's Sarah Everett, the minister's wife. Ruth and Christal are with me. Might we come in?"

She motioned to Aunt Ruth and Christal to follow her.

Mr. Lawrence was just as Christal and Isaac had left him only moments before, asleep in his chair. Aristotle screeched, but Aunt Ruth reached into her pocket and pulled out something that she held toward the bird.

Aristotle flapped over to her, snatched it out of her hand, and carried his prize again to the top of the bookcase.

"What on earth was that?" Christal asked, amazed.

"A slice of apple. I was knitting, and you know how much I enjoy a cut apple while I knit. It's much easier and less sticky to have it in pieces. Well, waste not, want not. I brought it with me when we came here. I know that Aristotle likes apples."

"How?" Christal couldn't keep the astonishment from her voice. "How did you know that?"

"Christal Maria Everett," her aunt admonished, "just because a woman might be old doesn't mean she's lost all her faculties. Or that she doesn't know someone. John Lawrence and I have known each other for many years, even before Aristotle came into his life. And do you know *why* Aristotle has such a spot in John's heart?"

Christal looked at the bird perched on the bookcase. His feathers were a splotchy mixture of brown and black, and in places they appeared to be thinner than others. His beak was chipped slightly, and one eye had a film over it.

Why the creature had a spot in anyone's heart was beyond her.

"Come into the kitchen with me, child, and you and I can tackle it while your mother attends to the living room. Sarah, you might want to consider cleaning the birdcage first and putting in some fresh seed. I think Aristotle might actually fly into it by himself if it's not so messy."

Mother smiled at Christal as Aunt Ruth marched into the kitchen. "Guess I'll start with the birdcage then!"

They moved quietly so as not to awaken Mr. Lawrence or startle the bird. Aunt Ruth began the process of heating water for washing the dishes as they both worked on the general disorder of the room.

"It looks like he would get started and then quit," Aunt Ruth said. "Of course he's so sick he probably has the energy of a footstool."

"A footstool?" Christal asked with a grin.

"Don't be impertinent," Aunt Ruth said with a mischievous glint in her eyes. "By the way, do you want to hear about Aristotle?" She picked up a stack of newspapers. "We can take care of these right now. It's only called 'news' when it's new. These probably date back to the Lincoln administration."

She handed the papers to Christal who stacked them by the door. They'd leave a few for cleaning the birdcage, but most of them would be thrown out.

Aunt Ruth ran her hand over the counter. "This needs a good cleaning, too. But about the bird. John was married to a beautiful woman, and he adored her. He was older than she was, maybe fifteen years, possibly twenty. I don't remember exactly. She got sick, though, very early in the marriage, and she didn't live."

"How sad!" Christal exclaimed.

"It was. For the longest time, an aura of melancholy surrounded him. He was there, but he wasn't, if you know what I mean. His heart wasn't in anything he did."

"He must have missed her terribly."

"Oh, he did. He was a good man, but the joy left him when she died. I'm not saying that he never laughed or smiled—he did indeed—but I could tell that he seemed to have buried himself with her."

Christal sighed.

"But then one day he found Aristotle in the yard. The bird was a tiny broken thing, and most of us who knew John thought it was a bad idea for him to get attached to it. It's quite hard to raise a bird anyway, but a wild bird that's just a baby and injured, too—well, we didn't see how the thing could survive. So we discouraged John."

"Wouldn't it be a good thing?" Christal asked, starting to mop the floor. "I'd think it might take his mind off his wife's death."

"Honey, nothing can take your mind off a spouse's death. It comes and sits in you and it never, ever leaves. It's been twenty-seven years since my Theo went to his reward, and there isn't a day I don't think of him. Anyway, we thought John had put all his hope in this little bird, and we knew he'd be devastated if it died, too, but the thing survived and has lived with him ever since."

"Since it's a wild bird, wouldn't it be better if it was outside?" Christal rinsed the mop in her bucket, and as she wrung it out, the water ran so dark it looked like mud.

She remembered her pet toad, and her counterargument that Jesus had been born in a stable, and the explanation her mother had given her that kings can live anywhere but wild animals must live outside.

Aristotle didn't seem like a king.

"I'd think it was unkind to keep the bird inside. It should have been outdoors, where it could fly free," Christal said, leaning down to get a spot she'd missed. "I think Aristotle would be happier if he had the entire neighborhood to annoy."

"He's got something wrong with his wing," Aunt Ruth told her as she attacked grime on the stove. "He can fly a little bit, but he would die outside. So John saved Aristotle, and I think Aristotle saved him."

Christal nodded and peeked around the corner. The bird had moved closer to her mother, who was carefully cleaning out the cage. Now that she understood why Aristotle meant so much to Mr. Lawrence, the bird didn't look quite as disreputable.

It flapped over to her mother, lit on her head, and nipped her ear. Her mother yelped softly with surprise and waved the bird away.

Christal shook her head. No matter what, the bird was cranky, even if it was beloved by Mr. Lawrence.

She and Aunt Ruth set to soaking and washing the dishes. It was quite a process, but apparently Aunt Ruth had never met a plate that she couldn't get clean. She scrubbed until it seemed the pattern might come off.

As Aunt Ruth washed and Christal dried, they talked about the weather and the preparations for Christmas that were already under way even though it was still October. Christal was used to planning for Christmas this early. That was the life of a minister's family. Having two holidays come so close together—Thanksgiving and Christmas, both of which required special services and celebrations—meant they had much to do to be ready.

A church member had proposed that the church supply a festive meal for a poor family or two at Christmas, and at the moment Papa was busily working on the details of such an arrangement.

"People don't always like to be helped," Aunt Ruth said as she handed a pan to Christal. "Here. I finally got the last bits off. I was nearly at the point of throwing it out and simply buying him a new one."

Aunt Ruth sometimes had the ability to carry at least two conversational threads at the same time. Christal had learned to wait it out if it got confusing. Her aunt would eventually resolve it.

"So we have to be careful when we choose this poor family, which is, of course, quite logical. No one wants to be categorized as 'that poor family,' especially then to become the ward of the church no less. So how do we do this without hurting their feelings? Careful, now, I believe that cup is Limoges. And it must be old. I wonder if it wasn't his wife's."

"Mother will know how to do it," Christal said. "She can do that kind of thing."

"The thing is," her aunt said as she wiped out the basin, "to be able to figure this out on your own without relying on her. You're getting old enough that you need to quit expecting her to do everything. Your mother is, without a doubt, the picture of tact, and she will have some way of making the family the church selects feel as if they've won a treasure. But what would *you* say, Christal?"

The question made Christal uneasy. She knew she didn't have her mother's diplomatic skills, and the thought of the possible missteps she could make terrified her. "I probably wouldn't say anything. Maybe, 'Here's some food.'"

Amusement flitted across Aunt Ruth's face. "And then when they asked where the food came from, what would you say?"

"I'd probably stammer out something like, 'People. It came from people.' And then I'd turn and hurry away."

"My dearest niece, you are charming, but you do lack your mother's poise, don't you? I don't think it's quite that simple. John Lawrence is snoozing away in the other room, but what happens when he wakes up and sees that three women have come into his house, uninvited, and cleaned it? What will you say?"

" 'Surprise'? Oh, I don't know. We don't want to say that his home is a mess, do we? But what *can* we say? Maybe we should just sneak out and let him wonder."

"And have him doubt his sanity? He knows what the house looked like when he fell asleep. Imagine his reaction if he wakes up and it's all cleaned."

"Like the shoemaker and the elves!" Christal thought of the fairy tale that had been her favorite when she was a child. She'd hated cleaning her bedroom, so the story of the elves who did the shoemaker's work while he slept had been quite appealing.

"I think he's a bit old for fairy tales. I wonder—"

What her aunt had been about to say was interrupted by a loud snort as John Lawrence woke up in the living room.

"Sarah Everett, what are you doing here?" he asked, his voice still slurred from sleep.

"Listen carefully," Aunt Ruth whispered in Christal's ear. "Learn from what she says."

They moved to the doorway where they could watch but not be seen by the elderly man.

Mother straightened the blanket over his feet. "You've been sick, you know, and my Christal came by with Isaac Bering to visit with you and Aristotle. Do you remember that?"

"Yes." His voice was raspy from the extensive coughing, but the hacking had stopped.

The medicine must be working, Christal thought.

"I wanted to see if there was something you needed, but you were asleep. I hope you don't mind that I let myself in. Christal and Ruth are with me, by the way." She motioned them into the room. "We wanted to visit with you. Aristotle was out of his cage, so I thought it was the perfect opportunity to clean it out."

He nodded, but he seemed a bit confused still.

"While we were waiting, we just puttered around a bit here and there, trying to make things a bit easier for you during your recovery."

"You didn't have to."

Mother patted his hand. "Maybe not, but you can't tell me that if you put three women in a house that's lived in by a man and his bird, that those three women aren't going to be fixing things. Remember when we had that door that wouldn't close? You had stopped by for something else, and when you saw it, you got your tools and dealt with it right then and there."

"Ah, I do remember. That was a long time ago." He put his head against the back of the chair and closed his eyes.

"But I still remember it." Mother smoothed back a strand of white hair that had fallen over his forehead. "One always remembers a kindness."

A smile drifted over his lips before he succumbed again to sleep.

Mother tucked the wrap under his feet again. "Sleep well, my friend."

With those words, the three women tiptoed out of his house and back into the October brightness.

"Are you going on to the library?" Mother asked.

Christal shook her head. What she had just learned today, about giving with kindness, was too big to dilute with a light fable or tale. She looped her arms through her mother's and aunt's. "Let's go home."

—

Isaac closed his Bible and laid it on the table in his room. He'd read through, yet again, the story in Mark of the woman who "suffered many things of many physicians" and who touched the hem of Jesus' clothing and was healed.

Jesus said to her, "Daughter, thy faith hath made thee whole; go in peace, and be whole of thy plague."

He leaned back and thought about those words. John Lawrence had the faith of many, yet he also was not young, and his body wasn't up to the fight that his illness was wreaking. Would his faith make him complete in heaven?

He knew the answer. He opened his Bible once more, but the autumn sun had diffused to twilight, and he struggled to make the words out in the dim surroundings. He could get up and light the lamp, but he wanted to sit and reflect.

Again he closed the Bible, this time holding it against his chest as he shut his eyes and thought.

This had been his first day in the practice of being a doctor. With his uncle, he had seen several patients, but John Lawrence was the one who had crawled inside his heart and stayed there. Perhaps it was because of the old friendship between his uncle and Mr. Lawrence.

Isaac knew that Uncle Alfred had sent him home with Mr. Lawrence for a reason, but he hadn't explained. And while he was certain his uncle hadn't set it up this way, it was interesting that his first patient was a man who was heaven-bound.

He remembered something his father had told him once, that medicine wasn't completely about a physical cure but about making people comfortable on their earthly journey to their reward. Often the two were one and the same, but not always.

Isaac shook his head. He needed to think about something else. He got up, lit the lamp, and picked up the volume his uncle had given him, the Jules Verne novel. Soon he was following the adventures of Phileas Fogg as he tried to circle the world in eighty days.

His mood brightened as he read eagerly, and when finally exhaustion forced him to lay the book aside, he understood why his uncle was so insistent that he develop an outlet like recreational reading. It would serve him well in future days like this.

Isaac got into bed and pulled the blankets up to his chin, staying still until his body warmed up. From below, the calming notes of a Brahms melody floated from the piano as his uncle played before he, too, went to sleep.

It had been quite a day, and as he drifted off, thoughts of a wild bird and an old man mingled with those of a young woman who had a smile like an angel. Yes, it had been quite a day.

Chapter 4

Autumn took its crimson and golden garments and left as November entered with the icy breath of winter. The first frosty flakes of snow fell, melting as they hit the still-warm earth; and then, as the days moved toward the year's end, bit by bit they accumulated into small white drifts along steps and roadsides, around trees and posts.

Christal walked a little faster as she headed toward the library. Her hands were shoved into her pockets because she had, as usual, forgotten her mittens. Aunt Ruth would undoubtedly find them on the floor by the front door and be ready to chide Christal when she got home—a well-deserved rebuke, Christal thought as a gust of wind blew tiny snow particles into her face and down the neck of her coat.

Yes, winter was definitely making an entrance.

At least the library would be warm, and she could shed her coat and warm her hands and devote the rest of the day to her reading. Her parents were on a mercy mission to a family in need of assistance, and she had the entire day to herself. She'd even brought an apple to eat so she wouldn't have to go home for lunch.

Today she had things to think about—or to avoid thinking about—and the library was the perfect place. It had become her second home once she'd gotten strong enough to walk the distance by herself, and she went at least once a week. The librarian teased her that one day she would have read every book there, and then what would she do?

Christal's innocent answer had made the librarian laugh: Weren't there more books being written, more books to buy?

The library was hushed when Christal entered it. She took a deep breath and filled her nostrils with the glorious smell of books. She headed right to her favorite section, the classic tales of other lands.

She ran her fingers over the golden lettering on the books' spines. Today she was in the mood for something exotic. What would it be? Egypt? The stories of the pharaohs and the sphinx were enticing, but she passed them up. Japan? The history of Commodore Perry's expedition there was exciting, but she had read it three times already. Italy? She loved the tales of ancient Rome, with gladiators and the Coliseum, but not today.

Her hand moved farther along, past the stories, past the poetry, until she came to the history section. She stopped at *Palmetto-Leaves*, a book by Harriet Beecher Stowe. Last year she'd read *Uncle Tom's Cabin*, and the story had moved her greatly. She seized on *Palmetto-Leaves* at once, and opened it and leafed through the pages.

It was about Florida, the St. Johns River, to be exact. She had no idea where the river was or if it was anywhere near Key West, where Isaac was from, but a few pages into the book was a map.

The map cut off the very bottom of Florida, which included Key West, she was sure. But she began to read, and from the first chapter, "Nobody's Dog," she was captured. Stowe was such a good writer that soon Christal was caught up in the book.

At last a rumble from her stomach brought her back from Florida and into Minnesota. Lunchtime.

She placed the book on the table with a whispered message to the librarian that she would be back to read further, and she stepped out into the glorious November noon. The snow had stopped and the sun shone brightly in a brilliant blue sky. November certainly could be a beautiful month, she thought.

She fished in her bag and withdrew a red apple that she bit into as she walked around the library. It was housed in a splendid building, the Ingersoll Block, and the library took up the entire second floor of the long, narrow structure.

On the main floor were doctors and dentists, those who didn't have home offices like Dr. Bering. She glanced in a window that was undraped to let in the noonday sun and saw a waiting room, its utilitarian furnishings not nearly as grand as those in Dr. Bering's office.

If she were a doctor, would she want to have her office in her home? She mulled it over as she strolled on slowly, enjoying her apple. There would be the issue of transportation, of course. In winter, travel to and from might be difficult, but on days like this, the early days of winter, being out in the sun was wonderful.

Dr. Bering's office had been in his house for so long, he'd probably never thought of moving it out. As it was, the house was still too large for him, even with his office in it. It was good that Isaac was there with him. He would be a great help in cases like John Lawrence's, where the patient became housebound.

She chewed away the last bits of apple from around the core as she thought about her life. It had been perfect, but it was starting to erode around the edges now that she was worried about Mr. Lawrence, whom she'd known for practically her whole life, and there was nothing she could do to help.

Spending her day in the library was not enough, and, in fact, she felt as if she were idling away her hours there. She should be thinking ahead.

What was her future like? She didn't believe in fortune-telling, but there were times when she'd like a peek into God's plan. What did He have in store for her? Certainly He didn't intend for her to spend the rest of her days in the library reading.

But what was she to do?

She ran through her options.

Could she be a doctor or a nurse and save lives? From what she had learned of the study of medicine from Isaac, she knew she couldn't concentrate to the degree necessary. At her hands, her patients would undoubtedly all fail and die.

She liked ice-skating, but there was no career in that, and besides she wasn't at all good at ice-skating. Her ankles flopped back and forth as if they were made of paper, unless she proceeded very slowly and cautiously.

Music was nice, but her singing voice was dreadful, and she didn't know how to play an instrument. As Dr. Bering had pointed out, she lacked the interest in learning.

Could she be a teacher? Perhaps, but the idea wasn't one she was especially drawn to.

An artist? Her drawings were unrecognizable. A cook? Not when she didn't know how to heat the cookstove. A seamstress? She'd have to be able to thread the sewing machine, or at the very least, a needle.

No, she did what she did best, spending her days in the covers of books at the library. A life of idle, self-centered nothingness.

For the past nine years, she'd taken advantage of her illness, although she hadn't done so consciously. Her parents were so glad to have her alive and well, after nearly losing her to death from scarlet fever and rheumatic fever, that they'd taken almost all responsibility away from her.

It had been too easy to coast along, spending days and then weeks and finally years of a life with no responsibility. The time had come for that to end.

She'd nibbled every possible piece of apple from the core, so she wrapped it carefully in her handkerchief and returned it to her bag. She'd throw it away later.

She returned to the library and gave the book back to the librarian. Maybe she'd come back to it another time, but for the moment, the story had lost its allure.

Slowly she put her coat back on and descended the stairs and went out into the November afternoon.

What was she going to do with her life?

She could be married, that much she knew. It was the usual path for women her age, but so far no one had asked for her hand. She didn't quite believe that she was destined to be an old spinster, but the truth was that she was showing about as much promise as a potential wife as an ice-skater or a cook.

For the past year or so, Aunt Ruth had been spending much of the time before church prodding Christal with her bony elbow, pointing out eligible bachelors. Sometimes Christal was sure that there must be something terribly wrong with her aunt's vision. Just two months ago, she had indicated a man who was twice Christal's age.

That wasn't how God meant for it to be done—Christal was sure of that. She wanted to find this man herself, and to fall in love and live happily ever after like her parents, who were still as openly in love now as they had ever been.

So what about Isaac? The question popped into her thoughts and refused to go away.

So what about Isaac? She let her mind drift over the question. She couldn't get as far as the idea of marrying him, but there was something different about him, something that wasn't like the boys and men she'd met in church.

It was too early to know how it would go with him—if there even was anything to happen. He was a new friend, and she was glad for that.

But if something *could* come of it, well, she would be interested in seeing how it would go.

Maybe there would be more to her life now than reading.

Having an interest in a fellow was new to her, and she had no idea what she was supposed to do.

She grinned. She could ask Aunt Ruth. Somehow she thought the older woman would have hours of advice.

They gathered again in Uncle Alfred's parlor, this time with a plate of gingerbread passing among them. All of them sat in the places they had before, Isaac noted with amusement, just as people sat in the same seats in church week after week.

Christal sat in the rocking chair, her feet tucked under her, and took a piece of gingerbread from the platter. "Thank you so much," she said with a sigh that radiated happiness. "My very favorite food in the world is your spice cookies, Dr. Bering, but your gingerbread comes in a close second." She took a bite and grinned. "They're both especially wonderful this time of year, warming me from the inside out."

"I heard some folks talking at the church today," Rev. Everett said, "that even more snow should come soon."

"Snow?" Isaac sat up straight.

He'd seen snow on the ground now, blown against the corners of the houses and in the cracks of the stone fences on his weekly walk to church, but he hadn't actually seen the snow come down.

The first flakes had fallen while he'd been inside, and he hadn't decided yet if he was glad he'd missed it or if he should have gone out and watched it float down and felt it on his skin. His desire to experience it warred with his concern about the cold. The only time he was truly warm here was when he sat directly in front of the fireplace, and then only one side of him got warm.

His uncle chuckled. "It is November, Isaac. We're heading into winter, and we can expect more snow."

"It gets quite cold here, doesn't it?" Isaac asked. He didn't want to seem like a weakling, worrying all the time about the winter ahead, but the fact was that he didn't truly know what he was in for. He took a measured sip of his tea then asked in a purposefully casual voice, "How cold does it get here, anyway?"

Rev. Everett shrugged. "It's not all that bad. We have houses and fireplaces and blankets, so we make it through all right. I'm sure your uncle will make sure you stay plenty warm here."

Aunt Ruth tapped on the floor with her cane. "The young man asked a question, and he deserves an answer. Alfred, tell him."

His uncle nodded. "You are right as usual, dear Ruth. Sometimes the temperatures do go quite low."

Christal leaned forward. "Like this past January. Remember that?"

"Now, Christal dear." Mrs. Everett frowned at her daughter. "That wasn't quite the average day. It's not fair to—"

Isaac took a deep breath. What was Christal about to say? He had to know. He exhaled slowly and asked. "How cold was it?"

Christal looked at everyone and grinned. "It was thirty-six below zero here in St. Paul."

"Thirty-six below zero." He repeated the words slowly. "Thirty. Six. Below. Zero. I can't even imagine what that's like."

"It's cold," Christal said, and everyone laughed. "But it wasn't as cold as it was in St. Cloud the same day. It was fifty below zero there."

"How do you manage when it's like that?" he asked. "Human skin begins to freeze at the same temperature water does, due to the fluid in the cells. If there is wind, we know that increases the danger of frostbite considerably."

He stopped when he realized that the others were staring at him, slight smiles forming on their faces.

"I am sounding like a textbook, aren't I?" he asked. "I am lecturing you all about frostbite, and yet I've never been anywhere that it was even a danger."

"Well, it's a danger here," Aunt Ruth said, "and I daresay you'll see your fair share of blackened fingers and toes."

Isaac bit back the fear that rumbled in his chest.

"Most of the folks here are pretty much aware how dangerous cold weather can be," his uncle said, "but Ruth is right. Every year I do see some frostbite."

"So is it that cold—what was it, fifty below? All winter long?"

"To be exact, the fifty below was in St. Cloud, which is west of us. We were only thirty-six below. But within three days the temperature rose to almost fifty degrees *above* zero." Rev. Everett smiled. "It was very odd."

Isaac's head spun. The numbers swirled around his brain like a bad dream. What had he undertaken?

"There is one advantage to this cold," Dr. Bering said. "The Winter Carnival! If it weren't for our legendary winters, we wouldn't have this opportunity. By the way, I've heard more about it."

Christal stopped chewing, the gingerbread halfway to her mouth. "Tell us!"

"They met on the second, and they've formed a committee."

Aunt Ruth snorted. "That ought to stop it on the spot."

"Oh, not this group," the doctor continued. "George Finch is heading it, and he's a powerhouse of a leader. So far about forty businessmen are on board."

"Who's George Finch?" Isaac asked.

"He's a top-notch leader in our community, and I'm mighty glad he's going to be leading the group. There's also his partner in the wholesale trade, and a banker and a real estate fellow, and many others. It's going to happen." Uncle Alfred folded his hands over his stomach. "And quickly."

"How quickly?" Christal's gingerbread was still poised midair, forgotten.

"Early in the year. I think they're hoping to have it in February. I don't know exactly."

"That's not very long. What are they planning to do in that short amount of time?" Aunt Ruth asked. "Put together a snow fort and have a snowball fight?"

"Snow fort? Not exactly. More like an ice palace."

"Ohhhh." Christal sighed, and a chunk of gingerbread fell onto her skirt, unnoticed. "An ice palace!" She wriggled excitedly. "Just think of it!"

"Christal Maria Everett, please watch yourself. You have gingerbread in your lap," Aunt Ruth said.

"Sorry." She picked it up with her free hand and popped the stray piece into her mouth.

Isaac held up his hand. "Could we stop for just a moment here? An ice palace? What does that mean?"

"In Montreal, they've been having a winter carnival for a while, but they've got smallpox there, so gathering people together isn't going to happen. The fellows who do the ice palace up there, the Hutchinson brothers, are already here, planning for our carnival's palace." His uncle beamed.

"Can they get it done in time?" Mrs. Everett asked.

Uncle Alfred shrugged. "I suppose. We'll have to see. They'll need help here, that's for certain."

They were going to build a palace out of ice. In Minnesota. In the middle of winter. They were insane. Isaac had no doubt about it now.

"Didn't you just tell me that this past New Year's Day it was a balmy thirty-six degrees below zero?" he asked. "I think I'd rather take my chances with small-pox. If the local people want a festival of some kind, why don't they do it in summer, when it's warm?"

"We have the state fair," Christal offered.

"Aren't there any buildings that could house a winter celebration? Surely there must be a large structure of some kind here that would work."

"The idea," his uncle said, "is to have it outdoors."

"Why?"

"Why not?" Uncle Alfred smiled at him.

"No, not 'why not?' Why? Why on earth would you—" Isaac shook his head.

"An ice palace would have to be outside. Otherwise it would melt," Christal said. Her eyes were glowing. "An ice palace!"

"One more time," Isaac said. "An ice palace is outside because it's got to be cold enough to stay frozen. Stay frozen. Did you hear me? Frozen! Who in their right mind would wander around outside to see a palace made of ice?"

"I would." Mrs. Everett spoke up. "I wonder how big it will be. Is the whole thing going to be made of ice?"

"Maybe there'll be a prince," Christal said, her eyes sparkling with laughter. "An ice prince, and—"

"You live in a world of stories," Aunt Ruth said. "There won't be a prince."

Rev. Everett held up his hand. "Not so fast. Christal isn't that far off with her idea. There will be a king and a queen. I heard about it myself at the church. They're Boreas Rex and Aurora, Queen of the Snows."

"Boreas and Aurora," Christal repeated. "What lovely names."

Isaac viewed his companions in the parlor, all apparently sane people who were now preparing to celebrate winter with an outdoor carnival. Could anything be more insane?

"Are these real people?" Isaac asked. "I mean, are there going to be real people crowned?"

"That's what I was told," the minister answered. "And a Fire King, too. He's the enemy of the King and Queen of the Snows."

Christal's face shone with excitement. "This is going to be so much fun!"

How people could enjoy themselves when they were nearly frozen to death was beyond Isaac's imagination. A festival of frostbite, that's what it would be. It would mean more work at his uncle's office. There would probably be a parade of folks with afflicted fingers and toes and noses during the carnival.

"It will be a great boon to the city," Rev. Everett said. "We need something to brighten up those long winter days."

Isaac noticed his uncle regarding him with a definite twinkle in his eyes. "Isaac, you're not quite ready for this, are you?"

He didn't know how to respond. As much as he wanted to argue the point with the Everetts, this wasn't something that was within his control.

Instead of answering, he merely wrung out a faint smile. It was a crazy idea, this Winter Carnival, but it wasn't his. He needed to let it go and to be supportive as best he could. Debating the merits of an outdoor celebration in the depth of winter wouldn't change anything.

Let it go; let it be, he reminded himself.

The conversation continued until at last Mrs. Everett pointed out that the hour was late, and with a flurry of coats and gloves and scarves, the minister's family was on their way home to the house next door.

His uncle put his arm over Isaac's shoulders as the two of them returned to collect the plates and tidy the parlor.

"Isaac," Uncle Alfred said, "I know it's difficult for you to understand what our life is like up here. But really, it's not that different from Key West. It's colder, of course, but other than that, people are the same wherever you go. They need something to enjoy, something to anticipate."

They could do that indoors, he thought. There was so much wrong with this idea. Not only the cold was a concern, but the fact that the entire carnival was to be put together so precipitously spelled certain failure. Haste did make waste. The proponents of the carnival were ambitious—perhaps too ambitious. The plan was to have this ready in three months?

But one of the lessons he had learned early on in his medical studies was that keeping silent was a talent, one that he had rarely used before embarking on his career. It was, his professor had told the class, the way that learning occurred. One must be silent to listen.

It had been a hard lesson. He had wanted to protest assignments as being overly long and convoluted, but after watching his classmates being chastised for weakness, he had trained himself to keep his opinions private.

He had learned much from his silence, more than he would have gained from speaking out as he'd often wanted to do. Even certain protocols of treatment, which had seemed laboriously involved and ineffective at first glance, had proven to be important ways of working through a particular illness or malady.

He called upon that now.

Uncle Alfred chuckled. "You're holding your tongue, aren't you? That is something you will need to do quite a bit, you know."

Isaac's stomach twisted uneasily. "I should have done that earlier tonight, shouldn't I?"

His uncle patted him on the back. "Just as you need to understand them, they need to understand you. And you have raised some good questions, and good questions need good answers. Let's hope that there are good answers."

The words reassured Isaac somewhat.

"Get some sleep, my boy," Uncle Alfred said. "Tomorrow comes quickly."

Isaac climbed the stairs to his room, feeling so completely awake that slumber seemed impossible.

He'd taken another of his uncle's books with him, this time a book by a man named Mark Twain. Uncle Alfred had said he'd find the book, *The Celebrated Jumping Frog of Calaveras County and Other Stories*, amusing. Perhaps he could lose himself in the stories. But as he readied himself for bed, the heavy weight of exhaustion fell on him.

He clambered under the covers as quickly as possible to avoid touching the cold wooden floor with his bare feet, his Bible in his hands. The lamp beside him illuminated the pages as he leafed through it in search of some wisdom. He especially liked the Psalms for their praise and comfort. Psalm 4:8 made him smile: *"I will both lay me down in peace, and sleep: for thou, Lord, only makest me dwell in safety."*

Even when it was thirty-six degrees below zero.

With the words of the psalmist in his mind, he closed his eyes, let a prayer settle over his heart, and gave the worries of the day to the Lord.

No music came into Christal's room tonight. The window was closed and latched, as if the early blasts of winter's chill might sneak under the wooden frame with icy fingers and raise the pane.

The evening's conversation swirled in her head, the words as thrilling as the notes of a symphony.

A winter carnival! With a king and a queen and a palace!

She couldn't sit. She walked over to the window and gazed out. The only light on in the house next door was in the parlor, and it soon was extinguished.

How could anyone sleep with this new knowledge?

The palace would be made of ice, her father had said. How would they do it? Would the builders use blocks of ice as if they were bricks? Would it be white when it was done, or would it be transparent?

How big was it going to be? What if it were as big as her house? Even as small as a dollhouse would be wonderful.

She'd never thought about a palace made of ice.

Aunt Ruth was right. It was like a story, one of the fairy tales that she read again and again at the library. But there had never been such a story as this one. And it would be real!

How could she wait?

An ice castle. A snow king and queen. The adversary of fire. It *was* like a story.

An idea flitted into her mind and batted against the edges of her imagination like a butterfly, faintly at first and then with increasing urgency. A story began to take shape.

Maybe she could be a writer! With her love of stories, she could do that. What would she need to do? She'd have to put these ideas down in words. How hard could it be?

She thought about it more, but it simply wouldn't go past the vague notion of the wonderful images, and she realized that without a plot, the pictures in her mind would stay that way—just pictures.

And she definitely wasn't an artist, so she couldn't transfer them from what she saw in her head to colorful designs on paper.

Christal sighed. She couldn't be a writer, and she couldn't be an artist.

What was she going to do?

The fact was that there weren't a lot of options available to women. Homemaker. Mother. Wife.

She knew that there were some careers open to her. There were writers. She considered Harriet Beecher Stowe, whose book she had been reading at the library. Now there was a woman who was a successful author. *Uncle Tom's Cabin* was a well-known and highly respected book.

There were a smattering of female artists, none of them as popular as their male counterparts, and only a few whose names were familiar to the populace of St. Paul.

It's not that I want to be famous, God, she prayed, *but I'm searching for something to make my life meaningful. I want to make the most of this time here on earth. I could use Your help. If I have a direction, could You guide me to it, please?*

What she really wanted from her life, though, was to make a difference somehow, like Isaac was doing, or was going to do. If only there were a way to somehow have an impact upon another person. Doctors did. Ministers like her father did.

As a woman, her choices were curtailed. Housekeeper, wife, mother. That about summed up her future.

Housekeeper? She looked around her room. Books and papers were piled haphazardly on the floor. Her clothing from the day was draped over the back of the chair. Her hairbrush was on the table, and one shoe was near the window and the other near the door, exactly where they had landed when she'd kicked them off after unbuttoning them.

Wife? Wouldn't she need a husband for that? And if it did happen—she tucked the bright image of Isaac far back into the distant recesses of her mind for the moment—she'd have to know how to do things like cook and sew.

Mother? She thought of her own sweet mother, how she offered advice, how she'd guided Christal through the perilous journey of childhood and into womanhood, how she'd taught her right from wrong. Being a mother was a job that required great things from a woman. Did she have what it would take?

She buried her face in her hands. It was hopeless.

Or was it?

She needed to focus. Even Mrs. Harriet Beecher Stowe, famous novelist though she was, knew how to cook a roast.

It was time she learned.

Chapter 5

Christal bounced into the kitchen the next morning, filled with resolve. She tied on an apron and said to her mother and aunt, "Teach me to make eggs."

"Only God can make an egg," her father said from behind the newspaper as Aunt Ruth tipped the teapot to fill up her cup.

It was an old joke, but she grinned.

"True, but I am going to make your breakfast egg."

Aunt Ruth stopped midpour. "Excuse me? You?"

"Yes. And I'm going to make the toast, too."

Mother came up behind her and touched her cheek gently. "Dear, I've already prepared breakfast. Your father's egg and his toast are done."

"But I wanted to—"

"Come and sit with us. Your oatmeal is waiting. I made it the way you like it, with brown sugar and cream. Here. Eat it while it's warm before it gets cold."

Her determination crumbled. She did like her oatmeal. Nice and hot, with a sprinkling of sweet brown sugar and a drizzle of cool cream. She started to sit down, but as she did, she remembered her resolution of the night before.

"I need to learn how to do it," she said, standing up again.

Her mother and Aunt Ruth exchanged surprised looks.

"To what do we owe this sudden burst of interest in cooking?" her aunt asked.

Christal stood as straight as she could. "The time has come. I'm old enough that I should know these things."

"Well," her mother said, "that's commendable."

"I'm ready to learn."

"And we are quite pleased," her father said, lowering the paper and folding it carefully, "but the fact is, Christal, breakfast is already made. Perhaps you could embark on breakfast tomorrow."

"You'd have to get up earlier," Aunt Ruth added. "Eggs don't cook themselves."

Mother smiled. "A hard-boiled egg, the way your father likes it, does take twenty-two minutes."

"Twenty-two minutes," Christal echoed faintly.

Her mother smiled. "Oatmeal requires only five minutes to prepare, and putting the toppings on it to make it special doesn't take long at all."

How was it possible that something as delicious as oatmeal took a fraction of the time that a hard-boiled egg did?

"If you're truly interested in learning to cook," her mother said, "you can help me with the noon meal. I'll be roasting a chicken. That's not at all difficult, and it would be a good place to start."

Roast chicken sounded good. She knew how to simply roast it, but her mother added a rub of herbs that made the chicken incredibly delicious.

"We're having the chicken and root vegetables," Mother continued, "and biscuits with gravy. But today we'll start with the chicken and carrots and potatoes. We'll deal with the biscuits another day."

"Not another day," Christal protested. "I want to learn it today."

"Rome wasn't built in a day," her father said as he stood up and carried his dishes from the table.

"I'm not building Rome. I just want to make a meal. All of it."

Papa smiled. "I'll let you womenfolk figure this out. I have a meeting at the church that I'll be late for if I don't hurry along. I'll see you all at noon."

After he left, Mother and Aunt Ruth began clearing the table. Christal scraped the last of her oatmeal from her bowl and stood up to help.

"I'm delighted to see that you've developed a desire to learn about meals," her aunt said as Christal reached for the creamer at the same time the elderly woman did, with the end result that the cream splashed across the linen tablecloth.

Tears stung Christal's eyes. She'd wasted the cream, and the tablecloth would have to be washed. She tried to help, but instead she made more work for her mother and aunt.

"I'm sorry," she said, untying the apron and slipping it over her head. She threw it on the counter in an untidy heap. "I'm so sorry."

Mother quickly came to her side and wrapped her in a soothing embrace. "Christal, my dearest Christal, it's all right."

"No, it isn't." Her voice was muffled against her mother's shoulder. "I've spilled the cream and soiled the tablecloth, and you all must think I am such a clumsy goose."

It was so tempting to let her mother spoil her more, to excuse her deficiencies, but she needed to be strong. She had so much to learn, and at the same time, she had to fight against her own tendency to take the easy way.

"There, there. The creamer was almost empty, and the tablecloth needed to be washed anyway," her mother murmured.

"We all make mistakes," Aunt Ruth said in her no-nonsense voice. "There's no use crying over spilt milk—or spilt cream. It doesn't put it back in the pitcher."

"I won't start preparing the chicken until midmorning," her mother said. "Why don't you go for a walk and get your head cleared, and when you come back, we can discuss what needs to be done to make a nice meal."

"We'll finish up here." Her aunt refolded the napkins at each chair.

Perhaps it was for the better, anyway. If she stayed, she would probably drop a plate or stab herself with a fork.

She fled the dining room and seized her coat from the rack in the front hall. Slipping into it as she left the house, she started up the street, following her usual path toward the library.

"Christal!" Isaac called to her from the doorway of Dr. Bering's house.

She swiped at her nose as surreptitiously as she could. Why was it that the slightest onset of tears made her nose run like a river?

"Yes?"

"Are you going by John Lawrence's house?"

"I wasn't planning on it. Why?" Of course he wanted her to stop and talk when her face was swollen and red from crying. She tucked her chin down and studied the ground beneath her feet as if it were the most fascinating thing in the world.

"Could you do me a favor?" He stepped away from the door a bit and shivered. "I have another bottle of medicine I wanted to get to him, but I don't want him to have to come here, not in this cold. I was going to take it to him, but my uncle had two patients show up this morning, and I'm really needed here."

"Sure, I can take it to him."

"Come on in, then, and I'll give it to you."

He waited until she arrived at the door before going back inside, even though he was in shirtsleeves.

The bottle was on the table by the door.

"He knows how much to take, but if you don't mind," he said, "I'd appreciate it if you could make sure he gets it in him as soon as possible. He told Uncle Alfred two days ago that he was running out, but he didn't come in to get it."

"You're worried, aren't you?" she asked softly.

He tried to look stalwart but failed. "I am," he said at last. "It's not like him."

"I'll take it right over."

"I appreciate it." He walked her to the door. "And Christal, thank you. I don't know how to repay you—"

"Repay me? For what?"

"For doing this. For caring."

"Here's how you can repay me. Pray for Mr. Lawrence."

"I do," he said. "I do."

She believed that he did.

He opened the door and said with delight, "It's snowing!"

"Just barely," she said, unable to keep the merriment from her voice. He sounded like the children in the church seeing the first snow of winter. They'd all run outside and stand like turkeys, stock-still, their heads back, with their mouths open to catch the flakes on their tongues.

"I've never seen it snow before," he said, his voice filled with awe.

"Oh, you have, too!" Christal rubbed her toe in the snow that had drifted up against the stoop. "See? Snow! You silly!"

He smiled at her. "I've never seen it as it was coming out of the sky. I've only seen the icy evidence."

"Well," she said, "you'll see it falling a lot. Wait until it snows big, fluffy, white flakes at sunset. That is absolutely beautiful."

"I can imagine." He wrapped his arms around his torso. "It's beautiful but cold. Brrr! You'd better button that coat! And don't you have any gloves?"

"Aunt Ruth told you to say that, didn't she?"

He laughed. "She's a smart woman."

"She is."

They stood together, unwilling to part, until at last he shivered wildly. She hadn't even thought about the fact that he was standing outside with her, and he was still in shirtsleeves.

She put her hand on his sleeve. It was slightly damp where the snow had fallen on it. "You're cold," she said, "and I need to get this to Mr. Lawrence."

"Yes," he agreed.

Light snowflakes fell on her eyelashes, and she blinked them away. With a quick nod and smile, she turned and ran down the steps.

As she scurried toward John Lawrence's house, she was aware of Isaac's gaze following her until she was out of his sight.

The day had greatly improved.

The more she knew of Isaac, the more she liked him. He was a caring man, and he was showing that he would probably be a doctor like his uncle, treating the human being as well as the disease.

Her fingers closed tightly over the bottle she was taking to Mr. Lawrence. His cough had punctuated the Sunday service so much that he'd finally had to leave and listen to the sermon from the vestibule. He didn't seem to be getting better.

Her feet sped toward his house, and soon she was at his front door, knocking. "Mr. Lawrence? Mr. Lawrence? It's Christal Everett. I have your medicine from Dr. Bering."

There was no response from inside, and she pounded on the door. "Mr. Lawrence? Mr. Lawrence? It's Christal Everett!"

A faint sound from within beckoned her to open the door a crack and call again. "Mr. Lawrence? Are you all right? Might I come in?"

A bird's screech from the living room brought her in to see John Lawrence slumped in his chair, his chest rising and falling violently as he gasped for air. From the top of the floor lamp, Aristotle hopped from one leg to the other nervously as she felt for the man's pulse. It was rapid and erratic.

"I'll be right back," she promised him.

She ran out of the house and down the streets until she reached the Bering house. Without knocking, she burst in.

Dr. Bering and Isaac looked up from a sheaf of papers in surprise. "Christal, child, what on earth is the matter?" Dr. Bering asked.

She panted, out of breath and unable to form the words. Instead, she pointed in the direction of the Lawrence residence.

"Your house? Something is wrong at your house?" the doctor guessed.

Isaac was already reaching for his coat. "It's John Lawrence, isn't it?"

Dr. Bering handed his nephew his bag. "Take this. You may need it. I have an appointment with a woman who is due to give birth soon, so I need to stay here. Do you know what to do, Isaac?"

Isaac nodded as he wound a muffler around his neck. "Body temperature, clear airway if necessary, start steam, inhalants as needed." He stared at his gloves. One was brown leather, the other a red and black knit. He shook his head and pulled them on. "I'll figure it out later."

"Have your mother and aunt meet him there," Dr. Bering said to Christal as Isaac left. "They'll know what to do."

Tears gathered in her eyes. "He's dying, isn't he?"

Dr. Bering patted her shoulder. "He may be. This is why I want your mother and aunt with Isaac."

"He'll know what to do, won't he?" She tried to keep the worry out of her voice but knew she failed.

"I have the greatest confidence in his abilities, but remember that this is new for Isaac. He's just now learning what it's like to work with real people with real problems, not those in the textbooks he had at school. He needs to have those around him who have experience with the ill."

She nodded, numb with the realization of what was happening.

"I understand," she whispered. "I'll get my mother and Aunt Ruth. I'm sure they'll know what to do."

As she started to leave, he called to her. "Christal, one more thing. Your father is a minister. You've been in the faith since the day you were born. You know what sickness is like, and you also know the strength of the human will. It's a gift from our Lord, this intense love we have for life, the way we cling to it and let go of it so reluctantly. Never underestimate that power."

"I know, and I believe in my heart and in my soul that the body does not last, but we do live on in His presence." She blinked as tears gathered in her eyes. "But it doesn't make it any easier."

He nodded. "I often think, when I see some of the things that befall our bodies, that we are perhaps fortunate to spend eternity without them."

"That's true."

"But let's not send our friend into heaven quite yet." He smiled at her.

She hugged him and hurried next door.

Her mother and Aunt Ruth were just finishing the breakfast dishes. Had all this happened in such a short time? It seemed as if the morning had been going on for quite a long time. She told them what was going on, and the two women quickly whipped off their aprons and walked quickly to the entryway for their wraps.

"Could you finish up for us, Christal?" her mother asked. "There isn't much left to do to bring the kitchen to rights. Just wiping off the last pans and putting away the cutlery."

"I will." Christal chewed on her lip. "He's going to be all right, isn't he? Mr. Lawrence, that is?"

Mother laid her gloves on the table in the hall and took both of Christal's hands in hers. "I hope so, but he is a very ill man, and he's a very old man. Those two factors don't bode well."

Aunt Ruth cleared her throat. "He's much older than I am, but I don't want to be clever about that and pretend that I am still young. I am not. When our bodies age, any sickness takes a greater toll on us than it does when we are young. We don't have quite the resources someone who is, say, in their twenties might have. We're weakening, and it's all part of God's plan."

Christal turned to her aunt, who stood tall and straight, as stately as ever. For the first time, she noticed the beginning of wrinkles on her face and neck, the white strands that sprinkled the upswept dark hair. Had she been so absorbed in herself that she hadn't noticed the changes in those around her?

Aunt Ruth settled her scarf and met Christal's gaze with her eyes still as sharp and shining as bright black buttons. "Don't worry, Christal. I am in excellent health. When the good Lord decides to take me, I suspect He will do so as quickly as possible, probably to avoid the potential that I might argue with Him otherwise. I do enjoy living, and I have no intention of leaving this earth anytime soon."

"We must hurry," Mother said. "Christal, I don't know how long we will be gone, so could you please stay? If we're not back when your father comes home for his noon meal, there is enough beef left that if sliced carefully, can serve both of you. A cold meal won't hurt either of you. There's bread in the box, of course. And butter in the—"

Aunt Ruth tapped her cane on the floor. "Sarah, if you insist upon giving the girl an inventory of what's in the kitchen, we may never get there. She is smart enough to figure it out herself."

"That's true." Mother kissed Christal's forehead. "I'm sorry about the cooking lesson being delayed, but I think you understand."

Christal nodded. There were a few things more important than a roast chicken.

The two women left, and suddenly the house, which Christal had lived in for most of her life, seemed large and empty. There was nothing to do except get busy.

She returned to the kitchen and picked up the apron she'd discarded earlier. Of course she had dropped it on the counter, but her mother had picked it up and hung it on the hook by the door.

She pulled it over her head and tied it in the back and looked at the task she'd been left.

There were two pans left to dry and a handful of forks and spoons to be put into the drawer. It would take her moments to finish that.

Maybe she should address the beef and the carrots that her mother had told her about. There was no use waiting until the very last minute.

She dug them out of the icebox and examined them. The piece of beef that her mother referred to didn't seem as if it would feed one person, let alone two. The carrots were fine, but her father couldn't have a meal of carrots only.

She took the towel from the rack and dried the remaining two pans, put them away, and sorted the forks and spoons into the appropriate slots in the cutlery drawer.

Again, she regarded the little bit of food that was available to her. Unless she was to serve her father a carrot sandwich, she'd have to think of something else.

She peeked in the icebox again. Ah. There it was. The solution.

⌒

"Inhale."

Isaac placed his hand on John Lawrence's chest. There was almost no muscle tone, and he could easily feel each rib as the man tried to breathe.

His uncle should have come. He wasn't prepared to see a patient on his own, especially one this ill. This was a doctor's realm, and he was a mere student.

From the kitchen came the subdued sounds of Mrs. Everett and Aunt Ruth as they tidied up the kitchen and boiled water to make steaming vats to place around the patient.

"Don't fight it. Go ahead," Isaac urged. "Breathe in, as deeply as you can."

"I'll cough," Mr. Lawrence said in a weak voice.

"Then cough. You need to. It's the way your body clears out the infection that's clogging your lungs. Take a deep breath, as full as you can. Go past the urge to cough."

"Can't." The older man bent over as a series of spasms jerked his torso.

He was clearly fighting the cough, and Isaac didn't blame him. Mr. Lawrence's throat was raw from it, and his entire being was simply tired of it.

Isaac knelt. "I want to make sure you're getting enough oxygen. The problem with what you have is that inhaling triggers the cough reflex, so you're breathing very shallowly. Let's try it two different ways. First, breathe in slowly."

Mr. Lawrence took a breath and stopped as a cough burst out.

"That's fine. Let's try this then," Isaac said. "Breathe in as rapidly and deeply as you can."

Mr. Lawrence tried it, and only at the end did he cough.

"Good! I'm not saying you can breathe like that all the time—it'd be a neat trick if you could, but you'd end up so light-headed you might faint—but I'd say every couple of minutes, if you could do that, your body would appreciate it."

For a few minutes, the two men breathed together, the strong lungs and the weak lungs, in unison as if one could lend the other some of his vigor.

"I do feel a bit better," the patient said at last.

Isaac laughed. "I'm not surprised. Our bodies need oxygen. It feeds our brains and our blood and our muscles. I wish I had some way to pipe it into you, but I don't."

As he settled the man into an upright position, pointing out that he'd be more likely to breathe better if he were sitting up straight, he talked to him about his illness.

"You have heavily congested lungs. I'd like to dry them out, but that very act of drying them out will cause increased coughing, and you're quite cachectic."

"Of course I am," Mr. Lawrence said with a little smile. "What on earth does that mean?"

"I'm sorry," Isaac answered, mentally reviewing one of the lessons of medical school, that a doctor should speak using words that the patient will understand and avoid terminology that is specific to physicians. "I mean simply that your body as a whole is suffering."

It wasn't a true definition. What it meant was that the patient was wasting away. His skin was thin, only a loose covering over his skeleton. He was so gaunt that every bone showed. There was no muscular definition.

It was the circular dilemma of a major illness. Because he was sick, his body was atrophying. And because it was atrophying, he couldn't fight the illness. He didn't have the strength.

"Your uncle and I have talked quite a bit about death. He has told me I'm dying." Mr. Lawrence's voice was reedy, like a child's.

"He did?" Isaac stopped midmotion. In his studies, he had been taught that one should never tell a patient that he was dying. One reason was that it might not be true, and the other was that patients often simply gave up upon hearing the news.

Mr. Lawrence's chuckle sounded like wind through dry grasses, and he stopped for a paroxysm of coughing "I'm sorry," he said at last. "I'll have to do that inhalation business you showed me."

Isaac nodded. "Indeed."

"You seemed surprised that your uncle was blunt with me. Am I right?"

Isaac pondered how to respond. He didn't want to make Uncle Alfred look bad in the eyes of his patient, but he was curious as to why he'd said such a thing. "You and my uncle go back quite a ways, I understand," he said at last, opting for a nonanswer.

"We do. I've got some illness in my lungs, and it's got one of those names that I couldn't pronounce for the life of me, no pun intended. But here's what else I know, and what your uncle knows. I'm eightysomething—I quit counting birthdays long ago—and I'm looking at heaven. As a matter of fact, I'm right at the gate. I can even peek through the slats and see the other side."

Isaac smiled at the old man's imagery.

"Everybody my age is nearing the end anyway, but when you're my age and sick. . ." Mr. Lawrence shrugged, and a round of coughing took over. "Your uncle is younger than I am, but he and I did indeed discuss being at our stage of life, when our bodies fail. We're like old wagons. Oh, maybe our wheels don't fall off, but the axle sure gets cracked. At some point, we're past the point of repair."

"Oh, I don't believe that," Isaac said heartily. "Medicine is doing quite a bit of wonderful things and soon—"

"Soon we'll live to be as old as Methuselah? What does the Bible say? How old was he?"

"Nine hundred sixty-nine years." Isaac grinned. "Everybody back then lived for a long time. Jared was 962 years old when he passed on. Lamech was 777 years old when he died."

Mr. Lawrence waved it away. "Older than I'd want to be. Can you imagine what a thousand-year-old man would look like? What could he do? Do I want a couple hundred years of mashed food?"

Aristotle, who'd been sleeping through most of the ministrations, woke up and flew across the room, raucously shrieking as he barely missed Isaac's head.

"And besides, unless my dear Aristotle can live long, too, why would I want to?"

Mr. Lawrence was smiling when he said it, but Isaac knew how attached he was to his bird. And the heart, when it lacked a reason to go on beating, often simply stopped.

"I reminded your uncle that although I may not last here on earth much longer, I have a home awaiting me in heaven," Mr. Lawrence continued. He wheezed and coughed, and Isaac knew the discussion was wearing him out. But it was all right. He needed to say what he was saying.

"That's very true."

"Is the minister's wife in the kitchen? Is that her I hear rattling around in there?"

"She and Ruth Everett are both in there."

"Will you ask Sarah to come out here?"

Isaac stood and went into the kitchen.

"How's he doing?" Mrs. Everett asked.

"He's very sick, but I think we can make him comfortable. He needs to have some nutrition for one thing, so if you could make some broth to start, that would be great. Of course, the steam pots will help clear the congestion, too."

"I can do that. I'll run home and get that chicken and start stewing it," Ruth said. "It'll make good stock and some healthy soup when he's up for it."

"That sounds good. Meanwhile," he said to Christal's mother, "he's asking for you."

"For me?"

She took off her apron and hurried into the parlor. "John, what can I do for you?"

"You're a Bible-toting woman."

"I believe you could call me that." She looked at Mr. Lawrence, her eyes brimming with amusement. "Just as you're a Bible-toting fellow."

"I am, but I'm too spent at the moment to locate what I want to hear now. Can you find me that part about what heaven is like? You know, the verses about our future homes being mansions?"

" 'In my Father's house are many mansions'?"

"That's the one. You don't need the Bible for this one, do you?"

"I don't. It's a beautiful passage. It's from John 14. 'Let not your heart be troubled: ye believe in God, believe also in me. In my Father's house are many mansions: if it were not so, I would have told you. I go to prepare a place for you. And if I go and prepare a place for you, I will come again, and receive you unto myself; that where I am, there ye may be also.' "

"I'm going there—you know that, don't you?" he asked.

Isaac stood off to the side, wanting to be respectful.

Mrs. Everett touched Mr. Lawrence's arm. "Oh, John, I hope we all are. We just arrive at different times."

"I'll be there before you."

She fussed with the cloth of his sleeve. "Maybe. God will take us when it's our time to go. Until then, though, we need to live as fully as we can here on earth."

Mr. Lawrence coughed, and Isaac reached out to give him his medicine. Mr. Lawrence held up his hand in objection.

"The medication will give you relief from the coughing," Isaac said.

"It makes me sleepy. I take it, and almost immediately I fall asleep."

"Yes, it will do that," Isaac answered. "It's formulated for that very purpose. It has an ingredient that lets you sleep."

"Lets me sleep? Makes me sleep!" Mr. Lawrence's words were grumbling, but a small smile twitched at the edges of his mouth.

"You need to rest." Isaac offered the spoon again, and the patient shook his head.

"I'll make sure he takes it," Christal's mother said.

"I'm going to get lectured, aren't I?" Mr. Lawrence asked mournfully.

"You are. You need to do exactly as the doctor orders. Take your medicine now. Later Ruth will bring you some broth, and I will sit here myself and make sure you drink it. After the broth, we'll graduate you to soup."

"And from there, on to pork chops!" Coughing caught at the laughter and stopped it.

"Yes, pork chops."

There was nothing more for Isaac to do at the moment. With the medicinal syrup at work in Mr. Lawrence's exhausted system, he'd soon sleep. Already the man's eyes were hooded with fatigue, and his breathing, with the coughing spasms eased, was regular and, Isaac was gratified to see, deeper, getting oxygen to his starved cells.

"You can go," Mrs. Everett said at last. "I'll stay with him."

"Thank you."

He knew that John Lawrence would be in good hands with her at his side. The woman had the soul of a saint. She could handle any emergency that came her way.

Christal's aunt came to the door between the living room and the dining room. "Isaac, I hate to take you away from the business of doctoring, but I'd like to get the chicken soup started so it's ready when John wakes up. Everything is here except the chicken." She chuckled. "It's pretty important to have chicken in your chicken soup. If you wouldn't mind, could you go to our house and pick up the chicken? Oh, and a few more potatoes and carrots. John's produce bin is looking a bit spare. Christal's home. She'll put it all in the stockpot for you."

Isaac's heart lightened. He knew what awaited him at the Everett house. Christal's buoyant good spirit, her indefatigable joy of living, and her bright happiness with life in general lifted his mood every time. After a struggle like today, he needed her effervescence.

He hurried his way there, smiling as he imagined her shining face.

At the house, he knocked on the door and waited, tapping his fingers against each other in anticipation.

There was no answer.

He knocked again. Still, no one came to the door.

His disposition lost its glow. She must have left the house.

Still, the chicken was needed. Perhaps she hadn't locked the door when she left? He turned the handle of the heavy door cautiously, and it swung open.

Immediately he reeled at the smell. It hung in the air, acrid and sharp. Something had been on fire.

"Christal? Christal?"

He clapped his hand over his nose and mouth and tried to breathe shallowly, which was nearly impossible in his abrupt state of panic.

"Christal?" he called again, and then, with more urgency, again. "Christal!"

His heart leaped into his throat and beat rapidly. Christal hadn't come to the door. Could it have been because she was unable to?

The thought stabbed him, and he nearly doubled over from the pain. But a rush of sudden energy gave wings to his feet, and he sprinted through the house, following the bitter cloud that hovered over his head. Within seconds he was at the source of the smell.

A haze hung in the kitchen, and the odor was dreadful. Christal stood at the counter, her hair sliding out of the braid at the back of her neck. Her apron was festooned with multicolored stains, and a smudge of black ran across her nose. A curl of carrot peel was stuck over her ear, and shreds of potato skins lay scattered around her feet.

At her side in an instant, he enveloped her in his arms, carrot peelings and all, and buried his face against the top of her head. "Christal, you're not injured, are you? Was there a fire? Were you burned? If you are, I could, you know, I'm a doctor, or almost, and—oh, my dear, my dear, my dear."

He knew he was babbling, but he couldn't stop. If anything had happened to her—it was too much to even consider.

"I'm fine." She sniffled against his chest.

Relief mingled with love, he murmured wordlessly as he held her against him. His mouth moved over her head in a series of kisses that flowed like water.

Dear God, thank You! She isn't injured, she isn't burned, and she's in my arms. Dearest God, thank You!

The smell was distinct around her, and even more so as he buried his lips into her hair.

"What's burned?" he asked, pulling back a bit. "It smells like—it smells like hair! Like burned hair!"

"It might be." Christal sniffed and wiped the back of her hand across her cheek, leaving yet another dark smear.

"Is it—*your* hair?" Isaac asked cautiously. The kitchen was a terrible mess. Bits and pieces of food were everywhere, and water pooled on the floor in front of the stove. And above it all, the sharp reek of burned hair permeated the air.

"Yes."

She turned and showed him the awful truth. A section of her hair, over her left eye, was singed off. A short bit, perhaps an inch and a half, stuck straight out, the ends ragged and uneven where they'd been burned.

"I made a little mistake. I'm not sure exactly how."

"Here, sit down." He guided her to the little table at the end of the counter and pulled out a chair for her and one for himself. "Can I get you a drink of water?"

She nodded and waved toward the counter. "I was going to make some tea."

"Did you burn your hair then?" he asked, getting up to find an empty cup and a tin of tea next to it. The water was hot on the back of the stove—probably, he thought, a way of keeping the room warm at the same time—and he opened drawers until he found a tea ball. He made a pot of tea and then poured them both cups.

She wrapped her hands around the cup as if seeking the warmth.

"What happened?" he asked again.

She looked at him, her blue eyes filled with tears. "I was burning the feathers off the chicken."

He had no idea what she was talking about. "Christal," he began, realizing he was in uncharted waters, "this chicken had feathers?"

"All chickens do," she said. She stared at him, as if he had taken total leave of his senses.

He tried to redeem himself. "Well, I know they start with feathers. I understand, however, that one plucks a chicken rather than burning the feathers off."

She nodded.

"And," he continued, "I don't know anything about cooking a chicken, but I'm pretty sure they come with their feathers already off. This one didn't?"

"Most of them. But my mother always burns off the pinfeathers," she said. "I've seen her. She singes them off."

"How?" He almost dreaded the answer.

"She uses a match."

"And you caught your hair on fire doing that?"

She shook her head. "No."

"Then how did you do it?"

She sighed. "I had peeled the potatoes and scraped the carrots. I was going to put them in the stockpot, but then I remembered that I'd done it backwards, that Mother always started the chicken first. So I pushed them aside, and I got the match, and I singed off the pinfeathers just fine."

He rested his chin on his hand. He adored this woman, but she was taking forever to get to the point. "And the fire?" he prompted.

She shrugged. "I got too close to the match, and the next thing I knew, I was on fire." She looked sadly at the disarray around her. "I made a mess—a mess of the kitchen and a mess of myself. And everything smells really bad, doesn't it?"

"I am not going to lie to you," he said, smiling at her. She really looked pitiful, sitting at the table, trying to stick her singed hair back into place and being quite unsuccessful. "Yes. Burned hair is quite, um, aromatic, shall we say?"

As much as he would have liked to linger and talk with her, he had a mission to fulfill—getting the chicken for Christal's aunt to make soup with. He spoke to her of it.

"Take it," Christal said, pushing the stockpot toward him. "You're lucky you got here when you did, or it would have been ruined."

He glanced inside and saw a sad-looking chicken, its skin charred here and there, evidence of her failed culinary efforts.

She sat up suddenly as the grandfather clock in the parlor chimed. "Oh no! Papa will be home in minutes, and look at this place! Look at me! Nothing is ready for him to eat!"

She leaped to her feet and began sweeping up the mess on the kitchen floor. "Put the vegetables in the pot and run the chicken to Aunt Ruth, please, and let me get this place put to rights!"

He took the heap of scraped carrots and potatoes, added them to the pot, and put the lid on the top. His muffler had gone awry, and he began to straighten it, turning to say good-bye to her.

She was on her knees on the floor again, trying to scoop up the fallen potato peelings, and from the audible sniffling, he knew she was crying again.

"Let me help." He dropped to the floor beside her and gathered up the scrapings for her.

"I wanted to help," she said, wiping the back of her hand across her eyes. "That's all I wanted to do today was help. Nobody wanted my help. Not you, not your uncle, not my mother, not my aunt, nobody. So I tried to do something on my own, something that would be helpful, and look what I did! And now you want to help me? I can't do anything on my own."

He took her hands in his, ignoring the stray peelings and scrapings that adorned their wrists and fingers. "Christal, it's a matter of learning," he said, "and that in itself has its own run of fits and starts. You'll learn to cook by your mistakes as well as your successes. I'm sure that's how your mother learned. We all do."

"My mother's perfect."

He chuckled. "She may be, but I suspect that she had her trials along the way, too. She has, I'm sure, burned toast and oversalted stew."

"Maybe," she said, her voice brimming with doubt, "but when I compare myself to her. . ."

He stood up. "I have to get this chicken to the Lawrence household, but before I go, I want to remind you that comparing yourself to your mother is probably not the best idea. She has much more experience than you do. I suspect that what makes us all better at everything we do is actually doing it, getting the experience."

"And praying that you don't catch anything on fire," she added morosely.

"That, too."

Together they added the last of the ingredients to the pot, a pungent onion and three smashed garlic cloves.

Within minutes, he was on his way to John Lawrence's house, the filled stockpot in his hands.

Mr. Lawrence still slept soundly, he was gratified to see. Mrs. Everett sat beside him, humming softly. Isaac handed the pot to Aunt Ruth, who made a face. "That's a strong onion!"

He breathed a sigh of relief. The onion had covered whatever smell of smoke might be lingering on him.

After reassuring himself that Mr. Lawrence was stable, he hurried back to his uncle's house.

He'd have to focus on the patients at hand and get his mind off the feeling of Christal in his arms.

He'd known her such a short time. He needed to rein in his feelings for her. She was a minister's daughter, after all, and although he'd never romanced one before, he was sure that the daughter of a churchly man would require a slower approach. Plus there was the fact that any courting would have to wait until he finished his studies.

Nevertheless, what had he done? He'd kissed her! Not on the lips, but that nuzzling the top of her head was kissing as sure as the sun rose each day.

He shouldn't have, but it seemed so right.

"How's John?" Uncle Alfred asked when Isaac entered the house, rubbing his hands together to warm them.

"He's congested, and his lungs are filling." The answer was short but to the point. The image of Christal was driven from his mind and replaced with the thin face of John Lawrence. "He's failing."

Isaac dropped onto the overstuffed chair and buried his face in his hands. "How do you do this, Uncle? How?"

Uncle Alfred walked to him and patted his shoulder. "In order to be strong in death, we have to believe in life. You believe in life, don't you?"

"Yes." His answer was muffled against his locked fingers as he willed himself not to cry.

The only sound was the ticking of the clock atop the cabinet. Isaac breathed deeply and sat up. It wouldn't do for him to lose control like this.

"Sometimes the patient will die. Despite our best efforts, despite our best medicines, the patient will die." His uncle sighed and stared hard into the fireplace. The dancing flames were reflected in his tired eyes. "Every time that happens, my faith is tested, Isaac. I wonder how a God who loves His people, a God who gave them life, can take it away from them, and often with great suffering."

Neither of them spoke. A log fell and sparked, sending tiny glimmers of light onto the hearth, where they burned out quickly.

It's a metaphor, Isaac mused. *We're like those little pieces of the log, beautiful and shining as we arc through the air, and yet we end as ashes on the brick, burned, with only the ash to show that we were ever there.*

"Except for memories," Dr. Bering said, and Isaac realized that he'd spoken his thoughts aloud. "People stay on in the lives of others. They've shaped the people around them by loving them, or, in some cases, by hating them—or perhaps worst of all, by their indifference."

Isaac frowned. Indifference?

"Ignoring the cries of your fellow human beings is reprehensible," his uncle continued. "It is a sin beyond sin. But fortunately, most of our lives are formed by the love around us. Parents who love us, siblings, relatives, friends, spouses—every time we are told we're loved, either in word or action, we are strengthened and bettered."

"Christal's mother and aunt are there with Mr. Lawrence, tidying and making chicken soup."

His uncle chuckled. "He's in good hands then. So what did you do to treat John?"

Isaac ran through the regimen he'd prescribed, and his uncle nodded approvingly. "Good. That's perfect."

Uncle Alfred motioned toward the examination room. "Now we go from near-death to near-life. I'd like you to meet Mrs. Bonds. I think we can expect a Christmas baby from her."

Christal bent down and swooped up the last stray carrot peeling before leaning against the stove and wiping her forehead. At last, the kitchen didn't show the signs of the chaos that had occurred. The smell of her burned hair still hung in the air a bit, but it was dissipating. She'd opened every window in the house, and a beeswax candle lit in the kitchen was helping to disperse the odor.

She tucked the burned part back into the other hair at her temple and pulled a pin out from the bun at the nape of her neck and used it to keep the short section in place. Stuck in at the right angle, the pin might hide the singed area well.

The memory of being held by Isaac flooded back, as real and palpable as if he were still there. She could feel the imprint of his fingers in her hair as he soothed her. Had he—had he kissed her head? Or had she wanted it so badly that she imagined it?

If he *had* kissed her—the thought made her smile.

She had liked it very much, being close to him. Maybe it might happen another time, and it might even be on the lips.

She hugged herself, as if doing so could keep the event fresh in her mind.

He'd kissed her! Or, she corrected herself, he maybe kissed her!

"Are you cold?" Her father spoke from the doorway of the kitchen, startling her so much that she nearly jumped.

She shook her head. "Sorry! I didn't hear you come in. I've got your meal all laid out. It's not much."

As they walked together into the dining room, she filled him in on the events of the day.

Her father frowned, but as he said the blessing over the food, he included the line, "And we pray for those who are sick and for those who tend to the sick."

They ate quickly, because, as he explained to her, the Christmas charity group was meeting and he had to return to the church.

"I'm hoping to get Isaac on the team," he said as he stood up after eating. "He'd be—oh! I nearly forgot. Come with me."

She followed her father to the entryway, where he reached into the pocket of his overcoat and handed her a small tin. "I don't know what this is about," he said. "Isaac stepped out of the door of his uncle's house and asked me to give you something. Then he went back inside and got this."

He put his coat on and wrapped a scarf around his neck. "I know, I know," he said with a grin. "I'd better button up, because if I don't, as sure as anything I'll see Aunt Ruth!"

With those words and a hasty peck on his daughter's forehead, Papa was gone.

She looked at the tin curiously. Ornate flowery golden letters spelled out GARDEN DELIGHT HAIR POMADE. She opened it, and a faintly familiar scent floated up.

Why did she know this aroma? Where had she smelled it before?

Chapter 6

The next two weeks were filled with a flurry of activity. Christal's usual trips to the library were curtailed as she worked on becoming knowledgeable about homemaking. She stood in the kitchen every morning and evening, trying to learn the fine art of cookery. Her motivation was real and her mother was patient, but there seemed to be so much to remember.

Baking soda and baking powder were actually two different products, and cream of tartar had nothing to do with cream. Egg whites were actually clear until they were cooked, and separating an egg required steady hands.

A pinch was bigger than a smidgen, and a sprinkle could mean one shake or two, depending on whether she was adding cinnamon, which required two shakes, or salt, which took only one.

Two cups made a pint—or was that a quart? Were there sixteen tablespoons to a cup measure? And which was the bigger one, the teaspoon or the tablespoon? The numbers spun in her head until she'd gotten the idea to write everything down in a little book she kept in her apron pocket—her own personal guide to the art of cookery.

At last the evening came when she leaned over the stove and pulled out a pork roast that was fragrant with herbs and oil. It was beautiful and smelled wonderful. The proof, of course, was with the tasting, and she held her breath as, at the dinner table, her father stood to slice into it with great ceremony.

He served each of them a piece, and as one, they all tried it.

The meat was done perfectly, tender and aromatic, and she smiled with relief as her family congratulated her. She felt ridiculously happy. She'd done it!

She'd never mentioned the incident with the chicken, although she suspected that her mother and aunt knew something was amiss from the burn marks on the bird, but neither had said a word. She'd managed to get the kitchen back to its usual pristine state by the time her father had gotten home, and had, in fact, made a quite passable lunch of cold beef with carrots and bread and butter for him.

They had just finished their meal of the pork she'd roasted and she was putting the dishes away when a knock sounded at the door.

"I'll get it," her father said.

The voices of their next-door neighbors carried into the kitchen.

"Isaac is here!" Christal said, untying her apron and flinging it onto the small table. She stopped and grinned sheepishly at her mother and aunt. "I know, I know. I'll hang it up."

She retrieved the apron and put it on the hook properly. She left the kitchen, then slowed, smoothing down the front of her dress and checking the hall mirror to make sure the burned lock of hair wasn't sticking straight out. From her position in the hallway, she could hear her mother and Aunt Ruth.

"She's learning quickly," Mother said, and Christal smiled at the pride in her mother's voice. She pulled herself up straighter and walked toward the parlor. "Something in her has changed, and I'm very pleased with what she's doing. Whatever her motivation is, it's working."

"She's in love," Aunt Ruth said, and Christal stopped so suddenly she almost tripped.

"Do you think so? They've just met, although—" Her mother's voice continued but became too faint for Christal to hear. She must have moved to the far side of the kitchen.

Aunt Ruth's voice was strong enough to carry, though. "I knew immediately when I met my Theo at the skating party that he was the one for me. And the minute Matthew laid eyes on you, dear Sarah, he was smitten and has remained so."

Her mother said something that Christal couldn't quite make out, and her aunt responded with vigor, "Love at first sight, or love at hundredth sight. It doesn't matter. Love is love."

Was it possible? She had barely seen Isaac since the fiasco with the chicken, and when they had been together, they had either been at church or in passing outside. She had finally convinced herself that the kisses on the top of her head had merely been flights of fancy and that she had imagined them.

The question was: Why had she imagined them? Could it have been because she wanted them so badly that she had let her mind create them?

Was it because she was in love with Isaac Bering?

Her heart fluttered a bit at the thought.

From the parlor she heard his laughter. Her pulse raced, and the palms of her hands grew sweaty.

Maybe her aunt was right, but that wasn't why she was learning the fine art of housekeeping—was it?

"Are you waiting for an invitation from the queen herself?" Her father stood at the door of the parlor. "Come on! Dr. Bering has brought more of the spice cookies you enjoy so much."

"I'll be in soon," she answered, marveling at how calm and collected she sounded. "If he has cookies, we'll need tea. I'll help get it ready."

"Don't take long!" he said before he vanished back into the parlor.

She turned to go back into the kitchen and met her mother and aunt on the way out. Her mother held a tray with a teapot and cups on it.

"How did you manage that?" she asked. "I just now said that—"

"Christal dear, what your mother heard was the sound of guests coming. One always prepares tea for guests," Aunt Ruth chided a bit harshly, and Christal felt herself coloring from the rebuke.

"It wasn't difficult to do," Mother said with her usual gentleness. "The water was already hot. Tea is the easiest beverage in the world to make, I believe."

"Christal, there is much you need to know." Her aunt's tone was brisk but loving. "This is simply a fact, something every woman should be aware of. It's a matter of etiquette."

"Men don't have to make tea," Christal muttered. "Don't they have to be polite?"

Her mother ducked her head, but not before Christal saw the smile on her face.

"Well, of course they do." Aunt Ruth put her arm around her niece's shoulders. "Don't you hear your father in there? He's making our guests feel welcome by talking to them. It's just Alfred and Isaac, but your father's had to develop the talent of carrying on a conversation with anyone and making them feel like they're his favorite people. Sometimes, Christal, what seems the easiest can be the hardest."

Christal's spirits flagged. Just as she took one step forward, she realized that there was a whole flight of steps ahead of her, like a stairway of life. How would she ever catch up? How many times had she seen her parents in exactly this situation, her father talking with the guests in the parlor as her mother made tea and served it? Yet she'd never taken notice of it.

She would never catch up. She should have started a long time ago, paying attention to the operations of the house.

Well, she'd gotten as far as learning to make a savory pork roast, and she already knew how to brew a pot of tea, and she was remembering to hang her apron on its hook when she was done, but that wouldn't be good enough when she had her own household to tend to, unless she and her husband wanted to live on pork and tea.

Her own household! Her husband!

Like wild butterflies, her thoughts flew back to Isaac. It was easy—too easy, perhaps—to imagine him in the role, sitting in his chair in the parlor reading the newspaper. Or across the table from her, eating his roast pork and drinking his tea. Or greeting her each morning with a kiss.

"If we're going to serve this tea, we really should be in the same room as our guests," her mother prompted, her eyes twinkling.

Her mother led them into the parlor. The men all stood when the women came in. Isaac looked directly at Christal, and suddenly she felt as awkward as a schoolgirl.

Is that what love is like, God? she asked silently. *Is it being flustered and tongue-tied around him?* She glanced over and noticed how her mother's eyes immediately focused on her father, and the slow smile that curved her lips spoke volumes—silently.

She couldn't stop herself from sliding her gaze over to Isaac, who now sat on the small sofa. Heat climbed up her neck and onto her cheeks in a sudden flush, and beads of sweat sprang out on her upper lip, and of course, the singed section of her hair chose that moment to escape the pins that held it back. She could see it on the periphery of her sight, its edges poking straight out as if it were waxed.

Isaac stood up so quickly that his shins knocked into the table in front of him, and Mother had to steady the cups she was in the process of placing there.

"I'm sorry," he said to her, and as he tried to assist, he succeeded only in clinking them together and dislodging them from their saucers.

"It's fine," Mother said. "No harm done."

He stepped away and sat back down self-consciously as she put the tray back to rights and then took her place beside her husband. "I'll—" he began, but Aunt Ruth interrupted him.

"Excuse me," she said, stepping around Christal and taking a seat in the chair covered in ruby-toned velvet.

Christal stared at her aunt. Plush and soft, with deeply carved wooden arms—the chair was always hers. Her aunt liked to sit on the small sofa near the fireplace. Where Isaac was now sitting. Where the only empty seat was. Where she was going to have to sit.

Apparently he realized it at the same time she did, for he stood up again and nodded as she crossed the room to join him.

They both sank to the sofa together, and Christal kept her body as rigid as possible, trying to avoid squishing herself against him. The sofa was small, though, and coziness was unavoidable.

She tried not to think about the fact that he was so close to her, so close that she had no choice but to let her elbow touch his. It was either that or she'd have to crane herself backward or hunker over forward. Well, she told herself, if it didn't bother him, it didn't bother her.

She was not a good liar.

This close to him, she could smell the clean fragrance of soap and bay rum. It certainly was an improvement over their encounter in the kitchen, when the air had been full of the awful smell of burned hair. Her fingers stole up to her temple, and she tucked the singed lock back under the safety of the hairpin that tried to conceal the damage.

The conversation drifted from one topic to another, until at last Dr. Bering asked if a family had been selected for the church's goodwill project.

Her father shook his head. "We had a family selected, but they left to go back to Indiana, so we're without one at the moment. We'll need to find someone else, and quickly."

Dr. Bering leaned back and laced his fingers across his stomach. "Could I make a suggestion? I have in mind a young couple expecting their first child. They're as poor as church mice but quite pleasant and kind. I don't believe they have a church home yet, so this would be a good way to reach out to them."

Papa nodded thoughtfully. "That sounds splendid. I'll stop in tomorrow morning, if you don't mind, and pick up the details."

"It would be perfect for the season, wouldn't it, Matthew?" Mother said softly. "So reminiscent of the first Christmas."

"Except this woman won't be giving birth in a stable, I can assure you of that," the doctor said with a deep chuckle. "Not in these days and times!"

"That new hospital is supposed to be quite the place, I understand," Papa said, and Aunt Ruth agreed.

"It's got the latest gizmos and gadgets, everything a doctor could want or need," she said, grinning at Dr. Bering. "All a physician has to do is push a button, and the machine takes it from there."

"Not exactly," Dr. Bering responded with a chortle. "And even if it were so, Ruth, someone still has to know which button to push!"

Christal's mind began to wander away from the subject of hospitals and charity cases. How could she concentrate on something like that when Isaac was so near that she could feel him breathing, the rise and fall of each inhalation and exhalation?

Usually the only time she was this close to a man who was not related to her was at church—and then only at the Christmas and Easter services, when the sanctuary was packed with visitors and with those who made the trek to worship on the holidays. Then the pews were filled to capacity with a suddenly large congregation.

That wasn't the same. This, no, this was different.

The sound of the others' voices was a background to her thoughts, and to the rhythm of Isaac's breathing.

She couldn't focus on anything except him.

Oh, this wasn't good. Not good at all.

Was this what God meant for her? Was she supposed to fall in love with Isaac Bering?

He seemed to be fond of her, if indeed her recollection of the time in the kitchen after the great hair catastrophe had occurred, and he had truly nuzzled her hair as he held her. The more she thought about it, the more likely it seemed that her memory was correct.

He laughed, and she nearly jumped out of her skin. What had someone said that was funny? She had totally lost the conversation.

"Wouldn't you agree?" her father asked her.

She had no idea what to say. What on earth were they talking about? Everyone was watching her, including Isaac, who had turned his head and was looking at her curiously.

"Well," she said slowly, hoping that if she were vague enough, no one would know she'd been woolgathering, "you know me."

"I believe we do," Aunt Ruth said sharply, "and I also believe that you were not paying attention, Christal."

She nodded guiltily. *Please don't let her ask me why I was off in dreamland, or what I was thinking about,* she prayed quickly. Her aunt was a wonderful woman, but sometimes she could ask the most embarrassing questions at the most inopportune times.

"To catch you up with the rest of us," Papa said quickly, as if to forestall anything Aunt Ruth might say, "we were discussing the newest plans for the Winter Carnival."

"Really?" She leaned forward eagerly, completely intent on the topic at hand.

Dr. Bering chuckled. "I thought that would bring you back to us. Yes, we're talking about the latest developments. The plans for the ice palace are being finalized."

"When is it going to be built?" Mother asked. "I'm surprised they haven't started yet."

The doctor shrugged. "My understanding is that they will assemble it shortly before the carnival itself. I suppose the very nature of the bricks dictates that. What if we had a thaw and it melted?"

"That's an excellent point," Papa said.

"But there is something that I do know," Dr. Bering continued. "Christal, I was just telling your family and Isaac that the committee is planning a series of parades, including a nighttime one."

"A parade!" She clasped her hands together delightedly. "Oh, I do love parades!"

"They're going to be quite an assortment, too, so that there'll be something for everyone."

"What will there be? Will the king and queen be there?"

"I suppose they will be. Right now the fellows are working on getting sports teams lined up." Dr. Bering reached for his teacup, which was dwarfed by his huge hands.

"Sports?" Isaac shook his head. "Like baseball? In winter?"

"Not baseball. They're thinking winter sports, like tobogganing or curling."

"Winter sports," Isaac repeated.

Christal grinned. She could tell he was unconvinced about the concept of winter games. "You don't sound as if you quite accept the notion of tobogganing or curling as a sport."

He tilted his head to the side, as if considering her words. "I don't know if it's so much that as it is that the term *winter sports* seems to be impossible."

"Oh, pshaw!" Aunt Ruth tapped her cane on the floor. "People can have an enjoyable time, with good clean fun, any time of the year. So it's snowing. Or not. What does it matter?"

"Now, Ruth," Dr. Bering admonished gently, "Isaac is new to St. Paul. He hasn't had the chance to learn everything about being up here, such as how people who live in cold climates manage to have sporting events year round."

"I certainly hope I'm not giving you all the impression that I'm opposed to anything having to do with cold or snow or winter," Isaac said. "Trust me, I am not. I'm going to be attempting to enjoy it all, even though it may be quite alien to a southern soul like myself. I'm afraid that I'm coming across as being cranky, and I'm not."

"We understand," Papa said. "This is quite a change for you in many ways, and climate is a major one. But I suspect you'll be fine. Say, Isaac, have you ever been to a curling tournament?"

Curling was one sport that Christal had never been able to appreciate, although her father enjoyed it. Still, it was fascinating to watch, even if she couldn't appreciate the subtleties of it.

"No," he said, "I've never seen it, but I know what it is. It's a Scottish sport, I understand, in which the players slide a handled stone down a sheet of ice, and they do all kinds of things to keep it going where it needs to go."

"That's an excellent description," Dr. Bering said.

"That's all I know," Isaac confessed. "Last Sunday some fellows at church commandeered me to try to get me interested, but they failed."

"Curling's very popular here," Papa said, "so at some point you'll undoubtedly find yourself at a bonspiel, which is what they call their competitions."

"As a spectator, not a participant," Isaac responded, his eyes twinkling golden in the lamplight.

"As all of us in this room are," Mother agreed.

"Excuse me," Dr. Bering said, hooking his thumbs under his suspenders. "I will have you all know that I was once on a curling team."

Aunt Ruth jabbed him with her cane. "You must not lie, Alfred."

"I'm not lying. It's the truth. A patient of mine was with one of the local clubs, and he invited me to give it a try. So I did."

"How did you like it?" Christal asked.

"I think I slid down the ice better than the stone did. It's amazing how quickly an overweight man can zip across a sheet of ice."

"Well, then, maybe you have a talent for it," she said.

"I don't think so. Apparently I wasn't supposed to cross the ice on my stomach, and you know, it's odd, but they never invited me back."

They all laughed, and Dr. Bering said, "I have so enjoyed my time here tonight, but my nephew and I must return to our own home and to sleep. Another day of keeping St. Paulites in good health awaits us both tomorrow."

At the door, Isaac hung back near Christal. "How's the cooking going?" he whispered.

"I've graduated from burning my hair to cutting my finger." She held up her bandaged forefinger.

"Ah," he said, and before she could react, he lifted the injured finger to his lips and kissed it. "The best medicine in the world."

With that, he turned and left.

And Christal knew she was in love.

The morning air was icy, and Isaac tiptoed to his slippers, trying to avoid too much skin contact with the cold floorboards.

He'd stayed up much too late reading. His uncle had started him on the habit of reading for leisure in the evening, and Christal had shown him the delights of the St. Paul Library, where he'd found a collection of short stories by Mr. Nathaniel Hawthorne that had turned out to be riveting.

He shivered as he got ready for the day ahead.

In one of his early classes he'd been taught that heat rises. If that was true, why on earth was his bedroom so incredibly chilly? He hurried into his clothes, anxious to get downstairs where the fireplace would already be stoked back into life and the rooms filled with heat.

He could smell breakfast. His uncle was a firm believer in the necessity of a big breakfast. Already, Isaac thought, as he had to yank on his trouser button at his waist, he was starting to fill out a bit too much with all this food.

Bacon, eggs, sausage, toast, and coffee—he could identify them all as he loped down the stairs.

"You know," he said to his uncle as he entered the kitchen and sat at the table, "I think a man could have breakfast for every meal and be quite happy."

Uncle Alfred poured him a cup of coffee and handed him the pitcher of cream. "I believe you're right. I suppose we start the day with the best so we can face what's ahead in good spirits."

He sat across from Isaac and said his usual, "Shall we?"

It was his signal that the time had come to say grace.

When Isaac was growing up, the grace had been a simple rhyme, said with habit and yet supported by belief. He'd never much thought about the words they'd used—"*Bless the food for our good. Guide our day in Your way*"—but subtly they had touched him.

His uncle, however, never used the same prayer twice. Each day it was different.

They both bowed their heads, and Uncle Alfred said the grace. "Today, dearest Lord, we will meet the sick who need Your healing touch. We will meet those in need who crave Your blessings. We will meet our friends in whom we see You. Keep us always mindful of You. May we be Your hands, Your feet, Your heart. Sanctify this food we are about to eat so that it may serve us as we serve You. We ask it in Your name. Amen."

Isaac raised his head and, as he reached for the platter of bacon, asked his uncle, "Did you ever consider the ministry? You are a powerful prayer, as they say."

Uncle Alfred took a bite of sausage, chewed, and swallowed, and then answered. "I guess you could say that my doctoring is my ministry. We teach by what we live, you know. I'm known as a devout Christian, and perhaps my example has given strength to those who have needed it the most."

"Like John Lawrence?"

"Ah, John." His uncle spread jam across a piece of toast. "John is a good man. His faith teaches me. It's pure and strong."

"He's a widower, isn't he? Did you know him then?"

Uncle Alfred nodded. "I did. I was just starting out in my practice, and I knew the woman he married actually better than I knew him at the time. We had been in school together. You know, there was quite an age difference between him and his wife. She was so young, which made it all that much sadder—if one can even measure one death sadder than another."

"I suppose his faith held him up then."

"No."

Isaac nearly dropped his fork. "No?"

"He was a mess when she died. He blamed God. He said that if God had been fair and just, He would have taken some criminal rather than her. Someone who didn't deserve to live. That either God had made a mistake or God was cruel."

"That seems rather. . .harsh."

"It seems rather honest, I'd say."

Isaac stared at his uncle. "What? How can you say that? That's terrible!" He knew he was sputtering, but he couldn't stop himself.

His uncle's large hands reached across the table and gripped Isaac's forearms. "Listen to me. This may be the most important thing you learn for a long time. Grief has its own voice. It's loud and practically shouts in your ear. It demands to be heard, and it must have its say."

"But to utter those things—" Isaac couldn't imagine it.

"Again, it's the voice of grief. God knows all about it."

"But now John is a stalwart Christian, isn't he?"

"He is."

"How did he work his way through it? How did he answer those questions?"

Uncle Alfred shrugged. "He came to his own peace with it. He struggled his way from the depths, and he climbed to the heights. I don't know what the resolution was, just that there was one. The rest is between the man and his God."

It made sense. "You're telling me to respect that, aren't you?"

His uncle smiled. "I am. The relationship between you and God is not the same as mine is with Him. We need to accept that and keep it front and center as we treat those who come to see us. Remember they're not just patients. They're people who are patients. People who are children of God."

"I see."

"And speaking of children of God, our first patient is Mrs. Bonds, who is about to present us with one of those children. I'm recommending to Matthew Everett that the church select her and her husband as their Christmas family—I refuse to call them a project—since they could use a little boost right now."

"What will this mean to her?" Isaac asked, finishing up the last strip of bacon.

"There will be food, of course, and clothing and bedding for the baby. I'm going to request that the church also take up an offering for them to help with whatever else they might need," his uncle said as he stood and began to clear the table.

"Don't they get any presents?"

His uncle stopped suddenly. "You're right! Presents! Isaac, you're brilliant!"

"I am?"

"Yes, you are. We've been thinking about what they need in terms of things, day-to-day things, and we should have been thinking about the things that make life brighter and better. I like that. I'll make sure that happens. Like a necklace for Mrs. Bonds, and for Mr. Bonds, what?"

Isaac shook his head. "I don't know. I've never met him."

"Give it some consideration, and let me know what you come up with."

They washed up the breakfast dishes, each deep in his own thoughts, and when at last they'd dried the last cup and hung the towels, they looked at each other with anticipation.

"Got anything?" Isaac asked.

Uncle Alfred swung his head back and forth. "Nope."

"We'll keep thinking on it then."

"We will," his uncle said as they left the kitchen. Then he stopped and slapped his hand on his forehead. "Well, of course! I've got the perfect solution! We'll ask Ruth. She'll know exactly what to do."

"Humph," Isaac said with a grin. "She'll buy them both jackets."

Chapter 7

Christmas flew in on the snowflakes—snowflakes that melted as fast as they fell. After a dive into temperatures that were well below zero, the thermometer rose just as rapidly as it had fallen, and the holiday was unseasonably warm.

"Isaac must truly think we are crazy to live here," Christal said to her mother as they prepared the Christmas dinner. "A seventy degree temperature hike in a matter of days!"

"He's bound to be happy now," Mother agreed. "Say, look at these pies. See how the crust is a nice golden color? You want to watch them closely and take them out just as they turn this shade. Any longer in the oven and the crust will be dry and tough."

Christal beamed at the pies. Her contribution had been to roll out the crusts under her mother's watchful eye. What had seemed so simple had ended up taking nearly an hour. First, the dough stuck alternately to the rolling pin and the board. Then it was too long and narrow to fit the pan, so she had to start all over. And twice it broke apart as it was being moved to the pan.

This wasn't the first time she'd tried to make pies, but today she'd persevered and hadn't abandoned the project and given it over to her mother to finish. That alone made her immeasurably pleased.

They were beautiful pies, even if the undercrust was patched together with a watered forefinger. The pumpkin pie's crust was crimped almost evenly. Christal had misjudged the circumference and the size of her thumb a little bit, so where the end met the beginning there was a bit of a clump. The apple pie's elegant *A*, carved on the top crust by her mother's artful hand, hid a great crack that appeared as Christal carefully laid the dough atop the filling.

"Pies are awfully hard to make at first," her mother told her, "but you've been marvelously patient, and I commend you."

The turkey was roasting itself, as Mother explained it. "The less you peek at it, the better. Let the steam build up in the oven to keep it tender and juicy. Every time you open the door, you release some of that moisture, so avoid it if you can."

Christal was surprised at how easily she was able to do more in the kitchen. She accomplished more and more of the tasks and had become comfortable with her mother's recipes that had challenged her—and defeated her—before.

Aunt Ruth had, for this meal's preparations, sat in the parlor with Papa, knitting and listening as he read aloud.

Christal beamed with pride as she called them in to dinner. The table was spread with a linen tablecloth, and they were using the best china.

In the middle of the table was the turkey, gloriously golden.

They sat together and held hands in a circle, and Papa said grace. "Bless us on this holy day, the day in which a new life began so long ago, and which begins in us anew. Today, and every day, may we know the spirit of Christmas in our hearts, the joyous excitement of life ahead. In Your holy name, we pray."

The dinner was wonderful, every single crumb and flake and slice of it.

The only improvement could have been the addition of the two bachelors next door, but as usual, Dr. Bering had insisted that he—and now Isaac—celebrate the holiday privately.

Afterward, they gathered in the parlor, where usually each person selected their favorite occupation. Christal read, her aunt knitted, her mother embroidered, and her father slept.

This time, when she had finished cleaning the kitchen and joined the others in the parlor, she sensed something was different. The knitting was laid aside, as was the embroidery, and her father was wide-awake.

"Christal dear, please sit." Her mother's voice was surprisingly nervous.

She slipped into her usual seat, but she couldn't slouch down into it as she often did. Something was going on.

"Today when I said the grace, I mentioned *the joyous excitement of life ahead*," her father said. "Do you remember that?"

She nodded, although the truth was that she had been so excited about the dinner she'd only listened to the prayer with half her mind.

Papa reached out and took her mother's hand. "We have an announcement to make." Her father paused. "This is something we've prayed about. We are planning to embark on an adventure. We're going to be missionaries!"

"We are?" Missionaries! She tried to take it all in. Her mother's face was creased with concern, and Christal stood to go to her side and give her a hug—although who she was reassuring, her mother or herself, she could not say.

"No, *we* are. *You* aren't." Her father's voice was subdued.

She stopped. "I'm not? I'm not going with you?"

"Christal, you can't go with us. We are considering a seven-year commitment." Mother reached out for her, but Christal stepped away.

"I could go."

"You can't."

"If you wanted me to go, I could go. You don't want me to come with you!"

The pain was so intense that the tears refused to fall. Her head felt like it would burst.

"It's not that, honey." Her mother shot a despairing look at her father. "We're going to a place that is so distant, so undeveloped, that you'd be miserable. There aren't libraries, no schools. The buildings are minimal, and we'd be building the only church. Plus, your health—"

"I want to go." A volcano of anger rose within her. "I am no longer sick. Will you never see that?"

She had never spoken to her parents like that, but they had never proposed anything quite as life shattering as this.

"Christal, no." Her father's words were quiet but firm.

Aunt Ruth stirred in her chair, and Christal spun around to look at her.

"What about Aunt Ruth? You're leaving her, too? Oh!" She sat down as she realized what the plan would be. "I see. Aunt Ruth and I will stay here." She smiled at her aunt.

Her parents shook their heads. "No," they said in unison.

"What about her then?" she cried. "Is *she* going with you?"

"I'm also going to be traveling," Aunt Ruth said, "but not with them."

"You're going by yourself?" This made no sense to her.

"No." Aunt Ruth touched her upswept hair self-consciously and sat a bit straighter.

"Then what?"

"I," Aunt Ruth said with a faint smile, "am going to be traveling with Alfred. We are getting married in April, and he and I will head off to Miami, where we'll get on a ship and head to Borneo and Egypt and Argentina, living the vagabond life."

"You and Dr. Bering? You're getting married? So, are you in love?" she blurted out.

Her aunt blushed, a charmingly youthful reaction. "Don't be impertinent, Christal Maria Everett."

"So, Mother and Papa, if you go to Bora-Bora or wherever, and Aunt Ruth goes to Cairo, where do I go?" She buried her face in her hands.

"Your father and I won't go until next fall at the very earliest," Mother said, getting out of her chair and coming to kneel at Christal's chair. She ran her hand over her daughter's hair. "We won't leave until you're settled."

"I will," said Aunt Ruth, bluntly. "No matter what, I've got a date to become Mrs. Alfred Bering on April 27, 1886, and then I'm on a train to Miami and then on a ship, destination: Borneo!"

Merry Christmas to me, Christal thought. *Merry Christmas, indeed!*

❧

"I think the Bonds family liked their gifts," Isaac said to his uncle as they retired to the chairs near the fireplace after their Christmas dinner. They had delivered the baskets of presents to the expectant couple before sitting down to their own meal.

"The idea of the book for Mr. Bonds was truly inspired. *Around the World in Eighty Days* by Mr. Jules Verne was an excellent choice."

"That's the book you gave me, you might remember." Isaac smiled. "I took it only because you're my uncle and I have the greatest respect for you, but I knew I wouldn't enjoy it. I was incredibly wrong."

"I'm glad you enjoyed it."

"I did. I've been reading every evening, mainly shorter works, but earlier this week I went to the library and borrowed *Twenty Thousand Leagues under the Sea* by him, too. I thought I'd start it today as a Christmas gift to myself."

"I like that idea. A good book on Christmas Day—excellent. I'm sure Mr. Bonds is sitting with the book open now. Didn't you think that Mrs. Bonds seemed to genuinely like the necklace Ruth selected for her?"

"She did. She put it right on. Did you notice that Ruth included scarves, hats, and mittens for both of them? She knitted them herself, along with a blanket and little socks for the baby." Isaac grinned. "If she'd had more time, she probably would have knitted them all jackets, too."

"True!"

"Well, they seemed to enjoy the day, even if the baby didn't make a Christmas appearance."

Uncle Alfred looked at the anniversary clock on the mantel. "It's not even seven o'clock yet. There are still five good hours left in the day."

"I am so stuffed," Isaac commented as he leaned back and sighed contentedly, "that I'm afraid she'd have to have that baby here. I don't think I could walk to our front door, let alone to her house. Do you think she could let herself in? And we could just tell her from our chairs what to do?"

His uncle chuckled and slid down into the chair, putting his feet up on the ottoman and undoing his collar button. "I don't think so. I'd never tell a woman in labor what to do. I let her tell me what to do. The body knows."

"I wonder if Christal and her family will come over tonight," Isaac said.

There was a pause before his uncle answered. "I don't think so."

"Why?"

"Well, it's Christmas."

"No." Isaac considered sitting up but decided that sprawling was easier. "I mean why the hesitation? What did you mean by that?"

"What did I mean when I didn't say something?"

"Yes. No. Oh, I don't know." The fire was warm and the food was settling so nicely that he wanted to just drift off to sleep.

"I suspect they're trying to calm Christal down. She's probably really upset." His uncle's voice was very soft, so soft that at first Isaac wasn't sure he'd heard it correctly—or at all.

"Upset?" Isaac struggled upright. "Why would Christal be upset?"

Uncle Alfred pulled himself to a sitting position. "Matthew and Sarah are leaving next fall to be missionaries, and in the spring Ruth and I are getting married and traveling the world."

This was not the kind of announcement one should try to assimilate when one had eaten entirely too much Christmas dinner, Isaac thought. One should be awake and alert and smart, not sleepy and lethargic and dull.

Missionaries? Married? Traveling the world?

The meaning began to sink in.

"Christal, too?" Christal was leaving? Moving away?

Another angle of the situation struck him, and the stupor began to wear off rapidly. "If you go, that means—"

His uncle nodded. "It does. You have to be ready to take over."

"How soon?"

"April 27th, eleven o'clock. That's the time that Ruth walks down that aisle and I officially retire from doctoring and start living my life with the woman I love."

"That's only four months away."

"Four months, one day, and sixteen hours, if my math still holds."

"I thought you said you'd be here for two years." Isaac swallowed, trying to force down the lump of fear that seemed to have grown in his throat.

"I will be, off and on. But for the most part, you'll be the doctor."

"I won't be ready! I can't—"

"You can, and you will. You have the knowledge and the book training. Now all you need is to fine-tune it with some understanding of how people get ill, and as importantly, how they recover."

He shook his head vehemently. "I can't—"

"I'll be coming back regularly—in between trips to far-off climes with my love, where we'll wear tropical flowers around our necks and play drums in the sand and get sunburned in January. And besides, I'm not leaving tomorrow."

Could he do it? Could he learn all he needed to know in that short amount of time?

And what about Christal? What would she do? Would she stay in St. Paul? What would he do if she didn't? What would he do?

He was a doctor—or almost one. He knew that the human heart was an organ, the same as a liver or a lung. It beat, in a generally regular pattern, from before birth and quit only when life on earth was done. Its job was to pump blood through the body's circulatory system.

That was all it did. It couldn't break. It couldn't feel emotions. Hearts weren't sorry or sad or devastated. Their owners were.

Like him.

Yet his heart was aching already. He couldn't lose her. He couldn't. Somehow he'd find a way to keep her here. He had to!

"She's not going with them," Uncle Alfred said from the depths of his chair. Isaac realized that his uncle had been studying him.

"She isn't?" His question came out in a high-pitched squeak, and he cleared his throat.

"No. Matthew and Sarah are going by themselves."

"So," he said, slowly, trying not to sound as excited as he felt, "Christal will be staying here?"

"That I couldn't tell you. I suppose that's Christal's decision."

"What would she do here? Would she have to find employment? Where would she live? Next door?"

His uncle shrugged. "I know the house belongs to the church, so I'd say that she couldn't live there unless she stayed on as a maid or a cook."

A maid or a cook? Christal?

"I suppose she could find work at the library here. She'd be a marvelous employee," Uncle Alfred mused. "She knows the books inside and out."

"Where would she live? In a boardinghouse?"

"That, or as a roomer somewhere."

He'd known her only two months, but he knew that she wouldn't be happy in either situation.

"They'll figure it out," Uncle Alfred said. "After all, Matthew and Sarah won't be leaving until early autumn. There's plenty of time. Plenty of time. Not to worry."

His uncle's voice trailed off as he drifted to sleep.

But Isaac was wide-awake. *Not to worry?* How could he not worry? He was worried about Christal, but he was also very concerned about himself. Was he ready to take over as a full-fledged doctor within a few months?

He put his hands together, palm to palm, and bent his head over so that his fingertips touched his brow.

When things seemed insurmountable, there was only one path. He took it. He began to pray.

It wasn't one of the beautiful prayers that came from his uncle's lips or the clear ones that he heard from Rev. Everett's pulpit each Sunday. It was a wordless mishmash of concerns, of cares, of wants, of needs, all laid at the table of Heaven. Soon it began to sift through, until he was left with one unavoidable fact.

He was in love with Christal, and he couldn't live without her. They belonged together. Perhaps, perhaps—he couldn't go further with the unspoken thought this early on, but it took up residence in his soul and settled in for a long stay.

His heart, that insensate organ he'd been mulling about earlier, did an odd little leap. It felt like joy.

~

Christal retired to her room as soon as she could. She wanted to take her aching head away from her parents and aunt, who were trying very hard to make her feel better—and failing miserably.

They all had plans. They all had something exciting and different to look forward to, but she didn't. She had nothing but a big open abyss.

They all assured her that they were not abandoning her. Her mother repeated that she wouldn't leave until Christal had a home and a source of income, but neither she nor Christal's father had any suggestions about that. She wasn't trained to teach. She'd make a miserable cook or maid. Perhaps she could find a job at the library. She could ask tomorrow.

They didn't understand that her distress wasn't just about not living in this house where she'd spent her entire life, or having to find employment in a world that didn't offer much to women. From now on she would be alone. For the next seven years, unless she opted to spend Christmas with her parents in their missionary home, they'd be apart for the holidays.

This would be the last time they celebrated Jesus' birth together.

Or at least the last time for a long time, she added as a hasty amendment to her stream of thought. She'd have a family, but they'd be gone.

Even Dr. Bering. It struck her like a bolt of lightning. Even Dr. Bering!

And if Dr. Bering left, would Isaac stay?

If he left, too—she couldn't bear it. She just couldn't.

A man shouted outside, and she raced to her window. Isaac stepped out of Dr. Bering's carriage.

The door of the house opened, and two men emerged—Dr. Bering and a man she didn't recognize but who looked terrified. His hat was askew, and his jacket flapped open in the night chill.

Isaac looked up at her window and waved at her, but his face was solemn. Something was going on.

She hadn't changed into her nightclothes yet, so she ran down the stairs, threw her jacket on—ignoring her aunt's pleas to button it—and sped to the carriage.

"Is everyone all right?" she asked breathlessly.

"My wife's having a baby!" the man she didn't recognize said.

"This is Mr. Bonds. Mr. Bonds, Christal Everett." Dr. Bering put his hand on the fellow's back. "My good man, let's get in the carriage and see about putting that baby into your arms as soon as possible."

Isaac was behind them, and she could see the anxiety on his face. "You'll be all right," she whispered, patting his arm.

"It's my first baby," he answered with a tight smile as he began to climb into the carriage. "I've never delivered a baby before. And this one is a Christmas baby. They say doctors never forget their first delivery."

"It'll be fine. Just fine. Go on now. I'll be praying."

He stopped midstep and smiled. "Thank you."

"Come on, Isaac! Babies wait for no one!" his uncle called from inside the carriage, and Isaac got behind the horses, pulling his doctor's bag inside with him, and picked up the reins.

The carriage clattered away, and Christal watched it, her heart riding with it.

The woman twisted in the bed, the blankets tangled around her arms and legs. Her face was dotted with sweat, and her husband stood at her side, wringing his hands together fiercely.

Isaac knew that labor was painful, but it was one thing to read about it on paper and another to see it in its vivid reality.

"Can't you help her?" Mr. Bonds asked, his voice hoarse with fear. "I know you wanted us to go to the hospital, but it was Christmas, you know, and we thought we'd spend this time alone, and the pains came faster and faster. . ."

"That's all right," Uncle Alfred said soothingly. "Women have been having babies in homes for hundreds and thousands of years. This baby will be just fine being born here."

The room was small and dark and lit only faintly with a single lamp. They hadn't covered this in medical school—delivering a baby in a room that was the size of a closet.

Nor had they told him what to do when he had to work with only the instruments in his doctor's bag. He hoped that if all went well, the only item he'd need would be the scissors to cut the cord.

The hospital would have been better. Now that those in medicine realized how much safer a hospital birth was, more women were using maternity hospitals. There was a new one in St. Paul, and his uncle was enthusiastic about it. But this baby was going to be born at home, not in the controlled surroundings of the hospital.

His uncle sat beside the woman on the bed. "Hello, Mrs. Bonds. It's almost time for you to see your child!"

She moaned in response, the sheets clutched in her white-knuckled grip.

"Can't you end the pain?" her husband asked. "Make it stop? I can't bear to watch her like this."

His voice was tense with unshed tears, and Uncle Alfred patted the worried man's hands. "The only thing that will make this stop will be the appearance of Baby Bonds. Are you ready to become a father tonight?"

"Yes." The man looked again at his wife and wiped the sweat from her forehead.

"Good. Now, Mr. Bonds—"

"Jeremy. Please call me Jeremy."

"Very well. Jeremy, you could be a great help if you'd gather some things for me. Some boiling water, and some chilled water. Some ammonia. A bar of soap, too, would help. And some cloths, please, preferably ones we can discard at the end of this."

"Why would we want to—" the husband began, and then he stopped. "Oh. Oh!"

He turned and slipped out of the room, his fingers still working wildly together.

"Why do we need ammonia?" Isaac asked.

"We don't. We needed him out of the room."

His uncle turned his attention to the woman on the bed. "Mrs. Bonds, I hope you don't mind my bringing in my nephew. Is it all right if he stays?"

She nodded. "This. Hurts. So. Much."

"I have heard that," Uncle Alfred said soothingly. "But the reward at the end is great."

"I have never had pain this bad in my entire life," Mrs. Bonds said, reaching out and gripping Isaac's hand so tightly that his knuckles cracked in protest. "This is—" She screamed as a contraction seized her.

"Your body is helping the baby come out," Uncle Alfred said. "It's all going as it should. Do you have a name for this child yet?"

"David if it's a boy, and Elizabeth if it's a girl." The woman panted and then tensed as another contraction took over. "How soon? How much longer?"

Uncle Alfred did a quick and discreet examination and smiled. "I think we're due for a baby very soon here. Go ahead and scream if you want, or—"

Her husband reentered the room. "I heard her scream again. That was right after the other one. She's—"

"She's having a baby, and we're getting closer." Uncle Alfred reached for a cloth and dipped it in the cool water and wiped it across her forehead and over her cheeks. "Go ahead and try to let your body have this baby. Don't fight the pain; it'll make it worse. Breathe, Mrs. Bonds. Breathe. In and out. That's right. If you do that during the contraction, it'll be better."

Her husband stood at the side. "I feel so helpless. I want to help her, and I can't. I don't have anything I can do to make it better. And I feel so guilty."

Isaac shot a look at his uncle. How would he deal with that?

Amazingly, his uncle laughed. "As well you might. But trust me when I tell you that in a very short time, this whole experience will be overshadowed by something that will amaze you beyond anything else. In just a few minutes—"

"Something, something, something is happening! Oh, it is!" Mrs. Bonds curled and straightened. "I think I'm—"

"Isaac, I think it's time. Are you ready? Let's deliver this baby!"

Uncle Alfred lifted the blanket, the woman screamed one more time, and Isaac helped a wet, wriggly baby into the world.

The baby was beautiful, perfect in every way. He handed the baby to his uncle, who wiped it with a cloth, checking it over as he did so.

"Congratulations! You two are the parents of a perfect baby boy. David, right?" Uncle Alfred laid the baby on Mrs. Bonds's chest and reached out as Isaac handed him the scissors. "Isaac, would you like to tie the cord?"

He couldn't make his hands stop shaking as he reached over and tied the cord on the baby, whose cries took over where his mother's left off.

His first birth. There was nothing as incredible as what he'd just seen.

"There's one more thing I always do when I deliver a baby," his uncle said.

"What's that?" Isaac looked around. What was left?

"I always offer thanks and ask the Lord's blessing."

"Please do," Mrs. Bonds said softly, her lips pressed against her baby's forehead.

The four of them encircled the newborn child, united in prayer. "Thank You, dearest Lord, for this gift of life, the ultimate gift of Christmas. Bless David through his years ahead, and guide his feet to walk in Your service, his hands to share Your abundance, and his lips to sing Your praises. In the name of all that is holy on this day of Christmas, amen."

"Amen." Isaac breathed. "Amen."

Chapter 8

"It was incredible!" Isaac enthused as they walked home from church together. Two weeks had passed since the birth of the Bonds baby, and he was still talking about it.

Christal tried to feel happy for him, but her own situation kept her outlook bleak. Her future was dim and dark and foreboding. At least that was the way it seemed.

She'd gone to the library to ask if she might find employment there, but the librarian had shaken his head. No jobs.

Her hands were jammed into her pockets and her scarf wound tightly around her neck, and she burrowed into the wool as if hiding from the world.

Her mood wasn't just about her. More than anything, she wanted her parents to be happy, and that would mean that they would go on this missionary sojourn. She could tell from their voices that it was important to them.

"So I think that I can do it. I'm really feeling energized. Maybe it's the new year; maybe it's that new baby. I don't know, but I'm happy!" Isaac threw his arms out wide, nearly knocking Christal into a leafless shrub. "Oh, I'm sorry!"

"That's all right," she said gloomily. "If I had a branch from that chokecherry bush stuck through my chest, maybe I could say things were looking better."

He stopped, faced her, and put his hands on her shoulders. "I'm sorry. I know that you're going through some dark times now, but trust me—they'll improve. There will be a solution."

She wanted to believe him, but his words were just the flat meaningless syllables she heard from her own family. *Trust*. Her ability to trust was being tested.

"What am I going to do? What?" She knew she was being fretful, but she couldn't help herself.

"Something will come along."

"It won't."

"Oh, Christal."

Suddenly his arms were around her, and his lips grazed the thin area of exposed skin between her eyebrows and the bottom brim of her knit hat.

She was so bundled up that she had no sense of where her body was, and there was just a bit of ice on the sidewalk. The next thing she knew, she and Isaac were tumbling down onto the ground.

Her hat had slid entirely down over her face, and her scarf was caught on the buttons of his overcoat.

Something scratched her neck under her coat collar, and she realized that they were at the base of the chokecherry and one of the branches was digging into her skin.

"I shouldn't have said anything about being impaled by the bush, because I am—" she said as she struggled to an upright position, tugging her hat back up. "Oh!"

His face was just inches from hers, his arms around her waist, and he grinned. "And I shouldn't have tried to kiss you."

Suddenly brave, she smiled. "I'm glad you did."

"I should do it again."

"Perhaps."

He bridged the short gap between them, and his lips touched hers.

The branch scratched more sharply at her neck, but she ignored it. He was kissing her, and for the moment the cares of her life fell away. Locked in his embrace, there was no one but the two of them, nothing but this kiss.

He pulled away. "I think this is not the place, sprawled here on the street, although I have to say I would happily stay here, frozen in your arms."

"We'd be the talk of the church, then, wouldn't we?" She unhooked her scarf from the front of his overcoat. "And we'd probably be famous. I can see the headline on the *Dispatch* now: 'MINISTER'S DAUGHTER GOES TO HEAVENLY REWARD WHILE SMOOCHING THE NEW DOCTOR ON THE STREET UNDER THE CHOKECHERRY BUSH.' "

"That's a long headline," Isaac said, grinning as he helped her to her feet.

"News like that doesn't come along every day here in St. Paul, you know." She dusted the snow off her elbows and what she could reach of the back of her coat.

"Well, since we're newsworthy now," he said, linking her arm in his, "I wonder if we could possibly consider going into full courting now?"

"Courting?" She swallowed hard. More than anything she wanted to look at him, but her head seemed locked into place, and her ability to speak was stifled. He was asking permission to court her! She had dreamed of this, hoped for this, wished for this; and now that the moment had arrived, she had no idea what she should say or do.

"Yes," he said, and she could hear the amusement behind the single word.

"I, well, yes, I suppose, we, I imagine, um, why not?"

"Not the most fervent avowal of interest that I've heard," he said, "but I'll take it."

She looked at him at last and saw again how kind he was. How happy he was. How gentle he was.

"How's this?" she said. "I would be delighted to be courted by you, Mr. Almost-Doctor Bering."

"Better. Much better. I'd kiss you again, but the neighbors would definitely be talking."

"They're already talking."

"Very well."

He leaned over and kissed her again, a proper and sedate kiss, yet warm in the brisk January air. She wanted to linger, but she knew they were already late for dinner.

He took her mittened hand in his as they walked the last steps to their block. He stayed with her, as he always did, until she arrived at the door of her house.

"Would you do me the favor of accompanying me to the Winter Carnival parade?" he asked.

"My, aren't we formal!"

"We're courting. That's the way it's done—I think. I've never courted a woman before."

"And I've never been courted." The heat climbing her cheeks told her she was blushing, but she didn't care.

"See? We're perfect for each other."

"Indeed."

"So will you?"

"Will I what?"

"Go to the Winter Carnival parade with me?"

"Yes, I will."

"Because we're courting?"

"Because we're courting."

He kissed the tip of her nose, winked, and left, taking her heart with him.

Sometimes, Isaac thought, in the bleakest of moments, God showed Himself the clearest.

His uncle had fallen asleep in the parlor, a book open on his chest, but Isaac was too excited to nap.

Was what he had done all right? Had he been too forward?

He hadn't been joking when he told her he was inexperienced with courting. He'd gone out with some young women, but nothing had been serious or lasted for long. He'd never let himself get involved with matters of the heart.

At first he'd been too immature to settle down, and he'd gone from one girl to another, enjoying each girl's company but never finding the desire to stay with any certain one. Then as he got older, his studies came first. He rarely left his room once classes were over for the day.

Now, as the inevitability of his future weighed in on him, he realized that he was, indeed, going to be a doctor, and furthermore, he did not want to be alone.

God gave Adam a helpmate in the Garden of Eden, and that had gotten the proverbial ball rolling for romance. What had always captured Isaac's interest in the story of Adam and Eve was the question: Did Adam and Eve love each other?

He thought the answer was yes, that when God created the first two, He created the first couple, and He created the first romantic love.

So Isaac had never considered that he would ever marry without a deep love. That was what God wanted. It was what Isaac wanted.

He'd known Christal only three months. He knew without a doubt that she was the one he wanted to spend the rest of his life with. But three months wasn't very long.

If her parents hadn't decided to go to a missionary post, and if his uncle hadn't decided to marry Ruth and travel around the world, things might have gone at a different pace. But those two factors moved everything along faster, and the next thing he knew, he was kissing Christal again.

The remembrance made him smile.

Kissing Christal was very nice. He hoped to do it again. And again. For the rest of his life.

It would be the answer to her problem, and to his.

He still had time to let the idea rumble around in his head for a while. Her parents wouldn't leave for eight months at the earliest. His uncle had said that his wedding to Ruth was scheduled for April. He didn't want to be hasty, though. What was that his mother used to say? *Marry in haste, repent at leisure.* He nodded slightly. It was best to be wise about this and not to rush into something he might rue later.

His uncle mumbled something in his sleep, and Isaac's attention turned to him.

Uncle Alfred was an amazing man. A skilled doctor, he'd built his talent not only on the knowledge of the human body, but as importantly, knowledge of the human soul.

He'd been single his entire life, choosing to marry only when retirement was possible. Isaac smiled as he realized that his uncle would approach marriage with the same single-mindedness, making it the center of his world, assigning it the utmost importance.

A thought struck him. His uncle had clearly separated the two, being a doctor and being a husband. Did he think it wasn't possible to be both at the same time?

He frowned as he considered that. He would be starting out as a new doctor.

Maybe the time was wrong to be courting anyone. A medical practice would take almost all of his energy, especially when he was following in the footsteps of someone as beloved as his uncle.

His uncle stirred again, and Isaac studied his face. Uncle Alfred's main diversion was reading, which he believed helped him in his doctoring. One of their earliest conversations, about the Jules Verne book, returned to him, and he could hear in his memory his uncle's words about how even science fiction helped him understand his patients.

But might it also be that such reading provided a very needed respite?

"Is something written on my face?" his uncle asked, startling Isaac so sharply that he jumped.

"You startled me."

Uncle Alfred sat up, his round face wreathed in good humor. "You've been staring at me so long that I was beginning to wonder if I had a story on there."

"No," Isaac answered. "I was just thinking."

"If you would like to talk, I would like to listen."

"I was thinking about love."

"Ah! An excellent topic."

Isaac mustered up all his courage. "Why did you never marry?"

His uncle smiled. "What do you think?"

"I don't know. That's why I was thinking."

"You're a smart young man. When you don't know something, you think. That is excellent. Too many people, when they don't know something, do just the opposite. They stop thinking."

Isaac tilted his head, his gaze steadily on his uncle. "Was it because you felt you couldn't practice medicine well and be married?"

Uncle Alfred chuckled. "There are plenty of doctors who are married, and they're fine physicians. No, Isaac, I didn't get married because I quite simply found no one who captured my heart to the extent that's necessary to have a successful marriage."

"But Ruth—oh!" Isaac leaned forward and lowered his voice. "Were you in love with her when she was married to her husband?"

"No," his uncle answered, "there's nothing as intriguing as that. The simple answer is this: Over the past year or so, Ruth and I've come to spend more time together, and we've found that we share many things, not the least of which is our faith in God. That smooths the way quite a bit."

He laid his book, which had been spread open across his chest, on the table beside him. "The more time I spent with her, the more I liked her, and that turned into deep respect and then love. In our case, love was the ripe fruit on the vine."

Isaac sighed. That was just the opposite of what he felt for Christal, which were the first eager buds, not the "ripe fruit" his uncle referred to.

His uncle put his head back and closed his eyes again. "Christal is a charming young woman. You are an intelligent young man, and I love both of you as if you were my own. But I'll tell you this."

He shifted in his chair. "One day you will grow old. You'll have wrinkles, and you won't be able to remember the name of your cousin in Baton Rouge, and she'll have aches and pains, and her hearing will fade. That's when you get to see the miracle of love. It does something to the eyes. She'll still be as beautiful as she is today. It does something to the memory. Old slights vanish into the mists of the past. It does something to the fingers. They gnarl and don't feel the roughness the years have wrought on the other's hand."

He didn't speak again, and Isaac thought his uncle had gone to sleep. Then, at last, he spoke once more.

"Marry her."

Excitement along the parade route was almost palpable. Talk of the carnival was everywhere—in church, in the shops, along the streets—and now that the opening was only two weeks away, hardly anyone spoke of anything else.

Plus, if there was one thing that the residents of St. Paul liked, it was a parade, and the organizers had scheduled them regularly until the first day of February, when the carnival began.

"This is the first parade of many before the carnival starts, my father told me this week," Christal said. "But I think it's going to be the biggest, except for the one on opening day, of course."

"It seems as if everybody in the city is here," Isaac commented.

It certainly looked liked it. The street was solidly lined with people who were anxious to see what the first parade of the season would be like.

"My parents are here," she said, craning her neck to see if she could find them, but there were so many people, she'd never locate them. "And I think Aunt Ruth and Dr. Bering are here, too."

"Oh, my uncle is, most definitely. He's very excited about this. I can't imagine that he'd miss it." He grinned at her. "He left before me, and he was wearing a heavy jacket, buttoned up, and a muffler and a big fur hat and thick mittens, so I'm guessing that Ruth is with him."

Christal laughed. "They'll be on some tropical isle, and she'll make him button up his sarong so he doesn't catch a chill."

"Sarongs have buttons?" The corners of his eyes crinkled with amusement.

"They will when Aunt Ruth finishes with them."

Standing there with Isaac, waiting for the parade to start, made the uncertainty of her future seem far off, nothing that she needed to worry about at the moment. Right now, her whole focus was the parade and Isaac and how wonderful she felt.

"Don't you think parades are the best thing ever?" she asked, wrapping her gloved hand around his arm.

"I've never been to a parade."

"What? How can that be?"

He turned to her and shrugged. "A parade just never came my way, I guess."

"You can't wait for a parade to come to you. You have to go to the parade."

She couldn't imagine never having seen a parade. In St. Paul they were fairly regular things, celebrating all kinds of events and people and companies, and she'd attended almost every one of them.

"I love parades, especially when the band comes by, marching together and playing at the same time. If I were in it, I'd probably tromp right into the fellow next to me. I don't see how they can do both and not topple all over each other." She shook her head.

The crowd shouted, and Christal leaned forward as far as she could, with Isaac holding on to her so she didn't fall.

The parade had started.

Leading the way was the police department, dressed warmly in their winter uniforms. They strode confidently, handsome and strong with their navy blue coats with brass buttons. Two of them were members of the church, and Christal waved at them.

Then came the parade marshal and his troupe. "He looks so proud," she said to Isaac, "doesn't he?"

"He looks cold," he said with a laugh. "But he's probably got a lot to be pleased with. He—"

The arrival of the Great Western Railroad band cut off whatever Isaac was about to say. Christal clapped along with the songs as they played their way down the street. The music filled the winter day with melodies and marches.

"Oh, look at her!" Christal said as the band passed them and a sleigh with Clemence Finch in it drew near. "She's the carnival queen, and the daughter of George Finch, the organizer."

Clemence Finch was beautiful as she waved at the people along the street. Her curls glowed like burnished gold under her hat, and her short red coat was bright in the sunshine.

"I've heard she's wearing the Nushka toboggan team's jacket," Isaac said.

Christal sighed. She knew she shouldn't be envious—it was a sin—but it must be so much fun to wear a jacket like that and ride in a sleigh in a parade and be the carnival queen. Some things, though, were simply out of the reach of a minister's daughter.

After the sleigh came the governor, the mayor, and other dignitaries, looking stiff and formal in their long coats. Yet under the stately top hats, Christal noticed, the men all beamed happily.

Then came the sports clubs. Snowshoe clubs, toboggan clubs, and ski clubs—they all celebrated winter with great gusto. One club, the Ice Bears, brought shotguns that they fired every few minutes into the air. Christal kept a watchful eye on them and held her hands over her ears as they walked past. It didn't seem safe at all, but no one else appeared to worry.

A huge sleigh, shaped like a ship, followed the clubs. Finally, the firemen, postmen, military men, and members of the horseshoe and curling clubs ended the parade.

Christal sighed happily. Here she was watching a parade with Isaac, the man who was courting her.

"What did you think of your first parade?" Christal asked him.

"It was amazing," Isaac said.

"Wasn't it?" Her mind was filled with the images and sounds from the parade. "I wouldn't have changed a thing."

"I would."

"What would you have changed?" she asked in astonishment.

He pretended to shiver. "I'd have had it indoors!"

Chapter 9

The days until the carnival were filled with parades and great speculation about the ice palace. Christal had heard murmurs about what it was going to be like, but none of it seemed to be at all possible. The construction was finally beginning, but the majority of it would be done quickly, right before the start of the carnival.

"An ice-skating rink?" Isaac said one evening as they sat in the parlor eating his uncle's gingerbread. Now that they were officially courting, the older family members left them alone more, although Christal had seen some inquisitive faces peeking around door frames throughout their evenings together.

"Maybe it's a very small ice-skating rink." Christal took a bite of the gingerbread.

"You mean the size of one that might be in someone's yard?" he asked.

"One summer when I was nine, one of my friends and I decided that we would make a wading pool behind our house. We dug and dug, and finally we had a fairly respectable hole."

"Your parents were supportive of it?"

"I'm not sure they understood the scope of our plan," she admitted. "Remember, this is me, the same person who had a pet toad. Anyway, we decided the pond needed fish, so we went down to the river, and after getting our clothes snagged on dead trees and our feet ripped up on rocks, we managed to capture a couple of little fish."

He leaned back, smiling as he listened.

"We got back to the house and realized that we had a bit of a problem. The water we'd put in our pool, all painstakingly carried bucket by bucket from the well, had run out. There was nothing there but a mud hole."

"That doesn't sound good," he commented.

"It wasn't. My parents got upset when they saw what a mess we'd created. They made us take the fish back to the river and let them go, and we tried to fill in the hole, but mud has a mind of its own. No matter how hard we tried, we couldn't get the ground level again."

"Especially if you're only nine years old."

"Exactly. Plus every time it rained, it got worse. It never dried out the rest of the summer. That winter, though, we had a wonderful area for ice-skating back there, so it wasn't a total loss."

"So you think that the ice-skating rink at the ice palace is going to be the same thing?" he asked.

"I think it'll be planned a bit better," she said, laughing.

Her father cleared his throat from the doorway. "We've had just about enough of hiding out in the kitchen. It's time for us to go home, Christal."

She popped the last of the gingerbread into her mouth. "Waste not, want not. But I'll still want more later on."

"Dr. Bering gave your mother a platter of it," Papa said, "so I think you'll live through the night. Isaac, you're going to the opening of the ice palace?"

"Christal and I are going to it as soon as the last patients leave. You know that I was a doubter all along, but I've been impressed so far with what I've heard and seen of the Winter Carnival. Tomorrow will be the pinnacle. First, though, we'll go to the last parade of the carnival. I hear it's going to be quite a spectacle."

"I've been told the same thing. Christal, shall we?"

As they proceeded to the entryway, Christal hung back to walk beside Isaac. Their fingertips brushed and intertwined.

Courting, she thought, was really quite wonderful.

"I'll see you tomorrow," he said at the door. "Finally, the carnival!"

As soon as she got home, she said good night to her family and went to her room. She had to be alone with her thoughts.

Had her life ever been such an odd mixture?

She was in love, and yet mixed in with her great happiness was great sadness. Within eight—no, seven!—months she would be on her own. A huge wall of loneliness loomed ahead of her. What would she do without her parents and her aunt? And Dr. Bering?

She probably could, if she fought hard enough, go with her parents on their missionary trip, but even as she considered the idea, she dismissed it. The reason was simple: If she were with her parents, she wouldn't be with Isaac.

She wanted them all to stay together, for everything to remain exactly as it was now. That would be perfect.

"Perfectly unrealistic," she said in disgust.

No, what was going to happen was going to happen, and she needed to acknowledge that.

Or she could not think about it at all. At least not tonight. Maybe after the carnival, when the world got bleak again, she would deal with it. Right now, though, life in St. Paul was exciting and vivid, and she was going to enjoy it.

She pulled a book off her shelf and plumped up the pillows on the bed before plopping down to read. It was a European legend in a collection of stories she had borrowed from the library, and in it there were a king and a queen and a prince and a princess and a palace. Within moments she had left frozen Minnesota and was on the French countryside, astride a white steed.

In this story, no one left the princess, and they all lived happily ever after.

She got to the end of the book, closed it, and clasped it to her chest. "God," she said softly, "do fairy tales ever come true? Or is that why they're called 'tales,' because they don't?"

⌒

"And so, we're off to the last parade of the carnival!" Isaac announced to his uncle. "I have to say I've become quite a fan of these events, but I am looking forward to viewing one in the summer! Are you ready? I'll go next door and—"

Ruth Everett burst in. "I'm sorry for not knocking, but it's John. Come quickly. I'll get Sarah, and we'll meet you there."

Isaac and his uncle looked at each other, and each seized his medical bag and threw on jackets and sped out the door, racing to John Lawrence's house.

The man was on his chair, his eyes shut. Aristotle flew from one corner of the room to the other, cawing with great agitation.

Uncle Alfred dropped to his knees beside Mr. Lawrence and put his fingers aside the sick man's throat. "His pulse is thready but there. Help me."

They lifted Mr. Lawrence and carried him to the couch where they stretched him out. Isaac straightened the sick man's arms and legs and rubbed them, trying to generate blood flow.

Uncle Alfred raised Mr. Lawrence's torso, placing pillows under his chest and head. He then covered his extremities with a light blanket. "Let's make it as easy for him as possible. He'll breathe more comfortably if he's on an incline, but you're right to massage his extremities."

With his stethoscope, Isaac checked the patient's heartbeat and respiration. "I don't know," he said to his uncle. "Would you listen?"

The older doctor did, and rocking back on heels, he said, "The congestion is thick."

"What do you think?" Isaac asked, afraid to hear the answer.

His uncle only shook his head.

Ruth came in with Mrs. Everett. "We'll be in the kitchen if you need anything. Tea? Coffee?"

"Tea would be good, thank you." Uncle Alfred's voice was calm, and Isaac was reminded of what one of his professors had said, warning them about upsetting the patient with their tone of voice. *Stay calm*, the professor had said, *to keep the patient calm.*

John Lawrence's breathing became labored, with longer periods between each inhalation. Isaac leaned over and again placed his stethoscope against the man's chest. The rattle was unmistakable. Isaac had read about it, the death rattle, but this was the first time he'd heard it.

Without a word, Uncle Alfred lifted the blanket that covered the man's feet. The skin was mottled, nearly blue and white. He met Isaac's eyes and rewrapped the man's feet.

"Lord of all we know, this is Your blessed servant, John Lawrence. He has been Your own from his first breath, and now as he undertakes his last journey to Your arms, we ask that You hold him tightly in Your arms. Cradle him now as You did when he came to us at his birth."

The man coughed a bit, and Uncle Alfred wiped his lips and swabbed his mouth with water.

Isaac took the old man's hand in his own. It was cold, an indication that Mr. Lawrence was nearing his final moments on earth. His eyes filled with tears. How could he let this man go, after all he had done to try to pull him through? How did his uncle do this, praying the patient into heaven? He knew that Mr. Lawrence was old, and that there wasn't anything they could have done to save him from death. Yet it didn't soften the loss. He barely knew Mr. Lawrence, but in the short time he had known him, he'd taken him to his heart because of the older man's gentle ways and true faith. Isaac truly believed that this man was going into heaven, that he was stepping upwards as the culmination of a life of faith, but how was he to manage? What was he supposed to do?

Uncle Alfred wiped the man's face again and hydrated his lips. "You've had a good life, John," he said, "and I know that you are bound for Glory. You—"

The man lifted his head, and his face broke into a beaming smile. "Maryanne!" he said in a long exhalation. He held the posture, and time stood still until at last he smiled even more widely and dropped back upon the pillow.

Uncle Alfred ran his fingers over the man's face and looked at Isaac. "It's all right to cry."

Isaac realized that his face was wet, and he put his head in the palms of his hands. Sob after sob wracked his body as he sat at the bedside.

His uncle stood and made his way around the bed to put his hands on Isaac's shoulders. "This seems like a loss, but it's a win. He's going to heaven. I know that. You know that."

Isaac reached out and touched Mr. Lawrence's face. So this was what death looked like. It looked quite a bit like life, as if he were still breathing.

"Uncle Alfred!" he shouted. "Uncle Alfred! He's not dead!"

"No," John Lawrence mumbled. "Not dead." He took a deep breath, coughed, and breathed again.

His uncle laughed and rubbed the wizened hands of the elderly man. "You old codger! I thought you'd gone to your heavenly reward!"

Mr. Lawrence opened his eyes a slit and smiled slightly.

"Do you know that you went right to that door of heaven, my friend? I suspect you even peeked in between the posts, just to see." Uncle Alfred laughed again. "I think you'll have many more days with us."

Ruth and Mrs. Everett rushed in from the kitchen. "What is all the noise about?"

Aristotle resumed his frantic flights across the room, squawking at the women.

"God wasn't quite ready for our friend." Uncle Alfred turned to Isaac. "Sometimes we're fooled as doctors. We think we know exactly how life is going to go, how death is going to go, and we are wrong. This is one of those instances. Remember that in all things, God is the One who is in control. He wasn't ready for John to advance to heaven. Not yet."

The crow flapped over to the couch and plucked a button off his owner's shirt.

"God looks after this crazy crow as much as He does his owner, and I guess He wasn't ready for one without the other," Ruth said with a fond smile.

"Aristotle," John Lawrence said, lifting his hand. The bird jumped onto it, bit the man's knuckle, and flew off to the top of the bookcase.

"That," said Mrs. Everett, "is love."

His uncle decided to stay a bit longer, and Christal's mother volunteered to sit with Mr. Lawrence. "You and Ruth go ahead," Mrs. Everett said. "Take Christal to the carnival."

The carnival! He'd forgotten all about it.

Ruth Everett had her hand on the door when he went to leave.

"To walk with you, Ruth Everett, I'll even button my coat and put on my hat and gloves."

Christal's aunt laughed. "You're a quick study, Isaac."

As they walked back together, she told him stories of her youth, of the good times they'd all had, ice-skating and sledding and having snowball fights.

"It was as if we were crazed to have our last moments of wildness before putting on the heavy garments of adulthood. We played, we gamboled. . ."

"You gambled?" He couldn't imagine her with a pair of dice or a deck of cards in her hand, not now, not as a young woman. "I can't see you at a game of chance, gambling."

She laughed. "Gamboled with an *o*. As in, we frolicked. We reveled. We celebrated whatever could be celebrated. And probably some things that couldn't. You know what it's like."

Actually, he didn't. Having spent his entire youth as a somber, study-absorbed child, going to college simply moved him to the next stage of the same behavior.

The thought of letting himself act so freely ran contrary to the way he was.

He couldn't gambol *or* gamble.

He realized that she was watching him with a puzzled look on her face. "You didn't, did you?"

He cleared his throat. "Didn't what?"

"Didn't enjoy the carefree days of childhood."

This was wrong. He drew himself up straighter and protested, "I did. I had a wonderful childhood."

"Oh, Isaac, I didn't mean that!" Her hand flew up to her neck and fluttered around the knot of the scarf like a wizened sparrow. Her face was wrinkled with concern. "I know your family was wonderful. Alfred has spoken often of the kindness of your mother and the love your father shared with his children."

"I was a somber child, and I am a somber adult," he said. "It just simply is not in my nature to be merry and convivial."

She stood on the street, studying him with her head cocked to one side, until at last she said, "Well, we will have to change that."

He felt himself sagging inside. He wasn't the center of attention at social gatherings; in fact, he was rarely at social gatherings. The most he could manage was church, and he shuddered as he recalled the first service he attended when he'd had to meet everyone. He'd made it through that situation only through the literal grace of God—and a certain scripture. The fact was that he didn't like wrestling with God. It was so much easier to stand firm on what was comfortable for him, to assert that this was, after all, the way God had made him and the way God had established the world around him.

He'd been ridiculously pleased, though, when he'd forced himself to greet the people at the church. To tell the truth, it wasn't as if he'd had any choice. Once Christal's father had announced his presence and invited them all to say hello to him, he'd had little opportunity to slide out unnoticed.

"Everybody needs to savor the gifts we've been given," Ruth said. "Even if we're just sitting in the sunshine or enjoying the grace of snowflakes floating to earth, we need to acknowledge and appreciate the wonders."

"I don't have time—" he began, but she interrupted him.

"Even a moment is enough. Understanding that simple beauty is really not simple at all is important. It comes from our Creator. Think, Isaac, if you had made a daisy, a little common daisy, wouldn't you be incredibly pleased? And wouldn't it be nice if someone said, 'Good job, Isaac'?"

They had come to the front of the Everett household, and he paused at the brick walkway. "I see your point," he said.

"Good. A little honest recognition of how complex the smallest part of our world is will make you truly awed."

Awed. That was exactly how he felt. Awed by the littlest detail, like a snow-flake, all the way to the greatest thing, like John Lawrence's near-death.

Awed by the creations of the Lord and the creations of man. Like the ice palace.

And parades. He thought of Christal's words: "You can't wait for a parade to come to you. You have to go to the parade." It was time for him to go to the parade, in more ways than one.

$\rightleftharpoons$

They missed the parade, but knowing that John Lawrence would live was worth it.

The sun was nearly set, and the sky was a vision of splendid oranges and purples and golds, like marbled fire, and the ice palace glittered in the late after-noon light. Visitors streamed toward it, drawn by the icy glory. It dominated most of Central Park with its wintry splendor.

Christal's steps slowed as she tried to take in the beauty of it. Her eyes didn't seem to be big enough to absorb it.

"It's incredible." She breathed at last.

Isaac took her mittened hand in his. "I've been reading about this in the newspaper and hearing people talk about it, but I didn't quite grasp what it was going to be like."

"How could anyone imagine something like this? It shimmers, doesn't it?"

"I know the statistics of it," he said, reaching in his pocket with his free hand. "I have it right here."

She tore her attention from the ice palace to look at him. "You have statistics in your pocket?"

"It was in the newspaper. I thought it would be interesting."

Had she hurt his feelings? She squeezed his fingers through their mittens. "It will be interesting. I was just teasing. Read on, please!"

"I won't read the entire thing, but here's the gist of it. The palace is built from twenty thousand blocks of ice, and the ice has been brought in from all around the area, even from Fargo, North Dakota."

"Why would they do that?" She turned back to study the ice castle, which shone with an iridescent gleam in the last vestiges of the afternoon sun.

He shook his head. "They needed the ice, I suppose, but I'd imagine that the folks in these other communities might have enjoyed being part of this."

"It's really much bigger than I'd ever dreamed it would be."

"According to the article, it's 189 feet long and 160 feet high. The central tower alone is 106 feet tall!"

The ice castle, silhouetted against the vermilion and scarlet sunset, was commanding. It glowed with the vivid reflected colors of the sun's last blaze, combined with the cool blues and purples and greens from within the ice itself.

"It's a frozen rainbow," she said, squeezing his hand tightly. "I've never seen anything like it."

She turned to look up at him. He was staring at the ice castle, his mouth open a bit, and his breath came out in short white puffs. He was no longer hunkered down inside his coat and muffler. Perhaps the scene in front of him was enough to make him forget how cold he was.

The last vestiges of light vanished beneath the horizon as the sun sank with its usual wintry suddenness, and Isaac sighed. "One of the oddest things about this area," he said, "is how quickly the sun sets. It lays out the most glorious palette, and then, just like that, it's done. Day is over and night begins."

"That's only in winter. In summer the sun takes a more leisurely stroll ending its daylight time, and the sunsets last longer. You'll see."

He looked at her and smiled. "I'm looking forward to that—and not just because it'll be warmer then!"

The ice palace suddenly began to glow from within, sending a kaleidoscope of color across the snow.

"Electric lights," he said to her. "There are electric lights in there. I have to see that!"

"I saw them at an exhibition last year. The fellow who was speaking claimed that there's no flame involved. It was quite amazing."

"It's the future, according to Uncle Alfred. One day that's how we'll be lighting our houses!"

She shook her head. How could anyone believe that? Light without a flame? Was it possible? And in their houses?

He tucked her arm closer to his body, and together they walked toward the palace. Around them a crowd of people surged forward, all of them headed in the same direction.

The evening was wrapped in magic. The palace seemed to be illuminated with its own radiance, still echoing the last moments of the sun's wild blaze.

" 'He casteth forth his ice like morsels: who can stand before his cold?' " she said softly.

She leaned against Isaac, taking advantage of the fur surrounding the hood of her coat to steal covert glances at him. His cheeks, above the swath of the muffler he'd wound around his neck, were reddened with the cold, and his nose was scarlet.

He wore a great fur hat that made her smile; it looked for all the world as if an oversized squirrel were perched upon his head. The poor man was dressed as if he were going on an Arctic expedition instead of just across the city.

Yet the ice palace had apparently made him temporarily, at least, forget his constant chilliness. He didn't walk bent over, as if he were trying to preserve every particle of heat possible. Instead, he stood straight and craned his neck out of the safety of the muffler to see the spectacle before him.

The crowd gave them no choice but to keep moving toward the arched entrance to the ice castle. A young woman dressed in a long white wool coat rimmed with white fur stood next to a portly gentleman in a dress overcoat. The buttons of his coat strained over his stomach, and he moved from foot to foot to keep warm, like Aristotle on his perch, Christal thought.

"Good evening!" the woman sang out. "Welcome to the Winter Carnival!"

She looked like the spirit of winter, garbed in pure white, her cheeks rosy in the cold, and she smiled widely at each person who entered the castle through the arch, motioning them in with a wave of her white-gloved hand.

The man, however, was clearly the gatekeeper, and pleasantries were at a minimum. "Twenty-five cents entry a head," he said mechanically. "Twenty-five cents."

Isaac held out two quarters, and coin and paper exchanged hands. "We've got our tickets," he said to her. "We can go in."

The young lady swept her hand toward the entrance. "Enjoy the ice palace!"

The castle was extraordinary from the outside, but inside it was stupendous. No matter where Christal looked, there was something unexpected, something wonderful.

A village of Sioux Indians was set up in one of the rooms. It was an entire encampment, and Christal's eyes couldn't stop looking at all of the details, from the tepee to the clothing. It was an astonishing display.

"They brought this all here and set it up? It looks so real!"

"It is real," Isaac said. "All of this is real."

Through the translucent walls of ice blocks, she could see people moving about. Everyone was clad in layers, and she wished she'd thought to bring her muff. Her fingertips were beginning to get numb even through the woolen mittens, but her whole arms could freeze and she wouldn't leave.

"There's the ice-skating rink," Isaac said, pointing.

"Papa told me that there are two ice-skating rinks, and a curling rink, too!" She shook her head. How could all this be? "Toboggan slides, too! I've never seen such a thing!"

"Look," Isaac said, pulling her in a different direction. "There are warming rooms! We can even buy food here!"

Christal couldn't take it all in. It was splendid beyond belief, right down to the crystalline walls and ceiling made of ice.

"It's so beautiful," she said.

Everywhere they turned, there was something else to see, each thing more amazing than the other. The dark of the night was chased away by the electric lights that punctuated the grand building, brightening every corner.

"Next week they're adding the items from the Adolphus Washington Greely Arctic expedition," Isaac said. "His sled will be here, and his journal, and even his gloves and his boots."

They strolled through the palace arm in arm.

She stopped suddenly and took off her mitten.

"What are you doing?" he asked in surprise.

She pressed her fingertips to a nearby wall, pulling them back only when the cold became too much to bear.

"Why did you do that?" he asked.

"It's like a dream. I had to make sure it's real."

"It's real," he said. "I'm thunderstruck—although that's probably not the right word to use in an ice palace. Whoever thought of this is a genius."

"A genius? So you've changed your mind? It's not as silly as you thought?"

"I was wrong." He laughed. "Those words don't come easily to me, understand, but they're true. This is beyond belief. It's like something from one of those fairy tales you like."

She shook her head. "Fairy tales have ogres and trolls in them."

He faced her and took her hands in his. "Let's make this a real fairy tale, Christal. This is a castle, and you're a princess. That much is true. Would you consider letting this very common man spend his life with you?"

Her breath caught in her throat. "You mean—?"

"In simple English, please marry me. I love you beyond all thought. Please, Christal, marry me."

The magic of the ice palace wrapped them in a glittering embrace.

"Yes," she said. "Yes."

Epilogue

From the church bulletin:

The congregation of Redeemer Church bids a fond farewell to Rev. Matthew Everett and his wife, Sarah, who have gone to Tahiti in the missionary service. As his last official act as minister of this church, Rev. Everett joined in holy matrimony his daughter, Christal Maria, and Dr. Isaac Tobias Bering.

A belated wish for Ruth and Alfred Bering, whom we have known and loved for many years, as they start the next chapter of their lives as husband and wife: May you always know sunshine.

It is written in the Bible: The greatest of these is love. And so it is.

2 ½ cups flour
1 teaspoon baking powder
½ teaspoon baking soda
¼ teaspoon salt
1 ½ teaspoons ground ginger
1 teaspoon cloves
1 teaspoon nutmeg
¾ teaspoon cinnamon
1 cup brown sugar
1 cup shortening
¼ cup molasses
1 egg
Extra sugar (about ½ cup) to roll the cookie dough in

Mix together dry ingredients and then add shortening, molasses, and egg. Shape dough into balls about 1 to 1¼ inches in diameter, and roll in extra sugar. Place on cookie sheet, tapping each cookie very slightly to flatten dough balls a bit, and bake at 350 degrees for eight minutes. Let cookies cool on cookie sheet. Makes about 40 cookies.

KIND-HEARTED
WOMAN

Dedication

To my good friend Colette Riely.
You are a truly kind-hearted woman.

Chapter 1

He has answered me! He can't live without me! He tells me that we belong together, that we will breathe and live and love as one. When I read his words, of how he will carry me away from this drudgery, I want to spin in the barnyard. Never mind the chickens. I am Cinderella, and this is no longer Minnesota, 1935, and the drought is only

Lolly Prescott smiled as she reread the words. He was wonderful, truly he was. He was everything she'd always wanted, everything she'd dreamed of. She shut her eyes and clutched the journal close to her. Her heart was in the paperbound volume, her secret love revealed.

Her reverie was broken by frantic barking from outside, signaling her brothers' arrival back from the fields. The family dog never let the two young men out of sight, and the beast barked the way some people talked—without end. If it weren't for the furry protective love Bruno provided, she would have long ago traded him in for something quieter.

She shoved the notebook into her apron pocket. The notebook had been a gift from her teacher when she graduated from high school. It was no bigger than a slice of bread, and was bound in plain brown card stock, but it had become her haven. Hurriedly she stuck the pencil into the bun straggling down her neck. She didn't dare let them know about her secret. They'd never give her a moment's peace—not that they did anyway, she thought, as the dog danced happily around her feet.

"George. Bud." She tried to calm her voice. "You're back early."

Her brothers threw their hats at the rack in the hallway, both of them missing the hooks and leaving the hats on the floor. Automatically she walked over, rescued the headwear from Bruno's playful tossing, and hung them properly.

"It's hotter than—" Bud began, but George prodded him with a warning shake of his head. Bud glared at his older brother. "What did you think I was going to say? Give me a little credit here, George."

"I know it's hot," Lolly said, trying to stave off the argument that would inevitably begin if her brothers weren't sidetracked. "This whole summer's been dreadful. Do either of you want a glass of water?"

"Is it boiling?" George asked, pulling a chair from the table and dropping into it.

"Not yet. Ask me again midafternoon. It just might be by then, especially if it sits in this kitchen." She poured water into a dish for Bruno, who promptly lapped the bowl dry.

"Awww, poor Lolly. Is my poor sister feeling put upon? Is it too hot in here? Want to try a turn in the fields? Think it's cooler there?"

"Stop your blathering, Bud. It's too hot for that kind of nonsense." George leaned back and put his arms over his head. "I wish the air wasn't so still today."

A fat fly buzzed sluggishly on the window ledge. She pushed a stray strand of hair, wet with sweat, back to the bun at the nape of her neck, but it promptly fell out again. "It might rain."

Bud hooted. "Might rain. Might snow. Hey, George, it might even hurricane!"

Lolly shut her eyes just long enough to send up a short prayer for patience. All these years of living with her two brothers, especially Bud, had given her plenty of practice in the art of the brief prayer.

Bud was nearly seventeen, but his impetuous energy made him seem younger. He sped through life without caution. When he was four, he jumped from the hayloft to see if he could fly. He couldn't, and the scar over his ear was silent testimony to that experiment.

At seven, he decided he wanted to know what it was like to drive the truck. They had to rebuild the chicken coop after that escapade.

Now, ten years later, he was still as rambunctious and uncontained as ever.

George, on the other hand, was a somber and proper fellow. He seemed to Lolly to be stolidly middle-aged rather than twenty-four. He was, Lolly had to admit, a bit boring.

"Anything coming up in that weed patch you call a garden?" Bud asked, interrupting her thoughts. "I'm about ready for some sweet corn and green beans and some big, ripe tomatoes. That's the stuff dreams are made of."

She rolled her eyes. "Dream on, then. So far I've got radishes. Want some radishes for dinner? How about for breakfast?"

"You two are crazy. Radishes just come up first. Give her some time, Bud."

George unfolded his lanky frame from the spindle chair and made his way to the door. "I'm soaked, and I smell like a barn. Just because I stink doesn't mean that the kitchen should, too. I'm going to clean up before dinner."

He preferred to use the pump outside to clean himself off rather than the sink inside after working in the fields, especially in summer when the water was cool from the well and evaporated almost immediately in the heat.

From her position in the kitchen, Lolly watched him at the pump. Lately the water hadn't been coming out of it as easily as before. No matter how hard she tried, there were times when she couldn't get any water out at all.

But George was stronger than she was, and water soon gushed out. That was a good sign. It meant that the water table was still high enough for them to use. Nevertheless, George, always careful, made sure that every drop went into the catch basin.

Her brothers were so different from each other. George lived by rules and expected everyone else to. Bud was a bundle of lightly packaged energy. There was nothing about the two that was alike, except their nearly obsessive sheltering of their sister.

As if she had anything to be sheltered against here in Valley Junction. Lolly resisted the urge to sigh. There wasn't a marriageable man within fifteen miles of her, unless she counted seven-year-old Adam Whitaker, or Nigel Prothus, who was well into his nineties.

One thing this drought had done was to take away what few choices she'd had. When she thought about it, a heavy blanket of sorrow lay across her. So she did the only smart thing. She didn't think about it at all, at least not unless she had to.

Usually there wasn't enough time to dwell on anything. Taking care of the farmhouse and the scattering of chickens took up most of her time.

She touched the little notebook hidden in her apron pocket. Everyone needed some kind of dream. Dreams were choices.

If anything, she needed the light that her dreams provided. She felt stuck, right in the middle, both in age and in managing her brothers. Stuck on the farm. Stuck with her brothers forever. Stuck with a dog that would not stop barking.

When her parents had died in an accident five years ago, the responsibility for the family had fallen directly on her young shoulders. She'd been barely fourteen at the time, and she'd grown up very quickly. Too quickly.

The fly on the windowsill stirred slightly, and she noticed others beside it, on the outside of the house. In the distance, somewhere near the river, a mourning dove called, and she lifted her head with hope. "Did you hear that?" she asked Bud.

He shook his head. "It's all folklore, and you know it."

"No, it isn't." One thing she'd inherited from her father's side of the family was the same streak of stubbornness that made Bud such a trial at times; except she'd learned—usually—to keep her composure. Bud, on the other hand, was pigheaded and strong willed, and it was only through the grace of God that he hadn't ended up in some kind of major trouble.

She could still hear her mother's advice as clearly as if she were speaking it beside her: *We choose our battles, Lolly-Dolly. Be wise.* So she crimped her mouth shut and turned away, back to the window.

It wasn't folklore. It was real. Flies congregated on walls and mourning doves cooed before rain.

Her heart lifted with a momentary anticipation. Maybe it would rain. She closed her eyes, linked her fingers together, and began to pray. *Rain. Please, dear God, let it rain. We need—*

Her conversation with God was interrupted as something pulled on the back of her head, and her hair tumbled down around her shoulders in a sticky mass.

"A pencil? Why do you have a pencil stuck in your hair?" Bud waved it just out of her reach. "Let me guess. You're writing a book! That's what my sister's doing. She's writing a book! Hey, George! Guess what Lolly's doing!"

Hot anger mingled with cold fear. She watched as Bud let the screen door slam on his way out, and listened as he told George, who shook his head soberly.

Her fingers closed around the notebook. There was no way she would share it with her brothers. She'd sooner eat every page than let them see its secrets.

She needed the comfort of her words. If she could build this story in her mind, it became, for a moment, a window. No, not a window. It became a door, a full-fledged exit from a relentless reality into something glorious and shining and beautiful.

Bud was talking animatedly to George, waving his hand in the air as if he were writing fanciful letters. His words floated to her through the torn screen door. "Look at me. I'm a famous writer. Here's my story. Once upon a time there was an ugly girl named Lolly."

"Cut it out," George said flatly. "Leave her alone."

Bruno barked at Bud, and her younger brother, diverted for the moment, threw a stick for the dog to retrieve.

Lolly let herself breathe easier.

He was just teasing. Of course he was. How could he possibly know? There was no way.

~

Colin Hammett stopped and leaned against a sun-bleached fence post. The sun was relentless in its assault. He pulled a grimy handkerchief from his pocket and wiped the sweat from his face.

There'll be times you'll try to remember this heat, Hammett, he reminded himself. *Mentally bottle this and put a strong cork in it, so when December rolls around with its bitter winds and its stinging snows, you'll have this summer's excess to warm your hands and your soul.*

He almost laughed aloud. All this time on the road alone was making him quite the poet. Next thing he knew, he'd be penning sonnets about stars and odes to squirrels.

He'd changed so much in the past two months. He rubbed his chin and grimaced at the growth of beard. How long had it been since he'd shaved? One week? Two?

He was a mess. There was no doubt about it. He'd thought that his time on the road would give him some time to think, to sort things out, but now he knew even less than he did before.

When he'd left New York, he hadn't had any idea at all what he was getting into. He knew he had to get away, and get away he did.

His life there had been good, too good. The challenges were few, mainly which tie to wear to which soiree.

His company, a family business, was still successful despite the hard financial times that others had experienced.

He dropped his pack and flexed his fingers. He was very tired, but he needed to remember why he was here. Consciously, he began to run the scene again in his mind.

He'd been in one of the poorer sections of the city, in a hurry, as always, to leave it. He'd volunteered to drop off a carton of food, donated by his church, at a soup kitchen.

That had been his life—not unaware of poverty but untouched by it. And always, always, he'd prayed for the poor. Perfunctory prayer perhaps, but there was a part of him that held back compassion. Was it possible that there were *no* jobs, no employment out in the world? It made no sense to him.

He'd been especially rushed that afternoon. An evening dinner with the mayor beckoned. A ragged man seated at the door of a shop caught his attention, and in his expression, Colin had seen not the vacant gaze of despair, but eyes full of—of something. He hadn't been able to put a name on it.

The action was easy. Reach in his pocket, pull out a handful of coins, toss off a quick "God bless you," and be on his way. He'd done it a million times.

But this was the millionth and one.

"God bless you," he'd said, and the man looked at him with what he now knew was dignity and responded, "Blessed is the man that trusteth in the Lord."

At first it hadn't made sense, and Colin had dismissed it as the ramblings of a vagrant. But the words had stayed with him, digging into his bones until he finally faced the truth: He hadn't trusted in anything, especially not in God. He saw how meaningless and empty his life was, and he vowed to quit letting his life be given to him on a silver platter. The only way to do it was to change it all. If he was going to understand the man on the street, he'd have to become the man on the street. It meant starting over, with nothing.

The prospect of change was exciting. He'd come back from his expedition a changed man, with a backpack of stories to tell.

He went home, threw a change of clothes in a bag, and headed off to find himself.

Now he wished he'd been a bit more circumspect in his actions.

As he'd done so many times before, he ran through the litany of what he'd do differently. He'd have brought more money, arranged for lodging, settled his meals, organized some transportation, even packed additional clothing. He lifted up his right foot and stared ruefully at the sole of his shoe. It flapped loose and had a hole in it the size of a silver dollar.

But haste has its own wings. He'd flown out of the city, vowing never to look back. Here he sat, somewhere in Minnesota, by the best of his reckonings, and without a penny to his name—and he was indeed looking back and reevaluating his actions.

The life of a rambler hadn't been as exciting and invigorating as he'd envisioned. He'd managed to cobble together enough food and shelter at each stop to make this adventure bearable. It hadn't been easy, but that was part of the challenge.

The road shimmered in front of him, and he reached for a fence post to steady himself. Each step was becoming harder to take. Maybe the end of the road was near for him.

He'd always claimed himself as a Christian. He was a bulwark of his church, in the front each Sunday. Tithing and singing and serving as the president of the men's league—it all counted, didn't it?

When he'd decided to adopt the life of a vagrant, it was to understand those less fortunate, to become aware of his own blessings, and to get closer to God. He had succeeded on the first two counts, but on the last one? Unless he counted that he was pretty much knocking on heaven's door at the moment, he'd have to say he'd failed.

He took the canteen out of his pack and raised it to take a drink. His hand shook, and the few precious drops of water remaining fell to the ground.

The moment had come to ask for help.

A few tears stung sharply at his eyes, and he dashed them away with the filthy handkerchief.

Help. He didn't want to ask anyone for anything, not anymore. That had been his motto, ever since his life—or lack of it—had sent him from the days that had been totally planned out, right into the dizzying unknown of a life on the road.

Only the weak asked for help. How many times had he heard that—or, God help him, how many times had he said that? Only the weak.

But he had to have something to drink, and soon. His lips were dried and cracked, and his tongue was so swollen that he could no longer sing his way along the road. Now the hymns were only in his mind, the lines and verses jumbled together. Just that afternoon he had tried to get through "Rock of Ages," and he struggled in the middle of the second verse as the lyrics left him.

Left him! He'd prided himself on his knowledge of hymns, and now that, too, was leaving him.

Something was happening to his head. Not only was he becoming wildly fanciful and horribly forgetful, he was having difficulty keeping his eyes focused on the road ahead.

Now there's a metaphor for you. The road ahead. How can I keep my eyes on the path before me when I can't even see where I'm going?

The brilliance of the sun was blinding. He blinked, and blinked again. But still he saw through a white veil of blazing sunlight.

His head felt like an oversized empty ball on the top of his body. He was floating.

Had it ever been this hot? This airless? The truth was that today was blistering and dry, just like the day before, and the day before that. *Rain* was the prayer on everyone's lips.

A verse from Jeremiah sprang into his head, the same one the man on the New York City street had said to him, and he said it aloud: "Blessed is the man that trusteth in the Lord, and whose hope the Lord is." There was more after it, something about a tree by a river, but he couldn't recall it at the moment.

He had to trust. God saw him, trudging along the road. God would see to him. God would provide. He had to trust in that, but he knew one other thing: He had to help himself, too.

He took one last swipe across his face with the grubby cloth and took a deep breath. *Pull it together. You have work to do.*

Resolutely, he balanced his bedroll on his back and took a tentative step. His knees turned to rubber, numbly refusing to hold up his body. The world swirled into a dust-colored spinning vortex, and his legs gave out from under him.

As he sank to the ground, a carving on the fence post spun by him. It was a roughly scratched outline of a cat.

Kind-hearted woman. That's what it meant. Some hobo before him had taken the time to alert others that this farm housed a woman who would feed the homeless.

That was what he needed, a kind-hearted woman.

As the clouds took over his brain entirely, he smiled. More words from the Jeremiah passage came to him: *"Heal me, O Lord, and I shall be healed; save me, and I shall be saved: for thou art my praise."*

⌒

"Lolly!"

Bud and George kicked open the screen door and made their way to the front room, where they dropped a man onto the sagging cushions of the worn old couch.

"Get some water," George said as he examined the man's face, lifting his eyelids and feeling his pulse in his neck. "He's still alive, but just barely. Hurry, Lolly."

As she picked up the pitcher from the kitchen table, the man groaned. She poured some water into a bowl and carried it to the living room, putting it on the table beside the couch.

"Here," she said, handing George a towel she'd snatched up from the kitchen. It was one she'd embroidered—a teakettle with a smiling face. It seemed so incongruous here with a stranger unconscious on her couch.

Beside them, on the shelf next to the crystal vase that had been their parents', a Bakelite clock ticked away the seconds.

George splashed the water on the man's face and dribbled a few drops into his mouth. "He's dehydrated," he announced. "Look at his lips, how dry they are. There's hardly any liquid in him at all."

"Yeah," Bud agreed. "His canteen was on the ground beside him, sis, empty and dry as one of Bruno's bones."

"He hasn't had enough food or water to keep body and soul together," Lolly said softly. "He's so thin."

"Look at this." George pinched a bit of the skin on the back of the man's hand. "See how it stays up in this peak? That means he's really parched."

Lolly checked on her own hand. The skin spread right back to its original state. "I didn't know that was how you tested for dehydration. How'd you know that, George?"

He shrugged. "It was in the chickens manual I got from the county. Figure a body's a body, whether it's a chicken or a man."

"Did it tell you how to treat it?" Bud asked as he studied the man on the couch.

"I know we shouldn't give him a lot of food and water all at once," George said. "Just give him a small amount at a time, even if he wakes up and asks for more."

"'Even if he wakes up'?" Lolly repeated. "He is going to wake up, isn't he? I mean, he's not going to, you know, well..."

"He'll be fine," Bud said, standing up and wiping his hands on his dungarees.

George moistened the tea towel embroidered with the smiling teakettle and wiped it across the man's face. "Why, he's just a young man," he said as the dirt came off. "No older than me."

Lolly's heart twisted as she looked from the man to her brothers. How lucky they were to be together, rather than living the life this poor man had been.

He groaned again, and the three stared at him.

"I believe we have company, Lolly," Bud said at last. "Bring out the fine china."

Chapter 2

Together. It is the most beautiful word in the English language. Together.
We are not meant to live apart, not when God has joined our hearts in
timeless love. We will grow together like the well-watered vine, climbing
up the trellis of the years. It is our destiny, our forever.

The three siblings stood around the worn sofa, watching intently as the man stirred. His face was ashen against the faded burgundy and green tapestry of the couch, his shoulders gaunt in the sunken cushions.

Breathe. Lolly stared at the man's chest, willing it to rise and fall. Breathe in. Breathe out. Breathe in. Breathe out. She realized she was inhaling and exhaling with him, as if her own strong lungs could give him air.

One of the neighbor's cows lowed from a far field. Bruno barked in response, and the chickens clucked among themselves.

The cows belonged to Ruth Gregory's family. George was, everyone assumed, going to marry Ruth one day, but he was slow to speak his piece. For the past three years, whenever he was in town, he'd dawdle at her café in town, sipping a cola. The cow was more vocal than he was, Lolly thought.

It seemed odd, almost as if there were two worlds existing side by side, the normal everyday one out in the field and the yard, and the drama unfolding in the house.

The stranger's mouth twitched, and his eyelids flew open, his gaze latching almost immediately onto Lolly. "Sah kaahraah aah," he said, his eyes, as dark brown as George's coffee, not moving away from hers.

"A cigarette!" Bud said under his voice. "The man wants a cigarette!"

"No, I think he said he wants a cigar." George frowned at the stranger.

"How do you get cigar out of 'Sah kaahraah aah'?" Bud argued. "He's clearly asking for a cigarette, aren't you, pal? Do you want a cigarette?"

"Or a cigar?" George persisted, leaning in toward the man.

"You want a cigarette, don't you?" Bud shook the stranger's elbow lightly. "A cigarette, right? See, he nodded."

"Oh, will you two stop?" Lolly said, pushing her brothers away. "You're taking up all of his air, and besides that, we don't have a cigar or a cigarette, so what does it matter?"

"I suppose," Bud grumbled, "although I'm sure that's what he said."

"Sah kaahraah aah," the stranger said again, and this time his mouth slid into a faint smile that held for a moment and then slipped away as his eyes shut again.

"Well, no cigar for you, mister," George said, "at least not until you get your strength back."

I'm going to need Your help here, Lolly prayed silently. *I've got a fellow here who is in terrible shape, and then, well, I've got my brothers.*

A flurry of barks from the door and a clatter of claws on the wooden floor announced the arrival of the dog. Bruno pushed his way in front of them and sniffed the stranger, starting at the top of his head, going all the way to his toes, and then back up again.

Before she could react, the dog licked the man's face enthusiastically. The stranger didn't even flinch as the huge dog's tongue left a trail of slobber through the dirt that still encrusted the man's face despite George's ministrations.

"Get back, Bruno! Honestly!" She tugged at him and pulled him away.

The dog flopped onto the floor, sprawling out as if his exertions had tired him out entirely.

Lolly shut her eyes. *See what I mean, God? Even the dog is a daily challenge for me.*

"I wonder where this fellow came from," Bud said. "He looks like he's been on the road for quite a while."

"I'm going to go back to the spot where we found him and poke around, see if there's something that might give us a clue as to who he is." George whistled and Bruno sprang to alertness. "Come on, boy. We've got some investigating to do."

"I'll come, too." Bud stopped and looked back and forth between his sister and the man on the couch. "You going to be all right?"

"I think so." Lolly looked at their guest. "He doesn't look like he's got the energy to swat a fly."

"Well, if he lives—" Bud began, but George walloped him in the shoulder, stopping the sentence if not the thought.

"He looks to be a tough sort," George said gruffly, looking away as he said the words.

Lolly turned her attention to the man on the couch. He looked anything but tough. His skin's underlying pallor lent a blue-white tinge to his sunburned face, and his breathing was shallow and rapid.

She touched the back of his wrist, carefully, tentatively, and his fingers twitched in response. She pulled her hand away and tucked it behind her back, as if hiding it would undo the action.

The man muttered something and jerked his head back and forth spasmodically.

Then he began to speak. Through his parched and split lips, unintelligible words, no more than broken syllables, spun out in a papery stream.

Lolly knew he wasn't talking to her. He couldn't even know that she was there, he was in such bad shape. His eyes clenched, as if squeezing away a bad image, but never opened.

Perhaps he was delirious. Her knowledge of medicine was minimal at best. The only things she'd had to deal with were the occasional colds, sore throats, and stomach distresses, and the treatment for those had been simply to let the illnesses run their courses.

Was that the wisest thing to do here? Should she call for the doctor? And how on earth would she pay for his visit?

She couldn't let the man simply die on her couch.

The only thing she could do was pray. She swallowed hard and put her hand on the man's chest—right over where she was pretty sure his heart was—shut her eyes, and prayed aloud: "Please, dearest God, make him well and whole. Please. Please, God. Bring him back to health."

She could feel each of his ribs as his chest rose and fell with every labored breath. He was as thin as his shirt.

She opened her eyes and looked at the man again. Whoever he was, he seemed to be teetering on the edge of life. "Stay alive," she whispered to him.

There had to be a reason God had brought him to their home. Maybe in time she'd know, but one thing she'd learned in her nineteen years was that God had His own timetable, and it might not be until she was in the great hereafter that she would learn the whys and why nots of life on this earth.

It wasn't that she didn't have questions. Why, for example, did good people suffer? Why did God let that happen? Why did their parents die so young?

Why was there drought? Why didn't He command the rain to fall? Why was the Depression tearing so many lives apart? And when people were hungry, why didn't He send down some of that manna?

She sat next to the couch, matching the rise and fall of his chest, breath for breath, willing him to keep inhaling and exhaling, until frenetic barking and loud voices announced that her brothers and the dog had come back.

"We found it!" Bud called from the doorway, then clapped his hand over his mouth as he glanced at the prone figure on the couch. "Is he dead?" he asked in a stage whisper.

George pushed him aside. "You have the manners of a coyote," he informed his brother, "and you smell just as bad." Then, gently, to his sister, "How's he doing?"

"The same. What did you find?"

"Wait until you see!" Bud slid across the floor to her. No matter how many times she'd told him to stop, he insisted on doing it. He'd never grow up. The boy was almost seventeen and still acting like an adolescent. Lolly despaired of his ever behaving like a grown-up.

Automatically she chided, "Slide across that floor one more time, and I'll polish out the scratches with your head."

He waved away her complaints and held out a pack. It was dusty and soiled, and Lolly drew back. It smelled like, well, like a man on the road would smell.

"And George has got the fella's bedroll."

Before Lolly could interrupt the inevitable, Bud dumped the contents of the pack on the floor next to the sofa, and George untied the bedroll and let it unfurl. The end struck the little table with the bowl of water they'd used to clean off the man's face, and she caught it before it spilled.

"You shouldn't be doing that," she said. "That's just wrong, going through his things like that."

"It's not like he's in any position to give us permission," George pointed out. "And this might give us some important information, like maybe he's got some disease or something that we should know about."

"Some disease? There's a cheerful thought." Lolly shook her head. "Even if he had a disease, we couldn't do anything about it."

"Oh, do you suppose?" Bud asked, stopping his investigation of the contents of the man's pack.

"Do I suppose what?" Lolly asked.

"What if he has one of those terrible diseases that's really catchable—"

"Contagious," George said.

"Contagious, and now we'll all get it and die? And they'll come to find out why we haven't been to town for a month, and they'll find our shriveled-up bodies, and they'll realize that there are four bodies and only three of us, and it'll be a huge mystery who the extra—"

God, isn't it enough that I have these two buffoons to watch over, and now You give me an unconscious man, too?

George rolled his eyes at his brother and gathered up the blanket and flattened pillow that had been in the stranger's sleeping bundle. "Nothing here. I'll put it out on the fence to air out. Lolly, maybe once the bedding isn't quite so pungent you can take a look at it and see if it's worth laundering."

"Take this extra shirt and pants with you," Bud said, tossing the offending items toward his brother. "They're a bit heavy on the stink, too."

George paused before leaving the room. "So was there anything of interest at all in the pack?"

Bud shook his head. "There isn't anything in there, really. One of those free Bibles they give away and a comb and a toothbrush. I know, I know. Take it out of the house, too. Who knows what all is crawling on it."

Lolly looked at the man on the couch. His breathing had deepened, but it was still erratic. "He looks to be about your size, George. Do you suppose you could clean him up a bit more and get him into some of your old clothes?"

"Sure. Let me get his stuff taken care of, and then Bud and I will work on him. Come on, Bud, help me out."

The brothers left the house, carrying the stranger's things with them, and she turned to their silent guest, humming as she studied his face. She ran through hymn after hymn, singing the words when she could remember them, and letting the melody carry the song when she couldn't recall the lines.

He looked so frail, so helpless, lying there. His dark hair made the ashen color of his skin even more pronounced. He must have been on the road a long time to be this thin. His wrist bones angled out. Had he been hungry? Had to go without meals? Been forced to beg for food?

She and her brothers constantly battled the curse of need. There was never enough money, or maybe only just enough to keep them one step ahead of losing the farm entirely. They were still safe from this gnawing want that was plaguing the nation. At the very least, they had food. It wasn't fancy, and there were times when it wasn't very good, but at least it was there.

Was that why he'd come here? She'd fed other travelers in need, but they'd always thanked her and gone on. None had stayed. Of course, this man didn't have the option of choosing to stay or leave.

The verse from Hebrews sprang to her mind: "*Be not forgetful to entertain strangers: for thereby some have entertained angels unawares.*"

"Is that what you are?" she asked softly. "Are you an angel?" She shook her head. "I somehow don't think so, but angel or not, you are welcome to stay here and recover. We will take care of you as long as you need, whatever your reason for rambling is."

The Bible was on the floor, right where Bud had left it. Typical of her brother, she thought, to leave it where it landed when he'd scrounged through the contents of the backpack.

More from idle habit than anything else, she opened the Bible—and saw a name written there in pencil. Colin Hammett.

"Is that your name? Colin?"

The figure on the couch didn't stir, and she picked up the pack to replace the Bible. It wasn't at all what she'd expected. The bag was made of fine leather and lined with beautiful lustrous fabric, although the piece hadn't weathered its time outside too well.

Someone must have taken pity on this man of the road and given him this bag to use. He certainly didn't seem the type to be able to afford it on his own.

135

One day he would tell her the story of his life. In order to do that, though, he'd have to wake up.

She sighed and looked at him. "One day at a time, Colin. One day at a time."

He wanted to open his eyes, to slide from this darkness back into the world. A woman's voice reached into the void, speaking his name. *"Colin."*

An incredible thirst reached into his mouth and down his throat. He wanted to speak, and he tried, but the motion made his lips sting with nearly unbearable pain, and he slipped back under the edges of the darkness.

Waves. Sound came in waves, muffled, as if he were under the water at Jones Beach on Long Island. He was swimming, gliding through the dark waters. Overhead he could hear the cadence of conversation but nothing came together to form recognizable words.

Except his name. *"Colin."*

Where was he? Who was speaking?

His brain wouldn't work, wouldn't stay on a thought. It skipped and skittered its way through his memories, searching for tags of something, anything, that could claim these sounds.

A dog barked. But that didn't make sense. It shouldn't be a dog. It should be a cat. A kind-hearted cat.

No, that wasn't right. Not a kind-hearted cat. A cat. A cat and a kind-hearted woman.

The barking was suddenly very close, and something slimy slurped across his face. Voices spoke sharply, and he was suddenly being lifted into the air.

His eyes sprang open, and the faces and shoulders of two young men were only inches from him.

"He's awake!" the older one said.

"Well, don't drop him," the other fellow said. "Lolly would kill us if we killed him, especially after we've saved him."

Every part of his head tried to piece together what his eyes and ears were telling him. None of this made sense.

"Lolly?" Colin croaked out.

"Hey, he's talking! Wait until Lolly hears about this! God does answer her prayers, I guess."

"Maybe she could pray us out of this drought, do you think?"

Colin had totally lost track of which one was speaking, as the exchange between the two men arced over his head.

"She hasn't left his side since he got here, except for now, of course."

Then a few of the stray bits clicked into place. A woman with long, light brown hair. Dark blue-gray eyes, the color of river-wet rocks. And a soft smile, a gentle touch, a quiet and true voice that sang—sang something he couldn't quite remember. But she had been there. "Ki-ha-wo?"

"What did I tell you, George?" the younger one asked. "He wants a cigarette."

Colin shook his head, an unfortunate action since it caused all the loosely connected fragments in his cranium to fly apart in a painful flurry. He shut his eyes again, closing out the world until the storm of pain could subside.

He was slipping back under the water at Jones Beach. The gentle waves were cool on his face, wet and refreshingly liquid. He could breathe under this water.

But first he had to say something, something that was very important. He struggled back to the surface and fought through the pounding that caromed around his skull.

He took a deep breath and focused every fragment into a fairly cohesive whole, and then he spoke. "Kind. Hearted. Woman."

Then, having said it, he let the water reclaim him.

~

"He was awake, I tell you, he was," Bud said to Lolly. "And he asked again for a cigarette."

George swatted at his brother. "He did not. He said something, but it didn't make any sense. He said, 'Kind-hearted woman.'"

"Kind-hearted woman?" Lolly looked at their guest, prone on the sagging old couch. His eyes were closed, but his mouth was open a bit and his breathing seemed to be not as labored. Perhaps her brothers' cleaning him up had helped. The dirt had been sponged away, his hair washed and combed, and he was garbed in an old work shirt and pants that once belonged to George. "Why would he say that?"

"He's loco," Bud said. "He smacked his head when he passed out and he's probably got amnesia."

"Oh yeah," George said. "I forgot to tell you. He's got a big swelling over his ear. His hair covers it, but we found it when we were washing him up."

"He kind of yelped when I touched it," Bud volunteered. "So George looked at it really close. There isn't any cut or anything, just a lump the size of your hand there. And it's an amazing color of purple, too."

Lolly knelt beside the sofa and gently pushed aside the man's hair. "His name is Colin," she said as she examined the wound. "Colin Hammett. I don't know if it's better or worse if there's no cut. At least it won't get infected, but it sure looks like he hit something pretty hard when he fell. I wonder what it was."

"He was over by the fence. Probably fell against the post. How do you know his name?" George frowned.

"I'm assuming it's his name. It's what's written on the flyleaf of that Bible." She smoothed the hair over the wounded scalp, taking care not to touch the swollen area. "He looks like a Colin. Did he have any other injuries?"

Her brothers shook their heads.

"Not that we could see, anyway," George contributed.

She bit her lip as she studied Colin's face. She knew absolutely nothing about medicine, but it did seem to her that he should have woken up. And since she knew now about the blow to his head, the stakes had been raised.

That much she was sure of. Head injuries could be deadly.

"We'd better get the doctor here." As soon as she said the words she knew that this was the right course, but how on earth would they pay for a doctor's visit? The only physician in Valley Junction was Dr. Greenleigh, whom Lolly knew solely from church. She had no idea how much he'd charge, but she suspected his services didn't come cheap.

"We can't afford a doctor," Bud said.

"We can't afford to let him die, either." George straightened their guest's collar. "I sure do hope that God is watching over this one. I really do."

You are, aren't You? Lolly asked God silently. *You are watching over him?*

She began praying in earnest, sometimes with words, sometimes without. George and Bud both left, and she only vaguely noticed. Colin had to live. He had to.

Shadows crossed the room. Sunset came late on summer nights, but it started to creep across the horizon when she heard the rumble of the truck pulling up in front, followed by the smoother motor of an automobile.

The door slammed, and footsteps hurried across the floor to the couch.

"Lolly, let me take a look." Dr. Greenleigh perched on the side of the sofa. "If you all don't mind, I'll need some privacy. I'll tell you as soon as I know anything."

The three siblings left the room and gathered in the kitchen. Bruno followed them and sprawled on the floor next to them, chewing on something.

Lolly reached down and took the doctor's handkerchief out of the dog's mouth. "Nasty, Bruno." She'd wash it before she returned it. That dog. . .

Sudden tears filled her eyes. "You stupid dog," she said, fighting back the sobs that were building inside her. "Can't even leave the doctor's hankie alone." She swabbed at her eyes. Silly, crying over something like a handkerchief.

"He'll be fine," George said, but Lolly noticed the way his fingers were white where he gripped the back of a chair. "He'll be fine."

Bud shook his head. "I hope so. I don't want to be gloomy about this, but he's in really bad shape."

She knew that, but hearing Bud say it so baldly rattled her with unexpected force. Their guest had to live. He had to.

Her eyes stung as she fought tears. She mopped them away with the back of her hand as she lost the fight and great watery drops slid down her cheeks.

George put his arm around Lolly's shoulders, and she leaned against him, grateful for his strength.

Dr. Greenleigh called them back into the living room. "What this fellow needs is water. Start small at first and then build up, for the next day or so. Clear soup if you have some. Then add in food, a bit at a time. He may be ravenous, but it won't do his stomach any good to eat a lot right away."

"Eat a lot right away?" Bud echoed. "He's not even awake. How can he eat?"

"Bud's got a point, in a way," Lolly said. "I think I'd be glad if he just woke up. Why won't he wake up?"

The doctor nodded. "Well, he's tired for one thing. Exhausted. I'd wager that he hasn't had a good, restful sleep in quite a while. But he's also got a head injury, and that's tiring in itself."

"I thought people weren't supposed to sleep if they got conked on the head," Bud said. "I'd always heard that you had to keep them awake."

"He doesn't have a concussion, so it doesn't matter. But that doesn't mean he's going to sail on through this. Head injuries are mighty dangerous things." He looked at each of them slowly, one at a time. "The greatest danger, I'm afraid, is that he may lose all or some of his memory."

"But it'll come back, his memory that is, won't it?" Lolly asked, her hands twisting in her apron.

The doctor shrugged. "We would hope. The brain is an incredible thing. It has the remarkable ability to heal or to re-create new paths that go around the damaged area. Having said that, I do caution you that I've seen my share of brain injuries, and some people never recover."

"You mean they die?" Bud asked.

The doctor faced him. "Or sometimes the body stays alive, but the brain doesn't—or at least not much more than is necessary to sustain life functions. I can't say which is worse. That's not my call."

No one spoke until at last the doctor said, "Lolly, George, Bud, I'd recommend you pay close attention to him, and that you pray. What medicine can't do, God can. It's in His hands."

"Thank you, Doctor," George said, as the physician clicked his medical bag shut and headed for the door. "How much do we owe you?"

The doctor paused and shook his head. "No charge. I can't imagine a more fortunate place for a man to almost die than here. If anyone can save him, the three of you can. The healing that's needed here isn't something medicine can do. No, it's up to you three—and God. I'll check back tomorrow."

The door closed behind him, and for a moment they stood in silence, stunned by the gravity of the task ahead.

"Well," George said, "no pressure on us, huh?"

Bruno barked at the doctor's car as it drove away. "He's quite the watchdog, that one," Bud said almost absentmindedly. "Barks when the doctor leaves."

"We should take turns watching over Colin," Lolly said. "If he wakes up—when he wakes up, someone needs to be at his side."

It was odd, she thought as she sat next to the couch later in the day, how things could change in a matter of minutes. And with those changes, how her perception shifted, too.

She'd felt caught, robbed of any choices she might make. And now, here with an injured stranger in her life, she was even more snared, unable to leave. But she no longer felt bound to the farm. She had a mission.

Chapter 3

He is beyond what I ever could have expected. If I could dream a love story, this would be it. With him at my side, I feel light and carefree. I waltz on rainbows; I skip on clouds. The world is glorious with color, and melody surrounds me. He holds my hand, and we face the future. . .as one.

Her head bobbled on her chest as she fought sleep. She was so tired. George had slept right through his shift with Colin, but she hadn't had the heart to wake him up. He worked so hard to keep the farm going, and doing that while keeping Bud in line—or as much in line as possible—was difficult, and she knew that.

But she had to stay awake. What if Colin woke up? She couldn't let herself succumb to sleep. She had to stay awake; she had to.

A touch on her arm startled her.

She must have drifted off. The sun was up, and the dog was snuffling around her feet.

"Sorry," George whispered. "I guess I overslept."

"How is he?" She looked over at Colin.

"Better. He stirred a bit as I came in here. I wouldn't be surprised to see our patient coming to later on today, maybe even this morning. Why don't you catch a few minutes by yourself? You know, swab off, drag a comb through your hair, that kind of thing. Maybe even pop on a clean dress."

She couldn't bear the thought of leaving Colin's side, not when he might be waking up at any moment. "I'm fine."

"No offense, sis," George said, "but you're not."

"No kidding," Bud added as he joined them. "You should take a run by a mirror sometime soon, and then tell me if that's the first thing you'd want to see if you were returning from the world of the nearly dead. You, dear Lolly, are a mess."

There was no point in taking offense at anything Bud blurted out. What his mind thought, his mouth said.

And, in this case at least, he was right, she realized when she caught a glimpse of herself in the mirror over the mantel. The bun at the nape of her neck had almost entirely worked its way free of the string she'd used to hold it back, and now lank locks straggled around her face. Her dress was wrinkled and soiled from the day before. She wasn't a sight for sore eyes as much as she was a sight to make eyes sore.

She filled the basin in the bathroom and dunked a washcloth in it and began to repair the damage as best she could. Soon her hair, still wet, was pulled back in a respectable braid that was tied with a piece of blue ribbon, and she smoothed down the blue and white dress she'd changed into.

"Better?" she asked as she reentered the room.

"Lolly, we have guests. More guests." Bud's voice let her know exactly what he thought of these visitors.

Two women stood up from leaning over the couch. From the stormy expression on George's face, she knew that he wasn't happy. Bruno was growling softly outside the screen door, obviously not pleased at being exiled.

Lolly's heart sank as she saw who was gathered around the couch. She wasn't ready for them. Even with a good night's sleep she wouldn't be a match for them.

Hildegard Hopper had been widowed so long that the townspeople disagreed whom she'd been married to. Whoever the mysterious Mr. Hopper had been, he hadn't lasted long into the marriage, but he'd managed to leave her well enough off that she'd never wanted for anything, even with the Depression nipping at everyone else's heels.

Today her substantial body was wrapped in a spotless ivory dress, and she wore matching shoes with tiny curved heels and open toes. An absurd hat made of a scrap of wool, some netting, and a miniature bird's nest was perched atop her waved auburn hair.

Amelia Kramer was a tiny little thing, just the opposite of Hildegard, and within her gray-curled head were filed the town's secrets. Like a miniature human sponge, she absorbed everything that was said or done around her. Amelia reminded Lolly of a moth that fluttered around the brighter light of Hildegard Hopper.

Amelia had also dressed up for the occasion of meeting the mysterious visitor. She had on her Sunday best, a navy blue two-piece suit. Lolly knew from the design that once it had been quite expensive, but the seams had been repaired so many times that the cut no longer retained its original sharpness.

"Eleanor!" Hildegard tippy-tapped over to Lolly in her impractical shoes and embraced Lolly in a deep hug. Lolly tried not to inhale too deeply; Hildegard did love her perfume.

She winced as the heady scent invaded her lungs. Everything about Hildegard was simply too much: too much perfume, too much money, too much artifice.

And she called her Eleanor. Nobody called Lolly *Eleanor*, not since the day she was born and George had called her Lolly. Lolly she'd become—forever.

Lolly broke from the hug and summoned a smile for the women. "How sweet of you to come. I wasn't expecting you, but—"

"Oh, you goose!" Hildegard gushed on. "Of course you weren't, but we just had to come and see for ourselves! You are so nice to take this man in when you have practically nothing to speak of to live on as it is, not with this terrible depression taking its dreadful toll on all of us!"

"So nice," Amelia echoed. "So nice."

Hildegard minced back to the couch. "He's such a handsome young man. If only his circumstances hadn't brought him here to this lowly place."

George cleared his throat, and Lolly could tell that politeness was arguing with his desire to tell Hildegard Hopper what he thought of her calling their home lowly.

Hildegard must have noticed, for she clapped one hand over her mouth. "Oh, my dears, I didn't mean that! I meant his poor, poor condition, the state of affairs that placed such a man on the road, forced him to become a vagabond and to live off the kindness of strangers who might well not be able to stretch their own meager means to include him."

"Very kind of you to see to his needs." Amelia nodded as she spoke.

"Oh, these woeful times!" Hildegard fanned her face with her fingertips. "There isn't a body in the whole of Minnesota who hasn't felt the dreadful strictures of this horrible mess the nation is in, with no jobs anywhere and no money! Why, just the other day I was commiserating with Reverend Wellman about the sad state of the collection plate. One can hardly hope to keep house and home together, let alone give, as we all should, for the Lord's good work. It's a piteous time, indeed."

Amelia tsked in agreement. "Indeed, Hildegard. Wise, wise words."

"This poor man is indeed fortunate to have found you. Do you know what his situation in life is?" Hildegard's eyebrows arched inquisitively at Lolly.

"His situation?" Lolly asked blankly. "I'm afraid I'm not following you."

"His past. You know, what he was, what he did, who his people were."

Lolly moved a bit closer to Colin, and she noticed that her brothers leaned in almost defensively, too. "I'm sure I don't know," she said, trying to keep the coolness in her voice to a socially acceptable level.

"We're just concerned," Hildegard said, heading for her with opened arms again, "for your safety. With just the three of you out here, all alone, so vulnerable, orphans, the lot of you—why, it pains my heart just to think of the consequences that might occur."

Lolly stepped aside to deflect most of the hug. "We'll be fine."

"He could be a criminal," Amelia said in a softly sinuous voice. It was, Lolly thought, what a snake would sound like if it could speak. The woman's eyes were bright with anticipation, as if she hoped she was right and Colin might slaughter them all in their sleep. What a wonderful story that would be.

It was definitely time for the two women to leave before she or her brothers said something they'd regret.

Lolly placed a gentle hand on each woman's elbow. "He is still quite weak, so I think I'll ask you to return later. We are limiting his visitors and trying to keep the room as quiet as possible. I think you understand." She continued to murmur until she had steered the women out of the room and to the door of Hildegard's DeSoto. Bruno kept a wary eye on the group from the shade of the cottonwoods, occasionally baring his teeth at the visitors.

Without giving either woman a chance to interrupt, Lolly's flow of words continued until the two women were seated in the vehicle.

"Perhaps another day? I hope so. Thank you so much for stopping by to see us. I hope you have a pleasant day."

She stood outside and watched as they drove away, perhaps, she admitted to herself, as much to make sure they were truly going.

When the last puff of road dust had vanished behind the stand of cottonwoods, she returned to the living room.

"How on earth did they know?" she asked her brothers.

"Well," Bud started out, and she knew she was in for a long story, "we went to the doctor's office to find him. You remember, you sent us to get him, so don't even think about blaming us."

"Bud—" she began, but he picked up his story, apparently anxious to clear his name.

"He wasn't there, so we went to the usual places we might find him. The bank, the post office, the church. Nobody'd seen him. George had to stop at the café, of course, and make lovey-dovey eyes at Ruth—"

"I did not!" his brother interjected, his face growing red at the mention of the young woman he'd been somewhat courting.

But Bud continued. "So by the time we got to Leubner's Store, word had spread that we were looking for him, and everybody of course thought you were sick or you'd cut off your hand or had died or something."

"Bud!" George broke in. "You can't tell a story straight for anything." He turned to his sister. "Let me tell what happened. We went into Leubner's, and we were asking if anyone had seen the doctor, and the next thing we knew, here he comes, wondering if you were all right."

"So," Bud interrupted, "we really did have to tell about this fellow here, and it couldn't be helped that Amelia the Snoop was there with her big old ears on; and next thing we know, everybody in town had heard."

Lolly sat down next to the couch. The smell of Hildegard's perfume hung heavy in the air, and she knew it also clung to her clean dress, courtesy of the hugs the older woman had given her.

"I don't like those two," Bud declared. "They were squeezing and poking our fellow, even wanted to look under his shirt to see how thin his arms were. I just don't like them at all."

"Oh, hush!" Lolly scolded. "You shouldn't say things like that."

"But if I say I do like them, I'm lying, and that's a sin, and you know it."

"You don't have to say anything about it at all. I don't recall anyone asking you what your feelings were about them." A bit of hair had fallen over Colin's forehead, and she brushed it away. She was feeling quite protective about him, and the fact was that she didn't want to share him with anyone else. Maybe later she would, but right now she wanted to make him better.

Bud shoved his hands in his pants pockets. "I guess I've got work to do outside. The farm isn't going to take care of itself, you know. Wheat won't grow on its own. Well, I guess it will, but I don't suppose anyone's got the eggs out of the henhouse yet, did they? Didn't think so." He whistled for the dog.

As he and George turned to leave, Lolly heard him mutter, "Hildegard Hopper. Bet that old woman's got a whetstone somewhere in that house that she sharpens her tongue on every morning."

Lolly looked down to hide her grin. It wouldn't do to let her brother see it. No, it wouldn't do at all.

Finally the room was quiet. Colin opened one eye a crack, just to make sure that they were gone.

He'd been asleep when suddenly a woman with a sharp voice like a cackling hen had bent over him, pinching his cheeks and pulling up his sleeve to examine his arm. Someone had pulled her away from him, but her voice clawed at his eardrums.

Her shrill voice kept on, until the woman with the gentle voice, the familiar voice, led her away. Her words were indistinct, but he could tell from her tone what she was doing.

Now they were gone, and the men, too. It was safe.

He opened his eyes. "Hello."

The young woman who'd floated in and out of his delirium jerked into alertness. "You're awake!"

"Sorry," he said. "I didn't mean to startle you."

That was what he tried to say, but it came out distorted. His words sounded thick and muffled. Something was wrong with his tongue. It seemed to be twice its normal size, and his lips didn't move like they were supposed to. He tried again.

"Excuse me. I'm having trouble speaking." The last words came out more like *lubble beeding*.

She leaned forward and ran her hand over his cheek. "Sssh. Let me get you a sip of water. That'll help."

She was the most beautiful woman he'd ever seen. Of course at the moment he couldn't recall any women he'd ever seen, but he was sure that when he could remember them, she would still rank at the top.

The water she dropped into his mouth from a spoon was like liquid grace. A few precious drops spilled out, and she caught them with her fingertip.

"Sit up." The words came out with remarkable clarity, and encouraged by that, he tried more. Slowly but distinctly the words formed. "I want to sit up."

"Are you sure?"

He started to nod but thought better of it when his head pounded in immediate response.

"I'll try," she said, and she leaned over. The smell of the sharp-voiced woman's perfume returned but under it was the soft aroma of soap, and a faint scent of shampoo.

She moved the pillows around and put her hands under his arms to lift him. "If I hurt you, let me know. I'll do my best not to, though. On the count of three? One. Two. *Three!*"

It felt wonderful to sit up at last. His body felt disconnected, as if his legs and his arms were no longer joined to his torso. He moved them experimentally and was relieved when feeling sparked back into the limbs.

"More water, please."

"Just a bit at a time, but yes, here's more."

She held the spoon to his lips again.

"I dreamed of water," he told her.

"I'm not surprised. You're quite dehydrated."

"I was swimming at Jones Beach."

She smiled. "I don't know what that is."

"It's on Long Island, in New York."

"That's quite far away." She lifted the spoon again. "More?"

"Yes, please. And I could breathe under water."

"Ah. That is quite a rare talent."

He was like a bottle uncorked. He couldn't stop talking, and the more he said, the easier it was. The words kept coming.

"You sang to me, didn't you?"

"Maybe. My brothers might argue if I sing or if I caterwaul, though."

"You sing. Like an angel."

She laughed at that, and the sound was like a crystal waterfall. "I think I should tell you that you hit your head pretty hard. I don't sound anything like an angel, I'm sure."

He couldn't stop looking at her. "What is your name?"

"Lolly. Lolly Prescott."

He nodded but checked the motion before it could set off the drums in his head. "Who's Eleanor?"

She grinned. "You were listening, weren't you?"

"Maybe."

"I'm Eleanor, but nobody calls me that, and neither will you. Not if you know what's good for you." She put another spoonful of water in his mouth.

"What happened?"

It felt as if he were waking up from a long sleep, which in fact, was probably true, he realized. Bit by bit his mind was starting to put all the little pieces together. But the effort of talking had worn him out, and he was glad to let Lolly speak for a while.

"My brothers, Bud and George, found you in the road behind our field. You were unconscious, and all you had with you was a backpack and a bedroll. They brought you to our house, and this is where you've been since yesterday, watched over by my brothers, our mutt of a dog, myself, and, of course, God. Somehow we managed to keep you alive. I think most of the credit goes to Him." Her lips curved into a slight smile. "All the credit goes to Him."

She settled back in the chair. "By the way, you're in Minnesota, not too far from Mankato. We're right along the Minnesota River. I don't know if you've ever been here before, but this is a lovely place, and I wouldn't trade it for all the riches of the city. The Minnesota is a golden river, especially in the fall when the leaves are touched with autumn and they fall into the water as it courses its way to meet up with other rivers, other streams. They're carried along like russet and bronze and copper boats, taking away the story of summer joy and making room for the icy splendor of winter."

Her words were spontaneous poetry, and he found himself hanging on every syllable. She sat back, and the images flowed from her like the current.

"You weren't too far from the river, and you may have heard the sound of it as it rushes toward Mankato, and then pushes up to join the Mississippi. I think it was calling you, and you heard its voice as it offered to give you relief from your thirst. When you're stronger, we can go to the riverside, and you can put your hand in the river, touch the water that saved your life. We will make little boats out of milkweed pods and send them on to Mankato and Minneapolis and on down to New Orleans."

He put his head back and shut his eyes again and listened. Her words flowed over him like the river, like the music of the river.

Chapter 4

Even though he has been away from me, away from my arms, away from my embrace, he has never left my heart. I think of him with each sunrise, and I pray for him at each sunset, and when the moon rises high into the sky, a pure pearl suspended against a velvet drop of ebony, I throw a kiss to the orb that watches over us both as surely as our Creator does. The universe wants us together, needs us to be together, as surely as we need each other.

The days passed, from June to July to August, with a wild energy. Lolly's garden grew straggly in the afternoon heat, but still she watered it each evening with hope. Bud pointed out to her that maybe she should start watering it during the afternoon, and that way the potatoes and carrots would already be boiled when she dug them up for dinner.

Colin got better quickly—the doctor attributed that to his youth and prior good health, but Lolly knew the real reason. God had meant for Colin to survive.

His memory was spotty. Sometimes he could recall an event down to the tiniest detail, and at other times, entire events seemed to be missing. And of course, in between were the spots where traces of his former life lurked, tantalizingly imperfect and incomplete.

The gaps in his recollection frustrated Lolly, but she held her impatience in check. His healing couldn't be hurried.

He had gotten, finally, to the point where he remembered parts of his life: his name, where he had lived, and so on. He had been in the family business in New York City, but exactly what that was, he couldn't totally identify. He'd told her he had brief flashes of a large building and desks and the distant sound of machinery, perhaps a printing company.

Trying to bring back the scenes of his past brought him to excruciating headaches, so they'd come to an easy accord: He would, at his own pace, explore the reaches of his memory, and she would listen as he shared the growing volume of his own history.

He had moved to the old house, a small building adjacent to the farmhouse. When her parents had first gotten married, they lived in the tiny place until their growing family needed more room, and they built the larger farmhouse. When Lolly was growing up, the old house had played many roles: a playroom, a place to dry pelts, a handy spot to store potatoes, and a catch-all for unused furniture. With the brothers' help, Colin repaired it and made it livable. It wasn't fancy, but it was good.

The wheat was starting to turn golden, baked too quickly under the summer sun, and he watched the crop as anxiously as George and Bud did, learning at their side the capriciousness of farming.

As soon as Colin had been able to, he'd joined them in worship at the little church in town. The townspeople of Valley Junction had taken to him, and with their usual good grace accepted him into the church community without reservation. Of course, Hildegard Hopper and Amelia Kramer were intensely interested in talking to him, but George and Bud were expert at moving him out of the women's sphere of nosiness. Her brothers knew how to keep the focus on worship.

Lolly was so glad to have them all together in God's presence each Sunday morning, and as this Sunday came with the usual August heat that shimmered from the ground to the sky, the church's windows were thrown open with the hope that can only come on Sunday that some breeze might find its way in. Ladies fanned themselves furiously, and men used prayer cards and announcement sheets, whatever they could find that made the still air move even a little bit.

Reverend Wellman was a tall, slender man with a slight limp. Born and raised in the area, he knew everyone and had an astonishing ability to tailor his sermons to the needs of the community—without casting an accusatory light on any member of the congregation.

His sermon was about the uniqueness of creation. Every one of us is different, he said.

He used the example of identical twins and told the story of his own brothers. No one, he said, could tell them apart. The doctor had marked them with his pen—A for the firstborn, and B for the second.

"Keep these marks on them," he'd told their mother and father. "That way you can tell them apart."

His mother had shaken her head. "I know them already."

The doctor tried some tests to prove to her the necessity of doing it his way. First, he had them dressed in matching buntings, with the marks covered.

She knew which was which.

He took them behind a curtain and she listened to their cries.

She knew.

He had her eyes covered, and laid each one in her arms.

She knew.

Now she was an elderly woman with failing eyesight, limited hearing, and a faltering gait. Her senses seemed to be abandoning her, yet she knew which son was which by touch alone, and sometimes by his mere presence in her room. She knew; even through the veil of the years, she knew.

That, Reverend Wellman said, was the way God knows His own. God wants us to seek out the qualities of each other that are special and to care for them, to know them the way God knows us.

Lolly sneaked a glance at Colin. He listened in rapt attention to the story the minister told, and when he'd finished with the sermon, Colin nodded, as if something had spoken to him.

The four of them sat together as they always did during every service, with Colin at Lolly's left side and Bud on her right, while George was perched on the edge of the pew.

Ruth, the woman who had George's attention—and his heart, if he'd ever admit it—sat across the aisle from him, her silvery blond hair glowing in the sunlight that poured through the open windows. Lolly suspected that George's attention wasn't always on the service. One day, she knew, either George would cross the aisle to sit with Ruth, or the reverse would happen, and she'd cross to sit with him, and they'd be as good as engaged.

Outside, Bruno snoozed in the shadow of the steps, keeping a wary eye open a crack in case an inattentive squirrel wandered too close.

Lolly had always enjoyed going to church. The music, the sermon, and the Gospel reading—all of those elements combined with the fellowship of the congregation kept the experience uplifting every week, a respite from the cares of the day.

Having Colin at her side made church even better. She told herself it was his strong baritone that the little church needed in the hymns, or his fervent *amen* at the end of the prayer, or his willingness to stay afterward and help straighten the sanctuary.

But she also treasured the way he held his Bible out to her so they could follow the Gospel reading together. Why it mattered so much, she couldn't say, but it did. When he was beside her, and they were sharing the Bible he'd had in his pack, she couldn't imagine a Sunday without him.

He was, as Reverend Wellman's sermon had illustrated, very special, not only to God but to her.

He was still a man of contradictions in so many ways, and he wasn't able to reconcile them all himself. The blankets in his bedroll, she'd discovered when she'd laundered them, were woven from what she presumed to be cashmere or something similar. She was guessing, of course, never having seen cashmere, but these blankets were softer than any she'd touched.

The pack he'd been carrying when her brothers found him was made of fine leather, and the lining, although faded from days on the road, was a thick silken fabric with a golden brocade pattern woven into it. It had to have cost a dear penny, too.

Yet inside was that same Bible he shared with her on Sundays, a free Bible that had been given to him on the road. One afternoon he'd told her how he'd come to have it.

Her mind wandered away from the closing hymn, as she remembered the story he'd shared with her.

He'd been on the road, hitchhiking when he could, but generally walking and riding on freight trains, and following a set of railroad tracks on the theory that they would, eventually, take him to a city of some substance.

Sure enough, at last he'd gotten to a town in the upper Midwest—he didn't know the name of it—where he'd met some fellows in the rail yard. As a group of ruffians surrounded him, he'd heard the soft swish of knives being opened.

Suddenly an arm came out of seemingly nowhere, and a loud voice announced, "I've got him now."

The thugs stopped their advance, and he was spirited out by his rescuer. It turned out that the fellow ran a flophouse for transients, and he'd put Colin up for the night.

But first he'd asked Colin if he was continuing on his travels, and Colin had said yes, he was. Would he like a road map? the man asked. Colin had nodded, and the man put a Bible in his hands, and said it was the best road map anyone could use.

It wasn't his first Bible. He remembered another one with pages he'd hesitated to turn because they were so thin they tore easily. He was almost afraid to touch it for fear of damaging the Word.

So this inelegant Bible, with its cardboard cover and thick rough pages, had been exactly what he'd needed.

He read it, he said, but not all of it, and he tended to turn to familiar passages, the comfort verses, he'd called them. Psalm 23. The Beatitudes. The Lord's Prayer. Those lines he knew.

He'd stopped speaking of it then. She suspected other memories were too nebulous to be shared, so she hadn't pried. In time he would remember—or he wouldn't. She couldn't change that, and she accepted it.

The benediction was pronounced, and the four of them filed out of the church.

George lingered for some small talk with Ruth by the front steps before joining the others.

"I'm sorry to say this in such a holy spot," Bud declared, "but that's not a nice place to be in August. It was so hot in there that the bird on Ruth's hat roasted, and it smelled so good that I was tempted to eat it."

"Oh, stop it," George growled. "That bird was made of wool, and you know it."

"I was simply making a point," Bud said. "You've got to admit that—"

"Boys, boys," Lolly chided, interrupting the inevitable argument. "Let's just get home. And Bud, watch what you say. That wasn't nice at all."

"How can I watch what I say? Words are invisible," he said as he climbed into the back of the truck. "I was just being honest. And by the way, I'm not going to crunch in the front with you. It's just too hot. Come on, Colin, you, too. It's more comfortable back here."

"When are you and Ruth going to go on a date or something?" Lolly asked her brother as he drove toward the farm.

George growled.

"Well, let me give you some female advice here. It's hard to get any kind of relationship going if all that happens is he looks at you. There's got to be more than that. Speak up."

"You're the big romance expert?" he asked. "Since when?"

"No, I'm not saying that. It's just that Ruth is nice, and I'd sure like to see you two together. But it doesn't look like it's going anywhere."

His eyes flickered over to her and he sighed. "I'll tell you what. I can't. I will not ask Ruth—or anyone—to share my life until I can take care of her the way a husband should. What would I do? Move her in with us? Or maybe we can boot Colin out of the old home place and she and I could set up house in there?"

"You could build a new house, George," she said. "There's nothing stopping you."

He didn't answer.

"Really," she persisted, "you could. Bud would help you. We can get the lumber here or maybe in Mankato, and with some nice new furniture, you'd be all set up."

"It isn't a good time."

"You're just shy." She loved to tease him about his slow courtship of Ruth.

"Things are too uncertain," he said, his mouth tightening, which always meant he was literally holding back his words. "The drought, the Depression."

"But we're okay. We've got—"

"We've got enough for us," he interrupted. He glanced in the mirror at Colin and Bud behind them, horsing around, and lowered his voice. "You know that having Colin here has been a blessing, for sure, but it's also stretched us to the limit. We don't have reserves for a wedding, a new house, for furniture, and probably for children. I'm not bringing someone as classy as Ruth is into our chaotic bit of paradise."

She touched his arm. She hadn't thought about that at all. "I shouldn't have said anything."

He lifted one shoulder and let it drop. "No problem. It's a mess for all of us."

The rest of the ride was silent except for Bud and Colin singing silly songs from the back of the truck.

The next day, the heat continued. She fanned herself as she stood in the kitchen by the open window and watched Colin with the chickens. Not a single breeze lifted the light curtain, and she felt a trail of sweat roll down her back.

She'd become used to seeing him in the farmyard, his dark brown hair under a worn straw hat as he strewed seed for the chickens, making *chhhkk, chhhkk, chhhkk* sounds at them while they scratched and picked their way through the bounty at his feet.

The chickens liked him, or so it seemed. Lolly shook her head at the thought. A chicken was a chicken, and it didn't do well for her to become attached to any animal on the farm that might end up on the table. Besides, chickens were such odd creatures, with their featherless feet and jerky head movements.

It had to rain, and soon. Even the light teasing showers that only misted the air would be welcome.

She didn't like weather like this, when the world seemed poised on the edge, as if waiting for whatever was coming.

It wasn't quite tornado weather. The sky was still too blue, not the sick green that indicated trouble was on the way, and the blanket of stillness that preceded a twister was absent. The chickens clucked and squawked territorially, Bruno barked in the distance at something—or nothing, knowing Bruno—and overhead a bird trilled out a melody.

But there were clouds. They were high and thin but they were there, and maybe, just maybe, they held moisture.

The sound of an automobile approaching intruded on the day. "Oh no, please don't let it be. . ." she said aloud as she wiped her hands on the dish towel. She hung it up again, making sure the smiling teapot faced outward as if encouraging her.

Hildegard Hopper's DeSoto pulled around the curve at the end of the yard and slid over the corner of Lolly's garden, crushing the tender trumpets of the petunias, the same kind of flower her mother had planted years ago and which Lolly tended lovingly. Hildegard continued on, apparently unaware of the damage she'd caused. Beside her in the front seat was perched her ever-present sidekick, Amelia Kramer.

"Oh Lord, You'd better give me some patience and quick!" Lolly said aloud. "Don't let me say anything I'm going to regret later on."

She ran a hurried hand over her hair. As usual, she hadn't done much more than pull it back and wind it into a haphazard bun. It shouldn't matter that her hair wasn't as styled as theirs, she knew that, but there was just something about the way they acted that made her feel insecure.

She went to the door and pulled it open, a falsely hearty smile on her face, but they weren't there. They had, she realized, gone around the side of the house and were standing on each side of Colin.

The chickens had scattered to the far sides of the yard, but they were edging back closer. The two women were, after all, standing in the midst of their meal.

Lolly saw what was going to happen only seconds before it did. There was no time to stop it.

One chicken stepped over to Hildegard's right foot, stared at it for a moment, and then bobbed its head down and pecked at the glittery bow on the vamp. A plump hen gazed at her reflection in Amelia's shiny patent leather sandals, and suddenly poked at it with her sharp beak.

The women's screams pierced the morning, and Lolly bit back a smile as she saw Colin trying to calm the women and the chickens. She rushed out and scooped up the two chickens and held them close to her as she tried to soothe them.

"Let me put them in the coop," she said over the loud protests of the chickens that wriggled fiercely in her arms, scratching her wrists and hands with their sharp claws. "I'll just be a moment. Colin, do you mind taking our guests inside and getting them settled while I see to things out here?"

He swept off the worn straw hat and bowed "I'd be delighted to. Ladies?" As he guided them into the house, she could hear him saying all the right things, tending to their own ruffled feathers.

She got the chickens settled and even gave them a little extra corn for their distress.

She could easily have stayed out there, relaxing under the cottonwood and listening to the leaves. When she'd been little, she had thought the cottonwoods were whispering prayers when their leaves rustled in the faint breeze—and for just a moment she lingered in the shade.

But the thought of Colin at the mercy of Hildegard Hopper and Amelia Kramer brought her up sharply and she hurried back inside.

The two women were seated on either side of Colin, and the questions, in soft little voices with very pointed words, were flying at him like arrows.

"Where did you come from?"

"Do you have a family?"

"How long were you on the road?"

"What is your livelihood?"

"Will you stay here through winter?"

"Are you going back on the road?"

Motionless, he wasn't responding, which made their questioning even sharper.

"What are your plans?"

"Are you a Lutheran or a Baptist?"

"What was in your pack?"

"Do you miss your vagabond ways?"

She took immediate pity on him. "Hildegard, Amelia, can I get you something to drink? Tea perhaps? I'd offer you coffee, but we don't drink that in the summer. My brothers find it too heavy when it's this warm. I have some no-bake bars I made that I think you'll enjoy. I made them from a recipe I cut out a long time ago from the Mankato newspaper."

She knew she was chattering but she couldn't bear it anymore, seeing him beset by the barrage of questions.

They were, truth to tell, good questions, questions that needed answers, but he didn't need to share all that with the women. They were simply being nosy and meddlesome, always in search of a good juicy rumor to share at the store or after church.

Of course, what the women didn't know, and what Lolly and her brothers had managed thus far to avoid sharing with the townspeople, was that Colin didn't really know the answers himself, not entirely anyway. Every day his memory got stronger, and every day a bit more of it came back.

He didn't need to have these women assaulting him with a volley of questions.

Fortunately they were easy to deflect, and for the moment their mission was set aside, although she was sure that they would not let it go unsatisfied. What they didn't get today, they would return for another day. Hildegard and Amelia were relentless in their quest for gossip.

But temporarily at least, the onslaught was stilled, and the four of them sat in the stifling living room and made polite conversation about the cookery. None too soon the two women called an end to their visit, and with promises of recipes for blond brownies and oatmeal raisin bar cookies to be exchanged for copies of Lolly's newspaper clipping.

When Hildegard and Amelia were safely on the road again, Lolly collapsed in the chair by the couch. "I'm sorry you had to endure that," she said. "Those two are unbearable at times."

"I'm the one who should be apologizing," he said. "I feel like I'm taking advantage of you and your family."

Bruno's barking and a flurry of chicken squawks ended the somber discussion. The dog had figured out how to open the door to the coop and had apparently done it again. From the noise, Lolly was sure he'd gone inside to annoy the hens.

"I'll take care of it," he said, rising quickly. "He's all bark and no bite, but I'm afraid those chickens aren't quite as polite. I'd better save that mongrel before he meets the same fate as Hildegard's shoes."

She stayed in the chair and enjoyed the last minutes of solitude before mayhem broke loose. If the dog was back, so were her brothers, and they'd be hungry.

After they ate, maybe they'd all leave together. They'd started taking Colin with them out to the field and the barn, and she'd begun writing in her notebook again. After their meal, maybe she'd have the chance to put a few more words in it.

"Lolly!"

The door slammed open and then shut again as George and Bud burst into the room. Colin, she could see through the window, was still outside, kneeling in front of Bruno as the chickens watched curiously.

The dog had something in his mouth, as usual, and Colin was coaxing it out of his jaws.

Lolly rolled her eyes as she recognized the bow from Hildegard's shoe. First pecked by chickens and then chewed on by the dog, the ornament was beyond saving. Colin looked up, caught her watching from the window, and held up the trophy with a grin.

"Lolly, let's eat!" George, she could see, had already washed his hands and face at the pump—a layer of grime circled his hairline and his wrists where he hadn't washed. Well, she told herself, at least he had washed some of the dirt off.

"What are we having? Not that meat loaf again! What did you put in it? Gopher?" Bud grinned goofily as he slid into a chair at the kitchen table.

Bruno darted in front of Colin as he entered the house. Soon the small kitchen was filled with four people and a dog, and chaos ruled again.

~~~

The never-ending job of fence repair called the three men to the edge of the farmstead.

Colin rode along with the brothers. He'd elected to sit in the back of the pickup truck with the dog rather than in the cab. It was hotter than an oven, but at least he got some air in his face, and he rather enjoyed bumping along the pitted road with Bruno for company.

Plus, riding in the back gave a fellow time to think about things that needed to be thought about. Like who he was.

Sure he knew his name was Colin Hammett. He'd led a life of comfort before this trip, but he only dimly remembered the details. His mind would find some piece of his former life, as he was calling it for lack of a better distinction, and sometimes the bit would take shape and become focused and grow, and he'd get another section of his past back.

Other times it was like trying to remember a dream. Details were slippery and would slither out of his reach when he'd try to grasp them.

He had so many questions. Why did he leave his life behind? He knew he had been well-off. The leather pack and the cashmere blankets he'd brought were proof of that. But why was he on the road? When he'd try to remember, his mind would almost let him get there, but it would stop just short of an answer.

Lolly and her brothers were terrific. They didn't push him but let him try to regain the lost ground on his own.

What an act of faith and trust that was! Could he have done the same, welcomed a stranger into his home as completely as they had?

The truck rumbled to a stop, and George and Bud got out.

"Fence work," George said. "Want to grab that toolbox, please?"

As far as Colin had been able to determine, fence posts worked themselves out of the ground at least once a week. They spent time every day riding the fence line and correcting the leaning posts, tightening wire where the fence was strung or replacing planks where the fence was lath.

"I don't know what we're keeping in," Bud grumbled as he wrestled with a post that refused to stay upright. "It's not like we have animals anymore, unless you count the chickens, and I don't know why you would."

"Eggs," George said around a mouthful of nails. "That's why Lolly keeps those nasty creatures around."

"Oh, they're not so bad," Colin said, trying to help Bud with the recalcitrant fence post. He told them the story of the chickens' reaction to the shoes worn by Hildegard and Amelia the day before. "I wouldn't be surprised if people all the way over in Minneapolis could have heard them, they were hollering so loud."

"I've just changed my opinion of chickens, then." Bud grinned at Colin.

"Bud," George chided, "watch what you say. Hildegard and Amelia have their good points. . .I'm sure."

They all laughed and returned to the business of fixing the fence.

His body was enjoying the labor. As the muscles flexed and tendons stretched, he felt better, and his recovery was speeding along. All that was left were a few missing pieces in his memory.

Sweat dripped off his chin. He leaned on the post while he swabbed it away with his handkerchief and took advantage of the respite to look around him.

This was beautiful country here. Admittedly the drought had taken its toll, but he could easily fill in the blanks and imagine the area with normal rain— and snow. The field was ringed with deep grasses that were looking somewhat parched at the moment, but he knew the trees, with deeper roots, had to be drawing water from the river to stay alive.

There was a metaphor somewhere in there but he was too engaged in the scene to work it through. Maybe he'd figure it out later.

Yes, this place should be beautiful, come fall. He didn't know much about trees, but he did recognize the characteristic shape of the maple leaf, and he knew how extraordinary they were in autumn. Mingled in with the—

"Hey, dreamer," Bud said, giving him a light bop on the shoulder, "want to help me out? Here, dream on this post now."

Bud's grin told him that he was teasing, and as he headed to the next tilted fence post, the dog followed, settling at last in Colin's shadow.

George came over to fix the wire twisted around the post. "Look at you. Earlier this summer you wouldn't have held up a post. It would have held you up."

"Once it knocked me out," Colin joked. "It's amazing what food and water and a place to sleep can do for a body." He paused, wondering if he should read more into what George said. Was he implying that the time had come to move on?

It probably had, in all honesty. And the thought of leaving here brought immediate pain.

He'd come to love this family who'd taken him in so easily and so completely. Even the dog that lay drooling on the toe of his boot had worked his way into his heart.

Lolly, though—how that woman had put her imprint on his soul. A stray thought intruded—*maybe you're falling in love with her*—but he dismissed it. He'd known her less than three months, hardly long enough for that.

There had been an emptiness in him, though, that had started to fill in. And somehow that had to do with Lolly.

George rewound the wire. "Well, we're—oh, will you look at this?"

He bent over and ran his fingers over the post. "Someone's gone and carved something on it."

"Let me see." Bud pushed George aside and leaned in close. "Yup. Someone's carved a cat here."

"A cat? Now, why on earth would someone do that?" George stood up and dusted his hands off on the back of his overalls. ·

"Kind-hearted woman." Suddenly doors flew open and windows came unshuttered in Colin's mind. "Kind-hearted woman," he repeated. "That's what I saw. This was the spot!"

The brothers, he realized, were standing stock-still, staring at him as if he'd totally gone around the bend.

"It's the hobo sign. It means that a woman lives here who will feed you. A kind-hearted woman."

"Who? Lolly?" Bud chortled. "Lolly is a kind-hearted woman? You sure didn't grow up with her."

"I think she's a kind-hearted woman," Colin said.

George held up his hand. "Wait. Say that again."

"Say what?"

"She's a kind-hearted woman," Colin repeated.

"That's what he was saying," George said to his brother. "When we brought him into the house, and he kept saying something, and you, doofus, thought he was saying 'cigarette.'"

"Who's the doofus?" Bud shot back. "You thought he was asking for a cigar."

"A cigar? I don't smoke," Colin said.

"You weren't very clear when you first got to our house," George explained, "and we misunderstood what you said. Just forget that part. So you were really saying *kind-hearted woman*! I would never have guessed."

Bud snorted. "Especially if he had met Lolly. Her heart's made of stones and thistles and barbed wire."

George shushed him and as the two brothers joshed with each other, Colin thought of Lolly and smiled. *Kind-hearted woman, indeed!*

⌒

That night, after the dishes were done and George and Bud were seated in front of the radio listening to the news, Colin and Lolly went for a walk. The sun was low but not set entirely.

"I want to show you something," Colin said to her, and he led her to the fence post with the carving on it. "This is where I hit my head."

She tilted her head in confusion. "Yes?"

"Look." He took her hand and traced the outline of the cat with the heart in it. "It's the kind-hearted woman sign."

"Who carved it? You?"

He laughed. "Lolly, if I'd carved it, you wouldn't be able to tell if it was a cat or an alligator. I don't know who carved it on here. Someone you'd helped before, I assume."

"Me?"

"Lolly, you're the kind-hearted woman. You're my kind-hearted woman."

⌒

She wrote quickly, leaning over the kitchen counter next to the cake that had just come out of the oven, pouring the words of her imaginary love onto the paper. For some people, perhaps such love existed, but there was no place in her life for flowery phrases and romantic gestures. Yet in her notebook, with a flourish of her pencil, her life could change.

She began again to write the story she wanted to live.

As the letters fell onto the paper, the Depression vanished. There was wealth in the land, waterfalls ran silver in the sunlight, flowers lifted sunny heads to the heavens and rejoiced.

And through it all she was happy.

Her hero had no name. Giving him a name would have grounded the dream, limited the scope so that it could never reach as far as it did now.

Her brothers would return soon, bringing both Colin and the dog with them, and her world would burst into crazed activity, with her brothers talking at the same time trying to tell her something they'd found that she probably didn't even care about, while Colin tried to help her finish supper preparations, and the dog ran in frantic circles around her feet on the off-chance she'd drop something edible.

Her heart flowed onto the page. Love lost, love found. It was the theme she knew really nothing about, but the drama appealed to the romantic in her.

There was a sound behind her, and she quickly closed the little book and stuffed it in her pocket.

"What are you doing?" Bud asked.

She shrugged. She couldn't lie, but on the other hand, she couldn't tell him the truth. He'd pester her forever.

"You were doing something."

"Don't be silly. I'm always doing something, you know that. Why, do you want to clean the counter for me? Is that what you're doing in here?" She'd learned a long time ago that the best way to get rid of her brothers was to ask them to do a household chore. They evaporated like water on a skillet in the face of a cleaning rag.

George and Colin were at the door. They had it cracked open, and the dog bounded in before she could stop him, a wriggling squirrel in his mouth. He dropped it cheerfully at her feet and chased it around the kitchen, barking as it climbed the Hoosier cabinet, leaped across to the curtains and pulled them down rod and all, ran over the counter, through the cake she'd set out to cool, and down the hall to the bedrooms.

"Bruno!" they shouted in unison. And while she tried to get Bruno out of the house—which he did not want to do, not with a squirrel running loose in the house, a squirrel that he had caught himself, no less—the men tried to shoo the equally excited animal out.

At last the squirrel had been rescued and released, the dog had been pacified with a beef bone, and Lolly slumped as she looked at the cake. The top of it had been torn apart when the squirrel had raced across it, and crumbs littered the countertop. No one could eat it now. She sighed and scraped it into the dog's dish.

Where was her hero when she needed him the most?

Chapter 5

The forest is fragranced with green. Deep moss cushions our path, and each
footstep releases lush, woodsy aromas that surround us. The trees are in
the height of summer glory, each leaf displaying its own variant of green.
From the jeweled shrubbery of emerald and jade to the graying patina of
lichen on the tree trunks to the dazzling brilliance of bright green grass in
a patch of sun through the canopy, we are blessed by the richness of the day,
we two, who stroll hand in hand.

August seemed to fly by on winged feet. Each sunlit hour passed entirely too quickly as summer breathed its most fiery breaths in the grand finale of the season.

Every day Colin got stronger, and every day Lolly became more attached to him. From being able to reach the bread plate on the highest cupboard shelf to holding the outside washbasin when she needed to empty it, he had become an integral part of her life.

The question that was never answered—because it was never asked—was what would happen in the future. Would he stay on with them? As much as she'd enjoy having him around, their lives couldn't stay this way forever. He was living in the old house, a temporary arrangement at best, but it was only a matter of time before the tongues in town would begin to wag, with Hildegard and Amelia leading the way.

And if he chose to leave? That was the worst outcome possible. Where would he go? Back on the road? Living from town to town, shivering his way across a wintry America in search of—in search of what?

She couldn't bear the thought of him leaving and going back to living as a vagabond. He was flourishing with them. Alone—why, who knew where that lifestyle could lead him?

Would he have a safe place to lay his head at night? Would he have enough to eat? Would he be safe?

Would he miss her?

She cut the thought before it went any further. It wasn't productive, and it could only make her sad. What she needed to do today was go into town and do some shopping. George told her the evening before that Martin Jorgens, the grocer, had asked him if she had any eggs she could sell him. He'd run short.

One thing her chickens did was lay eggs, and lots of them. She'd gathered them in a basket lined with a kitchen towel, and asked George to drive her to town.

Colin and Bud were out in the back with Bruno, ostensibly planning a tool-shed near the chicken coop, but she was sure they probably were just talking. There was no reason to interrupt them. Plus it was always simply easier to leave someone at home, or else Bruno would chase after the truck until one of her brothers took pity on him and let him ride in the bed of the truck—and then they had the dog to contend with for the rest of the day.

It wasn't going to be a long trip to town anyway. The eggs had to be delivered quickly, since in this heat they'd run the risk of spoiling. She'd do that first, and then stop at the drugstore to get some aspirin.

The trip to town was pleasant. George wasn't a big talker, so Lolly was able to roll the window down, lean her head out, and let the air blow on her face and just relax.

"You look just like Bruno right now," George said.

Lolly pulled her head back into the cab of the truck. "I do not."

"Well, okay, you're not drooling and you haven't barked at any squirrels, but you have the same blissful expression on your face that he does when he sticks his head out the window."

She laughed. "It does feel wonderful, George, and you should probably try it—sometime when you're not driving, of course. Especially when it's this hot, the wind on my face feels great." She had a sudden terrible thought. "Be honest. Does my hair look all right?"

He snorted. "As much as it ever does."

Trust a brother not to give an answer that told her anything. She tried to check her reflection in the mirror he had rigged up after nearly backing up over the minister one time, but he kept swatting her away. "You're going to make me drive off the road here. Hey, you're sticking your elbow in my ear. Ow! Stop it! Your hair's fine. It's growing on your head, it's not purple, what more do you want?"

"Forget it," she answered. He'd never understand.

"I'll be at Ruth's having a cola," he said. "Meet me there when you're through."

She suppressed a smile. Her brother spent a lot of time at Ruth's Café, most of it talking to Ruth. He could make a single cola last for hours if necessary, although she suspected that Ruth would freshen it as necessary to keep him here.

She waited until he'd parked the truck along the main street before giving her appearance a quick check. No one would ever beg to paint her portrait, but she was presentable.

With her basket of eggs balanced carefully on her arm, she entered the grocery store. The market wasn't crowded at all. Two women paused at the fruit and vegetable counter and casually examined the celery while chattering away.

Martin Jorgens greeted her. "Oh, Lolly, I'm so glad you're here. I'm down to the last egg. I hope you brought me at least a dozen."

"Two dozen, if that's all right."

She put the basket on the counter and carefully unfolded the towel that was tucked around the precious cargo. "They all look whole."

"Lucky, knowing the way George drives," Martin answered, and they both laughed. George was probably the most sedate driver in Valley Junction. She could probably have put the eggs on the hood of the truck while they rode into town, and the eggs would still be intact.

The women had stopped talking and looked over at her. She recognized them as wives of farmers on the northeast side of town. She didn't know them well, but she smiled and nodded at them. "Think it'll cool off ever?"

The women smiled back and one of them said, "I would hope so. Cooling off would do everyone good, I think," and the other woman laughed before turning her attention to a packet of carrots and saying something under her breath to her companion.

Lolly felt the blood rush to her face. She had no idea what prompted this from these women that she barely knew, but the condescension was obvious.

What could have brought this on? She checked to make sure the hem of her dress wasn't tucked up behind her and that her shoes matched.

The two women put their heads together and made a great act of pretending to discuss the carrots, but their gazes flitted back to Lolly and they snickered.

Then they laid down the carrots, and both women left together, still smiling over some shared secret.

Martin shook his head. "Biddies," he muttered as he took the eggs from the basket. "I'm surprised they don't cackle and lay their own eggs. Come in here every time their husbands visit town, and I've yet to sell them a thing. Apparently my products aren't as highfalutin as what they'd get in Mankato."

Lolly frowned. "I thought they were talking about me."

"Probably were," he said almost cheerfully. "Those two are the kind that aren't happy unless they have someone else's arm to chew on. Don't waste any time on them. They sure won't waste any on you, unless it's to find something to talk about."

"But that's hardly reassuring," she answered.

He shrugged. "Lolly, they will talk about you, I can guarantee that. They'll talk about me. They'll talk about Ruth over at the café, and Joe at the drugstore. If they see the minister, they'll talk about him, and if they don't see him, they'll still talk about him."

She laughed. "Point taken."

"Why some people have to be that way is beyond me. I figure I have enough to do chasing after my own life without getting that picky about everybody else's life, too. You know, if we all took a page from the Good Book and do unto others, the world would be a right friendlier place."

"Martin, I feel a lot better!"

She was much happier when she left, the coins from the sale of the eggs jingling in her dress pocket. When she got home, she'd put some aside and drop them into the glass jar she had hidden in the back of her closet. It wasn't the most original place to hide it, but her brothers weren't the most original thinkers, so she figured the money was safe.

What she was going to do with it, she had no idea, although the thought of a trip to Paris was lovely. At the rate she was going, she'd have enough saved to go by the time she was two hundred and three.

Her next stop was the drugstore. It was, as always, dark and fragrant with the scent of wintergreen and licorice and alcohol.

Joe Albee called a hello as she walked to the counter. The floor of the pharmacy was made of wide wooden planks and they creaked loudly under her feet. It was all part of the charm of the drugstore.

"What can I get you, Lolly?" he asked.

"Just a box of aspirin today," she answered.

"Those brothers of yours giving you a headache, are they?" He chuckled as he retrieved the aspirin for her.

"They wouldn't be my brothers if they weren't."

"Those two can do some pretty crazy things, that's for sure." He handed her the aspirin. "Here you go. Now, you try not to overheat, you hear me?"

She was probably reading too much into innocent conversations, she told herself as she walked toward the café. It was August after all, and it was hot, and people were trying to cool off.

If only she had her notebook with her! This would translate well into the emerging story she was writing. As soon as she got home, she would steal a few minutes away and write this part of the tale.

She strolled to the café, taking her time as she spun the story out in her mind. She was in no hurry. George always dallied at the café to talk to Ruth, and although he might bark at her about how slow she was, she knew he truly didn't mind.

Maybe she could take some time to window shop.

The display at Leubner's Store featured a woman's dress in a raucous pattern of yellow and red swirls. Just looking at it made Lolly dizzy. A brooch thick with faux gems caught the matching scarf flung dramatically over one shoulder.

It was undoubtedly out of the price range of most women in Valley Junction, but she knew what would happen.

The dress was one of a kind, the sign below it boasted. The designer's name wasn't one she'd heard of, but that didn't mean much. She wasn't up on the current fashion scene.

She had time, she realized, to step into Leubner's and see what the styles were. She made her own dresses, but maybe she could get a few ideas for updating her patterns.

The rotating blades on the ceiling moved the air in the store, but failed to cool it. A young woman stood behind the counter, a Chinese paper fan languidly waving in her hand.

"Afternoon!" she called. She was the daughter of the teacher in Valley Junction, a pretty young woman with elegantly straight hair as black as a raven's wing. She was in Bud's class at school, and had always struck Lolly as someone who seemed much older than she undoubtedly was.

"Good afternoon," Lolly replied.

"Can I show you something?"

"Well, I have to admit that I was drawn in by the dress in the window."

The young woman nodded. "It's already sold. But you can take a look at it if you want."

"Thanks, but it's not quite my style."

The clerk laughed. "It's almost no one's style."

Lolly didn't need to ask who had bought it, or why it was still on display if it had been sold, or what the sales clerk's comment meant.

The dress on the mannequin was very small. Only a tiny, quite petite woman could wear it.

But in two or three weeks, the dress, Lolly knew, would vanish from the store window and appear on the body of Hildegard Hopper.

The purpose of this artfully engineered ruse was common knowledge in Valley Junction. Hildegard had created it herself.

She had Leubner's send away for the dress in her size, and when it arrived, the smaller version would disappear. Hildegard had made the slight mistake of confiding her reasoning to one of the store's earlier and chattier clerks, who had almost immediately left the employ of Leubner's once the story escaped into the fast-moving environment of Valley Junction's rumor mill.

Hildegard's reasoning behind the scheme was this: People would think that Hildegard was wearing the smaller dress, and they would see her, then, as a less formidably sized woman.

The plan, of course, never worked, but no one dared tell Hildegard, and Lolly had to admit that the town took a very wrong pleasure in being in on the rather twisted workings of Hildegard Hopper's mind.

"Would you like to try something on?" the clerk asked. "You know that the trend now is neckline accents." She came from behind the counter and pulled out a green dress with white rickrack edging and an oversized flounce that surrounded the shoulders like a cape. "This, for example, is quite lovely. Look at the detail!"

Lolly glanced at the dress and ran her hand over the offerings in her size. None of them appealed to her.

"I'm not much on big bows and floppy collars," she confessed. "When I've tried to wear them, I feel like something isn't zipped or buttoned or tied."

The young woman laughed. She hung the dress up again and returned to her spot behind the counter. "I understand that. Say, can I ask you—are you Lolly Prescott?"

"I am."

"My name is Sarah Fallon. My mother was Bud's teacher a couple of years ago."

"I thought I recognized you. Please extend my sympathies to your mother; I can imagine Bud wasn't the most thoughtful student." Lolly abandoned the dresses with a sigh.

Sarah chuckled. "I liked him. We had some classes together this year. He adds energy to the class."

"That's one way to put it."

The clerk made a great show of wiping off the counter. "Is Bud seeing anyone?"

Lolly stopped. Could she be hearing this right? "Bud? My brother?"

She'd never thought of Bud in this context before, and definitely not with someone as stylish as Sarah. Lolly's mind tried to put her wild brother with this fashionable young lady, and failed.

Sarah continued to focus on the glass surface of the counter. "Bud makes me laugh. I like that. We're not exactly Jean Harlow and Clark Gable, but I don't think that matters."

Lolly laughed. "Him as Clark Gable? Never. Maybe one of the Marx brothers, though." She sorted through the jewelry display on the counter as she considered the idea of her brother as a matinee idol.

"So nobody can really blame you for what you did." Sarah smiled a bit awkwardly.

Lolly stopped investigating the necklaces and bracelets. "What I did? What did I do?"

Sarah shook her head. Her hands fluttered like dragonflies as she dismissed her own words. "Nothing. Just that you have that handsome man with you—what's his name?"

"Colin, and he's not my handsome anything. Well, he is handsome, but he's not mine." Lolly quit while what she said still made some sense. This was a conversation headed down a bad road. It was best to end it quickly.

The young woman smiled. "I understand. I sure don't blame you. We do what we need to, don't we?"

A customer entered the store, and Lolly fled, grateful for the interruption. She wasn't sure she wanted to hear what the young woman thought she'd done. This had all the markings of the gossip-mouths in town, two of them in particular.

She wanted to hurry home, back to the security of the farm—back to her trying brothers, a mysterious guest, an always-hungry dog, and chickens that attacked women's shoes. *That* was normal.

As she walked to the café, she focused on the idea of Bud and Sarah. Should she say anything to him? The temptation to rag him about it was nearly overwhelming, but she fought it. Maybe the best idea was to keep it to herself. Telling Bud about it would doom the relationship immediately. He'd undoubtedly do something like get gum stuck in that lovely hair. And if George got wind of it, he'd never let the subject die.

No, the best thing was to keep it to herself. Sometimes the young woman came to church. Maybe she could play matchmaker a bit.

The café was vacant, except for Ruth and George, and Ruth slid a cola down the counter to her with a practiced hand. "Here, honey," Ruth said. "Cool yourself down."

George shot the young woman a look that Lolly couldn't quite read, and he pushed his chair back suddenly.

Ruth flushed an immediate brick red. "I didn't mean—" she said, as the crimson deepened. "I meant—oh, you know I'd never—well, it's August—but not that—"

"Let's go," he said abruptly to Lolly. "I've got work to do."

"Can I at least have my drink?"

"No." George slammed a nickel on the counter. "Keep the change," he muttered.

"There's no change," Lolly began, but he pulled her by the elbow out of the café, without even a good-bye to Ruth.

When they were in the truck again, she turned to face her brother. "Well, that was rude," she said. "Is something wrong between you and Ruth? Did I walk into the middle of an argument?"

He didn't answer for a while, and then he simply said, "I'm taking you home." He was silent the entire ride home, and Lolly chewed on her lip nervously. This didn't bode well at all.

Chapter 6

Ahead of us there is a bridge. Under the slatted wood, water ripples over moss-covered rocks that line the river's edge and continue beneath the liquid surface. Trees arch overhead, shading us as we step onto the bridge. The planks creak as we pass over the bridge, but we hold onto each other's hands and tread carefully. The bridge sways, but still we know the alternative is to wade across the river—and we have no idea how deep the water is, how slick the moss is, and how sharp the stones are. "Take my hand," he invites. "Trust me."

Colin sat at the table, peeling potatoes for her. She'd tried to tell him that he didn't have to, but the repetitive motion was pleasant. After being on the road and then struggling to recover from acute memory loss, he was enjoying the experience of something as everyday as peeling potatoes.

Lolly's brothers were out at the shed. George had asked Colin to give him some time to talk to Bud alone, and Colin was glad to oblige.

Plus, he liked being around Lolly. She didn't have Bud's unbridled wildness or George's stodginess. Instead, she was calm and funny and capable. Lolly was the anchor in the family, although he was sure the brothers didn't recognize that.

He dropped a curl of potato skin and Bruno snapped it up.

Bit by bit his memory was returning. There were only a few gaps in it, and he sometimes wondered if they were there because he didn't want to remember it all.

He knew, for example, that he wasn't married. He did know that he had been employed in the publishing and printing business in New York City, although he was vague on the details. He had some remembrance of setting out on the road— and a man and a Bible verse that he only partially remembered but which Lolly'd helped him put together again. *"Blessed is the man that trusteth in the Lord."*

Did he trust in the Lord? It was a question that gnawed him, especially at bedtime, when his head was on the pillow but sleep was elusive in the August-hot night. He worried about himself and God. He longed for that same trust Lolly had, that God was in control, that He hadn't forgotten this depression-ridden country, that prosperity would return, if not in the form of material riches, then as a wealth of the spirit.

He could remember, now with startling clarity, the church he'd attended in New York City; and although his brain tried to block the images, he also remembered his pride, his *hubris*, as it was called, in how devout he was.

But now he knew that this had been only a surface faith, that he'd never truly taken the Bible completely to his heart.

So he read the Bible the man had given him not so long ago, and each time he found himself edging closer to understanding it, but he couldn't yet make the leap from knowing it to believing it. His head ached some nights trying to determine why he couldn't simply have a faith like Lolly's.

Here he'd thought he was the perfect Christian, and she'd shown him there was much more to it.

"Penny for your thoughts." Lolly's voice interrupted his musing.

He laughed. "That's about what they're worth."

"You looked so serious sitting there."

He could hear the concern rising in her voice. "Peeling potatoes is serious business," he answered lightly, hoping to allay her anxiety. "Are those carrots ready yet? I think it's about time to add them to the pot. Let me finish this spud. Is this about the right size you want them cut to?"

He continued to talk as he scooped up the potatoes and carried them to the large stewpot, in which meat cubes bubbled in a savory gravy. "Sure smells good," he said.

She moved aside to let him slide the potatoes in while she continued to stir. Today her hair was tied back with a red ribbon, limp from her work at the stove.

As they stood shoulder to shoulder at the stove, billows of pungent steam wrapped around them.

"You know, this is better than the most costly French perfume," he declared. "Actually, if Chanel had thought of it, she'd have bottled it."

On a whim, he seized her by the waist and whirled her around, setting her squarely in the middle of the room. "Lolly, let's capture this in a bottle, and we'll sell it and be millionaires! We'll travel to the south of France, and be the toast of Paris society, and we'll eat oysters and lobsters and steaks every day, served to us on the finest bone china. For dessert, we'll dip strawberries in chocolate and eat truffles with our fingers. What do you say? Shall we?"

Her face was only inches from his, and for a moment neither one of them spoke.

He realized, with some surprise, that it would be so easy to bridge that gap, put his lips on hers—and that he wanted to. But those inches might as well have been miles. He couldn't do that. He wouldn't do that, not until he knew her heart.

Plus, it wouldn't be right, not with him still living here.

He pulled his hands away from her waist and laughed, a bit rockily. "Maybe not. Somehow I don't think Eau de Beef Stew would be quite as popular as Chanel No. 5."

She smoothed the front of her apron. "Well," she said, "I suppose—"

Her words were cut short by a shrill "Yoo-hoo" from the open front door. The sound carried to the kitchen like a rusty saw on metal.

"Oh no. Please, no," she said under her breath. But he noticed that she had managed to create a smile as she walked to the door.

"We can tell that you're getting ready to eat," Hildegard began, and Colin forced himself not to roll his eyes. Why on earth would they come by at this time of day? Didn't they know that most people were getting ready to eat? In order for them to skip dinner, he realized, they must be on the trail of something more delicious than Lolly's stew.

"Yes, indeed, I'll be serving very soon," Lolly answered.

"What are you making for dinner?" Hildegard asked, sniffing the air and looking for all the world like Bruno, who sat at attention near Colin's feet, his snout poked upward and quivering in delight at the aromas swirling around him.

"Nothing more exciting than stew," Lolly said.

"You know, we heard the most interesting story today," Hildegard burbled. "Didn't we, Amelia?"

Her sidekick nodded enthusiastically. "Yes, we did. Very interesting, indeed."

"That's quite intriguing, and I'm sure we'd love to hear it, but—"

"Oh, you would enjoy this story, I'm sure of that. Wouldn't they enjoy it, Amelia?"

"Both of them would," Amelia agreed.

"Well, it will have to wait for another time, I'm sorry to say, unless of course—"

Colin's hands cramped from the fists he made. Certainly Lolly would invite them, out of politeness. They couldn't accept, could they?

They couldn't, Hildegard explained. They were just out for a drive and thought they'd stop by and say hello. But since they'd obviously caught Lolly and Colin at a bad time, they'd visit another time.

Don't turn around and look at me, Colin said to Lolly silently. *Don't give them the satisfaction.*

Lolly kept her composure and within seconds the women were on their way to Hildegard's DeSoto.

Colin smiled as Lolly adroitly maneuvered the two women into the car. She was quite a woman. If it had been up to him, he would have ushered them right out the back door, into the unwelcoming midst of the chickens.

"You know what they're doing, don't you?" Lolly said as she stared after the car. "They saw us, and they'll make the most of it."

"They saw nothing," he said with a confidence he didn't feel. "How could they have seen anything? We were in the kitchen. Plus, it's not like we were doing anything scandalous. If they had seen anything, it would have been nothing more than two friends who care for each other very much. What's newsworthy about that?"

She glanced at him over her shoulder. "In their hands, nothing becomes something very quickly."

"Perhaps."

"I wonder what the story was that they were talking about." She frowned. "Today in town, people were acting really odd."

"Here? In Valley Junction?" He laughed. "I'm sure it's just another of their tales, something little that they've made into national news. Call FDR himself, and have him put it in one of his Fireside Chats. Lolly, I suspect that almost everybody in Valley Junction knows what they're like, that their stories can't be trusted. I wouldn't worry. Maybe you could enjoy the notoriety, which I suspect will be short-lived without verification from another source."

She laughed. "I could enjoy notoriety? What a thought! Meanwhile, go get my brothers and tell them to get ready for supper. And tell them that their sister is notorious. They'll like that."

George and Bud were pulling down an old storage hut that had seen better days, with the plan that the wood could be used for other projects. Already a neat stack of boards was placed beside the partially razed lean-to.

Bruno accompanied Colin, staying close at his heels until he saw a butterfly that he chased and amazingly caught—and ate. That dog was an omnivore, for sure. There wasn't anything he wouldn't eat.

As Colin got nearer, he could hear George and Bud's words clearly.

"Bud, you shouldn't have done that. Ruth told me. The story had already gotten over to her."

"It was funny. You've got to give me that. I mean, *jeweled shrubbery?* When was the last time you saw a bush with diamonds hanging on it? You show it to me, because I'm tired of being poor. Let's harvest those diamonds!"

"Funny for you. Not funny for Lolly." George pounded a board free. "You have to think before you speak, little brother. This is really going to hurt her."

Colin's stomach tightened. This didn't sound at all good. He stepped behind the barn, just out of their direct sight, but where he could see and hear them. He didn't want to eavesdrop, but this didn't seem to be a conversation he could rightfully interrupt.

"Nah, she's a tough one. She'll be mad at me but she'll get over it, eventually. She's no little delicate flower waiting for her prince to come riding in." Bud snorted.

"She isn't? You read it. You know what she wrote. Put one and one together and see if you don't get two." George glared at his brother.

"Why wouldn't I get two? What do you get when you add one and one?"

George shook his head. "Honestly, some days I just don't know about you. I think you're putting one and one together and getting one and a half."

Bud stood up. "You're talking in riddles."

"I'm talking the truth here, Bud. You have to tell her."

"I don't want to." Bud kicked one of the loose boards, and the tidy pile fell apart. "She's going to be mad."

"You can be sure of that. Tonight, after dinner, you have to tell her what you did," George announced. "It's the right thing to do."

"You mean it's the scary thing to do. She's going to kill me."

"If you're lucky. If you're not lucky, she'll let you live and she'll make you suffer for a long, long time. Deservedly so, I might add." George began rebuilding the stack of boards. "You're going to be in big trouble, brother. Big trouble."

Colin coughed and crashed against the side of the barn, just to make noise to let them know he was near. Bruno, having finished eating the butterfly, stopped to bite off a dandelion and swallow it.

"Dinnertime," Colin called to the brothers. "Lolly made stew."

"I don't want to go," Bud began, but his brother grabbed him by the elbow and led him toward Colin, saying something that Colin couldn't make out. But by the set of George's jaw, he could guess the gist of it.

This was going to be an interesting night.

⌒

"That was excellent stew, dearest sister," Bud said after dinner. "Now I think I will end the meal with a nice stroll outside."

"Not so fast," George said. "Lolly, leave the bowls. Bud has something he wants to tell you."

"I can listen and start the dishes at the same time," she said. "You know I don't like to let them sit and get crusty. They're harder to wash that way."

"I suspect that you shouldn't have anything in your hands when you hear what Bud has to tell you. Bud, tell her. Now." George leaned back and crossed his arms over his chest.

Colin stood up and carried his dish to the sink. "I have the feeling that this is a family-only conversation, and I think I'll leave the three of you to sort it out."

"Do you know what's going on?" She took the bowl from him and rinsed it in the sink.

"No, I don't, and I undoubtedly don't need to know. I'll just head out and read for a while."

He left the kitchen, and when the screen door slammed and the sound of his whistling his way across the yard to the old house carried over the night air and through the open windows, she turned to her brothers.

"I don't want to hear this, do I?" she asked, as a feeling of dread clutched her stomach.

"No, you don't," Bud said, standing up and stretching, "which is why I'm going to take that walk."

"Sit." George seized Bud's belt and pulled his brother back into his chair. "Talk."

"Do I have to?" Bud wheedled. "I don't want to ruin a perfectly good dinner and a perfectly good evening with a perfectly horrible story."

"Ruin it." George glared at him.

"Well," Bud began, "it all started when I needed a blanket."

"A blanket? In this weather?" Lolly frowned at her brother. Had he totally lost his mind?

"*I* didn't need a blanket. But Floyd did."

"Floyd. Ah. That explains it. Who's Floyd?" This conversation was getting weirder by the minute, and from the grim expression on George's face and the worry on Bud's, she knew it wasn't going to get better.

"Floyd B. Olson."

"The governor of Minnesota needed a blanket from us?" Lolly put her face in her hands. This had to be a dream.

"No, silly. Floyd is the new rooster." Bud picked up a leftover roll and began to shred it.

"You named the rooster after the governor? Why would you do that?" she asked from between her fingers.

"Well, it would have been impolite to name him after the president. So I couldn't call him Franklin."

"Of course not." She had a terrible urge to laugh, but she didn't dare. This conversation was not headed in a humorous direction.

"Get on with the story," George growled.

"All right. I wanted a blanket for Floyd. He'd had a bit of a run-in with the old rooster, and he had a big scratch on his—"

"Bud!" George's voice was stern. "Watch it!"

"Well," Bud continued, his fingers still toying with the roll, "Floyd wouldn't be too comfortable sitting on the straw, so I had to get him something softer, and I knew there was one in your bedroom closet, and—"

She knew where this was going.

She flew out of her chair. "You did *not*! Tell me now that you did not read it!"

Bud made doughballs out of the now-destroyed roll. "Sure, I'll tell you that. I didn't read it."

"Bud," George growled warningly, "you can't run from this."

Her younger brother looked down and crumpled the rest of the roll. "Well, maybe I did."

She wanted to cry. Her beautiful dream story. Her escape from the financial mess the country was in and this hot, hot farm. Her window, however imaginary, out of a life that offered her no choices, no chances. It was gone, all gone.

Her brother had taken the beauty from her life as surely as if he'd gone after it with scissors and knives.

She took off her apron and then put it back on again. Everything was so mixed up now. She began to gather the remaining dishes from the table, so calm that it seemed as if something had died inside of her. Her life was flat. "I give up."

"Lolly, no." George's forehead crinkled.

"Well, why shouldn't I? I tried one little thing, one tiny little nothing thing. It didn't hurt anyone. It didn't do anything. But now, it's been taken from me."

"You can have it back," he said. "I put it in your room this afternoon."

"You don't get it, do you?" She leaned across the table, picking up the empty stew tureen and cradling it to her chest.

She sank back into her chair, putting the tureen in front of her. "That notebook was mine. Mine. It was the only thing I have that was mine. And now, you've destroyed it."

"I'm sorry, Lolly."

She didn't say anything. Her beautiful story, her one shining bit of beauty that she had created, was now tarnished. The anger that boiled inside her began to mourn the loss of her privacy. But Bud looked so miserable her heart began to relent. "I guess it could be worse," she said at last.

George touched her hand. "Sis, it can. Bud, finish the story."

"She's not near any knives, is she?" Bud asked.

"Not funny. Finish the story." George wrapped his hand around hers. "Lolly, in advance, I'm sorry. You did not deserve this."

The room was silent until at last Bud put the remaining bits of the roll down and stared at the crumbs.

"I told some people, and some other people were there, and I think they told some other people."

Lolly didn't need for him to tell her who they were. She already knew. She could sense the hands of Hildegard Hopper and Amelia Kramer in this.

God, this would be a good time to take me Home.

"I need to leave," she said. "Please excuse me."

George tightened his grip on her hand. "I hate to tell you this, but there's more. Bud, please continue."

"I might have sort of led these people to think that maybe there could be, well—I implied a little bit that Colin is your mail-order groom."

Chapter 7

The river twists and turns back onto itself, a golden ribbon in the fading summer sun. Soon the trees will be bare, and the leaves will float down the river, away from where they began and flourished. Winter's hoary head will claim even the river, then. He holds my hand one last time and promises me that tomorrow the sun will shine, the stars will twinkle, and the moon will glow. But we will not be together.

L olly sat on her bed. All the lights were extinguished, and she sat in the darkness and talked to God.

We've been through a lot together, You and I, and I've trusted You—and I still do. I don't understand why things happen the way they do. My parents should have lived longer. I miss them so much. Every day is a struggle to keep the family together. And now, this. I'm not asking You to explain it to me—although if You'd like to, I'm willing to listen—but I would like some guidance here. What do I do?

In the clear night, she could hear a dog barking from a neighboring farmstead, and Bruno's baying response. Beyond them, another dog howled. They were just like the rumor network in Valley Junction, she thought. From one dog to another, the story got spread.

Mail-order groom!

She hadn't been able to look at her brothers after Bud had told her the horrible news. She hadn't even done the dishes, but she'd heard her brothers in the kitchen taking care of cleaning up. Tomorrow she'd probably have to redo the dishes, or, she thought with some meanness, she could make Bud eat out of the dirty ones.

Had they said anything to Colin? What was his reaction? She groaned as she realized that not only did she have the townspeople to deal with, she had him, too.

Mail-order groom!

What had she said in the notebook that had led to it? Anything? Or had it been all Bud's overactive imagination?

She stood up and crossed the room to check in her closet. In the dark, she felt around the top shelf where the blanket had been, and her fingers found nothing.

The notebook was missing, but at this stage, it was all water under the bridge or whatever the appropriate metaphor was.

The notebook was gone, and with it, her reputation.

No wonder the women at the grocery store had been eyeing her with amusement. The druggist. The clerk at the clothing store. Even Ruth. To them she was a woman so desperate for love that she'd sent for a man to marry!

Hildegard and Amelia had probably taken the story and embroidered it even more. She didn't want to think what they might have done with it.

But her mind wouldn't let the fact rest and batted it around fruitlessly, like a cat playing with a toy mouse. A mail-order groom!

Her own brother had told the story, too, lending a great degree of credibility to it. So even if Colin were right, when he'd said earlier that the people of Valley Junction would simply dismiss Hildegard and Amelia's story as silly gossip, it circled back to that. Bud had started the story.

Plus, what would Colin think of the story? It would probably drive him out of town, away from her forever. She thought of Colin at the stewpot, then twirling her around with the lure of Eau de Beef Stew making them rich.

It was silly, so silly that it made her laugh through her heartache. Eau de Beef Stew!

They'd stood together, right there in the kitchen, his arms around her waist. She'd thought he was going to kiss her.

Even now, reliving it, she was amazed at how much she wanted him to.

She'd gone all these years without being kissed, except, of course, by her parents, and that one time behind the school when she was thirteen. It had been a quick, experimental peck on the cheek, given by a boy who had long ago moved away from Valley Junction, and whose name she'd forgotten.

But a real kiss—that was the stuff that she'd never let herself even dream of, except in her notebook. And at that moment in the kitchen, it had seemed like her creation and real life might actually meet.

No. It hadn't happened, and that told her everything. They had both been caught up in the moment—a dangerous thing, that—and it was better that it hadn't gone further.

Still, Eau de Beef Stew. It made her smile.

But like a drumbeat of a dirge, under the memory was this new twist, and it stripped away all of the sweetness and replaced it with a sour, spoiled taste.

She'd come so close to love, so close, and now it was slipping out of her grasp.

⌒

Colin had spent most of the night awake, trying to first of all, figure out what had happened, and second, how to deal with it. George had filled him in, feeling that it was only fair that he was aware what the situation was.

Here he'd worried about being a burden on the family economically, but this came out of nowhere and caught him off guard. Now his very presence had put Lolly in a socially precarious spot.

He was angry at Bud. Angry that he'd put Lolly in this position, angry he'd put him in it. Bud's impulsiveness was part of his charm, but there was nothing charming about what he had done.

Through the dark hours he'd tossed and turned, searching for a cool spot in the August heat and talking alternately to himself and to God.

He still wasn't totally accustomed to being this familiar with God—he was used to the formal tone of his church in the city, where the language of prayer employed *Thou* and *Thee* and, of course, *hast* and *shalt*. His time with the Prescott family, however, had made God more real to him, and he knew that no matter what words he used, God understood him, even if he didn't totally understand God.

It wasn't one of those electric moments, when the light came on and all things spiritual were clear. That would be nice, he had to acknowledge, but it didn't happen that way.

Instead, bit by bit he began to move, to edge, to creep into the light of the truth. And always, God was there, listening to him. Now it was time to listen to God.

The situation with Bud was dire. What was he to do about it? Something? Anything? Nothing?

Forgive. That was the only solution he could come up with, and it wasn't going to be easy. These wounds cut deep.

Forgiving seemed a lot easier in principle than it was in action. Bud was the kind of person who bumbled and blurted his way through life, and Colin was sure this wasn't the first time he'd done something hurtful to his family. But this one was possibly the most virulent blunder he'd made.

Maybe the best idea wasn't to forgive Bud, at least not right away. He certainly needed to understand how much his actions had hurt his sister. Bud needed to squirm under the hot light of his own shame.

Even as he thought it, he realized the herculean task ahead of him.

It was easy to be the forgiven one, but much more difficult to be the forgiver. *How do You do it, God? How do You forgive, and yet lead us to know better?*

He turned the question around in his mind, but still it made no more sense than it had initially.

The sun had begun its rosy climb over the horizon before he'd finally drifted off into an exhausted but fretful sleep.

Breakfast was a somber meal, with all of them eating in silence. Colin furtively watched the siblings as they bent over their food. No one really ate anything, and clearly appetites had suffered after the prior evening's disclosure.

Bud finally burst out, "All right! I am horrible! I am terrible! Hate me! I deserve it!" and ran from the kitchen.

Lolly moved as if to follow after him, but George stopped her. "Let him go."

"George, did you hear what he said? I can't let him—"

"Lolly, you have to let him feel the wrong. If you don't, he'll find a way to justify it, and he won't have learned anything. He'd probably do it again."

She sighed and rubbed her forehead. "This isn't easy," she said. "I don't know what to do."

If only life were written in pencil, Colin thought, he could take an eraser and undo all the missteps.

"George," she said to him, "there's something else. The notebook isn't in my room. He said he put it in there, but it's not on the shelf and not on my dresser."

"You know how he is," her brother said. "He gets mentally waylaid easily. He must have meant to put it in there, but I saw it on the floor next to his hat. And yes, I know his hat isn't supposed to be on the floor, and that's how I saw the notebook, when I was picking up his hat. I put it in your room on the chair."

"It wasn't there. You don't suppose he took it again, do you? Did he have it with him when he went to town?"

George grimaced. "He had it, of course. He, well, Lolly, he read some of it out loud in the bank."

She put her face in her hands and groaned.

"But he brought it home. That's when I saw it. It's here somewhere. You'll find it. Maybe you just picked it up without realizing it."

Lolly shrugged, and Colin's heart twisted at the hopelessness in the gesture. "It doesn't matter. What's done is done."

He started to move toward her, but George interrupted him.

"Colin, let's go work on that shed. I'd like to have it finished by supper." George stood up, and Colin followed suit.

Outside, George looked around. "I'll bet Bud went to the river."

"He'll be okay, won't he?" Colin couldn't keep the alarm out of his voice.

"Oh, I'm sure he will be. This isn't the first time he's done something goofy, as you might have guessed. It's just that this is probably the messiest."

They walked to the shed, neither one of them speaking much, as Bruno, mindless of the drama at play, chased insects through the grass.

George handed Colin a hammer, and they both began to dismantle the shed.

"I'm really sorry that Bud got you involved in this," George said at last. "It was bad enough that he did what he did to Lolly, but to haul you into it, too, well, that was really too much. Mail-order groom, indeed."

Colin smacked the plank over the window sill and then pried the nails out carefully before dropping them in the can that George had for that purpose. "I've been called worse," he said at last.

George swung his head slowly from side to side. "Maybe. But how on earth he came up with that story about you being a mail-order groom is beyond me."

"What, you don't think somebody would send away for me?" Colin grinned. They laughed.

"I'm a bit concerned that the notebook is missing. Are you sure you moved it to her room?" Colin asked as he carefully removed a bent nail from the window frame.

"I'm sure of it. I put it on the chair in Lolly's room. I figured enough of this tomfoolery had gone on, so let's just get this thing out of circulation."

"Smart. Well, she's sure to find it soon." Colin wiped sweat off his forehead. "I can't believe it's so hot this early. Doesn't bode well for the afternoon."

"We'll probably be baked alive. Since the shed is in the sunlight, let's work on this until noon, and then we can find something else to do in the afternoon."

"Do you ever think about just sitting under a tree and, oh, reading some afternoon?" Colin asked. "I don't think I've ever seen you when you're not doing something here."

"Time is all I've got," George replied somewhat cryptically.

Bruno bounded over to them, a treasure of some kind in his jaws that he dropped at George's feet.

The black-and-white furry creature lifted its tail, identified itself, and ran back into the underbrush.

"It isn't! Please tell me it isn't what I think it is?" Colin drew back as the smell hit him.

"I'm sorry, but it is." George clapped his handkerchief over his nose. "I don't think either of us got that stink on us, do you?"

"I can't tell," Colin said. The smell seemed to permeate everything.

"Hold onto Bruno," George said. "I'll be right back."

The smell was overpowering, and Bruno put his head down and wiped his snout across the scrubby grass, making high-pitched moaning sounds as he did.

"I sure don't blame you, dog," Colin said, trying to breathe as shallowly as possible. "That's nasty."

George returned with two large buckets. "I've got the stuff in here to take care of skunk stink. Take him to the old cattle tank."

The watering tank was empty, except for two grasshoppers and a rather bored-looking toad hiding in the scattering of leaves.

"Come on, boy," George said to the dog. "You know the routine. In."

The dog jumped into the tank, startling the grasshoppers and the toad into activity. He stopped his whimpering and watched them curiously before trying to catch them.

Colin rescued the creatures from Bruno's paws and set them free.

"This isn't the first time this has happened," George said as he emptied the buckets of two large bottles, a box, and a carton of soap. He dumped the first bottle in one bucket and shook in the contents of the box and stirred it with his hand.

Then he swished the bar of soap through the mixture until it was foamy. He repeated the entire process with the second bucket. "Bruno is a two-bucket dog," he explained. "Now to get this smell out. This ought to do it."

"What goes into it?" Colin asked, leaning over to see.

"It's truly the kitchen sink potion, except that Lolly would never allow me to do this in the kitchen. Heinz white vinegar. Arm & Hammer baking soda. And good old Fels-Naptha soap."

"And it works?" Colin watched as Bruno sat in the tank, letting George wash him.

"Sure. The key," George said, as he scrubbed the dog with the concoction, "is to get to him right away, before the stink has a chance to set. Skunk'll do that. If you don't clean him up then and there. . ." George shook his head sadly at the thought.

"Why do you do it in the tank? Why not just on the ground?" Colin asked. This was fascinating.

"Because there's a water connection here, and it usually works. It lets me rinse him—" George lifted his hand to point to the pipe, and Bruno seized the chance.

With one leap, he slid free—his fur slicked with the soap—and ran away. Colin started to chase after him, but George called him back. "He's just going to the river. He'll swim in it for a while to get the soap out." He chuckled. "Can't say that he'll smell much better, though. The river is a bit heady this time of year. And speaking of heady, we'd better lather up, too, or Lolly'll have us eating by the barn for the next week or two."

The two of them used the rest of the compound and washed themselves off, even sudsing up their shirts and dungarees.

"Better?" Colin asked, taking a whiff of his shirtsleeve. He couldn't tell if the odor was gone or not.

"Just in case, I think we'd better head down to the river and wash off. Lolly won't want us in the house reeking like this. Of course, after being in the river we won't smell like roses, but it's better than this."

Plus they'd be able to check on Bud, Colin thought.

Lolly was coming out of the house as they walked past, a load of laundry in her hands. "Where are you fellows going?"

"The river," George called back.

"Did you get Bruno cleaned up?" she asked. "You know, I spend more on vinegar and soda and Fels-Naptha on that dog than I do on the rest of us. You're going down to the river to rinse off, I hope, before you bring those clothes back in here. You going to go fishing, too?"

George looked at Colin and for the first time that day, grinned. "What a great idea. Let's grab the poles and see if we can't catch us something."

"You know," Colin said as they got the poles and a pail from the barn, "I'm a bit surprised that we haven't done this before."

George chuckled. "If you'd seen Bud and me try to fish, you'd understand. We're farmers, not fishermen. You asked if I ever take any time off. This is about as close as I get to not doing anything. The fish and I have a deal. I don't bother them and they don't bother me."

"You don't bait your hook?"

"Oh, it's baited but the fish don't care. They either ignore it or eat it right off the hook."

After a quick discussion about what kind of bait was best—George nixed the idea of worms, claiming that doughballs made from bread were just as good since they weren't going to catch anything anyway, so why sacrifice a perfectly good worm's life?—they made a trip into the house to get some bread. Lolly gave them the heel of the loaf from the day before, explaining she had a fresh loaf in the oven, and the two men headed down to the river.

Bud was indeed at the riverside. He'd been in the water already, swimming and working off a head of steam apparently, for he was now sprawled at the shoreline, his shirt and pants still a bit damp. Bruno was splashing happily in the river.

Bud scrambled to his feet when he saw them. "The dog found himself a skunk, huh? When I saw him tearing through the trees, lathered up like that, I figured he'd either finally gone entirely mad or met himself a skunk."

George looked at him steadily before speaking. "You ran away from us."

Bud shook his head and studied his bare toes that dug into the wet ground at the edge of the river. "I ran away from myself."

"Did it work?" George asked him.

Colin began to step back from them, to move out of this very personal conversation, but George touched his arm. "Stay. You have a stake in this, too."

"No," Bud said. "No matter where I went, I was there. I wasn't getting away from anything. Not that I went anywhere anyway. Just here. But I thought about going somewhere, like Colin did. But I'd still be with me. So I decided to stay. I mean, I was here anyway."

George nodded seriously, but Colin thought he saw a twinkle in the older brother's eyes. "I can't believe it, but I think that made sense in a Bud sort of way."

"Yup," Bud said. "I swam for a while, prayed a little bit, and then I sort of drowsed off."

"Well, we came here to go fishing," Colin said.

"Did you bring me a pole, too?" Bud asked.

George tossed him one, and soon the three of them were sitting on the ramshackle pier, lines in the water. Overhead in the trees, a cluster of birds chatted with each other, and the leaves rustled in the faint breeze against a cloudless sky.

The river made little splashing noises when it spilled onto the shore, and Bruno crashed through the underbrush in search of something interesting.

Sometimes, Colin thought, there was nothing as companionable as silence. It was when people chose not to speak that was telling. He'd known men who would have been unable to tolerate this stillness, who would have found it necessary to fill it up with words.

But silence wasn't a void, not always, and definitely not now. Bud and George's acceptance—and apparent appreciation—of the hush identified them as two who were in touch with their environment and who were able to find harmony in nature.

It was, Colin knew, a rare gift.

Nobody spoke of the thing that Bud had done. Perhaps this was the best way to manage it, Colin thought. Repent in silence, and forgive in silence. Bud certainly seemed a bit more sedate in his behavior. Perhaps he had learned something.

"I should fix this pier," George said, "but for as little as we use it, it seems like such a waste of time."

"It's beautiful down here," Colin said, "so peaceful."

Lolly scrambled down the incline to the shore and stopped suddenly. "Oh, you're all here." She had a fishing pole in her hand, and she stood stock-still, her eyes locked on Bud. "I didn't know—"

The moment hung awkwardly, the pain the family felt spread open and revealed in front of Colin.

Without saying more, she sat beside Colin. She pinched her nose as Bruno joyfully came over to see her, and snuffled around her. "Oh, I can still smell skunk on you! Get away from me."

"Here, boy." George threw a stick into the river and Bruno raced after it. "Sorry, Lolly. I'll keep him out of the house until he's not so awful-smelling."

"You do that. That mongrel's never going to learn about skunks, I'm afraid."

"He had this one in his mouth, and he brought it over to us," Colin explained.

"Wonderful. I gather it was still alive?"

"Quite."

He watched as she rolled a piece of bread into a ball and stuck it on her hook.

"You fish, too?" he asked.

"She's the best of all of us," Bud declared, and Colin breathed easier as she smiled at her brother. Forgiveness came easily to this family, but then, he thought, with a brother like Bud, she probably got a lot of practice.

Bruno came out of the water and settled in the shade—upwind, Colin noted with some amusement.

There was something about fishing that brought people together, he thought. They sat, quietly, letting their hooks sit in the water until whatever bait was on it had surely gone, but not caring. It was being together that mattered.

"Lolly, I'm sorry. I really am," Bud said at last in a low voice. "I act without thinking a lot, and I say things without thinking, too. Actually sometimes I think that I don't think much."

They laughed.

"Bud, I do wish that you wouldn't be so impetuous, but that's part of what makes you who you are," she said. "Someday, I think you'll find a way to harness all that energy you have, and it'll be wonderful; but right now, there are days when I could throttle you."

"There are days when I could throttle myself," Bud said.

This was the right place for him to be, Colin thought as his line floated in the water—at this very moment, in this very spot, with these very people. God was good.

He knew he should think about returning to New York City, to take his place back in the world of commerce; but now, sitting on a pier, dangling a line in the Minnesota River on a late summer afternoon seemed much more important. The broken links in his memory were almost all mended now, and the spiritual quest that had sent him on his way was nearly complete.

Yet he couldn't bear to leave. Not yet. Maybe not ever.

"This is one of the grand days of summer," Lolly said. "I can feel it in the air off the water. It's like the river is telling us to enjoy this, to store up this warmth, because it's getting to the end. Too soon it'll be September."

September! How long had he been there?

As if reading his mind, she mused, "And to think that it's been just three months, hasn't it, since Colin arrived at our doorstep."

Bud snorted. "Arrived at our fence post, you mean."

Colin shifted uneasily. This conversation had to happen eventually, but he was not looking forward to it at all. He led into it as obliquely as he could. Maybe that would make it easier, although he doubted it.

He took a piece of bread and kneaded it into a ball to be used for bait. He dropped it into the pail and began another one. That one joined the first, and then another and another, and soon the small pail began to fill up.

This was not something he wanted to discuss, but this was as good a time as any, with all of them sitting in the sunlight on the river, fishing poles in their hands.

"You three saved my life."

Bruno left his spot in the shade and trotted over and plopped at his side, dropping a soggy offering of some kind of lake weed at Colin's feet. The smell of the skunk was dissipating a bit, so maybe the dog hadn't received a direct hit after all. Colin reached over and patted the dog's side. "Sorry. You four. Without you, I'd have probably died back there on the road behind your farm."

"It was an honor," George said.

"An honor?" Colin stopped rubbing Bruno's stomach and faced George. "Hardly! I've been a dreadful inconvenience. We all know that these times are making everyone's pocketbook thinner by the day, and yet you took me in, and if you've complained, you haven't done it where I've heard you."

Lolly jiggled her fishing line in the sunlit water. "There's no point in complaining. We don't much believe in it."

Bud snorted. "Remember that the next time you whine about my leaving my socks on the kitchen floor."

"Well, socks on the kitchen floor would make anyone complain. That's unsanitary," Lolly responded.

"Like someone's going to eat off the floor. Even Bruno doesn't do that, do you, big boy?" Bud nudged the dog, who opened one eye slightly before going back to sleep.

"Bruno would eat anything, anywhere, and you know it," George interjected. "The only thing the mutt won't eat is rocks, and even that's just a matter of time. He chewed the handle right off my toolbox last week. And today I had to pull one of your socks out of his mouth. I don't know where he found it."

"On the kitchen floor! I told you. It's disgusting. They smell, for one thing; and for another thing, if you don't pick them up, I have to. And that's nasty. I have to touch your stinky socks with the hands I use to make our dinner, and—"

"Enough!" George thundered. Bruno scrambled to his feet, nearly knocking over the makeshift bait can, and barked. "Bud, just put your socks in the laundry like any other human being. Lolly isn't your servant. And Lolly, don't pick them up any more. Just leave them there until he takes care of them."

"But he won't. And I need to be in the kitchen to cook."

"Then kick them out of the way. . ."

Colin let the argument flow around him like the waters of the river. He knew that they weren't really angry. In fact, it was satisfying, being in a family—

He broke off the thought before it could go any further. This wasn't his family, not really.

He wanted them to be.

The idea struck him with the force of a locomotive. He wanted to be part of this family.

He looked at them, one by one.

Bud's energy. George's stalwartness. Lolly's—Lolly's loveliness.

She was beautiful, but not in a big city sort of way. She wasn't the kind to go smearing on makeup or dolling up her hair with fake waves or color. What she had came from within.

Was it the result of her unshakable faith? Was it the magic that made her eyes sparkle, far beyond what any cosmetic could supply?

And that was one of the reasons he didn't want to leave Valley Junction. He'd wanted to make his life matter, to have meaning, and now, as he watched the sunlight play across Lolly's hair like dappled gold, he wondered how much further he'd have to go.

Maybe he'd already found it, and he was so jaded he didn't really see it?

"Pull it in! Pull it in! You've got something! Oh, for crying out loud, let me have it!" Bud reached across him and snatched the fishing pole and began reeling like mad. "Oh, this has got to be a big one. It's really fighting."

"A big boot, probably." Colin stood and cheered as Bud fought with whatever was on the other end.

Bud's face grew red with the effort, as he walked backward, trying to work the line, until the pole dipped almost to the water's surface. Suddenly it sprang back, nearly knocking Bud into a startled Bruno, who barked furiously at the empty fishing line and the water.

"Well, that was fun," Bud said as he got back to his feet.

"Fun to watch, too," George said. "If I were a wagering man, I'd say that you were snared on a log in there. The lower the water gets, the more debris we'll be catching."

"We won't think about that," Colin declared. "For the record, that was the biggest fish ever caught in Minnesota, and it merely broke free at the last moment."

"A log fish," Lolly said.

He grinned at her. "I never said what kind of record it was, did I?"

Bruno spied something in the river. His nose quivered, his front paw lifted, and his tail raised like a flag. For a moment he was motionless, and then he shot off, splashing into the water and flailing and spattering until Colin tensed, getting ready to go in after him.

Suddenly the dog emerged and trotted victoriously over to George. A catfish almost as long as he was flapped wildly in his jaws and then fell silent.

"Crazy dog caught a fish!" Bud said. "We can't catch anything with fishing lines and hooks and baits, and this mutt dives in and catches a giant fish with his teeth. Where's the fairness in that?"

"Come on," George said, taking the fish from the dog. "This was your fish, Colin. It's still got the hook in its mouth. Bruno just brought it in for you. I guess we're having catfish for dinner. Lolly, we'll see you and Colin later."

"Who's going to clean this stupid fish? I'm not going to," Bud began as they headed toward the house. "How come I always have to do the dirty jobs around here? Why don't Lolly and Colin have to—"

His voice faded away as they walked through the trees lining the river.

"There's that complaining thing again," Lolly said. "That boy's mouth goes all the time."

"He's a good kid. Energetic." He picked up the fishing pole with the broken line and rewound it.

Lolly laughed. "Definitely energetic. I wish I had even a particle of his liveliness. I feel like a slug around him sometimes."

"I feel like a slug today, that's for sure. Hey, Lolly. Look over there, toward the west. Doesn't it look like there might be some weather coming our way?"

"Could be. Oh, some rain would be so nice. Maybe this heat would break then."

"Well, until then, I'm going into the water." He slid off the pier and, bending his knees, let himself sink up to his chin. George was right. The river was quite shallow there. Now that he wasn't on the platform any more, he could see the watermarks on pilings. They were mute testimony to the falling levels.

He pulled himself back out and sprawled on the pier, letting the sun dry his clothes on him. "I could stay here forever."

"Then do."

He struggled upright. "Lolly, as much as I want to, I can't."

She turned her head, but not before he saw the flicker of pain that twisted her face. "Then don't."

"I don't want to keep taking advantage of you." He sought the words that simply would not come, and he shrugged helplessly.

"You're not taking advantage of us," she said, her words tight in the summer afternoon. "You work."

"Not well." He tried a laugh but it faded on his lips. "I'm not a farmer, Lolly. I'm a businessman."

"Well, that explains it. You can't be a farmer and a businessman? I suppose not, not in these times." She still wouldn't look at him.

He took her hands. They were rough, the fingernails split. A scratch ran across the back of one of them, and he ran his thumb down the raised red welt. "Lolly, I want to stay. I do. I don't want to leave you."

She turned at last. Her eyes brimmed with tears. "But you're going to, aren't you?"

The world spun crazily. He couldn't.

He had her in his arms, and her face was in his shoulder, and his hand was in her hair, and then his lips were on her cheek, and on her mouth, and she was kissing him back, and everything changed.

He couldn't live without her. He just couldn't.

Lolly paused, trying to identify the sound. Bruno was outside barking at something, a series of sharp excited yips—so whatever she heard, he did, too.

Ping. Ping. Pingpingping. Ping. Ping.

It couldn't be. Could it?

She wiped her hands on her apron and ran out the door. Her brothers and Colin met her by the coop.

"It's raining!"

"It really is!"

The four of them stood in the yard, their faces up to heaven, and let the droplets fall on their faces.

"Thank You, God!" she called out. "Thank You!"

Rain! Had anything ever felt as good?

She smiled as the drops soaked her. Yes, something had.

Colin had kissed her.

Chapter 8

The last days of summer are filled with promises—promises given and promises kept. These days are precious, the final hurrah of the sun's bright fire. He takes me in his arms, and he vows the great promises of summer. We speak of stories that will keep us warm through winter's cold blast, of kisses that can catch snowflakes, of love that knows no end. He promises he will stay...

Bliss. That was what this was all about, Lolly thought. Just bliss. The chickens clucked happily as Colin spread corn for them. He'd learned quite a bit since his arrival there. She smiled as she remembered the first time he'd fed the chickens. He'd dropped the feed in a circle around him and found himself surrounded by a tight ring of hungry poultry that would not move for anything.

He'd had to stand there, motionless, until they'd finished their meal.

But now he knew how to do it so he wasn't hemmed in. Maybe he could be both a businessman and a farmer.

She scolded herself at the thought. *One kiss, and you've got yourself married off. Hold on, Lolly! He isn't your mail-order groom!*

Still, it was nice to dream. Now that the joy of the notebook was taken away—she didn't even know where it had gone—she'd had to keep her story going in her head. It had taken a very interesting turn recently, too, she thought.

She smiled at the dish towel with the happy teakettle embroidered on it. She smiled at the hairbrush. She smiled at the petunias, now perky after the rain.

She smiled through church, even beaming at Hildegard Hopper and Amelia Kramer, who looked at her with ill-disguised interest. Reverend Wellman's sermon, about the meaning of grace, seemed absolutely on track, and Lolly's heart swelled with love for all her fellow human beings. The hymns were all familiar ones, and she sang with enthusiasm.

After the service had ended, Hildegard and Amelia made a beeline for her, exclaiming over the rain and how it must have truly benefited Lolly's petunias.

"So," Hildegard said, the magenta flower on her hat quivering as she took one of Lolly's elbows and Amelia, in her usual navy blue dress, took the other, "are we having a nice dinner today?"

"We?" Lolly didn't remember inviting them, but she felt so good that she was ready to serve soup and sandwiches to the entire world. "Of course, you're invi—"

George swooped in, leaving Ruth standing in front of the church with an amused expression on her face, and rescued Lolly from the two women. "Dear sister, I'm so sorry to interrupt this conversation, but we really must go. Bud needs to get home. The chickens, you know."

The two women recoiled in horror at the mention of the chickens. Bud shook his head and pointed out loudly that Colin had already fed them, but George was insistent and hustled them all into the truck. Bruno, who'd been sleeping under the truck, jumped in the back.

"Why did you do that?" she asked, so squished into the seat that she could feel Bud's ribs on one side and George's belt on the other. There really wasn't room for all four of them in the cab. "We were chatting so nicely and—"

"There's no such thing as a nice chat with those two," George said, frowning at the road. "Plus you were just on the verge of asking them to come to dinner."

Pandemonium broke out in the truck as Bud began railing about Hildegard and Amelia, Colin tried to calm him down, George started yelling at Lolly about her lapse in good judgment, and Lolly hollered back at him. Bruno howled over the entire thing.

At last they pulled up in front of the farm. As they spilled out, Bud said grumpily, "It's a good thing we're too poor to be fat, or we'd never fit in there."

"Finally," Lolly said, grinning again. "Something positive to say about being broke!"

After their dinner, Colin helped Lolly clear the table. "I'll dry," he offered as she filled the sink with dishes.

She felt that all-over smile coming on again. He needed a haircut. His dark brown hair was spilling over his shirt collar at the nape of his neck, and he had a little puff of soapsuds on one cheek. She'd never seen anyone as handsome as he was. Mail-order groom? Sure! She'd have picked him immediately from the catalog—if that was indeed how someone would get a mail-order groom.

George stood at the door. His face was solemn. "Can you two come into the living room, please?"

"You sound so serious," she said. "Just let me finish—"

"Now."

She'd never seen him look so grave, nor heard him speak so abruptly.

"Colin, come on." She took her apron off and hung it over the back of the chair.

Bud was already in the living room, and from the baffled expression on his face, she could tell he didn't know what this was about either.

George pulled his chair closer to the little table. In his hand was a ledger. Lolly recognized it. It was the same one that their parents had used. They'd just started it when they'd died, and George had used it ever since.

He opened the ledger and sighed.

"I hate to say this. I've gone over the numbers again and again. I was up all night praying, trying to decide if this was the right thing to do."

As he paused, Lolly studied her brother's face. Dark circles rimmed his eyes, and lines were etched deeply between his eyebrows into a constant frown. He looked exhausted.

Colin moved closer to her, as if offering her support.

"Go on," she said to her brother.

"The wheat isn't going to come in at all where I'd hoped it would. There just wasn't enough moisture this year. We'll be lucky if we break even."

"But the harvest isn't in," Colin said. "Maybe it could rebound."

George shook his head. "The kernels are shriveled. You can walk through the fields and hear it, that rattling sound. The stalks are like the skeletons of the wheat. We can't do it. I can't keep the farm together any longer."

"What are you saying?" she asked, unable to take in what her ears were hearing.

"I'm saying that we're going to have to sell it." His shoulders slumped. "That is, assuming we can even find a buyer."

"But I don't understand," Bud said. "I thought we owned the farm, that it was paid for."

"It is," George answered. "But we're in debt for the other things. We haven't made a profit in a couple of years. Honestly, I don't think anyone has."

Lolly put her face in her hands. This was horrible, beyond understanding. How could this have happened?

Colin put his hand on her back and murmured something reassuringly. "There's no other way?" he asked George.

George pushed the ledger to him. "You're a businessman. Take a look and see if you can see an escape route. I sure can't."

Bud looked at Lolly, and in his eyes she knew was reflected her own fear. "Colin will find something. Just watch, he will."

She knew what the answer was going to be—it would be the same for them as it was for thousands of others. They were going to lose their home.

Everything that their parents had sacrificed for, everything the three children had worked for with the goal of keeping the farm as their home—it was all going to be lost to creditors.

It was an entirely too-familiar saga.

She stood up and walked back to the kitchen. There were dishes to be washed.

Dishes that would be sold and put into cupboards that would belong to someone else. Spoons and forks and knives laid into drawers that would be used by another set of hands.

It all seemed unreal, like a dream that she would wake up from at any moment and wonder about. Like a replay of that horrible day five years ago, when George had told them that their parents had died. Time ceased making sense as her mind tried to sort through this life-changing news.

A horn outside announced visitors.

"Get rid of them," Bud said to her from the doorway of the kitchen. "This isn't the time for guests."

Her mind wouldn't form a coherent thought. All she could think of was that she was losing the farm.

She pasted on a smile and went outside. The two women had the doors to the DeSoto open, and Hildegard was heaving herself out with effort as Amelia delicately swung her legs onto the ground.

Hildegard immediately began fanning her face with her hand. "Whew! It's muggy down here by the river." Beads of sweat populated her forehead and cheeks. "I'd have thought the rain would have taken care of that, but it's still so close."

"I don't think it's this bad in town," Amelia contributed, her face screwed into a dainty frown. "It's probably all these trees and plants and such."

Lolly held up her hand. "I'm sorry, but this isn't a good time for a visit."

Hildegard's gloved hand flew to her rather substantial chest and with a great show of concern, she asked, "Is everyone all right? No one is sick, I hope! Oh, my goodness!"

The woman was a terrible actress, Lolly thought. Her false sincerity would fool no one.

"One person falls ill, and the next thing you know, everyone in town is sick, too," Amelia said. "That's the way plagues start."

Hildegard nodded so vehemently that the feather in her hat bobbed crazily. "The plague. Like the flu epidemic in '18. Of course, you're too young to remember that, Lolly."

"No, Hildegard dear, she wouldn't even have been born then," Amelia said.

"I was born in 1916," Lolly said, wondering why she was even part of this absurd conversation. What did it matter how old she was during the flu epidemic?

"Nevertheless, we learned then, didn't we? One cough in church. That's all it takes." Amelia fairly quivered with self-righteousness.

"Who coughed in church?" Hildegard looked alarmed.

"No one coughed in church," Lolly said, but the older woman was not going to be swayed from the idea.

"Was it Bud? George? Colin?" Hildegard leaned forward eagerly. "Is Colin the one who's ill? Oh, poor thing! I'd better see to him right now."

She began to bustle toward the door, despite Lolly's protestations. "No one is sick! That's not it at all! Please, stop! No one is ill!"

"But you said that Colin had the flu," Amelia said, her lips pursing in disapproval. "And on a Sunday, too. Not nice to lie on a Sunday." She shook a gloved finger in Lolly's face.

"I didn't—" Lolly began, but a great ruckus from the back interrupted her.

"Lolly! The chickens!"

Colin tore around the house, a frantic chicken in his grasp. Its wings flapped wildly, and feathers floated around him.

The two women retreated immediately to the DeSoto, and as Hildegard pulled out of the driveway, she called out, "Colin, you shouldn't be out, not as sick as you are! Fluids, that's the answer. Fluids and sleep."

The chicken calmed down as soon as the automobile cruised out of sight behind the bend in the road, and Colin put it back on the ground. It immediately picked its way back to the yard behind the house.

"What was that all about?" She pointed at the chicken, which paused to shake its feathers into place.

"I thought you could use some help, so I intervened with the chicken."

"What was wrong with it? It sure was upset."

He grinned. "I was hugging it. Chickens don't like to be hugged."

"Ah." She stood still, unsure what to do next.

"They don't like to be hugged, but I do," he said, and he opened his arms.

She stood in his embrace, drawing strength from him. She could feel his heart beating, the rhythm regular and strong. With each breath his chest rose and fell, while his fingers wrapped themselves in her hair, and the bun loosened, the ribbon sliding off, and she didn't care.

When she was in his arms, there were no money worries. The farm was safe. Her future was secured. If only she could stay there forever.

If only.

She could hear her brothers in the background, and she didn't care. This moment was hers and Colin's.

He kissed the top of her head and hugged her tightly. "You're so much nicer than a chicken to hug."

"You say the sweetest things," she answered.

"They call me sugar mouth," he murmured.

"They do?" She felt the smile begin again as she lifted her head for what she knew was coming.

Kissing. What a wonderful thing it was, she thought as their lips met. She understood now why it was so valued—and why it was so dangerous.

She didn't want for it to end, but something sharp jabbed into her foot, and she screamed against his mouth.

"I'm sorry!" he said, pulling away immediately, but she shook her head and looked down.

Around them were many of the chickens, pecking at their feet. She soon realized why.

"Colin, I hate to say this, but I believe we're standing on an anthill."

As if to prove the truth of her words, two chickens picked off more of the little black insects from her feet, and the rooster, Floyd, strutted over to see what the buffet was all about. He started in on Colin's feet, his beak tapping rapidly on Colin's shoes.

"You know," he said with a laugh as he shooed the birds and they scattered, "I thought your brothers would be our chaperones, but they're ignoring us. The chickens, though—do you suppose they don't want us kissing?"

"They'd better watch it or they'll end up as fried chicken," she said, reluctant to leave the harbor of his arms.

A stray breeze picked up a strand of her hair and ruffled it. He smoothed it back into place and kissed her forehead. "You're tough. But I like that. We need to—"

"Colin and Lolly are kissing, Colin and Lolly are kissing!" Bud sang from behind the chicken coop. Bruno dashed out and ran in circles around them, barking happily.

"Stop it, Bud," she said. "That's terribly rude. And childish. And stupid. And hush up, Bruno. Just because you're with Bud doesn't mean you have to act like him."

"George wants you to quit smooching and come inside," her brother said, ignoring her little tirade. "He wants to talk to you some more. Probably about the farm."

~

George was standing at the window, looking out over the farm. "Even if Colin can find some little bit of something I've overlooked—and I don't see how, not as often as I've gone over the accounts—we're going to have to figure out what to do. First off, like I said, selling the farm is going to have to happen."

"How much do we owe?" Lolly asked.

Her older brother shook his head. "It's not that. We really don't owe anything except taxes and a small bill at the store in town."

"Then we could cut back," Bud said.

George sighed and rubbed his forehead. "We've cut our electricity use to almost nothing. Our food is pretty much what we get from the garden here, and what we don't grow, Lolly gets through trade with the store for the eggs."

"So what's the problem?" Bud asked. "If we're okay, why can't we just stay on the farm?"

"There's more than that. There's gasoline for the truck—it's not much, but it still has to be paid. Things break and have to be replaced. And let's not forget that winter is coming, and this farm's income comes to a complete halt then. How can we heat this place? And food? Lolly can put some aside with canning and such, but nowhere near enough to get us through a Minnesota winter. Even if I cut down every single tree on the property, it won't keep us warm until next summer."

She had never heard George say so much at one time.

"There are programs," Colin said, "new things the government is trying. Like the Works Project. Have you looked into that?"

"I sure don't want to have to rely on the government," George said, clearly uncomfortable with the idea that he hadn't been able to provide himself.

"I think they're doing something in Mankato," Lolly said, "but that's probably too far away. There's no way to live here in Valley Junction and work in Mankato. And in the winter—" She shuddered. "That would be a terrible drive to have to make every day."

"The bad state the economy is in has got to end, I'm sure of that," George said. "I'd hoped we could wait it out by being prudent with what we had, but we ran out of steam before it did."

"The drought hasn't helped a thing, either." Lolly thought of the carrots that she'd dug up last night. The downpour hadn't done much to help the shriveled roots that looked more like tiny gnarled orange fingers than like the plump carrots they should have been.

"But it's got to break. I really think that it'll end soon." Colin's voice rang out confidently in the small room. "God won't let this go on forever."

Bud shook his head. "I don't know. I know it's not true, but doesn't it sometimes seem like God has forgotten us? That maybe there's a little stretch of the U.S.A. that He's missed? A place called Minnesota?"

"It's everywhere," George said gloomily. "Not just here."

She'd never heard them talk like this before, and her soul stung with their pain.

It did seem like they'd been forgotten, but she'd never gotten to the stage they were at, where they were actually doubting God.

"God is with us," she said gently. "He is. He was with us before, through those terrible days five years ago, when we thought the world was over."

"We were right, apparently," Bud muttered.

"You don't really believe that, do you?" she asked him, covering his hand with hers. She knew he didn't think it was true. This was just Bud's way, to blurt out whatever crossed his mind.

"Nah, I guess not," he admitted. "But you've got to admit that God sure does like to test us a lot. And I don't know why."

"That's what faith is all about," Lolly said. "It's being sure that even if we don't understand why things are happening the way they do, that we know there's a purpose, a goal. God understands suffering. We just have to trust that this is going to work out. We need faith."

"Oh, I guess I've got faith, all right," Bud said. "I do know that there's more to our lives than this particular moment, and in twenty or forty or fifty years, I'll probably look back on this and say, 'My, but didn't we have fun.' Still, I'll tell you what, if God would like to put a gold mine in our backyard today, I'd be fine with that!"

They all laughed at Bud's honesty.

"I suppose there's always the chance that could happen," Colin said, "but I kind of think we shouldn't wait for it. Barring a gold mine under the chicken coop, the government will help out more. It has to. There's too much at stake." Bruno sat up, his tail thumping in anticipation. "S-t-a-k-e, you goofy dog, not s-t-e-a-k."

"Like we've seen s-t-e-a-k around here lately," Bud said morosely.

"The time will come when you will eat steak, and maybe you won't have diamond-encrusted belts and shirts made of silk, but you'll be fine. I just know you will."

George sighed. "I'm glad you can be that certain, and while I do trust the Lord, I'm still going to want to see a real dollar now and then."

Lolly's stomach twisted. This wasn't just a theoretical discussion about the effects of this economic Depression. This was real life, *her* life.

They were going to lose the farm, the place that had been their home for their entire lives, the fields that their parents had nurtured and cared for, the house that her father—and mother—had built with their own hands, knowing that a family not only needed each other but something to call their own. They'd chosen land.

"Mom and Dad bought this land and built the old house and then this house themselves," she said softly. "Mom had been saving her sewing money in a baking soda box in her stockings drawer. Remember how she told the story? Then one day she didn't get the drawer all the way shut, and their cat pulled the drawer out, found the box and chewed on it. She laughed and said that was one time when she was lucky that she didn't get paid in paper money. The cat couldn't hurt the coins, just the box."

George picked up the story. "Dad had tucked away his 'summer money'— the extra that he got from clearing out the gophers on the neighbor's farm. After they knew they were going to get married, they each lived at home and worked, Mom as a teacher and Dad as a clerk at a grocery store, and they saved every penny. They had already chosen this piece of land and drawn up the plans for the house, down to what doorknobs they wanted. That's what they saved for."

"Mom told me that they added that to the money they got from their wedding. They were counting every penny." Bud chuckled. "She said she was horribly disappointed when the banker and his wife gave them the crystal vase. They were so focused on saving money for a home that she didn't realize how expensive that vase was."

"That's the vase," Lolly said, pointing it out on the corner shelf. "How it's made it through three children and a rambunctious dog or two without even a chip in it is amazing."

"This is the only way we were allowed to look at it." Bud stood up and walked over to the shelf. He put his hands behind his back and laced his fingers together, and Lolly laughed at the memory.

"Our hands had to be locked together behind us," she said. "That way, she told us, they couldn't get in trouble. She used to say, 'One hand watches the other,' which made Dad laugh every time. It wasn't until I got older that I realized she was making a play on words for 'One hand washes the other.'"

"I still don't get it," Bud said as he walked back to his chair.

Colin grinned at Lolly as her brother continued, "Well, do you? One hand does wash the other." He shrugged his shoulders in defeat. "So why do people keep saying it?"

"It means that if you do something nice for me, I will probably do something nice for you," George said. "It's not about washing your hands."

"Then why—oh, never mind." Bud reached down and took a soggy piece of brown cloth out of Bruno's mouth. "Does anyone know what this used to be?"

"I'm pretty sure it's my work glove," Colin said, waving away the wet scrap of fabric that Bud offered him. "No thanks. Bruno can have it. It doesn't seem to have all the fingers on it anymore, so I can't think it's worth saving."

Lolly stood up and directed Bruno to the door. "Out. Now."

"Come on, Lolly," Bud said. "He wasn't doing anything."

"Right. Not much. Just drooling on the floor and leaving shreds of Colin's glove under the table." She scowled at her brother.

"So?"

"So do you think he's going to pick the pieces up?"

"Just leave them there. He'll eat them sooner or later," Bud answered cheerfully. "Or you can grind them up and use them in our meat loaf."

Meat loaf. The world was falling apart and her brother was talking about work gloves and meat loaf!

Colin walked down to the river. The recent rain seemed to have revitalized the mosquitoes, and he swatted them away impatiently.

George's news put an entirely different face on his situation. The mail-order groom fiasco was reduced to just that—a fiasco. They could live through that. This was more important.

A sense of urgency pounded through him, even if the Prescott family seemed to be resigned to the loss. There had to be some way to save this farm. There was a family heritage on the line. He couldn't let it go without doing something.

The family needed some way of sustaining itself until the economy righted itself. It might be a year. It might be ten.

What could he do to help them? He had money back in New York. Or at least he might have. When he'd left in June, he hadn't exactly taken care of all the loose ends that would result from his sudden departure. No, he'd just assumed someone would clean up after him. He shook his head as he thought back to the life he had led.

But the point was that he had been financially secure. He had money. The problem was how to get it to them. He knew they wouldn't accept it from him, even as a loan, and certainly not as a gift.

No, it had to be more than that.

He sat on the pier, and immediately the swarm of mosquitoes surrounded his head and arms. God must have had something in mind for them, but right now Colin couldn't see the purpose. They were like the Depression and the drought. Somehow they fit into God's grand plan, but just how, he couldn't see.

One thing was becoming very clear. He couldn't stay here. Every bit of food he ate and every drop of water he used in washing hastened the demise of their home. He had to leave, and quickly.

Unless he could help them.

He weighed his options, such as they were, and only one option seemed possible.

If he was going to find a way to help them, he couldn't do it here. Perhaps if he went back to New York, he might be able to think of something.

Plus there was the very real fact that his separation from Lolly might make him work even that much harder to resolve the problem.

The mosquitoes were relentless. They bit through his clothes, attacked his eyelids, and crawled along his ears.

"This might help," Lolly said as she sat down beside him. "It's a mixture I make up, but mainly it's just citronella oil. We use it when the mosquitoes are bad, like they are now."

She opened a small bottle and poured some out in her hand. With practiced moves, she wiped it over his face and the back of his neck, and then his hands. "Run your hands over your trousers and ankles, too," she advised.

Almost instantly the pesky insects dispersed. "Thanks," he said, as she recapped the bottle and put it back into her pocket. "They were about to send me back to the house. I don't think I could have borne being out here with them much longer."

Lolly's legs dangled over the edge of the pier, and she swung them back and forth. "They can be insistent, that's for sure."

"That's true."

The sun was high in the sky, baking off the last remnants of the rain from the day before. Only along the water's edge, where the sun hadn't penetrated entirely through the woods, had he been able to smell the humid reminder of the shower.

"It's very pretty here," he said, watching the river's surface reflect the bright daylight in a mottled display of gold and bronze and taupe.

"I love September trees, but they're a bit sad, you know."

"September trees are sad?" He glanced at her, but she was smiling faintly at the opposite shoreline.

"Of course. This is the end of summer, the last stretch of time when they know they'll have their leaves. Come October, the leaves will begin to fall, not a lot at first, but it'll start." She stopped suddenly, and he thought he knew why.

"Are you thinking about this October?" he asked.

She nodded, and he saw a tear slide down her cheek. "I know what I have to do, except I don't know how to do it. Everything in my life is changing. I don't even know if we'll stay here in Valley Junction."

"Will you all stay together?" he asked, putting his hand over hers.

"I don't know. George is very fond of Ruth, and I'd thought they'd end up getting married eventually—once he knew I was seen to." Her face reddened, and she added very quickly, "But without a home or a job, that won't happen. He wouldn't ask her to live on Relief."

She sniffled, and he handed her his handkerchief. She took it and wiped the tears away, even as new ones were replacing them.

He didn't interrupt as she continued.

"And Bud—I don't know what we'll do about Bud. He's a bit of a loose cannon, if you know what I mean. He's a good kid, but he needs someone with him to keep him contained. So I guess that he'll go with either Bud or me, or both of us."

She shook her head. "We'll all be together still, I guess. I have no skills, and neither does Bud. George can do all sorts of things, but it's a matter of someone hiring him. And what are we supposed to do? Just go on the road, like hoboes?"

She gasped. "Oh, I didn't mean that! Colin, please, please, forgive me!"

He rubbed the back of her hand with his thumb, and looked into her river-dark eyes. "Not a problem."

She still looked so horrified at what she'd said that he laughed. "Lolly dear, please stop worrying. I wasn't offended by what you said. I know what you meant. Having to sell the farm is traumatic. It's not just a loss of some property. It's a loss of an entire lifestyle." Lolly still appeared so aghast at her words that he did the only thing he could reasonably do. He took her in his arms and kissed her.

Again, and again, and again.

He was never going to leave.

They walked back to the house, their fingers intertwined. Although they hadn't spoken of love, Lolly knew that for her, at least, her heart had been given over entirely. She loved him, and yet she was afraid of it.

Yesterday, it had been different. Yesterday, the Depression hadn't come up to their door and walked right in. Yesterday, their tomorrows were the next step in the line of years.

They stopped on the edge of the field. The farm was framed in golden sunlight, set against a backdrop of a natural shelterbelt. From here, no one could tell that the world had ground to a sudden and ugly stop at this very spot.

Even love couldn't cushion this blow.

"It's beautiful," he said, his grip tightening on her hand.

"I want to remember it always, just the way it is now," she whispered. "One day I will tell my children about this place, about the love that was built into the floorboards and the walls and the ceilings, and about how a man came here, at the end, and what he brought to my life."

As long as he stood beside her, she was strong.

"You saved my life," he said. "In so many ways, you saved me. My kind-hearted woman."

He let go of her hand and spread his fingers across her cheeks. His thumbs ran over the bones under her eyes, and traced down the side of her face. "Lolly," he said. "Lolly."

She was astonished to see his eyes brimming with unshed tears.

"What's wrong?" she asked, and then she laughed shakily. "Aside from knowing that we're losing our home?"

"How can our lives be so beautiful, and yet so torn apart? How can I choose this day to tell you, when I know that your world has been pulled from under you—"

He paused.

"Tell me what?" she prompted.

"That I love you."

Chapter 9

The last days of summer slip through my fingers like kernels of wheat, dried in the sun. So this is the harvest of my love? Lonely days become even lonelier. Once one knows love, a spot becomes created for it in the heart, and whenever love is gone, that place is an aching abyss. My soul aches for him. My heart cries for the love we knew. Where does love go? Does it die, like the last grasses of August?

I told her that I love her." There. The words were out in the open, ready to take on their own life.

He felt better, knowing that he wasn't keeping a secret from Lolly's brothers. It had kept him sleepless almost every night for the past two weeks, worrying about whether it was right not to let them in on his feelings for their sister.

"No fooling!" Bud clapped Colin on the back.

"What did she say?" George asked, not looking up from the pile of boards from the back barn that he was pulling nails from. Not having been used in several years, it had fallen into disrepair. Now that the utility shed was down, he was attacking the back barn, too. "Bud, you have to be more careful when you put the lumber over here. If you don't take the nails out first, someone, like me, is going to step on one and drive it right through his shoe."

"Sure." Bud pulled another board off the nearly dismantled barn and tossed it toward George.

"Didn't you hear me? Look at this!" George held the offending board in front of him and pointed at a nail sticking out from the side of it. "Take the nail out before you put the board on the pile. Put the nail in the can." He shook the can of nails. "Here. Goes in here."

"Why don't you show me how?" Bud asked with a sideways grin at Colin. "Show me what you mean."

"Yeah, you think I'm going to fall for that?" his brother grumbled as he pulled the nail out and dropped it into the can and then neatly placed the board on the stack.

"You just did." Bud laughed and George rolled his eyes.

He couldn't leave this family, Colin thought. He'd have to think of some way to stay here and help support them, both financially and emotionally. He owed them at least that much.

And the fact was that he was in love with Lolly. It still took him by surprise how quick and effective the process had been. He had, truth be told, lost his heart when he'd opened his eyes and seen her leaning over him, her hair that would not stay put falling around her face, her dark gray eyes searching his face, her fair brow furrowed with concern.

She had, from that day on, moved into his heart, completely and fully. How could he even think about leaving here? About leaving her?

"So what are your intentions toward my sister?" Bud asked as he tugged yet another board free and pitched it, nails still in it, onto the pile that George had just straightened. George rocked back on his heels and glared at Bud.

"What?" Bud asked George innocently.

George didn't answer. Instead he dramatically picked up the board, removed the nails, and one by one, dropped each nail into the can. Then he carefully placed the plank onto the pile and returned to his work.

"Slow learner," Bud said to Colin out of the corner of his mouth.

"Let's do this," Colin offered. "You pull the board out. Hand it to me. I'll take the nails out and put them in the can. I'll give the board to George, and he can put it on the stack."

"Assembly line," George said. "Brilliant. I feel silly that I didn't think of it earlier myself."

"And he calls himself the smart one," Bud said with a wink.

"Did *you* think of it?" George snapped back. "Ah. I thought not."

"See? He thought not. That means he doesn't think."

The back-and-forth between the two brothers lent an air of normalcy to the day, so much so that he was caught off guard when Bud picked up the earlier thread of conversation. "Are you going to tell us what she said when you told her you loved her?"

"A gentleman doesn't kiss and tell," George said almost primly.

"Yeah, but we're talking about Colin now."

"I honestly don't remember what she said," Colin said as he took the next board from Bud. "Maybe nothing."

"You weren't kissing her, were you?" George asked, leaning on the plank that Colin handed him.

"Maybe." Colin wiped his face with his handkerchief. It was one thing to tell George and Bud that he was in love with Lolly. It was another thing entirely to discuss the kiss. That was private and pure. "Here's the deal. I do love Lolly. I know I haven't known her long enough to dare to ask her to marry me, and maybe that's not where this will go, but she is special to me."

"I'm not sure the timing on this is good," George said, his face serious.

"The timing is terrible," Colin admitted. "I had no intention of telling her what my feelings were. The words just took wing and flew right out of my mouth."

"And how did you feel afterwards?" George kept his gaze steadily on Colin's face.

"Like a weight had been lifted off my shoulders. Off my heart. I knew it was the right thing to say."

"I see." Lolly's older brother returned to the lumber stack. "I'd say it's the real thing then."

"Listen to him." Bud joined the discussion. "Mr. Expert-in-Love himself. You learn all this from Ruth?"

His older brother abandoned the woodpile and approached Bud, his eyes blazing with anger. "You leave Ruth out of this."

Colin understood George's fury. The decision to sell the farm had taken his future away from him, and without even the basics of a home and a job, he certainly couldn't pursue the young woman's affections.

"Fine, fine!" Bud lifted his hands in surrender.

George stood still, his face reddened with emotion, until at last he turned, knocking over the can of nails, and stalked away, his hands shoved into his pants pockets.

"What was that all about?" Bud asked, watching his brother leave. "I didn't mean anything by it."

"I'm guessing that he is quite in love with Ruth, and that he's quite committed to her and to being with her." Colin knelt down and began to pick up the scattered nails.

"That's for sure. Have you ever seen him at the café? I practically have to pull him out of there with a towrope to get him to go."

"How does Ruth feel about him?"

"Oh, she's just as goo-goo about him as he is about her."

"They might have been making plans for a life together, or maybe they were just thinking about it, wouldn't you say?"

"Sure."

"I'm wondering," Colin said carefully, "if the prospect of losing the farm has destroyed their dreams."

The fact was that he had studied the ledger George had kept. How Lolly's brother had managed to keep them all on the farm without going into debt was nothing short of a miracle.

But it seemed that the time for miracles on this farm had come to an end. There were precious few pennies on this farm, and he could see no way to squeeze any more out of them than George already had.

He wasn't used to praying, at least not like Reverend Wellman, with *Thou* and *Thee* and *wilt*. The best he could do was tell God what he wanted and leave the rest up to the Divine.

On Sunday, Reverend Wellman had preached about the plow. You could pray for a plow, and maybe a friend lends you one, or a neighbor moves and gives you his. You strike it rich and buy a plow. So you've got a plow.

But that doesn't mean your fields are plowed, and that's what matters.

You've got to put your back into the work, the minister had told them, and do it. That's how God works through you. He gives you the plow—the capability—and it's up to you to use that plow.

Even as he changed the subject to the heat, and as he and Bud exchanged predictions on if and when it might break, a wordless prayer circled through his heart—one that asked for help, for relief, for grace, and for mercy.

And for a solution.

Bruno circled her feet, his toenails clicking on the linoleum, as Lolly cut the beans for the hot dish, a mixture of pasta and vegetables and leftover beef. If she diced everything a bit finer, the vegetables didn't look so peaked and the meat went a little further.

"If I carve any more corners off the food," she said aloud to the dog, "there won't be anything left."

For the past hour, she'd heard the men talking outside. They were too far away to make out individual words. Just the ribbon of sound floated to her.

Now they had stopped, and she couldn't hear the sound of the hammer on the wood of the outbuilding they were taking down.

"They probably went swimming," she said as she leaned over and lit the stove. "I don't know why I'm doing this. It's so hot I could put it on the counter and it'd bake up just fine."

Bruno yawned loudly, and she gave him the bone from the roast. "Here you go, you goofy mutt." He snapped it up in his jaws and carried it under the table, where he plopped down and chewed on it.

There wasn't much meat on the bone at all. She'd taken every possible scrap off it already, but she knew the dog would carry the bone around for days, protectively guarding it against any and all threats.

"Don't worry," she said. "I won't fight you for it. And I don't think anyone else will, either."

She tucked her hair back into the bun. One of these days she'd go ahead and bob it, just cut the whole scraggly thing off and be done with it. She looked longingly at the kitchen shears, but satisfied herself with twirling it in a loose knot and retying it.

She walked through the house, straightening a pillow on the couch, wiping down the shelves by the window. She paused at the crystal vase and she carefully took it down and sat with it on the sofa, cradling the precious object in her lap.

With the edge of her apron, she cleaned the dust from the etched surface. She licked the tip of her finger and ran it around the edge, and was rewarded with a shrill sound that brought Bruno running, the bone clenched in his jaws.

"Sorry," she said, laughing as he hid under the table. He stared out at her with suspicious eyes. "Didn't like that, I gather?"

"Didn't like what?" Colin asked as he entered the room and sat beside her. "He doesn't like crystal?"

"I made it sing, like this." She wet her finger and ringed the top of the vase, again producing the piercing note.

"That's singing?" Colin asked, wrinkling his nose. "I'm with you, Bruno. That hurts my ears."

Lolly put the vase back on the table. "Here it is. The best thing we own. I wonder what it would fetch if we sold it."

"Not much, I'm afraid," he said. "You're better off to hold on to it and the memories that go with it. Those are priceless, you know."

"I don't need priceless. I need something with a price."

She didn't mean to sound glum, but it was unavoidable. She'd carried the news of the impending sale with her for over two weeks now. It was like a heavy cloak, settling on her shoulders and weighing her down. Every once in a while she'd forget, but something would remind her and again, she'd feel the pressure.

She stood up and put the vase back on the shelf. "*Pfft*," she said. "After all these years of dusting this vase, I thought I might get something in exchange." She tried for a cheerfulness she didn't feel.

"We'll figure something out," he said from the couch.

"I like that. *We.*"

"George is going in to Mankato on Friday, he says. He's going to check into that program the government has now, and he's also going to see if there's any kind of help the family can get in the interim."

"Relief? We're going to have to go on Relief?" Her shoulders sagged in defeat and she leaned against the wall.

George had once characterized Relief as the last door in the hall, the one you thought was an exit but was instead another office. They had vowed never to take advantage of it—but they hadn't envisioned their situation getting so desperate.

"Relief isn't a bad thing," Colin said. "The economy's condition is a bad thing. The drought is a bad thing. But Relief isn't."

"I can't do this. I just can't do this anymore." She buried her face in her hands.

She felt his arms go around her, and she leaned into his welcome strength. "Don't cry," he whispered as he stroked her hair. "We can make do. Don't cry."

"I'm not crying." Her words were muffled against his shirt collar. She breathed in his scent, a mixture of sun and sweat. "I'm too drained to cry. It seems like everything is make do, make do, make do. I've cut the carrots for dinner so tiny they're nothing more than little orange flakes. The meat in the hot dish is there in name only. Tonight we can play a game called Find the Beef. I used the last of the noodles, and I don't know what I'm going to do tomorrow."

He held her tighter.

"And I've just lied," she said to him.

"You lied?" She could hear the surprise in his voice.

"I *am* crying."

She knew she was getting his shirt wet with her tears, but once they started, she couldn't stop them. She cried out all the grief, all the anger, all the frustration, all the hurt, until finally her head ached.

She pulled back and said, shakily, "I need a handkerchief."

"Here, take mine."

She shook her head. "I have my own." She managed a weak smile. "These days, it doesn't do to be without, you know."

"I suppose."

His chest was so comfortable, she didn't want to leave the safe enclosure of his arms, and she leaned against him while she fished in her pocket for her handkerchief.

"Let's go for a walk," he suggested. "You can bring your hankie."

"Am I going to need it?"

"Only if the vision of a broken down barn brings you to tears."

She had no idea what he was talking about. She knew that he and her brothers had been pulling down the back barn, but why would he want her to go see it now?

Not that it mattered. She would have followed him to Timbuktu if he'd asked her.

He led her, holding her hand, out to the spot where they'd been working. Most of the outbuilding had been taken apart, and she saw the sure hand of her brother George in the neatness of the work site. The wood was piled in a tidy stack, the nails were contained in an old coffee tin, and the tools were out of sight, probably safely stowed in his toolbox in the barn.

"What do you see here?" he asked her, as he stood behind her, his hands on her shoulders.

"I see some trees and a sky and a back barn that, if you all had just waited a week or two, probably would have fallen down of its own accord."

He chuckled. "It was fairly awful."

"It was originally meant to store wagon equipment, but when we got the truck, George sold the horse and the wagon and its accoutrements, which is what he called the reins and the harness and all that. Big fancy word, but George likes fancy words."

Colin smiled as she continued, "Lately it's housed a skunk or two—I think you've already met one—and a possum, and batches and batches of field mice, and a hornets' nest every year."

"So it's the local zoo?"

"You could say that. It's a definite improvement having it come down. Now I won't have to worry about what tenant is going to come out and greet me as I walk by." She shuddered as an old memory resurfaced. "There was even a snake in there once. Nonvenomous, Bud said—as he waved it in my face, of course—but still scary."

"Ah, typical Bud. So you see an old barn that needed to come down—and it is, bit by bit—and what else do you see?"

"I see the wood and the nails. George, always the thrifty one, will never throw away something even as little as a nail. I've seen him pound one straight to use again in a fence or something."

"Do you know what I see?" he asked as his fingers tightened on her shoulders. "I see hope. I see a family that won't stop believing and trusting in the future, so much so that they'll take down an old building and make plans for a new one."

"But he started this earlier," Lolly began, "before we knew that we'd have to sell the farm."

Colin leaned in, so close to her that his breath tickled her ear. "Do you really think he hasn't known this for some time? That he hasn't been trying to find a way out of it? But more importantly, once he decided that he couldn't save the farm, he continued on with this. Do you know what we're going to do with this lumber?"

Her head was spinning, not only with what he was telling her, but the very fact that he was so close to her.

"He's going to build a new shed, a toolshed."

"He says that, but I think it's just talk," she answered.

"No, he's got the plans all drawn up and ready to go. And he's talking about how he can store his tools in it. Lolly, is this the voice of a man who's given up hope?"

She couldn't bear it any more. She was tired of trying to stay upbeat and positive, when it was clear to her that their options were not just limited, but gone.

She twisted out of his hold and turned to face him. "You say this over and over, but here's the truth. Unless someone comes up with a way to save this farm, it's done. We can talk about having faith and having hope and all those pretty words, but we're like Bruno with that bone. All the meat is gone. It's just a bone. We can chew on it and chew on it and chew on it, *but it's just a bone.*"

Her chest hurt so bad she thought it would split open. "I've lived here my whole life. My entire past is here. I have nothing else. Nothing! There isn't anything romantic about poverty, and I think you, of all people, should know that. Look at you, sent out on the road with only a change of clothes and a bedroll."

"But it was my choice."

"Choice! You really don't understand, do you? There isn't any thing called 'choice' any longer! There isn't enough money here, and without money, Colin, all options are closed. If you can't pay for a place to live, then you're homeless. If you can't pay for food to eat, you're hungry. Where's the choice in that?"

She didn't even bother to swab away the tears that coursed down her cheeks freely. "They don't call it a Depression because everybody's having such a swell time."

With those words, she turned and marched back into the house, hating the way her life had turned against her.

He stood in the clearing, his hands still open as if at any moment she might walk back into his embrace. His ears still rang with her words, sharp and direct.

She was right. It was fine for him to mouth platitudes about keeping her faith and having trust and all that, but there was a time, he knew, to put some muscle behind the plow God had given him, just as the minister had said in the service on Sunday. He had to push it forward to make it work.

What could he do?

Bruno was snuffling around in the foundation of the old barn, and Colin kept a wary eye on him. He wasn't too fond of any of the animals that Lolly had mentioned, particularly snakes, and Bruno had already proven his talent at rousting animals from the shed with the skunk.

The dog pawed away a loose brick and picked something up in his teeth. Every muscle in Colin's body prepared for immediate flight as the mutt headed his way.

But it wasn't an animal. It was a notebook, rubbed over with dirt. The cover was partially ripped away, and it was, of course, damp with dog drool. He could see that Bruno had created his own stash of treasures—a sock, three feathers, a piece of rubber that must have been a tire, a bone, a gnawed candle, and of course, the notebook.

Bruno must have taken it from the house and brought it out to the barn and buried it.

Colin opened it and began to read.

It was a charming story, beautifully told. He understood immediately what he had in his hand.

It was Lolly's story.

Chapter 10

I thought my dreams were safe with him. And perhaps they are. But I have no idea where he has taken them. Across the ocean to enchanting Paris? To a mountaintop in exotic Asia? Into a pyramid in Egypt? I hope he takes good care of them, for these dreams are fragile things. And they are mine.

Dinner was a quiet meal, without much discussion.

George was angry with Bud, who was angry that George was angry. Lolly sighed. They'd been through this many times before. Eventually the whole thing would evaporate and life would go on as if nothing had ever happened.

It drove her crazy.

Colin seemed preoccupied. Occasionally he would lift his head and smile vaguely at her, and then lapse back into his own thoughts.

She shouldn't have snapped at him that afternoon. He was only trying to help, but she had reached the end of her patience. And she had to admit that nothing she said was untrue. It might have benefited from some editing of the tone, admittedly, but the facts themselves were indisputable.

He was probably hurt, and that unfocused smile was simply his way of dealing with her dreadful tirade. After dinner she'd try to catch some time with him alone and apologize. That would undoubtedly go a long way to heal his ruffled feathers.

She beamed happily at him, content with her decision, and let the dinner ride on in silence.

After the last noodle had been eaten, she cleared the table and prepared to wash the dishes. Usually Colin helped her, but tonight he wasn't there, and bless his heart, she thought, who could blame him?

No, definitely an apology was in order. It wouldn't solve the problem of the farm, but at least her heart would be happier.

She hummed contentedly while she straightened the kitchen. She hung the dish towel so that the smiling teakettle she'd embroidered faced outward. The plates and cups and silverware were washed and dried and put away, and the counters wiped off.

With one last unnecessary pass at the immaculate stovetop, she took off her apron, looped it over the hook on the broom closet door, and retied her hair.

She took a deep breath and entered the living room. "Colin, I'm sor—"

Her toe caught on the edge of the throw rug, and she tripped. Everything slowed down so that she caught the entire fall in amazing detail: stumbling on the rug, splaying across a sleeping Bruno who barked sharply at her for interrupting his dog dreams, sliding across the floor on her knees and chin, and coming to a halt against the edge of the sofa.

"And that's why they call it a *throw* rug," Bud quipped as he sprang to help her up.

"Are you all right?" George said.

"You're bleeding." Bud held up his hand and showed her the smears.

"Is anything broken?" George held her elbow, steadying her.

"Just my pride."

"Oh, that," Bud said dismissively.

"Where's Colin?" she asked, as she finally realized that this had all been for naught, since he wasn't in the room.

"I don't know." George looked around, as if realizing for the first time that Colin wasn't there. "I don't know that he came in here after supper."

"He did, but then he went to his room in the old house," Bud volunteered. Then he leered at his sister. "Maybe he is your mail-order groom after all. Did you want to go for a long walk in the moonlight? A little hand-holding? Kissy-kissy? Smooch-smooch?"

With all the dignity she could muster, she left the room and went into her bedroom. There was no way she was going to get to talk to Colin, not while her brothers were around.

She didn't miss her notebook as much as she'd thought she would. She had the real thing here in her home.

She sprawled on her bed and let her mind wander to the subject she enjoyed the most—Colin.

If only this stupid Depression hadn't interfered. He could have found work in Valley Junction, or even stayed and helped with the farm, freeing George to marry Ruth if he wished. Bud—well, she'd never figured out a solution for Bud. At some point he'd find a girl in the area and settle down. The problem with him was the settling down part.

She'd never thought she'd find love here and had long ago resigned herself to being a spinster and living out the rest of her days keeping Bud in line.

But now she had Colin. She loved him. She needed him.

What if he chooses to leave? Resolutely she tried to push the idea out of her mind, but it stayed just inside the fringes. There was no reason he should stay, and in fact, every reason for him to go.

He could take her with him.

Her brain began to play with the thought. They could go somewhere else.

Now that the farm was going to be sold, she had no reason to stay in Valley Junction. In fact, she would probably have to move and find a job. Of course her first thought was that she could go to St. Paul or Minneapolis, but why should she limit herself?

The economy was hurting there, too, but at least in a city they'd have a fighting chance at earning a living.

Perhaps this was a blessing in disguise. The cost was horrendous, but maybe there was a silver lining in this dark cloud.

She'd asked for this, longed for this, ached for this, and now she had it.

Freedom.

She laced her fingers behind her head and lay back on the pillow and stared at the ceiling. The more she played out the scenario in her mind, the more she liked it. Yes, it was absolutely possible.

She and Colin would move to the city.

George and Ruth could take the profit from the farm—assuming anyone would buy it—and start again, here or somewhere else.

And Bud? He was the wild card in the lot, but she knew even that would resolve itself.

God would help her sort this all out. He didn't create problems that His people couldn't solve.

With those plans floating through her mind like butterflies, she fell asleep.

The sun hadn't come up yet, but he couldn't wait. Once again he rolled up two blankets with rope and stowed a change of clothes and his Bible in his backpack.

In this hour before sunrise, the farm was silent except for the last sounds of the night birds calling to each other from the cottonwoods. The chickens were tucked in the coop, sleeping soundly in their straw nests.

Bruno sprang to his feet, his nails scrabbling across the kitchen linoleum as Colin tiptoed through the room.

Colin knelt and scratched the dog's head. "Take care of them for me, will you please? Especially Lolly."

He stood up and surveyed the room where he'd spent so many enjoyable hours with Lolly, falling in love with her as she peeled the carrots that never seemed to grow completely, or as she stood over a basin full of soapy water and dishes, her hair that couldn't stay in place escaping into those eyes as dark as wet granite.

Every part of his being screamed at him: *Stay!* His heart spoke the loudest. But he couldn't. He needed to leave, to go back to where he'd begun.

He had work to do.

His heart wanted to stay here, tucked in the curve of the Minnesota River, where within a couple of weeks the first gilt of autumn would touch the landscape. He wanted to sit on the pier with Lolly, enjoying October crisp mornings when the sun was as golden as the leaves, against a backdrop of clear blue sky.

And then to watch the first snowflakes fall. . .together. To stand in the warmth of the farmhouse and watch the winter put on an icy mantle, or to walk in the snow, their footsteps marking where they had been, and only their love deciding where they should go.

To await spring with its burst of brilliant new green, the first shoots of life to appear after the winterkill on the land.

He sighed. It was not to be.

He'd come in search of God, in search of meaning, and he had found it. He realized at last that it was very simple.

All he'd had to do was open his heart and let God bloom. God had been there all along. He had just been waiting.

He shifted his backpack onto his shoulders and settled the bedroll.

This was so difficult to do.

And so necessary.

"Good-bye, Lolly," he said into the dark. "God bless you."

With that, he turned and left the house, shutting the door very quietly behind him, and walked down the road, headed toward the future.

⌒

The chickens squawked and clucked and complained loudly, and Lolly smiled as she tied her apron on. Colin had probably just walked by. The silly birds had decided that whenever he appeared, it was time for him to feed them.

And, soft touch that he was, he almost always did, even if it was only a few kernels as a treat.

She went to the window to call him in for morning coffee. It was weak, to be sure, but it was coffee.

The chickens, though, weren't being fed. Instead, they were milling around anxiously, pecking at the bare ground as if that would make the food appear.

Where was Colin?

Bud slid into the kitchen with his usual carelessness, and she automatically chided him. "Can't you just walk into a room? You know, one foot in front of the other like a normal person?"

"Aw, Lolly, you know I don't do imitations." He picked up a cup and poured from the coffeepot. "I thought we were having coffee now."

"We are."

"So what is this?"

"Coffee."

"No, I mean really. What is it?"

She sighed. "It's coffee."

"Coffee is brown. This isn't brown. It's beige."

"I had to make it a little bit weak."

George joined them at that moment. "Any coffee left?"

Bud hooted. "Depends on what you call 'coffee.' There's some stuff left that Lolly brewed up, but it's a stretch to call it coffee."

George poured himself a cup. "It is kind of, well, transparent, Lolly."

"I'm trying to make it stretch until I can get into town with some more eggs."

"So what do you suppose is better, brother of mine," Bud asked as he pulled a chair out from the table and sat backwards on it, "five cups of weak coffee, or two cups of good coffee?"

"I don't know, Bud." George dished up scrambled eggs from the skillet and joined him at the table, but with his chair facing forward. "You tell me, as I'm sure you will."

"Sounds like somebody got up on the wrong side of the bed today."

Bud was in one of his taunting moods, Lolly realized. That was going to make the day all that much more difficult. When he was like this, especially first thing in the morning, it set the tone for George, who liked to eat his breakfast in grumpy silence.

"Where's Colin?" George asked, interrupting Bud's discussion of coffee.

"I don't know," Lolly said, frowning at her own cup of coffee. Maybe she had been a bit too light-handed with the ground beans. This looked a lot more like tea. She took an experimental sip. It tasted like hot water with a faint aroma of coffee. "Isn't he with you?"

"I haven't seen him," George said.

"Me, either."

"Those fool chickens are about to drive me insane, too," George said, sending a dark look in the general direction of the henhouse. "Colin needs to get up and feed them."

It wasn't like Colin to ignore the chickens, Lolly thought. Something was wrong.

"Would one of you do me a favor and check the old house?"

"Why?" Bud asked as he reached over to George's plate and speared a forkful of eggs.

"Get your own!" George growled.

"It's easier to just eat off yours," Bud said.

"Stop!" Lolly came around the corner of the counter. "Just stop it, please!

213

You two don't need to argue about every little thing that comes your way. I want one of you to go check on Colin and—"

She frowned as an ominous *crunch* behind her broke into her rant. "Bruno, you didn't!"

"Oh, he did," Bud said.

The dog had gotten into the garbage and pulled out the eggshells and was contentedly munching away on them.

"Nasty dog!" She leaned down and forced Bruno's jaws open and pulled out what she could of the shells. "Now you'll probably get sick."

She cleaned up the shells that were spilled on the floor, and when she stood up, George was standing beside her.

His face was solemn. "Lolly, Colin's not in his room."

"He's probably out in the back somewhere." She dropped the shells back into the garbage. "Bad dog!" she said, shaking her finger at Bruno. "No more garbage!"

"Lolly, I think he's gone."

"Gone?"

She froze, her finger still pointed at the dog.

"Gone. His bed is made, and his pack and bedroll are gone."

How could he be gone? How could he? She braced herself against the counter with both hands. "He's gone?"

George nodded. "I'm sorry. Sis, I'm really sorry."

"He's just outside somewhere. He can't have left."

"Lolly, he's gone."

"Then there's a note. Let's look for a note."

"No note. I already checked."

"Why would he leave? Why wouldn't he stay? He'll be back. He will. You just wait and see."

He didn't say anything. But she saw the answer in his eyes.

Whatever was left of her world shattered. She turned around and slammed her fist into the countertop. "This is not fair! Not fair!"

"Lolly. . ." George tried to put his arm around her, but she shook it off.

"First God takes both Mom and Dad and leaves us here on the farm. Then He brings a drought to the land, and if that's not enough, a Depression, too. My name gets smeared all across Valley Junction—"

"Actually," Bud interjected, "that was my fault. Not God's."

"Whatever. He could have stopped you. He could have tripped you when you were reaching for that blanket for the governor rooster. He could have had George run over a nail and get a flat tire. He could have made you decide that for once you'd keep your mouth shut."

"Eleanor Ann Prescott!" George barked. "No more!"

"And He could have let Colin stay here."

The rage in Lolly dissipated, and she slid down to the floor. "I'm out of fight. I can't go on anymore. We don't have enough money for even a halfway decent cup of coffee today. What are we going to do for dinner tomorrow?"

"We have the chickens," Bud said.

"We can't eat eggs forever," she pointed out.

"Not just the eggs," George said.

"Oh, this is exactly what I mean! If we eat the chickens, there won't be any more eggs. Do you see? I'm sorry I yelled at God. I am. But I just don't know what to do."

"We aren't totally out of options," George said. "In Mankato—"

"I want to be here. I want to be here with Colin."

"Well," Bud said, "I know what I'm going to do. I'm going to find Colin and make him answer to me, that's what I'm going to do."

"You're right, you know that, little brother? We saved that fellow's life! We did!" George pushed back his plate angrily. "We saved his life, and we took him into our home, and we fed him, and gave him clothes, and let our sister fall in love, and—"

What were they saying?

Lolly raised her head. "Wait just a second. You let me fall in love? Are you both insane? I think I can fall in love on my own, thank you very much."

"But he told us that he told you that he loved you," Bud said.

"He told you that, did he?" Cold fury was beginning to displace hurt. "What else did he tell you about us?"

Bud screwed his face into a thoughtful frown. "Well, George asked him if he'd kissed you, and—"

"You did *not*!" She nearly flew to her feet. "Tell me you didn't do that."

"Well, I might have." George at least had the good grace to look uncomfortable.

"And what did he say?"

"He didn't really say anything. He didn't seem to be a kiss-and-tell kind of guy."

Lolly snorted. "More like a kiss-and-leave kind of guy."

George pushed his chair back with force. "So he did. He did kiss you."

She put her hands over her forehead. What on earth had she done to deserve this from her brothers? Wasn't anything going to go her way?

"I am going to find a place where no one will bother me for a while," she said, with as much dignity as she could muster. "I need to be alone for a while. But first I am going to feed the chickens."

She straightened her apron, tucked her hair back into the bun, and left the room. Her brothers' words carried through the open doorway.

"Which way do you suppose he went?"

"If we take the back road, we can probably catch him before he gets to Mankato."

"Unless he's going west. But why would he go west?"

"He's from New York. He's wending his sorry way back there."

"But he was going west when we found him."

"Well, it's heading into winter. He'll probably want to go home."

"Let's do the back road."

"We'll find him and bring him back here and make him marry Lolly."

That was entirely too much.

She spun on her heel and turned back into the kitchen. "Don't do me any favors. I don't want him."

Bud narrowed his eyes. "But we do, Lolly. Boy, do we ever!"

Colin saw the truck as it came down the road, and he ducked into the underbrush, rolling down a slight embankment as he lost his balance with the pack and bedroll strapped to his back. He could easily see Lolly's brothers in the front of the truck. From the way Bud was leaning out the window, scanning the sides of the road, and the forward thrust of George's chin as he hunkered over the steering wheel, it was clear they knew he was gone—and they were furious.

He couldn't blame them. But this was a way for them to weather the situation, and as difficult as it was, he had to leave. They had given him his life back. He owed them this much.

The last missing bits of his life had all come together, and with them, the answer.

It would work. It had to.

Chapter 11

*Farewell. It means, literally, travel safely. Be healthy. Enjoy your trip.
And don't forget about the one who loves you, the one who stays behind,
holding her heart in her hands because it doesn't fit inside her any more.
Farewell. Go with my love.*

Lolly and her brothers rode into Valley Junction Sunday morning. Without Colin in the truck, the three of them were able to sit without being crammed together. Lolly held her own Bible now, one that she'd gotten from her parents when she passed her confirmation class. The days of sharing Colin's Bible were gone.

As soon as she stepped out of the truck, Hildegard Hopper hobbled toward the truck in shoes that were clearly too small for her. Her feet bulged over the tops of them, and she winced with each step. Lolly had to admit that they were beautiful, though. Made of a soft shell pink leather with a pearl fan on each toe, they must have cost a fortune. *Or at least a month's grocery bill,* Lolly thought a bit jealously.

Amelia Kramer followed in Hildegard's wake like a small, drab rowboat. Her eyes were bright with anticipation, and both women smiled toothily.

"Why, Eleanor," Hildegard said, and Lolly flinched, "I see it's just the three of you today."

"Yes, it is."

"We left the dog at home," Bud said.

Lolly pinched his side so hard he yelped, and he looked at her with a fake wide-eyed innocence that she was sure didn't fool the two women for a moment. "Why did you do that? It's true. Bruno's at home. So it's just you, George, and me."

"Do you know why I like you so much, Bud?" Hildegard asked, as Amelia nodded enthusiastically behind her.

"We really like you," Amelia echoed.

Why do they call him Bud, and me Eleanor? Lolly wondered. *They must not know that his real name is—*

She suppressed the thought, realizing that it might actually have some bargaining power with her brother. She could threaten to tell the two women what his real name was. Bud hated it and wouldn't let anyone use it.

"Why do you like Bud so much?" she asked, wanting to deflect their attention onto her much more worthy brother.

"He is just so cute and so clever," Hildegard said, beaming at him. "And such a good boy, coming to church every Sunday."

"Very good boy," Amelia repeated.

"All three of the Prescotts come every week, don't they, Amelia?" Hildegard asked.

"They do."

"But for a while they had someone else with them, if I'm not mistaken." Amelia took a step closer.

If the woman had antennae like a beetle, I'm sure they'd be wiggling like mad, Lolly thought as she took a corollary step back.

"A man, Hildegard," Amelia contributed. "A man, named Collier? Colbert? Something like that?"

"You know exactly what his name was," Bud said.

"Oh my, do I now?" Hildegard touched her fingertip to her mouth in artificial coyness. "What was the name of Lolly's mail-order groom? Oh! I wasn't supposed to mention that, was I? Silly me."

"His name was Quincy," Bud said. "Quincy Peapod Featherbee the Third."

Lolly almost choked. She pinched him again, but he ignored her warning and plunged on ahead.

"Yes, Quincy, or QPF the Third as we liked to call him, was a splendid fellow. Sailed in one day on a clipper ship, right on the Minnesota River, it was, and stopped for tea. His ship, sadly, sailed without him, but they finally realized he was missing and they came back for him. We miss him terribly, especially his strawberry and cream cheese sandwiches. Now, if you'll excuse us, it's time for worship."

Bud took Lolly's left elbow, and George took her right, and together they walked into the church.

When they were seated, Lolly scolded her brother in a whisper. "What on earth was that about? Now it'll be even worse. I thought that everyone had let the mail-order groom thing pass, and now this. We'll be the laughingstock of the town."

Then she turned to George. "And you! You just stood there like a big old goose and didn't say a word! What's the matter with you?"

"I didn't hear you say anything," he pointed out.

"Well, I didn't, but I was pinching him." She settled in her seat, her back straight and her hands folded over her purse.

"Oh, well, that makes all the difference in the world," George said. "You were pinching him."

"Is that a bit of sarcasm I hear?"

"It's a lot of sarcasm." He leaned closer. "Don't you see the method in his madness? What do you suppose are the chances of us being corralled by those two again, either here or at our house? I think he might have just finished it."

"Or finished us," Lolly said.

She only half-listened to the sermon, paid a bit of attention to the hymns, and listlessly followed the readings. She was tired. Tired of constantly fighting with her brothers, fighting with Hildegard and Amelia, tired of fighting the constant lack of money, tired of fighting loneliness and hopelessness. Just tired.

Once again she was trapped, trapped without options, without choices. Without hope.

As they were leaving the church, she felt a touch on her arm. It was Dr. Greenleigh, the man who had first examined Colin.

"I don't see your young man with you today," the doctor said.

"First off, I don't think he's my young man," Lolly retorted.

"Fair enough. I was just concerned because he's always here with you at services." Dr. Greenleigh's friendly face creased with a frown, and Lolly reproached herself for being so rude.

"Actually, he's gone again." The words came out smoothly, and she congratulated herself on how normal they sounded.

"Oh, good. So you did exactly the right thing, provided the correct amount of care, and got him healthy again. To be honest, I had my doubts at first that he would survive."

She drew back in shock. "You did? But you didn't say anything."

"You know," he said, "as a doctor I get to see a lot that surprises me. People who should by all rights be dead from an injury will live and you'd never know they'd had any kind of trauma. Of course, I see the other way, too, when death is unexpected."

"That's true enough, I suppose," she answered.

"But that's taught me the greatest lesson ever. I didn't read it in a medical book or hear it in a lecture. No, I learned it from my patients. And do you know what that lesson is?"

She shook her head.

"It's that you can never underestimate the power of the human spirit, of its desire to live and soar as close to the angels as it can. That, I suspect, is what healed the man who collapsed on your property."

"It was the strength of his soul," she said almost to herself. "That's it, isn't it?"

"Don't discount the role of support. Just like when you might need someone's arm to lean on when you're walking on an icy stretch, that's very important for survival. Without you, he probably would have died. You were the support he needed."

He patted her on the arm. "You were the hands of God."

She stood in the shadow of the church, mulling over what he had said, and she kept coming up against something. She didn't much like the way she had been acting since Colin left. Her words were snappish, and her patience was short while her anger was long.

She needed to guard her heart, that much was common sense, but she didn't need to encase it in cement and then make everyone around her suffer because it hurt. She was focusing on the wrong thing.

She had done what she needed to. Colin was alive because of her.

Take the victory, she told herself. *You didn't lose. You won. Take the victory.*

Colin was out of practice. He'd lost his ability to duck around rail yard guards and hide behind boxcars. He'd managed most of his travels from New York City by bartering rides when his feet had given out and he wasn't able to walk anymore. He'd do some cleaning up for the yardmaster in exchange for the man's silence about his presence in the boxcar.

But not all yardmasters were amenable to this, and out of necessity he'd developed an ability to find an empty railway car in the dark to sleep in, and if it had taken him farther along on his destination, so much the better. At first it hadn't bothered him. It was one more exciting step in the life he'd taken on that fateful day when he left his home.

He remembered how, as the days wore on and the thrill wore thin, he spent long hours debating the rights and wrongs of what he was doing. Riding the rails, he told himself, was the hobo's life. That's what they did. But on the other hand, it didn't seem right to tag along without paying in some fashion, even if the ride was in a dusty closed car.

He wasn't going to do that this time. It had been too early in the day to reach anyone in New York to see if some money could be wired to him.

If only he had waited longer. He'd chased sleep all night, until he'd made his decision to leave in the early trickle of morning light. His impetuosity had put him back on the rails. He had no choice except to go back, at least part of the way, the same way he'd come out, as a vagabond.

Still, when he got to Minneapolis he'd try to contact his company in New York. Let them know he was alive. Tell them he was all right. Ask for money.

He smiled wryly as he thought of the reaction that call would bring. Would they even believe him?

Night fell earlier in September than it had in June when he came out to Minnesota, and his judgment was off on which train went where and when—because now he was going in the opposite direction.

He climbed into an empty boxcar and curled up in the corner. Once he got some sleep, he'd probably figure this out.

This wasn't at all the same trip. He'd heard some talk in the railway station in Mankato of cold moving through. It would probably pursue him all the way to the East Coast.

This time of year, the temperatures and precipitation could be unpredictable. It often swung from the shirtsleeves of summer warmth to the first cold breath of winter—within a day or two.

"You going far?" A voice spoke from the opposite corner of the boxcar, and he realized he wasn't alone. It was so completely dark in the boxcar that he hadn't even noticed someone else sharing the space with him.

"To New York City. What about you?"

"I want to go someplace warm for winter. I'd like to see Virginia. Tennessee. Louisiana. And Florida. Oh, I'd like to go to Florida someday. Wait, I got a picture to show you." Some scuffling in the vicinity of the voice followed, and a match scratched into light, revealing a man with a heavy growth of beard, his glasses taped together, and wearing a red plaid flannel shirt that was more hole than cloth. He lit the stub end of a candle with the match and scuttled over toward Colin. "See this?"

He handed Colin a postcard of a palm tree on a shoreline. A couple played volleyball while the sun shone off a pristine sand beach and the turquoise-tinted water. "Don't it look like a place a fella should be? And look. See? On the back. There's writing. It says *'Dear Grandpa, Come to Florida and we will get seashells. I love you. Imogene'* She wrote that herself, my Imogene did."

The card was addressed to Grady Shields, General Delivery, Omaha, Nebraska. "It's really lovely, and your granddaughter strikes me as a charming girl. So your name's Grady, is it?"

The man sat back on his haunches. "How did you know that?"

"It says so right here." Colin pointed to the address and Grady nodded.

"Oh, right. I'd forgotten about that."

The man couldn't read. Colin had figured that out when the words weren't exactly the same as what he'd said. The gist was the same, but the words were different enough to clue him in to the fact that Grady might be illiterate. The actual words were, *"Dear Grandpa, You can come to Florida and we can find seashells. I love you. Imogene."*

"Does this train go to Florida?" Colin weighed the advisability of trusting a man who couldn't read.

Grady shook his head. "Nope. Goes to Chicago and then heads off toward Indianapolis and on to Nashville."

"Nashville is south."

"My Imogene isn't in Nashville."

The cars shuddered a bit as the train came to life, ready for its travels, and Grady blew out the candle. "Just in case," he said cryptically.

As the train rattled its way out of the station, Colin asked, over the grind of the wheels, "When did you last see Imogene?"

"Oh, I'd say going on four years now. I've had this card for about two of those four. It's as precious to me as my own blood."

Colin closed his eyes as the motion of the train hypnotically swayed him back and forth in a regular rhythm. "Are you a Christian, Grady?" he asked at last.

"Why, yes indeed, I am. I count myself among those who love the Lord, yes I do."

"Do you know the Lord's Prayer?"

"Yes, I do."

"The Twenty-third Psalm?"

"That's *'The Lord is my shepherd,'* ain't it?"

"It is. Do you know it by heart?"

"Parts of it but not all of it. Why are you asking all these questions? You planning to put me on the stage in some Sunday school pageant? Dress me up in a bathrobe and have me be one of the Wise Men? Want me to sing 'Jesus Loves Me,' too?" Grady's rusty laugh echoed in the empty boxcar.

Colin joined in the laughter. It felt good to laugh with Grady.

"The reason I'm asking," he clarified, "is that I'm thinking you might be wanting to perk up your reading skills before you get to Imogene's house, am I right?"

There was a long silence from Grady, and Colin feared he'd offended him. Then Grady spoke. "I can't read at all. Not even a single word. I was raised on a farm back in the olden days, as Imogene calls them, and we got a little bit of schooling but not much. I can cipher a tad, but reading was one of those school subjects that just didn't stick in this poor brain."

"You can't read at all?"

"Not a word, not a syllable, not a letter. Oh, I ain't proud of that, let me tell you, no sirree, but facts is facts, and the fact here is that I just couldn't learn."

Colin was grateful for the darkness. He didn't know if Grady would speak so freely in the daylight. "How do you know which train to get on, then? Do you ask? Don't you run the risk of them getting suspicious?"

"*Pffft.* Most of the rail yard people don't care as long as you're neat and tidy and don't leave a mess in the car for them to clean up. Like me, for example. Tidy Grady. Nobody bothers me because I also help them when I can."

"One hand watches the other." Colin smiled in the inky train car.

"Huh?"

"Oh, just something a dear friend told me."

"How dear are we talking about?" Grady asked.

"Very dear."

"And you're going home to her now?"

"No. I've got some things to do before I can ask her to settle in with me."

"Don't wait too long," Grady advised. "Hearts change."

Colin didn't answer. It was his greatest fear, and it, more than anything, would keep him away.

He changed the subject, this time to the conditions at the various railroad stations, and as Grady talked, he put his head back and thought about how his life had taken yet another odd twist. Here he was, once again, riding in boxcars, he who had less than a year ago been driven wherever he wanted to go.

But now he had a new idea, how to make this time on the rails truly blessed. The phone call to New York could wait. This was more important. He had work to do in that boxcar.

⌒

"Here."

Bud tossed something to her when he walked in the door. It landed on the counter and slid across the length, nearly knocking over the cup of tea she'd just made and landing at her feet.

She bent over and picked it up.

It was a new notebook. This one had pink roses scaling a trellis on the off-white cover. And in the middle it said Mankato Hotel.

"Very pretty, Bud. Thanks!" She tucked it into her pocket. She'd have to think about this, using a new notebook. What was that old adage? Once burned, twice shy? It certainly fit this scenario.

"Well, aren't you going to ask me what I'm doing with a notebook from the Mankato Hotel? Aren't you even a little bit curious? Don't you want to know if I went to Mankato, and how I got there, and what I did? And why I ended up at the hotel there?"

"Actually," she said with a smile, "I didn't even know you were gone."

"Okay, I wasn't gone. I didn't go to Mankato. But I saw this notebook at the post office, and I said that I had a sister who sure liked to write romantic stuff down and the fellow gave it to me. Then we got to talking, and he said I could come to Mankato and he'd see about getting me some work. So I didn't go yet, but I am going to."

"Really, Bud?" Something somewhere in the area of her heart ached with a sudden heavy burden. "You want to move to Mankato?"

He wrapped his body around a chair in a motion that, if she'd tried it, would have caused severe damage to her hips and torso. "I don't want to, but this poverty stuff is about to make me loony. I love this place as much as you do, but we can't do it, sis. We just can't."

She leaned across the counter, her hands cradled around her hot cup of tea. "I know."

In a rare show of brotherly affection, he patted her arm. "You know that he'll find you no matter where you are, don't you?"

He had, with that single sentence and the unnamed pronoun, identified yet another basis for her not wanting to leave. As irrational as it might be—Colin hadn't given any indication that he'd be coming back—her heart still clung to the awkward hope.

How *would* he find her if she went with her brothers somewhere else? It wasn't like she could leave a note on the door for him.

She missed him terribly. The thought of going through life without him was depressing for her to consider.

Bruno padded over to lie at her feet, a half-eaten shoe hanging from his jaws. Grateful for the change in focus, she asked her brother, "Do you suppose that there's a chance our dog is part goat?"

"I think he's kind of lonely," he answered. "Think about it."

"Oh, because Colin's gone?"

"Never mind him. I think he misses Hildegard Hopper and Amelia Kramer and their shoes!"

Chapter 12

I can't forget him, and when I sleep, I find him. We run through frosted fields, leaving copper footprints on the silvered landscape. Always we hold hands, as if that will keep us together when this earthly sphere drives us apart. Our fingers are locked together in an endless lover's knot, now and forever. I can't let go.

The grasses were crisping, and ice had begun to creep along the edges of the river in sheltered areas. In the waters along the edge, crystal touched fallen leaves, and the world glittered its way into winter.

Lolly walked down to the pier by herself. They were moving out the next week, into Mankato, where George and Bud had both found small jobs work, George as a handyman at the teachers college and Bud as a busboy at the hotel restaurant. Neither job offered more than a day-to-day offer of employment, but, as Bud said, that was better than a poke in the eye.

She'd go along with them. Perhaps she could clean houses or work as a cook's assistant.

And the farm would stay right where it was, but there wouldn't be anyone in it to love it. George had figured out more numbers and come up with what he called the If Budget. *If* he and Bud worked at least six days out of every week, and *if* they were paid promptly, and *if* the apartment he'd found was all right, and *if* the cost of everything stayed right where it was at the moment, they could keep the farm. There were more *if*s, but Lolly's head spun with this short list.

There was one more *if* on his list. It was the big one. *If* the nation's economy didn't get any worse. That was the one item that drove everything else.

She didn't want to leave the farm. It was everything to her. Her entire life had been spent on the land, and the river that flowed through it was like her own blood.

Thanksgiving was coming up, and then Christmas, and the thought of spending those holidays in a tiny apartment made her heart sink. She'd asked George about the possibility of at least coming out to the farm for the holidays, and he'd thought about it and decided that if there was enough money to put gasoline in the truck and enough wood stored at the farm to heat the house with the fireplace, then yes, they could.

It was a small sparkle, but it was good. Bud had been chopping firewood all week, without his usual snappish commentaries, so she knew it was important to him, too.

The house was packed, for the most part. The crystal vase was cradled in layers of blankets and would ride to Mankato on Lolly's lap, and the housewares had been divided between the two homes. The furniture was staying at the farm because the apartment was furnished and taking the sagging old tapestry couch wouldn't be worth it, assuming it would even make the trip without falling apart.

The apartment was small. One bedroom with a curtain dividing it from the rest of the place. Privacy was available only in the cramped bathroom. The first time she'd seen the tiny room, Lolly had stood in the doorway, amazed at the way the sink, bathtub, toilet, and a cabinet dovetailed into the space that effectively.

The kitchen, which George had tried to tell her was efficient—"Look, you don't even have to move! From one spot you can reach the stove, the icebox, the cabinets, and the sink!"—was dark but clean. They gave her the bedroom and with an elaborate arrangement of one brother on the couch and one on a pallet on the floor, with a rotating schedule of who got the couch and who was forced to sleep on the floor, they took the living room. Bruno, of course, got his choice. He was too big to argue with.

Again, it was Bud who summed it up best. "The nice thing about living in a Depression is that we don't have anything, so this fits us just perfect!"

Mankato was interesting, but she did not want to leave the farm, especially now when all around her, the change of the season was in full bore, the trees now in resplendent crimson, elegant gold, and fiery auburn.

At least this was, for the moment, still hers, and as long as things went the way George had outlined them, she would still be able to come to the farm.

The sun had melted the early morning frost, leaving the pier dark with moisture. She stepped out on it and sat on the edge and remembered the day they all went fishing and Bruno caught the catfish. On this pier, Colin had kissed her for the very first time.

And on this pier, he had kissed her for the very last time.

She didn't write in the notebook that Bud had brought her. She'd tried, but her fingers would freeze up when she opened to a new page. Now the story ran only in her mind, and there were times when it was all that kept her going.

~

Each night, Colin and Grady leaned over Colin's Bible. As they would say the familiar words of the Lord's Prayer or the Twenty-third Psalm, they would follow along on the page, matching word for sound. And when they tired of that, with a short piece of a pencil, Colin taught Grady the letters for his name.

"I'm going to learn this for Imogene," Grady said. "If it's all right with you,

I'll ride with you until I get this in my brain. I have to do this for my Imogene."

One cold afternoon, Colin and Grady took refuge in the station in Pittsburgh. Colin found an abandoned newspaper and spread it out in front of them.

"Let's do the headline together," he said. " 'President. Roosevelt. Visits. . .' "

Grady stood and paced nervously and then sat back down.

"Something under your skin?" Colin asked curiously as his new friend fidgeted.

"I'm tired of living like this, always on the move. I want to find a place, settle down, maybe try the family thing again." Grady touched his chest pocket where Colin knew the postcard from his granddaughter was. "I've let too many people go unloved. That's wrong, and I've got to make it right. It's been good knowing you, and thank you for trying to teach this old grizzled head how to read. At the very least, I can read some of the Bible."

"You don't have a Bible, do you?" Colin asked; and when Grady shook his head no, Colin reached into his pack and pulled out his. "Here, take this."

"You're giving me your Bible?" Grady looked at Colin in surprise.

It was the Bible that had been given to him when he'd been on the road before and so in need of the Word, and now, it seemed right to pass it on to another traveler who would also benefit.

"Are you sure?" Grady asked. "I'd be honored to carry it, knowing how it came into your possession."

"I'm sure. Here, let's do this."

They opened the Bible, and under the name Colin Hammett, the new owner wrote in labored but proud letters, GRADY SHIELDS.

Bible in hand, Grady touched his fingers to his forehead, turned, and was lost in the crowd.

Colin watched him go, sending a prayer with him. *Pad his footsteps with peace. Reunite him with love.*

He looked at the posted schedule board. If he hurried, he could slip out and catch the next train to New York City.

It was amazing, he thought as he settled himself in for the long ride, how someone who'd come into his life for such a brief time had given him direction. People like Grady were truly gifts.

He must have been truly exhausted, for when he awoke, the train was slowing down, pulling into the yard. He yawned and stretched, and when he stepped out, a familiar cityscape surrounded him.

Pulling his pack and bedroll onto his back, he headed for the neighborhood he knew so well.

It was quite a long walk, but he jogged along happily. It was good to be home.

At last he came to the building where his apartment was. The doorman stopped him. "You have business here?"

"I live here."

"We don't have bums living here. Go peddle your papers elsewhere!" The doorman lifted his whistle, ready to call for police assistance.

"No, I live here. I'm Colin Hammett."

"Mr. Hammett disappeared—oh, sir!" The doorman's face split into a wide beam, and Colin could tell he had stopped just short of hugging him. "It's good to have you back. My, you're looking a bit, well—"

"Ragged?" Colin laughed. "Just let me in so I can bathe and shave and change my clothes. Oh, it's so good to be home!"

His apartment hadn't changed at all. The maid service had come in and cleaned regularly, and even fresh towels were laid out in the bathroom. It was obvious that they had been ready for him to come back at any moment.

Within an hour, he was comfortable again and ready to head off to his office.

The doorman called for a driver, and as Colin rode the once-again familiar road to his business, he realized how truly changed he was. The people on the streets, hurrying toward their jobs or home after a day of labor, or those who had no employment and were going door to door, office to office, seeking anything— they now were real to him.

The office staff fell silent when he entered the room. And then, pandemonium broke loose. "Mr. Hammett is back!"

His cousin, Ralph, came out of the main office. "Colin!" The two embraced and then, after speaking to the staff and shaking hands with each one, Colin followed his cousin into the inner office.

"Where have you been? What happened?" his cousin began as they sat on opposite sides of his desk.

"I've been living in Minnesota after having my memory erased on a fence post. That's the short version," Colin said.

"The short version?" Ralph raised his eyebrows. "How much time should I set aside for the long version? This sounds like a story I want to hear."

"And it's a story I want to tell."

Ralph leaned across the desk. "What happened, Colin? Why did you leave so suddenly? One afternoon you simply came in here, told me you were off in search of yourself. You didn't contact me at all to let me know you were all right. Do you have any idea how worried I was? How worried we all were?"

"I'm sorry. It was thoughtless of me." Colin rubbed his forehead. "I'm so sorry."

"I think you should begin that long story now. I think I deserve it."

Night was darkening the sky in the window behind Ralph by the time Colin finished.

Ralph leaned back, his fingers laced behind his head. "Of course we want to help them. But what can we do, short of sending them money, which I'm glad to do."

Colin reached into his pocket and pulled out Lolly's notebook. "Take a look at this and tell me what you think."

His cousin opened it and began to scan it. Soon, though, he was reading in earnest, and at last, he put it down in front of him. "Amazing. Who is this writer?"

"She's the woman who saved me, and she is as incredible as her writing."

"Can we get her?"

"Let's talk, Ralph," Colin said.

When he left two hours later, night had wrapped the city in darkness, punctuated by the bright stars of streetlights and marquees, and he had a thick envelope in his hand and a smile on his face. Two days after that, he was at the Grand Central Terminal buying a ticket—destination, Minnesota. This time, there was no bedroll, no backpack.

"It's good to be back here again," Bud said as he laid another log on the fire. "I've missed this old farm."

"It is nice, isn't it?" George sat down on the couch, sinking down as the cushions sagged.

"I like being able to move my arms like this," Lolly swung them around in crazy windmills. "I can't do that in the apartment without taking out a window or pulling down a towel rack or knocking the pictures off the wall."

"There's no time like Thanksgiving to come home," George said. "I look at these doors and these shelves and these walls and I think, my parents did this, with their own hands."

They didn't speak for a while. This was probably going to be the last time they'd gather like this at the farm.

The If Budget hadn't worked out. The jobs that George and Bud had were too irregularly scheduled, and they simply didn't make enough money. Plus the rent on the tiny apartment was going up.

They needed cash, and the only way they could see to do it was to put the farm on the market. It might sell, or it might not.

For Lolly, either way was a nightmare.

"Good dinner," George said.

Bruno raised his head and dropped it again, as if the effort to move were too great. He'd shared the meal with them, including two of the cobs from the corn that Lolly caught him trying to escape with.

"I'm tired of chicken," Bud complained, but Lolly wasn't in the mood to argue with him. Of course he was tired of chicken. That was all they could afford.

They'd had to sell her chickens when they moved into town, and the farm was remarkably quiet without the hens and the rooster constantly squawking and crowing.

"I could stay here forever," George said from the depths of the sofa.

"Of course you could, " Bud shot back. "You can't get out of it. It's kind of like a conversation with Hildegard and Amelia."

They had just started to laugh when they heard a car pull up and a knock on the door.

"Oh no!" Bud said. "They're here!"

"Lolly, get rid of them," George said.

"You get rid of them," she told him. "Why do I always have to do it?"

"Because I can't get up, that's why."

She sighed and went to the door, mentally composing lines of conversation that would encourage the two women to leave.

Whatever would have possessed them to come on a holiday evening?

She opened the door and screamed as the snowy figure grabbed her and swung her around and around and around.

Bud tore into the room, with Bruno hot on his heels, a treasured corncob in his teeth.

Bud yelled and Bruno barked as Lolly cried and laughed and cried some more.

George, finally motivated to extricate himself from the couch, joined them and boomed, "Colin!" He stood, and with his arms crossed over his chest and his heavy sweater, he looked as formidable as a prizefighter. "At last. Now, come in and explain yourself."

Bud stood beside him, his hands jammed onto his waist. "You owe us at least that," he growled. "You owe Lolly that."

"Can't you see he's been traveling?" Lolly said. "Let him get his bearings again, and then you two can start grilling him. I have a few questions for him myself."

Finally, with a cup of warm tea in his hands and them all gathered in the kitchen around the table, he told them the story of finding the notebook and taking it to the publishing company.

"Apparently Bruno felt you weren't feeding him enough tires and feathers and books and such, so he'd started his own treasure chest of gastronomical delights out there where the back barn was. That's where I found your notebook, Lolly."

"My notebook?" Lolly asked, feeling dull but very happy.

"Your notebook. Bruno buried it where we took down the barn. He had quite the collection there. I know you'll be delighted to know that your notebook ranked right up there with some feathers and a sock and a chewed candle stub in his doggy mind."

"Oh, my." Lolly looked at the dog that was now happily licking the snow off Colin's boots. "He had it."

"He did. So I left here—"

Remembered pain washed over her. "Why did you just leave like that? Didn't you know that it would hurt?"

"Hurt?"

"To have you simply take off like that."

George nodded. "You could have at least left a note."

"I did. You didn't see it? I put it on the table in the kitchen, and then I said good-bye to Bruno...."

Realization struck them all at once, and all four of them turned to look at the dog. He'd left Colin's shoes and returned to his corncob and the fireplace, where he promptly fell asleep.

"I wonder if a certain overgrown mutt might have had something to do with its disappearance," George said.

Bruno sighed in his sleep and moved his corncob closer to him so that his chin was resting on it.

"So back to the notebook," Bud prompted.

"You know that my family owns a publishing company," Colin continued. "Not a big one, mind you, but when I read your notebook—"

"You read it!" Lolly sighed. "Well, why not. At this stage, it's probably public record, thanks to Bud."

"Hey!" Bud objected. "I said I was sorry."

"It doesn't undo what you did."

"You keep bringing it up, and I'll quit being sorry."

"That's what I mean. Living with you is a trial."

"Living with *you* is the crime."

"Stop!" George pounded the table with his hammy fist. "You two are the arguingest folks. Now stop so Colin can get on with what he has to say."

Lolly shot Bud one last *I'm not happy* glare, and he made a face at her.

Colin grinned and continued with his story. "I took your notebook back to New York and showed it to my cousin, and he suggested that we publish it as part of our Fairy Dreams line. Your notebook fits right into it."

"So what does that mean?" George asked, his face serious.

"It means we want Lolly to expand the book, and we'll publish it. To that end, I have a contract for you. We think it'll be a big hit."

She shook her head. "I'm not a writer."

He held up the notebook. "This says you are."

She looked at her brothers. "What do you think?"

"It's your decision," George said. "I think it's worth looking into."

"If someone is willing to pay you money for pink roses and lavender ponies or whatever this stuff is that you write, I say go for it." Bud grinned. "Actually, what I say is take the money and don't look back."

Money. She looked around the farmhouse, which had seemed so forlorn when they'd first arrived, before they filled it with voices and warmth and food.

"Is there money with this contract?" she asked. "I don't mean to be crude about it, but—"

"There is a modest amount as an advance. There should be royalties, too, once the book is published and sells enough to recoup the advance."

"Would it be enough that we could stay here?"

"As I said, it's modest, but you should be comfortable for the rest of the year. At least until next spring."

"Is it enough for all of us to stay here?"

He touched her hand, very lightly. "We should probably talk about what you mean by 'all of us.'"

Her heart shivered. His gaze caught and held hers, and without looking away, she said, "Go outside, Bud and George."

"Why should I have to—" Bud began his litany of complaint, but George hustled him into his coat.

"Why don't you and I go take a look at that old barn and see how it's doing?" George asked his brother.

"Well, this is stupid. There's going to be snow all over it. We won't be able to see anything. Let's look at it tomorrow. I just got nice and warm, and I don't want to lea—"

George yanked his brother toward the door. "Again, for the twelve hundred millionth time, I apologize for my brother. You two take as long as you need and give us a holler when you're ready for us to come in."

When they'd left, Colin took her hand in his and dropped to the floor on one knee. Bruno woke up again and brought the chewed corncob to Colin.

"Ewww," Lolly said, kicking it out of the way. "They should have taken you, too, dumb dog."

"Lolly, put simply, I love you. I want to spend my entire life with you. Will you marry me?"

He reached into his pocket and pulled out a small box. Bruno stuck his snout right on it, but Colin adroitly pushed him away. "This isn't for you."

Lolly opened the box. Inside was nestled a ring, a layered combination of gold and silver with a diamond centered squarely on top of it. "Oh, Colin!"

"If you say yes, we can get married at any time. Tomorrow or next year or a decade from now. Whatever you say, my kind-hearted woman."

"I say yes," she said. "Yes to both contracts. Yes, yes, yes, yes, yes!"

She flung her arms around his shoulders, and he stood, holding her and kissing her. "Let them stay outside for a few more minutes," she said at last. "We have a lot of catching up to do."

Epilogue

We are together at last, forever. Spring is the time of new beginnings, and we have chosen to unite our lives as life touches the earth again, as it does each year to remind us that God's love never leaves us, never forgets us, never overlooks us. We are His. We belong to Him. He has given us this love, and we consecrate this union to Him.

From the *Mankato Free Press*:

Eleanor Ann Prescott and Colin Edward Hammett, both currently of Valley Junction, Minnesota, were joined in Holy Matrimony on April 2, 1936, in the Community Church, Reverend William Wellman presiding.

Miss Prescott was presented for marriage by her brothers, George and Barnaby. Ruth Gregory was her attendant.

A dinner was served after the ceremony at the home of the bride.

Mr. and Mrs. Hammett will be at home on the Prescott family farm following a honeymoon trip to New York City.

The honeymoon in New York City had been wonderful. Lolly had met Colin's family and the details of opening a Minneapolis branch of the company were in the works. Within a few months they'd be moving there, but now she was back at home in Valley Junction, as Mrs. Colin Prescott.

The old house was actually cozy once Colin and her brothers finished the work in it. It had taken them all winter to refurbish it, but now it was charming. It was small but as Colin said, as long as Bruno stayed in the main house, it was large enough.

The thought of starting her married life in the same tiny house where her parents had begun theirs was wonderful. She couldn't imagine a better place.

As a wedding gift, she'd embroidered the Bible verse that had started Colin on the journey that led him to their home. It had taken two months and was a bit uneven in places where she'd had to undo the stitching several times, but it was truly a labor of love. George framed it and hung it in the dining room.

Blessed is the man that trusteth in the Lord, and whose hope the Lord is.
For he shall be as a tree planted by the waters, and that spreadeth out her
roots by the river, and shall not see when heat cometh, but her leaf shall be
green; and shall not be careful in the year of drought, neither shall cease
from yielding fruit. JEREMIAH 17:7–8

"We got you something, too," Bud said. "Bring it in, George."

"You could help," his brother said through clenched teeth.

"I could. But I'm not." Bud grinned cheerfully at Lolly.

George muttered as he muscled a small table from the corner. "We took the fence post with the cat carved on it and made it into the base of this table. See?"

Lolly sank to her knees and traced the outline of the cat. "Kind-hearted woman. I love it! Thanks so much, you two!"

"It was my idea," Bud said.

"I did the work," George countered. "You couldn't be bothered to—"

"Oh, you did not do the work. I did it. You were busy making googly eyes at Ruth and sucking down colas and planning your own wedding while I was at the hardware store getting the sanding—"

"Stop!" Colin held up his hand, laughing. "We get the idea. It's from both of you."

Lolly interrupted. "Wait. Did I hear the word *wedding*?"

"You did. We're planning for October, when the harvest will be over. You and Colin will be in Minneapolis by then, so we can live in our house. Bud can stay with us, too."

Lolly threw her arms around her older brother. "I'm so glad!"

"If I tell you that I'm taking Sarah Fallon to the church social next week, would I get a hug, too?" Bud asked.

"Of course!" She followed through on her promise and nearly choked when Bud squeezed her so hard he lifted her right off the floor.

"We have something else, too," George said, handing Lolly a large flat packet.

She opened it. "Look, Colin!" It was their marriage license, framed and under glass.

"It's got the glass over it," Bud said, "so Bruno can't eat it."

The dog cocked his ear at the mention of his name.

"Let's put it here," she said as she put it over the fireplace. "Safe and sound, so nobody will knock into it. And where Bruno can't possibly reach it!"

The dog sighed and lay down to sleep, but if anyone had been watching, they'd have noticed that one eye didn't close all the way but was instead tracking a path from the table to the couch to the fireplace—all to check out the treat that was hanging over it.

REMEMBRANCE

Dedication

To Kevin, always...and forever

Chapter 1

On the way to Remembrance, Minnesota
January 1886

Eliza Davis drew her coat a little closer around her. The early winter night closed in on the darkened railroad car like a thick woolen wrap. The *chicketta-ticketta* of the wheels clicked out a regular beat, but she couldn't sleep. Snow flurries, lit by starlight, fluffed beside the windows as the train sped onward.

Home. She was going home. There was a good feeling about this, something that almost kindled the dead corner of her heart where love had once lived.

No one knew she was coming. She'd done the only thing she could think of in the thin dawn hours in the cold room where she'd lived in St. Paul. She hadn't packed, other than snatching the worn Bible from the table, seizing a few last-minute items from her bureau, and throwing some clothing into the big carpetbag that belonged to her father.

Haste had been of utmost importance—at least at the time it had seemed so. Now that miles separated her from Blaine Loring, she was already feeling calmer.

He became everything to her, and everything became his. It was a dangerous combination.

How had her life spiraled so badly out of control?

At first, her plan to establish herself as a fine seamstress in St. Paul had gone well. She quickly found employment as an assistant to one of the most respected tailoring establishments in the growing city. Her skills quickly took her far. She opened her own business within a short time, sewing fancy dresses for the women of wealth who appreciated her attention to the tiniest details.

Soon she met some of the most well-known people in Minnesota's capital, and the stars in her eyes grew bigger and brighter, blinding her to the reality of her world.

Blaine Loring slithered into her life, saw her glittering ambition, and stole her heart. He had money to spend, and spend he did. Whenever he came into the tailor shop, he'd slip a gift to her, once a fine silk scarf as soft and delicate as a windswept whisper, once a tiny gold locket on a thin linked chain.

He had promises, one after the other, and with their power, she let herself be swept along like a leaf on a wild torrent. She wouldn't stay a seamstress, he told her again and again. She was too good for that. Her place was on Summit Avenue, the splendid street in St. Paul lined with the largest, stateliest houses she'd ever seen.

For a while, she let herself believe that she might actually one day be a fine lady on Summit Avenue. One foot inside the mansions lining the street set that desire firmly upon her heart. She'd never seen such sumptuous homes, such tasteful wealth.

Earlier this evening it had all come to an end.

Eliza shifted uncomfortably on the cracked leather seat of the train. It was a horrible memory.

She simply went to return a paper she found on the floor of the shop after he left, a list of investors she knew he needed for a meeting that night, and found him shadowed in the back door of the club he frequented, his arms wrapped around a young woman as he murmured familiar words to her.

That had been bad enough, but then—

She paused in her mental recitation of the night, not wanting to go further but unable to stop, and the images continued.

She must have gasped, because he turned to her, and in the faint reflection of the moon, his eyes hardened to coal.

"You!" he snarled, and then he laughed, a humorless sound that made the young woman in his embrace giggle. "You have more alley cat in you than I'd guessed, following me the way you do. Shoo! Scat!"

His words threw ice shards into her soul, and she ran back to her room, tossed some of her belongings into a bag, and went to the train station.

"Where to?" the agent asked, and the answer rose quickly to her lips.

"Remembrance." She hadn't been there for years, but it was the only other place she knew as her home, besides St. Paul. Her memories of it were warm and comforting.

Yes, she was headed in the right direction, back to Remembrance, back to the home in the north woods of Minnesota where the world was small and safe and God-fearing.

The train swayed as a gust of wind struck them. Eliza glanced outside. The snowflakes were coming faster, and no longer falling straight down.

She shut her eyes for a quick prayer. *Please, God, calm the winds. I can't be delayed in getting home.*

She was going home, laden not with success but with secrets, secrets that could change the way they viewed her.

Remembrance was on the edge of the prairie, where the land suddenly turned to forest. She loved that about the little town, how it had the best of both possible worlds. The prairie land stretched to the west, all the way to the horizon, and the forests sprang up to the east, each tree reaching for heaven.

When she left fifteen years ago, summer had just touched the prairie with newborn green. Baby rabbits bounced across the open lands, growing, well fed on the fresh grasses and budding flowers.

But it hadn't held any happiness for her father, not after her mother got sick, and he traded in the clean country town for a city clogged with soot and grime. Oh, not all of it, she had to admit. Parts of St. Paul were lovely—amazingly so, in fact.

"Excuse me." The older woman across the aisle from her spoke softly so as not to wake the others. "Would you like a muffin? I have extra, and the trip is long yet."

Eliza shook her head. "No, thank you. I don't seem to have an appetite at the moment."

The woman nodded sympathetically. "Traveling does that."

Eliza sized her up quickly. She looked safe. One thing she'd discovered quickly about Blaine was that his friends usually looked as sleazy as they were. Why hadn't she seen that earlier?

But she reminded herself that this was probably all part of God's plan. She couldn't see it now, but at some point, everything would make sense. That was one promise she could believe.

Her stomach growled loudly, reminding her that she hadn't eaten in several hours.

The woman smiled encouragingly and offered the pastry again. "Please, help yourself."

"Thank you very much," Eliza said, accepting the muffin. It smelled wonderful.

"Are you going far?"

"I'm going to Remembrance. I do appreciate the muffin. I don't know when I'd be able to eat, now that I think about it. I hadn't planned that far ahead."

The woman nodded but didn't inquire.

"Remembrance is small, too small to have a restaurant like I'd find in St. Paul. There are seven buildings downtown," Eliza said, nearly reciting it as a litany. "One is white-painted wood, and one is new-lumber brown, and one is grayed from the wind. Two are red brick. The other two are brown and gray speckled brick. There is a church, and a school, and a general store. A doctor's office, a bank, and a station. The last one is still empty."

"Not anymore." Her traveling companion spoke.

"You know Remembrance?" Eliza sat up. There was something in the Bible about news from home, how good it felt. It seemed as if her heart were being washed.

"I'm on my way to Remembrance myself. I'm Hyacinth Mason."

Eliza relaxed at the friendliness of the woman's voice. "It's good to meet you, Mrs. Mason."

"Please, call me Hyacinth. I'm expecting we'll be friends in Remembrance."

The warmth of her voice reminded Eliza how much more Blaine had stolen from her—her friends. She hadn't had a true friend since she'd met Blaine. With him, everything and everyone was business. All of her friendships, under his guidance, were mined as investment possibilities.

"I hope so. It's been awhile since I've been to Remembrance," Eliza said. "Do you live there now?"

The woman smiled, and suddenly she looked years younger than her true age, which Eliza estimated to be around fifty-five or sixty. "I'm on my way to meet someone. I'm hoping that he and I might find a life together."

"Excuse me?" The woman's words made no sense to Eliza.

Hyacinth smiled. "We haven't met face-to-face. I'm from Chicago. We've corresponded for some time, though, and he convinced me to come join him in Remembrance. If all goes well, we plan to get married."

"You came from Illinois to marry someone you haven't met?" Eliza couldn't stop the question. It seemed too outrageous. Marrying someone, anyone, was massively important, even if you'd known the person all your life. She knew that well enough herself. But marrying someone you'd never met. . . !

"I knew his heart, and that was the most important thing." Hyacinth looked at Eliza and laughed. "I can see by your face that you are unconvinced. Haven't you ever been in love?"

Eliza's face burned. This was a question she would not, or maybe could not, answer. Instead, she focused on breaking off a bit of the muffin and chewing it slowly. "I have loved," she stated simply.

Suddenly exhaustion washed over her, and she rested her head against the railroad car's seat. Hyacinth smiled gently at her and patted her hand. "I can see you're tired, my dear. Remembrance isn't far away, perhaps two hours more. Go ahead and rest. Get some sleep."

It should have been no surprise, the way God put Hyacinth Mason in the same car with her. She was the perfect traveling companion, calm and caring and watchful.

Blaine Loring stole Eliza's few last moments of wakefulness. He quickly swept into her life like the winter wind, and equally quickly swept away her heart. . .and her good sense. His elegant clothing and regal demeanor bore an aura of glamour, and like a moth to the flame, she was drawn to the small light they offered.

A way out of a life of dressmaking. An exit from the mundane. Excitement. That was what she had wished for. That was, unfortunately, exactly what she had gotten.

Silas paced edgily. The thin boards of the station didn't do much to protect him from the cold or the hungry wind that sought and found each crack in the walls.

This was a bad idea. In a world filled with good ideas, why did his uncle have to choose this? People didn't fall in love with words on the page. That was ridiculous. Usually his uncle was a sane, normal man. Love did something terrible to him.

Now Uncle Edward was at home, his foot swathed in a bandage. He'd been adding some furbelow over the frame of the front door—a carved piece of plaster flowers, most odd—when he lost his balance and tumbled to the floor, snapping his ankle when he hit the floor.

And Silas blamed it all on love. It made idiots of perfectly normal people. Now someone like himself, who was undertaking a serious program of study, *Professor Barkley's Patented Five Year Plan for Success*, would never make such a mistake. He sighed and thanked the Lord for leading him to the small booklet, which he found stuck in the desk drawer in his room at his uncle's house.

Hyacinth. What kind of name was that? She was undoubtedly some fortune hunter, a woman of insubstantial means, out to make her way on the coattails of his uncle's hard work.

The wind increased its howl, and Silas instinctively shrugged deeper into his buffalo robe. At least Uncle Edward had the sense to live in town. He wouldn't want to face the prairie on a night like this, when the sky and the earth blended into one whirling stretch of white.

He'd asked his uncle to describe his mail-order bride, but all he'd gotten in response was a rather coy reminder that Hyacinth wasn't his bride yet. This was, as Uncle Edward pointed out, simply an extended visit, with perhaps an eye on potential matrimony.

Silas was not fooled. Potential matrimony, indeed. His uncle planned to marry Hyacinth. Perhaps the only question was whether Hyacinth planned to marry his uncle.

It was enough to curdle his blood. Love. Who needed it?

Over the whine of the wind, the train shrilled the announcement that it was headed into town.

Usually it was a lonesome sound as the train whistle cut across the prairie, but tonight its sound filled the snow-locked town with life. Tonight the train would stop in Remembrance.

He stopped his striding back and forth. If he kept this up, he'd wear a hole in the floorboards.

The train chugged its way to a stop, and he got ready to brave the cold. . . and Hyacinth.

He raised the collar of his coat and tucked his chin down deep inside the rich brown fur. He'd smelled better things than this buffalo robe, but nothing could beat it for warmth.

He opened the door of the station to go out and carry in Hyacinth's bags. A woman like her would probably expect that. She was undoubtedly too fragile to see to her own baggage.

A gust of wind blew in, and a young woman staggered in on its force, right into the front of his buffalo robe. Instinctively he reached out to steady her, and for just a minute he allowed himself to revel in the sensation of holding a woman in his arms—even if they were separated by a good two inches of wild fur and thick woolen fabric.

She smelled better than his coat, too. It took him a moment to realize that she smelled like blueberries and. . .what was that indefinable smell? Ah, soap.

How on earth did she manage to smell like blueberries? She looked up at him, and he knew the answer. A crumb was somehow attached to her cheek—how it managed to stay in the wind was a mystery. It had been a long time since he'd eaten a blueberry muffin.

He tried not to think about that, or about the scent of soap, or the way she felt in his arms.

She must be Hyacinth.

His hands fell away from her as if her arms were on fire.

His first thought was that Uncle Edward had been miraculously—undeservedly—blessed. She was beautiful, her fragile beauty shining through her exhaustion. The deep circles under her eyes only highlighted the blue that he knew would be bright when unclouded by fatigue.

"Excuse me." A voice behind her spoke, and a woman, her ebony hair edged with silver, leaned over the young lady's shoulder. Her eyes were worried. "I'm looking for Edward Collier. I understood he would be here." The last words were more a question than a statement.

The pieces of the world fell into place, and he was absurdly glad to have the knowledge that the damsel with the enchanting blue eyes was not his uncle's mail-order bride.

His relief had nothing to do with the rosy cheeks and the bright pink lips. Professor Barkley discouraged romantic entanglements, so love was definitely not going to have a place in Silas Collier's heart. No, not at all.

Chapter 2

Eliza smoothed the front of her coat, her nervous fingers wiping away the imprint of this man's embrace. The last time—the only time—she'd been that close to a man's chest, she had been struggling for her honor. The memory brought a quick, sour taste to her mouth.

But she felt she could trust this fellow. His cinnamon-colored hair was neatly trimmed, and his buffalo robe must have been chosen for function rather than style. His face, reddened with embarrassment, indicated that he was not the same kind of beast that Blaine Loring was—*he* would have taken full advantage of having a woman clasped that tightly to him.

This man's forehead was furrowed with confusion. He took off his wire-rimmed glasses, wiped them, and stuck them back on his nose. Then he cleared his throat. "Excuse me. My name is Silas Collier, and I am to meet a Mrs. Hyacinth Mason. Might either of you be Mrs. Mason?"

Hyacinth stepped forward. "I'm Hyacinth Mason. Edward Collier—"

A man, his hair the same dark gold as Silas's but lightened with gray, laboriously hobbled toward them, his face glowing with obvious anticipation. He looked vaguely familiar; Eliza must have known him when she was a child. "Hyacinth? Hyacinth? Is it truly you?" His leg and ankle were wrapped, and he balanced himself—badly—with a wooden crutch.

"Uncle Edward, didn't I tell you to stay home?" Silas reached to help him but was waved away impatiently.

"How could I stay away from seeing my Hyacinth? Hyacinth, oh, Hyacinth, how long I have waited for this moment!" The older man's eyes glowed.

Eliza couldn't keep her eyes off the unfolding scene. It was like something out of a book, a story of love lost and found and told with great drama.

Hyacinth ran toward the man. "Edward? Oh, Edward, what has happened to your precious limb?"

Silas coughed. " 'Precious limb'?"

Eliza couldn't help herself. She knew she shouldn't find this so funny, but she was so tired that she had no self-control left. *Precious limb, indeed.* She choked back her laughter and tried to hide it in a series of coughs that probably fooled no one.

"Crazy woman," Silas muttered.

She leaned over and said, in a stage whisper, "Hyacinth seems very smitten."

Silas shook his head, as the older couple cooed over each other like love-struck teenagers. "I can't think this is a good thing."

"What, that his precious limb is broken?"

"That, and the fact that he's so overtaken with the idea of having found his true helpmate in Hyacinth that he's been remodeling the house, which was just fine to begin with, and two days ago he took a dive off a ladder while installing a decorative doodad on the door and managed to crack his 'precious limb.'"

"The limb will heal," she said gently.

"Do hearts?" he responded cryptically.

She didn't have an answer for that.

The couple on the other side of the station stood up, their arms linked together, and slowly made their way toward Silas and Eliza.

"Mrs. Mason, we've arranged to have you stay at Mrs. Adams's Boardinghouse. I'm sorry, I didn't know your daughter was coming, too."

"Oh, bless your heart, as honored as I'd be to have her as my own, she and I just met on the train." Hyacinth reached over and squeezed Eliza's arm as Silas reached for her bag. "I'm hoping that she and I will become good friends, and that she'll become a part of the Collier family, too."

Eliza froze, and even without moving her eyes, she saw Silas's reaction. He, too, stopped mid-motion, his arm halfway to her bag, his mouth agape.

Hyacinth broke the ice of the moment by laughing. "Well, that's not exactly what I meant. Of course we don't want her to be part of the family." She stopped as Silas stood up, his face flooded with crimson. "That's not right. I mean she could be, and— Oh, someone give me a shovel. I'm digging this hole way too fast!"

Eliza swallowed. This wasn't going at all the way she'd featured it would. In her hurried plans, she'd imagined that she'd come to Remembrance and hide while she gathered her dreams about her. She hadn't even thought where she might stay.

"Actually, I'll be on my way now—" she began, but Silas interrupted her.

"Please, allow me. The boardinghouse is just across the road and down a bit, and I'm taking Mrs. Mason there anyway, so one more in the wagon is no trouble." He picked up Hyacinth's bag in one hand and hers in the other, and once again, his warm golden eyes met hers. "So, Miss—" He stopped. "I'm sorry, I don't know your name."

"Davis. Eliza Davis. And I'm pleased to meet you."

Color washed over his face. "Thank you. I'm glad to meet you, too." He cleared his throat. "Shall we go?"

They left the little station and went outside. Snowflakes sparkled through the air, turning to water as soon as they touched her skin. Silas helped her into the wagon and handed her a lap robe to cover her legs and feet. She tucked herself under as much as she could, burying her hands in the blanket's warmth. She sat, trying to ignore the couple behind her as they spoke soft words that lilted in the night air.

Beside her, Silas stared straight ahead as he led the horse away from the station and down the snow-covered road.

The incongruity of her situation was almost overwhelming. Within twenty-four hours, or just a bit over it, she'd watched her romance destroyed, abandoned her home and business, left the city she'd called home for fifteen years, returned to a place she obviously hadn't remembered at all well, and now she was sitting in a wagon with people she didn't know, being led to a place she'd never seen.

She'd had no plans at all when she'd left the city in a heartbroken rush, and headed for what seemed to be home—to Remembrance.

Under the cover of darkness, she peeked at Silas. He could be a murderer for all she knew, and she'd willingly gotten in the wagon with him and let him take her to a place she knew nothing about, where she would stay. She had clearly gone off her bearings to trust him so completely, but there was just something about him, something about those cider-colored eyes behind the staid wire-rimmed glasses, that made her feel comfortable with her decision to go with him.

She was in Remembrance. She hugged the thought to her.

Remembrance!

Her eyes couldn't take in enough of the small town. It had changed so much since she'd left, and what she hadn't been old enough to recall, her mind created. The school had seemed big, but now it looked small. The white house on the corner with the blue shutters—hadn't that been a small reddish house before? And she didn't remember the mercantile being on that street at all.

The moon was almost full, illuminating the town as they drove to the boardinghouse.

It wasn't far. Soon Silas brought the wagon to a stop and leaped out.

"My uncle and I would be pleased to have both of you come to supper tomorrow evening," he said as he lifted the bags from the wagon. "By the way, if you've a mind to attend services in the morning, the church is not at all far from Mrs. Adams's place. She usually brings over the churchgoers."

Edward snorted. "*Usually?* Humph. Like they have a choice."

Eliza sat in the wagon, reluctant to leave the comfortable cocoon of the lap robe, and studied the building where she'd begin her new life in Remembrance.

The boardinghouse was large, its white paint reflecting the moon's glow with a dazzling brilliance. Blue shutters framed wide windows that were draped with patterned curtains. One curtain fluttered a bit. Someone inside had taken notice of their arrival.

"I don't intend to carry you in." Silas's voice broke her reverie, and she laughed.

"I suppose!" She took Silas's hand almost absently as she got out of the wagon and, while Hyacinth and Edward murmured reluctant good-nights, she walked up the steps to the front door, with Silas behind her, bearing the bags.

Mrs. Adams met them there, a single lantern illuminating the entry to the boardinghouse. Her steel gray hair bristled out at odd angles, and her barely stifled yawn indicated that they'd woken her up.

"I'll take them from here," Mrs. Adams said, reaching for the bags and taking one in each hand. "You know my rules, Silas Collier. There'll be no men in this house this time of night. Good evening."

He barely had a chance to lift his hand in farewell before the door slammed on him. "Too late for gentlemen to be here," Mrs. Adams grumbled. "I run a decent house here, and there'll be none of that, thank you very much. By the way, I don't rent rooms to just anyone."

The landlady sighed and walked over to a tall desk near the front door. She unlocked the desk and removed a ledger book. "I'm going to need some information about you both. Who you are, and how long you plan to stay. Lodging is fifty cents a week, in advance. Hyacinth Mason, I have your particulars, but not yours." She stared at Eliza. "Who are you?"

"I'm Eliza Davis, and I will need a room until I find a place to live." Eliza had no idea what else she should say.

Mrs. Adams nodded, her gaze still locked onto Eliza's face. Perspiration began to break out under Eliza's coat. It was horribly uncomfortable, being overtly examined like this.

"You're going to stay in Remembrance?" Mrs. Adams said at last.

"I hope to."

"I see. Well, fill this out." She pushed the ledger toward Eliza and watched as Eliza filled in her name and address.

"St. Paul, I see," Mrs. Adams said, looking at the entry.

"I've left there. That was my last address."

For a moment, the landlady didn't speak, and then she said, "Payment in advance," and held out her hand.

Eliza opened her coin purse and withdrew fifty cents. Mrs. Adams took it, along with Hyacinth's money, and the coins vanished into a tin in the desk. The woman closed the desk and locked it.

"Now, I'll take you to your rooms. You two are my only boarders at the moment, so there's no hiding in the crowd. Your rooms are on the second floor,

Mrs. Mason, you're first on the left, and Miss Davis, you're next to her. Here are the rules. Breakfast is served at seven. On the dot. You're late, you've missed it. Dinner is at noon. Supper at six. I don't tolerate stragglers."

As the three of them climbed the stairs, Mrs. Adams continued. "These doors lock at nine each night. You're not in by then, you're out. I'll have your bags packed and on the front steps by sunrise the next morning."

A pin had worked its way free from the stiff gray hair coiled at the nape of the landlady's neck, and Eliza watched it in fascination as it swung back and forth, keeping time with Mrs. Adams's verbal list.

"Church every Sunday. Bell rings at eight, service begins half an hour later. You're expected to be there," she continued with her list as they neared the top of the stairs. The hairpin had nearly worked its way free. "No men guests, except in the parlor, and then just on Saturday and Sunday afternoons between three and five. Dress and act modestly, and that means no taking the Lord's name in vain. Those are the rules."

The silver hairpin dangled dangerously, and just as it was about to tumble down the collar of Mrs. Adams's blue calico wrapper, the woman dropped the bags at the first door and reached up to resecure the wayward pin. "And no animals, not a cat, not a dog, not a chicken."

Eliza looked at Hyacinth, which was a mistake. Hyacinth rolled her eyes, and a stream of laughter began to bubble up. She disguised it with a quick cough, which apparently didn't fool Mrs. Adams, who harrumphed.

"You don't have to stay here. But I'll warn you, I'm the only boardinghouse in town."

"Yes, ma'am," Eliza said meekly. She didn't trust herself to say more.

"You have my word, Mrs. Adams," Hyacinth said.

Mrs. Adams turned and faced Hyacinth. "You're that mail-order woman."

"I have been corresponding with Mr. Edward Collier." The color rose in Hyacinth's face.

"Humph." Mrs. Adams considered her guest silently before turning to open the door. "I don't hold with that kind of nonsense, but you're old enough to know better, and I do not meddle in things that are not my business. This is your room. And yours, miss, is next to hers."

"Come see me when you're settled," Hyacinth whispered behind the landlady's broad back before disappearing into her room.

Mrs. Adams led Eliza to the next door. "I didn't catch your purpose in being in Remembrance."

You sly thing, Eliza thought, but she simply answered, "I used to live here."

"Davis is your name, correct? The only Davis family I remember left several years ago. Somebody got sick. The father?"

"No, my mother. We left here to get her medical treatment in St. Paul, but it wasn't successful. She passed away shortly after that." Eliza swallowed. How often was she going to have to relive this? There were undoubtedly people in Remembrance who knew her parents. She'd been only a child when she lived here and hadn't paid much attention to the adults, preferring to play with her dolls and cats. Plus, fifteen years of absence placed a blur over names and faces.

"I'm sorry to hear that." Mrs. Adams opened the door to Eliza's room. "This room will be yours."

She carried Eliza's bag in and placed it by the foot of the bed. Then she brushed her hand over the bureau, wiping away an invisible speck of dust, and said as she left, "Have a pleasant sleep. Breakfast at seven, church after eight."

Eliza surveyed her surroundings. This would be her new home for a while.

The room at the Mrs. Adams's Boardinghouse was clean, if a bit small. Next to her bed was a bright rag rug, its colorful scraps circling into a kaleidoscope of color. A white-painted nightstand was nearby, and Eliza smiled as she noticed the Bible centered squarely on the top. She could imagine Mrs. Adams placing it there, as if commanding the guest to read it.

She opened the carpetbag, and the clean scent of soap rose from it. One of the women she'd sewn for told her to tuck a cake of soap in her clothing and one in her carpetbag to keep her clothing smelling fresh, and she'd done so ever since. It was better than perfume.

She hung the few dresses she'd brought with her in the armoire, placed her toiletries on the bureau, and tucked her sewing kit in the top drawer of the chest. It was her prized possession—that bag with the assortment of needles and threads and the scissors that were kept knife-sharp. The kit had given her employment before, and it needed to again. She gave it one final tap before closing the drawer.

If only she'd been able to bring her sewing machine! She'd just gotten it a few months ago, but in her hurry to leave, she'd left it in the shop.

For a moment, she stood in the middle of the room. She had done it. She had left St. Paul, left Blaine and his loathsome lies, and come back to Remembrance. Now, her life was going to start anew.

She already had a friend. Two, if she could count Silas, but she wasn't sure she could. He hadn't seemed happy to see them at the station—in fact, if she were a wagering woman she might bet that he'd have been happier if he'd gone to meet the train and they hadn't stepped off.

Still, he looked nice. He certainly didn't have the oily charm of Blaine—the thought almost made her laugh aloud as she recalled how ungraciously Silas had met them—but there was still something basically nice. He didn't seem comfortable being ungracious, maybe that was it.

Or perhaps she was trying to find something to like in somebody, anybody, to counteract the distress Blaine caused her.

Eliza wanted to freshen up a bit before visiting with Hyacinth, so she poured a bit of water from the pitcher over her hands and splashed it on her face. It was cold—of course—and invigorating.

She turned to the mirror, and what she saw there confirmed her worst fears. Four hours of traveling hadn't done her hair any favors. The braid that was wrapped into a knot at the back of her neck was still in place, but all around her face the shorter bits of hair had escaped, surrounding her head with a brown frizzy cloud that made her look as if she'd just woken up. The bow had come untied and straggled down the side of her neck in a trail of wrinkled blue velvet.

Great. Just great. Her first introduction to Remembrance and she looked totally disreputable.

She tried to slick her hair into place. Her hair had been the source of constant struggle since she was born. It was thick and curly and brown, not a pretty brown, she thought, but rather a floorboard brown. With all the wonderful things God could have topped her head with, why this? It was especially unfair here in Minnesota, where most women had Scandinavian hair, blond and straight.

No, not blond nor auburn nor even ebony black. Her hair was the color of wooden planks.

She gave up and went to Hyacinth's room.

"I thought perhaps you weren't coming," the older woman greeted her.

"I was lamenting my hair. You have such pretty hair, jet with ivory streaks." Eliza plopped on the chair.

Hyacinth laughed. "You make it sound so poetic. I like that. So, dear, what do you think of Remembrance so far? Is it at all what you expected?"

"I lived here so long ago," Eliza said honestly, "that what I expected was impossible. I know that the town couldn't stay the same way just because I left it, even if in my mind it was so."

"Well said. Tomorrow would you like to visit your old home again? We could explore together a bit after church."

"You'll want to spend that time with Edward. I can venture forth on my own. Somehow I don't think I'll get lost in Remembrance." A yawn took her by surprise. "Oh, I am so sorry! That came out of nowhere!"

"You get some sleep. We'll talk more tomorrow. Good night—and I'm glad I met you." Hyacinth gave her a quick hug. "Sweet dreams."

Back in her room, she began to unwind her disobedient hair, but her fingers were clumsy from lack of sleep. She hadn't realized until now just how tired she was, but as soon as she sank onto the bed to remove her shoes, the urge to put her head atop the pillow, on the crisp white case edged with green crocheted lace, and pull the green-spotted quilt over her head was nearly irresistible. She fought the fatigue and managed her before-bed rituals, slipping on a white cotton nightgown and hurrying under the covers.

She thought of the Bible as she gave in to her exhaustion, but her hands wouldn't—no, couldn't—make another motion. Instead, she began to recite the twenty-third Psalm from memory, her lips moving as she breathed the words that had always been such comfort. "The Lord is my shepherd; I shall not want. He maketh me to lie down. . ."

Eliza smiled. That was true. It might be a green quilt rather than a green pasture, but already her soul was feeling better.

Every muscle in her body screamed for sleep. Her nerves were stretched as far as they could go, but even the psalm couldn't bring the respite she needed. No matter what she tried, she could not sleep. Her body was ready, but her brain was still wide-awake.

She got out of the bed and dug into her satchel until she found the blue knit slippers she'd brought. At one point, she'd planned them for her trousseau, but that dream withered just hours ago, when she saw Blaine Loring with the other woman.

Now they were simply slippers to keep her feet warm against the cold.

She padded to the window. The snow cover reflected the partial moonlight, brightening the darkness. The snow had tapered off, with only a few scattered flakes gliding slowly through the air.

From her vantage point on the second floor, she could see Remembrance laid out below her. It looked peaceful, serene. It had changed so much since she'd left. How old was she then? Nine? Ten? Her father packed them up and moved them to St. Paul, searching for the ever-elusive cure for her mother's illness. When she'd died two months later, he began searching for a home for his soul, moving with his daughter again and again until he gave up and breathed his last. He was buried in St. Paul, next to his beloved wife.

Eliza put her head down on the chilly windowsill and let the pain wash over her. It was so unfair. She'd lost everything she loved, everyone she loved.

Someday she would cry about it all. Someday. Right now she needed to step back and study her life, to see if she could determine God's promised path. It was there. She couldn't see it now, but it was there.

A huge yawn overtook her. Whatever God meant for her future, it was going to have to wait. Right now He wanted her to get some sleep.

As she stood up, a figure moved, a dark silhouette against the whitened backdrop of the new snowfall. The man walked along the town square, his footprints showing gray in the snow. Around he went, until at last he turned toward the line of houses lining the street and vanished around the corner.

Could it be Silas, out for a late evening stroll? She shivered and scurried toward the warmth of the bed. Some people might enjoy a winter night in Minnesota, but not her—at least not when she was this desperately tired.

She slid into the bed and dutifully prayed her bedtime verse that she had ended each day with for as long as she could remember. "Thank You for Your gifts I pray, thank You for this special day, for the morning light and the evening star, and bless those who love us near and far."

*

The morning light spilled into the kitchen of the Collier house. Silas poured a cup of coffee and took it into the parlor. He'd rebuilt the fire in the stove, and the bright flames were taking the chill off the start of the day. His coat had fallen from the hook by the door. He must have hung it too hastily when he returned last night. Four times around the town square, trying to think through what couldn't be thought through, and then trying to rid his mind of the topic entirely.

It'd been a fool's errand.

Sunday mornings were special. He liked the slow start, the quiet hours that preceded the church service.

Now maybe things would change. He shook his head. No, there was no *maybe* about it. Things would change.

He sipped the coffee, staring out the window. From where he stood, he could see the edge of the boardinghouse. There were two women there who were about to turn his life topsy-turvy. He knew what Hyacinth's role would be—but what about Eliza's? There was something about her that intrigued him.

He shrugged. There was no use in overthinking this. He'd make better use of his time getting ready for church.

He made it to the top stair when his uncle called out from his bedroom. "Silas!"

He opened the door and looked in. "Are you feeling all right? Does your ankle hurt? I told you that you shouldn't have gone to the train station with me last night."

Uncle Edward waved away his question. "*Pfft*. It's just a bone. I would have walked through hot lava to see her at long last. Isn't she wonderful?" He smiled dreamily.

Silas didn't answer right away. On one hand, he had some doubts—no, cancel that, he had a whole wagonful of doubts—about someone who would move to be near someone she hadn't even met, someone she might, in fact, marry.

On the other hand, he had enough respect for his uncle not to willingly hurt his feelings, so he didn't want to blurt out his true feelings.

And on still another hand—he chuckled slightly at the realization he had three hands going in this internal argument—he was not about to lie. He didn't like falsehoods, and lying on a Sunday seemed especially dreadful.

At last he settled for a noncommittal and truthful, "She seems quite interesting."

His uncle boosted himself up straighter in the bed. "Say, did I hear you leave last night? Were you out for a late night stroll?"

"Yes, sir. My legs needed some stretching." It wasn't a lie. It felt wonderful to go for a walk and let his muscles get some exercise.

"I know what you mean, son. If it weren't for this cracked-up leg, I might have joined you." Edward sat up, carefully maneuvering his swaddled ankle around the blankets. "Hyacinth is quite a woman, isn't she?"

He did not want to talk about it. This woman was the cause of everything that had gone wrong. If it hadn't been for Hyacinth, Uncle Edward wouldn't have been renovating a perfectly good house. He wouldn't have decided to put up that ridiculous plaster bouquet on the door, and he certainly wouldn't have let himself lose his balance and fall off the ladder and break his ankle.

He knew that men did the most ridiculous things for women. Not him, though. He'd keep his head—or better still, never fall in love to begin with. What a silly notion it was. Why, Professor Barkley advised great control in matters of the heart.

Unfortunately, his uncle was not a student of Professor Barkley and fell headfirst into this middle-aged amour.

But the fact of the matter was that what had happened had happened and wasn't about to unhappen. So he smiled at Uncle Edward. "Indeed."

"I'm going to church with you," his uncle announced, swinging his legs over the side of the bed and grimacing.

"Are you sure that's a good idea?" Silas frowned. "We got a good snow last night. You shouldn't even have gone last night to the station."

Uncle Edward shot him a look that brooked no argument. "I am going to church, and I am going to sit with my beloved."

"Well," Silas said, "let's get you up and presentable because I do believe that your beloved won't want you until you've shaved and washed." He grinned. "And changed out of your nightshirt."

Soon the two of them were headed for the church, Silas walking slowly beside his uncle in case he slipped. Luckily the church was just around the corner, but still the trip seemed to take forever.

Down the road they could see the two boarders from Mrs. Adams's house heading toward church, with Mrs. Adams herself leading the way like a plump mother hen.

He smiled as he noticed Eliza and Hyacinth trailing immediately behind the matronly woman, no more than an arm's reach away from the landlady. He knew that Mrs. Adams put them there to make sure they approached the house of worship with the proper decorum.

His uncle stepped forward, sliding a bit on the icy step in the entrance of the church. Silas caught him before he could fall. "Careful," he warned, but Uncle Edward ignored him.

"Hyacinth dear!" he called. "Lambkins!"

If only there were a hole nearby, he could sink into it, Silas thought. His uncle had clearly gone around the bend mentally. If he were going to be acting like a love-stricken fool, the least he could do was behave that way in the privacy of his own home, not out in the public like this—and definitely not while Silas was standing beside him.

Hyacinth waved enthusiastically. "Darling!"

He couldn't help it. He looked at Eliza, who was, to his horror, gazing straight at him, a smile dimpling her cheeks with humor. Mentally he consulted with Professor Barkley—and drew a blank. If the good teacher dealt with such issues, it must be later on in the course of study.

"*Expect the unexpected.*" That one had been last week, and was perhaps applicable for this situation. It struck him as odd when he'd read it then, and now, when the time came to put Professor Barkley's principle into action, it fell short. How could he expect the unexpected? If he could expect it, it wouldn't be unexpected.

Furthermore, Professor Barkley urged him to prepare for the unexpected so that when it did come his way, he'd be ready for it. Silas snorted to himself. Hardly possible!

Eliza came up the walk to the church's entrance, avoiding the reunion of Edward and Hyacinth. He automatically reached out to help her across the icy spot where his uncle had almost lost his bearings, and the sight of her small, gloved hand against the woolen cloth of his overcoat did something odd to his knees.

Professor Barkley had clearly never dealt with a female hand on his coat, or he would have made that the first chapter of his book.

A little part of him that was rampantly vain was pleased that he'd worn his good overcoat this morning rather than the buffalo robe, which could get quite pungent in close quarters.

A group of children clattered in front of them, while a man with sunken and bloodshot eyes tried ineffectively to round them up.

"Good morning, Jack," Silas said to him, nabbing a young boy as he raced by and slinging him to his shoulder. "Here, I've got Mark."

"Thanks, Silas. All right, children, we are in God's house. Let's be worshipful," Jack said to his children.

Each child, from the oldest to the youngest, put their hands together and walked reverently down the aisle.

"That's Jack Robbins," Silas whispered. "Poor fellow has his hands full, that's for sure, what with six children and a wife who's been sick all winter. He's a good man, and makes sure his children get to church each Sunday."

"I remember him! They lived on the other side of Remembrance, and he was older than I was, maybe three or four years ahead of me in school, but I recall that he was kind and helped the younger children who had trouble understanding their sums."

"You remember him?" Silas asked, stopping so suddenly that Eliza nearly tripped. "I didn't realize you had ever lived here in Remembrance."

"That was fifteen years ago. I don't remember much about it, to be honest. Your uncle looks a bit familiar, but I don't recall Mrs. Adams, who says she knew my parents. I was just a child." She laughed softly. "Somehow grown-ups weren't nearly as important as my cats."

Silas tapped his uncle on the shoulder. "Miss Davis here used to live in Remembrance. Did you know that?"

Edward turned to her slowly, obviously reluctant to take his gaze off his new love. "Oh, that's very nice."

Silas rolled his eyes. There was clearly going to be no talking to his uncle until the man came to his senses—*if* he came to his senses.

So Eliza had lived in Remembrance before and had come back. He asked the question that arose naturally. "Are you going to stay here?"

"Perhaps," she responded lightly. He was unable to pursue the matter further as Reverend Tupper began the call to worship, and they hurried to their seats.

The four of them—Silas, Eliza, Hyacinth, and Edward—sat together during the service. As soon as Reverend Tupper announced the Gospel for the day, Silas squirmed. Matthew 22 was the parable of the wedding feast.

Why couldn't the minister have chosen something else? Lepers or wars or burning bushes would have been good. Why the wedding feast?

The rosy-cheeked minister, as short and round as a pumpkin, described the wedding feast. To Silas's right, Uncle Edward and Hyacinth beamed at each other happily. He glanced surreptitiously at Eliza. She looked ahead, her gaze steadily on Reverend Tupper.

Silas didn't want to hear about a wedding feast, or anything else to do with weddings. Out of the corner of his eye, he saw Edward reach for Hyacinth's hand. This was getting worse.

He'd hoped that his uncle would see the light of reality and come to his senses. How could a grown man, usually so stalwart and intelligent, fall in love through a series of letters?

He didn't like being embarrassed by Edward's behavior, either. Life was hard enough as it was, without being plagued by something so totally out of his control. Maybe, he considered with a quick hope, his uncle had some kind of dementia that led him to this foolish relationship.

The minister reminded the congregation that the parable was about the kingdom of God. He leaned forward, his face beaming with the joy of his message, as he exhorted them to come to the banquet.

Then, with his usual good humor, he ended the service by noting that dinner with pie and coffee would be served by the Women's League. "Different banquet, same theory. Please choose to come," he quipped.

The back of the church had been turned into a temporary dining room. As usual, the other members of the congregation served the Robbins children first, and Silas caught the littlest boy's wobbling plate before it slipped to the floor. "Do you do this every week?" Eliza asked Silas as she accepted a dish heaped with ham and beans.

"In the summer it's easier. We sit outside. We try to do it every week, yes. There's a very active Women's League." He glanced over at Hyacinth and his uncle, bent over a plate. "Mrs. Mason will have to join."

"Have to join? You make it sound like it's a requirement."

"It is, in a way. This church was built with great enthusiasm and optimism. You'll note that it seats about one hundred and seventy people. One hundred and eighty if they're family." He grinned. "But at the moment, there are only one hundred people or so in Remembrance proper, and that includes the very old and the very young and a few dogs and cats. The church needs everyone participating."

"Including Hyacinth."

He didn't want to argue the point, and in fact, he wasn't sure that she did, either. He speared a piece of ham, stuck it in his mouth, and chewed thoughtfully. He wanted to answer her as honestly as possible. "They'll take to her like barn swallows to the wind, as my father used to say. You know that saying, 'Many hands make light work'? Well, it's true. The more people who pitch in, the better the outcome. Anyone who volunteers to help in any capacity is welcome here. Plus she'll make friends in the Women's League. Good friends."

"That's true." Eliza seemed to understand what he was saying, which oddly mattered to him—quite a bit.

Reverend Tupper joined them and introduced himself. "I hope you'll be with us quite a while," he said to Eliza.

"I'm enjoying my time here," she said, rather neatly avoiding a direct answer, Silas noted.

"And how did you come to choose Remembrance?" the minister continued.

"Remembrance chose me, I'd say," she responded with a smile. "I lived here when I was a child, but my parents and I moved to St. Paul when my mother became ill. It was quite awhile ago, and both of my parents have passed on now, but I was ready to see what became of Remembrance."

Silas realized he was as anxious to hear more as the minister was.

Reverend Tupper began to speak, but another parishioner tugged at his elbow with a request about the stove. "We'll discuss more later, I do hope," he finished.

"I'm sure we will," she answered.

"He's a bit inquisitive," Silas told her as he handed his empty plate to one of the women at the table and took up the piece of apple pie she handed him, "but it's to his advantage. He knows his flock as well as any good shepherd."

"Oh, I don't deny him that," she said, "and in fact, I'd have liked to have visited with him some more. I wanted to ask him about the Gospel reading he used."

"The wedding banquet story? What was your question?"

"I always felt bad for the guest who didn't have the right clothes," Eliza said. "I know it's a parable, but to be thrown out simply because he wasn't dressed appropriately—doesn't that seem a bit harsh?"

Her question caught him off guard. "Harsh? I hadn't thought about it. But if you're invited to a wedding by a king, wouldn't you wear your finest?"

"What if it were his finest?" she persisted.

"Well," Silas hedged, aware that he was well out of his theological waters, "the Bible does say that the man was supposed to have worn his wedding garment, not that I'm at all sure what a wedding garment would have been in that time..."

She laughed. "I imagine I take it a bit more literally than most, being a dressmaker."

"Truly? You're a dressmaker? Why then, would you come to Remembrance? Oh, I know what you said to Reverend Tupper, but wouldn't you have more business in St. Paul?"

Was he mistaken, or did her expression falter? "My business was prospering in St. Paul, but I was drawn to a smaller community, a closer community, like Remembrance. I have good memories of living here, even if they're a bit faded and dusty themselves."

He led her to two chairs that had become vacant when the occupants left the church. "Did you not enjoy St. Paul? I'd think a city would be exciting."

She shrugged, but he saw a flash of something—pain?—across her face. "Exciting? Oh yes. It was very exciting, but I got to the point where I was abandoning my upbringing and turning my back on God." Again, the flicker of hurt flared in her eyes "I lost the person I was, and I knew I needed to regain her. That is why I returned to Remembrance."

He touched her arm, his large hand on her pale blue sleeve, and he was again struck by the comparison of the earlier image of her delicate hand on his overcoat. She was so small that he felt like a lumbering giant next to her.

"I'm glad you did."

Chapter 3

A knock on Eliza's door was followed by, "Eliza dear, are you ready to go?" She practically flew to the door to let Hyacinth in. "I am. Did you talk to Mrs. Adams about our going to supper at the Collier house? What did she say?"

"Of course she was a bit put out since she'd already planned the meal, although our saving grace was that she hadn't actually prepared it yet. By the way, Eliza, she has her ideas of what ladies do and what gentlemen do and what courting is all about and—"

"Courting? Courting? Who's courting me? Silas? Oh, honestly!" Eliza shook her head with exasperation.

Hyacinth sat on the edge of the bed and pulled Eliza down beside her. "It sounds strange to you, and yes, to me, too, but we have to remember where we are. You're not living on your own in St. Paul anymore, and I'm not in Chicago."

"I can take care of myself," Eliza protested.

"You can, of course." Hyacinth's words were soothing. "As can I. We both know that.

"But the fact is that we need to be a bit inconspicuous at first. Not, of course," she hurriedly added, "that either of us has anything to be ashamed of."

Eliza looked down. She wasn't ready yet to tell anyone the soil upon her life.

"Have you ever had a cat, Eliza?"

She snapped her head up. What on earth was the woman talking about? "Yes, I've had a cat."

"How many?"

"I had one. His name was Tim. And then I got another one, Hannah."

"But Tim was first, right? And then Hannah?"

"Yes, but I don't see—" Eliza drummed her fingertips silently on the quilt. What did this have to do with Mrs. Adams?

"Hear me out. How did Hannah react when she came to the house? How did she treat Tim?"

"She was very quiet and hid most of the time, and then slowly she came out from under the bed and behind the couch and sat with us, until she and Tim were the best of friends—oh! I see!"

"Exactly," Hyacinth said as she stood up. "Hannah fit in by lying low and not

260

fighting with Tim. That gave Tim the time that he needed to get to know her, and it let Hannah figure out what was what. It made the adjustment as painless as possible."

"So that's what we need to do?" Eliza asked. "We need to be Hannah to Mrs. Adams's Tim."

"That's one way to put it," Hyacinth said, with a smile. "For the moment, unless our landlady—or anyone—becomes totally outrageous, we'll abide by the rules. They're strict, I'll give you that, but not without reason, I'm sure."

Her advice made sense. Yet, Eliza thought as they left the boardinghouse with Mrs. Adams's frowning face watching them from the window, it was a bit too much. Well, she thought philosophically, she could try. It wasn't as if she'd live in the boardinghouse forever.

There wasn't a cloud in the sky, and the air was icily crisp. Eliza tugged her scarf up tighter around her face, and then dug her hands into the muff she'd brought along. With no wind to lash at their faces, this was the perfect day to explore a wintry Remembrance.

"Do you remember where you lived?" Hyacinth asked as they headed to their right.

"I thought I did, but it feels like somebody rearranged all the houses. I was sure it was down this road, but these other homes weren't here so everything looks different. I'm not sure."

For fifteen years, she'd built the town in her mind, and rebuilt it and rebuilt it. It was the home where she went in her dreams, it was the place she fled to in her memory when she was feeling alone, it was the solace she sought when her soul ached. She knew exactly what it looked like, right down to the snow-covered branches outside the church.

"We can find it, I'm sure," Hyacinth declared. "We'll wander until we do. How long can it take us, anyway? Remembrance isn't that big."

The town had changed much, but the core was still essentially the same, Eliza realized as they walked along the snow-packed roads, stopping only to exclaim over a bright blue doorway or a stained-glass transom. There was a pride evident in Remembrance, a sense of community that she had been too young to notice as a child, but which she saw in the tender care the Robbins family received at the church.

"This is it."

There, in front of her, was the house she and her parents had lived in. In many ways, it hadn't changed much. The clapboards were white and the shutters were black, and the red flower boxes were still in the front.

In other ways, though, it was completely transformed. She and her father left with the house wrapped in the dark specter of illness. The rooms themselves hung heavy with sadness. Now it seemed to sparkle with renewed life. Signs of children were obvious: a wagon abandoned near a bush and filled with snow, a doll propped in one window and a cloth dog in another. A room had been added to the side, and bushes had been planted on each side of the front door.

"How are you feeling?" Hyacinth asked softly.

Eliza shook her head. "I don't know. Not bad, I know that. I was so heartbroken when we left here. I think we both knew that my mother wouldn't live, but there was that glimmer of hope that maybe a doctor in the city could save her, and we chased that hope. I'm glad to see that the house isn't so depressed—oh, now I'm being silly. How can a house be depressed?"

Hyacinth shrugged. "That probably falls under the heading of 'mysterious ways.' I imagine that, at the very least, when your mother was so ill, when you knew she was dying, you saw things differently. I know that's what happened when my Matthew passed on. I felt as if God threw a black veil over everything. Nothing looked the same, nothing smelled the same, nothing tasted the same."

Her words shot Eliza back into the past, into the days of pain. Losing her father was still a raw grief, too. "Exactly."

She was suddenly transported back to Remembrance fifteen years ago. It was the start of a summer filled with promise. Eliza had loved summer, loved the juicy strawberries, the sweet corn, the little fish that nibbled on her feet when she waded in the river.

And then her mother got very sick. Days and nights were indistinguishable, as the curtained windows blocked out any bit of sunshine that her mother might have found painful. It happened so quickly that it seemed like a dream, one that she'd wake up from and her mother would be well and they'd be on their way to the berry patch to get the best selection before the birds got there.

The fever stole not only her mother but it also snatched away her father's smile and stripped her young life of joy.

Tears burned at her eyelids as the horrible pain returned full force, undiluted by the years. She missed her mother desperately, grieved for her father anew.

They began to walk on, and Hyacinth spoke. "I felt as if my heart had been slashed by a great knife. It hurt so bad, as a matter of fact, that I thought I was dying, too, and I actually went to the doctor. He said that yes, I was sick—heartsick—and the only way to recover was to grieve Matthew with my whole being and move on."

"That seems a bit, I don't know, callous," Eliza ventured.

"Not really, although at the time I thought he was horrible to even suggest such a thing. No, I must say that I've never forgotten Matthew. Never. I also had to forgive him for dying—and come to terms with the fact that God took him from me."

"How did you do that?" Eliza found herself clinging to every word. "Did you forgive God?"

Hyacinth laughed. "Oh, my dear, one doesn't forgive God! We can understand Him a bit more, but I wouldn't call it 'forgiving.' I wish Matthew hadn't died, but he did, and now it's time for me to let myself love again."

"And that's why you're in Remembrance."

"That's right. Edward and I have a mutual friend who thought we'd enjoy each other's company. He introduced us by a letter, and Edward and I took it from there. I came to love him so much." Hyacinth's face grew soft. "He is a good man."

"But what about Matthew? How can you love twice?"

Hyacinth put her arm around Eliza. "That is the most astonishing thing. God created this fragile thing called a heart, and then gave it the most amazing ability—the capacity for love that expands as needed."

"But hearts can be wounded. And sometimes they don't recover." She thought of her father, who never healed from his beloved wife's death.

"There's the mystery—because sometimes they do. Sometimes they do."

Eliza pondered what Hyacinth said. Her own heart had been pounded terribly, and letting herself love again was too great a risk.

Oh, she was simply being silly. Moving to Remembrance had pretty much taken care of that danger. How many eligible men were even available? This was a small town, after all.

They were about to complete their survey of Remembrance, having come nearly full circle in their tour, when Hyacinth pointed out a small house behind the mercantile. "If I remember correctly, this is the house I'll be renting. Let's go peek in the windows."

"Are you sure we can? What if it isn't the right place?" Eliza asked nervously.

"Oh, I'm sure it's right. Edward described it well enough in the letters. He said it had a birdbath in the front, and do you see any others with a birdbath? And he said it was behind the store, and this is. And it certainly looks empty."

Eliza trailed after Hyacinth. She'd feel a bit better if she knew for sure—

A small body cannonballed into her. "Got you!" the reedy voice shouted as the boy's arms wrapped around her legs.

She recognized one of the Robbins boys. He couldn't have been more than six years old. "You startled me!" she said, snatching off his knit cap and ruffling his hair. "What are you doing?"

The boy took the cap back and shoved it on his head. "I'm protecting this for Mr. Collier," he said, throwing his chest out proudly. "He asked me to keep an eye on it, and I am."

Eliza knelt in front of the child. "Do you know why? Because Mrs. Mason here is going to move into it."

"Oh." His face sagged. "I'm so sorry, ladies. I thought you might be robbers."

"Well, we could have been," Hyacinth said, joining them. "You were certainly Johnny-on-the-spot with paying attention, too."

"My name's not Johnny. It's Paul."

"I see." Eliza fought back a smile. He was so serious. "I'm glad to meet you, Paul. I believe I saw you in church this morning."

"Yes, ma'am, I was there. Say, I'm sorry I tackled you like that. Do you think Mr. Collier will be mad at me?"

"You did a good job, Paul," Eliza said. "And no, he won't be angry. If anything, he'll be proud of how vigilant you were."

"You must live near here," Hyacinth said.

"Yes, ma'am." He pointed to a house two lots down. "You should come visit us sometime."

"We will," Eliza said, rising to her feet and brushing the snow off the front of her coat. "We'll see you again soon!"

As they walked toward the Collier house, they chuckled over the little boy's solemn caretaking of the house. "At least I know I'll be safe when I live there," Hyacinth said.

Edward and Silas lived on the other side of the town square.

The Collier house looked much like the others on the street, "tall and thin," as Hyacinth described it, built to take advantage of the fact that heat would rise in the cold winter months, thus warming the upper story a bit more.

Silas met them at the door, with Edward peering over his shoulder, his excitement nearly palpable.

Something utterly delicious scented the air. "I hope you both like chicken pie," Silas said as he took their coats. "Uncle Edward is a talented cook."

"But he's using a crutch!" Hyacinth objected, scurrying into the kitchen.

Silas looked at Eliza, and they chorused softly, "His precious limb!"

"I suspect they'll be in there a bit, finishing up the dinner, and fussing over each other," Silas said, "so let's sit in here."

The front room was small but neat. A grandfather clock ticked in the corner, and the fireplace crackled as a log fell.

Near the fireplace were two chairs covered in slick damask. Eliza sat in one and had to grip the arms to keep seated on the stiff cushion. "One of Uncle Edward's projects to prepare for Hyacinth," he said as he sat in the other chair. Eliza noticed that he, too, held onto the arms. "New upholstery. He's sure they'll become more comfortable as time goes on."

I should certainly hope so! Eliza thought, but aloud she merely said, "They will get broken in soon enough."

Most of the furnishings in the room did seem new or refurbished, and even the ruinous plaster molding of a bouquet of flowers had been successfully nailed in place, undoubtedly the work of the more-focused Silas.

"The house is truly finished beautifully," Eliza said. "I understand that you and your uncle both have excellent carpentry skills." Mrs. Adams had filled her in on that. "Have you always been interested in woodworking?"

"It's something my uncle and I share." Silas stared contemplatively into the fire. "I grew up outside of Crookston—do you know where that is?"

She nodded. Much larger than Remembrance, Crookston was near the border of the Dakota Territory.

"My family moved back to Pennsylvania when I was thirteen, and instead of going with them, I came here, to apprentice with Uncle Edward."

This would explain why she and Silas hadn't met when she'd lived here. He didn't arrive until several years after she'd moved away.

"Did you want to be a carpenter?"

He looked directly at her with clear surprise. "What an odd question."

"One that's worth asking, I believe."

For a moment, he didn't answer. Then he replied, "I was thirteen. All I knew was that I didn't want to move to Pennsylvania. My father was planning to take over his father's printing company, and I couldn't think of anything more dreadful than that."

She chuckled. "Ah, the unerring wisdom of youth."

"Truly. Uncle Edward offered to take me and teach me woodworking, and it was here in this house and in the shop in the back that I found my calling. Carpentry is—well, let's just say that he taught me well."

"Then this time has worked out for both of you."

He shrugged. "According to my uncle, I have a talent for wood. Of course, he could be saying that only because I'm his nephew."

"Or he could be saying it because it's true."

He took off his glasses and cleaned them carefully, even though Eliza suspected there wasn't a spot on them. Silas didn't seem to be the kind to appreciate compliments.

"Whatever his reason, I'm here and I'm now a carpenter. Life has a way of changing when you least expect it."

"That's a good way of looking at it," Eliza said. He had no way of knowing how applicable his words were to her life, too. "Then you're staying on to work with your uncle?"

His lips tightened slightly. "I don't believe so. Remembrance is a small town, and there really isn't a need for two carpenters here."

"But if Hyacinth stays—"

"But if Hyacinth stays, my uncle will need to retain the business. Having another person in the household—" He broke off before he could finish what he was saying, but she understood. The problem was one facing all the small towns that were starting up: finding an income that would support a family, no matter how large or how small.

"Reverend Tupper has asked me to talk about something with you," he said, suddenly changing subjects. "There's a family in Remembrance who has fallen on some hard times. You saw the father and his children today in church. Jack Robbins is the fellow's name."

"Ah, yes." Eliza told him, in light words, of their encounter with Paul.

"Yes," Silas said with a slight smile. "Paul is very responsible. I'll have to tell him how much I appreciate his apprehension of the possible criminals today. He's a good child, but in danger of being old beyond his years."

He told her more of the situation at the Robbins house. Mary Robbins was quite ill, and Jack was having to let his own work drop to care for her and their family.

"That can be quite difficult," she said, thinking back to her own childhood and the similar circumstances she lived with.

"Indeed it can. The church is helping as best it can, and Reverend Tupper has inquired if you might be able to help with some of your needlework skills. The older women in the church can—and have—done quite a bit, but there is much more." Silas sighed. "There are six children in the family, and they're growing so very quickly."

"As children are wont to do."

"True. I'm going in this next week to do some repairs in the house. Might you—"

"Yes."

"You will?" The relief in his voice was clear. "That's wonderful!"

At that moment, the door to the kitchen burst open, and Hyacinth ran out, a smoking pan in her hands. "Coming through!" she sang as she raced across the room and out the front door. Within seconds she returned, without the pan in her hands, but her eyes were twinkling. "We won't be having turnips tonight."

Edward's face peeked around the corner of the door, and he grinned.

"I am not going to ask what that was about," Silas said. "Eliza, I do believe we'd better head toward the dining room before the rest of the dinner goes up in flames."

The dinner, which Silas had been dreading, passed, and he actually enjoyed it. He could have managed nicely without Uncle Edward pointing out how well Silas and Eliza were getting along, how their friendship was blossoming, how they'd be working together for the Robbins family, even how they both liked chicken pie. He'd stopped short of carving their initials in the tree by the front door.

Now Eliza and Hyacinth had gone back to Mrs. Adams, and Uncle Edward was inside, puttering around and setting things back in order, while Silas stood in the winter moonlight.

But things couldn't go back into order. Not now.

A snowflake fell on his cheek, and then another and another. He looked at the moon in the cloudless sky. When he was little, he thought that God lived there, so far away, but he came to know over the years that He was never further than Silas's thoughts.

He'd only known Eliza for twenty-four hours, and while he was not a believer in love at first sight, he did believe in the power of friendship, and that's exactly what he was labeling this as. Hadn't Professor Barkley himself endorsed friendship?

Maybe he needed a friend, and that's what he was finding in Eliza. He hadn't had anyone he could consider a friend—someone to laugh with, someone to share secret jokes with. Someone who found "precious limb" as funny as he did.

A gust of wind whipped around the edge of the house, and he shivered. It was time to go back inside and put this day to rest.

Uncle Edward had finished his final touches in the kitchen and was hobbling up the stairs, one awkward step at a time. Silas rushed to his rescue.

"Why don't you let me fix a bed downstairs," he said, "so you don't have to do this every night?"

His uncle shook his head. "There's nothing like a fellow's own bed. Just lead me to it. I know I've got some sweet dreams ahead of me." He winked at Silas. "You, too, I suspect."

"Humph. I'll be dreaming of turnips that someone managed to burn, that's what I'll be dreaming about. That smell will take weeks to go away."

"You think I did it because I don't like turnips, don't you?"

Silas grinned. "Maybe."

"There are some things that are more important than turnips, Silas. Love is."

Silas patted his uncle on the shoulder. "That's true. Now get some sleep."

In the haven of his own room, Silas eagerly turned to the day's lesson in *Professor Barkley's Patented Five Year Plan for Success*. Sunday, he read, was meant to be a day of rest and reflection. And how did a man do that? Planning ahead, Professor Barkley counseled. Prepare for the Holy Day by gathering your clothes, cooking your food in advance, and laying out the items you would need so they would be at hand.

Planning ahead? Professor Barkley should try living in this house.

The lesson also included the admonition to read the Good Book daily and to commit a Bible verse to memory each day.

Silas's eyes threatened to shut before he could finish the day's directive, but he forced himself to read on. The recommended verse for him to learn was John 8:32: *"And ye shall know the truth, and the truth shall make you free."*

Easy. Easy to memorize, easy to understand.

He ran through his evening prayer and slid under the covers.

The truth. It was easy. . .wasn't it?

Chapter 4

Eliza tucked the last strand of hair into the bun coiled at the nape of her neck. Trying to make it stay was a losing battle, but if she didn't turn too quickly, and if she was careful removing her knit scarf, the lock might stay in place.

As if to taunt her, the wayward strand immediately slid out, but before she could do battle with it again, someone knocked on her door. She abandoned the tussle with her hair and opened the door.

Mrs. Adams stood there, her arms crossed over her calicoed chest. "Silas Collier is downstairs. He said he'll walk with you over to the church."

"Good. Thank you for letting me know. I'll be right down." Eliza reached for her coat, but Mrs. Adams didn't move. Obviously she had more to say. Eliza suppressed a smile. Mrs. Adams always had more to say.

"He didn't tell me, but I heard at the market this morning that you have volunteered to help the Robbins family out." The crusty demeanor softened. "Thank you."

Then the grumpy bearing was right back in place. "Don't forget. Dinner is at noon. Prompt. I don't hold the food for anybody."

"Thank you so much, I will remember."

"You've got a bit of hair that's gone awry," Mrs. Adams commented, as if the lock had itself violated one of her many rules. Perhaps reassuring herself that her own steely gray hair was safely confined within the limits of the braided circle at the nape of her neck, she ran her hand over the sides of the constrained hair. She smiled, maybe a bit smugly, Eliza thought, as her fingers found no stray tresses.

Eliza tucked the errant strand back into place and snatched up her coat and her sewing bag. "Thank you, Mrs. Adams. I don't know if I'll be back for dinner at noon or not. Silas and I are meeting Reverend Tupper in the church first." She paused. Should she ask? "I'm not quite sure what to expect when I get over to the Robbins's home."

"Expect a mess," the woman said succinctly. "The family needs help."

Mrs. Adams, Eliza had already found out, was more than willing to share what she knew. Perhaps she could give her some more information about what to expect at the Robbins's house.

"How long has Mrs. Robbins been ill?" Eliza asked.

269

"Several months, but when she fell ill, it was quick and terrible. Most of us didn't expect her to survive, to tell you the truth. She was very close to death's door." Mrs. Adams shook her head sadly.

Memories of her own mother's illness made Eliza's stomach clench. "But Mrs. Robbins is getting better, isn't she?"

Mrs. Adams didn't answer immediately, as if considering her answer. "She's alive," she said at last. "She's alive."

They left the room, and Eliza followed Mrs. Adams's heavy tread down the stairs.

"Silas is in the parlor," Mrs. Adams said, "waiting for you."

He rose when she entered the parlor, Mrs. Adams trailing closely behind her. "Just a minute." The older woman suddenly turned and bustled out of the room.

"What was that about?" Eliza asked as Silas helped her into her coat. "That woman has more surprises than Christmas."

"I have no idea," he answered.

Mrs. Adams returned quickly, a basket in her hands. It was covered with a large white napkin, neatly tucked in around the edges. She held it out to Silas. "Here. It should feed the lot of you."

As he took it from her, the warm aroma of baked turkey arose from it. "Mrs. Adams, you want me to take this with me?" he asked.

"Why else would I have given it to you?" she answered with a sniff. "It certainly seems obvious that your work crew would get a lot more done, and the Robbins family might have a decent meal, if you ate this over there."

"This is what you were going to serve for dinner today, isn't it?" Eliza asked, finally catching on to what Mrs. Adams had done. "What a wonderfully sweet thing to do!"

"Sweet? Well." Mrs. Adams seemed taken aback, as if no one had called her *sweet* in a long time—if ever. "I can make another dinner. Not turkey, mind you, but I can put together a nice potato and ham hot dish in its place. Mrs. Mason and I will enjoy that just as much."

"The family will certainly enjoy this. Thank you, Mrs. Adams," Silas said. "Eliza, we need to go."

The temperature had dropped overnight, and the wind had picked up. Conversation was impossible as Eliza tucked her chin deep inside her knitted scarf, covering as much of her face as she could with it. The wind was bitter, tugging at her skirts until they whipped around her ankles tightly.

The warmth of the church was welcome. Reverend Tupper had a small fire burning in the iron stove at the front of the church, and she held her hands out toward the flames.

"Thank you for sharing your talents with the family," he said to Eliza, who could only chatter wordlessly in response, her face was so frozen. "The Robbins house is not far away, but I'll give you a chance to thaw out a bit first. Silas, might I borrow you for a moment? I'd like you to look at the back window...."

Their voices grew fainter as they walked away from her. Eliza huddled near the stove, letting the heat radiate into her body. It wasn't far to walk, but the wind was brutal, making every foot seem like a mile.

She looked around the church. When she'd lived here, the church had been smaller, not much larger than some of the original houses the settlers built. The community added onto it, even expanding the sanctuary. She ran her hand over the altar, undoubtedly crafted by one of townsmen, perhaps Edward or Silas even. It was smooth and polished, and ornamented with an iron cross centered on a white cloth, the edges touched with lace.

In a low murmur from the back of the church, she could hear the men's voices.

What an odd journey this had been. Within a week, she abandoned the life she'd been building—she'd *thought* she'd been building, she corrected herself—and had come back, full circle, to where she began.

It surprised her at first that no one seemed to recognize her name—no one except Mrs. Adams, of course—but she'd already realized that many people came to and left Remembrance, not having found the financial relief they'd been expecting here. Her family had been one in a steady stream of temporary residents.

In her memory, Remembrance staged itself as larger and grander, but in retrospect, she had to admit that nostalgia had put a gleam on the little town that was her own creation. It was, simply, the place she had been happiest.

Here her mother had been well, here her father had laughed, here she had played in the grass of the prairie.

But it had all been fleeting. When they left, they took everything. Her father emptied the house of its furniture and its quilts and its pictures, and sold it and the parcel of land it sat on to the next man ready to believe the promises of this new town in the north of the state. Now the woods surrounding it had become fields, and in time, the fields would become towns, more towns like Remembrance. Some would survive. Some wouldn't.

From the corner where the men spoke, she heard laughter. It was like music. There hadn't been much laughter with Blaine Loring. He was an intense man. It was, as he told her patiently one day, how he became wealthy. His single-focus approach to whatever he was doing meant that his project succeeded, but it also meant that there were casualties along the way. But he never concerned himself with that.

If she had paid attention to his words then, she might have spared herself becoming one of those very casualties.

Silas, on the other hand, had a genteel side. Even though she had just met him, when she was with him she felt different. She sought for a word to describe it but came up blank. The closest she came was "equal." Blaine kept her on edge, worried that he might find something to disapprove of in her style, her manner, her words. She didn't feel that way with Silas.

He was—a friend. That was it. And it was wonderful. She needed friends.

He and Reverend Tupper called to her. It was time to bundle up again and go to the Robbins's home.

Her scarf fell off, and as she replaced it over her head, she thought of what her hair must look like—probably more was out of the bun than in it at this point. She should just give up and let it go wherever it wanted. It would anyway.

They left the church, and Eliza followed the two men. The weather wasn't improving, she thought as they struggled through the pillow drifts that criss-crossed the road, little fingers of snow that would, with any encouragement from the elements, soon become full-blown snowdrifts. But she'd said she'd help, and she wouldn't go back on her word.

Soon they slowed in front of the white house Paul had pointed out. "It's seen better days," Silas said charitably.

In fact, the steps were slanted, one shutter swung free, and the paint was peeling badly. "Those we'll take care of when spring comes," Reverend Tupper said. "Let's go inside and see what we can do today."

The inside of the house was in better shape. Paul ran to meet them and take their coats, and she heard Silas say to him, "Say, I hear that you were quite observant at the house yesterday. Good job, Paul. I'm proud of you."

Once the coats were off and hung on the coat rack, the children clustered around Silas and peered into the basket containing the turkey dinner, their shouts of glee almost drowning out Jack Robbins's greeting.

"Children," he said, clapping his hands and getting his offspring's attention, "I think we should all introduce ourselves to Miss Davis. I'll start. Miss Davis, I'm Jack Robbins. I think we knew each other a long time ago. It's good to have you back in Remembrance."

The children immediately formed a line, and the oldest boy stepped forward. "I'm Luke. I'm ten."

"You know me. I'm Paul and this is my twin brother Peter, and he's six." The children snickered, and Paul flushed. "We're both six."

"He's silly," said the next to the last child. "I'm Brian, and I'm four, and this is my brother Mark. He's two."

A girl with shy eyes was last. "I'm Analia. I'm five."

"I'm pleased to meet you all," Eliza said, a bit surprised at how much she meant it. She hadn't been around children much, but this group had already shown itself to be special. The few times she had needed to work with children nearby, they hadn't been this well behaved at all.

Within minutes, the turkey was put aside for dinner, safely out of the reach of eager little hands.

"Would you like to meet my wife?" Jack asked.

"Yes, I certainly would," Eliza responded. She tried to tuck her hair back into place, but as usual, it wouldn't stay.

Mary Robbins was a slight thing, very pale and thin, and almost lost in the bedcovers which were tousled and twisted.

She reached a gaunt hand to Eliza. "I'm glad to meet you," she said, her voice as soft and faint as a whisper. "I understand you're a dressmaker and that you've come to help my children not look so much like ragamuffins." She coughed and sank back onto the pillow as if the short conversation exhausted her.

"It's my pleasure. I enjoy sewing. There's something relaxing about it."

Mary's hands plucked uselessly at a blanket that had slipped down. "Would you like me to fix your bedding?" Eliza asked.

The ill woman nodded. "Please."

Eliza straightened the blankets and fluffed the pillows. "There. Now I'd better see what's awaiting me in the mending basket. It's been a delight to meet you."

Mary smiled. "God bless you, Miss Davis."

Eliza touched the woman's hand. "Please, call me Eliza, and I am already blessed."

Reverend Tupper and Jack came into the room, and Eliza left to begin on the sewing.

She and Silas soon settled themselves by the fire. Eliza had a basket of shirts that needed to be mended or cut down, and she studied them carefully, evaluating each one.

He was repairing some of the boys' boots. "I've never done this before, but it's not horribly difficult," he told her as he squinted at the instep of one. "With six children, and five of them boys, I guess boots need to have a longer life than usual."

"Strikes me that it's a lot like basic sewing, isn't it?" She flexed her fingers. The cold had made them clumsy at first, but as they warmed up, the feeling had returned. She turned the red plaid shirt to see if there was any way to salvage it for one more wearer.

"If there's more to it than that, I'm lost," he admitted. "But so far it's been a simple matter of thick thread, a stout needle, and a load of patience."

"That's why I sew." She took up her shears and cut the shirt smaller. "This'll have to be redone. It's torn along the seams. I think this may be the last go-round for this shirt. It's so thin that it's almost transparent. But yes, I do like to sew because I'm so impatient."

He laid the shoe down and stared at her, the flames of the fire reflecting in his pale brown eyes. "That seems odd. Wouldn't it be the other way around? I'd think you'd have to be a patient person to sew."

Eliza laughed. "I wish it were so! I'm very impatient with many things, but sewing makes me slow down, and it gives me time to think."

"What do you think about?"

"Of course I think about the project. I love to watch the flat material become a dress or a shirt or a pair of trousers. There's such a sense of success about it when it's going well. And when it isn't going well, of course I get frustrated, but I view it like a puzzle, and I can almost always resolve it. I also pray a lot when I sew."

"Really?" He cut the thread he was using and tested the seam. "Good. It'll hold."

"On the long stretches, where I'm finishing a seam or hemming a skirt, I talk to God a lot. The even stitching is the perfect backdrop for prayer. Don't you pray while you work? Or maybe that's not a good idea. You might fall off a ladder."

"And break my precious limb," he finished for her. They both laughed. "I usually pray in the morning and at night before I go to bed, and I say grace before I eat, of course. I also pray during the course of the day, mainly when I have a challenge or I want to take up a cause with God. I must sound like God's neediest child sometimes!"

She spread the pieces of the now cut-up shirt out on the table in front of her. "I'll be praying that this comes together all right. Well, with five boys in the family, it ought to fit one of them."

Jack called them in to eat. The turkey that Mrs. Adams had sent over was carved, and a bowl of potatoes and gravy was placed next to a platter of corn.

The children rushed in, each taking what was clearly their designated spot at the table, from the oldest to the youngest.

"Please, have a seat," Jack said. "I've got two extra chairs here."

"What about Mary? And Reverend Tupper?" Eliza asked.

Jack's face softened. "I always feed Mary first. She ate fairly well today, thanks to this delicious food. The Reverend has gone on to his home, so it's just us."

Silas pulled out a chair for her, and then sat on her left. Analia was on her right.

"Time for grace," Paul said. "Hold Mr. Collier's hand, Miss Davis. That's how we pray, holding hands."

Peter snickered.

"Not like that, silly," interjected Brian. "They're praying hands, not I-love-you hands."

Silas coughed, and Eliza looked down to hide her smile. She took Analia's hand first and then reached for Silas's. Analia's were warm and sticky, and Silas's were dry and firm.

"Children, hush," Jack said. "Silas, would you say our blessing?"

"Dearest Lord, we thank You for Your gifts, for food, for friendship, for eternal life. May we always keep you close. Amen."

"That was sure short," Paul said. "Reverend Tupper goes on so long the meat gets cold."

The other children shushed him, and the dishes were passed from one to another.

The dinner was excellent and the children well behaved, but Eliza was aware of Silas next to her throughout the meal. *Not I-love-you hands, indeed!*

They spent the rest of the day working together quietly, until at last they decided to quit. Reverend Tupper had already gone back to the church, so they walked together back to the boardinghouse. The sun had set, and the wind had died down. The snow had ended, but a light crystalline shimmer made the air sparkle in the moonlight.

Fairy dust, her mother had called it, and it did look as magical as that. This was the backdrop of beautiful dreams, in which anything could happen.

"I love this," she said, sweeping her hand in front of her. "I'm sure there's some scientific name for the phenomenon—"

He began to interrupt, but she put a gloved hand over his lips. "I don't want to know. It's so beautiful, these tiny speckles of ice floating in the air."

They walked in silence to the boardinghouse, watching the interplay of the crystals and the moonlight. At last, as they reached the door, Eliza paused, reluctant to let the magic end.

"Eliza—" Silas began, but whatever he was about to say was lost as the door flew open and Hyacinth and Edward burst out.

"We're getting married!" Hyacinth sang. "We've decided that we like each other as much in person as we did in letters, so we're going to get married as soon as Edward heals."

"I want to be able to carry my bride across the threshold," Uncle Edward said. "That's the only reason I'd delay matrimony with my Winter Butterfly."

Winter Butterfly? Eliza let it go and hugged her new friend. "That's wonderful!" she said. "Isn't it, Silas?"

He hadn't moved until she spoke. Then he shook his uncle's hand. "Absolutely grand. Absolutely grand."

That moment of hesitation spoke volumes, and Eliza noticed the fleeting disappointment on Hyacinth's and Edward's faces. His approval mattered so much to them.

She diverted them with questions about the upcoming nuptials. Had they spoken to Reverend Tupper? What about a reception afterward? A wedding dress?

"I want you to make the dress," Hyacinth said, her eyes again bright with excitement. "I know just what I want, too. Yellow silk—"

"Yellow silk?" Eliza's thoughts flew to the impracticality of yellow silk in the midst of winter. "Are you sure? Perhaps a soft woolen or even satin, although even one snowflake could spot it forever, would be better."

"She wants yellow silk? Yellow silk she shall have!" Uncle Edward boomed.

Silas stood aside as the wedding plans were quickly spun into place. His lips tightly compressed, his dissatisfaction was evident.

At last he spoke. "I am going home now. Uncle, are you coming with me?"

Uncle Edward turned toward Hyacinth. "The hour is late, dearest. I shall see you on the morrow."

Silas rolled his eyes. "When did you turn into Shakespeare? Honestly!"

"That's not Shakespeare," his uncle responded. "As much as you read, you should know that."

The two quibbled the entire way out of the boardinghouse, and their words carried across the open air as they headed to their house.

"I can't help but feel I'm at the center of some discord between Edward and Silas," Hyacinth said as she shut the front door of the boardinghouse. "Silas doesn't seem to be happy about my marrying his uncle."

Mrs. Adams came into the room and moved around the edges, straightening an antimacassar, adjusting a doily, wiping imaginary dust from a small round table. "Oh, don't mind me," she said. "I'm just tidying up."

A nod of Hyacinth's head indicated that they should go upstairs where they could talk in private, and Eliza followed her into the older woman's room, where Hyacinth sank onto the bed with an exasperated sigh.

"What do you think, Eliza? Silas doesn't seem to be as, well, enthusiastic as I'd hoped he would be."

Eliza detested being caught in the middle, and yet she saw no way to avoid it here unless she spoke carefully. Quickly she prayed for God to guide her words. "I don't know that he has anything against you, Hyacinth. Of course he is concerned. You have to admit that you and Edward met in an unconventional way. You can't blame him for being cautious. He loves his uncle, and he wants to make sure he's doing the right thing."

Hyacinth flung herself back, her arms outstretched. "I *am* the right thing!

Why can't he see that?"

"Well," Eliza began, feeling for all the world like she was picking her way through a field of thistles, "I suspect he doesn't know you yet. And he may be concerned that his uncle doesn't know you well enough. Yet."

"But he does. There's nothing hidden in my past. I've led my life as a good Christian woman. I tell you, Eliza, he could hire a detective and I'd come up as clean as new linen. How many women could say that?"

Eliza flinched. It seemed like Blaine Loring had reached into her and seized her heart with his sin-stained fingers. She felt as if she'd never be clean again. The only relief she had was that she hadn't let his advances progress. She had always stopped him. No, the spot on her soul was what she had done to others, on his cue.

Hyacinth switched to the happier topic of her wedding plans, and Eliza let her mind continue to revisit the specter of Blaine Loring. How could she have let herself believe his lies?

Was it wrong to trust so completely? The Bible did caution about this. Matthew 10:16 came easily to her mind: *"Behold, I send you forth as sheep in the midst of wolves: be ye therefore wise as serpents, and harmless as doves."*

"You're not listening," Hyacinth said accusingly, with a playful glint in her eyes, her earlier distress clearly laid aside.

"I must be tired," Eliza said. It was true. She was. It had been a long day with many unexpected twists and turns.

Back in her room, she got ready for bed quickly. Once she'd buried herself under the quilt and the extra blanket from the chest at the bottom of the mattress—the night was indeed cold—she closed her eyes and thought again about the verse.

Sheep. Wolves. Serpents. Doves. It was quite a menagerie for so few words but its meaning was clear. If only she'd heeded it earlier.

She said her prayers and turned over, ready to sleep, when one final thought crossed her mind. *Harmless as doves.* It was beautiful. She could do that. She could be as harmless as a dove.

⌒

Silas helped his uncle to his bedroom, noting that each evening the trip seemed to get easier. His ankle was healing.

"I'd like to talk to you before we turn in, Silas," Uncle Edward said as he hobbled into his room. "Have a seat."

Silas sank into the chair beside the small table in his uncle's room. Fortunately it wasn't one that Uncle Edward had recovered in his remodeling frenzy, so he was in no imminent danger of sliding off.

His uncle patted Silas's shoulder, and for the first time, Silas noticed how rheumatism had swollen the joints. Carpentry must be painful for him.

"Silas, don't be too harsh with Hyacinth and me. I do love her."

"Of course you do."

Edward sighed. "I do. I don't expect you to understand, Silas, at least not in your brain. Please try to understand in your heart. I never married, you know that. I told myself that was fine, and I guess it was. I had the carpentry business, but after a while, it all wears thin. I don't know how to explain it."

"You don't need to." The last thing he wanted was to hear his uncle wax rhapsodic about his Chicago sweetheart.

"I do need to. You've been like a son to me. But I'd like a wife. I want to be loved, to be held in a woman's embrace. I want to wake up to the smell of lilacs on my pillow. I want—"

The smell of lilacs. Or soap, like Eliza. In a town that often didn't smell very good at all, a woman's scent had great power.

He was getting as fanciful as his uncle.

He could understand the need to be loved, but what if Hyacinth wasn't the right one? His uncle had spent his entire life single. Was he leaping headfirst into trouble by choosing the first woman he courted?

It all seemed so impetuous. And impetuous meant silly.

"Good night." Silas left his uncle's bedroom, shutting the door and heading to his own room.

What a day! He had worried about his own future, what he would do if Hyacinth came into the household, and now, all of his concerns about that disappeared. Like early snowflakes that evaporated before landing on the ground, the burden he'd carried about his livelihood vanished.

He would have the carpentry business. His financial future was settled. The irony of it struck him—if Hyacinth hadn't come into his uncle's life, this security might have remained elusive.

Nothing was going to ever be the same in his life again, and he had to admit that some of that came from a woman named Eliza.

She fit in so easily at church and with the Robbins family. Eliza had a rare talent for gentleness and yet he also saw a great source of strength. He had never met anyone quite like her.

Eager to get his mind off the strange turn of events, he opened *Professor Barkley's Patented Five Year Plan for Success*. He was supposed to be reading these in the morning, not the evening, and he felt a twinge of guilt about that. Tomorrow he'd change.

The day's study was about trust. Professor Barkley pointed out that one must trust in the Lord's guidance rather than the often-faulty perceptions of man. He cited some direct advice from the Bible, which was the verse for the day. It was Proverbs 3:5–6: *"Trust in the Lord with all thine heart; and lean not unto thine own understanding. In all thy ways acknowledge him, and he shall direct thy paths."*

Silas shut the book. It was excellent advice but, like much excellent advice, hard to put into action.

He wondered how Eliza fit into God's ways for him. The thought carried him into sleep, and sleep carried him into dreams, dreams sprinkled with a magical glimmer.

Chapter 5

Time was flying by. Eliza counted the days she'd been in Remembrance—almost three weeks now. She'd been so busy at the Robbins's house that she'd barely had time to think.

Hyacinth handed the platter of hotcakes to Eliza. "I could eat all of these, they're so good, but I'd be waddling down the aisle if I do. You'd better take them."

"If one of us has to be waddling around, it might as well be me." Eliza took another hotcake. They *were* good.

"Tell me about yesterday. How was it?" Hyacinth took a sip of her tea as she waited for Eliza's answer.

"The family certainly does need help. The mother is so sick, and the father is stretched as far as he can go, I'm afraid. I spent all of my time there trying to do something with the children's clothing. They have six children, and five of them are boys."

"How sad. Were you able to mend the clothing?"

Sudden tears crowded behind Eliza's eyes, and she made a great point of buttering the hotcakes. Finally she said, "I did what I could. The youngest one, poor thing, is getting the worst of it. By the time the clothing gets to him, the material in the shirts and trousers is worn almost through. It seems like as soon as I mend something, it comes back to me with more repair needed. The fabric is simply giving out."

"Can we get some more yardage from the mercantile?" Hyacinth asked. "I'd like to help in some way, but I'm not a seamstress and I'm not a carpenter, and it's been a long time since I've been around children, but I could buy several yards if that would help."

"It would! Hyacinth, you're a blessing for all of us."

Her offer was the answer to a prayer. Eliza had spent several days at the Robbins's house, dissecting shirt after shirt to make them last for one more wearer, one more season. Just the day before, as she stitched a side seam, the back split open, it was so worn. Her sewing was slow. Not only was she hampered by the lack of her sewing machine, she was frustrated by the condition of the fabric. Some of it was so thin that it almost came apart in her hands.

"Let's go over as soon as the store opens, then, and we can select some new fabric," Hyacinth said, her face glowing as she planned the trip. "And let's make sure the littlest boy gets a new shirt. Actually, let's see if we can't find enough for everyone to have something new."

"It'll mean so much to them." The family had done with so little for so long that the new clothing—from new fabric—would be a real treat for them.

The woman truly had a heart of gold, Eliza thought. She'd make sure that Silas knew about Hyacinth's offer. Maybe that would help him see her in a better light.

"As much as I like Mrs. Adams, and I do like her and she certainly can cook circles around me," Hyacinth said as they left the boardinghouse, "I'm not complaining, mind you, or maybe I am, but I'm feeling a bit stifled with Mrs. Adams always looking over my shoulder. I'm used to living on my own, having no one to answer to but myself and God.

"You have the housewith the bird bath," Eliza pointed out.

"Well, I'm not in the house yet, am I? We're stuck forever in the boardinghouse. We'll grow old together there, you and I. But we'll have our breakfast at seven, our dinner at noon, and our supper at six. And between three and five on Saturdays and Sundays, we can receive gentlemen callers in the parlor. Oh, we have a grand life ahead of us, Eliza."

They stopped and peeked in the window at the small house. "I think I'm going to have a talk with Edward about this," Hyacinth declared. "It doesn't look as if a single thing has been done to it."

Eliza stood on her tiptoes and stared through the grimy panes. "It does need a good cleaning."

Hyacinth shook her head and sighed. "Something has to be done."

After one last look through the window, they left the house and headed for the store.

Walking into the mercantile was like stepping into a kaleidoscope. Dazzling in the early morning sunlight, colors were jumbled together. Green pickles in brown barrels and red licorice in rainbowed glass. Silvery nails and bronze tacks. Pink combs and yellow brushes. In the sewing section, spools of ribbons slid on a rod, spilling out in a rainbow of bright stripes; bolts of calico leaned against workaday chambray and broadcloth; thread glowed in multi-hued splendor.

"I suppose this is nothing like you're used to," Hyacinth whispered as they approached the fabric. "The shops in St. Paul must be fantastic."

Eliza pulled a strand of chocolate brown ribbon between her fingers. Its velvety texture would make a striking detail on a winter dress. "I generally didn't have the option of selecting the material. I did to-order dressmaking."

"Look at this pattern, these tiny blue flowers against the cream. Wouldn't it be the perfect material for a young girl's dress?"

It would look striking with Analia's chestnut hair. Eliza thought of the girl with the sad eyes, and an idea came to her. Analia was so quiet that it was easy to forget her as she curled in the corner with her books and dolls, especially with five boisterous brothers demanding attention.

Eliza looked at Hyacinth, now leafing through a copy of *Godey's* that she suspected was quite out-of-date, and had an idea.

"I'll be going over to the Robbins home again later today. Why don't you come with me? I'll need to take more measurements and do a bit of fitting work, and I can always use some help."

Hyacinth put down the magazine. "I don't know a thing about it, but that's never stopped me before," she declared.

Eliza smiled. Hyacinth's ready good humor was going to be a blessing to her as she remade her life in Remembrance.

They selected utilitarian thick cotton to make trousers for the boys, bright plaids for shirts to replace the faded and worn ones Eliza had been trying to repair, and the blue and cream floral as well as a soft pink and white striped fabric for dresses for Analia. At the last minute, Hyacinth added a delicate spring green flannel for a nightgown for Mary.

"Do you want a peppermint stick?" Hyacinth asked as they approached the cash register. "I confess I have a weakness for them." She picked one out of the glass jar on the counter. "One for you, too?"

"Of course! Peppermint and snow. They go together, don't they?"

At last they left the store, their bulky packages balanced carefully, and they picked their way across the snowy road to the Robbins's house. "We should have gotten Silas to help us," Hyacinth panted as one of the bundles nearly slipped out of her grasp.

"He's already there. They started early because they're working in the pantry area today, putting up new shelves, and want to get them done by the end of the week." She tucked her chin deeper into her scarf.

"Will it take that long? I'd think they could do that in a day or two."

Eliza laughed. "Not with five boys eager to 'help.' That makes every project last even longer."

"I suppose it would. My son Thomas nearly drove his father to the madhouse, dogging his every footstep. He wanted to know what every seed was that his father planted, how long it took to come through the earth, how seeds ate—"

"How seeds ate? What kind of question is that?"

"A Thomas question. He was full of them. How do seeds eat? Do caterpillars dream while they're in the cocoon, and do they dream caterpillar dreams or butterfly dreams? He teaches at a college in New York now."

"You must be very proud of him."

"I am. Oh, I am."

"This is the house, by the way," Eliza said.

"I'm so glad. My fingers are frozen into immovable sticks. I'm going to have to knit some warmer mittens, and soon!"

They were met at the door by all of the children. "What did you bring?" they chimed.

"Nothing more exciting than fabric, I'm sorry to say," Eliza said. "Let's go to the table and open these packages and you can take a look at what your new clothes will be made out of."

The children danced happily to the table and began opening the packages. Brian, the four-year-old, whooped. "Are these for us? There are—let me count. One, two, three, four, five, six, seven, eight, nine, ten, eleven! Eleven peppermint sticks."

"Silly." Luke, his older brother, took the candies away from him and put them back inside the wrapping. "That doesn't even make sense. There are six of us children, and Mother and Father. That's eight."

Hyacinth laughed. "And Mr. Collier and Miss Davis and myself. That makes eleven. Here, my darlings, one for each of you, one for your father, one for your mother, and please take one to Mr. Collier, also. But don't spoil your dinner!" Hyacinth's last words were lost to the shouts of joy from the children as they each took a peppermint stick and then argued over who would take the others to the adults. The littlest ones were victorious, and soon all of them, adults and children alike, held a candy stick.

Silas popped out from the pantry area. His hair was liberally dusted with sawdust, and his face had a big smear of something dark on it. A peppermint stick stuck out of his mouth like a striped cigar. "What a treat!" he exclaimed. "Thank you so much! I haven't had one of these in years."

"Hyacinth got them," Eliza said. "The *children* are certainly enjoying theirs." She couldn't resist just a bit of teasing.

"You don't have one?" he countered, coming close enough that she could smell the clean aroma of newly sawed wood mingled with the crisp scent of peppermint. A few shavings fell from his arm as he pointed to her hand, which held her own peppermint stick. "Let me guess. You're a savorer, someone who makes the candy last as long as possible. This peppermint stick will probably last you a week."

She could feel the flush that crept up her neck. "Well, yes. That way I can enjoy it longer."

"But this way—" He took a bite from his with a great *crunch*. "This way, you get the full effects of the mint. And you get to chew it. That, my dear girl, is the way to eat a peppermint stick."

Eliza cleared her throat. "I shall certainly keep that in mind." Gratefully she seized on the conversation happening behind her.

Hyacinth and Analia were examining the opened packets from the store. Analia's small fingers caressed the striped fabric. "Do you like it?" Hyacinth asked quietly. "It's going to look so pretty with your dark hair and eyes."

"It looks like my peppermint stick."

"Oh, it does! It's pink and white, isn't it?" Hyacinth looked at Eliza and winked. "Let's ask Miss Davis if she might do this first then."

Analia shook her head. "No."

Eliza knelt down. "No? Analia, why not? You'll look like a princess in it."

"Make my mother's gown first. Please."

Everything seemed to slow. Even the clock's ticking lagged. Eliza blinked back the tears that stung her eyes. She wrapped Analia in her arms and held her closely against her. "Honey, I will. Your mother's first, and then yours. You are such a sweet, thoughtful girl."

Something in her heart moved as if a piece that had been broken slid back into place.

"Why don't you come with me?" Hyacinth said, holding out her hand to Analia at last. "Let's braid your hair, and then why don't you and I go in and visit with your mother for a while? We'll have some lady talk."

Eliza worked near the window, cutting and pinning the pale green fabric for Mary Robbins's nightgown. She wished she'd been able to bring her sewing machine with her from St. Paul, but it was at the shop, and she had left it behind. Sewing went so much faster with the machine. She'd be able to have all the clothing made in a third of the time it would take her to hand stitch it.

As it was, all this sewing was going to take at least a month and a half. With a sewing machine, she could probably get it done in two weeks. Then she'd feel better taking some extra care with the hand finishing, making sure everything was exactly right.

Still, speed came with a price. Here, she'd be around Silas. And, she had to admit as she bent over the green cloth, she was enjoying it. There was something about that solemn expression that could suddenly open with a smile that she looked forward to seeing every day.

Remembrance was fitting her quite well. She might just stay.

⌒

"Yes, I went over there," Silas said to his uncle for what seemed like the twentieth time in the last half hour. "Yes. I gave them the message. Yes, they said they'd come."

Uncle Edward struggled to his feet and limped over to the window. "You're sure?"

"Yes! And use your cane, please! I don't want you falling and breaking your other precious limb."

"My *what*?" his uncle boomed.

"Oh, never mind." Silas knew he was snappish but was just cranky enough not to care. God must be challenging him all the time, he thought, to be more accepting of change because He certainly provided enough learning experiences.

Even Professor Barkley seemed in on it. The day's lesson was titled, "How to Take Control of the Future." They'd already covered that earlier, with the "Expect the Unexpected" lesson. Today Professor Barkley advised that although one cannot control the future—it is, after all, written by God's hand—one can prepare for what lies ahead.

He mulled it over, just as he had the earlier lesson. Professor Barkley clearly didn't consider them to be the same subjects, so what was Silas missing? Maybe if one could expect what they weren't expecting, they could control what they couldn't control?

It made his head hurt.

Everything in his life was beyond his control.

From the time he chose to come to live with his uncle as a young lad, he had been like a leaf in a stream, sent whichever way the current sent him. He had two choices: printing or carpentry.

The oddest part was that he found he possessed a true talent for carpentry. It was, as Uncle Edward was wont to remind him, a sacred profession, too, for the blessed Jesus had Himself been a carpenter.

Then his uncle had delivered the biggest surprise: He was hoping to marry someone he'd never met, never even seen.

The surprises just kept on. The broken ankle. The arrival of Hyacinth—and Eliza. Oh, Professor Barkley had let him down this time. Even he couldn't have been prepared for any of this.

"I see them!" Uncle Edward crowed, and he hobbled happily to the front door.

Eliza and Hyacinth entered the house with a covered basket that emitted the heavenly aroma of cinnamon and brown sugar. Uncle Edward investigated the contents greedily. "Good! Cookies! I've got just the platter for them—" His sentence trailed off as he and Hyacinth left the room.

"Did you make them?" Silas asked Eliza.

"Do you really think that Mrs. Adams would let me in her kitchen?" Eliza began to unwind her scarf. "Ha!"

He helped her out of her coat, breathing in her clean scent and trying to ignore the little curl that had escaped the thick bun and spiraled down her neck behind her ear, the wayward coil as brown as the cinnamon-dusted cookies she carried in.

She turned back to him, automatically touching her hair to straighten it, and he almost sighed aloud when her fingers found the lock and pressed it back into the bun. "Honestly, sometimes I think you men are the lucky ones with the short hair. There are days when I would love to just chop this all off!"

Before he could respond, Hyacinth rejoined them, carrying a tray with cups of tea and the cookies. "We'll have them in here," Uncle Edward said, who was right behind her, "and take advantage of the fireplace and the sunshine."

Silas removed the newspaper from the seat beside him and tossed it onto the small reading table. Eliza immediately picked it up. "I haven't seen a newspaper since I came here!" she said. "Oh, it's from Duluth."

"My darling Hyacinth and I are dreaming of making our nest there," Uncle Edward said, beaming at his bride-to-be. "We'll live in our cottage by the sea—"

"Lake Superior is not a sea," Silas interjected, not liking his petulant tone but unable to stop himself. "It's a Great Lake. There are five of them. Lake Superior. Lake Huron. Lake Michigan. Lake Ontario. Lake Erie."

"Then we'll live in our cottage by the Great Lake," Uncle Edward said, obviously annoyed with his nephew. "Happy?"

"I'm just pointing out to you that Duluth isn't on a sea. That's all. It's on Lake Superior." Silas scowled.

"Wait!" Eliza waved her hands in front of her. "Stop! I don't care if Duluth is on the edge of the Arctic Ocean or the Nile River. What does it matter?"

"Indeed." Uncle Edward picked up the newspaper. "I've been having this sent to me. It's a dandy paper, too. Not only does it keep me up on what's happening there, it's got news from the rest of the state. Here's a bit about the St. Paul Ice Carnival. Now there's some spectacular thinking going on in the capital."

Hyacinth read over his shoulder. "What an interesting idea! There are all sorts of things planned, even a palace made entirely of ice! Eliza, have you heard of this?"

Eliza nodded. "The minister of the church I went to in St. Paul, Reverend Everett, told me about it. They're quite excited about it. His daughter, Christal, was a friend of mine, and she was very interested in it. I'll have to have her tell me all about it, the next time I see her."

"And here's another story of interest," Edward said, reading further. "Down in Mankato, along the Minnesota River, they're building a new courthouse."

Silas yawned. "All very interesting, Uncle."

"Not wild enough for you?" his uncle asked with a sharp glare at Silas. "Then maybe you'll like this story. Some sly trickster in St. Paul has been discovered taking advantage of the maidenly workforce there. Apparently he coaxes them into believing he's in love with them by filling their minds with pledges of a secure monetary future while—"

Eliza gasped, and her hand moved quickly to her throat. "No!"

Silas leaped up and went to her, kneeling in front of her. "Eliza, are you feeling unwell?"

All the color drained from her face, and her breathing was shallow. He put his fingers over her wrist and frowned.

"Your pulse is racing. Eliza! Are you all right?" he asked again, this time a bit louder.

"I'm fine," she said, fluttering her hand in front of her face. "I feel like such a goose for alarming you. I couldn't help but think that I used to live in St. Paul, and it was probably only His mercies that I escaped this beast. What was his name again, Edward?"

"Let me see." Uncle Edward scanned the article. "Oh yes, here it is. The scoundrel's name is Loring. Blaine Loring."

Chapter 6

Eliza forced herself to breathe normally. She was here, safe, in Remembrance. There was nothing to tie her to this monster anymore. She thought he was merely a two-timing Lothario—and that had cut deeply, right into her heart—and now she was learning he was also a criminal. She was lucky to have gotten away from him before he dragged her into his sordid activities.

Her mind busily tried to sort the new information out, even as those around her continued to speak, their voices muted as the pounding in her head grew. What she had done—that was legitimate. It had to be.

"The story becomes more interesting," Uncle Edward said. "Listen to this: 'Loring is assumed to have taken financial as well as romantic liberties with the young women by conniving them into investing in a complicated scheme in which only he benefits. Apparently the young women, who are maids and seamstresses and nannies, were encouraged by Loring's empty words to take part in his malevolent plan, turning their savings over to him. How Loring was able to exact the exchange of money for promises, and at such magnitude, has not been discovered, but an investigation is underway, and authorities have vowed that all parties will be prosecuted to the full extent of the law.'"

"Oh, Eliza, I am so glad you didn't get mixed up with this nasty fellow," Hyacinth said as she stirred sugar into her tea. "He sounds like just the kind of person who could easily ruin your life."

Eliza's heart pounded so loudly she thought that certainly they all could hear it. The kind of person who could easily ruin her life? Indeed.

"Not our Eliza!" Uncle Edward scoffed. "Why, she's too intelligent to get sucked into one of those setups. And that's just what it is. A setup. Some man with absolutely no moral backbone wastes all of the brains God gave him by trying to figure how to get rich without putting forth any effort, when in reality, it's probably more work that way than it would be if he'd just gone out and gotten a job, like the rest of the world."

"Now, dearest Edward, calm down. That Loring man is an animal, and I'm glad that his fiendish design is coming down around his head. Have another cookie."

Have another cookie. If only it could be that easy. Eliza wanted to put her hands over her ears and stop the rushing sound that kept echoing in her head.

This was far worse than finding the man she loved in the arms of another woman. Far worse than finding out that he hadn't cared at all for her.

How could she not have seen it? She let herself get so caught up in his web of false flattery that she hadn't seen the truth, even when it was right in front of her.

She was a lowly seamstress; he was a wealthy investor. She had been so blinded by his attention to her that she'd never wondered what such an apparently rich and influential man would see in her.

All the signs were there from the beginning.

He sought her out. His gifts were not from his heart but from his plan—to get her so overcome with the glitter that she wouldn't see the tarnish.

She'd walked right into his treachery. He had an investment opportunity, he told her, that he wanted to open to the young women in service to the wealthy. It was a way for them to improve their lots in life—the same way, he so winningly pointed out—that the rich got richer, through investment.

He'd sounded as if he thought only of these poor girls, and his false altruism made him even more appealing to her.

So she very helpfully went out and encouraged these same women to give him their money.

How could she have been so stupid?

She had been his accomplice in this horrible plot. Now she knew why he had been so interested in her. She'd been so blind, so willing to believe his oily lies that she fell right into his trap.

"We're so lucky to be in Remembrance, away from people like that," Hyacinth said, shuddering. "Can you imagine how those poor women feel?"

Edward nodded. "There are some men who feel that innocence is a challenge."

"Absolutely," Hyacinth agreed, "and too often we assume that innocence is a physical matter, when in fact true innocence lives in the soul, far beyond the reach of such men."

Silas dismissed the entire conversation. "Certainly we can discuss something other than this beast in St. Paul. He isn't worthy of our words."

Eliza swallowed hard and stared out the window. Snow had started to fall again, a very pretty snow for the onset of evening. Oversized white fluffs that drifted slowly were silhouetted against the deep twilight-blue sky, undisturbed by even the faintest touch of wind.

The snow would quickly cover the disturbed and uneven patches where boys had had snowball fights, or the mud-colored ruts in the road that would be reformed into treacherous muck in the spring melt. All they'd see tomorrow would be smooth unbroken snow, clean and fresh.

"Eliza?"

She realized that the others were watching her expectantly, waiting for an answer to a question she hadn't heard. "I'm sorry. I'm afraid you've caught me daydreaming." She managed a light laugh that didn't sound to her as if it would fool anyone.

"I mentioned the house by the mercantile," Hyacinth said, "and I said we'd stopped by and nothing seemed to have been touched in it."

"It seemed quite abandoned." Eliza seized on the chance to discuss a different subject. "The only footsteps in the snow were ours, so clearly no one else had been by recently."

Edward buried his face in the newspaper again. "Here's more news of interest. Apparently the precipitation in Duluth last month—"

Silas, Eliza realized, was no longer slouched in the chair. He was sitting up, staring at his uncle sharply.

"The house by the mercantile?" Silas repeated. "What house? Not the old Lindstrom house!"

"Well," his uncle replied, only half-lowering the paper, "it's a good sturdy house."

"Would you like to fill me in on this, Uncle?"

"It's a good, solid house."

"So is this one."

"It's an investment."

Eliza trembled at the term. If she never heard of investments again, it would be fine with her.

"Are you telling me," Silas continued in the same low voice, "that you're thinking of buying it?"

The newspaper went back up.

"Uncle Edward, what aren't you telling me?"

The silence from behind the newspaper seemed to grow.

Silas sat back and sighed. "You already bought it. That's just foolish. You bought it just so Hyacinth would have a place to stay?" He paused. "Or for me to stay? Is that it?"

"Not exactly." Edward folded the paper neatly, obviously stalling for time. Then he looked at his nephew. "I've owned it for a while. I keep meaning to get over there and work on it but—" He motioned toward his ankle. "It seems like it's always been one thing or another."

"Why on earth, though?"

"The Lindstroms, you know, left, and their daughter and her husband moved in, but he got that job in Chicago, and they moved, and an older man moved in, but he got so he couldn't walk and his grandchildren came and got him, and then that kind young man stayed until—"

"I know all this. What I don't know is why you now own it."

"Because that young fellow was in love with a woman living in Rochester, and he couldn't bear to be apart from her, and he wanted to go to be with her, and I bought the house so he'd have the money to go up to Rochester and be with her. There. That's it. I'm a romantic old sap."

"I see. Well."

"And it worked out perfectly, because all we have to do is fix it up a bit, and it'll be just right for what we need now."

"What kind of shape is it in?" Silas asked. "Nobody's lived in it since, when, late October? November? It'll need some work."

"I don't rightly know," Edward said. "I meant to go over there but then I got busy and one thing led to another and then next thing I knew I was flying off the ladder and cracking the bone in my ankle here. I guess I got excited about Petunia Blossom coming out to Remembrance and just kind of forgot."

Petunia Blossom. Now there was a new one. Even in her distress, it made Eliza smile.

"Before you plan further," Silas interjected, "let me go over and take a look at it. The house may not be sound anymore."

"Good idea," Edward said. "You're right. A house is an investment, and we need to keep that in mind. It's quite unfortunate that those poor young women in St. Paul hadn't done that before giving that reprobate their money. If they'd been a bit wiser, they wouldn't be in the situation they are today. Makes me wonder, though, if there wasn't some kind of an insider involved, someone who'd be able to convince these women that their money was safe."

It was too much for her.

"Excuse me," she said, standing rather quickly. "I don't feel at all well, and I think I'd better go back to the boardinghouse. Please excuse me."

She knew that they were staring at her, astonished at the sudden change in her, but she had to leave. She needed to be alone and work this out. She had to talk to God—and to herself.

Buttoning her coat as she closed the door behind her, she was only slightly aware that the soft snow had now turned to sleet. Nothing in the present mattered. Only the past was important today.

She strode, blindly, down the road and across the town square to the boardinghouse.

"Did they like the cookies—" Mrs. Adams began when Eliza pushed the front door open, but she could only duck her head and run up the stairs to her room.

Please, don't let anyone knock on my door and ask if I'm all right, she pleaded with God as she slipped out of her coat and let it fall to the floor. *I can't talk to anyone. I can't. Only You.*

She went to her favorite spot in the room, the window seat, and put her head on the cool wooden ledge.

Help me, she pleaded. *Dearest God, what should I do?*

The past began to march past her in a lurid parade. Blaine Loring, dressed as he always was, in an impeccable suit with a gold tiepin, courting her with flowers and poetry and trinkets. He loved her so much, he'd told her, that not only would he line her path with rose petals, he'd do the same with her friends.

All they had to do—

She stopped. The memory was like a knife jabbed deeply into her heart, but she forced herself to go on.

All they had to do was give him part of their wages, meager though they might be, and he'd invest them in a no-fail venture that would double, triple, or even quadruple their portions. One day, he told her, her friends could hire their current employers to be *their* maids, *their* seamstresses, *their* nannies.

It was a delicious lure, and she fell for it. For the next eighteen months, she encouraged her friends to turn over as much of their earnings to him as they could. Week after week, month after month, they all scraped yet another layer off their expenses, because they had been assured of a return that would make it all worthwhile.

Apparently this was the biggest of his lies. And worst of all, she'd pledged that his honesty was unquestionable, and because of that—because of *that*—they trusted him with their money.

Her father raised her to be as straight with people as possible. She thought she had been, but she believed the lies, too.

Fool. That's what she was, a fool.

God, please help me. Please. I don't know what to do. Please.

It was the only prayer she could come up with. Visions of the young women who so innocently handed over their savings floated in front of her eyes. Penny by penny, nickel by nickel, she had helped him rob them.

The verse from Matthew floated back into her mind: *"Behold, I send you forth as sheep in the midst of wolves: be ye therefore wise as serpents, and harmless as doves."*

There was the warning, right in front of her. Every word, every single word, applied to what happened. Yet still she hadn't seen it, her head had been so completely turned with his fancy words and slick phrases.

She hadn't been harmless. That was what would haunt her.

Would they ever forgive her? Could she ever forgive herself?

Maybe in a legal world, she wasn't guilty of anything except misguided faith. She sat up abruptly. What was it that Edward read from the newspaper? Something about the authorities planning to search for Blaine Loring's accomplices?

She couldn't breathe as she realized what that meant.

The police wanted her, too.

⸺

Silas paced in his room. He was done with the unexpected. It never seemed to be good news, and the events of the day proved it once again. He watched Eliza as his uncle read the news aloud, and he'd seen her reaction. Then when Edward brought up the subject again, she grew as pale as the snow-covered lawn and fled from the house. It was clear what had happened.

She'd invested heavily in this crook's scheme and gauging from her reaction, she'd lost quite a lot of money in it. He rubbed his forehead and frowned.

Was there anything he could do to help her? He wasn't a rich man, but he wasn't poor either. Yet somehow, offering her money seemed wrong. Even though his intentions were the best, considering how she'd lost her investment, his move might be misread.

He could wait for her to broach the subject herself. Immediately he rejected that idea. She wasn't the kind to do that. She was undoubtedly embarrassed by what happened.

What *had* happened, anyway? The newspaper provided only the vaguest skeleton of events. He wanted to know how she came to be involved and how deeply she was affected.

He needed to know how much was her money—and how much was her heart.

Silas walked to the window and looked out. He couldn't see the boarding-house, but he knew where it was—just beyond that set of trees and that cluster of houses, down the road and around the corner.

Tonight it felt as if it were at the end of the universe.

The clock downstairs chimed twice. Two a.m. He'd be a wreck in the morning if he didn't get some sleep.

He climbed into bed and, as always, reviewed Professor Barkley's memory verse for the day. It was Proverbs 25:25: *"As cold waters to a thirsty soul, so is good news from a far country."*

There certainly was news from a far country—that is, if one considered Duluth and St. Paul "far countries" rather than "far cities"—but how this could possibly be considered "good news" was beyond him.

He gave up trying to make sense of it and, as he succumbed to sleep, a prayer for Eliza was on his lips. . .and his heart.

Chapter 7

The days marched forward relentlessly, with no respite in sight. When Eliza did sleep, it was too lightly to be restorative. She spent most of the nights in a drowsy torpor, too anxious to sleep and too tired to rouse herself.

A tentative knock on the door startled Eliza. She sat up and stretched, every muscle in her back and neck screaming in protest. She must have finally fallen asleep at the window seat, her head cradled on her arm.

This had to end—soon. For almost two weeks the guilt had been building until her stomach throbbed from it, her head shrieked in pain, and her soul was sick. She tried to reason her way out of it, to convince herself that she couldn't be held accountable for something she didn't know about, but it didn't help. All she could think about were the women who gave Blaine Loring their money, simply because they trusted her.

Maybe in a court of law she wouldn't be considered responsible, but she couldn't shake the knowledge of her culpability.

She stood and made her way to the door. Hyacinth stood there, a steaming cup of tea and a plate of toast in her hands. "How are you feeling?"

Hyacinth didn't need to say more. Eliza knew that the older woman's eyes had scanned her room and had seen the bed still not slept in, had taken note of her clothing that she had worn the day before and which was now quite wrinkled.

She'd only gone out when absolutely necessary, pleading a headache the week before when church time came around. It wasn't a lie. Her temples pounded from lack of sleep and worry.

"Are you sick?" Hyacinth persisted gently. "Should I find a doctor?"

Eliza shook her head. "No, no doctor."

"Do you want to talk about it?"

It wasn't an easy question to answer. She did want to, but not yet. Not until she had sorted through everything that was plaguing her.

"Dear, if you do decide you want a sympathetic ear, I've got two. Take it on your own time. Are you hungry? Mrs. Adams sent this up."

The tea and toast smelled heavenly, and she gratefully took them. "I'm sorry," she managed to say, working the words past the dry lump in her throat that wouldn't go away. "It's not that I'm trying to avoid you, or anyone, for that matter. I've got something sitting heavily on my mind."

Hyacinth patted her arm. "You take your time. But if you want to go to church with us, taking your time isn't an option. We're leaving on the dot of eight, you know, which is in twenty minutes."

Time with God in His own house sounded like a wonderful idea. She spoke around the pulsing throb that settled behind her ears. "I'll hurry."

"Good," Hyacinth pronounced. "I'm glad."

As soon as the older woman left, Eliza hurried to get ready for worship. In between bits of toast and sips of tea, she washed her face, rebraided her hair, and changed her dress.

Soon she was walking down the road to the church with Hyacinth and Mrs. Adams. The temperature had risen, and with the sun shining so brightly, she could almost smell spring ahead.

At the front of the church, the weather was the topic of conversation.

"It's the January thaw," one man said. "It happens every year. It's just running late a bit. Doesn't mean a thing. Soon enough the temperature will drop and we'll be shivering again."

"Of course it's the January thaw," another answered, "but it's God's way of saying that the winter will end and that spring will come."

"Science versus poetry," Hyacinth murmured to Eliza. "It's a battle that will never end."

"I hope poetry wins." Being able to walk outside without burying her face in her scarf was liberating. With the sun on her face, she managed to let herself relax and enjoy the brief walk.

Hyacinth led her right to the pew where Silas and Edward were sitting. Both men looked at her with concern but neither said a word. Never before had Eliza appreciated silence so much.

"Today's sermon is about housekeeping," Reverend Tupper began. "Spiritual housekeeping, that is. It comes right from the fifty-first Psalm: 'Create in me a clean heart, O God.' I'd like us all to think about how clean our hearts are. Do you need to do some spiritual housekeeping?"

Eliza leaned forward. The words were startlingly apropos, and she clung onto every one.

"The psalmist seems to be telling us that God can do it for us," the minister continued. "Is he saying that God is like a hired man, maybe a butler sweeping the crumbs away from our banquet of a sinful life? 'Create in me a clean heart, O God.' What do those words mean? We tell God what to do, and He does it? We want Him to take away our sins, and He does it? Is this verse a command to God?"

The answer came to her so clearly that she thought she must have spoken it aloud. It wasn't a command; it was a plea. She wanted a clean heart. Desperately.

Reverend Tupper continued. "This is a very personal verse. I imagine that every one of you is sitting in your pew, interpreting the words' meaning as they apply to your own life's needs, and for each of us, that meaning will be different. These words strike right to the need of the human existence."

Behind her, a sleeping child awoke and was promptly quieted by its mother. Other than that, the church was silent as the congregation listened intently.

" 'Create in me a clean heart.' The words sum up the earthly situation and the basic quest of the Christian. We're all looking to make our hearts clean. But how? Is it God's responsibility? Let's read further."

He opened his worn Bible and read the entire psalm aloud. "Notice that the psalmist asks God to wash him, to purge him. He asks God not to put him aside, and not to hold back His love. 'Restore unto me the joy of thy salvation,' he begs. He needs God. He knows God, but something has come between him and the Lord. He's penitent, and he wants to make it right."

The minister closed the Bible. "This psalm addresses the importance of coming before God Himself, and asking His help. Isn't that," Reverend Tupper said softly, "what we need to do? All of us? He knows it. We just have to ask."

She did want a clean heart. She knew that only God could make it happen— but she had to be repentant. She had to ask for it. She had to want it with all her being. It wasn't just going to happen.

But what was she supposed to do? What did God want her to do? How, exactly, was she to do her own spiritual housecleaning?

The sermon was over, and the congregation stood to sing the final hymn. She sang the words but her mind was still on the sermon. The hymn ended, the blessing was given, and she didn't move, too absorbed in her self-questioning.

Hyacinth nudged her. "I think the service is over."

Eliza came back to earth with a start. "Of course. I'm sorry. I was completely lost in thought."

"That's the way a good sermon should end," Edward declared stoutly. "It's like a solid meal for the soul that lasts all week long."

"I like that." Eliza turned to Silas. "Your uncle has a way with words, doesn't he?"

Silas made a sound like a cross between a snort and a sniff. "He's quite the Nathaniel Hawthorne, that one."

If she hadn't been in church, she might have argued his attitude, but the aura of thoughtful worship held her tightly, and she was not going to let it go. Instead, she paused to let an elderly woman step in front of her, taking advantage of the break to focus away from Silas's sneering words.

"Sorry."

The word was muttered so low, that for a moment she wasn't sure if she'd imagined it. A quick glance over her shoulder showed that Silas had, in fact, spoken.

"It's just that—" he began, but he let his voice trail off and he shook his head. "Sorry," he repeated as the cluster of worshipers in the aisle began to move again.

She might have pursued it further had not she heard her name called.

"Miss Davis! Mrs. Mason!" Mrs. Adams bustled through the congregation still waiting to leave the sanctuary.

Eliza stopped, but Hyacinth had already moved out of the church ahead of her with Edward.

"Miss Davis, I would like to discuss something with you and Mrs. Mason. You are coming back for dinner, are you not? You're not going to the Collier house."

Eliza noticed it wasn't a question, but rather a statement. "I hadn't—" she began, and Mrs. Adams nodded.

"I'd like to meet with you after dinner today." She buttoned her coat to the top, wrapped her scarf around her neck, and tugged on her gloves. "I wouldn't miss it."

And with those enigmatic words, the landlady left Eliza and Silas.

"Well," Eliza said. "We've been told—something, I just don't know what."

"What have you done? Have you and Hyacinth been acting wild?"

"You needn't sound so hopeful," Eliza said. "I'm afraid we've done nothing more dangerous than shop for fabric, walk about Remembrance, and spend time at the Robbins home."

Unless, she realized as soon as she'd spoken, Mrs. Adams had heard about what had happened in St. Paul. But she'd never have been able to connect it with Eliza.

A thought leaped into her mind with such force that Eliza stopped suddenly, and Silas ran right into her. Guilt gnawed so deeply that it was beginning to erode her common sense.

The sole way out of letting Blaine Loring's vileness win was to fight back, and the only weapon she had was the truth.

A clean heart.

She knew what she had to do, and she was going to do it. The rhythmic coursing in her head began to fade as hope replaced it.

Eliza barely heard Silas's good-bye, scarcely registered Hyacinth's chatter as they returned to the boardinghouse. Her mind was full of what she had to do, and her thoughts were racing to determine how to proceed.

She ate automatically as she mentally sorted through approaches to deal with her guilt, and at the end of the meal, Mrs. Adams reminded them to stay.

"I've come to a decision," the landlady announced. "It wasn't an easy one to make, but it's the right one. I have a daughter in Mankato, you know, and I'm going to move there to live with her."

"You have a daughter?" Eliza asked, coming out of her fog. The thought of Mrs. Adams having a family had never even crossed her mind.

"Yes, I have a daughter. And a son, too. He's in Minneapolis. But the point is that I'll be moving in with Ella and closing the boardinghouse."

"That's wonderful," Hyacinth said. "I mean that you're moving in with your daughter, not closing the boardinghouse. When is this going to happen?"

"In two weeks, if the weather holds. Ella and her husband will come up here and pack my belongings. I'll be living with them, so some of the furniture will be sold, I imagine."

The full import of what Mrs. Adams was saying sank in. Eliza would be without a home soon. Her stomach cramped at the thought.

Mrs. Adams crossed her arms over her broad chest and frowned. "Are you still planning then to take the old Lindstrom place?"

"The small house with the birdbath behind the store? Yes, when it's ready, which should be within a few days," Hyacinth answered. "I'll be leaving here and moving in there, so this should work out perfectly."

This couldn't be real. What was going to happen to her? Eliza's fingers curled into tight fists. Where could she go? Not back to St. Paul, certainly.

Hyacinth looked at Eliza. "If Eliza is willing, she can stay with me. We can be bachelor girls together."

Eliza sighed happily. *Thank You, Lord!* It was the answer to her prayer—or at least one of them.

This was the perfect solution, even if it was only temporary. Until she got things squared away in St. Paul, much of her life would be short-term solutions to long-term problems.

She heard only faintly the plans of the two older women to move some of the extra furniture from the boardinghouse into their new home. If but for a little while, she had some time.

Now she had to use it wisely.

~

Silas blew out the lamp and stood at the window, staring toward the boardinghouse. Word had filtered back to him what Mrs. Adams wanted to talk to Eliza and Hyacinth about.

To be honest, he wouldn't miss the cantankerous landlady. Her stinginess was legendary in Remembrance. She could squeeze a penny and get a dollar, as Silas overheard one day in the general store, where apparently she'd taken the store owner to task for charging the same for two apples, when one was clearly larger than the other.

What was the matter with the world anyway? It seemed to get crazier every day. People couldn't stop fighting, and it escalated from arguing about the cost of an apple to major conflicts like the war that split the country in two just two decades ago.

If everybody would just learn the basic rules of conduct for life, things would go much easier. They weren't difficult.

The world was getting wilder, and it wasn't just the young people who were out of control. Older people were, too. One had only to look at Edward and Hyacinth to see a shining example of that. His parents raised him to know the rules and to obey them, and now, God rest their souls, their influence lived on.

He liked rules. They contained behavior, kept unruliness in check, and were, all in all, a superb way of ordering one's life.

But even he wasn't as bound by them as Mrs. Adams was. If she had her way, single people would spend each day in contemplation and prayer, with only two hours on Sunday for relaxation.

How was a fellow to court a girl with those rules?

Silas froze. *Undo that thought. Scratch it out.*

He didn't mean he would court a girl. Oh, not at all! He had better things to do than that. Professor Barkley addressed this repeatedly, so much so that Silas could quote him word for word. But just to be sure, he picked up the *Patented Five Year Plan for Success* and reread it:

> *A romantic entanglement is just that, an entanglement. It becomes a knot that cannot be loosened. Beware of such a thing. Look instead for a friend-ship, a good, deep friendship that runs as pure and true as an underground stream. That is to be valued. The Good Book says, "A friend loveth at all times."*

The Bible had always been a reliable set of rules. You couldn't top the Ten Commandments for clear regulations on how to live. Those commandments, added to *"Thou shalt love the Lord thy God with all thy heart, and with all thy soul, and with all thy strength"* summed up an outline for an ethical life.

Ethical and uncomplicated. Unfortunately they weren't the same. If everyone lived by the rules, life would be so much easier than it was now.

For one thing, his uncle wouldn't be marrying someone he'd wooed across the country, someone with the improbable name of Hyacinth. What kind of name was Hyacinth anyway? What was wrong with a good solid name like Mary or Catherine or Sarah?

Or Eliza. He knew he was in dangerous territory with her. He was old enough to realize what was going on. He'd had girlfriends before, when he'd been a raw teenage boy. But now, it was different. He thought of her entirely too much, and lately he'd been revisiting their first meeting, when she had fallen into his arms, smelling of blueberries and soap.

She'd felt much too good in his arms. It would be easy to let his heart lead him right to her, to let himself go ahead and fall in love with her, but there was something in the way.

For one thing, he had too many unanswered questions about her life before she came here. Of course, he hadn't actually asked any of these questions, he had to admit, but maybe the time had come to do so.

He should make a list.

He padded over to the small table and found a pen and a piece of paper, and he sat down.

First order of business, he told himself, in making any list was to label it neatly. And so he did. *Questions for Miss Eliza Davis.*

Already he felt better. He did like lists.

He continued, buoyed by knowing that this would help. He wrote the first question.

1. Why did you leave St. Paul?

She'd already told him a bit, but he needed more information. Moving, as he well knew, wasn't a process to be undertaken lightly. It was dreadful, all the sorting and packing, and then the actual move itself, followed by more unpacking and resorting. Nobody did it unless there was no other option. Eliza hadn't brought much with her—just that large carpetbag—but as far as he knew, maybe she didn't have any furniture to bring with her. Plus there was the awkward matter of the scoundrel that she'd had some kind of encounter with. He'd like to know more about that.

2. Why did you come back to Remembrance?

Again, she'd told him somewhat superficially, but he wanted more detail. She'd left here when she was a child. What were her memories of Remembrance that drew her back? He smiled, satisfied that this was an extraordinarily good question.

3. Do you intend to stay in Remembrance? Why?

That was actually two questions, but they needed each other.

4. What makes you happiest? What has made you cry? What do you need? Do you like me?

The last question slipped in, and he caught it before he wrote it down.

He carefully folded the paper and put it in his Bible. He'd take another look at it tomorrow.

Silas extinguished the lamp, knelt beside the bed, said his prayers of thanksgiving—Professor Barkley noted that one must always acknowledge all gifts—and moved on to his prayers of intercession. As always, the Robbins family was front and center. He didn't understand why God had done what He had done, but the Lord was sovereign and to be trusted.

His prayers for Eliza meandered off track into prayers that were more for him than her. She needed to stay—he needed her to stay. She needed to feel safe—he needed to reassure her. She needed to be loved—and he loved her.

If he hadn't been so tired, he might have fought the last one. But it sat right in his mind, a thought as warm and comfortable as hot cocoa. He let it stay.

He closed with requesting blessings on those near and far—he'd long ago figured that ought to cover everyone and everything—and got into bed.

A list. He had made a list. He smiled. This was the way to proceed. A list.

Chapter 8

I hope that's all right with you," Hyacinth said to Eliza as they sat in the parlor of the boardinghouse. "It just came to me that it would work out for both of us, and you know how I am. My mind thinks it, and my mouth says it."

Eliza reached over and squeezed Hyacinth's hand. "You have no idea how much I appreciate it. When Mrs. Adams said she was closing the boardinghouse in two weeks, I thought I might end up homeless."

"Don't worry about that. I'd never let it happen." Hyacinth's eyes twinkled dangerously. "There's a young man in Remembrance who seems quite taken with you, and I'd like to see the two of you together."

Heat shot up Eliza's neck and into her face, and she knew she was blushing. "I don't think so."

"It would be wonderful. We could have a double wedding, and—"

"Oh, stop it!" Eliza interjected, laughing. "We're just friends."

Hyacinth nodded. "You are, and that's the best way to start a lifelong relationship. You need the basis of friendship—you need to like each other as well as love each other."

"Is that the way your marriage was?" Eliza asked softly.

"It was. He was my best friend, and I knew I could trust him with my heart. So I did."

"It must have been very hard when he died."

Tears filled Hyacinth's eyes. "Even now, it still hurts so bad that there are times I think I can't bear it. And when he died, and our son was so young, I didn't know how I could go on another day."

"But you did."

"I did. I had to. Thomas, our son, had to. We had to go on living even when my husband couldn't."

"You must be proud of your son."

"I am. When his father died, he took up the farm work. He was probably old enough by most people's standards—he was twelve—but he was my little boy. I wish you could have seen him, standing behind that big plow, trying to guide it through the packed earth while the patient horses walked just a bit slower, as if they knew that it wasn't Matthew behind the plow, but Thomas." Her eyes glowed with the memory.

"Might I ask another question?" Eliza ventured.

"You can ask. Until I hear the question, I don't know if I'll answer."

"What does your son think of you marrying Edward?"

"He has some hesitation, which I understand." Hyacinth smoothed the fabric of her dress over her lap, and a slight smile curved her lips. "Of course, no one is good enough for me in his mind. But he wants me to be happy, and he understands that, even though this hasn't been the most conventional courtship, it works for us."

A movement outside the window of the parlor caught Eliza's attention. "Silas is here." She clapped her hand over her mouth. "I wonder if he's expecting me to go to the Robbins house today."

"I want to go over there again," Hyacinth said. "Analia needs someone to brush her hair and fix it for her. And so does Mary Robbins. I'm not an expert at it, but I do like doing it."

"That would be wonderful! I know Analia really enjoyed your 'lady time.' Mary's asked about you, too. Plus you'd get to see what's happening with the material you purchased. You'd be very welcome there."

"If Silas agrees. Honestly, sometimes I just don't know about that one."

As soon as Silas entered the parlor, with Mrs. Adams watchfully behind him, Hyacinth asked if she might go over.

"Absolutely," he said. "I was just there, as a matter of fact. The boys are having a heyday making swords out of leftover pieces of wood from the banister we replaced, and the poor little girl is stuck with a book in the corner, looking a bit overwhelmed. I don't think she's very interested in swords, and I suspect she'd like some female company."

Hyacinth stood up immediately. "I'll go over now."

"While you're there, Eliza and I will go check on the house where you'll be staying to see what's left to be done," Silas said.

"You mean Birdbath House?" Hyacinth asked with a wink at Eliza.

"Birdbath House?" Silas looked at them blankly. "It's the old Lindstrom place."

"The Lindstroms have been gone from Remembrance for almost seven years," Mrs. Adams said from the doorway.

"Then it shouldn't be called the old Lindstrom place, should it?" Eliza asked, joining in. "It should be called the new Mason place, or the Mason-Davis place."

"Or Birdbath House, since it has a birdbath." Hyacinth was buttoning her coat as she spoke.

"But what if the birdbath falls over, or is taken off the property?" Silas asked.

"Then it'll be the old Birdbath House, won't it?" Hyacinth chuckled. "Or Remembrance could give in and number the houses, and it'll be something as prosaic as 13 Oak Street."

Her laughter ringing behind her, Hyacinth swept out of the boardinghouse.

"It's not too cold outside," Silas said, "but it'll be cold at the house—Birdbath House, I guess I need to start calling it, although I've never heard of anything quite so silly. We'll need to check the stove and the fireplace while we're there to make sure nothing is blocked, no nests in the stovepipe or the flue."

Mrs. Adams cleared her throat. "I don't believe that a man and woman should be alone until they're married."

Silas sputtered wordlessly, and Eliza took his arm and smiled at the landlady. "We're only going to inspect and clean the house. Marriage hardly seems necessary for that."

Mrs. Adams stepped aside as they left, her disapproval following them out the door.

"I shouldn't have said that," Eliza said. "She means well."

"I imagine you'll be glad to leave there," Silas said as they headed out into the sunny afternoon. "It must be like living under a magnifying glass. She watches everything that you do."

"She does have definite ideas of right and wrong," Eliza said, loosening her muffler a bit. With the sun beaming overhead, the air seemed warm. "According to her, though, mostly everything is wrong. I appreciate the way she takes care of us, although I feel like a chicken that has hatched but the mother hen still insists on sitting on it."

He grinned. "What an image! I think she'd probably suffocate you."

"It feels like it sometimes."

The walk to the small house was short, and they were soon there.

The snow had begun to melt from the roof, and a steady drip from the corner suggested that some repair might be necessary on the eaves. He opened the door for her.

It was definitely a small house. The rooms were tiny, with barely enough space to fit the dusty couch and the single wooden chair in the front room, and the two bedrooms each contained a small bed and bureau, which took up most of the space. The kitchen was oddly shaped, running along the entire back of the house, like a long narrow corridor.

"This was added on later," he said before she could ask the question. "If I'd built it, I believe I might have made it a foot or two wider, but what's done is done. I could take down this outer wall here, though, and expand this part."

Silas walked through the house, muttering about the changes that needed to be made.

The scent of old wallboards and wood smoke mingled with the slightly sour smell of a house that hadn't been aired out recently. The furniture had seen better days, to say the least. The textured tapestry of the sofa was worn in the shape of bodies that had sat in the same spot for years. Eliza ran her hand over the arm of the couch, and a tiny mouse scurried out from under the throw pillow.

"We will bring a cat in," Silas said, and she suppressed a smile at the little shiver of revulsion that he unsuccessfully hid. He looked for all the world as if he'd like to have fled from the room, back into the outdoors where mice crept and hid in bushes and rocks, not in the furniture.

"Not a fan of mice, are you?" she asked.

His laugh sounded a bit choked. "Who is? No, we'll bring in a cat."

"Can I keep it?"

"The mouse or the cat?"

Eliza had to grin. "The cat. Or will we be borrowing it?"

"There are enough barn cats in this neck of woods that I think we can accommodate you with a cat of your own. For a while, it was quite the booming industry, selling mousers to the townspeople, but nowadays, the farmers are just as happy to give you a kitten or two."

A cat. Eliza wanted to hug herself. She loved cats, but she hadn't had one since Tim and Hannah, the two she'd had when she lived in Remembrance. She gave them away when she left, and it broke her young girl's heart.

Now she'd have a cat again, at least for a while.

Silas was examining the stove. "It looks like it's been cleaned out, so I think it'll hold a good fire for you and Hyacinth." He looked doubtfully at the sofa. "Are you going to want to keep this furniture?"

She shook her head. One thing she knew for sure was that if she saw one mouse, there were another ninety-nine she didn't see. "I want to share the house with Hyacinth, not the rodents, and I suspect they've made their own homes in the furniture. We've already talked to Mrs. Adams about taking some of her furniture."

"Excellent idea." He grinned impishly. "And somehow I don't think that she allows mice in her house."

If the sofa was this bad, she could only imagine what shape the beds were in. The thought of mice living in the mattress beneath her would keep her from ever sleeping in this house. They'd undoubtedly burrowed their way in and made nests.

She shuddered at the thought. Yes, a much better idea was to jettison the furnishings that were there and replace them with ones from the boardinghouse.

"Hyacinth and I will talk to Mrs. Adams this afternoon about the furniture. Do you think you can bring in a cat as soon as possible?" A shadow darted along the corner of the room. "Preferably a hungry cat. A very big, very hungry cat."

"I know a fellow outside of town who's got just the creature for you. Big ugly thing."

"Who, the cat or the fellow?"

He laughed. "I meant the cat, but he's not much to look at either. Say, why don't you come with me? We can go now, and you can meet both of them—the man and the cat."

A ride in the country sounded wonderful, and soon they were both wrapped in thick blankets in his wagon, bouncing along the still-frozen ruts of the road out of Remembrance. "You'll like Carl," Silas said, speaking loudly over the creaks of the wheels. "He's a good Norwegian, a real honest sort. He doesn't come into town much, but every once in a while he'll show up at church or for a social or something."

Soon he pulled into a small farm, and a man in a thick jacket came out from the barn to greet them. "Howdy now," he said, his voice thickly accented with a Nordic lilt. "What brings you out today?"

"This is Eliza Davis," Silas said, "and she needs a cat. She's moving into the old Lindstrom place, and there are mice in it."

The large blond man nodded. *"Uff da."* Eliza didn't speak Norwegian, but she knew what that meant. It was the catchall phrase that roughly translated to *Oh my.* "Do you want to borrow Slick Tom, or do you want a kitten?"

"Slick Tom?" Eliza asked, and Carl nodded.

"I'll be right back." He disappeared into the barn and emerged a few minutes later with a gigantic yellow cat draped over his arm. "This is Slick Tom." The cat opened its eyes sleepily at the mention of its name.

One of Slick Tom's ears was half gone, and his back was striped with scars, visible through his scruffy fur. She reached out and touched his head, and the cat produced a purr that must have been audible the next farmyard over.

"He's wonderful," she murmured.

"Yah, he is a good mouser," Carl said. "I'll send him back with you, and he'll have the place cleared out in two days. You might want to get a kitten, too, though. All the kits are from Slick Tom, so they've got his talent." He handed Slick Tom to Silas, who looked as if he'd just been given a crocodile.

Carl grinned at Eliza. "Silas ain't much for cats."

"His loss," she said, hiding her amusement as best she could when Slick Tom stuck his gigantic head under Silas's chin and sighed with pleasure.

Again Carl went into the barn, and this time he came out with a gray-striped kitten. "This is a girl. She'll be a good hunter. You can tell by the ears, you know."

"Of course," she murmured, although she had no idea what that meant. She was too enchanted with the kitten that curled up against her chest.

"Your good mousers will have large ears," Carl explained. "Helps them hear the mice. Now here's what you do. Put them both in the house. Slick Tom knows what to do, and by the time he's got all the mice out, this little gray will have learned from him. Bring him back, and you can keep the girl."

Silas helped her into the wagon and handed her Slick Tom. Immediately the oversized cat curled up into a ball on her lap while the kitten chewed on the button of her coat.

Two cats on her lap, and Silas at her side. Life was lovely.

⌒

Silas opened the door of Birdbath House. Twilight had crept early across the land, and the hard chill of the night was settling in.

"Here, kitty-kitty-kitty," he called, feeling like an idiot. But one couldn't exactly talk to a cat like one would to, say, a business associate. He tried it. "Good evening, Mr. Slick Tom and Miss, I'm sorry I didn't catch your name earlier. Has the day been profitable?"

He lit the lamp that was on the table, and a circle of light illuminated the room. "Oh, I shouldn't have done that."

The day's catch was laid out in a tidy line with the two cats, the big yellow one and the little gray one, sitting proudly beside the row. He patted each cat awkwardly on the head, told them each what good hunters they were, and left them to their spoils. He'd check the next day to make sure the harvest was taken care of before bringing Eliza over.

Eliza. How easily—and how completely—she had moved into his life. She was a complication he never foresaw, despite Professor Barkley's warnings about being prepared for the unexpected.

What would he have done if he had known she was coming into his life? What if he *had* been able to expect the unexpected?

He shook his head. Much more thinking like this, and he'd be as loony as his uncle.

Love was what it was. There was no use complicating it by trying to figure out the *how* or the *why*. Just the *who* was enough.

Suddenly Slick Tom sailed through the air and pounced on something. As the cat came back, the prize dangling in his mouth, Silas decided he'd continue this train of thought in the safety of his own rodent-free home.

Until Slick Tom finished the job here, Silas knew he wouldn't be lingering at Birdbath House.

⌒

Eliza watched Silas as he read. They were waiting for Hyacinth and Edward to return from a short walk. Edward rarely used the cane, and soon he wouldn't need it at all.

Silas had picked up a treatise on the properties of knowledge. It seemed too thin to cover the topic at all well, but she kept that to herself.

He'd offered her a newspaper, or another book, but she refused. What she needed to say would make concentration impossible.

"Silas," she said, twisting in the seat uncomfortably, "I need to talk to you." She clenched her fingers around the arms of the chair, not to keep her on the slippery cushion but to keep her from fleeing the house.

He raised his head from his book and slowly focused on her. She'd come to anticipate that expression with delight. He had the ability to completely immerse himself in whatever he read, and he moved so slowly into the world of reality.

"Yes?" He took his wire-rimmed glasses off.

"I have to—" She stopped. "I must— I need to—"

He smiled slightly. "Then by all means, you should."

"When I was in St. Paul, I knew Blaine Loring." The words sprang out.

"Blaine Loring?" He put his glasses back on, as if they helped him understand her better. "The name is somewhat familiar, but I can't place it right now."

God, help me, please. Obviously she'd need some divine help if she were to tell him the whole sordid story.

She squeezed the arms of the chair even tighter. "He's the man that Edward read about from the paper. He took money from young women in St. Paul, claiming he was going to invest it for them, when in fact, he didn't."

Silas's brow wrinkled with concern. "Oh, Eliza, he took advantage of you, too? I was afraid of that."

"Well, yes." This was not getting any easier.

"How much did you lose?"

She lowered her head. "I didn't lose any money," she whispered at last, the hand of guilt wrapped firmly around her heart.

"I don't understand."

Eliza swallowed hard. There was nothing to do at this stage but to barrel on through. "I thought Blaine and I were in love. He could charm the wool off a sheep."

"The wool off a sheep?" he asked blankly.

"It's a phrase my father used to describe someone who could talk people out of whatever he wanted. That was Blaine Loring. His 'love' for me was only a cover."

Silas's lips thinned to a hard line. "Are you telling me that Loring took liberties with you? That he abused your innocence?"

Eliza's face flushed even hotter. "No! Not that! I mean that he saw in me someone who could help him with his snake oil plan. He made me think that he loved me, and I was so gullible that I believed him."

"Eliza," Silas said, leaning closer, "we should thank God that you weren't prey to his swindle. I'm sure that you weren't the only one he charmed."

"Probably. But I might be the only one who helped him with his con game."

She put her head in her hands.

"You helped him? How?" Disbelief rang in his voice.

She wanted to get up, to run from this house, to leave Remembrance. This had been a terrible, terrible idea.

"I was the go-between. I convinced the other women in service to the wealthy families in St. Paul to give their money to him. He had a plan, he said, that would let them double, triple, maybe quadruple what they'd given him."

"How much money—how many of these women are we talking about?"

Eliza blinked back the tears that stung her eyes. "I don't know how much money. How many women did I bring to this? Twenty-five, maybe thirty."

She didn't want to revive the memory of how she'd taken advantage of these women for him, how she sacrificed their friendships. He changed her enough that she stopped seeing them as friends. Instead, they'd all become investors. That made him happy—and she recreated her life just to keep him happy.

"What did you tell them?" he asked stiffly. "Did you tell them that investments aren't sure things?"

"No. I told them there was no risk at all. That's what he told me, and that's what I told them." Her stomach twisted. "How could I have been so foolish?"

"And what did he promise you? Some of the money? A cut of the profits?"

"No! I did it because I thought we'd be together. I did it because I thought I loved him. I did it because I thought he loved me." Her voice caught in a sob.

Silas was silent. The ticking of the clock on the mantel was the only sound.

"Do you see what I've done?" she asked him, the words ragged as she tried to talk around the pain. "I helped him. I did. And—God forgive me—I hurt my friends. And what do I have left? Only guilt."

Her fingers gripped the arms of the chair. "I don't know much about the law, but I suspect that what he did was illegal. Silas, do you see? I helped him. I helped him! That makes me an accomplice."

He stared past her, his face a stony mask.

"Say something," she begged.

He stood up and turned to leave the room.

"Please. You must say something." She knew she was pleading, but it meant so much to her. "Say you hate me. Say I disgust you. Say—please say you forgive me."

He stopped. When he spoke, he was still facing the door, not her. "I don't hate you. I don't find you disgusting. I have one question for you, though."

"What is it?"

"If you believed him, if you thought what you offered your friends was a true investment, why didn't you invest in it, too?"

Her breath froze in her chest. Why, indeed, hadn't she? The answer was too horrible to consider.

He left the room. She was left alone by the fireplace, but she was colder than she could ever have imagined. Even the flames burning behind the hearth couldn't warm the iciness that had enclosed her heart with his final words.

She stood up, got her wrap from the coat tree by the front door, and let herself out. The sun was shining brightly, and the winter birds were singing, but she was only vaguely aware of them.

When she'd come to Remembrance, she'd run away from everything associated with Blaine Loring—or so she thought. But she hadn't been able to escape the stain that was on her soul.

She needed somebody to forgive her. Silas? God? Herself?

⌒

"So I've got my eye on the ruby ring I saw advertised in the Duluth paper," Edward said at the dinner table. "I think Hyacinth would like it, don't you?"

"Yes." Silas shoved the piece of potato through the gravy on his plate until it came apart.

"I'd like to go to Duluth fairly soon to look at it. Would you like to go?"

"Yes." A green bean began to make the same trip through the gravy.

"Good. And we'll look into getting a panda as a pet and riding grasshoppers onto the moon."

"That would be fine."

"Silas, would you pay attention? You haven't heard a word I've said, have you?" Edward frowned at his nephew.

"I heard," Silas protested. "A ring, Duluth, and—oh, I don't know. Sorry, I wasn't focusing."

"What's wrong? You've been in a slump all evening."

Silas shoved his plate away. The dinner was undoubtedly tasty, but it all sat like dry cardboard in his mouth. "Guess I'm not hungry."

"Guess you're in love."

"In love? With whom?" Silas glared at his uncle. Truly he had lost his mind. Eliza was—well, she was Eliza.

His uncle smiled. "I'd say that Eliza Davis has done a job on your heart."

Silas snorted. "You are mistaken. Eliza has done nothing to my heart, nothing at all."

"Love doesn't have to be this painful experience you're making it out to be. Let yourself enjoy it."

"The way you are?" Silas snapped. "You and Hyacinth? Are you insane?"

Uncle Edward nodded happily. "Yes, indeed. Insane with love."

"I don't believe you're saying this." Silas pushed his chair away from the table so furiously that it fell over. "Just because you and Hyacinth act like a couple of moonstruck youngsters doesn't mean that everyone has to be in love. I'm not in love with Eliza. Not at all."

He slammed his napkin onto the table and stalked out of the dining room.

In love with Eliza. What an inane thing to say. How could he love someone who had participated in such a blackguardly deal as she did, bilking young women out of their savings? Here he'd thought she was innocent, when in fact she was completely the opposite.

He went up to his bedroom, the only place in the house where he was guaranteed a modicum of privacy.

In love with Eliza. Humph.

Some time with the Word might settle his spirit. He sat at his table and opened his Bible, and as he did so, a piece of blue paper fluttered to the ground.

It was the list. What a silly piece of business that had been. He was such a fool to have been taken in by her.

Had it been just yesterday that he'd written it? He couldn't stop himself from unfolding the list and rereading it.

Why did you leave St. Paul? He didn't need to ask that question anymore. He had the answer.

Why did you come back to Remembrance? He could figure that one out on his own. She was running, trying to escape the proverbial long arm of the law.

Do you intend to stay in Remembrance? Why? Again, that had become quite clear. Remembrance was a tiny dot on a map. No one would think to look for her here.

What makes you happiest? What has made you cry? What do you need? He didn't even want to know the answers to these questions, but they answered themselves anyway. Swindling people made her happy. Getting caught made her cry. She needed someone to hide her.

Then there was the question he hadn't written on the paper, only in his mind. *Do you like me?*

He buried his face in his hands.

Why had God done this to him? Why had God let him fall in love with a criminal?

His pulse hammered in his temples. No, no, no.

He had just admitted it to himself. He was in love with her. Despite the litany of reasons he shouldn't love her, he did. It made the pain that much worse.

Darkness washed into his room, and still he sat at the table, stricken by the realization—and the nasty corollary that came with it. He loved her, and he couldn't. He could not love someone who was as morally flawed as she was.

So this was what heartache was, he thought almost detachedly. No wonder the poets wrote of it and the musicians sang of it.

What was he to do? Professor Barkley hadn't dealt with this, but he also

311

repeatedly warned against the knotty experience of love. There was no point in consulting the *Five Year Plan* to see what counsel the professor would give.

He opened his Bible and found the comfort verse of the Lord's Prayer in the book of Matthew. The triumph of the last lines, *"For thine is the kingdom, and the power, and the glory, for ever,"* never failed to elevate his mood. That was the promise of the prayer.

With a start, he noticed the two verses that follow the Lord's Prayer: *"For if ye forgive men their trespasses, your heavenly Father will also forgive you: But if ye forgive not men their trespasses, neither will your Father forgive your trespasses."*

How could he have missed the lines before? It was as if God was speaking directly to him, pointing out the divinity of forgiveness, and the necessity of the act of forgiveness.

He had refused to forgive Eliza. Clearly he was wrong. He recalled the words of the sermon Reverend Tupper had preached. Forgiveness was the first step to renewing the relationship between God and himself, to restore the bond of Creator and creation. Now it was his turn to work on his own "clean heart."

And it was time to start learning how to love.

Chapter 9

"We're all going to the Robbins's house today," Hyacinth announced the next morning at breakfast. "Eliza dear, are you sure you're not sick? Your eyes are bloodshot."

"I'll be fine. I can't guarantee how straight my seams will be, though." Eliza manufactured a smile. The last thing she wanted to do was to be around Silas, but Analia's striped dress was so close to being done that she could probably finish it today.

She had no choice. She had to go.

Actually it was probably not going to be a problem anyway. The way Silas had walked from her, oozing disapproval, meant that he probably would manage to stay as far away from her as he could.

"We're meeting at Edward and Silas's house," Hyacinth continued. "Edward wants to show me something." She leaned over and in a conspiratorial whisper said, "I think it's a ring."

Eliza mustered up all the enthusiasm she could. Even if her life had fallen into shreds, she needed to be upbeat about her friend's romance. "Did he get it? What does it look like?"

"I don't think he has it yet. We'll see when we get over there."

I don't want to do this. I don't want to do this. I don't want to do this. The silent words echoed through Eliza's mind as she and Hyacinth walked over to the Collier house.

Edward sat by the window, his ever-present Duluth newspaper in his hands, but this time it was folded open to a particular page. "Hyacinth, my Morning Flower!"

Silas looked at the ceiling and rolled his eyes as he mouthed, *My Morning Flower?*

Edward was showing Hyacinth an advertisement in the paper. "Do you like it?" he asked, and in response got a loud kiss from her. He winked at Eliza. "I guess she does!"

Hyacinth danced over to Eliza and held the paper out. "Look at this ring! Isn't it beautiful? It's to be my wedding ring!"

It was indeed a lovely ring, but Eliza's eyes were riveted on the story beside the advertisement. It was a short news story, stating simply that without further evidence, the case against Blaine Loring would be dropped.

Had Silas seen it? She must know.

"Let's leave the lovebirds alone for a moment," she suggested to him. "I'd like some tea before we go to the Robbins house."

"Of course." Silas looked confused but followed her into the kitchen.

"Did you read the paper?" she asked without preamble as he put some water on to boil.

"My uncle showed me the advertisement for the ring if that's what you mean. Why, do you think that she really won't like it?"

Eliza shook her head vigorously. "Not the ring. It's beautiful, and she'll wear it proudly. No, I mean the story next to it."

"I guess I was too busy watching Uncle Edward extol the virtues of the ring. Why?"

"The case against Blaine is going to be dropped for lack of evidence."

He froze. "That would be a good thing for you," he said, overly polite. "It lets you off."

"No, it's not a good thing for anyone. I wasn't part of this, not knowingly at any rate. You have to believe me. I want him to go to jail for what he did. If he isn't prosecuted, he'll do it again."

He had to believe her, had to understand what happened. He had no idea the pain she was in, how it was eating at her.

"So what do you intend to do about it?" He measured tea into a strainer and laid it over a cup.

"What can I do?" She clutched his arm. "Really, Silas, what can I do?"

"You could provide a statement."

She shook her head. "I've already thought of that, but it won't work. St. Paul isn't like Remembrance. No one is going to believe me. I'm just the voice of a young workingwoman, one who has been spurned, no less. Do you think my testimony would carry any weight?"

"So what's your solution, then? Either you do something, or you don't."

"It's not that simple."

"Isn't it?"

He picked up a pencil and one of his uncle's old newspapers, and in large strokes, drew a square. In it he wrote *Problem*. Under it he added two slanting lines, labeled *Do something* and *Do nothing*.

"But do what?" she asked impatiently. Sometimes he was so analytical that he couldn't see that reality and logic were often on two different planes entirely.

"You go to the police. You tell them what you know, and justice will take its due course." He spoke plainly and flatly, as if he were explaining it to a child.

"You're a man, Silas, a man with some status. You're respected for your gender and your career at the very least. I'm a woman, a seamstress, and as if that weren't bad enough, he rejected me. I'm the cast-off woman, so whatever I say will be dismissed as my attempt at retribution."

"Really, Eliza. You've certainly got this thought through." His voice was cold.

"Don't you understand that you could tell the police what happened, and you'd be believed? I doubt that I would. Think about it, Silas. Think about it!"

"You want me to testify for you?"

Oh, he was so maddening. "No, I don't."

The teakettle whistled, and he took it off the flame and poured the water over the tea in the strainer. "Eliza, it really is as simple as I've shown you. Now you have to decide which of these"—he moved the teacup aside and ran his finger over the diagram—"you will do."

There was no point in going further with him. Any discussion simply cemented his concept of her as being a willing participant in the sordid situation.

"You're right," she said. She picked the cup from the table and swirled the steaming tea in it, anything to keep him from seeing how badly her hands were shaking. She couldn't bear to look at him. If he saw the hot anger in her eyes, he'd once again misinterpret it.

All she'd wanted was support from him. That's what friends did. Was it too much to ask of him? Apparently so. She'd failed whatever test of logic and reasoning he'd set up, and that failure was enough for him to sever their friendship.

What he hadn't bargained for, though, was that by his very actions, he failed her test—her test of friendship, of caring, of love.

She gulped the tea, ignoring the burning path it seared in her mouth and throat. This was the least of her concerns.

"I'm ready to leave now."

As she began to step out of the kitchen, he put a restraining hand on her arm. "Wait. I don't think we've finished here."

"Oh, we've finished. I have nothing more to say. Now I will go to do what I know how to do—sew. I am going to stitch down seams and make buttonholes in five shirts and hem a dress. I will do it well, and I will do it now, because I am leaving."

"I don't mean to—" He held out his hand as if to stop her.

"I don't care. Maybe I will care tonight and maybe I will tomorrow, but right now I don't. You let me down. I wanted you to be there for me, to listen, to help me see my way through this mess, but you don't want to hear anything except your simplistic little diagram." She strode back into the room and seized it from the table and shook it in front of him. "Two lines. That's all. Two lines. Do you really think life is made that way? Two lines? Two completely straight lines?"

She could hear herself. She was out of control, raging at him. He stared at her, his astonishment so clear it might as well have been written on his face.

She couldn't stop. "The crux of the matter here is that I needed you, and you not only refused to support me, you turned away. Even if you think I am the worst sinner in the world, even if my soul is stained so badly that it reeks of transgression, who are you to dismiss me?" Tears crowded into her eyes. "I thought we were friends. I thought we were—"

In one step, he had her in his arms, his lips buried in her hair, half-kissing, half-murmuring reassurances. She leaned against him, knowing that the tears, which were now flowing freely, were soaking into his shirt. He smelled of clean cotton, a bit of wood smoke, and shaving cream. He smelled of strength.

Their words tumbled over each other's until they could no longer tell which one was speaking.

"I'm sorry. . .always. . .forever. . .love you."

She'd needed this. Tenderness wasn't Blaine Loring's style, to say the least.

But being held by Silas was comforting, and his energy flowed into her.

How long had it been since she'd felt this safe, this protected? She didn't want to move. If she could stay right where she was, enclosed in Silas's embrace, the world could spin on in its crazy course, and it wouldn't touch her.

A chorus of less-than-subtle coughs from the doorway told her they weren't alone. She and Silas sprang apart quickly.

"Now there are a couple of guilty looking mugs," Edward said, grinning.

"Guilty? I'd say happy." Hyacinth beamed at them both.

Eliza glanced at Silas. His face was bright red. "We need to get to the Robbins house," he said almost gruffly, without even a glance at Eliza.

The feeling of well-being evaporated. The moment of tenderness was short-lived, and he was back to being distant.

"We're going to have to have a talk, you and I," Edward said, putting his arm around his nephew as they headed for the door. "You're missing something here, something pretty important."

Hyacinth hung back and let the men leave the room. Then she looped her arm through Eliza's. "Men," she said in a conspiratorial whisper. "Some of them are like horses."

"Horses?" Eliza stared at her friend. "What are you talking about?"

"You have to train a horse," Hyacinth said, "and you have to train a man, too. My Matthew was just like Silas at the beginning. He had an incredible mind for the business of running the farm. He knew where every penny went. Nothing escaped him. Nothing except how to love."

"But shouldn't it come naturally?"

"Honey, Matthew loved me. I never had a moment's doubt about that, but he wasn't good at all with understanding that love is like a busy city street. Traffic goes both ways. To him, and from him. To me, and from me. Once he learned that I needed love from him, and I don't just mean kissing and hugging—I mean the special look over a shared memory, or a wildflower picked because he knew I'd like it, or making a cup of tea for me without my having to ask for it—then our marriage became extraordinary."

"I can't train Silas. The fact is, he isn't a horse. What do I do, tempt him with a handful of oats?"

Hyacinth laughed. "Now that I'd like to see. Eliza, you're misunderstanding me. Silas's heart isn't prepared for love. I think he's been completely blindsided by you. His heart will have to soften to let you into it. Right now he's resisting loving you. It couldn't be more obvious if he plastered a sign on the door of the mercantile. When I say you need to train him, I mean you need to help him open his heart so that the two of you can have the greatest love possible."

Eliza put her hands over her ears. "Stop! I can't change Silas. You know what he's like. You might as well be telling me to flap my arms and fly to the moon."

"I know it seems that way, but you can do it."

Eliza shook her head. "I don't want to. You're presuming I want Silas to love me. Well, I don't. I don't love him, and he doesn't love me."

"Eliza, that's not true."

She couldn't tell anymore. Her heart had been so battered with Blaine Loring that she thought it might never recover. Just minutes ago, Silas had held her tightly and said something about love—and then promptly rejected her again.

Hyacinth sighed. "Young love. It's never easy."

"It's not love. Haven't you watched him around me? He doesn't love me."

"Oh, I've watched both of you, and he does love you. He's sneaky about it, and he doesn't let you see it, and he's fighting it with everything he's got and whatever else he can borrow, but he's smitten."

Eliza shook her head. "You're seeing what you want to see. You're in love with Edward, and you want Silas and me to be in love."

"I do like a good love story," Hyacinth said, "and I'm a sap for a happy ending."

A good love story and a happy ending. Both seemed impossible.

"We'd better get going," Eliza said. "Buttonholes await."

~

There was no need to think about anything at the Robbins house, Silas thought. To tell the truth, there was no way to think, not with the chaos of six children eddying around him. Today they seemed especially rambunctious.

He'd put his hammer down to pick up the try square. The top of the cupboard seemed a bit off, and he wanted to make sure it was straight. He'd put the try square out of the reach of the children, who found the metal and rosewood tool to be fascinating. When he returned the try square to the toolbox and reached again for the hammer, it was gone, taken by a curious boy who was pounding a large nail into the middle of the board that was to be the center of the cupboard door.

Only by the grace of God had he not lost his temper. The board had been rendered unusable by the nail protruding from it, and he'd dug through the other pieces of wood to see if something else would work, and of course, he hadn't found a thing.

Now he rocked back on his heels, studying the partially assembled door and trying to figure out how to redeem the thing. He'd had the whole thing planned out, with every detail laid out so that no wood was wasted. Now not only was an expensive piece of wood wasted, but he'd have to buy more, and it wouldn't match. . . .

This was frustrating.

He was trying to help, but there were so many impediments. No wonder Jack hadn't been able to keep up with the household repairs. Who could?

A small arm snaked around his shoulders, and a sticky mouth pressed against his cheek. "It's a pretty door," little Mark said, his two-year-old body leaning against Silas's. "When I grow up, I want to be a wood-pounder like you."

His anger evaporated. A wood-pounder!

"You'll be a great wood-pounder," he said, hugging the boy back.

"Do you like my shirt?" Mark asked, puffing his chest out as much as he could. "Miss Davis just finished it, and she said I look very handsome indeed."

Silas glanced up, but Eliza was bent over another shirt, her bottom lip caught in her teeth as she worked. The sunlight caught a light reddish tinge of her hair, making it almost bronze. A single lock of hair had escaped the coiled bun at the back of her neck, and she pushed it out of the way, only to have it fall right back down again.

"Miss Davis knows fashion," Silas said, "so if she said you're very handsome in the shirt, then, my man, you are."

"I'm going to show my mother," the boy said, and with one last admiring look at the cupboard door, he darted off.

The boy certainly was a charmer, and he was obviously delighted with his new shirt. Silas peeked at Eliza again. She was sewing a button on a shirt that was a larger copy of Mark's. What a blessing she had been to this family.

He wasn't going to think about her now. He couldn't. For one thing, he needed to solve the puzzle of the wood.

Silas studied the wood laid out before him, trying to see if there was any solution to the problem. But he had planned precisely, and losing the big piece in the middle meant that it couldn't be done.

"Silas!" His uncle's voice boomed across the room.

"Uncle Edward?" He stood up, wincing as he realized his foot had gone to sleep. "What are you doing here?"

"I've got cabin fever. In case you hadn't noticed, my boy, this has been a long winter. My foot is almost healed, and I felt like a walk. So I thought I'd come over and see if I could help."

"Hyacinth is with Mrs. Robbins. Little Mark just ran in to show her his new shirt that Eliza made."

Uncle Edward picked his way carefully over to Silas's side. "You've got a lot of projects going on at once. Not being critical here, just commenting. . . ."

"It's true." Silas moved the stack of wood aside to make a path for his uncle. "I'm doing the cupboard now. It'll go right over here by the window."

"You trued it, didn't you?" Uncle Edward looked at the partially assembled piece. "It looks perfectly square."

"I put the try square on it again just a bit ago. I wanted to make sure it was perfect before I went any further."

"Excellent."

Uncle Edward's words meant much to Silas. He took great pride in his carpentry, and in the past months he'd taught Silas to do the same, even if it meant taking longer in the preparation.

"I do have a problem." Silas held up the board with the nail sticking out of it.

His uncle laughed. "I don't believe I've ever seen woodworking quite like that. Whatever possessed you to do that?"

"I can't take credit for it. I suspect one of the younger carpenters — or woodpounders, as Mark calls us—is responsible. Here's the situation: I have exactly enough wood, and my plan was—"

He explained it to his uncle, and when he had finished, he watched his uncle mentally analyze the dilemma.

"Hand me a pencil and paper," Uncle Edward said at last. "How about if you do this, and this, and this. You can lay the wood in at an angle. It's going to be more work, and you'll have to make sure you get the angle exactly the same on each piece, but you can do it if you use the miter square." He picked up the tool, like the try square but with the rosewood piece set at a slant. "It'll actually be very intriguing if you do it this way."

Uncle Edward was right. It was even more striking when the wood was placed in the door in an angular pattern. Still, he looked at his own plans, with the long slabs of wood placed in strict vertical lines, and he hated to let them go. But he had no choice.

He thanked his uncle, who stayed and watched and advised for a while before touring the rest of the house with Jack Robbins. Silas worked carefully and efficiently, and by the end of the afternoon, when night had stolen the daylight from the room, he lifted the finished piece into place.

"I like the design," Eliza said, as she came over to examine the new cupboard. "I know you had to change it, but it worked out."

"It did, didn't it?"

"Edward and Hyacinth have already left. I hope you don't mind walking with me." Was it his imagination, or did she stumble over the sentence?

"I don't mind." He hated the way the words came out, stiff and unwieldy.

They left the Robbins house and made their way without speaking to the boardinghouse. The silence was so heavy it was choking. He made an attempt at small talk. "When do you plan to move into the house?"

"Mrs. Adams hopes to leave in a week, so we will probably go in three or four days, depending on when her children arrive. Her daughter and her husband and her son will all be here to help her. They'll move the furniture we're taking into the house."

"And the cat?"

"Tiger is spending her days in the house, catching whatever mice might be bold enough to come in, although the Robbins children really like it when she comes with me. They must tucker her out pretty good. Whenever I go to leave, she's in with Mary, sound asleep."

He laughed. "Six children wear me out!"

"If she spends the day at Birdbath House, we go over at night and bring her to the boardinghouse. Mrs. Adams was fine with that, which surprised me. She told us initially that we couldn't have animals in the house. I believe her exact words were, 'No animals, not a cat, not a dog, not a chicken.'"

"A chicken?"

"I didn't ask. Well, maybe she's just ready to leave and that's why she lets Tiger stay."

"Maybe. Would you like to get the cat now? It'll save you an extra trip this evening." *And it'll give me more time with you,* he added mentally. Maybe he'd find a way to talk to her without sounding as if he'd been dipped in wax.

"If you don't mind, that would be wonderful."

Birdbath House was deeply shadowed, but the little cat was easy to find. She was waiting at the door for them and mewed when she saw Eliza. Eliza swept the kitten up and tucked her into her scarf. "I think she's hungry. Mrs. Adams saves her scraps of meat, and Tiger has become quite a fan of her cooking. I'd always heard that a cat won't mouse if it's fed, but apparently that's not true. Mrs. Adams told me that, and of course she's right."

He reached for the doorknob as she turned, and they met, their faces only inches apart. Automatically he put his hands on her shoulders to steady her, and for a moment, he couldn't move.

His silly chart that he had drawn out earlier reappeared in his mind, only this time in the box was written: *Kiss Her?* and from the bottom of it came two lines. One said *Yes*, and one said *No*.

His words came back to haunt him. It was simple, he had said. One path or the other.

Her eyes were deep blue in the faint light of the dying moon, and her lips were open just a bit.

He could kiss her. He wanted to, so very badly. But was it the right thing to do?

The image of that inane diagram flashed in front of him again. Yes? No? He chose, and he leaned forward, and she leaned forward, until their lips were almost touching. Suddenly with a flash of fur and tiny sharp claws, the cat squeezed free from between them, hissed angrily at him, and shot onto Eliza's shoulder.

"Who knew our chaperone would be so small?" she said, laughing somewhat shakily.

"And so effective." He touched her chin where Tiger had dug her claws in while making her getaway. "I think you're bleeding."

"Oh, great. Well, Silas, I do believe this is our cue to leave." She stepped back and peeled the cat from her shoulder and tucked her again into her scarf. "I need to get to the boardinghouse before Tiger here decides to eat my ear off or something."

"Eliza, we need to talk."

"Not now," she said, opening the door and stepping out into the winter night. "I'm not ready, and neither are you. We both have some deep praying to do. Today our emotions did our thinking. Maybe after we've had some food and some sleep and some prayer, we'll be able to use our brains, too."

He could only nod.

They didn't speak again until they came to the steps of the boardinghouse.

"Eliza," he said, clutching his hands together so they wouldn't reach out for her, "I meant it."

She stopped. "Meant what?"

"I meant it when I said I love you."

And with those words, he turned and walked away.

He knew what he had to do. He had to quit trying to figure it out, trying to justify it, or even trying to make sense of it all—whatever "it" was. Instead he needed to trust in the Lord and let his heart be open to His will.

Love was like the cupboard. He had his plan, his plan didn't work, and he found out that there was another plan that was even better than his. If it worked with cupboards, why wouldn't it work with love?

In his tired mind, it made sense.

Chapter 10

He loved her, did he? Could life become any more confused?

Eliza sat down at the table in her room and tried to think it through. If she was going to let herself fall in love with Silas—*as if that ship hadn't already sailed,* she added wryly—she was going to have to do something about the situation with Blaine Loring.

She slammed her fist on the table so hard that Tiger woke from her catnap with a start. She reached over and reassured the kitten, which promptly fell back asleep. It wasn't fair. She shouldn't have to still be dealing with the leftovers from that horrid situation. She should be done with it.

She was completely blameless, after all. She'd had no idea what he'd been doing with his nefarious plan.

Or had she?

She forced herself to revisit the earlier days of their romance, when he told her about his investment business. If it was a success, he'd be rich. She would have a fine house, lovely clothes, the chance to travel around the world.

Eliza rubbed her forehead with her fingertips as if she could erase those images. She'd been so young then, so innocent, so guileless. She'd been only a pawn in his evil business, drawn in by his alluring promises.

Suddenly she sat up as she realized the truth. She had to have known, but she'd managed to lie to herself, too. She wasn't stupid. She'd known, even then, that the money couldn't go in that many directions. The dollars that the nannies and cooks gave her couldn't make them and Blaine and her wealthy. Promises? No, lies.

She'd told herself she believed them because she wanted to, she had to. If she'd acknowledged the truth, that he was a crook, she would have had to commit to a life of thievery and deceit or give up Blaine Loring.

She had known, and she had continued.

Silas had seen it immediately. The day she poured out her heart to him, confessing her involvement with Blaine's scheme, he said he had one question for her—why hadn't she invested, too?

Was she stupid? Ignorant? Or had she purposely looked the other way? On some level, she'd known.

The realization was dreadful.

Her heart ached as she took in the consequences of the choice she'd made. So many lives had been hurt, so many dreams shattered and yet he was going to walk away, with no penalty of any kind. *Why would he?* she asked herself bitterly. The women had paid the price already.

She took out a sheet of paper and a pencil, and redrew the diagram Silas had made. *Problem?* And then, *Do nothing* and *Do something.*

She stared at what she had drawn. *Do nothing. Do something.* Did she really have any choice?

She slashed an *X* through *Do nothing* and penned a circle around *Do something.* The choice was made.

The time had come to take back her life, to rid herself of Blaine Loring's specter forever. She would go back to St. Paul.

There was time to catch the train through Remembrance. She still had some cash with her, though it was running low, and it should be enough to get her to the city again. She'd have to pack quickly, though.

She took her bag from the bottom of the armoire and opened it, getting ready to place into it two or three of her nicer dresses. The ivory wool was probably the best to wear before the police. It was a copy of one she'd made for the wife of a wealthy retailer, and it looked elegantly respectable.

She took the jacket off the hanger and folded it carefully. She wouldn't have time to steam it out later. As she opened the case wider to put the jacket in, she noticed a piece of paper sticking out from the bottom section of the bag.

She pulled it out, and her fingers trembled as she recognized Blaine's handwriting. She scanned through it and recognized what it was.

It was the list of investors she'd gone to deliver that fateful night in St. Paul. She'd been so horrified at the sight of him with another woman that she ran back home without giving it to him. Then she packed so quickly that she must have mindlessly put it in the bag.

She sat down and looked at what she held in her hands. It was more than a list of investors. It was a roster of all the women who had invested in his plan, with the amount they'd given him. According to the document, a ship was due to arrive in the Great Lakes with a cargo of fine porcelain, and the women as investors were owners of the contents, which would be sold at a great profit in Duluth.

There was something terribly wrong with that list. She studied it and read through it again and again, trying to decode what the problem was.

The names and numbers swam in front of her eyes until they quit making any sense at all.

14%
19%
17%
21%
15%
8%
13%
11%
20%

It just didn't add up. How could that be? Just that single column—and there were more—added up to 138 percent. There couldn't be 138 percent.

She must have added wrong. She checked her totals again. Still, the numbers added up to 138 percent. But the largest it could be was 100 percent.

There was only one delivery of porcelain that he sold portions to. All the women invested in the same shipment. It was like a bad mathematics problem but this time, she understood. It meant that—

She froze as she realized what he had done. He hadn't just stolen the money. No, this was more elaborate than that.

Fortunately his ego had been bigger than his brain, and he wrote everything down, probably so he could look at the numbers and enjoy how he outsmarted the women. He was such a small, little man, she realized. So small.

But his beautifully formatted list told the story that the police would want to hear. If they wouldn't listen to her, maybe they would listen to Blaine Loring himself—or at least his handwritten columns of proof.

She added together all the numbers, and found that in the end, he had promised nearly 350 percent of the profits to his investors. He promised a return that couldn't happen. He had vastly oversold the shipment—if indeed there ever was one.

He had, with great calculation, set out to take money from those who could spare it the least, and, even worse, he kept meticulous records of all the transactions.

Eliza bolted to her feet, once again startling the cat. "Tiger," she crowed happily, lifting the kitten to her face, "that's it! He kept records! He did! And do you know what? I have them! I have them, Tiger! *I have them!*"

She pulled on her coat and carefully put the piece of paper in her pocket. She'd find a safer place for it later. Right now she had to run over and tell Silas right away.

Her feet barely skimmed the stairs as she sped down out of the boarding-house. Vaguely she heard Mrs. Adams calling her, but she merely waved over her shoulder.

This was too important.

The lights were on in the Collier house, and she could see Silas and Edward inside. She pounded on the door, and when Silas opened it, she hugged him. "I've got it!"

From the other side of the room, Edward chuckled. "Well, if you've got it, share it!"

"Look!" She took the list out of her purse and waved it in front of Silas's face. "Look! It's Blaine's record of his transactions! I've got the proof!"

"Whoa, slow down!" Silas said. "What record? Proof of what?"

There was a knock at the door, and Hyacinth joined them. She was out of breath and quite red. "I am in no shape to go running after you, Eliza, so this had better be important. You scared me to death, running out like that."

"Oh, it's important all right," Eliza said. "Let's sit and talk."

The four of them sat at the table in the kitchen, the list in front of them. "I found this in my bag. Blaine left it in my shop, and he told me that he had an important investors meeting that evening, so I took it to his home. Unfortunately—or fortunately, I should say—I found him with another woman, and I raced home, packed my things, and left. This was in the bottom of my bag, and I didn't see it until tonight."

"Why did you have your bag out tonight?" Silas asked. "Were you—were you leaving?"

"For a while. I decided to go to St. Paul and at least tell what I knew. Silas, I think I did know, but I just didn't want to admit it, and I was coming back. Do you want me to?"

Edward shook his head. "Did you just say everything backwards? That made no sense at all."

Eliza and Silas stared at him. "She was going to give a statement in St. Paul about what she knew concerning Blaine Loring, the fellow that bilked all those young women out of their savings," Silas said. "She now thinks she knew all along what was going on. She was planning to come back to Remembrance after her statement, and yes, I want her to come back. You didn't follow all that?"

"You two are definitely meant for each other," Hyacinth said. "Nobody else could understand you. But go on. Edward and I will try to stay with you."

"Take a look at these registers," Eliza said. "If you add up the percentages, instead of coming to 100 percent, they total almost 350 percent. Do you see what he did? You can't sell 350 percent of anything because there isn't 350 percent. There can't be more than 100 percent."

"Intriguing," Edward said.

"I see," Silas said. "But what I don't understand is why he was so careless with this list at your shop. He undoubtedly considered you to be into the scheme, too."

Eliza shook her head. "I don't think so. Blaine must not have thought I could read. After all, most of the household help who'd invested couldn't read. I'm sure he showed them these lists, and the numbers, and they wouldn't have understood what they were looking at, just that they were getting back a lot of money—which of course, they were not."

"But you could read." Edward beamed happily at her.

"I can read and write and add and subtract and multiply and divide. And do percentages. But of course that wouldn't have even occurred to Blaine. He was so egotistical he'd never have even considered that someone as lowly as a seamstress could, in fact, read and understand this list."

"He sounds like quite a piece of work, this fellow does," Edward commented.

"Oh, he was that and then some. I am well rid of him."

Silas frowned. "It's not going to be easy for you. You'll probably come under a good deal of scrutiny yourself, and you may have to answer to exactly what you knew and when. Are you ready for it?"

"I have to do what I have to do." Eliza's stomach twisted as she considered what kinds of questions she might face in St. Paul. "I don't know that I'm ready for it, or even if I ever would be. But it's something I must do, and since I have this list, which is about as close to any proof as we're ever going to get, I'd say I have the responsibility to share it with the authorities."

"You could be arrested." Silas's voice cracked. "Did you think of that?"

"Of course I did. What Blaine did was horrible, and I feel guilty beyond belief for my part in it. I will do whatever I need to do to make things right."

They were brave words, but inside Eliza was quivering at the thought that her path might end in a cell. The time had come, though, for her to stop running and to put things right, not just for her but for the women he had stolen the money from.

"When do we leave?" Silas asked.

"You're going with me? You don't have to. You have things to do here in Remembrance."

"Eliza, of course I want to go with you. If you don't want me to go, you just have to say the word."

"Well, you have the Robbins house to work on, and Edward here, with his precious limb and all. . . ."

"My what?" Edward interjected. "What on earth are you talking about? My precious limb? Could you two go back to English, please?"

"No, Silas, you should stay here. Your uncle needs you. I can go to St. Paul by myself. I used to live there, you know." As much as she would like his presence, she knew this was something she had to do on her own.

"I'll go with her," Hyacinth announced. "You two need to stay here and watch Tiger, and finish up Birdbath House so we can move in. Mrs. Adams is getting nervous. I think she's convinced herself that we're coming with her to move in with her precious daughter Ella."

"You'll be all right, alone in the city?" Edward asked Hyacinth, grasping her hand and gazing into her eyes.

"Pudding Plum, we'll be fine."

Pudding Plum? Silas and Eliza mouthed in unison.

"We'll try to leave tomorrow," Eliza said. "Will you tell the Robbins family that I'll be back soon? If you two really want to help, you could sew the buttonholes on Luke's shirt and finish hemming Analia's dress."

"We'll watch the cat," Edward said. "I think everyone would be happiest if we left the sewing to you."

"Sounds reasonable," Eliza said, chuckling. "But I'd better get back to the boardinghouse and get ready for this trip."

"I'll walk you over there," Silas said. "Uncle Edward, you'll see Hyacinth home?"

"Of course," Edward replied. "I think I can hobble over there and back. Eliza, in case I don't see you before you leave, my prayers are with you."

"Thanks, Edward. I know I'll need them."

As they walked slowly toward the boardinghouse, Eliza took a deep breath. "There, can you smell it? It's not the January thaw this time. It's the real thing. Spring is coming. I can already smell the rain and the trees and the grass."

"I'm ready for winter to end," Silas said, taking her hand. "I don't mean just the calendar's winter either. My own winter has gone on long enough. It's time for me to find spring."

"I understand exactly," Eliza said. "I've been living in pain of one sort or the other for too long, and I've made mistakes because of it. I really need to know, Silas—can you forgive me?"

He squeezed her hand. "Being a Christian means agreeing to forgive. I've really had to work on that, because for me, anyway, it's the hardest part of following Jesus. I have to forgive. The Bible demands it of me. I fought it and fought it, but no matter how hard I struggled, I came right back to it. I have to do it. It's a gift that I get, and it's a gift I can give."

"I think it's the closest we can get to grace," she said softly. "God gives it to us freely, and we need to be able to do it, too. But it's difficult."

Silas stopped and faced her. "Eliza, I'll be honest with you. Your relationship with Blaine Loring frightened me, not just about the fact that he was a criminal, but that he was able to so completely take you over. I've never been in a romance before." He cleared his throat. "I don't think I could make you love me so much that you'd forget everything for me. I don't think I'd want to."

"God gave me a brain," she said. "I forgot to use it when I was with Blaine. I was young and I was foolish and I was so very needy. I was the perfect target for him. I don't want to be a target again."

"What do you want from the man who loves you?"

"I want him to tell me he loves me. I want him to hold me in his arms. I want him to respect me and love me and trust me and care for me."

His eyes softened in the moonlight that filtered through the trees, and as they stood together, arms around each other, Eliza knew she was home.

━━

"This has been quite an exciting time," Uncle Edward said as the train pulled away, bearing Eliza and Hyacinth on their way to St. Paul. "Eliza certainly is brave, going to the capital to give her statement. It would have been so much easier for her if she'd just let the whole thing go, but that's not our Eliza's way, is it?"

"I'm so very proud of her. I wish I were going there with her." He touched his mouth, where just minutes earlier Eliza had placed a going-away kiss. "I want her back here with me, safe and sound."

They began to walk back to their house. One of the things that Silas loved about this part of the state was that spring bounded in and pushed winter out. That was what was happening. Oh, there would still be skirmishes—there was almost always a spring blizzard or two—but for the moment, the sun was out, the air was warming, and even the birds sounded more chipper than usual.

It would have been a good day to take a walk with his Eliza.

"How do you think she's coping with all of this?" his uncle asked. His limp was almost gone, and he could now walk without expending most of his energy. Today he wasn't even using a cane.

"She was used so badly by this scoundrel, and I know she's having a hard time forgiving herself for her part in the plot. She's run through an entire laundry list of *ifs*. What if she hadn't been so eager to move up in the world? What if she hadn't taken so readily to his proposal that she solicit these young women for their money?" Silas stopped, but only for a moment. There was more. "What if she hadn't found him with that other woman? Might she have stayed with him, blinded by what she thought was love, until she was entwined in his corruption?"

"If she hadn't come across them locked in an embrace, she could have stayed with him and gotten even more deeply involved, that's true," Edward considered. "Perhaps it's best that she did see that, even though it hurt her terribly. God was truly looking out for her. It does seem that sometimes He takes us through the valley only to show us the sunshine, doesn't it?"

Silas looked at his uncle. "You've become quite the poet recently."

Edward shrugged. "Blame it on love, I suppose. You'll probably take up the lute and start composing romantic ballads yourself, and I'll have to listen to you all hours of the day and night, strumming and singing your heart out."

"I don't think so," Silas said with a grin. "I'd never subject you to my singing."

"It's good to see you like this," his uncle said. "There's so much joy in being in love. I'm glad you've found it. Eliza is a wonderful woman."

Their path took them near Birdbath House, and they stopped in to see what was left to be done. Tiger, who was at the Collier house while Eliza and Hyacinth were gone, had clearly done her job well. There was no evidence of mice.

"You know what we should do?" Edward said as they walked through the house. "Let's get this ready for them so when they come home they can move right in. We just have some cleaning and painting to do, and get this old furniture out and move the new in from the boardinghouse."

"That's all we have to do? All?" Silas surveyed the house. "I suppose I could—we *could*—in two or three days if I didn't go to the Robbins house."

"Cleaning should be the first item on the agenda." Edward ran his finger over the windowsill and held up the grimy proof. "As far as the Robbins family goes, they might like a break from the constant hammering and sawing. You'll catch up."

His uncle had an excellent point.

"All right, let's do it."

For the rest of the afternoon, the two men scrubbed and swept and polished and wiped, until the house glistened. Silas leaned against the doorjamb. It was really quite amazing what they had accomplished. "Tomorrow we'll move the old furniture out. Then we'll move the items from Mrs. Adams's place in here."

"So you think two more days?"

"That should do it. We'll be quite the pair when Eliza and Hyacinth come back into town. We'll be achingly stiff and sore."

"But it'll be worth it. I can't wait to see my Petunia Blossom's face when she realizes she can stay in Birdbath House."

"*Petunia Blossom?* You're saying Hyacinth is a Petunia Blossom? Is that even botanically possible?"

Edward winked at him. "Poetic license, Silas. Poetic license."

Silas laughed.

Edward mopped the sweat from his forehead as they packed up to leave the house. "I'm clearly not as young as I once was—or as I thought I was. Whew!"

Silas studied him covertly. His uncle's knuckles were swollen with arthritis, and during this short stint of cleaning, he'd managed to cut his thumb fairly deeply, and one fingernail was going to be black after he'd dropped a picture frame on it.

It wasn't right. People you loved weren't supposed to get old and weak.

"I know, Silas." His uncle's voice was soft and understanding. "I'm not what I used to be, not on the outside, and you know, not even on the inside. Each whack I take on the outside teaches me something on the inside. That's how life goes."

"Uncle Edward—"

His uncle held up his hand and stemmed Silas's objection. "I need to say this. As you know, I'll be taking Hyacinth as my bride soon—and yes, I know you don't approve of it, but I know what's in my heart and hers, so we are getting married whether you're there or not. Over the years, I've gotten a fairly profitable carpentry business built up."

"You do excellent work, Uncle." Silas picked up a pail and began spreading out the wet rags over the edge of it.

"When I manage to stay on the ladder. Which brings me to the next point. I'm looking at some changes, not just with my marrying Hyacinth. Silas, I'm offering you the business. I'm not getting any younger, and the time has come for me to have whatever adventures are ahead, to enjoy them while I can."

"But—"

"The right answer is, 'thank you,'" Edward said. "Not 'but.' You're a good carpenter, and you've become like my own son. I'm proud to pass the business on to you. . .if you want it. I'm hoping you'll say yes."

Silas put the pail down and looked at his uncle. In his face he saw the man who took in the untaught teenager, spent hour after hour, day after day, teaching him the ways of the wood, and all the time putting his own life on hold.

Was he the reason his uncle had never married before?

"Thank you," he said, and reached out, giving his uncle a long-overdue hug.

⌒

Silas looked up at the stars. His uncle had already gone to bed, and Silas was a bit concerned about the way Edward had winced on the stairs. He'd done too much too soon.

The stairs hadn't been easy for him, either, and he was thirty-something years younger than his uncle. They'd worked hard and they'd worked long today, and now they were going to pay for it.

Silas groaned as he thought of what he'd feel like in the morning. And he'd scheduled them to move the furniture out!

Would he be able to sleep tonight? His body needed rest, but his mind wouldn't stop turning over the conversation at Birdbath House.

He had the carpentry business. His future was secured.

He picked up *Professor Barkley's Patented Five Year Plan for Success*. What did the professor have in store for him today? He opened and began to read.

What have you left undone? Is there something that you've been ignoring because you simply don't want to see it? Maybe it's a pile of papers on your desk. Or a stain on the rug near the door? That missing button on your coat?

Or is it more than that? Is there an apology you've been avoiding? Do you have some anger that you need to diffuse? Some ill will that's taken root in your soul so deeply that it's going to be painful to pull it out?

Today, deal with what you have put aside for later. It is later.

Memory verse—"Proverbs 3:27: Withhold not good from them to whom it is due, when it is in the power of thine hand to do it."

Well, that was an odd little entry, and it certainly didn't fit into the day, not at all.

He read through the memory verse until he had it learned, and then, after his prayers, he slipped into his bed. As he fell into sleep, Professor Barkley's words taunted him. What had he left undone?

It was, he decided, another one of the professor's puzzles. Remembering what one had forgotten was about as easy as expecting the unexpected.

He'd never figure it out.

Chapter 11

Eliza and Hyacinth stood in front of the police station. A light spring snow was falling that melted as soon as it touched the ground. "I don't know if this is the right place or not," Eliza said, "but there's only one way to find out. Are you ready?"

"Let's say a prayer first," Hyacinth suggested, and the two women stepped to the side and, holding hands, dropped their heads. "Dearest God, we ask that You guide Eliza's words and actions now, in His name, Amen."

Eliza laughed. "Short but effective."

"We can hope. Shall we go in?"

After being sent from one desk to another and speaking to a series of law enforcement officials, they finally ended up speaking to the chief of police, a kind-looking man with a thick white moustache. He listened closely to Eliza and asked questions, but mainly he let her tell her story.

She handed him the list of the names of the "investors" and their promised returns and watched as he studied it. At last he nodded. "This appears to be exactly the document we need. With the name of the unfortunates he took advantage of, we'll be able to gather even more witnesses."

"I wish something could be done for these young women who were taken advantage of," Eliza said. "I know they'll all be grateful to see him behind bars, but that's a small cold comfort when you've lost your money."

The chief smiled. "Come to find out, Loring has quite the eye for art. His collection is worth quite a bit of money. I wouldn't be at all surprised to hear the court order it to be sold, and the profits distributed among the women. After all, it was their money that purchased the items." He smiled at her. "I believe that would be equitable."

She nodded. "I see. I'm glad to hear that. It makes this all a bit easier to accept, knowing that my friends will see at least some recouping of their losses."

He stood up. "Thank you very much for coming forward, Miss Davis. You are extraordinarily brave."

He shook her hand, and then Hyacinth's, and guided them to the exit. Eliza paused for a moment, long enough to let her knees stop shaking, and she heard the chief call to the captain, "Come to my office. We've got him now! Loring is ours!"

She looked at Hyacinth and smiled. "He believed me."

"You must feel relieved that it's all over," Hyacinth said to her.

"It's not quite over. I have some apologies to make."

Eliza led Hyacinth to her old neighborhood. Most of the women she knew were still there, and to her delight, they listened readily to her story and forgave her. "We knew your heart," one of them, a soft-spoken nanny, said to her. "You would never have hurt us on purpose."

"I have some things of yours," another said, her apron and cap indicating kitchen service. "We heard that the Loring fellow was going to go through your shop and your home—what he was looking for, I don't know, but it wasn't right. So some of us went to the shop and some to your quarters, and we got out what we could."

A third woman, her hands crusted from the harsh soaps she used to clean, added, "His men aren't so tough. They took one look at us, and they tucked tail and ran, like a bunch of mangy curs."

The group laughed, and the cook led them to the storeroom where in a box were Eliza's clothes, all neatly folded, and the rest of her sewing materials. "And behind here, I've got your machine." The cook opened a cupboard, and in it sat Eliza's sewing machine, dismantled to fit, but all there.

"You are all absolutely the best!" Eliza hugged each one of them. "I'll take these with me now, but you all must promise me that if you ever can get to Remembrance, you'll come and see me. Promise?"

There was nothing quite like good friends, she thought as she surveyed the group of women she'd known before, and Hyacinth, who came all this way for her. Friends made all the difference.

And now it was time for her to be a friend, as she took Hyacinth to her favorite store to buy some lovely yellow silk for her wedding dress, white lace bands for the sleeves and neck, and pearl buttons to march down the back in a tidy row. She couldn't wait to start on it.

As she sat on the train coming back, Hyacinth snoring softly at her side, she took stock of herself. She was finally happy, and her spiritual housecleaning was well underway. She'd cleared out the dirt and the webs and flung open the doors to let the sunshine in.

Her life was taking shape at last.

⌒

"Do you see them yet?"

"No, Silas, not yet." Uncle Edward walked with only a faint limp, but today he was using the cane again. All the bustle to get the house ready for the women had taken its toll. "But soon. I think I heard it a minute ago."

The station was empty. There wasn't much call for the train to stop in

Remembrance. Usually materials for the store were the only reason that the train even slowed down.

"Silas, since your own dear father long ago left this earth for his heavenly reward, I feel I should be the one to talk to you about love."

Silas laughed. "You? But you're Pudding Plum, as I recall. It seems to me that anyone who lets himself be called Pudding Plum is in no position to advise anyone else."

"You'll see, Silas. One day Eliza will call you something equally as ridiculous, like Lovey Lamb, and you'll absolutely melt. That's the way it is with love."

"Lovey Lamb?" Silas shuddered. "Oh, spare me!"

"I'm serious. If anyone else were to call you that, you'd probably straighten him right out. But because it's the woman you love, you'll smile and get fluttery and although you'll be as embarrassed as anything, you'll treasure it."

"I can't see Eliza doing that."

"Just wait. You never know. You'll be at church or with a customer, and she'll come in and she'll call you Lovey Lamb, and you'll want to sink through the floor—but you'll be as proud as anything that it's *you* she called Lovey Lamb."

"Lovey Lamb? Honestly, Uncle Edward, Eliza?"

His uncle chuckled. "Maybe not. But, Silas, you need to be able to have fun with the woman you love. Enjoy her company. Share laughter. Have secret jokes that belong to just the two of you. Remember that in marriage, two have become one."

"Uncle Edward, aren't you jumping ahead just a little bit? Or maybe a whole lot? You've got Eliza and me getting married. Don't you think we ought to court a little while?" Silas grinned.

The sound of the train came closer.

"Isn't that what you two have been doing?" his uncle responded. "You two learn to talk and laugh and not get so caught up in your own pride, and you'll be ready to marry."

"I think I'll wait a little bit, if you don't mind."

"You know what you need to do?" Uncle Edward asked.

The *chicketta-ticketta* of the train grew even louder, and his heart beat faster at the thought that she'd soon be in Remembrance.

"What do I need to do, Uncle?" Silas asked.

The train was too loud for him to hear his answer clearly, but it sounded for all the world like, "Kiss her."

He was never one to ignore good advice. The minute she stepped onto the platform, he swung her into his arms and kissed her squarely on the lips.

For a kiss that was tinged with locomotive smoke and grit, it wasn't bad at all. But just in case it could get better, he kissed her again. And again. And again.

The children crowded around Eliza. "This is a sewing machine," she said, letting them each look at it. "When I move the crank on this wheel like this, see how the needle goes up and down?"

The children were transfixed by the machine that Eliza set up in the Robbins home for the day. Silas carried it over in its wooden carrying case. They'd never seen anything like it. Analia stood at Eliza's shoulder, Tiger cradled in her arms.

"But just having the needle go up and down isn't enough with a machine, even though it is with hand sewing. For a machine to make a stitch, two threads are required, and that's what this little shuttle under here is for. It loops with the thread from up above to make the stitch. Now watch. I'm going to sew this seam."

She put the gown she was making for Mrs. Robbins in place and within a minute had the seam sewn. "Compare that to how long it takes me to hand stitch a seam, and you can understand why we take very good care of our sewing machines."

"Wouldn't it be nice," Silas said from the other side of the room where he was still putting up cupboards, "if someday someone would invent a machine that could put nails in place as easily as that puts stitches in? Then I could stand here, and instead of hammering in each nail, I could simply *pop-pop-pop-pop* them into place."

"Not likely to ever happen," Luke commented. "That's just dangerous."

Eliza looked up and smiled surreptitiously at Silas. Luke was very sweet, but very ten years old. He was at the age in which he knew it all, or at least most of it.

"Well, if they do invent a nail machine, I'll be the first in line to buy one. This hammering all day long is really hard on my arms." He rubbed his right shoulder.

"If you need help," little Mark offered, "I'm very good at pounding nails."

"Thank you, Mark. I'll keep that in mind."

The staccato hammering and the whirr of the sewing machine blended to make a solid background noise that, at least momentarily, drowned out the constant chatter of the children.

Having the machine back made so much difference, she thought, as the boys' shirts almost finished themselves. This had to be one of the best inventions created.

Once her world had tilted upside down. Now it was being righted, and it was wonderful. She took stock of all that had happened for the good.

She had fallen in love. That was the best, of course. When she first met him, he'd been so solemn, his eyes studiously serious behind his wire-rimmed glasses. Now, he'd come out of his own shadow, and she enjoyed being with him so much that loving him came easily.

She had a friend. How could she have gone on without Hyacinth at her side, advising and supporting her all the way? She had a sewing machine. She had a cat. She even had a house now, at least for a while. Hyacinth had added some charming touches to Birdbath House, so it truly felt like home.

Plus spring was definitely in the air. The snow and ice had begun to melt at an amazing rate, so that walking under any eaves or awnings meant sure splatters of water on one's head. Even the birds seemed happier.

Mary Robbins had actually gotten out of bed and come into the front room twice. The doctor told her that if she continued to regain her strength, she'd be back to health by summer's end.

Tomorrow Eliza would start on Hyacinth's wedding dress. The date was set for the first Sunday in June, right after the church services. All of Remembrance was invited, and even Mrs. Adams said she'd try to come back for it. She'd left four days ago, and Hyacinth and Eliza were reveling in having their dinner at 12:01 or even 12:02.

All in all, everything was perfect. Couldn't be better. Nothing to change.

Hyacinth came out of Mary's room after visiting with her, and Eliza stopped the machine to talk to her. Hyacinth smiled widely. "I think Mary's going to come to the wedding! She said she wants to but she doesn't have anything to wear. Eliza, do you think you could—"

Silas's nail-pounding stopped, and he laid the hammer on the table with a bit more emphasis than necessary.

"Eliza, I'm going to talk to Edward. I'll see you back at Birdbath House," Hyacinth said in a low voice, her eyes guardedly watching Silas.

Eliza nodded.

A pin that had been stuck into the fabric imperfectly worked its way loose and jabbed her finger. A bright spot of blood appeared, and she wiped it away before it could spot the fabric.

She needed to pay closer attention. That was simply a pin, but if she were careless around the machine, she could do much worse damage to her hands. She hadn't had it happen, but she'd seen it often enough with the other seamstresses, their hands riddled with scars from just such accidents.

It was a good thing this was Saturday. Tomorrow she'd be able to sit in church, soaking up the Word, and generally getting good with the Lord again. Sundays were her day of rejuvenation, and she certainly needed it.

Silas had stopped hammering and was now measuring the hinge placement. He measured, marked, re-measured, re-marked, over and over until at last he gave up with a sigh.

"How close are you to being done?" he asked.

"I can finish these shirts at home. There's just a bit left on each. Want to help me take the machine to the wagon?"

He strode over and began to insert the machine into its wooden table case with quick short movements. She clamped her lips together and folded the remaining items to take with her, and stopped into Mary's room to retrieve the cat.

The woman was sitting up in bed, looking better than she had all winter. Her hair was washed and braided, the work of Hyacinth who made sure that Mary looked as good—or better—than she felt.

"I hear you would like a new dress," Eliza said as she unhooked Tiger's claws from the blanket. "Any particular color or style?"

"You've already done too much," Mary protested, but Eliza waved her objection away.

"Making a dress is very easy for me. It won't take long at all. Just tell me what color you'd like. You can't have yellow since Hyacinth will be wearing a stunning yellow wedding dress. Red might be a bit too vivid, and black's harsh. How about a sky blue or a summer green or even a lilac or lavender?"

"Oh, I do like lavender. Let me get Jack in here to pay you—"

"No, no payment. I brought back my sewing machine and trunk that I left in St. Paul, and there's a nice length of fabric that I think will be perfect on you. The background is lavender, and there are tiny sprigs of flowers in creamy ivory. So, the next question is the style. What would you like?"

"Can you select something for me? You have so much more experience than I have."

"It would be an honor."

Eliza carried the cat to the wagon, and when they got in, Silas burst out with, "I'm sorry. I just can't deal with them getting married. I think it's wrong."

She faced him square on. "Get over it. They're in love. What's wrong with that?"

"We've already gone over this. They met through letters. She came out here without having ever even seen him. Don't you think that's odd?" He frowned.

"It's not the way I would do it, but on the other hand, I'm not Hyacinth. I'm not an older widow whose options for finding love again are limited."

"But to do it that way?"

"What do you care how they met? It's working out. Take a look at them, Silas. Pudding Plum is madly in love with his Morning Flower. Sappy, I agree, but look at how contented they are. Who cares how they got there? Why are you so upset?"

"I'm afraid," he said at last, "that I'm to blame for this. If Uncle Edward hadn't taken me in when I was a young man, he would have had time to meet someone else, and he'd have gotten married and—"

"He *might* have met someone. He *might* have gotten married." She shook her head. "Besides, everything is turning out just fine. He's retiring—and getting off ladders—and he's passing the carpentry business on to you. He's in love. What's wrong with that? It sounds good to me."

His lips tightened again into that expression that she'd seen way too much of, and she knew what it meant. He had an opinion, and he was going to hold onto it until it was forced out of his grasp.

"It's not the way we do things here," he said.

"It's not the way anybody does things—except for these two. Just be glad for them. They found each other, and I can't imagine two people who seem to be better suited for each other than them."

It was true. They were completely and totally ideal as a couple.

"I don't want him to be hurt," he said after a long silence.

"I don't think he will be," she replied honestly. "I suspect that your treatment of the woman he loves hurts him more than anything right now."

He stared straight ahead, his jaw clenched.

"Just take me home, Silas," she finished gently. "Help me unload the sewing machine and get it set up in Birdbath House, and you can go think about this. It's really vital for you to work this out inside your soul." She took a deep breath. "Until you do, I don't think you and I can go further. It's too big and too important for you to walk around with this weight in your heart."

He said no more than the necessary words as he set up her machine in the house for her and left again. She stood at the window and watched him go. He'd never looked so lonely.

And she'd never felt so lonely.

⌐

He'd gotten far behind with his readings from *Professor Barkley's Patented Five Year Plan for Success*, and he took the book out to catch up. Perhaps the professor had some advice for him.

But the daily lessons were more of the same. *"Be careful what you say."* He tried to be cautious with his speech. If he felt he was losing control, he simply opted for silence. *"Be kind to those less fortunate."* Look at how much time he spent at the Robbins house. *"Pray for peace."* Well, that was a given.

Could it be that Professor Barkley was getting—more predictable?

Maybe it was time for another list. He did enjoy lists. He glanced at his Bible, where his list of questions for Eliza was safely tucked away. Maybe his lists weren't always as helpful as he hoped, but they helped him organize his thoughts.

He made two columns on a piece of paper. One column he titled, *Yeas*. The other, *Nays*.

He worked on his columns until he could come up with nothing else, and he leaned back and studied the results.

Under the *Yeas* were two entries: *They seem to love each other*, and *They seem to make each other happy*.

Under the *Nays* were also two entries: *They don't really know each other*, and *They act crazy.*

So it hadn't been a particularly fruitful exercise. He expected more from it. His head wasn't any clearer than before. He wadded up the list and threw it toward the wastebasket, missing it entirely—something, he noted wryly, he had done a lot of lately.

He lowered his head and stared at the wall. Since when did someone have to like everybody? Well, there was of course the biblical injunction that *"Thou shalt love thy neighbour as thyself,"* but did that really apply here? He searched for the phrase in his Bible, and soon sat back, shaking his head.

It was from Matthew 22, the same chapter that Reverend Tupper had used as his text in church awhile back. The verse about loving his neighbor came after the wedding feast story, and according to Jesus, it was a foundational premise. He read it again:

> *Then one of them, which was a lawyer, asked him a question, tempting him, and saying, Master, which is the great commandment in the law? Jesus said unto him, Thou shalt love the Lord thy God with all thy heart, and with all thy soul, and with all thy mind. This is the first and great commandment. And the second is like unto it, Thou shalt love thy neighbour as thyself. On these two commandments hang all the law and the prophets.*

That last line laid a heavy responsibility on him. Clearly the charge to love others wasn't minor at all. Jesus compared it to loving God Himself.

His head started to hurt. Being a Christian was getting increasingly complicated. If Hyacinth and Eliza hadn't shown up in Remembrance, he might have been able to sail on through the rest of his life without these challenges. But now, having heard the Word on the subject, he had no choice but adapt his life.

That meant loving Hyacinth. Was it possible? If God insisted, could he?

He got up from the table and laid his weary body on his bed. Why did life have to be so complicated? His head pounded even harder. His eyes closed against the pain, and at last he slipped into a restless sleep.

His fitful dreams were interrupted by his uncle hollering up the stairs at him. "Are you going to church or have you turned into a heathen?" Silas's eyes flew open to glaring daylight and he groaned. If his uncle was already up and anxious about church, he must have overslept. He swung his legs over the side of the bed and stood up, automatically checking the weather outside his window as he did so.

It was a beautiful Sunday morning, and he winced at the sun's beams. The way he felt, at the very least the weather could have cooperated and produced some thundering clouds to gray up the sky.

But Sunday was Sunday, and he didn't miss church. He cleaned himself quickly and pulled on good clothes and headed downstairs. His uncle was already at the stove, and he handed Silas a plate of ham and eggs.

"Wolf this down and let's get going. I don't want to be late."

Silas ate as quickly as he could, and soon the two men were headed into the church.

Edward of course greeted Hyacinth enthusiastically. Today, she was his Sparkling Sunday Sunbeam. Silas tried very hard not to react. He was going to make every attempt to be kind to her.

Eliza was polite but guarded as he slid into the pew next to her. "Let's talk after church," he whispered to her as they stood for the first hymn, and she nodded. He had no idea what he was going to say to her. Perhaps something would come to him during church.

He sat back in the pew, mulling over the upcoming discussion with Eliza, when the sermon began. Reverend Tupper was in fine form, delivering a rousing sermon based upon Proverbs 22:24. Silas found himself listening intently, and he hung on every word.

"Make no friendship with an angry man." As the minister proceeded to explain the wisdom of the proverb, why one should choose one's companions carefully, Silas considered another angle of it.

What if he was the angry man?

Certainly he'd been polite enough—outwardly—with his uncle's romance, but lately he'd become aware that it had blown into something more virulent. He'd become angry about it.

Was Eliza thinking the same thing? Was she concerned about the man next to her, the man she'd professed to love? He was the angry man—and the Bible warned others about him.

He felt as if he'd been brought up sharp in front of God and had been found wanting.

But what was he to do? He had to make some change, somehow. He needed to let the anger go. The fact was, though, that it was one thing to be aware of it, but something else entirely to be able to do it.

He squeezed his eyes shut and prayed, asking God to take away his anger, to clean his heart of these negative emotions. If he was going to be able to love, he had to have an anger-free heart.

He prayed longer. More intently. He didn't want to carry this burden of hate any longer. He wanted it gone.

The fact was, he realized as he continued to petition God, he nurtured his dislike of Hyacinth. He looked for fault at every turn. His scorn became his pet, his companion, and he elevated it into a consuming passion that froze his heart to her. In other words, it had nothing to do with Hyacinth, and everything to do with him. His heart was in desperate need of a good housecleaning. He opened the darkness of his soul to the light of God's goodness and aired out every corner.

Bit by bit, he felt the ice leave the haven he'd given it in his heart, and his soul was filled again with joy.

After church, he and Eliza walked the short distance to Birdbath House. The snow was almost gone, and they had to pick their way through the rutted mud.

"I was the angry man," he said, "but I've made a commitment not to be. You were right. I needed to let go of my dislike of Hyacinth. For one thing, I was so concerned about my own future here in Remembrance that I let my worries overtake my senses. Plus I was being too protective of my uncle, and he is, after all, quite the grown man and able to make his own decisions. I still think it's a crazy way to find someone to love, but if it worked, then praise God."

"I'm glad," she said, taking his arm as they reached a particularly muddy area. "I do think you'll find Hyacinth to be quite a wonderful woman, very worthy of your uncle's love."

"You mean Pudding Plum and—what did he call her this morning?—Sparkling Sunday Sunbeam are meant for each other?"

"I do."

"Are we?" He held his breath, waiting for her answer.

She stopped and put her hands on each side of his face. "We are." She stood on tiptoe and kissed him. "And I promise I'll never call you names like that. Not Honey Bee. Not Darling Dumpling. And never," she finished, grinning impishly, "Lovey Lamb."

Chapter 12

I told her about it," Uncle Edward confessed when Silas asked him how she knew about "Lovey Lamb" from the earlier conversation the men had. "I thought she might find a time to use it," he added, grinning, "and I gather she did."

Silas laughed. "She did. But she did promise never to call me Lovey Lamb, so in the long run it was worth it."

His uncle shook his head. "Never underestimate the power of a bit of silly affection."

"Why, Uncle, you sound like quite the romantic expert," Silas quipped, raising his eyebrows in mock surprise. "For someone who avoided marriage for your entire life thus far, you sure do seem to know the secrets of a happy relationship. Is there something you haven't told me?"

Uncle Edward chuckled. "Probably. Oh, speaking of things I haven't told you, Hyacinth and I've decided not to move to Duluth, but to stay here."

"I'm delighted, of course, to hear that you'll stay here, but I thought your dream was to move to Duluth," Silas said. He marveled at his calm. Whatever the change in plans boded for his life, God was in charge.

His uncle shrugged. "Remembrance is home. Besides, moving is work for people my age, and I don't think I'm up for it. Plus I can do my work here as well as I could in Duluth."

"I thought you were retiring." Silas frowned. His uncle's hands weren't as steady as they used to be, and in woodworking, steady hands were all-important. It simply wasn't safe for Uncle Edward to continue to work with the sharp tools, and making his products to his demanding standards would be difficult.

"Oh, I'm giving the carpentry business over to you, no doubt about that. I mean my writing. I can do that anywhere."

"Writing?" Silas gaped at his uncle. "You want to be a writer? I had no idea!"

"Oh, I already am. About ten years ago I wrote some silly thing called *Professor Barkley's Patented Five Year Plan for Success*." Uncle Edward frowned a bit. "This is one of those things I didn't tell you, apparently. Well, it wasn't some grand production. I put all the sensible advice I could come up with into a book, and it sold, oh, maybe fifteen or twenty copies." He grinned. "I think I might rewrite it, update it for the new era, you know."

"You wrote it? You're Professor Barkley?"

His uncle laughed. "You can't tell me you've heard of it."

"Heard of it? I've been reading it every night for the past nine months. I found a copy in my room when I moved the nightstand—it was under the drawer in it, wedged in there pretty soundly."

"Oh, that's where I put the book. I looked all over the place for it. I think it's time for a revision, don't you?"

Silas laughed. "You might consider taking out all the warnings about romantic entanglements."

"You're right. I need to encourage love. After all, doesn't the Good Book say in the Song of Solomon, 'This is my beloved, and this is my friend'? How can anyone have a plan for success without including love?"

How, indeed? How, indeed!

⁓

Snowflakes sparkled in the moonlight as Eliza and Silas lingered outside Birdbath House. Hyacinth and Edward were inside, cleaning up after the dinner the four of them had shared.

"What do you think Mrs. Adams would say about that?" he asked, indicating the silhouettes of the older couple in the window as they shared a quick kiss over a pan of dishes.

"I think she'd say they should get married, and quickly."

Eliza felt as full as a cat. If she were able, she would have purred. The dinner of roast chicken and biscuits had been delicious, and sleep threatened to overtake her. She fought back a yawn. Had she ever been this happy?

"That's a splendid idea." He put his hands on her shoulders and turned her to face him. "Eliza, shall we make it a double wedding?"

Her sleepiness vanished. "A double—do you mean—are you saying what I think you're saying?"

"I should do this properly." He dropped to one knee and took her gloved hand in his. "We haven't known each other long, but the heart has its own schedule. I've loved you from the first time I saw you. You were scented with blueberries and soap, and you literally fell into my arms. I want you by my side—and in my arms—for the rest of my life."

She couldn't answer. Her heart caromed in her chest, coming to land squarely in her throat.

"I thought that *Professor Barkley's Patented Five Year Plan for Success* was going to revolutionize my life, but it didn't take into account one thing—and that was love."

"Professor Barkley's what?"

He waved her question away. "I'll explain later. So, Eliza, will you?"

"Will I—?" The snowflakes spun in a dizzying whirl of fairy dust.

"Oh, I still haven't asked you, have I?" Silas's cider-colored eyes shone behind his glasses. "Eliza, will you marry me?"

Everything changed. The moon glowed brighter; the stars glittered with a brilliant light. The leafless tree branches waved their approval in the evening breeze, and the flutter of wings and the hoot of an owl became a melody that floated on the night air.

"Yes," she responded, not sure if she were whispering or shouting. "Yes, yes, yes!"

He rose to his feet and wrapped her in his arms. "I love you, Eliza. Here, with God as my witness, I promise to love you always. Our love together, our life together, is just beginning."

A double wedding. What could be more perfect?

"You're sure, aren't you?" Uncle Edward asked his nephew.

"I am." Silas leaned against the doorjamb. It had been a magical evening, and he was reluctant to let it end. After he and Eliza had told Hyacinth and his uncle the news of their engagement and suggested the double wedding, the plans began to spin out from all four of them with great speed.

An August wedding, they decided, would be ideal. They wouldn't be rushing into their marriages, and they would have time to finalize living arrangements and the transfer of the business.

They'd be married, of course, in the church in Remembrance, with Hyacinth and Edward taking a long honeymoon trip to Duluth. The lakeshore would be a nice setting for a post-wedding vacation.

"How could two bachelors-for-life like ourselves have ended up with such extraordinary women?" Uncle Edward mused. "In this great huge world, and in this tiny little town, how did such a marvelous thing happen?"

Sometimes, Silas thought, a Patented Five Year Plan was a good thing, but even Professor Barkley couldn't create a better system than their heavenly Father already had.

Silas looked upward and smiled. "God knows. God knows."

Bees buzzed lazily in the hot August sun, but inside the church, Eliza was in a tizzy. Just minutes ago she'd had her bouquet of flowers, tied with blue string to match the new Bible Silas had given her as a wedding gift. But now the flowers were gone, and the ceremony was about to start.

"Look again," she told Hyacinth. "Maybe I left them in the wagon?"

"They're not there. I already looked. Are you sure you brought them with you?"

"I know I did. I had them with me when I got in, because a bee was overly interested in the daisies so I battled it the entire way over." Eliza put her hands on her hips and surveyed the back of the church. "They can't be that hard to find. This church isn't very big."

A sound under the pew made the two women step backward. They'd had the doors open for almost an hour now, and obviously some animal had joined them.

"Oh, please don't let it be a skunk," Eliza said. "Can you imagine what would happen if—"

At that moment Tiger stepped out, pulling the now bedraggled bouquet in her teeth. Eliza reached down and rescued the flowers. "How did you get over here?" she asked as she picked the cat up.

A small face poked around the corner. "I thought Tiger should be here," little Mark Robbins said. "I'll bet Tiger hasn't been to any weddings."

"There's a reason for that," Eliza said. "Did you go over to Birdbath House to get her?"

He shook his head solemnly. "I think she has a secret door or something because she keeps getting out and coming to our house. I tell her she's not supposed to do that, but she doesn't listen. I think maybe it's because she likes my mother. Or me."

She had a sudden inspiration. "Mark, do you know what a wedding gift is?"

"I sure do." His face fell. "I don't have one for you."

"But I have for *you*! Mark, do you think you could take care of Tiger for always?"

"You're giving her to me? Really?"

"She's for all of you. She's now Tiger Robbins. Isn't that a great name?"

The little boy hugged the cat. "Thank you, Miss Davis! Oh, you still are Miss Davis, aren't you? You're not Mrs. Collier yet?"

"I'm still Miss Davis. But you'd better run home. You've got to come back here with your family for my wedding! And make sure that Tiger doesn't get out again."

He left, grinning from ear to ear and talking constantly to the cat. "And you can sleep in my bed on Tuesdays, and Brian's on Wednesdays. . . ."

Hyacinth smiled. "You're giving up Tiger?"

"She's over there all the time anyway, so I might as well. Plus we got another wedding present last night. Carl brought us Slick Tom. Apparently the cat liked living in town and has moped around since we took him back to the farm, so he's ours now. Just let any mouse try to drop by for a visit!"

Suddenly the church began to fill with sound as the wedding guests arrived. Hyacinth and Eliza hustled into the tiny room at the back.

"Not too much longer," Hyacinth said. "Honey, are you through trying to shred that bouquet?"

"First the cat, and now me." Eliza's fingers trembled as she tried to save the bouquet. "Hyacinth, were you this nervous before your wedding to Mr. Mason?"

"My knees were knocking together so hard I was sure people could hear them," the older woman said. "I was so fidgety that I didn't even remember the ceremony. Suddenly someone was pronouncing us man and wife, and that was it. I guess I promised the usual things, although I could have vowed to plow the fields all the days of my life, since I didn't hear any of it."

Eliza moaned. "Oh, I am so nervous!"

"There, there," Hyacinth said soothingly. "Soon it'll all be done with, and you'll go on as Mrs. Silas Collier, and I'll be Mrs. Edward Collier."

"It has a lovely sound, doesn't it?" Eliza laid the repaired bouquet on the Bible. "Any last-minute tips for me?"

"Love is fun. There's less of the drama that came during courtship, and you'll find yourself being settled in. It's good. Enjoy yourself, Eliza. Silas is a good man."

Sounds at the door announced that the wedding would shortly be underway. "Hyacinth, I have never been so scared in my life." Eliza picked up the bouquet and knotted and reknotted the ribbons.

Reverend Tupper popped his head in. "I think it's time we proceeded with the ceremony."

One last hug, and the two brides stood together, their hands clasped together. *I'm getting married,* Eliza said to herself. *I'm getting married! Thank You, dearest God, for bringing Silas and me together.* Hyacinth squeezed her hand, and Eliza added, *And for giving Hyacinth and Edward to each other.*

The Robbins family, including Mary in her lavender dress with the ivory flowers, clattered in, despite the father's admonitions for silence. "Sorry," he said in a low voice. "That cat—"

"No need to explain," Hyacinth said with a laugh.

Eliza noted the suspicious bulge in Mark's shirt. Tiger apparently had made it to the ceremony after all. She chose to ignore the furry guest. "We haven't started yet. Analia, here's your basket. Remember, you lead us off."

Analia went first, dropping wildflower petals along the aisle of the church. Behind her floated Hyacinth, resplendent in her yellow silk dress with the lace edging and pearl buttons.

Eliza followed her. Now she knew why brides carried bouquets. It gave them something to hold onto so their hands could stop shaking.

Silas stepped from the side and met her in front of the altar. Her husband.

The wedding ceremony was a blur. Suddenly Reverend Tupper declared them to be husband and wife, Silas was kissing her, and she was married.

Just like that.

"I think Hyacinth got her good love story and her happy ending," Eliza said after the wedding, when they waved good-bye to Edward and Hyacinth, who were leaving for their honeymoon in Duluth. "What more could anyone want?"

"We do have it good," he said, putting his arm around her waist. "Think how well it all turned out. Edward and Hyacinth aren't moving to Duluth after all. They'll stay here. I like that."

As the wagon carrying Hyacinth and Edward disappeared in the distance, they walked back to the house.

"You know," Silas said, "they're so happy together, even if they do get silly sometimes. I guess that's a blessing of its own, isn't it?"

"Speaking of silly, what did you do with *Professor Barkley's Patented Five Year Plan for Success?*"

He leaned over and kissed her. "I've got my own plan for success. It's called love."

NOT a prof. soldier !

MEMOIRS OF AN INFANTRY OFFICER

SIEGFRIED SASSOON was born in 1886 and educated at Clare College, Cambridge. While serving in the trenches during the First World War, he began to write poetry, and in 1917, while convalescing from wounds incurred during the fighting, he wrote a declaration against the war, for which he was sent to be treated for neurasthenia. Sassoon's literary reputation grew after the war, and he is now known as one of the great World War I poets. His semiautobiographical George Sherston trilogy, which includes *Memoirs of a Fox-Hunting Man* (1928), *Memoirs of an Infantry Officer* (1930), and *Sherston's Progress* (1936), was incredibly successful during his lifetime. He published several more volumes of autobiography before his death in 1967.

PAUL FUSSELL was born in 1925 and fought in World War II, where the death of a close friend on the battlefield next to him deeply affected his life and work, and eventually led to his writing the classic *The Great War and Modern Memory*, which won both the National Book Award for Arts and Letters and the National Book Critics Circle Award for Criticism. He edited *Sassoon's Long Journey* for Oxford University Press and wrote or edited over twenty other books in his lifetime. He died in May 2012.

SIEGFRIED SASSOON

Memoirs of an Infantry Officer

Introduction by
PAUL FUSSELL

PENGUIN BOOKS

PENGUIN BOOKS
Published by the Penguin Group
Penguin Group (USA) Inc., 375 Hudson Street,
New York, New York 10014, USA

USA | Canada | UK | Ireland | Australia | New Zealand | India | South Africa | China
Penguin Books Ltd, Registered Offices: 80 Strand, London WC2R 0RL, England
For more information about the Penguin Group visit penguin.com

First published in Great Britain by Faber and Faber Limited 1930
First published in the United States of America by Coward, McCann, Inc. 1930
This edition with an introduction by Paul Fussell published in Penguin Books 2013

Introduction by Paul Fussell from *Siegfried Sassoon's Long Journey:
Selections from the Sherston Memoirs*, edited by Paul Fussell (1983).
Reprinted by permission of Oxford University Press (USA).

LIBRARY OF CONGRESS CATALOGING-IN-PUBLICATION DATA
Sassoon, Siegfried, 1886–1967.
Memoirs of an infantry officer / Siegfried Sassoon ; introduction by Paul Fussell.
pages ; cm.—(Penguin classics)
ISBN 978-0-14-310716-3
1. World War, 1914–1918—Fiction. I. Title.
PR6037.A86M36 2013
823'.912—dc23   2013000418

Printed in the United States of America
5   7   9   10   8   6

Contents

Introduction

The First World War, which lasted more than four years and killed seventeen million people, scored across twentieth-century history a deep dividing line, ugly as the scar of its own trenches. Before the war, the world could seem safely stabilized by monarchies, religious certainties, and patriotic pieties. But afterwards, the world appears recognizably "modern," its institutions precarious, its faith feeble, its choices risky, its very landscapes perverted into the Waste Land. No one contemplating the events of 1914–1918 in relation to the years preceding can quite escape this sense of experience divided into "before" and "after." Thus J. B. Priestley comparing the First War with the Second: "I think the First War cut deeper and played more tricks with time because it was first. . . . If you were born in 1894, as I was, you suddenly saw a great jagged crack in the looking-glass. After that your mind could not escape from the idea of a world that ended in 1914 and another one that began about 1919, with a wilderness of smoke and fury, outside sensible time, lying between them." One reason we understand so readily this scheme of before and after is that we have been taught it by the young writers who found in the First World War their first important literary material and who addressed it with the thrill of discovery that has kept their works fresh and powerful. Writing within their various national styles, Henri Barbusse in France, Erich Maria Remarque in Germany, and Hemingway in America earned their earliest reputations by exploiting this theme of before and after. In England, Edmund Blunden, Robert Graves, and Siegfried Sassoon did the same. All would agree with Priestley who says, "I left one world to spend an exile in limbo, came out of it to find myself in another world."

Why does Siegfried Sassoon seem so quintessentially English? One reason, surely, is his almost erotic fondness for the pastoral countryside. Another is his devotion to horses and horse culture. Another is his being equally skilled in prose and verse while declining to raise a clamor in either. And finally, there is his preference for experience over abstract thought, or, to put it more bluntly, his lack of interest in ideas. "My brain," he says, "absorbs facts singly, and the process of relating them to one another has always been difficult." When a reviewer observed of his book of poems *Counter-Attack* (1918) that Sassoon seemed "entirely devoid of intellectual edge," he commented: "But I could have told him that myself." What interests Sassoon instead is appearances, the look of things, especially the look of things in a past affectionately remembered, or even ambiguously remembered: "Oh yes, I see it all, from A to Z!" he says of the front line, recalling it with mingled love and horror at the end of these memoirs. These books emphasize Sassoon's distinction as an observer and evoker of visible objects, both in peace and war. If the war came close to exterminating Sassoon, it also educated him, teaching him, he writes, "one useful lesson—that on the whole it was very nice to be alive at all." It also developed in him "the habit of observing things with more receptiveness and accuracy than I had ever attempted to do in my undisciplined past."

The countryside he liked to feel alive in was the Weald of Kent, the wooded and agricultural part of that county southeast of London. He was born there in 1886, one of three brothers. His brother Hamo was to be killed at Gallipoli in 1915. The house of his well-to-do family stood at the edge of the green in the village of Matfield (here, in these fictionalized memoirs, "Butley"), a few miles from Tunbridge Wells. When Siegfried was five, his Spanish-Jewish father left his wife and died soon after. The boy grew up protected and encouraged by his mother, who had artistic and literary relatives. She knew critics and editors like Edmund Gosse and Edward Marsh, who interested themselves both in the boy and in his early verses. (The "Aunt Evelyn" of these memoirs is a fiction.) He went to Marlborough College (here, "Ballboro"), whose headmaster told him as he left, "Try to be more sensible." He proceeded to Clare College, Cambridge, where he began reading law but shifted to history and finally to nothing at all, leaving after four terms and returning to Kent. Delighted to be reinstalled at home, far from demands that he think, he collected books, read (with heavy emphasis on the hunting whimsies of R. S. Surtees), played cricket and golf, fox-hunted, and mooned shyly about, versifying in the vague sentimental mode customary in pre-war minor poetry. Between the ages of nineteen and twenty-six he published privately nine volumes of dreamy romantic verse, a fact he omits entirely from the "outdoor" version of his life he presents here.

This idyll was ended by the outbreak of war on August 4, 1914. He was healthy, naïve, unthinkingly patriotic, and horsy, and by August 5 he was in the uniform of a cavalry trooper. He was twenty-eight years old. Soon he transferred to the infantry and became a second lieutenant in the Royal Welch Fusiliers. Before long he was in action in France, where his initial enthusiasm gradually yielded to outrage as he learned that the war was not at all the heroic, high-minded operation pictured by propaganda. He was a brave and able officer, and his men, with many of whom he was in love, liked him for his kindness to them. One remembers: "It was only once in a blue moon that we had an officer like Mr. Sassoon." He turned fierce after his friend, fellow-officer David Thomas ("Dick Tiltwood"), was killed. Lieutenant D. C. Thomas had been Sassoon's current ideal companion, a Galahad figure,

> One whose yellow head was kissed
> By the gods, who thought about him
> Till they couldn't do without him.

("There is no doubt that I am still a Pre-Raphaelite," Sassoon once wrote in his diary.)

Conceiving that the cause of David's death was the Germans

rather than the war, Sassoon set himself to avenge him by bolder and bolder forays against the enemy. These helped earn him the nickname "Mad Jack" from his platoon. He won the Military Cross for bringing in wounded under fire, and he was soon wounded in the shoulder himself. While convalescing at home, pity for his men grew on him, together with a conviction that the war was a fraud, a swindle practiced on the troops by bellicose civilians at home and their viceregents, the staff, safely ensconced back at the Base. He began writing anti-homefront poems satirizing the cruelty and complacency of those whose relation to the war was rather forensic than empirical. These poems were very different from the ones he'd written before the war. Then, he had been content to turn out courteous little verses like this:

NIMROD IN SEPTEMBER

When half the drowsy world's abed
And misty morning rises red,
With jollity of horn and lusty cheer,
Young Nimrod urges on his dwindling rout;
Along the yellowing coverts we can hear
His horse's hoofs thud hither and about:
In mulberry coat he rides and makes
Huge clamour in the sultry brakes.

Before the war his poems had celebrated Dryads, "roundelays and jocund airs," dulcimers and shoon, daffodillies, shepherds, and "ye patient kine." Indeed, as the eminent pastoralist Edmund Blunden once said, "No poet of twentieth-century England . . . was originally more romantic and floral than young Siegfried Sassoon from Kent." But now he unleashed a talent for irony and satire and contumely that had been sleeping all during his pastoral youth:

"TIIEY"

The Bishop tells us: "When the boys come back
They will not be the same; for they'll have fought
In a just cause: they lead the last attack
On Anti-Christ; their comrades' blood has bought
New right to breed an honourable race,
They have challenged Death and dared him face to face."

"We're none of us the same!" the boys reply.
"For George lost both his legs; and Bill's stone blind;
Poor Jim's shot through the lungs and like to die;
And Bert's gone syphilitic: you'll not find
A chap who's served that hasn't found *some* change."
And the Bishop said: "The ways of God are strange!"

(As Wilfred Owen noticed, "Sassoon admires Thos. Hardy more than anybody living.")

In the blank verse in which formerly he had described rural delights he now delivered outdoor views of a different sort:

We'd gained our first objective hours before
While dawn broke like a face with blinking eyes,
Pallid, unshaved and thirsty, blind with smoke.
Things seemed all right at first. We held their line,
With bombers posted, Lewis guns well placed,
And clink of shovels deepening the shallow trench.
    The place was rotten with dead; green clumsy legs
    High-booted, sprawled and grovelled along the saps
    And trunks, face downward, in the sucking mud,
    Wallowed like trodden sand-bags loosely filled;
    And naked sodden buttocks, mats of hair,
    Bulged, clotted heads slept in the plastering slime.
    And then the rain began—the jolly old rain!

Back home the recruiting posters depicted women proudly watching the troops march away ("Women of Britain Say—

'GO!'"), and Phyllis Dare's music-hall song was heard everywhere:

> Oh, we don't want to lose you,
> But we think you ought to go;
> For your King and your Country
> Both need you so.
>
> We shall want you and miss you,
> But with all our might and main
> We will thank you, cheer you, kiss you,
> When you come back again.

Sassoon's response:

GLORY OF WOMEN

> You love us when we're heroes, home on leave,
> Or wounded in a mentionable place.
> You worship decorations; you believe
> That chivalry redeems the war's disgrace.
> You make us shells. You listen with delight,
> By tales of dirt and danger fondly thrilled.
> You crown our distant ardours while we fight,
> And mourn our laurelled memories when we're killed.
> You can't believe that British troops "retire"
> When hell's last horror breaks them, and they run,
> Trampling the terrible corpses—blind with blood.
>   O German mother dreaming by the fire,
>   While you are knitting socks to send your son
>   His face is trodden deeper in the mud.

Popular as poems like these were with the young avant-
garde back in London, they scandalized the respectable. The
critic John Middleton Murry found Sassoon's performances
"verses, . . . not poetry," mere "violent journalism": "He has no
calm," Murry wrote, "therefore he conveys no terror; he has

no harmony, therefore he cannot pierce us with the anguish of discord." Indeed, "Mr. Sassoon's mind is a chaos." Not certain whether to back this horse or not, Gosse straddled the critical fence, saying of Sassoon's *The Old Huntsman and Other Poems* (1917): "His temper is not altogether to be applauded, for such sentiments must tend to relax the effort of the struggle, yet they can hardly be reproved when conducted with so much honesty and courage. . . ." One might imagine that the scandal produced by Sassoon's anti-war poems would have been noticed everywhere in lettered England. But two years after the Armistice Rider Haggard confesses that he's never heard of Siegfried Sassoon and wonders whether he's not just another "Jew of the advanced school," like Bakst, Epstein, or Proust. Urged by an acquaintance to read Sassoon's poems, he finally does so, to find them "feeble and depressing rubbish."

But Sassoon was maturing an outrage more offensive than a few poems calling into question the official, sanitized view of the war. In July 1917, encouraged by H. W. Massingham ("Markington"), editor of the liberal weekly the *Nation*, and Bertrand Russell ("Thornton Tyrell"), he set off his own bombshell. He published his famous document "A Soldier's Declaration," in which he explained "his grounds for refusing to serve further in the army":

> I am making this statement as an act of wilful defiance of military authority, because I believe that the war is being deliberately prolonged by those who have the power to end it.
>
> I am a soldier, convinced that I am acting on behalf of soldiers. I believe that this war, upon which I entered as a war of defence and liberation, has now become a war of aggression and conquest. I believe that the purposes for which I and my fellow-soldiers entered upon this war should have been so clearly stated as to have made it impossible to change them, and that, had this been done, the objects which actuated us would now be attainable by negotiation.
>
> I have seen and endured the sufferings of the troops, and I can no longer be a party to prolong these sufferings for ends which I believe to be evil and unjust.

I am not protesting against the conduct of the war, but against the political errors and insincerities for which the fighting men are being sacrificed.

On behalf of those who are suffering now I make this protest against the deception which is being practiced on them; also I believe that I may help to destroy the callous complacence with which the majority of those at home regard the continuance of agonies which they do not share, and which they have not sufficient imagination to realize.

S. SASSOON.

He expected to be court-martialed for this, the attendant publicity, he hoped, adding force to the tiny public sentiment in favor of ending the war through a negotiated peace. Instead, assisted by his friend and fellow Royal Welch Fusilier Robert Graves ("David Cromlech"), he was sent by the authorities before a medical board, as if anyone voicing such pacific sentiments must be deranged. The medical officers found him overstrained and consigned him to a comfortable army mental hospital, Craiglockhart (here, "Slateford"), near Edinburgh.

In the hospital he met a poetical fan of his, Lieutenant Wilfred Owen, currently being treated for combat neurasthenia. Owen's enthusiasm for Sassoon's poetry and person was unbounded. He wrote his mother: "I have just been reading Siegfried Sassoon, and am feeling at a very high pitch of emotion. Nothing like his trench life sketches has ever been written or ever will be written." Owen quickly sought out his idol and sent this report to a friend: "He is very tall and stately, with a fine firm chisel'd (how's that?) head, ordinary short brown hair. The general expression of his face is one of boredom. . . . The last thing he said was 'Sweat your guts out writing poetry.' 'Eh?' says I. 'Sweat your guts out, I say!' He also warned me against early publishing. . . . He himself is thirty! Looks under 25!" (Typically, in the horsy *Memoirs of George Sherston* Sassoon says nothing about this meeting, while dealing with it extensively in his report on his literary life, *Siegfried's Journey*.)

In the hospital, guilt at the ease and safety he had purchased by his gesture of disobedience began to trouble him, and he finally persuaded his psychiatrist to let him go back to the war. His psychiatrist was Dr. W. H. R. Rivers (1864–1922), the well-known Cambridge physiologist and anthropologist, a bachelor 53-year-old Royal Army Medical Corps captain when Sassoon encountered him. In one sense Rivers is the real hero of "George Sherston's" memoirs, and the only person whose name Sassoon has not changed. His memory was a lifelong presence for Sassoon, who much later, in 1952, wrote in his diary: "I should like to meet Rivers in 'the next world.' It is difficult to believe that such a man as he could be extinguished." Sped on his way by Rivers, he returned to active service, at first in Egypt and Palestine. But he was transferred back to the Western Front after the German attack of March 1918, and in July he was wounded again, this time in the head, and sent home for good.

After the war he found himself caught up in London literary life, especially that branch of it espousing a genteel socialism, and for a time he worked as literary editor of the socialist *Daily Herald*. But when he was alone he was trembly and tired, afflicted by nightmares of the war. He felt a vague impulse to write something more sustained than lyric poems but wasn't certain what it should be. A long poem? A play? Or did he have a talent for prose? For fiction? For memoir? Later, he remembered talking with Gosse shortly after the Armistice:

> During our talk he strongly urged me to undertake a long poem which would serve as a peg on which—for the general public—my reputation would hang. He suggested that I might draw on my sporting experiences for typical country figures—the squire, the doctor, the parson, and so on. He was, of course, partly influenced by anxiety that I should divert my mind from the war. At the time I thought the idea unworthy of serious consideration.

Too much, perhaps, like a replay of George Crabbe's *The Parish Register* and *The Borough*. But Gosse's suggestion, if mistaken in its particulars, proved fruitful as Sassoon continued to meditate what he should write. As he tells his diary late one night in March 1921:

> I walked back from the Reform [Club] under a black but starful sky, feeling dangerously confident in myself and the masterpiece that I'll be writing five, ten, fifteen, or twenty years hence. That masterpiece has become a perfectly definite object in my existence, but it is curious, and rather disquieting, that I always dream of it as a novel or a prose drama, rather than as a poem or series of poems. . . . The theme of my "masterpiece" demands great art and great qualities of another kind.

It's clear that he's thinking of writing a book registering subtly and in the process justifying his homosexuality. His masterpiece, he says,

> is to be one of the stepping-stones across the raging (or lethargic) river of intolerance which divides creatures of my temperament from a free and unsecretive existence among their fellow-men. . . . O, that unwritten book! Its difficulties are overwhelming.

Eighteen months later he's still obsessed with this urgent but cloudy project. "My whole life has become involved," he says, "in an internal resolve to prepare my mind for a big effort of creation. I want to write a book called *The Man Who Loved the World*, in which I will embody my whole passionate emotionalism toward every experience which collides with my poetic sensitiveness." But alas, "At present I have not any idea of the architectural plan of this edifice."

But finally he got it: he would write a fictionalized autobiography elegizing his young friends killed in the war. "The dead . . . are more real than the living," he wrote in his diary in 1922, "because they are complete." At the same time he would try to understand what the events of 1914–1918 had done to him and his pre-war world, what their relation was, if any, to that pastoral quietude so rudely displaced. Knowing

now what he wanted to do, in 1926 he embarked on twenty
years of obsessive prose writing. In six volumes of artful memoirs he revisited the war and lovingly recovered the contrasting
scene of gentle self-indulgence and pastoral beauty preceding
it. At first uncertain of the value of his work, he sent some
manuscript pages to Gosse, who replied: "I think you will be
anxious for a word from me, and so I write provisionally to
say that I am delighted with it so far. There is no question at
all that you must go on steadily. It will be an extraordinarily
original book. . . ." But as further pages arrived, Gosse was
moved to reprehend a part of Sassoon he's always been uncomfortable with, his impulse to irony and self-distrust: "You are
not called upon," he reminded Siegfried, "to draw a sarcastic
picture of a slack and idle young man. . . . Remember, no satire and no sneering!"

The first volume, *Memoirs of a Fox-Hunting Man*, was published in 1928, a moment which brought forth two other classics
of innocence savaged by twentieth-century events, Blunden's
memoir *Undertones of War* and, in Germany, Remarque's novel
Im Westen Nichts Neues. Two years later, just as Graves was
publishing *Good-Bye to All That* and Hemingway *A Farewell
to Arms*, Sassoon brought out his second volume, *Memoirs of
an Infantry Officer*. And in 1936 *Sherston's Progress* com-
pleted the trilogy he finally titled *The Memoirs of George
Sherston*.

The story he tells here is that of a shy, awkward, extremely
limited young country gentleman acquainted only with hunting and cricket and golf who learns about the greater adult
world the hardest way—by perceiving and absorbing the
details of its most shocking war. One irony is that Sherston is
removed from the aimlessness of his rural life not by, say, a
career in the City, which before the war might have been
thought the appropriate antidote to idleness; he's removed
from it by an alternative quite needlessly excessive, the hell of
the trenches. The action of *The Memoirs of George Sherston*
is the transformation of a boy into a man, able at last to transfer his affection for horses first to people, and finally to principles. But this transformation is slow and belated. Sherston is

over thirty before he begins to master the facts of life, instructed at one point by seeing "an English soldier lying by the road with a horribly smashed head." Only now is he able to perceive that "life, for the majority of the population, is an unlovely struggle against unfair odds, culminating in a cheap funeral." One reason Sherston learns so slowly is that his character is so inconsistent and unfixed. He is never certain what he is. "He varied," Graves remembers, "between happy warrior and bitter pacifist." And his company second-in-command, Vivian de Sola Pinto ("Velmore"), notes a similar confusion. "It seemed to me a strange paradox," he recalls, "that the author of these poems [in *Counter-Attack*] full of burning indignation against war's cruelty should also be a first-rate soldier and a most aggressive company commander." It is out of such queer antitheses and ironies that Sassoon constructs these memoirs.

Of course every account of front-line experience in the First World War is necessarily ironic because such experience was so much worse than anyone expected. If in *Good-Bye to All That* Graves's irony is broad and rowdy, in *The Memoirs of George Sherston* Sassoon's is quiet and subtle. An example is the way he deals with the theme of horses and warfare, which is to say the way he relates the war part of his memoirs to the earlier pastoral part. In a quiet way, the memoirs become an ironic disclosure of the fate of cavalry—the traditional important military arm in the world before the war—in the new, quite unanticipated war of static confrontation across a pocked, pitted, and impassable No Man's Land. In Sherston's youth the cavalry was virtually the equivalent of the Army. But the machine gun and massed artillery changed all that, and almost all the one million horses used by the British army were put to work ignominiously behind the lines only, hauling rations and ammunitions. And a half-million were killed even then. What happened to the pre-war cavalry tradition for both Allies and Central Powers can be inferred from the production figures for machine guns. In 1915, the British manufactured 1,700. In 1916, 9,600. In 1917, 19,000. The war was inexorably becoming a heavy duty enterprise, and the swank of cavalry was only one of the colorful things it swept away.

Once this trilogy of memoirs was finished, Sassoon began another set. As if dissatisfied now with the degree of fiction he'd imposed on his experience, he began reviving the past all over again, writing now what he calls his "real auto-biography," this time as "Siegfried Sassoon" rather than "George Sherston." The result was a second trilogy, more true to fact this time, comprising *The Old Century and Seven More Years* (1938), *The Weald of Youth* (1942), and *Siegfried's Progress* (1945). But remote from fact as here and there it may be, the earlier trilogy seems the more persuasive of the two attempts to capture the past. "I am a firm believer in the *Memoirs*," Sassoon once said.

If Sherston was depicted as an athletic, non-literary youth, in the second trilogy Sassoon reveals himself more accurately as a poet extremely ambitious of success among the artistically powerful of London. "Sherston," he says, "was a simplified version of my 'outdoor self.' He was denied the complex advantage of being a soldier poet." But both characters, representing the two sides of himself he was never sure cohered into a whole, are notable for modesty and understatement, as well as a certain "chuckle-headed inconsistency," as he puts it. But smile as he may with amusement and pity at his former self, Sassoon's lifetime devotion to the young man he once was has something undeniably narcissistic about it, and in this he resembles another cunning twentieth-century memoirist, Christopher Isherwood. Both have created careers by plowing and re-plowing their variously furtive pasts, revealing something different with each rendering. Isherwood's shameful-proud relation to "Christopher" is similar to Siegfried's relation to "George." Thus Sassoon writes in his diary, "What it amounts to is this, that I must behave naturally, keeping one side of my mind aloof, a watchful critic. One part of me . . . is the player on the stage. But I must also be the audience, and not an indulgent one either." It is this very self-conscious awareness of himself as a performer uttering lines that gives much of *The Memoirs of George Sherston* its special quality, as in the scene in the hospital where he indicates the different things appropriate for him to utter in front of various audiences.

Aesthetes and hearties: that opposition, still a popular jocular way for university students to divide each other up, seemed in Sassoon's day a significant set of polar categories, and it was natural for him to conceive of the range of his own character by means of that formula. The polarities of horseman and artist are nicely indicated by two adjacent diary entries he made in 1920:

> Oct 20   Bought mare.
> Oct 27   Bought Pickering Aldine poets (53 vols)

and a little later he writes, "Inconsistency—double life—as usual. . . ." What he has done in *The Memoirs of George Sherston* is to objectify one-half of the creature leading this double life, the half identifiable as the sensitive but mindless athlete, and separate it from the other half, that of the much-cossetted aspirant poet, taken up by Lady Ottoline Morrell, Robert Ross, and other useful figures of the salons. Aestheticism, the actual milieu of his family and friends, vanishes from George Sherston's story. Hence the unsophisticated Aunt Evelyn replaces his actual mother and aunt and uncle, respectively painter, editor, and sculptor. Why does he jettison this Pateresque aspect of himself and his environs? Because, I think, he hopes to show the effect of the war on a more representative and ordinary man, not the man of sensibility and privilege he actually was—rich, literary, musical, arty, careerist. *The Memoirs* is in part a thirties pacifist document, like Vera Brittain's *Testament of Youth* (1933); and for it to work it must persuade the reader that the condition of the protagonist is not excessively distant from his own.

During the thirties Sassoon, active in pacifist causes, was distressed to witness Europe moving steadily toward war again. In 1933, at the age of forty-seven, he married and had one son,

George. He continued to write poetry, but most critics found this later work feeble compared with his performance as a "war poet." "My renown as a W.P.," he observed, "has now become a positive burden to me." In 1957 he became a Roman Catholic, and in 1967 he died at the age of eighty. But as he seemed to recognize himself, the interesting part of his life was the earlier part, which he revisited repeatedly, recalling twice over in superb prose the Edwardian and Georgian world of his youth and the war that shattered it forever.

PAUL FUSSELL
Princeton
July 1983

Memoirs of an
Infantry Officer

PART ONE

AT THE ARMY
SCHOOL

1

I have said that Spring arrived late in 1916, and that up in the trenches opposite Mametz it seemed as though Winter would last for ever. I also stated that *as for me, I had more or less made up my mind to die because in the circumstances there didn't seem anything else to be done*. Well, we came back to Morlancourt after Easter, and on the same evening a message from the Orderly Room instructed me to proceed to the Fourth Army School next morning for a month's refresher-course. Perhaps Colonel Kinjack had heard that I'd been looking for trouble. Anyhow, my personal grievance against the Germans was interrupted for at least four weeks, and a motor-bus carried me away from all possibility of dying a murky death in the mine-craters.

Barton saw me off at the crossroads in the middle of the village. It was a fine day and he had recovered his good spirits. 'Lucky Kangaroo – to be hopping away for a holiday!' he exclaimed, as I climbed into the elderly bus. My servant Flook hoisted up my bulging valise, wiped his red face with his sleeve, and followed me to the roof. 'Mind and keep Mr Sherston well polished up and punctual on parade, Flook!' said Barton. Flook grinned; and away we went. Looking back, I saw Barton's good-natured face, with the early sun shining on his glasses.

There were several of us on board (each Battalion in our Brigade was sending two officers) and we must have stopped at the next village to pick up a few more. But memory tries to misinform me that Flook and I were alone on that omnibus, with a fresh breeze in our faces and our minds 'making a separate peace' with the late April landscape. With sober satisfaction I watched a train moving out of a station with rumble and clank of wheels while we waited at the crossing gates. Children in a village street surprised me: I saw a little one fall, to be gathered, dusted, cuffed and cherished by its mother. Up in the line one somehow lost touch with such humanities.

The War was abundantly visible in supply-convoys, artillery horse-lines, in the dirty white tents of a Red Cross camp, or in troops going placidly to their billets. But everyone seemed to be off duty; spring had arrived and the fruit trees were in blossom; breezes ruffled the reedy pools and creeks along the Somme, and here and there a peaceful fisherman forgot that he was a soldier on active service. I had been in close contact with trench warfare, and here was a demonstration of its contrast with cosy civilian comfort. One had to find things out as one goes along, I thought; and I was whole-heartedly grateful for the green grass and a miller's wagon with four horses, and the spire of Amiens Cathedral rising above the congregated roofs of an undamaged city.

The Fourth Army School was at Flixécourt, a clean little town exactly halfway between Amiens and Abbeville. Between Flixécourt and the War (which for my locally experienced mind meant the Fricourt trenches) there were more than thirty English miles. Mentally, the distance became immeasurable during my first days at the School. Parades and lectures were all in the day's work, but they failed to convince me of their affinity with our long days and nights in the Front Line. For instance, although I was closely acquainted with the mine-craters in the Fricourt sector, I would have welcomed a few practical hints on how to patrol those God-forsaken cavities. But the Army School instructors were all in favour of Open Warfare, which was sure to come soon, they said. They had learnt all about it in peace-time; it was essential that we should be taught to 'think in terms of mobility'. So we solved tactical schemes in which the enemy was reported to have occupied some village several miles away, and with pencil and paper made arrangements for unflurried defence or blank-cartridged skirmishing in a land of field-day make-believe.

Sometimes a renowned big-game hunter gave us demonstrations of the art of sniping. He was genial and enthusiastic; but I was no good at rifle-shooting, and as far as I was concerned he would have been more profitably employed in reducing the numerical strength of the enemy. He was an expert on loop-holes and telescopic-sights; but telescopic-sights were a luxury seldom enjoyed by an infantry battalion in the trenches.

The Commandant of the School was a tremendous worker and everyone liked him. His motto was 'always do your utmost', but I dare say that if he had been asked his private opinion he would have admitted that the School was in reality only a holi-day for officers and N.C.O.s who needed a rest. It certainly seemed so to me when I awoke on the first morning and became conscious of my clean little room with its tiled floor and shut-tered windows. I knew that the morning was fine; voices passed outside; sparrows chirped and starlings whistled; the bell in the church tower tolled and a clock struck the quarters. Flook entered with my Sam Browne belt and a jug of hot water. He remarked that we'd come to the right place, for once, and regret-ted that we weren't there for the duration. Wiping my face after a satisfactory shave, I stared out of the window; on the other side of the street a blossoming apple-tree leant over an old gar-den wall, and I could see the friendly red roof of a dovecot. It was a luxury to be alone, with plenty of space for my portable property. There was a small table on which I could arrange my few books. Hardy's *Far from the Madding Crowd* was one of them. Also Lamb's *Essays* and *Mr Sponge's Sporting Tour*. Books about England were all that I wanted. I decided to do plenty of solid reading at the Army School.

Near by was the Mess Room where fourteen of us had our meals. A jolly-faced Captain from the Ulster Division had un-dertaken the office of Mess President and everyone was talk-ative and friendly. With half an hour to spare after breakfast, I strolled up the hill and smoked my pipe under a quick-set hedge. Loosening my belt, I looked at a chestnut tree in full leaf and listened to the perfect performance of a nightingale. Such things seemed miraculous after the desolation of the trenches. Never before had I been so intensely aware of what it meant to be young and healthy in fine weather at the outset of

summer. The untroubled notes of the nightingale made the
Army School seem like some fortunate colony which was, for
the sake of appearances, pretending to assist the struggle from
afar. It feels as if it's a place where I might get a chance to call
my soul my own, I thought, as I went down the hill to my first
parade. If only they don't chivvy us about too much, I added. . . .
It was not unlike the first day of a public school term, and my
form-master (we were divided into classes of twenty-eight) was
a youngish Major in the Oxford and Bucks Light Infantry. He
was an even-tempered man, pleasant to obey, and specially likeable through a certain shyness of manner. I cannot remember
that any of us caused him any annoyance, though he more than
once asked me to try and be less absent-minded. Later in the
year he was commanding a battalion and I don't doubt that he
did it excellently.

Every afternoon at half-past five the School assembled to listen to a lecture. Eyeing an audience of about 300 officers and
N.C.O.s, I improved my knowledge of regimental badges, which
seemed somehow to affect the personality of the wearer. A
lion, a lamb, a dragon or an antelope, a crown, a harp, a tiger
or a sphinx, these devices differentiated men in more ways than
one. But the regimental names were probably the potent factor,
and my meditations while waiting for the lecturer would lead
me along pleasant associative lanes connected with the English
counties – the difference between Durham and Devon for instance. There was food for thought also in the fact of sitting
between a Connaught Ranger and a Seaforth Highlander,
though both were likely to have been born in Middlesex.
Queer, too, was the whole scene in that schoolroom, containing as it did a splendid sample of the Fourth Army which began
the Somme Battle a couple of months afterwards. It was one of
those peaceful war pictures which have vanished for ever and
are rarely recovered even in imaginative retrospect.

My woolgatherings were cut short when the lecturer cleared
his throat; the human significance of the audience was obliterated then, and its outlook on life became restricted to destruction and defence. A gas expert from G.H.Q. would inform us

that 'gas was still in its infancy'. (Most of us were either dead or disabled before gas had had time to grow up.) An urbane Artillery General assured us that high explosive would be our best friend in future battles, and his ingratiating voice made us unmindful, for the moment, that explosives often arrived from the wrong direction. But the star turn in the schoolroom was a massive sandy-haired Highland Major whose subject was 'The Spirit of the Bayonet'. Though at that time undecorated, he was afterwards awarded the D.S.O. for lecturing. He took as his text a few leading points from the *Manual of Bayonet Training*.

To attack with the bayonet effectively requires Good Direction, Strength and Quickness, during a state of wild excitement and probably physical exhaustion. The bayonet is essentially an offensive weapon. In a bayonet assault all ranks go forward to kill or be killed, and only those who have developed skill and strength by constant training will be able to kill. The spirit of the bayonet must be inculcated into all ranks, so that they go forward with that aggressive determination and confidence of superiority born of continual practice, without which a bayonet assault will not be effective.

He spoke with homicidal eloquence, keeping the game alive with genial and well-judged jokes. He had a Sergeant to assist him. The Sergeant, a tall sinewy machine, had been trained to such a pitch of frightfulness that at a moment's warning he could divest himself of all semblance of humanity. With rifle and bayonet he illustrated the Major's ferocious aphorisms, including facial expression. When told to 'put on the killing face', he did so, combining it with an ultra-vindictive attitude. 'To instil fear into the opponent' was one of the Major's main maxims. Man, it seemed, had been created to jab the life out of Germans. To hear the Major talk, one might have thought that he did it himself every day before breakfast. His final words were: 'Remember that every Boche you fellows kill is a point scored to our side; every Boche you kill brings victory one minute nearer and shortens the war by one minute. Kill them! Kill them! There's only one good Boche, and that's a dead one!'

Afterwards I went up the hill to my favourite sanctuary, a

wood of hazels and beeches. The evening air smelt of wet mould and wet leaves; the trees were misty-green; the church bell was tolling in the town, and smoke rose from the roofs. Peace was there in the twilight of that prophetic foreign spring. But the lecturer's voice still battered on my brain. 'The bullet and the bayonet are brother and sister.' 'If you don't kill him, he'll kill you.' 'Stick him between the eyes, in the throat, in the chest.' 'Don't waste good steel. Six inches are enough. What's the use of a foot of steel sticking out at the back of a man's neck? Three inches will do for him; when he coughs, go and look for another.'

But what about being shot at.

2

Whatever my private feelings may have been after the Major's lecture, the next morning saw me practising bayonet-fighting. It was all in the day's work; short points, long points, parries, jabs, plus the always-to-be-remembered importance of 'a quick with-drawal'. Capering over the obstacles of the assault course and prodding sacks of straw was healthy exercise; the admirable sergeant-instructor was polite and unformidable, and as I didn't want him to think me a dud officer, I did my best to become pro-ficient. Obviously it would have been both futile and inexpedient to moralize about bayonet-fighting at an Army School.

There is a sense of recovered happiness in the glimpse I catch of myself coming out of my cottage door with a rifle slung on my shoulder. There was nothing wrong with life on those fine mornings when the air smelt so fresh and my body was young and vigorous, and I hurried down the white road, along the empty street, and up the hill to our training ground. I was like a boy going to early school, except that no bell was ringing, and instead of Thucydides or Virgil, I carried a gun. Forget-ting, for the moment, that I was at the Front to be shot at, I could almost congratulate myself on having a holiday in France without paying for it.

I also remember how I went one afternoon to have a hot

bath in the Jute Mill. The water was poured into a dyeing vat. Remembering that I had a bath may not be of much interest to anyone, but it was a good bath, and it is my own story that I am trying to tell, and as such it must be received; those who expect a universalization of the Great War must look for it elsewhere. Here they will only find an attempt to show its effect on a somewhat solitary-minded young man.

At that time I was comfortably aware that the British Expeditionary Force in France was a prosperous concern. I have already remarked that the officers and N.C.O.s at the School epitomized a resolute mass of undamaged material; equally impressive was the equine abundance which I observed one afternoon when we were on our way to a 'demonstration' at the Army Bombing School. Hundreds of light and heavy draft horses were drawn up along a road for an inspection by the Commander-in-Chief (a bodily presence which the infantry mind could not easily imagine). The horses, attached to their appropriate vehicles and shining in their summer coats, looked a picture of sleekness and strength. They were of all sorts and sizes but their power and compactness was uniform. The horsehood of England was there with every buckle of its harness brightened. There weren't many mules among them, for mules were mostly with the Artillery, and this was a slap-up Army Service Corps parade, obviously the climax of several weeks' preparation. I wished that I could have spent the afternoon inspecting them; but I was only a second-lieutenant, and the bus carried me on to study explosions and smoke-clouds, and to hear a lecture about the tactical employment of the Mills' bomb.

News of the Battalion came from the Quartermaster, to whom I had sent an account of my 'cushy' existence. Dottrell wrote that things had been quiet up in the Line, but advised me to make the most of my rest-cure, adding that he'd always noticed that the further you got from the front line the further you got from the War. In accordance with my instructions he was making good progress with the box of kippers (which Aunt Evelyn sent me twice a month); ditto the Devonshire cream, though some of it hadn't stood the journey well. His letter put me in the right frame of mind for returning to tours of trenches, though I should be sorry to say good-bye to young Allgood, with whom I was spending most of my spare time.

Allgood was quiet, thoughtful, and fond of watching birds. We had been to the same public school, though there were nearly ten years between us. He told me that he hoped to be a historian, and I listened respectfully while he talked about the Romans in Early Britain, which was his favourite subject. It was easy to imagine him as an undergraduate at Cambridge; travelling in Germany during the Long Vacation and taking a good Degree. But his Degree had been postponed indefinitely. He said he'd always wanted to go to Germany, and there seemed nothing incongruous in the remark; for the moment I forgot that every German we killed was a point scored to our side. Allgood never grumbled about the war, for he was a gentle soul, willing to take his share in it, though obviously unsuited to homicide. But there was an expression of veiled melancholy on his face, as if he were inwardly warned that he would never see his home in Wiltshire again. A couple of months afterwards I saw his name in one of the long lists of killed, and it seemed to me that I had expected it.

Our last day at the School was hot and cloudless. In the morning English and French Generals rolled up in their cars; there must have been about a hundred of them; it was not unlike an army of uniformed Uncles on Prize-giving Day. There were no prizes, naturally. But we did our best to show them how efficient we were, by running round the assault course in teams, stabbing the straw sacks. We also competed in putting up screw-pickets and barbed wire with rapidity and precision. Our exertions ended with a march past the Army Commander, and then we fell out to witness the explosion of two small mines. Earth and chalk heaved up at the blue sky, the ground vibrated, and there was a noise like a mad rainstorm, caused by the whizzing descent of clods and stones and the hiss of smaller particles. Finally, a fountain of dingy smoke arose and drifted away from the débris, and the Generals retired to have luncheon in the white château; and there, let us hope, they let their belts out a hole or two and allowed themselves a little relaxation from intellectual effort. Allgood said that he thought the French Generals looked much brainier than the British ones; but I told him that they must be cleverer than they looked, and anyhow, they'd all got plenty of medal-ribbons.

PART TWO

THE RAID

1

Adventure.

I came back from the Army School at the end of a hot Saturday afternoon. The bus turned off the bumpy main road from Cor-bie and began to crawl down a steep winding lane. I looked, and there was Morlancourt in the hollow. On the whole I con-sidered myself lucky to be returning to a place where I knew my way about. It was no use regretting the little room at Flixé-court where I had been able to sit alone every night, reading a good book and calling my soul my own. . . . Distant hills and hazy valleys were dazzled with sunrays and the glaring beams made a fiery mist in the foreground. It was jolly fine country, I thought. I had become quite fond of it, and the end-of-the-world along the horizon had some obscure hold over my mind which drew my eyes to it almost eagerly, for I could still think of trench warfare as an adventure. The horizon was quiet just now, as if the dragons which lived there were dozing.

The Battalion was out of the line, and I felt almost glad to be back as I walked up to our old Company Mess with Flook carrying my valise on his back. Flook and I were very good friends, and his vigilance for my personal comfort was such that I could more easily imagine him using his rifle in defence of my valise than against the Germans.

Nobody was in when I got to our billets, but the place had improved since I last saw it; the horse-chestnut in front of the house was in flower and there were a few peonies and pink roses in the neglected little garden at the back.

Dusk had fallen when I returned from a stroll in the fields; the candles were lit, there was a smell of cooking, and the ser-vants were clattering tin plates in the sizzling kitchen. Durley,

Birdie Mansfield, and young Ormand were sitting round the
table, with a new officer who was meekly reading the newspaper which served as tablecloth. They all looked glum, but my
advent caused some pumped-up cheeriness, and I was introduced to the newcomer whose name was Fewnings. (He wore
spectacles and in private life had been a schoolmaster.) Not
much was said until the end of the steak and onions; by then
Mansfield had lowered the level of the whisky bottle by a couple of inches, while the rest of us drank lime-juice. Tinned
peaches appeared, and I inquired where Barton was – with an
uneasy feeling that something might have happened to him.
Ormand replied that the old man was dining at Battalion
Headquarters. 'And skiting to Kinjack about the Raid, I'll bet,'
added Mansfield, tipping some more whisky into his mug.
'The Raid!' I exclaimed, suddenly excited, 'I haven't heard a
word about it.' 'Well, you're the only human being in this
Brigade who hasn't heard about it.' (Mansfield's remarks were
emphasized by the usual epithets.) 'But what about it? Was
it a success?' 'Holy Christ! Was it a success? The Kangaroo
wants to know if it was a success!' He puffed out his plump
cheeks and gazed at the others. 'This god-damned Raid's been
a funny story for the last fortnight, and we've done everything
except send word over to the Fritzes to say what time we're
coming; and now it's fixed up for next Thursday, and Barton's
hoping to get a D.S.O. out of it for his executive ability. I wish
he'd arrange to go and fetch his (something) D.S.O. for himself!' From this I deduced that poor Birdie was to be in charge
of the Raiding Party, and I soon knew all there was to be
known. Ormand, who had obviously heard more than enough
lately, took himself off, vocally announcing that he was 'Gil-
bert the filbert, the Nut with a K, the pride of Piccadilly, the
blasé roué'.

Barton was still up at Headquarters when I went across the
road to my billet. Flook had spread my 'flea-bag' on the tiled
floor, and I had soon slipped into it and blown out my candle.
Durley, on the other side of the room, was asleep in a few minutes, for he'd been out late on a working-party the night before.

I was now full of information about the Raid, and I could think of nothing else. My month at Flixécourt was already obliterated. While I was away I had almost forgotten about the Raid; but it seemed now that I'd always regarded it as my private property, for when it had begun to be a probability in April, Barton had said that I should be sure to take charge of it. My feeling was much the same as it would have been if I had owned a horse and then been told that someone else was to ride it in a race.

Six years before I had been ambitious of winning races because that had seemed a significant way of demonstrating my equality with my contemporaries. And now I wanted to make the World War serve a similar purpose, for if only I could get a Military Cross I should feel comparatively safe and confident. (At that time the Doctor was the only man in the Battalion who'd got one.) Trench warfare was mostly monotonous drudgery, and I preferred the exciting idea of crossing the mine-craters and getting into the German front line. In my simple-minded way I had identified myself with that strip of no-man's-land opposite Bois Français; and the mine-craters had always fascinated me, though I'd often feared that they'd be the death of me.

Mansfield had gloomily remarked that he'd something-well go on the razzle if he got through Thursday night with his procreative powers unimpaired. Wondering why he had been selected for the job, I wished I could take his place. I knew that he had more common-sense ability than I had, but he was podgily built and had never been an expert at crawling among shell-holes in the dark. He and Ormand and Corporal O'Brien had done two patrols last week but the bright moonlight had prevented them from properly inspecting the German wire. Birdie's language about moonlight and snipers was a masterpiece, but he hadn't a ghost of an idea whether we could get through the Boche wire. Nevertheless I felt that if I'd been there the patrolling would have been profitable, moon or no moon. I wouldn't mind going up there and doing it now, I thought, for I was wide-awake and full of energy after my easy life at the Army School. . . . *Doing it now?* The line was quiet to-night. Now and again the tapping of a machine-gun. But the demented night-life was going on all the time and the unsleeping strangeness of it struck my mind silent for a moment, as I visualized a wiring-party standing stock still while a flare quivered and sank, silvering the bleached sandbags of the redoubt.

Warm and secure, I listened to the gentle whisper of the aspens outside the window, and the fear of death and the horror of mutilation took hold of my heart. Durley was muttering in his sleep, something rapid and incoherent, and then telling someone to get a move on; the war didn't allow people many pleasant dreams. It was difficult to imagine old Julian killing a German, even with an anonymous bullet. I didn't want to kill any Germans myself, but one had to kill people in self-defence. Revolver shooting wasn't so bad, and as for bombs, you just chucked them and hoped for the best. Anyhow I meant to ask Kinjack to let me go on the Raid. Supposing he *ordered* me to go on it? How should I feel about it then? No good thinking any more about it now. With some such ponderings as these I sighed and fell asleep.

2

Next morning I went to the other end of the village to have a chat with my friend the Quartermaster. Leaning against a bit of broken wall outside his billet, we exchanged a few observations about the larger aspects of the war and the possibilities of peace. Joe was pessimistic as ever, airing his customary criticisms of profiteers, politicians, and those whose military duties compelled them to remain at the Base and in other back areas. He said that the permanent staff at Fourth Army Headquarters now numbered anything up to four thousand. With a ribald metaphor he speculated on what they did with themselves all day. I said that some of them were busy at the Army School. Joe supposed there was no likelihood of their opening a rest-cure for Quartermasters.

When I asked his opinion about the Raid he looked serious, for he liked Mansfield and knew his value as an officer. 'From all I hear, Kangar,' he said, 'it's a baddish place for a show of that kind, but you know the ground better than I do. My own opinion is that the Boches would have come across themselves before now if they'd thought it worth trying. But Brigade have got the idea of a raid hot and strong, and they've nothing to lose by it one way or the other, except a few of our men.' I asked if these raids weren't a more or less new notion, and he told me that our Battalion had done several small ones up in Flanders during the first winter; Winchell, our late Colonel, had led one when he was still a company commander. The idea had been revived early this year, when some Canadian toughs had pulled off a fine effort, and since then such entertainments had become popular with the Staff. Our Second Battalion had done one, about a month ago, up at Cuinchy; their Quartermaster had sent Joe the details; five officers and sixty men went across, but casualties were numerous and no prisoners were brought back. He sighed and lit a cigarette. 'It's always the good lads who volunteer for these shows. One of the Transport men wanted to send his name in for this one; but I told him to think of his poor unfortunate wife, and we're pushing him off on a transport-course to learn cold-shoeing.'

Prodding the ground with my stick, I stared at the Transport lines below us – a few dirty white bell-tents and the limbers and wagons and picketed horses. I could see the horses' tails switching and the men stooping to groom their legs. Bees hummed in the neglected little garden; red and grey roofs clustered round the square church tower; everything looked Sunday-like and contented with the fine weather. When I divulged my idea of asking Kinjack to let me go on the Raid, Joe remarked that he'd guessed as much, and advised me to keep quiet about it as there was still a chance that it might be washed out. Kinjack wasn't keen about it and had talked pretty straight to the Brigade Major; he was never afraid of giving the brass-hats a bit of his mind. So I promised to say nothing till the last moment, and old Joe ended by reminding

me that we'd all be over the top in a month or two. But I
thought, as I walked away, how silly it would be if I got laid
out by a stray bullet, or a rifle-grenade, or one of those clumsy
'canisters' that came over in the evening dusk with a little trail
of sparks behind them.

We went into the line again on Tuesday. For the first three days
Barton's Company was in reserve at 71. North, which was an
assortment of dug-outs and earth-covered shelters about a thousand yards behind the front line. I never heard anyone ask the
origin of its name, which for most of us had meant shivering
boredom at regular intervals since January. Some map-making
expert had christened it coldly, and it had unexpectedly failed
to get itself called the Elephant and Castle or Hampton Court.
Anyhow it was a safe and busy suburb of the front line, for the
dug-outs were hidden by sloping ground and nicely tucked
away under a steep bank. Shells dropped short or went well
over; and as the days of aeroplane aggressiveness had not yet
arrived, we could move about by daylight with moderate freedom. A little way down the road the Quartermaster-sergeant
ruled the ration dump, and every evening Dottrell arrived with
the ration-limbers. There, too, was the dressing station where
Dick Tiltwood had died a couple of months ago; it seemed longer than that, I thought, as I passed it with my platoon and
received a cheery greeting from our Medical Officer, who
could always make one feel that Harley Street was still within
reach.

The road which passed 71. North had once led to Fricourt;
now it skulked along to the British Front Line, wandered evilly
across no-man's-land, and then gave itself up to the Germans. In spite of this, the road had for me a queer daylight
magic, especially in summer. Though grass-patched and derelict, something of its humanity remained. I imagined everyday
rural life going along it in pre-war weather, until this business-
like open-air inferno made it an impossibility for a French
farmer to jog into Fricourt in his hooded cart.

There was a single line railway on the other side of the road,
but the only idea which it suggested to Barton was that if the

war lasted a few more years we should be coming to the trenches every day by train like city men going to the office. He was due for leave next week and his mind was already half in England. The Raid wasn't mentioned now, and there was little to be done about it except wait for Thursday night. Mansfield had become loquacious about his past life, as though he were making a general audit of his existence. I remember him talking about the hard times he'd had in Canada, and how he used to get a meal for twelve cents. In the meantime I made a few notes in my diary.

'*Tuesday evening, 8.30. At Bécordel crossroads.* On a working party. A small bushy tree against a pale yellow sky; slate roofs gleaming in the half-light. A noise of carts coming along with rations. Occasional bang of our guns close to the village. The church tower, gloomy, only the front remains; more than half of it shot away and most of the church. In the foreground two broken barns with skeleton roofs. A quiet cool evening after a shower. Stars coming out. The R.E. stores are dumped around French soldier-cemetery. Voices of men in the dusk. Dull rattle of machine-guns on the left. Talking to a Northumberland Fusilier officer who drops aitches. Too dark to write. . . .

'*Wednesday, 6.15 p.m. On Crawley Ridge.* Ormand up here in the Redoubt with a few men. I relieve him while he goes down to get his dinner. Very still evening; sun rather hazy. Looking across to Fricourt; trench mortars bursting in the cemetery; dull white smoke slowly floats away over grey-green grass with buttercups and saffron weeds. Fricourt; a huddle of reddish roofs; skeleton village; church tower, almost demolished, a white patch against green of Fricourt wood (full of German batteries). North, up the hill, white seams and heapings of trenches dug in chalk. Sky full of lark songs. Sometimes you can count thirty slowly and hear no sound of a shot; then the muffled pop of a rifle or a slamming 5.9 or one of our 18-pounders. Then a burst of machine-gun fire. Westward the yellow sky with a web of filmy cloud half across the sun; the ridges with blurred outlines of trees. An aeroplane droning overhead. A thistle sprouting through the chalk on the parapet; a cockchafer sailing through the air. Down the hill, the

Bray-Fricourt road, white and hard. A partridge flies away, calling. Lush grass and crops of nettles; a large black slug out for his evening walk (doing nearly a mile a month).'

3

At ten o'clock on Thursday night I was alone with Durley in the sack-cloth smelling dug-out at 71. North. Rain was falling steadily. Everything felt fateful and final. A solitary candle stood on the table in its own grease, and by its golden glimmer I had just written a farewell letter to Aunt Evelyn. I did not read it through, and I am glad I cannot do so now, for it was in the 'happy warrior' style and my own fine feelings took precedence of hers. It was not humanly possible for me to wonder what Aunt Evelyn was doing while I wrote; to have done so would have cramped my style. But it is possible that she was calling her black Persian cat in from the dripping summer garden; when it scampered in from the darkness she would dry it carefully with a towel, whistling under her breath, while she did so, some indeterminate tune. Poor Aunt Evelyn was still comfortingly convinced that I was transport officer, though I had given up that job nearly three months ago. Having licked and fastened the flimsy envelope I handed it to Durley, with a premonition that it would be posted. Durley received it with appropriate gravity.

In the meantime Mansfield was making a final reconnaissance of the ground with Sergeant Miles and Corporal O'Brien, while Barton (unaware of my intentions) was administering a drop of whisky to the raiding party in the large dug-out just along the road. It was time to be moving; so I took off my tunic, slipped my old raincoat on over my leather waistcoat, dumped my tin hat on my head, and picked up my nail-studded knobkerrie. Good old Durley wished me luck and economically blew out the candle. As we went along the road he remarked that it was lucky the night was dark and rainy.

Entering the other dug-out I was slightly startled, for I had forgotten that the raiders were to have blacked faces (to avoid the danger of their mistaking one another for Germans). Exchanging boisterous jokes, they were putting the finishing touches to their make-up with bits of burnt cork. Showing the whites of their eyes and pretending not to recognize one another, those twenty-five shiny-faced nigger minstrels might almost have been getting ready for a concert. Everyone seemed to expect the entertainment to be a roaring success. But there were no looking-glasses or banjos, and they were brandishing knobkerries, stuffing Mills' bombs into their pockets and hatchets into their belts, and 'Who's for a Blighty one to-night?' was the stock joke (if such a well-worn wish could be called a joke).

At 10.30 there was a sudden silence, and Barton told me to take the party up to Battalion Headquarters. It surprises me when I remember that I set off without having had a drink, but I have always disliked the flavour of whisky, and in those days the helpfulness of alcohol in human affairs was a fact which had not yet been brought home to me. The raiders had been given only a small quantity, but it was enough to hearten them as they sploshed up the communication trench. None of us could know how insignificant we were in the so-called 'Great Adventure' which was sending up its uneasy flares along the Western Front. No doubt we thought ourselves something very special. But what we thought never mattered; nor does it matter what sort of an inflated fool I was when I blundered into Kinjack's Headquarters at Maple Redoubt to report the presence of the raiders and ask whether I might go across with them. 'Certainly not,' said the Colonel, 'your job is to stop in our trench and count the men as they come back.' He spoke with emphasis and he was not a man who expected to have to say a thing twice. We stared at one another for a moment; some freak of my brain made me remember that in peace time he had been an enthusiastic rose-grower – had won prizes with his roses, in fact; for he was a married man and had lived in a little house near the barracks.

My thought was nipped in the bud by his peremptory voice telling Major Robson, his second-in-command, to push off with the party. We were about 400 yards from the front line, and Robson now led us across the open to a point in the support trench, from which a red electric torch winked to guide us. Then up a trench to the starting point, the men's feet clumping and drumming on the duck-boards. This noise, plus the clinking and drumming and creaking of weapons and equipment, suggested to my strained expectancy that the enemy would be well warned of our arrival. Mansfield and his two confederates now loomed squatly above us on the parapet; they had been laying a guiding line of lime across the craters. A gap had been cut in our wire, and it was believed that some sort of damage had been done to the German wire which had been 'strafed' by trench mortars during the day.

The raiders were divided into four parties of five men; operation orders had optimistically assumed that the hostile trenches would be entered without difficulty; 'A' party would go to the left, 'B' party to the right, and so on and so forth. The object of the raid was to enter the enemy loop on the edge of the crater; to enter Kiel Trench at two points; to examine the portions of trench thus isolated, capture prisoners, bomb dug-outs, and kill Germans. An 'evacuating party' (seven men carrying two ten-foot ladders and a red flash lamp) followed the others. The ladders were considered important, as the German front trench was believed to be deep and therefore difficult to get out of in a hurry. There were two mine-craters a few yards from our parapet; these craters were about fifty yards in diameter and about fifty feet deep; their sides were steep and composed of thin soft soil; there was water at the bottom of them. Our men crossed by a narrow bridge of earth between the craters; the distance to the German wire was about sixty yards.

It was now midnight. The five parties had vanished into the darkness on all fours. It was raining quietly and persistently. I sat on the parapet waiting for something to happen. Except for two men at a sentry post near by (they were now only spectators) there seemed to be no one about. 'They'll never keep that —— inside the trench,' muttered the sentry to his mate and even at that tense moment I valued the compliment. Major

Robson and the stretcher-bearers had been called away by a message. There must be some trouble further along, I thought, wondering what it could be, for I hadn't heard a sound. Now and again I looked at my luminous watch. Five, ten, fifteen minutes passed in ominous silence. An occasional flare, never near our craters, revealed the streaming rain, blanched the tangles of wire that wound away into the gloom, and came to nothing, bringing down the night. Unable to remain inactive any longer, I crawled a little way out. As I went, a few shells began to drone across in their leisurely way. Our communication trench was being shelled. I joined the evacuating party; they were lying on the lip of the left-hand crater. A flare fizzed up, and I could see the rest of the men lying down, straight across the ridge, and was able to exchange a grimace with one of the black-faced ladder-carriers. Then some 'whizz-bangs' rushed over to our front trench; one or two fell on the craters; this made the obstinate silence of Kiel Trench more menacing. Soon afterwards one of the bayonet men came crawling rapidly back. I followed him to our trench where he whispered his message. 'They can't get through the second belt of wire; O'Brien says it's a washout; they're all going to throw a bomb and retire.'

I suppose I ought to have tried to get the ladder-carriers in before the trouble started; but the idea didn't strike me as I waited with bumping heart; and almost immediately the explosions began. A bomb burst in the water of the left-hand crater, sending up a phosphorescent spume. Then a concentration of angry flashes, thudding bangs, and cracking shots broke itself up in a hubbub and scurry, groans and curses, and stampeding confusion. Stumbling figures loomed up from below, scrambling clumsily over the parapet; black faces and whites of eyes showed grotesque in the antagonistic shining of alarm flares. Dodging to and fro, I counted fourteen men in; they all blundered away down the trench. I went out, found Mansfield badly hit, and left him with two others who soon got him in. Other wounded men were crawling back. Among them was a grey-haired lance-corporal, who had one of his feet almost blown off; I half carried him in, and when he was

sitting on the firestep he said: 'Thank God Almighty for this;
I've been waiting eighteen months for it, and now I can go
home.' I told him we'd get him away on a stretcher soon, and
then he muttered: 'Mick O'Brien's somewhere down in the
craters.'

All this had been quick work and not at all what I'd expected.
Things were slowing down now. The excitement was finished,
and O'Brien was somewhere down in the craters. The bombing
and rifle fire had slackened when I started out to look for him.
I went mechanically, as though I were drowning myself in the
darkness. This is no fun at all, was my only thought as I groped
my way down the soft clogging side of the left-hand crater; no
fun at all, for they were still chucking an occasional bomb and
firing circumspectly. I could hear the reloading click of rifle
bolts on the lip of the crater above me as I crawled along with
mud-clogged fingers, or crouched and held my breath painfully. Bullets hit the water and little showers of earth pattered
down from the banks. I knew that nothing in my previous
experience of patrolling had ever been so grim as this, and I lay
quite still for a bit, miserably wondering whether my number
was up; then I remembered that I was wearing my pre-war
raincoat; I could feel the pipe and tobacco pouch in my pocket
and somehow this made me less forlorn, though life seemed
much further away than the low mumble of voices in our
trench. A flare would have helped my searchings, but they had
stopped sending them up; pawing the loose earth and dragging
my legs after me, I worked my way round the crater. O'Brien
wasn't there, so I got across into the other one, which was even
more precipitous and squashy. Down there I discovered him.
Another man was crouching beside him, wounded in one arm
and patiently waiting for help. O'Brien moaned when I touched
him; he seemed to have been hit in several places. His companion whispered huskily: 'Get a rope.' As I clambered heavily up
the bank I noticed that it had stopped raining. Robson was
peering out of the trench; he sent someone for a rope, urging
him to be quick for already there was a faint beginning of daylight. With the rope, and a man to help, I got back to O'Brien,
and we lifted him up the side of the crater.

It was heavy work, for he was tall and powerfully built, and the soft earth gave way under our feet as we lugged and hoisted the limp shattered body. The Germans must have seen us in the half light, but they had stopped firing; perhaps they felt sorry for us.

At last we lowered him over the parapet. A stretcher-bearer bent over him and then straightened himself, taking off his helmet with a gesture that vaguely surprised me by its reverent simplicity. O'Brien had been one of the best men in our Company. I looked down at him and then turned away; the face was grotesquely terrible, smeared with last night's burnt cork, the forehead matted with a tangle of dark hair.

I had now accounted for everyone. Two killed and ten wounded was the only result of the raid. In the other Company sector the Germans had blown in one of our mine-galleries, and about thirty of the tunnelling company had been gassed or buried. Robson had been called there with the stretcher-bearers just as the raid began.

Nothing now remained for me to do except to see Kinjack on my way back. Entering his dug-out I looked at him with less diffidence than I'd ever done before. He was sitting on his plank bed, wearing a brown woollen cap with a tuft on the top. His blond face was haggard; the last few hours had been no fun for him either. This was a Kinjack I'd never met before, and it was the first time I had ever shared any human equality with him. He spoke kindly to me in his rough way, and in doing so made me very thankful that I had done what I could to tidy up the mess in no-man's-land.

Larks were shrilling in the drizzling sky as I went down to 71. North. I felt a wild exultation. Behind me were the horror and the darkness. Kinjack had thanked me. It was splendid to be still alive, I thought, as I strode down the hill, skirting shell-holes and jumping over communication trenches, for I wasn't in a mood to bother about going along wet ditches. The landscape loomed around me, and the landscape was life, stretching away and away into freedom. Even the dreary little warren at 71. North seemed to await me with a welcome, and Flook was ready with some hot tea. Soon I was jabbering excitedly to

Durley and old man Barton, who told me that the Doctor said Mansfield was a touch and go case, but already rejoicing at the prospect of getting across to Blighty, and cursing the bad wire-cutters which had been served out for the raid. I prided myself on having pulled off something rather heroic; but when all was said and done it was only the sort of thing which people often did during a fire or a railway accident.

Nothing important had happened on the British Front that night, so we were rewarded by a mention in the G.H.Q. *communiqué*. *'At Mametz we raided hostile trenches. Our party entered without difficulty and maintained a spirited bombing fight, and finally withdrew at the end of twenty-five minutes.'* This was their way of telling England. Aunt Evelyn probably read it automatically in her *Morning Post*, unaware that this minor event had almost caused her to receive a farewell letter from me. The next night our Company was in the front line and I recovered three hatchets and a knobkerrie from no-man's-land. Curiously enough, I hadn't yet seen a German. I had seen dim figures on my dark patrols; but no human faces.

PART THREE

BEFORE THE PUSH

1

One evening about a fortnight later I was down in that too familiar front-line dug-out with Barton, who had just returned from leave and was unable to disguise his depression. I wasn't feeling over bright myself after tramping to and fro in the gluey trenches all day. A little rain made a big difference to life up there, and the weather had been wet enough to make the duckboards wobble when one stepped on them. I'd got sore feet and a trench mouth and food tasted filthy. And the Boche trench-mortars had been strafing us more than usual that evening. Probably I've been smoking too much lately, I thought, knocking my pipe out against one of the wooden props which held up the cramped little den, and staring irritably at my mud-encumbered boots, for I was always trying to keep squalor at bay, and the discomfort of feeling dirty and tickly all over was almost as bad as a bombardment. It certainly wasn't much of a place to be low-spirited in, so I tried reading the paper which the Company-Sergeant-Major had just delivered when he came down for the rum ration. The rum jar lived under Barton's bed; having been poured into some tin receptacle, the rum was carried cautiously upstairs to be tipped into the men's tea-dixies.

'Fancy Kitchener being drowned in the North Sea!' I remarked, looking up from the *Daily Mail* which was making the most of that historic event. (It seemed a long time since I rode past his park wall in Kent when I was with the Yeomanry; it would be two years next September, though it wasn't much use looking as far ahead as that, with all these preparations going on for the 'Big Push'.) Barton was scribbling away with

his indelible pencil – filling in all that bosh which made Brigade think they were busy. 'If you want my opinion,' he grumbled, 'I believe those damned Irish had a hand in Kitchener
being drowned. I'd like to see that fatuous island of theirs sunk
under the sea.' Barton had an irrational dislike of the Irish,
and he always blamed anything on them if he could. He
wouldn't even admit that Ireland was an agricultural country,
and since the Easter Rebellion in Dublin it wasn't safe to show
him a bottle of Irish whisky. 'I've never met an Irishman with
any more sense than that mouse!' he exclaimed. A mouse was
standing on its head in the sugar basin, which was made of
metal and contained soft sugar. He eyed the mouse morosely,
as though accusing it of Irish ancestry. 'This time three nights
ago my wife and I were having dinner at the Café Royal.
Upstairs at the Café Royal – best food in London, and as good
as ever even now. I tell you, Kangar, it's too much of a bloody
contrast, coming back to all this.' There was a muffled 'Wump'
and both candles went out. Something heavy had burst outside our door. Lighting the candles, I thought I'd just as soon
be upstairs as down in this musty limbo. In about an hour I
should be out with the wiring-party, dumping concertina wire
in the shell-holes along the edge of the craters. I wondered if
I should ever get a Blighty wound. One of our best officers
had been hit last night while out with the wirers. This was
Bill Eaves, who had been a Classical Scholar at Cambridge
and had won medals there for writing Greek and Latin epi-
grams. Now he'd got a nice bullet wound in the shoulder,
with the muscles damaged enough to keep him in England
several months. And two nights ago Ormand and a Sandhurst
boy named Harris had been hit while on a working party.
Ormand's was a 'cushy' shell splinter; but Harris had got his
knee smashed up, and the doctor said he would probably be
out of the war for good. It was funny to think of young Harris
being hit in the first twenty-four hours of his first tour of
trenches.

Anyhow we were due for Divisional Rest, which would take
us to the back area for three weeks, and the clogging monotony of life in the line would be cleaned out of our minds. And

you never knew – perhaps the war would end in those three weeks. The troops were beginning to need a rest badly, for most of them had been doing tours of trenches ever since the end of January, and even when we were at Morlancourt there was a working party every second night, which meant being out from seven o'clock till after midnight. And Miles, my platoon sergeant, hadn't been quite his usual self since the raid; but he'd been in France nearly a year, which was longer than most men could stick such a life. The chances are, I thought, that if Sergeant Miles is still here a few months hence, and I'm not, some fresh young officer from England will be accusing him of being windy. Sooner or later I should get windy myself. It was only a question of time. But could this sort of thing be measured by ordinary time, I wondered (as I lay on a bunk wishing to God Barton would stop blowing on his spectacles, which surely didn't need all that polishing). No; one couldn't reckon the effect of the war on people by weeks and months. I'd noticed that boys under twenty stood it worst, especially when the weather was bad. Mud and boredom and discomfort seemed to take all the guts out of them. If an officer crumpled up, Kinjack sent him home as useless, with a confidential report. Several such officers were usually drifting about at the Depot, and most of them ended up with safe jobs in England. But if a man became a dud in the ranks, he just remained where he was until he was killed or wounded. Delicate discrimination about private soldiers wasn't possible. A 'number nine pill' was all they could hope for if they went sick. Barton sometimes told me that I was too easy-going with the men when we were out of the Line, but it often seemed to me that I was asking them to do more than could be fairly expected of them. It's queer, I thought, how little one really knows about the men. In the Line one finds out which are the duds, and one builds up a sort of comradeship with the tough and willing ones. But back in billets the gap widens and one can't do much to cheer them up. I could never understand how they managed to keep as cheery as they did through such drudgery and discomfort, with nothing to look forward to but going over the top or being moved up to Flanders again.

Next evening, just before stand-to, I was watching a smoulder-
ing sunset and thinking that the sky was one of the redeeming
features of the war. Behind the support line where I stood, the
shell-pitted ground sloped sombrely into the dusk; the dis-
tances were blue and solemn, with a few trees grouped on a
ridge, dark against the deep-glowing embers of another day
endured. It was looking westward, away from the war, and the
evening star twinkled serenely. Guns were grumbling miles
away. Cartwheels could be heard on the roads behind Fricourt; it still made me feel strange when I remembered that
they were German cartwheels.

Moments like those are unreproducible when I look back
and try to recover their living texture. One's mind eliminates
boredom and physical discomfort, retaining an incomplete
impression of a strange, intense, and unique experience. If
there be such a thing as ghostly revisitation of this earth, and
if ghosts can traverse time and choose their ground, I would
return to the Bois Français sector as it was then. But since I
always assume that spectral presences have lost their sense of
smell (and I am equally uncertain about their auditory equipment) such hauntings might be as inadequate as those which
now absorb my mental energy. For trench life was an existence
saturated by the external senses; and although our actions were
domineered over by military discipline, our animal instincts
were always uppermost. While I stood there then, I had no
desire to diagnose my environment. Freedom from its oppres-
siveness was what I longed for. Listening to the German cartwheels rumbling remotely, I thought of an old German governess
I had known, and how she used to talk about 'dear old Moltke
and Bismarck' and her quiet home in Westphalia where her
father had been a Protestant pastor. I wondered what sort of a
place Westphalia was, and wished I'd seen more of the world
before it became so busy with bloodshed. For until I came out
to the war I had only the haziest notion of anything outside
England.

Well, here I was, and my incomplete life might end any minute; for although the evening air was as quiet as a cathedral, a

canister soon came over quite near enough to shatter my meditations with its unholy crash and cloud of black smoke. A rat
scampered across the tin cans and burst sandbags, and trench
atmosphere reasserted itself in a smell of chloride of lime. On
my way to the dug-out, to fetch my revolver and attend the
twilight ceremony of stand-to and rifle inspection, I heard the
voice of Flook; just round a bend of the support trench he was
asking one of the company bombers if he'd seen his officer
bloke go along that way. Flook was in a hurry to tell me that I
was to go on leave. I didn't wait to inspect my platoon's rifles
and not many minutes later I was on my way down the Old
Kent Road trench. Maple Redoubt was getting its usual evening bombardment, and as a man had been killed by a whizz-
bang in the Old Kent Road a few minutes earlier, I was glad
when I was riding back to Morlancourt with Dottrell; glad,
too, to be driving to Méricourt station behind the sluggish
pony next morning; to hear the mellow bells of Rouen on the
evening air while the leave train stood still for half an hour
before making up its mind to lumber on to Havre. And thus
the gradations of thankfulness continued, until I found myself
in a quiet house in Kensington where I was staying the night
with an old friend of Aunt Evelyn's.

To be there, on a fine Sunday evening in June, with the
drawing-room windows open and someone playing the piano
next door, was an experience which now seemed as queer as
the unnatural conditions I had returned from. Books, pictures,
furniture, all seemed kind and permanent and unrelated to
the present time and its troubles. I felt detached from my
surroundings – rather as if I were in a doctor's waiting-room,
expecting to be informed that I had some incurable disease.
The sound of the piano suggesed that the specialist had a
happy home life of his own, but it had no connection with my
coming and going. A sense of gentle security pervaded the
room; but I could no longer call my life my own. The pensive
music had caught me off my guard; I was only an intruder
from the Western Front. But the room contained one object
which unexpectedly reminded me of the trenches – a silent
canary in a cage. I had seen canaries in cages being carried by

the men of the tunnelling company when they emerged from
their mine galleries.

2

Correspondingly queer (though I didn't consciously observe it
at the time) was the experience of returning to France after
sleeping seven nights in a proper bed and wearing civilian
clothes. The personal implications were obvious, since everybody at home seemed to know that the long-planned offensive
was due to 'kick off' at the end of June. Officers going on leave
had been cautioned to say nothing about it, but even Aunt Evelyn was aware of the impending onslaught. I was disinclined to
talk about the trenches; nevertheless I permitted myself to
drop a few heavy hints. No one had any notion what the Big
Push would be like, except that it would be much bigger than
anything which had happened before. And somehow those
previous battles hadn't divulged themselves very distinctly to
anyone except the actual participators, who had so far proved
inarticulate reporters.

As regards my own adventures, I had decided to say nothing
to my aunt about the raid. Nevertheless it all slipped out on
the second evening, probably after she had been telling me
how splendidly Mrs Ampney's nephew had done out in Mesopotamia. Also I didn't omit to mention that I had been recommended for a Military Cross. 'But I thought you were only
looking after the horses,' she expostulated, clutching my hand;
her anxious face made me wish I'd held my tongue about it. Of
course, Aunt Evelyn wanted me to do well in the war, but she
couldn't enjoy being reminded that 'do be careful to wear your
warm overcoat, dearie', was no precaution against German
bombs and bullets. Afterwards I excused myself by thinking
that she was bound to find out sooner or later, especially if I
got killed.

Next day I walked across the fields to Butley and had tea with
my old friend Captain Huxtable. I found him chubby-cheeked as

ever, and keeping up what might be called a Justice of the Peace attitude towards the war. Any able-bodied man not serving in H.M. Forces should be required to show a thundering good reason for it, and the sooner conscription came in the better. That was his opinion; in the meantime he was working his farm with two elderly men and a boy; 'and that's about all an old crock like me can do for his country.' I gave him to understand that it was a jolly fine life out at the Front, and, for the moment, I probably believed what I was saying. I wasn't going to wreck my leave with facing facts, and I'd succeeded in convincing myself that I really wanted to go back. Captain Huxtable and I decided, between us, that the Push would finish the war by Christmas. While we talked, pacing to and fro in the garden, with his surly black retriever at our heels, the rooks cawed applaudingly in the clump of elms near by as though all were well with England on that June afternoon. I knew that the Captain would have asked nothing better than to go over the top with his old regiment, if only he'd been thirty years younger, and I wished I could have told him so, when we were standing at his gate. But English reticence prohibited all that sort of thing, and I merely remarked that Aunt Evelyn's lightning-conductor had been blown off the chimney in the spring and she said it wasn't worth while having it put up again. He laughed and said she must be getting war-weary; she had always been so particular about the lightning-conductor. 'We old 'uns can't expect to be feeling very cock-a-hoop in these days,' he added, wrinkling up his shrewd and kindly little eyes and giving my hand a farewell squeeze which meant more than he could say aloud.

When Aunt Evelyn wondered whether I'd like anyone to come to dinner on my last evening (she called it Friday night) I replied that I'd rather we were alone. There were very few to ask, and, as she said, people were difficult to get hold of nowadays. So, after a dinner which included two of my favourite puddings, we made the best of a bad job by playing cribbage (a game we had been addicted to when I was at home for my school holidays) while the black Persian cat washed his face

with his paw and blinked contentedly at the fire which had
been lit though there was no need for it, the night being warm
and still. We also had the grey parrot brought up from the
kitchen. Clinging sideways to the bars of his cage Popsy
seemed less aware of the war than anyone I'd met. But perhaps
he sensed the pang I felt when saying good-bye to him next
morning; parrots understand more than they pretend to, and
this one had always liked me. He wasn't much of a talker,
though he could imitate Aunt Evelyn calling the cats.

Next morning she contrived to be stoically chatty until I
had seen her turn back to the house door and the village taxi
was rattling me down the hill. She had sensibly refrained from
coming up to London to see me off. But at Waterloo Station I
was visibly reminded that going back for the Push was rather
rough on one's relations, however incapable they might be of
sharing the experience. There were two leave trains and I
watched the people coming away after the first one had gone
out. Some sauntered away with assumed unconcern; they chatted and smiled. Others hurried past me with a crucified look; I
noticed a well-dressed woman biting her gloved fingers; her
eyes stared fixedly; she was returning alone to a silent house
on a fine Sunday afternoon.

But I had nobody to see me off, so I could settle myself in
the corner of a carriage, light my pipe and open a Sunday
paper (though goodness knows what it contained, apart from
communiqués, casualty lists, and reassuring news from Gali-
cia, Bukovina, and other opaque arenas of war). It would have
been nice to read the first-class cricket averages for a change,
and their absence was an apt epitome of the life we were condemned to. While the train hurried out of London I watched
the flitting gardens of suburban houses. In my fox-hunting
days I had scorned the suburbs, but now there was something
positively alluring in the spectacle of a City man taking it easy
on his little lawn at Surbiton. Woking Cemetery was a less
attractive scene, and my eyes recoiled from it to reassure themselves that my parcels were still safe on the rack, for those parcels were the important outcome of my prevous day's shopping.

Armed with Aunt Evelyn's membership ticket (posted back

to her afterwards) I had invaded the Army and Navy Stores
and procured a superb salmon, two bottles of old brandy, an
automatic pistol, and two pairs of wire-cutters with rubber-
covered handles. The salmon was now my chief concern. I was
concerned about its future freshness, for I had overstayed my
leave by twenty-four hours. A rich restaurant dinner followed
by a mechanical drawing-room comedy hadn't made the risk
of Kinjack's displeasure seem worth while; but I felt that the
salmon spelt safety at Battalion Headquarters. Probably the word
smelt also entered my apprehensive mind. The brandy claimed
that it had been born in 1838, so one day more or less couldn't
affect its condition, as long as I kept an eye on it (for such bottles were liable to lose themselves on a leave boat). The wire-
cutters were my private contribution to the Great Offensive. I
had often cursed the savage bluntness of our Company's wire-
cutters, and it occurred to me, in the Army and Navy Stores,
that if we were going over the top we might want to cut our
own wire first, to say nothing of the German wire (although
our artillery would have made holes in that, I hoped). So I
bought these very civilized ones, which looked almost too good
for the Front Line. The man in the Weapon Department at the
Stores had been persuasive about a periscope (probably pris-
matic) but I came to the conclusion that a periscope was a back
number in my case. I shouldn't be in the trench long enough to
need it. Apart from the wire-cutters and the pistol, all other
'trench requisites' appeared redundant. I couldn't see myself
leading my platoon with *Mortleman's Patent Sound Absorbers*
plugged in my ears, and a combined Compass-Barometer also
failed to attract me. The automatic pistol wasn't 'warranted to
stop a man', but it could be slipped into the pocket. It was only
a plaything, but I was weary of my Colt revolver, with which I
knew I couldn't hit anything, although I had blazed it off a few
times in the dark when I was pretending to be important in
no-man's-land. The only object I could be sure of hitting was
myself, and I decided (in the Army and Navy Stores) that I
might conceivably find it necessary to put myself out of my misery, if the worst came to the worst and I was lying out in a
shell-hole with something more serious than a Blighty wound.

To blow one's brains out with that clumsy Colt was unthinkable. The automatic pistol, on the other hand, was quite a
charming little weapon. Not that I'd ever been fond of fire-
arms. I had never shot at a bird or an animal in my life, though
I'd often felt that my position as a sportsman would be stronger
if I were 'a good man with a gun'.

The truth was that the only explosive weapon I owned
before the war was a toy pistol which made a noise but dis-
charged nothing. Sitting in the wrong-way leave train I remembered how, when about nine years old, I used to go up to the
little sweet shop in the village and buy 'three penn'orth of per-
cussion caps' for my pistol; and how the buxom old woman
used to ask briskly, 'Anything else today, Master George?'
Whereupon I would be compelled to decide between clove and
peppermint bulls' eyes, with a bar of chocolate-cream to make
it up to sixpence. Twenty years was a long time ago; but
already the village green as I saw it last week was beginning to
seem almost as remote. . . . However, it was no use dreaming
about all that now; Kinjack's salmon was my immediate problem, and as soon as I was on board the crowded boat, I consulted an obliging steward and my fishy insurance policy was
providentially accommodated in the cold-storage cupboard.
Consequently my mind was unperturbed when we steamed
out of Southampton Water. I watched the woods on the Isle of
Wight, hazily receding in the heat. And when the Isle of Wight
was out of sight – well, there was nothing to be done about it.

At Havre I was instructed, by the all-knowing authority
responsible for my return, to get out of the train at Corbie.
Havre was a glitter of lights winking on dark slabbing water.
Soon the glumly-laden train was groaning away from the
wharves, and we nodded and snored through the night. Daylight came, and we crawled past green landscapes blurred with
drizzling rain. Of my compartment companions I remember
nothing except that one of them talked irrepressibly about his
father's farm in Suffolk. His father, he said, owned a bull who
had produced sixty black and white calves. This information was
received with apathy. The Battalion was at Bussy, a three-mile

walk in late afternoon sunshine. I kept to the shady side of
the road, for the salmon in its hamper was still my constant
care. Bussy came in sight as a pleasant little place on a tributary of the Ancre. A few of our men were bathing, and I
thought how young and light-hearted they looked, splashing
one another and shouting as they rocked a crazy boat under
some lofty poplars that shivered in a sunset breeze. How different to the trudging figures in full marching order; and how
difficult to embody them in the crouching imprisonment of
trench warfare!

With an unsoldierly sigh I picked up my packages and plodded on in search of C Company, who were billeted in some
buildings round a friendly farmhouse. There I found Flook
and despatched him to Kinjack's Headquarters with the hamper and a bottle of brandy. Barton, to whom I entrusted the
second bottle, told me that I was a cunning old Kangaroo, and
then regaled me with all the rumours about next week's operations. 'The bombardment begins on Saturday,' he said, 'so
we're having Battalion Sports tomorrow, in case we get moved
back to Morlancourt.' Then Durley came in with Jenkins, one
of the new officers who had been posted to the Battalion while
I was away. Fewnings, the gentle ex-schoolmaster, had been
appointed Lewis gun officer, but still messed with us; he now
entered with the air of a man who had been teaching Euclid
and Algebra all day. The Brigadier, he remarked, had ticked
him off that afternoon, because he was wearing a light-
coloured shirt; but no fault had been found with his Lewis gun
team organization, and, as he remarked, it wouldn't make
much odds what sort of shirt he was wearing in a week or two.
Neither Durley nor I had ever been favoured with a word from
our Brigadier, perhaps because our shirts were the orthodox
colour. It was odd, how seldom those graduated autocrats
found time to realize that a few kind words could make a platoon commander consider them jolly good Generals.

But there was harmony in our Company Mess, as if our certainty of a volcanic future had put an end to the occasional
squabblings which occurred when we were on one another's
nerves. A rank animal healthiness pervaded our existence during

those days of busy living and inward foreboding. The behaviour of our servants expressed it; they were competing for the favours of a handsome young woman in the farmhouse, and a comedy of primitive courtship was being enacted in the kitchen. Death would be lying in wait for the troops next week, and now the flavour of life was doubly strong. As I went to my room across the road, the cool night smelt of mown grass and leafy gardens. Away toward Corbie there was the sound of a train, and bull-frogs croaked continuously in the marshes along the river. I wasn't sorry to be back; I was sure of that; we'd all got to go through it, and I was trying to convert the idea of death in battle into an emotional experience. Courage, I argued, is a beautiful thing, and next week's attack is what I have been waiting for since I first joined the army. I am happy to-night, and I don't suppose I'll be dead in a month's time. Going into my billet I almost fell over a goat which was tethered among some currant bushes in the garden.

Five days passed us by. We did easy field-training; the Battalion Sports were a great success, and we were defeated, in an officers' tug-of-war, by our 9th Battalion who were resting a few miles away. Saturday evening brought a feeling of finality, for we were moving up to Morlancourt on Monday and the intense bombardment had begun that morning. Barton and I (and our bottle of '38 brandy) dined at Battalion Headquarters. Kinjack was full of confidence; he told us that the French were holding on well at Verdun, which would make all the difference. But the doctor looked thoughtful, and even the brandy couldn't make Barton optimistic about his ability to command a company in open warfare.

PART FOUR

BATTLE

1

On the morning of a Battalion move I made it my business to keep out of the way until the last moment. At the end of a march I had my definite duties, but before we started Barton was always in such a stew that my absence was a positive advantage to him. So on Monday, after bolting my breakfast while Flook waited to pack the mugs and plates in the mess-box, I left Barton shouting irritably for the Sergeant-Major and wandered away to sit by the river until the whistles began to blow. Durley and Jenkins had gone to make sure that the billets were being left clean and tidy. In the green orchard behind the farm buildings the men were putting their kits together, their voices sounding as jolly as though they were off for a summer holiday. For me it was a luxury to be alone for a few minutes, watching the yellow irises, and the ribbon weeds that swayed like fishes in the dimpling stream. I was sorry to be saying good-bye to the Marais and its grey-green pools and creeks and the congregation of poplar stems that upheld a cool whispering roof. Water-haunting birds whistled and piped, swinging on the bulrushes and tufted reeds, and a tribe of little green and gold frogs hopped about in the grass without caring whether they arrived anywhere. All this was obviously preferable to a battle, and it was a perfect morning to be reading a book beside the river.

But on the horizon the bombardment bumped and thudded in a continuous bubbling grumble. After a long stare at sun-flecked foliage and idly reflective alleys I bustled back to the farmyard to find my platoon all present and correct. Before I'd finished my formal inspection Barton emerged from the house with bulging

pockets, his burly figure hung like a Christmas tree with haversack, water-bottle, revolver, field-glasses, gas-mask, map-case,
and other oddments. The Battalion moved off at eight o'clock;
by twelve-thirty it was at Morlancourt, which was now congested with infantry and supply columns, and 'lousy with guns'
as the saying was. A colony of camouflage-daubed tents had
sprung up close to the village; this was the New Main Dressing
Station. We were in our usual billets—Durley and I in the room
containing a representation of the Eiffel Tower and a ludicrous
oleograph of our Saviour preaching from a boat, which we
always referred to as jocular Jesus. After a sultry dinner, the day
ended with torrents of rain. While I lay on the floor in my flea-
bag the blackness of the night framed in the window was lit with
incessant glare and flash of guns. But I fell asleep to the sound of
full gutters and rainwater gurgling and trickling into a well; and
those were comfortable noises, for they signified that I had a
roof over my head. As for my flea-bag, it was no hardship; I have
never slept more soundly in any bed.

Operation Orders were circulated next morning. They notified
us that Thursday was 'Z' (or zero) day. The Seventh Division
Battle Plan didn't look aggressively unpleasant on paper as I
transcribed it into my notebook. Rose Trench, Orchard Alley,
Apple Alley, and Willow Avenue, were among the first objectives in our sector, and my mind very properly insisted on their
gentler associations. Nevertheless this topographical Arcadia
was to be seized, cleared, and occupied when the historic
moment arrived and in conjunction with the French the Fourth
Army took the offensive, establishing as a primary objective a
line Montauban-Pozières, passing to the south of Mametz
Wood. There wasn't going to be any mistake about it this time.
We decided, with quite a glow of excitement, that the Fourth
Army was going to fairly wipe the floor with the Boches. In the
meantime our Corps Intelligence Summary (known as *Comic
Cuts*) reported on June 27th that three enemy balloons had
been set on fire and destroyed on the previous afternoon; also
that a large number of enemy batteries had been silenced by
our artillery. The anonymous humorist who compiled *Comic*

Cuts was also able to announce that the Russians had captured a redoubt and some heavy guns at Czartovijsk, which, he explained, was forty-four miles north-east of Luck. At Martin-puich a large yellowish explosion had been observed. On Tues-day afternoon I went up to the Line with Durley on some preliminary errand, for we were to relieve a battalion of the Border Regiment next day, in the sector in front of Fricourt Cemetery. Our Batteries were firing strenuously all along the countryside, with very little retaliation.

As we passed the gun-pits where some Heavies were hidden in a hollow called Gibraltar, I remarked on a sickly sweet smell which I attributed to the yellow weeds which were abundant there, but Durley explained that it was the lingering aroma of gas-shells. When we rode down the slope to 71. North, that familiar resort appeared much the same as usual, except for the impressive accumulations of war material which were dumped along the road. Durley remarked that he supposed the old spot would never be the same again after this week; and already it seemed to us as if the old days when Mansfield and Ormand were with our company had become an experience to be looked back on with regret. The Bois Français sector had been a sort of vil-lage, but we should soon be leaving it behind us in our vindictive explorations of Rose Trench, Apple Alley, and Willow Avenue.

On our way up to the Front Line we met a staff-officer who was wearing well-cut riding boots and evidently in a hurry to rejoin his horse. Larks were rejoicing aloft, and the usual sym-bolic scarlet poppies lolled over the sides of the communication trench; but he squeezed past us without so much as a nod, for the afternoon was too noisy to be idyllic, in spite of the larks and poppies which were so popular with war-correspondents. 'I suppose those brass-hats do know a hell of a lot about it all, don't they, Julian?' I queried. Durley replied that he hoped they'd learnt something since last autumn when they'd allowed the infantry to educate themselves at Loos, regardless of expense. 'They've got to learn their job as they go along, like the rest of us,' he added sagely. Five sausage balloons were vis-ible beyond the sky-line, peacefully tethered to their mother earth. It was our duty to desire their destruction, and to believe that Corps Intelligence had the matter well in hand. What we did up in the Front Line I don't remember; but while we were remounting our horses at 71. North two privates were engaged in a good-humoured scuffle; one had the other's head under his arm. Why should I remember that and forget so much else?

Wednesday morning was miserably wet. Junior officers, being at a loss to know where to put themselves, were continually meeting one another along the muddy street, and gathering in groups to exchange cheerful remarks; there was little else to be done, and solitude produced the sinking sensation appropriate to the circumstances. The men were in their billets, and they too were keeping their spirits up as vocally as they could. At noon Barton came back from the Colonel's final conference of company commanders. A couple of hours later the anti-climax arrived. We were told that all arrangements for the show were in temporary abeyance. A popular song, *All dressed up and nowhere to go*, provided the obvious comment, and our confidence in Operation Orders oozed away. Was it the wet weather, we wondered, or had the artillery preparation been inadequate? Uncertainty ended with an inanimate message; we were to go up to the line that evening. The attack was postponed forty-eight hours. No one knew why.

At five o'clock C Company fell in, about eighty strong. The men were without packs; they carried extra ammunition, two Mills' bombs, two smoke helmets, and a waterproof sheet with a jersey rolled inside; their emergency rations consisted of two tins of bully beef, eight hard biscuits, and canteens packed with grocery ration. In spite of the anti-climax (which had made us feel that perhaps this was only going to be a second edition of the Battle of Loos) my personal impression was that we were setting out for the other end of nowhere. I had slipped a book into my haversack and it was a comfort to be carrying it, for Thomas Hardy's England was between its covers. But if any familiar quotation was in my mind during the bustle of departure, it may well have been 'we brought nothing into this world, and it is certain we can carry nothing out of it'. We had trudged that way up to the Citadel and 71. North many times before;

but never in such a blood-red light as now, when we halted with
the sunset behind us and the whole sky mountainous with the
magnificence of retreating rainclouds. Tours of trenches had
been routine, with an ordinary chance of casualties. But this
time we seemed to have left Morlancourt behind us for ever,
and even a single company of Flintshire Fusiliers (with a ten
minute interval between it and B and D Companies) was justified in feeling that the eyes of Europe were upon it. As for
myself, I felt nothing worth recording – merely a sense of being
irrevocably involved in something bigger than had ever happened before. And the symbolism of the sunset was wasted on
the rank and file, who were concerned with the not infrequent
badness of their boots, the discomfort caused by perspiration,
and the toils and troubles of keeping pace with what was
required of them till further notice. By nine o'clock we had
relieved the Border Regiment. The mud was bad, but the sky
was clear. The bombardment went on steadily, with periods of
intensity; but that infernal shindy was taken for granted and
was an aid to optimism. I felt rather lonely without Durley, who
had been left behind with the dozen officers who were in reserve.

New Trench, which we took over, had been a good deal
knocked about, but we passed an unharassed night. We were
opposite Sunken Road Trench, which was 300 yards away up a
slope. Gaps had been cut in our wire for the attacking battalion to pass through. Early on the next afternoon Kinjack came
up to inspect the gaps. With the assistance of his big periscope
he soon discovered that the wire wasn't properly cut. It must be
done that night, he said. Barton brought me the news. I was
huddled up in a little dog-kennel of a dug-out, reading *Tess of
the D'Urbervilles* and trying to forget about the shells which
were hurrying and hurrooshing overhead. I was meditating
about England, visualizing a grey day down in Sussex; dark
green woodlands with pigeons circling above the tree-tops;
dogs barking, cocks crowing, and all the casual tappings and
twinklings of the countryside. I thought of the huntsman walking out in his long white coat with the hounds; of Parson Colwood pulling up weeds in his garden till tea-time; of Captain
Huxtable helping his men get in the last load of hay while a

shower of rain moved along the blurred Weald below his meadows. It was for all that, I supposed, that I was in the front-line
with soaked feet, trench mouth, and feeling short of sleep, for
the previous night had been vigilant though uneventful. Barton's head and shoulders butting past the gas-blanket in the
dug-out doorway wrecked my reverie; he wanted me to come
out and have a squint at the uncut wire, which was no day
dream since it was going to affect the fortunes of a still undi-
minished New Army Battalion. Putting *Tess* in my pocket, I
followed him to the fire-trench, which was cumbered with gas-
cylinders and boxes of smoke-bombs. A smoke-cloud was to be
let off later in the afternoon, for no special reason (except, perhaps, to make us cough and wipe our eyes, since what wind
there was blew the smoke along our trench). Shells were banging away on the rising ground behind Fricourt and the low ride
of Contalmaison. A young yellow-hammer was fluttering about
in the trench, and I wondered how it had got there: it seemed
out of place, perching on a body which lay trussed in a waterproof sheet. As for the gaps in the wire, they looked too bad for
words and only one night remained for widening them.

When I was back in the dug-out I found myself fingering
with pardonable pride my two pairs of wire-cutters from the
Army and Navy Stores. It is possible that I over-estimated
their usefulness, but their presence did seem providential. Any
fool could foresee what happened when troops got bunched up
as they left their trench for a daylight attack; and I knew that,
in spite of obstinate indentations to the source of supplies, we
hadn't got a decent pair of wire-cutters in the Battalion.

The big-bugs back at Brigade and Divisional H.Q. were
studying trench-maps with corrugated brows, for the 'greatest
battle in history' was timed to explode on Saturday morning.
They were too busy to concern themselves with the ant-like
activities of individual platoon commanders, and if they sent a
sympathetic Staff Captain up to have a look round he couldn't
produce wire-cutters like a conjurer. But the fact remained
that insistence on small (and often irrelevant) details was a
proverbial characteristic of Staff organization, and on the eve
of battle poor old Barton would probably be filling in a 'return'

stating how many men in his company had got varicose veins or married their deceased wife's sister. In the mean-time my casual purchase at 'the Stores' had, perhaps, lessened the likelihood of the Manchesters getting bunched up and mown down by machine-guns when they went over the top to attack Sunken Road Trench. And what would the Manchesters say about the Flintshire Fusiliers if the wire wasn't properly cut? So it seemed to me that our prestige as a Regular Battalion had been entrusted to my care on a front of several hundred yards.

Anyhow, I was ready with my party as soon as it began to be dark. There were only eight of them (mostly from the other companies) and we were unable to do anything before midnight owing to rather lively shelling. I remember waiting there in the gloom and watching an unearthly little conflagration caused by some phosphorus bombs up the hill on our right. When we did get started I soon discovered that cutting tangles of barbed wire in the dark in a desperate hurry is a job that needs ingenuity, even when your wire-cutters have rubber-covered handles and are fresh from the Army and Navy Stores. More than once we were driven in by shells which landed in front of our trench (some of them were our own dropping short); two men were wounded and some of the others were reluctant to resume work. In the first greying of dawn only three of us were still at it. Kendle (a nineteen year old lance-corporal from my platoon) and Worgan (one of the tough characters of our company) were slicing away for all they were worth; but as the light increased I began to realize the unimpressive effect of the snippings and snatchings which had made such a mess of our leather gloves. We had been working three and a half hours but the hedge hadn't suffered much damage, it seemed. Kendle disappeared into the trench and sauntered back to me, puffing a surreptitious Woodbine. I was making a last onslaught on a clawing thicket which couldn't have been more hostile if it had been put there by the Germans. 'We can't do any more in this daylight,' said Kendle. I straightened my stiff and weary back and looked at him. His jaunty fag-smoking demeanour and freckled boyish face seemed to defy the darkness we had emerged from. That moment has impressed itself strongly on my memory; young Kendle was remarkable for his cheerfulness and courage, and his cheeky jokes. Many a company had its Kendle, until the war broke his spirit. . . . The large solicitous countenance of old man Barton now appeared above the parapet; with almost aunt-like anxiety he urged us to come in before we got sniped. But there had been no sniping that night, and the machine-gun at Wing Corner had been silent. Wing Corner was at the edge of the skeleton village of Fricourt, whose ruinous church tower was now distinctly visible against the dark green woods. The Germans, coming up from their foundering dug-outs, would soon be staring grimly across at us while they waited for the relentless bombardment to begin again. As we got down into the trench young Kendle remarked that my new wire-cutters were a fair treat.

Next day, in warm and breezy weather, we moved to our battle-assembly position. For C Company 'battle-assembly position' meant being broken up into ammunition carrying parties, while Barton, Jenkins, and myself occupied an inglorious dug-out in the support line. The Manchesters were due to relieve us at 9 a.m., but there was still no sign of them at 10.30, so Barton, who was in a free and easy mood (caused by our immunity from to-morrow's attack), led the company away and left New Trench to look after itself. I had made up my mind to have another cut at the wire, which I now regarded with personal enmity, enjoying at the same time a self-admiring belief that much depended on my efforts. Worgan stayed behind with me. Kendle was unwilling to be left out of the adventure, but two of us would be less conspicuous than three, and my feeling for Kendle was somewhat protective. It was queer to be in an empty front-line trench on a fine morning, with everything quite peaceful after a violent early bombardment. Queerer still to be creeping about in the long grass (which might well have been longer, I thought) and shearing savagely at the tangles which had bewildered us in the dark but were now at our mercy. As Worgan said, we were giving it a proper hair-cut this journey.

Lying on my stomach I glanced now and again at the hostile

slope which overlooked us, wondering whether anyone would take a pot-shot at us, or speculating on a possible visitation of machine-gun bullets from Wing Corner. Barton's ignorance of what we were doing made it seem like an escapade, and the excitement was by no means disagreeable. It was rather like going out to weed a neglected garden after being warned that there might be a tiger among the gooseberry bushes. I should have been astonished if someone could have told me that I was an interesting example of human egotism. Yet such was the truth. I was cutting the wire by daylight because commonsense warned me that the lives of several hundred soldiers might depend on it being done properly. I was excited and pleased with myself while I was doing it. And I had entirely forgotten that tomorrow six Army Corps would attack, and whatever else happened, a tragic slaughter was inevitable. But if I had been intelligent enough to realize all that, my talents would have been serving in some more exalted place, probably Corps Intelligence Headquarters. Anyhow, at the end of an hour and a half the gaps were real good ones, and Barton's red face and glittering pince-nez were bobbing up and down beyond the parapet with *sotto-voce* incitements to prudence. Soon afterwards we dropped into the trench and the Manchesters began to arrive. It had been great fun, I said, flourishing my wire-cutters.

Early in the afternoon the Doctor bustled up from Battalion Head-quarters to tell me that my M.C. had come through. This gratifying little event increased my blindness to the blood-stained future. Homeliness and humanity beamed in Barton's congratulations; and the little doctor, who would soon be dressing the wounds of moaning men, unpicked his own faded medal-ribbon, produced a needle and thread, and sewed the white and purple portent on to my tunic. For the rest of the day and, indeed, for the remainder of my military career, the left side of my chest was more often in my mind than the right – a habit which was common to a multitude of wearers of Military Cross ribbons. Books about war psychology ought to contain a chapter on 'medal reflexes' and 'decoration complexes'. Much might be written, even here, about medals and their stimulating effect on those who really risked their lives for them. But the safest thing to be said is that nobody knew how much a decoration was worth except the man who received it. Outwardly the distribution of them became more and more fortuitous and debased as the War went on; and no one knew it better than the infantry, who rightly insisted that medal-ribbons earned at the Base ought to be a different colour.

But I must return to June 30th, which ended with a sullen bombardment from the British guns and a congestion of troops in the support-trench outside our dug-out. They had lost their way, and I remember how the exhausted men propped them-selves against the sides of the trench while their exasperated Adjutant and a confused civilian Colonel grumbled to Barton about the ambiguity of their operation orders. They were to attack on our left, and they vanished in that direction, leaving me with my Military Cross and a foreboding that disaster awaited them. Since they came within the limited zone of my observations I can record the fact that they left their trench early next morning at a wrong zero hour and got badly cut up by the artillery support which ought to have made things easy for them.

2

On July the first the weather, after an early morning mist, was of the kind commonly called heavenly. Down in our frowsty cellar we breakfasted at six, unwashed and apprehensive. Our table, appropriately enough, was an empty ammunition box. At six-forty-five the final bombardment began, and there was nothing for us to do except sit round our candle until the tornado ended. For more than forty minutes the air vibrated and the earth rocked and shuddered. Through the sustained uproar the tap and rattle of machine-guns could be identified; but except for the whistle of bullets no retaliation came our way until a few 5.9 shells shook the roof of our dug-out. Barton and I sat speechless, deafened and stupefied by the seismic state of affairs, and when he lit a cigarette the match flame staggered crazily. Afterwards I asked him what he had been thinking about. His reply was 'Carpet slippers and kettle-holders'. My own mind had been working in much the same style, for during that cannonading cataclysm the following refrain was running in my head:

> They come as a boon and a blessing to men,
> The Something, the Owl, and the Waverley Pen.

For the life of me I couldn't remember what the first one was called. Was it the Shakespeare? Was it the Dickens? Anyhow it was an advertisement which I'd often seen in smoky railway stations. Then the bombardment lifted and lessened, our vertigo abated, and we looked at one another in dazed relief. Two Brigades of our Division were now going over the top on our right. Our Brigade was to attack 'when the main assault had reached its final objective'. In our fortunate role of privileged spectators Barton and I went up the stairs to see what we could from Kingston Road Trench. We left Jenkins crouching in a corner, where he remained most of the day. His haggard blinking face haunts my memory. He was an example of the paralysing effect which such an experience could produce on a nervous system sensitive to noise, for he was a good officer both before and afterwards. I felt no sympathy for him at the time, but I do now. From the support-trench, which Barton called 'our opera box', I observed as much of the battle as the formation of the country allowed, the rising ground on the right making it impossible to see anything of the attack towards Mametz. A small shiny black notebook contains my pencilled particulars, and nothing will be gained by embroidering them with afterthoughts. I cannot turn my field-glasses on to the past.

7.45. The barrage is now working to the right of Fricourt and beyond. I can see the 21st Division advancing about three-quarters of a mile away on the left and a few Germans coming to meet them, apparently surrendering. Our men in small parties (not extended in line) go steadily on to the German front-line. Brilliant sunshine and a haze of smoke drifting along the landscape. Some Yorkshires a little way below on the left, watching the show and cheering as if at a football match. The noise almost as bad as ever.

9.30. Came back to the dug-out and had a shave. 21st Division still going across the open, apparently without casualties. The sunlight flashes on bayonets as the tiny figures move quietly forward and disappear beyond mounds of trench débris. A few runners come back and ammunition parties go across. Trench-mortars are knocking hell out of Sunken Road Trench and the ground where the Manchesters will attack soon. Noise not so bad now and very little retaliation.

9.50. Fricourt half-hidden by clouds of drifting smoke, blue, pinkish and grey. Shrapnel bursting in small bluish-white puffs with tiny flashes. The birds seem bewildered; a lark begins to go up and then flies feebly along, thinking better of it. Others flutter above the trench with querulous cries, weak on the wing. I can see seven of our balloons, on the right. On the left our men still filing across in twenties and thirties. Another huge explosion in Fricourt and a cloud of brown-pink smoke. Some bursts are yellowish.

10.5. I can see the Manchesters down in New Trench, getting ready to go over. Figures filing down the trench. Two of them have gone out to look at our wire gaps! Have just eaten my last orange. . . . I am staring at a sunlit picture of Hell, and still the breeze shakes the yellow weeds, and the poppies glow under Crawley Ridge where some shells fell a few minutes ago. Manchesters are sending forward some scouts. A bayonet glitters. A runner comes back across the open to their Battalion Headquarters close here on the right. 21st Division still trotting along the skyline toward La Boisselle. Barrage going strong to the right of Contalmaison Ridge. Heavy shelling toward Mametz.

12.15. Quieter the last two hours. Manchesters still waiting. Germans putting over a few shrapnel shells. Silly if I got hit! Weather cloudless and hot. A lark singing confidently overhead.

1.30. Manchesters attack at 2.30. Mametz and Montauban reported taken. Mametz consolidated.

2.30. Manchesters left New Trench and apparently took Sunken Road Trench, bearing rather to the right. Could see

about 400. Many walked casually across with sloped arms.
There were about forty casualties on the left (from machine-gun
in Fricourt). Through my glasses I could see one man moving his
left arm up and down as he lay on his side; his face was a crimson patch. Others lay still in the sunlight while the swarm of figures disappeared over the hill. Fricourt was a cloud of pinkish
smoke. Lively machine-gun fire on the far side of the hill. At 2.50
no one to be seen in no-man's-land except the casualties (about
half-way across). Our dug-out shelled again since 2.30.

5.0. I saw about thirty of our A Company crawl across to
Sunken Road from New Trench. Germans put a few big shells
on the Cemetery and traversed Kingston Road with machine-
gun. Manchester wounded still out there. Remainder of A
Company went across – about 100 altogether. Manchesters
reported held up in Bois Français Support. Their Colonel went
across and was killed.

8.0. Staff Captain of our Brigade has been along. Told Barton that Seventh Division has reached its objectives with some
difficulty, except on this Brigade front. Manchesters are in
trouble, and Fricourt attack has failed. Several hundred prisoners brought in on our sector.

9.30. Our A Company holds Rectangle and Sunken Road.
Jenkins gone off in charge of a carrying-party. Seemed all
right again. C Company now reduced to six runners, two
stretcher-bearers, Company Sergeant-Major, signallers, and
Barton's servant. Flook away on carrying-party. Sky cloudy
westward. Red sunset. Heavy gun-fire on the left.

2.30. (Next afternoon.) Adjutant has just been up here,
excited, optimistic, and unshaven. He went across last night to
ginger up A Company who did very well, thanks to the bombers. About 40 casualties; only 4 killed. Fricourt and Rose Trench
occupied this morning without resistance. I am now lying out
in front of our trench in the long grass, basking in sunshine
where yesterday there were bullets. Our new front-line on the
hill is being shelled. Fricourt is full of troops wandering about
in search of souvenirs. The village was a ruin and is now a dust
heap. A gunner (Forward Observation Officer) has just been
along here with a German helmet in his hand. Said Fricourt is

full of dead; he saw one officer lying across a smashed machine-gun with his head bashed in – 'a fine looking chap,' he said, with some emotion, which rather surprised me.

8.15. Queer feeling, seeing people moving about freely between here and Fricourt. Dumps being made. Shacks and shelters being put up under skeleton trees and all sorts of transport arriving at Cemetery Cross Roads. We stay here till to-morrow morning. Feel a bit of a fraud.

3

Early next morning we took leave of our subterranean sanctuary in Kingston Road, joined the Battalion at 71. North, and marched a couple of miles to a concentration point between Mametz and Carnoy. There, in a wide hollow, the four units of our Brigade piled arms, lay down on the grass, and took their boots off. Most of them had been without sleep for two nights and the immediate forecast was 'murky'. But every man had a waterproof sheet to sit on, helmets were exchanged for woollen caps, unshaven faces felt gratitude for generous sunshine, and bare feet stretched contented toes. Our Division having done well, there was a confident feeling in the air. But we had heard of partial and complete failures in other parts of the line, and the name of Gommecourt had already reached us with ugly implications. It was obvious that some of us would soon be lacing up our boots for the last time, and the current rumour, 'They say we've got to attack some Wood or other', could not fail to cause an uneasy visceral sensation. However, one felt that big things were happening, and my Military Cross was a comfort to me. It was a definite personal possession to be lived up to, I thought. I watched the men dozing in odd ungainly attitudes, half listened to their talk about the souvenirs they'd picked up in the German trenches, or stared at some captured guns being brought down the lane which led to Mametz.

A few of the men were wandering about, and my meditations were disturbed by Kinjack, who had given orders that everyone was to rest all day. 'Tell those men to lie down,' he shouted, adding – as he returned to his bivouac on the slope – 'The bastards'll be glad to before they're much older.' It was believed that his brusque manners had prevented him getting promotion, but everyone knew that it would be a bad day for the Battalion when Kinjack got his Brigade.

Evening fell calm and overcast, with a blurred orange sunset. Sitting among rank grass and thistles I stared pensively down at the four battalions grouped in the hollow. Thin smoke rose from the little bivouac fires which had been used for tea making; among the gruff murmuring which came up with the smoke, the nasal chant of a mouth organ did its best to 'keep the home fires burning'. In front of the hollow the open ground sloped treeless to Bazentin Ridge, dull green and striped with seams of trenches cut in the chalky soil. Field-guns were firing on the right and some aeroplanes hummed overhead. Beyond that hill our future awaited us. There would be no turning back from it. . . . I would have liked Flook to bring me an orange, but he was away with Jenkins and the carrying-party, and oranges were almost as remote as the sunset. Poor Flook will be awfully worried about not being with his officer bloke, I thought, imagining his stolid red face puffing along under a box of ammunition. . . . I went down the hill just in time to hear that we'd got orders to go up and dig a trench somewhere in front of Mametz.

For a few minutes the hollow was full of the subdued hubbub and commotion of troops getting into their equipment. Two battalions had been called out; the Royal Irish moved off ahead of us. As we went up the lane toward Mametz I felt that I was leaving all my previous war experience behind me. For the first time I was among the débris of an attack. After going a very short distance we made the first of many halts, and I saw, arranged by the roadside, about fifty of the British dead. Many of them were Gordon Highlanders. There were Devons and South Staffordshires among them, but they were beyond regimental rivalry now – their fingers mingled in blood-stained bunches, as though acknowledging the companionship of death. There was much battle gear lying about, and some dead horses. There were rags and shreds of clothing, boots riddled and torn, and when we came to the old German front-line, a sour pervasive stench which differed from anything my nostrils had known before. Meanwhile we made our continually retarded progress up the hill, and I scrutinized these battle effects with partially complacent curiosity. I wanted to be able to say that I had seen 'the horrors of war'; and here they were, nearly three days old.

No one in the glumly halted column knew what was delaying us. After four hours we had only progressed 1,500 yards and were among some ruined buildings on the outskirts of the village. I have dim remembrance of the strangeness of the place and our uneasy dawdling in its midnight desolation. Kinjack was somewhere ahead of us with a guide. The guide, having presumably lost his way, was having a much hotter time than we were. So far we had done nothing except file past a tool-dump, where the men had collected picks, shovels, coils of wire, and corkscrew stakes. At 2 a.m. we really began to move, passing through Mametz and along a communication trench. There were some badly mangled bodies about. Although I'd been with the Battalion nearly eight months, these were the first newly dead Germans I had seen. It gave me a bit of a shock when I saw, in the glimmer of daybreak, a dumpy, baggy-trousered man lying half sideways with one elbow up as if defending his lolling head; the face was grey and waxen, with a stiff little moustache; he looked like a ghastly doll, grotesque and undignified. Beside him was a scorched and mutilated figure whose contorted attitude revealed bristly cheeks, a grinning blood-smeared mouth and clenched teeth. These dead were unlike our own; perhaps it was the strange uniform, perhaps their look of butchered hostility. Anyhow they were one with the little trench direction boards whose unfamiliar lettering seemed to epitomize that queer feeling I used to have when I stared across no-man's-land, ignorant of the humanity which was on the other side.

Leaving the trench we filed across the open hillside with Mametz Wood looming on the opposite slope. It was a dense wood of old trees and undergrowth. The Staff of our Division had assumed that the near side was now unoccupied. But as soon as we had halted in a sunken road an uproar broke out at the edge of the wood, which demonstrated with machine-guns and bombs that the Staff had guessed wrong.

Kinjack promptly ordered A Company forward to get in touch with the Royal Irish, whose covering parties were having a bombing fight in the Wood. Our men were fired on as they went along the road and forced to take cover in a quarry. I remember feeling nervous and incompetent while I wondered what on earth I should do if called on to lead a party out 'into the blue'. But the clouds were now reddening, and we were fed up with the whole performance. Messages went back and our guns chucked a lot of shrapnel which burst over the near side of the Wood and enabled the Irish to withdraw. We then, as Kinjack described it afterwards, 'did a guy'; but it was a slow one for we weren't back at our camping ground until 8.30 a.m. The expedition had lasted nearly eleven hours and we had walked less than three miles, which was about all we could congratulate ourselves on. The Royal Irish had had sixty casualties; we had one killed and four wounded. From a military point of view the operations had enabled the Staff to discover that Mametz Wood was still full of Germans, so that it was impossible to dig a trench on the bluff within fifty yards of it, as had been suggested. It was obvious now that a few strong patrols could have clarified the situation more economically than 1,000 men with picks and shovels. The necessary information had been obtained, however, and the Staff could hardly be expected to go up and investigate such enigmas for themselves. But this sort of warfare was a new experience for all of us, and the difficulties of extempore organization must have been considerable.

During the morning we were a silent battalion, except for snoring. Some eight-inch guns were firing about 200 yards from the hollow, but our slumbers were inured to noises which would have kept us wide awake in civilian life. We were lucky to be dry, for the sky was overcast. At one o'clock our old enemy the rain arrived in full force. Four hours' deluge left the troops drenched and disconsolate, and then Dottrell made one of his providential appearances with the rations. Dixies of hot tea, and the rum issue, made all the difference to our outlook. It seemed to me

that the Quartermaster symbolized that region of temporary
security which awaited us when our present adversities were
ended. He had a cheery word for everyone, and his jocularity
was judicious. What were the jokes he made, I wonder? Their
helpfulness must be taken for granted. I can only remember his
chaffing an officer named Woolman, whose dumpy figure had
bulged abnormally since we came up to the battle area. Woolman's young lady in England had sent him a bullet-proof waistcoat; so far it had only caused its wearer to perspire profusely;
and although reputed to be extremely vulnerable, it had inspired
a humorist in his company to refer to him as 'Asbestos Bill'.

Time seems to have obliterated the laughter of the war. I cannot hear it in my head. How strange such laughter would sound,
could I but recover it as it was on such an evening as I am
describing, when we all knew that we'd got to do an attack that
night; for short-sighted Barton and the other company commanders had just returned from a reconnaissance of the ground
which had left them little wiser than when they started. In the
meantime we'd got some rum inside us and could find something to laugh about. Our laughter leapt up, like the flames of
camp fires in the dusk, soon to be stamped out, or extinguished
by our impartial opponent, the rain. The consoling apparition
of Dottrell departed, and I don't suppose he did much laughing
once he was alone with his homeward rattling limbers.

Zero hour was forty-five minutes after midnight. Two companies were to attack on a 600-yard front and the Royal Irish
were to do the same on our right. Barton's company was to be
in reserve; owing to the absence of the carrying-party it could
only muster about thirty men.

At nine o'clock we started up the sunken road to Mametz.
As a result of the rain, yesterday's dry going had been trodden
to a quagmire. Progress was slow owing to the congestion of
troops in front. We had only a couple of thousand yards to go,
but at one time it seemed unlikely that the assaulting companies would be in position by zero hour. It was pitch dark as we
struggled through the mud, and we got there with fifteen minutes to spare, having taken three and a half hours to go a mile
and a quarter.

Barton arranged his men along a shallow support trench on the edge of Bottom Wood, which was a copse just to the left of the ground we'd visited the night before. Almost at once the short preliminary bombardment began and the darkness became diabolic with the din and flash of the old old story. Not for the first time – I wondered whether shells ever collided in the air. Silence and suspense came after. Barton and I talked in undertones; he thought I'd better borrow his electric torch and find out the nearest way to Battalion Headquarters.

Everyone was anonymous in the dark, but 'It's me, Kendle, sir,' from a looming figure beside me implied an intention to share my explorations. We groped our way into the wood, and very soon I muttered that unless we were careful we'd get lost, which was true enough, for my sense of direction had already become uncertain. While we hesitated, some shells exploded all round us in the undergrowth with an effect of crashing stupidity. But we laughed, encouraging each other with mutual bravado, until we found a path. Along this path came someone in a hurry. He bumped into me and I flashed the torch on his face. He was an officer who had joined us the week before. He had now lost all control of himself and I gathered from his incoherent utterances that he was on his way to Headquarters to tell Kinjack that his Company hadn't moved yet because they didn't know which way to go to find the Germans. This wasn't surprising; but I felt alarmed about his reception at Headquarters, for Kinjack had already got an idea that this poor devil was 'cold-footed'. So, with an assumption of ferocity, I pulled out my automatic pistol, gripped him by the shoulder, and told him that if he didn't go straight back to 'Asbestos Bill' I'd shoot him, adding that Kinjack would certainly shoot him if he rolled up at Headquarters with such a story and in such a state of 'wind-up'. This sobered him and he took my advice, though I doubt whether he did any damage to the Germans. (Ten days later he was killed in what I can only call a *bona fide* manner.) So far, I thought, my contribution to this attack is a queer one; I have saved one of our officers from being court-martialled for cowardice. I then remarked to Kendle that this seemed to be the shortest way to Battalion Headquarters and we found our own way back to Barton without further incident. I told Barton that 'Asbestos Bill' seemed to be marking time, in spite of his bullet-proof waistcoat.

The men were sitting on the rough-hewn fire-step, and soon we were all dozing. Barton's bulky figure nodded beside me, and Kendle fell fast asleep with his head against my shoulder. We remained like this until my luminous watch indicated twenty past two. Then a runner arrived with a verbal message. 'C Company bombers to go up at once.' With a dozen men behind me I followed him through Bottom Wood. Darkness was giving way to unrevealing twilight as we emerged from the trees and went up a shell-pitted slope. It was about 500 yards across the open to the newly captured Quadrangle Trench. Just before we got there a second runner overtook us to say that my bombers were to go back again. I sent them back. I cannot say why I went on myself; but I did, and Kendle stayed with me.

There wasn't much wire in front of Quadrangle Trench. I entered it at a strong point on the extreme left and found three officers sitting on the fire-step with hunched shoulders and glum unenterprising faces. Two others had gone away wounded. I was told that Edmunds, the Battalion Observation Officer, had gone down to explain the situation to Kinjack; we were in touch with the Northumberland Fusiliers on our left. Nevertheless I felt that there must be something to be done. Exploring to the right I found young Fernby, whose demeanour was a contrast to the apathetic trio in the sand-bagged strong-point. Fernby had only been out from England a few weeks but he appeared quite at home in his new surroundings. His face showed that he was exulting in the fact that he didn't feel afraid. He told me that no one knew what had happened on our right; the Royal Irish were believed to have failed. We went along the trench which was less than waist deep. The Germans had evidently been digging when we attacked, and had left their packs and other equipment ranged along the reverse edge of the trench. I stared about me; the smoke-drifted twilight was alive with intense movement, and there was a wild strangeness in the scene which somehow excited me. Our men seemed a bit out of hand and I couldn't see any of the responsible N.C.O.s; some of the troops were firing excitedly at the Wood; others were rummaging in the German packs. Fernby said that we were being sniped from the trees on both sides. Mametz Wood was a menacing wall of gloom, and now an outburst of rapid thudding explosions began from that direction. There was a sap from the Quadrangle to the Wood, and along this the Germans were bombing. In all this confusion I formed the obvious notion that we ought to be deepening the trench. Daylight would be on us at once, and we were along a slope exposed to enfilade fire from the Wood. I told Fernby to make the men dig for all they were worth, and went to the right with Kendle. The Germans had left a lot of shovels, but we were making no use of them. Two tough-looking privates were disputing the ownership of a pair of field-glasses, so I pulled out my pistol and urged them, with ferocious objurations, to chuck all that fooling and dig. I seemed to be getting pretty handy with my pistol, I thought, for the conditions in Quadrangle Trench were giving me a sort of angry impetus. In some places it was only a foot deep, and already men were lying wounded and killed by sniping. There were high-booted German bodies, too, and in the blear beginning of day-light they seemed as much the victims of a catastrophe as the men who had attacked them. As I stepped over one of the Germans an impulse made me lift him up from the miserable ditch. Propped against the bank, his blond face was undisfigured, except by the mud which I wiped from his eyes and mouth with my coat sleeve. He'd evidently been killed while digging, for his tunic was knotted loosely about his shoulders. He didn't look to be more than eighteen. Hoisting him a little higher, I thought what a gentle face he had, and remembered that this was the first time I'd ever touched one of our enemies with my hands. Perhaps I had some dim sense of the futility which had put an end to this good-looking youth. Anyhow I hadn't expected the Battle of the Somme to be quite like this. . . . Kendle, who had been trying to do something for a badly wounded man, now rejoined me, and we continued, mostly on all fours, along the dwindling trench. We passed no

CRAWL

one until we came to a bombing post – three serious-minded men who said that no one had been further than that yet. Being in an exploring frame of mind, I took a bag of bombs and crawled another sixty or seventy yards with Kendle close behind me. The trench became a shallow groove and ended where the ground overlooked a little valley along which there was a light railway line. We stared across at the Wood. From the other side of the valley came an occasional rifle-shot, and a helmet bobbed up for a moment. Kendle remarked that from that point anyone could see into the whole of our trench on the slope behind us. I said we must have our strong-post here and told him to go back for the bombers and a Lewis gun. I felt adventurous and it seemed as if Kendle and I were having great fun together. Kendle thought so too. The helmet bobbed up again. 'I'll just have a shot at him,' he said, wriggling away from the crumbling bank which gave us cover. At this moment Fernby appeared with two men and a Lewis gun. Kendle was half kneeling against some broken ground; I remember seeing him push his tin hat back from his forehead and then raise himself a few inches to take aim. After firing once he looked at us with a lively smile; a second later he fell sideways. A blotchy mark showed where the bullet had hit him just above the eyes.

The circumstances being what they were, I had no justification for feeling either shocked or astonished by the sudden extinction of Lance-Corporal Kendle. But after blank awareness that he was killed, all feelings tightened and contracted to a single intention – to 'settle that sniper' on the other side of the valley. If I had stopped to think, I shouldn't have gone at all. As it was, I discarded my tin hat and equipment, slung a bag of bombs across my shoulder, abruptly informed Fernby that I was going to find out who *was* there, and set off at a downhill double. While I was running I pulled the safety-pin out of a Mills' bomb; my right hand being loaded, I did the same for my left. I mention this because I was obliged to extract the second safety-pin with my teeth, and the grating sensation reminded me that I was half way across and not so reckless as I had been when I started. I was even a little out of breath as I trotted up the opposite slope. Just before I arrived at the top I slowed up and threw my two bombs. Then I rushed at the bank, vaguely expecting some sort of scuffle with my imagined enemy. I had lost my temper with the man who had shot Kendle; quite unexpectedly, I found myself looking down into a well-conducted trench with a great many Germans in it. Fortunately for me, they were already retreating. It had not occurred to them that they were being attacked by a single fool; and Fernby, with presence of mind which probably saved me, had covered my advance by traversing the top of the trench with his Lewis gun. I slung a few more bombs, but they fell short of the clumsy field-grey figures, some of whom half turned to fire their rifles over the left shoulder as they ran across the open toward the wood, while a crowd of jostling helmets vanished along the trench. Idiotically elated, I stood there with my finger in my right ear and emitted a series of 'view-holloas' (a gesture which ought to win the approval of people who still regard war as a form of outdoor sport). Having thus failed to commit suicide, I proceeded to occupy the trench – that is to say, I sat down on the fire-step, very much out of breath, and hoped to God the Germans wouldn't come back again.

The trench was deep and roomy, with a fine view of our men in the Quadrangle, but I had no idea what to do now I had got possession of it. The word 'consolidation' passed through my mind; but I couldn't consolidate by myself. Naturally, I didn't under-estimate the magnitude of my achievement in capturing the trench on which the Royal Irish had made a frontal attack in the dark. Nevertheless, although still unable to see that my success was only a lucky accident, I felt a bit queer in my solitude, so I reinforced my courage by counting the sets of equipment which had been left behind. There were between forty and fifty packs, tidily arranged in a row – a fact which I often mentioned (quite casually) when describing my exploit afterwards. There was the doorway of a dug-out, but I only peered in at it, feeling safer above ground. Then, with apprehensive caution, I explored about half way to the Wood without finding any dead bodies. Apparently no one was any the worse for my little bombing demonstration. Perhaps I was disappointed by this, though the discovery of a dead or wounded enemy might have caused a revival of humane emotion. Returning to the sniping post at the end of the trench I meditated for a few minutes, somewhat like a boy who has caught a fish too big to carry home (if such an improbable event has ever happened). Finally I took a deep breath and ran headlong back by the way I'd come.

Little Fernby's anxious face awaited me, and I flopped down beside him with an outburst of hysterical laughter. When he'd heard my story he asked whether we oughtn't to send a party across to occupy the trench, but I said that the Germans would be bound to come back quite soon. Moreover my rapid return had attracted the attention of a machine-gun which was now firing angrily along the valley from a position in front of the Wood. In my excitement I had forgotten about Kendle. The sight of his body gave me a bit of a shock. His face had gone a bluish colour; I told one of the bombers to cover it with something. Then I put on my web-equipment and its attachments, took a pull at my water-bottle, for my mouth had become suddenly intolerably dry, and set off on my return journey, leaving Fernby to look after the bombing post. It was now six o'clock in the morning, and a weary business it is, to be remembering and writing it down. There was nothing likeable about the Quadrangle, though it was comfortable, from what I have heard, compared with the hell which it became a few days afterwards. Alternately crouching and crawling, I worked my way back. I passed the young German whose body I had rescued from disfigurement a couple of hours before. He was down in the mud again and someone had trodden on his face. It disheartened me to see him, though his body had now lost all touch with life and was part of the wastage of the war. He and Kendle had cancelled one another out in the process called 'attrition of manpower'. Further along I found one of our men dying slowly with a hole in his forehead. His eyes were open and he breathed with a horrible snoring sound. Close by him knelt two of his former mates; one of them was hacking at the ground with an entrenching tool while the other scooped the earth out of the trench with his hands. They weren't worrying about souvenirs now.

Disregarding a written order from Barton, telling me to return, I remained up in Quadrangle Trench all the morning.

The enemy made a few attempts to bomb their way up the sap from the Wood and in that restricted area I continued to expend energy which was a result of strained nerves. I mention this because, as the day went on, I definitely wanted to kill someone at close quarters. If this meant that I was really becoming a good 'fighting man', I can only suggest that, as a human being, I was both exhausted and exasperated. My courage was of the cock-fighting kind. Cock-fighting is illegal in England, but in July, 1916 the man who could boast that he'd killed a German in the Battle of the Somme would have been patted on the back by a bishop in a hospital ward.

German stick-bombs were easy to avoid; they took eight seconds to explode, and the throwers didn't hang on to them many seconds after pulling the string. Anyhow, my feverish performances were concluded by a peremptory message from Battalion H.Q. and I went down to Bottom Wood by a half-dug communication trench whose existence I have only this moment remembered (which shows how difficult it is to recover the details of war experience).

It was nearly two o'clock, and the daylight was devoid of mystery when I arrived at Kinjack's headquarters. The circumstances now made it permissible for me to feel tired and hungry, but for the moment I rather expected congratulations. My expectation was an error. Kinjack sat glowering in a surface dug-out in a sand-pit at the edge of Bottom Wood. I went in from the sunlight. The overworked Adjutant eyed me sadly from a corner of an ammunition box table covered with a grey blanket, and the Colonel's face caused me to feel like a newly captured prisoner. Angrily he asked why I hadn't come back with my company bombers in the early morning. I said I'd stayed up there to see what was happening. Why hadn't I consolidated Wood Trench? Why the hell hadn't I sent back a message to let him know that it had been occupied? I made no attempt to answer these conundrums. Obviously I'd made a mess of the whole affair. The Corps Artillery bombardment had been held up for three hours because Kinjack couldn't report that 'my patrol' had returned to Quadrangle Trench, and altogether he couldn't be blamed for feeling annoyed with me, especially as he'd been ticked off over the telephone by the Brigadier (in Morse Code dots and dashes, I suppose). I looked at him with a sulky grin, and went along to Barton with a splitting headache and a notion that I ought to be thankful that I was back at all.

In the evening we were relieved. The incoming battalion numbered more than double our own strength (we were less than 400) and they were unseasoned New Army troops. Our little trench under the trees was inundated by a jostling company of exclamatory Welshmen. Kinjack would have called them a panicky rabble. They were mostly undersized men, and as I watched them arriving at the first stage of their battle experience I had a sense of their victimization. A little platoon officer was settling his men down with a valiant show of self-assurance. For the sake of appearances, orders of some kind had to be given, though in reality there was nothing to do except sit down and hope it wouldn't rain. He spoke sharply to some of them, and I felt that they were like a lot of children. It was going to be a bad look-out for two such bewildered companies, huddled up in the Quadrangle, which had been over-garrisoned by our own comparatively small contingent. Visualizing that forlorn crowd of khaki figures under the twilight of the trees, I can believe that I saw then, for the first time, how blindly war destroys its victims. The sun had gone down on my own reckless brandishings, and I understood the doomed condition of these half trained civilians who had been sent up to attack the Wood. As we moved out, Barton exclaimed, 'By God, Kangar, I'm sorry for those poor devils!' Dimly he pitied them, as well he might. Two days later the Welsh Division, of which they were a unit, was involved in massacre and confusion. Our own occupation of Quadrangle Trench was only a prelude to that pandemonium which converted the green thickets of Mametz Wood to a desolation of skeleton trees and blackening bodies.

In the meantime we willingly left them to their troubles and marched back twelve miles to peace and safety. Mametz was being heavily shelled when we stumbled wearily through its ruins, but we got off lightly, though the first four miles took us four hours, owing to congestion of transport and artillery on the roads round Fricourt. On the hill above Bécordel we dozed for an hour in long wet grass, with stars overhead and guns booming and flashing in the valleys below. Then, in the first glimmer of a cold misty dawn, we trudged on to Heilly. We were there by eight o'clock, in hot sunshine. Our camp was on a marsh by the river Ancre – not a good camp when it rained (as it did before long) but a much pleasanter place than the Somme battlefield. . . . After three hours' sleep I was roused by Flook. All officers were required to attend the Brigadier's conference. At this function there was no need for me to open my mouth, except for an occasional yawn. Kinjack favoured me with a good-humoured grin. He only made one further comment on my non-consolidation of that fortuitously captured trench. He would probably leave me out of the 'next show' as a punishment, he said. Some people asserted that he had no sense of humour, but I venture to disagree with them.

4

Nobody had any illusions about the duration of our holiday at Heilly. Our Division had been congratulated by the Commander-in-Chief, and our Brigadier had made it clear that further efforts would be required of us in the near future. In the meantime the troops contrived to be cheerful; to be away from the battle and in a good village was all that mattered, for the moment. Our casualties had not been heavy (we had lost about 100 men but only a dozen of them had been killed). There was some grumbling on the second day, which was a wet one and reduced our camp to its natural condition – a swamp; but the Army Commander paid us a brief (and mercifully informal) visit, and this glimpse of his geniality made the men feel that they had done creditably. Nevertheless, as he squelched among the brown tents in his boots and spurs, more than one voice might have been heard muttering, 'Why couldn't the old—— have dumped us in a drier spot?' But the Fourth Army figurehead may well have been absent-minded that afternoon, since the Welsh Division had attacked Mametz Wood earlier in the day, and he must already have been digesting the first reports, which reached us in wild rumours next morning.

Basking in the sunshine after breakfast with Barton and Durley, I felt that to-day was all that concerned us. If there had been a disastrous muddle, with troops stampeding under machine-gun fire, it was twelve miles away and no business of ours until we were called upon to carry on the good work. There were no parades today, and we were going into Amiens for lunch – Dottrell and the Adjutant with us. Barton, with a brown field-service notebook on his knee, was writing a letter to his wife. 'Do you always light your pipe with your left hand, Kangar?' he asked, looking up as he tore another leaf out. I replied that I supposed so, though I'd never noticed it before. Then I rambled on for a bit about how unobservant one could be. I said (knowing that old man Barton liked hearing about such things) 'We've got a grandfather clock in the hall at home and for years and years I thought the maker's name was *Thos. Verney, London.* Then one day I decided to give the old brass face a polish up and I found that it was *Thos. Vernon, Ludlow!*' Barton thought this a pleasing coincidence because he lived in Shropshire and had been to Ludlow Races. A square mile of Shropshire, he asserted, was worth the whole of France. Durley (who was reading *Great Expectations* with a face that expressed release from reality) put in a mild plea for Stoke Newington, which was where he lived; it contained several quaint old corners if you knew where to look for them, and must, he said, have been quite a sleepy sort of place in Dickens's days. Reverting to my original topic, I remarked, 'We've got an old barometer, too, but it never works. Ever since I can remember, it's pointed to *Expect Wet from N.E.* Last time I was on leave I noticed that it's not *Expect* but *Except* – though goodness knows what that means!' My companions, who were disinclined to be talkative, assured me that with such a brain I ought to be on the Staff.

Strolling under the aspens that shivered and twinkled by the river, I allowed myself a little day dream, based on the leisurely ticking of the old Ludlow clock. . . . Was it only three weeks ago that I had been standing there at the foot of the staircase, between the barometer and the clock, on just such a fine summer morning as this? Upstairs in the bathroom Aunt Evelyn was putting sweet-peas and roses in water, humming to herself while she arranged them to her liking. Visualizing the bathroom with its copper bath and basin (which 'took such a lot of cleaning'), its lead floor, and the blue and white Dutch tiles along the walls, and the elder tree outside the window, I found these familiar objects almost as dear to me as Aunt Evelyn herself, since they were one with her in my mind (though for years she'd been talking about doing away with the copper bath and basin).

Even now, perhaps, she was once again carrying a bowl of roses down to the drawing-room while the clock ticked slow, and the parrot whistled, and the cook chopped something on the kitchen table. There might also be the short-winded snorting of a traction-engine labouring up the hill outside the house. . . . Meeting a traction-engine had been quite an event in my childhood, when I was out for rides on my first pony. And the thought of the cook suggested the gardener clumping in with a trug of vegetables, and the gardener suggested birds in the strawberry nets, and altogether there was no definite end to that sort of day dream of an England where there was no war on and the village cricket ground was still being mown by a man who didn't know that he would some day join 'the Buffs', migrate to Mesopotamia, and march to Bagdad.

Amiens was eleven miles away and the horses none too sound; but Dottrell had arranged for us to motor the last seven of the miles – the former Quartermaster of our battalion (who had been Quartermaster at Fourth Army Headquarters ever since the Fourth Army had existed) having promised to lend us his car. So there was nothing wrong with the world as the five of us jogged along, and I allowed myself a momentary illusion that we were riding clean away from the War. Looking across a spacious and untroubled landscape chequered with ripening corn

pretend.

and blood-red clover, I wondered how that calm and beneficent light could be spreading as far as the battle zone. But a Staff car overtook us, and as it whirled importantly past in a cloud of dust I caught sight of a handcuffed German prisoner – soon to provide material for an optimistic paragraph in Corps Intelligence Summary, and to add his story to the omniscience of the powers who now issued operation orders with the assertion that we were 'pursuing a beaten enemy'. Soon we were at Querrieux, a big village cosily over-populated by the Fourth Army Staff. As we passed the General's white château Dottrell speculated ironically on the average income of his personal staff, adding that they must suffer terribly from insomnia with so many guns firing fifteen miles away. Leaving our horses to make the most of a Fourth Army feed, we went indoors to pay our respects to the opulent Quartermaster, who had retired from Battalion duties after the First Battle of Ypres. He assured us that he could easily spare his car for a few hours since he had the use of two; whereupon Dottrell said he'd been wondering how he managed to get on with only one car.

In Amiens, at the well-known Godbert Restaurant, we lunched like dukes in a green-shuttered private room. 'God only knows when we'll see a clean tablecloth again,' remarked Barton, as he ordered langoustes, roast duck, and two bottles of their best 'bubbly'. Heaven knows what else the meal contained; but I remember talking with a loosened tongue about sport, and old Joe telling us how he narrowly escaped being reduced to the ranks for 'making a book' when the Battalion was stationed in Ireland before the war. 'There were some fine riders in the regiment then; they talked and thought about nothing but hunting, racing, and polo,' he said; adding that it was lucky for some of us that horsemanship wasn't needed for winning the war, since most mounted officers now looked as if they were either rowing a boat or riding a bicycle uphill. Finally, when with flushed faces we sauntered out into the sunshine, he remarked that he'd half a mind to go and look for a young lady to make his wife jealous. I said that there was always the cathedral to look at, and discovered that I'd unintentionally made a very good joke.

5

Two days later we vacated the camp at Heilly. The aspens by the river were shivering and showing the whites of their leaves, and it was good-bye to their cool showery sound when we marched away in our own dust at four o'clock on a glaring bright afternoon. The aspens waited, with their indifferent welcome, for some other dead beat and diminished battalion. Such was their habit, and so the war went on. It must be difficult, for those who did not experience it, to imagine the sensation of returning to a battle area, particularly when one started from a safe place like Heilly. Replenished by an unpromising draft from a home service battalion, our unit was well rested and, supposedly, as keen as mustard. Anyhow it suited everyone, including the troops themselves, to believe that victory was somewhere within sight. Retrospectively, however, I find it difficult to conceive them as an optimistic body of men, and it is certain that if the men of the new draft had any illusions about modern warfare, they would shortly lose them.

My exiguous diary has preserved a few details of that nine-mile march. Field-Marshal Haig passed us in his motor; and I saw a doctor in a long white coat standing in the church door at Morlancourt. Passing through the village, we went on by a track, known as 'the Red Road', arrived at the Citadel 'in rich yellow evening light', and bivouacked on the hill behind the Fricourt road. Two hours later we 'stood-to', and then started for Mametz, only to be brought back again after going half a mile. I fell asleep to the sound of heavy firing toward La Boisselle, rattling limbers on the Citadel road, and men shouting and looking for their kits in the dark. There are worse things than falling asleep under a summer sky. One awoke stiff and cold, but with a head miraculously clear.

Next day I moved to the Transport Lines, a couple of miles back, for I was one of eight officers kept in reserve. There I existed monotonously while the Battalion was engaged in the Battle of Bazentin Ridge. My boredom was combined with

Boredom

suspense, for after the first attack I might be sent for at any moment, so I could never wander far from the Transport Lines.

The battle didn't begin till Friday at dawn, so on Thursday Durley and I were free and we went up to look at the old Front Line. We agreed that it felt queer to be walking along no-man's-land and inspecting the old German trenches in a half-holiday mood. The ground was littered with unused ammunition, and a spirit of mischievous destruction possessed us. Pitching Stokes mortar shells down the dark and forbidding stairs of German dug-outs, we revelled in the boom of subterranean explosions. For a few minutes we felt as if we were getting a bit of our own back for what we'd endured opposite those trenches, and we chanced to be near the mine craters where the raid had failed. But soon we were being shouted at by an indignant Salvage Corps Officer, and we decamped before he could identify us. Thus we 'put the lid on' our days and nights in the Bois Français sector, which was now nothing but a few hundred yards of waste ground – a jumble of derelict wire, meaningless ditches, and craters no longer formidable. There seemed no sense in the toil that had heaped those mounds of bleaching sandbags, and even the 1st of July had become an improbable memory, now that the dead bodies had been cleared away. Rank thistles were already thriving among the rusty rifles, torn clothing, and abandoned equipment of those who had fallen a couple of weeks ago.

That evening we heard that our Second Battalion had bivouacked about half a mile from the camp. Their Division had been brought down from Flanders and was on its way up to Bazentin. Returning from an after dinner stroll I found that several Second Battalion officers had come to visit us. It was almost dark; these officers were standing outside our tent with Durley and the others, and it sounded as if they were keeping up their courage with the volubility usual among soldiers who knew that they would soon be in an attack. Among them, big and impulsive, was David Cromlech, who had been with our Battalion for three months of the previous winter. As I approached the group I recognized his voice with a shock of delighted surprise. He and I had never been in the same Company, but we were close friends, although somehow or other I have hitherto left him out of my story. On this occasion his face was only dimly discernible, so I will not describe it, though it was a remarkable one. An instinct for aloofness which is part of my character caused me to remain in the background for a minute or two, and I now overheard his desperately cheerful ejaculations with that indefinite pang of affection often felt by a detached observer of such spontaneous behaviour. When I joined the group we had so much to tell one another that I very soon went back with him to his tentless hillside. On the way I gave him a breathless account of my adventures up at Mametz Wood, but neither of us really wanted to talk about the Somme Battle. We should probably get more than enough of it before we'd finished. He had only just joined the Second Battalion, and I was eager to hear about England. The men of his platoon were lying down a little way off; but soon their recumbent mutterings had ceased, and all around us in the gloom were sleeping soldiers and the pyramids of piled rifles. We knew that this might be our last meeting, and gradually an ultimate strangeness and simplicity overshadowed and contained our low-voiced colloquies. We talked of the wonderful things we'd do after the war; for to me David had often seemed to belong less to my war experience than to the freedom which would come after it. He had dropped his defensive exuberance now, and I felt that he was rather luckless and lonely – too young to be killed up on Bazentin Ridge. It was midnight when I left him. First thing in the morning I hurried up the hill in hope of seeing him again. Scarcely a trace remained of the battalion which had bivouacked there, and I couldn't so much as identify the spot where we'd sat on his ground sheet, until I discovered a scrap of silver paper which might possibly have belonged to the packet of chocolate we had munched while he was telling me about the month's holiday he'd had in Wales after he came out of hospital.

When I got back to our tent in the Transport Lines I found everyone in a state of excitement. Dottrell and the ration party had returned from their all-night pilgrimage with information about yesterday's attack. The Brigade had reached its first objectives. Two of our officers had been killed and several wounded. Old man Barton had got a nice comfortable one in the shoulder. Hawkes (a reliable and efficient chap who belonged to one of the other companies) had been sent for to take command of C Company, and was even now completing his rapid but methodical preparations for departure.

The reserve Echelon was an arid and irksome place to be loafing about in. Time hung heavy on our hands and we spent a lot of it lying in the tent on our outspread valises. During the sluggish mid-afternoon of the same Saturday I was thus occupied in economizing my energies. Durley had nicknamed our party 'the eight little nigger boys', and there were now only seven of us. Most of them were feeling more talkative than I was, and it happened that I emerged from a snooze to hear them discussing 'that queer bird Cromlech'. Their comments reminded me, not for the first time, of the diversified impressions which David made upon his fellow Fusiliers.

At his best I'd always found him an ideal companion, although his opinions were often disconcerting. But no one was worse than he was at hitting it off with officers who distrusted cleverness and disliked unreserved utterances. In fact he was a positive expert at putting people's backs up unintentionally. He was with our Second Battalion for a few months before they transferred him to 'the First', and during that period the Colonel was heard to remark that young Cromlech threw his tongue a hell of a lot too much, and that it was about time he gave up reading Shakespeare and took to using soap and water. He had, however, added, 'I'm agreeably surprised to find that he isn't windy in trenches.'

David certainly was deplorably untidy, and his absent-mindedness when off duty was another propensity which made him unpopular. Also, as I have already hinted, he wasn't good at being 'seen but not heard'. 'Far too fond of butting in with his opinion before he's been asked for it,' was often his only reward for an intelligent suggestion. Even Birdie Mansfield (who had knocked about the world too much to be intolerant) was once heard to exclaim, 'Unless you watch it, my

son, you'll grow up into the most bumptious young prig God
ever invented!' – this protest being a result of David's assertion
that all sports except boxing, football and rock climbing were
snobbish and silly.

From the floor of the tent, Holman (a spick and span boy who
had been to Sandhurst and hadn't yet discovered that it was
unwise to look down on temporary officers who 'wouldn't have
been wanted in the Regiment in peace time') was now saying,
'Anyhow, I was at Clitherland with him last month, and he fairly
got on people's nerves with his hot air about the Battle of Loos,
and his brainwaves about who really wrote the Bible.' Durley
then philosophically observed, 'Old Longneck certainly isn't the
sort of man you meet every day. I can't always follow his theories
myself, but I don't mind betting that he'll go a long way – provided he isn't pushing up daisies when Peace breaks out.' Holman (who had only been with us a few days and soon became
more democratic) brushed Durley's defence aside with 'The
blighter's never satisfied unless he's turning something upside
down. I actually heard him say that Homer was a woman. Can
you beat that? And if you'll believe me he had the darned sauce
to give me a sort of pi-jaw about going out with girls in Liverpool. If you ask me, I think he's a rotten outsider, and the sooner
he's pushing up daisies the better.' Whereupon Perrin (a quiet
man of thirty-five who was sitting in a corner writing to his wife)
stopped the discussion by saying, 'Oh, dry up, Holman! For all
we know the poor devil may be dead by now.'

Late that night I was lying in the tent with *The Return of the
Native* on my knee. The others were asleep, but my candle still
guttered on the shell-box at my elbow. No one had mumbled
'For Christ's sake put that light out'; which was lucky, for I felt
very wide awake. How were things going at Bazentin, I wondered? And should I be sent for to-morrow? A sort of numb
funkiness invaded me. I didn't want to die – not before I'd finished reading *The Return of the Native* anyhow. 'The quick-
silvery glaze on the rivers and pools vanished; from broad
mirrors of light they changed to lustreless sheets of lead.' The
words fitted my mood; but there was more in them than that.

I wanted to explore the book slowly. It made me long for England, and it made the War seem waste of time. Ever since my existence became precarious I had realized how little I'd used my brains in peace time, and now I was always trying to keep my mind from stagnation. But it wasn't easy to think one's own thoughts while on active service, and the outlook of my companions was mostly mechanical; they dulled everything with commonplace chatter and made even the vividness of the War ordinary. My encounter with David Cromlech – after three months' separation – had reawakened my relish for liveliness and originality. But I had no assurance of ever seeing him again, or of meeting anyone who could stir up my dormant apprehensions as he did. Was it a mistake, I wondered, to try and keep intelligence alive when I could no longer call my life my own? In the brown twilight of the tent I sat pondering with my one golden candle flame beside me. Last night's talk with David now assumed a somewhat ghostlike character. The sky had been starless and clouded and the air so still that a lighted match needed no hand to shield it. Ghosts don't strike matches, of course; and I knew that I'd smoked my pipe, and watched David's face – sallow, crooked, and whimsical – when he lit a cigarette. There must have been the usual noises going on; but they were as much a part of our surroundings as the weather, and it was easy to imagine that the silence had been unbroken by the banging of field batteries and the remote tack-tack of rifles and machine-guns. Had that sombre episode been some premonition of our both getting killed? For the country had loomed limitless and strange and sullenly imbued with the Stygian significance of the War. And the soldiers who slept around us in their hundreds – were they not like the dead, among whom in some dim region where time survived in ghostly remembrances, we two could still cheat ourselves with hopes and forecasts of a future exempt from antagonisms and perplexities? . . . On some such sonorous cadence as this my thoughts halted. Well, poor old David was up in the battle; perhaps my mind was somehow in touch with his (though he would have disparaged my 'fine style', I thought). More rationally reflective, I looked at my companions, rolled in their

Hidden purpose

blankets, their faces turned to the earth or hidden by the folds. I thought of the doom that was always near them now, and how I might see them lying dead, with all their jollity silenced, and their talk, which had made me impatient, ended for ever. I looked at gallant young Fernby; and Durley, that kind and sensitive soul; and my own despondency and discontent released me. I couldn't save them, but at least I could share the dangers and discomforts they endured. 'Outside in the gloom the guns are shaking the hills and making lurid flashes along the alleys. Inevitably, the War blunders on; but among the snoring sleepers I have had my little moment of magnanimity. What I feel is no more than the candle which makes tottering shadows in the tent. Yet it is something, perhaps, that one man can be awake there, though he can find no meaning in the immense destruction which he blindly accepts as part of some hidden purpose.' . . . Thus (rather portentously, perhaps) I recorded in my diary the outcome of my ruminations.

For another five days my war experience continued to mark time in that curious camp. I call the camp curious, for it seemed so, even then. There was a makeshift effect of men coming and going, loading and unloading limbers and wagons, carrying fodder, shouting at horses and mules, attending to fires, and causing a smell of cooking. A whiff from a certain sort of wood fire could make me see that camp clearly now, since it was strewn and piled with empty shell-boxes which were used for fuel, as well as for building bivouacs. Along the road from Fricourt to Méaulte, infantry columns continually came and went, processions of prisoners were brought down, and small parties of 'walking wounded' straggled thankfully toward the Casualty Clearing Station. The worn landscape looked parched and shabby; only the poppies made harsh spots of red, matching the head caps of the Indian cavalry who were camped near by.

Among all this activity time passed sluggishly for me. Inside our tent I used to stare at the camouflage paint smears which showed through the canvas, formulating patterns and pictures among which the whiteness of the sky showed in gaps and rents. The paint smears were like ungainly birds with wide spread wings, fishes floating, monkeys in scarecrow trees, or anything else my idle brain cared to contrive. In one corner a fight was going on (in a Futuristic style) and a figure brandished a club while his adversary took a side-leap, losing an arm and a leg from a bomb explosion. Then someone would darken the doorway with a rumour that the Battalion had been moved up to attack High Wood – a new name, and soon afterwards an ugly one. Night would fall, with the others playing 'Nap' and talking stale war stuff out of the *Daily Mail,* and the servants singing by a bright shell-box fire in the gusty twilight. And I would think about driving home from cricket matches before the War, wondering whether I'd ever go back to that sort of thing again.

I remember another evening (it was the last one I spent in that place) when the weather seemed awaiting some spectacular event in this world of blundering warfare. Or was it as though the desolation of numberless deaths had halted the clouded sky to an attitude of brooding inertia? I looked across at Albert; its tall trees were flat grey-blue outlines, and the broken tower of the basilica might have been a gigantic clump of foliage. Above this landscape of massed stillness and smoky silhouettes the observation balloons were swaying slowly, their noses pointing toward the line of battle. Only the distant thud of gun-fire disturbed the silence – like someone kicking footballs – a soft bumping, miles away. Walking along by the river I passed the horse-lines of the Indian cavalry; the barley field above couldn't raise a rustle, so still was the air. Low in the west, pale orange beams were streaming down on the country that receded with a sort of rich regretful beauty, like the background of a painted masterpiece. For me that evening expressed the indeterminate tragedy which was moving, with agony on agony, toward the autumn.

I leant on a wooden bridge, gazing down into the dark green glooms of the weedy little river, but my thoughts were powerless against unhappiness so huge. I couldn't alter European history, or order the artillery to stop firing. I could stare at the War as I stared at the sultry sky, longing for life and freedom and vaguely altruistic about my fellow-victims. But a second-lieutenant could attempt nothing – except to satisfy his superior officers;

and altogether, I concluded, Armageddon was too immense for my solitary understanding. Then the sun came out for a last reddening look at the War, and I turned back to the camp with its clustering tents and crackling fires. I finished the day jawing to young Fernby about fox-hunting.

The Division had now been in action for a week. Next day they were to be relieved. Late in the afternoon Dottrell moved the Transport back about three miles, to a hill above Dernancourt. Thankful for something to do at last, I busied myself with the putting up of tents. When that was done I watched the sun going down in glory beyond the main road to Amiens. The horizon trees were dark blue against the glare, and the dust of the road floated in wreaths; motor-lorries crept continuously by, while the long shadows of trees made a sort of mirage on the golden haze of the dust. The country along the river swarmed with camps, but the low sun made it all seem pleasant and peaceful. After nightfall the landscape glowed and glinted with camp-fires, and a red half-moon appeared to bless the combatant armies with neutral beams. Then we were told to shift the tents higher up the hill and I became active again; for the Battalion was expected about midnight. After this little emergency scramble I went down to the crossroads with Dottrell, and there we waited hour after hour. The Quartermaster was in a state of subdued anxiety, for he'd been unable to get up to Battalion Headquarters for the last two days. We sat among some barley on the bank above the road, and as time passed we conversed companionably, keeping ourselves awake with an occasional drop of rum from his flask. I always enjoyed being with Dottrell, and that night the husky-voiced old campaigner was more eloquent than he realized. In the simplicity of his talk there was a universal tone which seemed to be summing up all the enduring experience of an Infantry Division. For him it was a big thing for the Battalion to be coming back from a battle, though, as he said, it was a new Battalion every few months now.

An hour before dawn the road was still an empty picture of moonlight. The distant gun-fire had crashed and rumbled all

night, muffled and terrific with immense flashes, like waves of
some tumult of water rolling along the horizon. Now there
came an interval of silence in which I heard a horse neigh,
shrill and scared and lonely. Then the procession of the returning troops began. The camp-fires were burning low when the
grinding jolting column lumbered back. The field guns came
first, with nodding men sitting stiffly on weary horses, followed by wagons and limbers and field-kitchens. After this
rumble of wheels came the infantry, shambling, limping, straggling and out of step. If anyone spoke it was only a muttered
word, and the mounted officers rode as if asleep. The men had
carried their emergency water in petrol-cans, against which
bayonets made a hollow clink; except for the shuffling of feet,
this was the only sound. Thus, with an almost spectral appearance, the lurching brown figures flitted past with slung rifles
and heads bent forward under basin-helmets. Moonlight and
dawn began to mingle, and I could see the barley swaying
indolently against the sky. A train groaned along the riverside,
sending up a cloud of whitish fiery smoke against the gloom of
the trees. The Flintshire Fusiliers were a long time arriving.
On the hill behind us the kite balloon swayed slowly upward
with straining ropes, its looming bulbous body reflecting the
first pallor of daybreak. Then, as if answering our expectancy,
a remote skirling of bagpipes began, and the Gordon Highlanders hobbled in. But we had been sitting at the crossroads
nearly six hours, and faces were recognizable, when Dottrell
hailed our leading Company.

Soon they had dispersed and settled down on the hillside,
and were asleep in the daylight which made everything seem
ordinary. None the less I had seen something that night which
overawed me. It was all in the day's work – an exhausted Division returning from the Somme Offensive – but for me it was
as though I had watched an army of ghosts. It was as though I
had seen the War as it might be envisioned by the mind of
some epic poet a hundred years hence.

PART FIVE

ESCAPE

1

On Saturday afternoon we made a short train journey and then marched four easy miles to a village called La Chaussée. Twenty-four hours' rest and a shave had worked the usual miracle with the troops (psychological recovery was a problem which no one had time to recognize as existent) and now we were away from the Line for at least a fortnight. It was a dusty golden evening, and the road led us through quiet green country. Delusively harmonious, perhaps, is that retrospective picture of the Battalion marching at case along an unfrequented road, at the end of a July afternoon, with Colonel Kinjack riding rather absent-mindedly in front, or pulling up to watch us go past him – his face thoughtful and indulgent and expressing something of the pride and satisfaction which he felt.

So it will go on, I thought; in and out, in and out, till something happens to me. We had come along the same road last January. Only five officers of that lot were with us now: not many of them had been killed, but they had 'faded away' somehow or other, and my awareness of this created a deceptive sense of 'the good old days'. Yesterday afternoon I'd heard that Cromlech had been killed up at High Wood. This piece of news had stupefied me, but the pain hadn't begun to make itself felt yet, and there was no spare time for personal grief when the Battalion was getting ready to move back to Divisional Rest. To have thought about Cromlech would have been calamitous. 'Rotten business about poor old "Longneck",' was the only comment that Durley, Dottrell and the others allowed themselves. And after all he wasn't the only one who'd gone west lately. It was queer how the men seemed to take

their victimization for granted. In and out; in and out; singing
and whistling, the column swayed in front of me, much the
same length as usual, for we'd had less than a hundred casualties up at Bazentin. But it was a case of every man for himself,
and the corporate effect was optimistic and untroubled. A
London editor driving along the road in a Staff car would have
remarked that the spirit of the troops was amazing. And so it
was. But somehow the newspaper men always kept the horrifying realities of the War out of their articles, for it was unpa-
triotic to be bitter, and the dead were assumed to be gloriously
happy. However, it was no use worrying about all that; I was
part of the Battalion, and now I'd got to see about getting the
men settled into billets.

Some Australians had been in the billets at La Chaussée and
(if they will pardon me for saying so) had left them in a very
bad state. Sanitation had been neglected, and the inhabitants
were complaining furiously that their furniture had been used
for firewood. Did the Australians leave anything else behind
them, I wonder? For some of them had been in Gallipoli, and
it is possible that dysentery germs were part of the legacy they
left us.

The fact remains that I awoke on Monday morning feeling
far from well and, after a mechanical effort to go on parade in
a glare of sunlight, took refuge in the cavernous bedroom
which I occupied alone. Feeling worse and worse, in the evening I remembered that I possessed a thermometer, which had
been handed over to me when I was Transport Officer. I had
never taken the temperatures of any of the horses, but I now
experimented shakily on myself. When I saw that it indicated
105° I decided that the thing was out of order; but next morning I was confusedly aware that Flook had fetched the doctor,
and by the afternoon I was unbelievably at the New Zealand
Hospital, which was in a substantial old building in the middle of Amiens.

The advantages of being ill were only too obvious. Lying
awake in the large lofty ward on my fourth night, I was aware
that I was feeling rather run down, but much better – almost

too well, in fact. That evening my temperature had been normal, which reminded me that this change from active service
to invalidism was an acute psychological experience. The door
to safety was half open, and though an impartial New Zealand doctor decided one's destiny, there was a not unnatural
impulse to fight for one's own life instead of against the Germans. Less than two weeks ago I'd been sitting in a tent thinking noble thoughts about sharing the adversities of my fellow
Fusiliers. But that emotional defence wouldn't work now, and
the unutterable words 'wangle my way home' forced their way
obstinately to the foreground, supported by a crowd of smug-
faced excuses.

Durley and the Adjutant had visited me that afternoon; they'd
joked with me about how well I was looking. While they were
with me I had talked about coming back in a few days, and I'd
genuinely felt as if I wanted to. But they took my fortitude
away with them, and now I was foreseeing that another night's
rest would make me look indecently healthy for a man in a
hospital. 'I suppose they'll all think I'm swinging the lead,' I
thought. Turning the last few months over in my mind, I
argued with myself that I had done all that was expected of
me. 'Oh God,' I prayed, 'do get me sent down to the Base!' (How
often was that petition whispered during the War?) To-day I
had seen young Allgood's name in the Roll of Honour – a bit
of news which had slammed the door on my four weeks at the
Army School and provided me with a secondary sorrow, for I
was already feeling sufficiently miserable about my friend
Cromlech. I sympathized with myself about Allgood, for I had
been fond of him. But he was only one among thousands of
promising young men who had gone west since the 1st of July.
Sooner or later I should probably get killed too. A breath of
wind stirred the curtains, blowing them inward from the tall
windows with a rustling sigh. The wind came from the direction of the Somme, and I could hear the remote thudding of
the guns. Everyone in the ward seemed to be asleep except the
boy whose bed had screens round it. The screens were red and
a light glowed through them. Ever since he was brought in he'd
been continually calling to the nurse on duty. Throughout the

day this had gradually got on everyone's nerves, for the ward
was already full of uncontrollable gasps and groans. Once I
had caught a glimpse of his white face and miserable eyes.
Whatever sort of wound he'd got he was making the most of it,
had been the opinion of the man next to me (who had himself
got more than he wanted, in both legs). But he must be jolly
bad, I thought now, as the Sister came from behind the screen
again. His voice went on, in the low, rapid, even tone of delirium. Sometimes I could catch what he said, troubled and
unhappy and complaining. Someone called Dicky was on his
mind, and he kept on crying out to Dicky. 'Don't go out,
Dicky; they snipe like hell!' And then, 'Curse the Wood. . . .
Dicky, you fool, don't go out!' . . . All the horror of the Somme
attacks was in that raving; all the darkness and the dreadful
daylight. . . . I watched the Sister come back with a white-
coated doctor; the screen glowed comfortingly; soon the dis-
quieting voice became inaudible and I fell asleep. Next morning
the screens had vanished; the bed was empty, and ready for
someone else.

Not that day, but the next one, my supplication to the Almighty
was put to the test. The doctor came along the ward on his
cheerful morning inspection. Arriving at my bed he asked how
I was feeling. I stared up at him, incapable of asserting that I
felt ill and unwilling to admit that I felt well. Fortunately he
didn't expect a reply. 'Well, we'll have to be moving you on,'
he said with a smile; and before my heart had time to beat
again he turned to the nurse with, 'Put him down for the afternoon train.' The nurse made a note of it, and my mind uttered
a spontaneous Magnificat. Now, with any luck, I thought, I'll
get a couple of weeks at one of those hospitals on the coast, at
Étretat or Le Tréport, probably. The idea of reading a book by
the seaside was blissful. No one could blame me for that, and
I should be back with the Battalion by the end of August, if
not earlier.

   In my hurried exodus from my billet at La Chaussée, some
of my belongings had been left behind, and good old Flook
had brought them to the hospital next day. He had come

treading in with clumsy embarrassment to deposit the packful of oddments by my bed, announcing in a hoarse undertone, 'Ah've brought the stoof,' and telling me that the lads in C Company were hoping to see me back soon. Somehow Flook, with his rough and ready devotion, had seemed my strongest link with the Battalion. When I shook his hand and said good-bye, he winked and advised me, confidentially, not to be in too much of a hurry about getting back. A good rest would do me no harm, he said; but as he tiptoed away I wondered when he himself would get a holiday, and whether he would ever return to his signal-box on the railway.

The details of my journey to the Base were as follows. First of all I was carried carefully down the stairs on a stretcher (though I could easily have walked to the ambulance, or even to the railway station, if such an effort had been demanded of me). Then the ambulance took me to Corbie, and from there the train (with 450 casualties on board) rumbled sedately to Rouen; we did the sixty miles in ten hours, and at two o'clock in the morning I was carried into No. 2 Red Cross Hospital. I remember that particular hospital with affection. During the morning a genial doctor came along and had a look at me. 'Well, me lad, what's wrong with you?' he asked. 'They call it enteritis,' I replied, with an indefinite grin. He had a newspaper in his hand as he glanced at the descriptive chart behind my bed. My name caused him to consult *The Times*. 'Is this you?' he asked. Sure enough, my name was there, in a list of Military Crosses which chanced to have appeared that day. The doctor patted me on the shoulder and informed me that I should be going across to England next day. Good luck had 'wangled me home'. Even now I cannot think of that moment without believing that I was involved in one of the lesser miracles of the Great War. For I am certain that I should have remained at Rouen if that observant and kind-hearted doctor hadn't noticed my name among the decorations. And in that case I should have been back with the Battalion in nice time for their operations at Delville Wood, which might quite conceivably have qualified my name for a place on the Butley village War Memorial.

Paradise

The Hospital Ship left Rouen about midday. While we steamed
down the Seine in fine weather I lay watching the landscape
through a porthole with a sense of thankfulness which differed from any I had ever known before. A label was attached
to me; I have kept that label, and it is in my left hand as I write
these words. It is marked *Army Form W* 3083, though in
shape and substance it is an ordinary civilian luggage label. It
is stamped *Lying Train and Ship* in blue letters, with *Sick
P.U.O.* on the other side. On the boat, my idle brain wondered
what *P.U.O.* meant. There must, I thought, be a disease beginning with P. Perhaps it was 'Polypipsis unknown origin'. Between
Rouen and Havre I devised several feebly funny solutions, such
as 'Perfectly undamaged officer'. But my final choice was 'Poorly
until October'.

At noon next day we reached Southampton. Nothing could
be better than this, I thought, while being carried undeservedly from the ship to the train; and I could find no fault with
Hampshire's quiet cornfields and unwarlike woods in the
drowsy August afternoon. At first I guessed that we were on
our way to London; but when the journey showed signs of
cross-countrihood I preferred not to be told where we were
going. Recumbent, I gazed gloatingly at England. Peaceable
stay-at-homes waved to the Red Cross Train, standing still to
watch it pass. It was nice to think that I'd been fighting for
them, though exactly what I'd done to help them was difficult
to define. An elderly man, cycling along a dusty road in a dark
blue suit and a straw hat, removed one hand from the handle-
bars to wave comprehensive gratitude. Everything seemed
happy and homely. I was delivered from the idea of death, and
that other thing which had haunted me, the dread of being
blinded. I closed contented eyes, became sleepy, and awoke to
find myself at Oxford. By five o'clock I was in a small white
room on the ground floor of Somerville College. Listening to
the tranquil tolling of Oxford bells and someone strumming
melodiously on a piano across the lawn, with a glimpse of tall
chestnut trees swaying against the blue sky, I whispered the
word Paradise. Had I earned it? I was too grateful to care.

2

In Oxford lived Mr Farrell, an old friend of Aunt Evelyn's. Some years before the War he had lived near Butley, and he now came to pay me an afternoon visit at the Hospital, where I was reclining under a tree on the lawn, still keeping up appearances as an invalid officer. He sat beside me and we conversed rather laboriously about Aunt Evelyn and her neighbourhood. He was Irish and a voluble talker, but he seemed to have lost much of his former vivacity. I noticed that he was careful to keep the conversation safely on this side of the Channel, probably out of consideration for my feelings, although I wouldn't have minded telling him a thing or two about the Somme. Mr Farrell was a retired Civil Servant and an authority on Military Records. He had written the lives of several famous Generals and an official History of the Indian Mutiny. But he showed no curiosity about the military operations of the moment. He was over seventy, and his face was unlit and fatigued as he talked about food restrictions in England. 'Sugar is getting scarce,' he remarked, 'but that doesn't affect me; my doctor knocked me off sugar several years ago.' I looked at his noticeably brown teeth, and then averted my eyes as if he could read my thoughts, for I was remembering how Aunt Evelyn used to scold me for calling him 'sugar-teeth'; his untidy teeth did look like lumps of sugar soaked in tea. . . .

Dear old Mr Farrell, with his red tie and the cameo ring round it, and his silver hair and ragged tobacco-stained moustache! As his large form lumbered away across the lawn, I thought that his clothes had got too big for him, though he'd always worn them rather baggy. Could it be possible that scrupulous people at home were getting thin while the soldiers got fat on their good rations at the Front? I began to suspect that England wasn't quite what it used to be. But my mind soon wandered indolently into the past which the veteran military historian had brought with him into the college garden. I remembered summer evenings when I was a little boy overhearing, from in bed upstairs, the mumble of voices down in the drawing-room, where Aunt Evelyn was having an after-dinner chat with Mr Farrell and Captain Huxtable, who had walked across the fields from Butley in the twilight. Sometimes I tiptoed down the stairs and listened at the door (rather hoping to hear them saying something complimentary about myself) but they were nearly always gassing about politics, or India. Mr Farrell had been in India for ages, and Captain Huxtable had been out there too; and Aunt Evelyn loved to hear about it. When we went to see Mr Farrell he used to show us delightful old books with coloured plates of Indian scenes. What queer old codgers they were, sipping tea and puffing their cigars (which smelt quite nice) and talking all that rot about Lord Salisbury and his Government. 'Her-her-her,' laughed Mr Farrell whenever he finished another of his funny stories which always ended with what someone had said to someone else or how he'd scored off someone at his club. They'd go on talking just the same, whatever happened; even if a Death's Head Hawk Moth flew into the room they wouldn't be a bit excited about it. It would be rather fun, I thought, if I were to fire my percussion-cap pistol outside the drawing-room door, just to give them a surprise. As I crept upstairs again in my nightgown, I wondered if I should ever be like that myself. . . . Mr Farrell was fond of playing tennis; he used to serve underhand, holding the ball a few inches above the ground as he struck it. . . .

Emerging from my retrospective reverie, I felt that this war had made the past seem very peculiar. People weren't the same as they used to be, or else I had changed. Was it because I had experienced something that they couldn't share or imagine? Mr Farrell had seemed diffident that afternoon, almost as if he were talking to a survivor from an incomprehensible disaster. Looking round me I began to feel that I wanted to be in some place where I needn't be reminded of the War all the time. For instance, there was that tall well-preserved man pushing his son very slowly across the lawn in a long wheeled bed. The son was sallow and sulky, as he well might be, having lost one of his legs. The father was all solicitude, but somehow I inferred that the pair of them hadn't hit it off too well before the War.

More than once I had seen the son look at his father as though
he disliked him. But the father was proud of his disabled son,
and I heard him telling one of the nurses how splendidly the
boy had done in the Gommecourt attack, showing her a letter,
too, probably from the boy's colonel. I wondered whether he
had ever allowed himself to find out that the Gommecourt
show had been nothing but a massacre of good troops. Probably he kept a war map with little flags on it; when Mametz
Wood was reported as captured he moved a little flag an inch
forward after breakfast. For him the Wood was a small green
patch on a piece of paper. For the Welsh Division it had been a
bloody nightmare. . . . 'Is the sun too strong for you here,
Arthur?' Arthur shakes his head and frowns up at the sky.
Then the father, with his neatly-trimmed beard and elegant
buff linen waistcoat, begins to read him Haig's latest despatch.
'There is strong evidence that the enemy forces engaged on the
battle-front have been severely shaken by the repeated successes gained by ourselves and our Allies. . . . ' The level culti-
vated voice palavers on until the nurse approaches brightly
with a spouted feeding-cup. 'Time for some more beef-tea!'
Nourishment is administered under approving parental eyes.

3

During my last week I was allowed out of the hospital in the
afternoons, and I used to go up the Cherwell in a canoe. I
found this recreation rather heavy work, for the water was a
jungle of weeds and on the higher reaches progress had become
almost impossible. Certainly the Great War had made a difference to the charming River Cherwell. But I had been feeling
much more cheerful lately, for my friend Cromlech had risen
again from the dead. I had seen his name in the newspaper list
of killed, but soon afterwards someone telegraphed to tell me
that he was in a London hospital and going on well. For fully
a fortnight I had accustomed myself to the idea that his dead
body was somewhere among the Somme shell-holes and it was

a queer experience, to be disentangling myself from the mental obituary notices which I had evolved out of my luminous memories of our companionship in the First Battalion. 'Silly old devil,' I thought affectionately; 'he always manages to do things differently from other people.'

By the end of August I was back at Butley with a month's sick leave and the possibility of an extension. So for the first week or two I forgot the future and enjoyed being made a fuss of by Aunt Evelyn. My outlook on the War was limited to the Battalion I had served with. After being kept out of the Line for nearly five weeks, they were expecting to be moved up at any moment. This news came in a letter from Durley. Suppressing such disquietude as it caused me, I put the letter in my pocket and went out to potter round the garden. It was a fine early September morning – almost my favourite sort of weather, I thought. The garden was getting wild and overgrown, for there was only one old man working in it now. The day before I had begun an attempt to recivilize the tangled tennis-lawn, but it had been too much like canoeing on the Cherwell, and to-day I decided to cut dead wood out of the cedar. While I climbed about in the tree with a bill-hook in my hand I could hear old Huckett trundling the water-tank along the kitchen garden. Then Aunt Evelyn came along with her flower-basket full of dahlias; while she was gazing up at me another brittle bough cracked and fell scaring one of the cats who followed her about. She begged me to be careful, adding that it would be no joke to tumble out of such a big tree.

Later in the morning I visited the stables. Stagnation had settled there; nettles were thick under the apple-trees and the old mowing-machine pony grazed in shaggy solitude. In Dixon's little harness room, saddles were getting mouldy and there were rust-spots on the bits and stirrup-irons which he had kept so bright. A tin of *Harvey's Hoof Ointment* had obviously been there since 1914. It would take Dixon a long time to get the place straightened up, I thought, forgetting for a moment that he'd been dead six months. . . . It wasn't much fun, mooning about the stables. But a robin trilled his little autumn song from an apple-tree; beyond the fruit-laden

branches I could see the sunlit untroubled Weald, and I looked
lovingly at the cowls of hop-kilns which twinkled across those
miles that were the country of my childhood. I could smell
autumn in the air, too, and I thought I must try to get a few
days' cubbing before I go back to the Depot. Down in Sussex
there were a few people who would willingly lend me a horse,
and I decided to write to old Colonel Hesmon about it. I went
up to the schoolroom to do this; rummaging in a drawer for
some note-paper, I discovered a little pocket mirror – a relic of
my days in the ranks of the Yeomanry. Handling it absent-
mindedly, I found myself using it to decipher the blotting
paper, which had evidently been on the table some time, for
the handwriting was Stephen Colwood's. '*P.S. The Old
Guvnor is squaring up my annual indebtedness. Isn't he a
brick?*' Stephen must have scribbled that when he was staying
with us in the summer of 1914. Probably he had been writing
to his soldier brother in Ireland. I imagined him adding the
postscript and blotting it quickly. Queer how the past crops
up, I thought, sadly, for my experience of such poignant associations was 'still in its infancy', as someone had said of Poison
Gas when lecturing to cannon-fodder at the Army School.

Remembering myself at that particular moment, I realize
the difficulty of recapturing war-time atmosphere as it was in
England then. A war historian would inform us that 'the earlier excitement and suspense had now abated, and the nation
had settled down to its organization of man-power and munition making'. I want to recover something more intimate than
that, but I can't swear to anything unusual at Butley except a
derelict cricket field, the absence of most of the younger inhabitants, and a certain amount of talk about food prospects for
the winter. Two of our nearest neighbours had lost their only
sons, and with them their main interest in life; but such trage-
dies as those remained intimate and unobtrusive. Ladies
worked at the Local Hospital and elderly gentlemen superin-
tended Recruiting Centres and Tribunals; but there was little
outward change and no military training-camp within a radius
of ten miles. So I think I am accurate when I say that Aunt
Evelyn was jogging along much as usual (now that her mind

was temporarily at rest about my own active service career).
She was, of course, a bit intolerant about the Germans, having
swallowed all the stories about atrocities in Belgium. It was
her duty, as a patriotic Englishwoman, to agree with a certain
prelate when he preached the axiom that 'every man who
killed a German was performing a Christian act'. Nevertheless, if Aunt Evelyn had found a wounded Prussian when she
was on her way to the post office, she would undoubtedly have
behaved with her natural humanity (combined with enthusiasm for administering first aid). In the meantime we avoided
controversial topics (such as that all Germans were fiends in
human form) and while I was writing my letter to Colonel
Hesmon she entered the schoolroom with her arms full of lavender which she strewed along the floor under the window.
The sun would dry it nicely there, she said, adding that I must
find her a very dull old party nowadays, since she had no conversation and seemed to spend all her time trying to catch a
new housemaid. I assured her that it was a great relief after
being incessantly ordered about in the Army, to be with someone who had no conversation.

But after dinner that evening I did find myself a bit dull, so I
walked across the fields for a chat with Protheroe, a middle-
aged bachelor who lived in a modest old house with his quiet
sister. Before I started my aunt implored me to be careful
about extinguishing the oil lamp in the drawing-room when I
got back. Oil lamps were far from safe – downright dangerous, in fact!

The night was very still; as I went along the field path I was
almost sure I could hear the guns. Not that I wanted to; but
the newspapers reported that a new offensive had been started
at Guillemont, and I couldn't help feeling that our Division
was in it. (I still thought of it as 'our Division'.) Our village
was quiet enough, anyhow, and so was Protheroe's white-
faced house, with its creaking gate and red-blinded windows. I
rapped with the knocker and Miss Protheroe came to the door,
quite surprised to see me, though I'd seen her a few hours
before when she called to return last month's *Blackwood's
Magazine*. Protheroe was in the middle of a game of chess

with the village doctor, a reticent little man whose smallest
actions were always extremely deliberate. The doctor would
make up his mind to move one of his men, grasp it resolutely,
become hesitative, release it, and then begin his cogitative
chin-rubbing and eye-puckering all over again, while Protheroe drummed his fingers on the table and stared at a moth
which was bumping softly against the ceiling of the snug little parlour, and his sister, with gentle careworn face, knitted
something woollen for the brother who, though past forty, was
serving as a corporal in the infantry in France. My arrival put
a stop to the doctor's perplexities; and since I was welcomed
rather as a returned hero, I was inclined to be hearty. I slapped
Protheroe on the back, told him he'd got the best dug-out in
Butley, and allowed myself to be encouraged to discuss the
War. I admitted that it was pretty bad out there, with an inward feeling that such horrors as I had been obliged to witness
were now something to be proud of. I even went so far as to
assert that I wouldn't have missed this War for anything. It
brought things home to one somehow, I remarked, frowning
portentously as I lit my pipe, and forgetting for the moment
what a mercy it had been when it brought me home myself. Oh
yes, I knew all about the Battle of the Somme, and could assure
them that we should be in Bapaume by October. Replying to
their tributary questions, I felt that they envied me my experience.

   While I was on my way home, I felt elated at having outgrown the parish boundaries of Butley. After all, it was a big
thing, to have been in the thick of a European War, and my
peace-time existence had been idle and purposeless. It was bad
luck on Protheroe and the doctor; they must hate being left out
of it. . . . I suppose one must give this damned War its due, I
thought, as I sat in the schoolroom with one candle burning.
I felt comfortable, for Miss Protheroe had made me a cup of
cocoa. I took Durley's letter out of my pocket and had another
look at it; but it wasn't easy to speculate on its implications.
The War's all right as long as one doesn't get killed or smashed
up, I decided, blowing out the candle so that I could watch the
moonlight which latticed the floor with shadows of the leaded

windows. Where the moonbeams lay thickest they touched the litter of drying lavender. I opened the window and sniffed the autumn-smelling air. An owl hooted in the garden, and I could hear a train going along the Weald. Probably a hospital-train from Dover, I thought, as I closed the window and creaked upstairs on tiptoe so as not to disturb Aunt Evelyn.

About a week afterwards I received two letters from Dottrell, written on consecutive days, but delivered by the same post. The first one began: 'The old Batt. is having a rough time. We were up in the front a week ago, and lost 200 men in three days. The aid-post, a bit of a dug-out hastily made, was blown in. At the time it contained 5 wounded men, 5 stretcher-bearers, and the doctor. All were killed except the Doc. who was buried in the débris. He was so badly shaken when dug out that he had to be sent down, and will probably be in England by now. It is a hell of a place up there. The Batt. is attacking to-day. I hope they have better luck. The outlook is not rosy. Very glad to hear you are sitting up and taking nourishment. A lot of our best men have been knocked out recently. We shall soon want another Battn. All the boys send their love and best wishes in which your humble heartily joins.'

The second letter, which I chanced to open and read first, was the worst of the two.

'Dear Kangaroo. . . . Just a line to let you know what rotten bad luck we had yesterday. We attacked Ginchy with a very weak Battn. (about 300) and captured the place but were forced out of half of it – due to the usual thing. Poor Edmunds was killed leading his Coy. Also Perrin. Durley was badly wounded, in neck and chest, I think. It is terrible to think of these two splendid chaps being cut off, but I hope Durley pulls through. Asbestos Bill died of wounds. Fernby, who was O.C. Bombers, very badly hit and not expected to live. Several others you don't know also killed. Only two officers got back without being hit. C.S.M. Miles and Danby both killed. The Battn. is *not now* over strength for rations! The rest of the Brigade suffered in proportion. Will write later. Very busy.' . . .

I walked about the room, whistling and putting the pictures

see
p. 186

straight. Then the gong rang for luncheon. Aunt Evelyn drew
my attention to the figs, which were the best we'd had off the
old tree that autumn.

4

October brought an extension of my sick leave and some
mornings with the hounds. By the time I received another letter from Dottrell, Delville Wood had more or less buried its
dead, in my mind if not altogether in reality. The old Quartermaster let off steam in a good grumble from which I quote a
specimen.

'Well, we have been out at rest about 10 kilos from the place
we were at last Xmas. We expected to be there three weeks but
after 8 days have had sudden orders to move to the old spot
with a *Why*. Kinjack left us to take command of a Brigade; a
great loss to the Battn. They all come and go; stay in the Batt.
long enough to get something out of it, and then disappear and
will hardly give a thought to the men and officers who were
the means of getting them higher rank. It's a selfish world, my
friend. All successive C.O.'s beg me to stay with the old Battalion they love so well. I do. So do they, till they get a better job.
They neither know nor care what happens to me (who at their
special request have stuck to "the dear old Corps") when I
leave the Service on a pension of 30s. a week.'

I am afraid I wasn't worrying overmuch about 'the dear old
Corps' myself, while out with the Ringwell Hounds on Colonel Hesmon's horses. In spite of the War, hunting was being
carried on comfortably, though few people came out. 'The
game was being kept alive for the sake of the boys at the Front',
who certainly enjoyed the idea (if they happened to be keen
fox-hunters and were still alive to appreciate the effort made
on their behalf). As for me, I was armed with my uniform and
the protective colouring of my Military Cross, and no one

could do enough for me. I stayed as long as I liked with Moffat, the genial man who now combined the offices of Master and Secretary, and for a few weeks the pre-war past appeared to have been conjured up for my special benefit. It was difficult to believe that the misty autumn mornings, which made me free of those well-known woods and farms and downs, were simultaneously shedding an irrelevant brightness on the Ypres Salient and on Joe Dottrell riding wearily back with the ration-party somewhere near Plug Street Wood. I don't think I could see it quite like that at the time. What I am writing now is the result of a bird's-eye view of the past, and the cub-hunting subaltern I see there is part of the 'selfish world' to which his attention had been drawn. He is listening to Colonel Hesmon while the hounds are being blown out of a big wood – hearing how well young Winchell has done with his Brigade (without wondering how many of them have been 'blown out' of their trenches) and being assured by the loquacious old Colonel that the German Count who used to live at Puxford Park was undoubtedly a spy and only hunted with the Ringwell for that reason; the Colonel now regretted that he didn't ride over to Puxford Park and break all the windows before war was declared. He also declared that any man under forty who wasn't wearing the King's uniform was nothing but a damned shirker. I remarked to Moffat afterwards that the Colonel seemed to be overdoing it a bit about the War. Moffat told me that the old boy was known to have practised revolver shooting in his garden, addressing insults to individual tree trunks and thus ventilating his opinion of Germany as a whole. He had been much the same about vulpicides and socialists in peace time. 'It's very odd; for Hesmon's an extraordinary kind-hearted man,' said Moffat, who himself regarded the War as an unmitigated nuisance, but didn't waste his energy abusing it or anybody else. He had enough to do already, for he found it far from easy to keep the Hunt on its legs, and what the hounds would get to eat next year he really didn't know. He added that 'the Missus's dachshunds only just escaped being interned as enemy aliens'.

VIP

———

Sport in Sussex was only a makeshift exhilaration, and early
in November I went to London for a final Medical Board. At
the Caxton Hall in Westminster I spent a few minutes gazing
funereally round an empty waiting-room. Above the fireplace
(there was no fire) hung a neatly-framed notice for the benefit
of all whom it might concern. It stated the scale of prices for
artificial limbs, with instructions as to how officers could
obtain them free of cost. The room contained no other ornament. While I was adjusting my mind to what a journalist
might have called 'the grim humour' of this footnote to Army
life, a Girl Guide stepped in to say that Colonel Crossbones (or
whatever his cognomen was) would see me now. A few formal-
ities 'put paid to' my period of freedom, and I pretended to be
feeling pleased as I walked away from Westminster, though
wondering whether the politicians had any expectations that
hostilities would be concluded by Christmas, and eyeing the
Admiralty with a notion that it must be rather nice to be in the
Navy.

Good-byes began all over again. A last day with the Ringwell
ended at the crossroads by the old Harcombe point to point
course. I went one way and the hounds went another. Jogging
down the lane, they disappeared in the drizzling dusk. Moffat's 'Best of luck, old boy!' left me to ride on, alone with the
creak of the saddle. I was due back at the Depot next day, but
we'd had a good woodland hunt with one quite nice bit in the
open, and I'd jumped a lot of timber and thoroughly enjoyed
my day. Staring at the dim brown landscape I decided that the
War was worth while if it was being carried on to safeguard
this sort of thing. Was it? I wondered; and if a doubt arose it
was dismissed before it had been formulated. Riding into
Downfield where I was leaving the horse which had been lent
me, I remembered how I'd slept on the floor of the Town Hall
on the day war was declared. Two years and three months ago
I had enlisted for 'three years or the duration'. It was beginning
to look as if I had enlisted for a lifetime (though the word was
one which had seen better days). Under the looming shadow of

the hills the lights of the town twinkled cosily. But a distant
bugle-call from some camp seemed to be summoning the last
reluctant farm labourer. 'You'll all have to go in the end,' it
seemed to say, and the comfortless call was being sounded far
across Europe. . . .

On my way home in the train I read about Roumania in the
paper. Everyone, Aunt Evelyn included, had been delighted
when Roumania came in on our side in August. But the results
had not been reassuring. I couldn't help feeling annoyed with
the Roumanian Army for allowing their country to be overrun
by the Germans. They really might have put up a better show
than that!

PART SIX

AT THE DEPOT

Clitherland Camp.

Clitherland camp had acquired a look of coercive stability; but this was only natural, since for more than eighteen months it had been manufacturing Flintshire Fusiliers, many of whom it was now sending back to the Front for the second and third time. The Camp was as much an essential co-operator in the national effort as Brotherhood & Co.'s explosive factory, which flared and seethed and reeked with poisonous vapours a few hundred yards away. The third winter of the War had settled down on the lines of huts with calamitous drabness; fog-bleared sunsets were succeeded by cavernous and dispiriting nights when there was nothing to do and nowhere to do it.

Crouching as close as I could to the smoky stove in my hut I heard the wind moaning around the roof, feet clumping cheerlessly along the boards of the passage, and all the systematized noises and clatterings and bugle-blowings of the Camp. Factory-hooters and ship's fog-horns out on the Mersey sometimes combined in huge unhappy dissonances; their sound seemed one with the smoke-drifted munition works, the rubble of industrial suburbs, and the canal that crawled squalidly out into blighted and forbidding farmlands which were only waiting to be built over.

Except for the permanent staff, there weren't many officers I had known before this winter. But I shared my hut with David Cromlech, who was well enough to be able to play an energetic game of football, in spite of having had a bit of shell through his right lung. Bill Eaves, the Cambridge scholar, had also returned and was quietly making the most of his few remaining months. (He was killed in February while leading a little local attack.) And there was young Ormand, too, pulling wry faces about his next Medical Board, which would be sure to pass him for General Service. I could talk to these three about 'old times with the First Battalion', and those times had already acquired a delusive unobnoxiousness, compared with what was in store for us; for the 'Big Push' of last summer and autumn had now found a successor in 'the Spring Offensive' (which was, of course, going to 'get the Boches on the run').

Mess, at eight o'clock, was a function which could be used for filling up an hour and a half. While Ormand was making his periodic remark – that his only reason for wanting to go out again was that it would enable him to pay off his overdraft at Cox's Bank – my eyes would wander up to the top table where the Colonel sat among those good-natured easy-going Majors who might well have adopted as their motto the ditty sung by the troops: 'We're here because we're here because we're here because we're here.' At nine-thirty the Colonel went to the ante-room for his game of Bridge. But the second-in-command, Major Macartney, would sit on long afterwards, listening to one or two of his cronies and slowly imbibing port with a hand that trembled nervously. Probably his mind was often back in Ireland, snipe shooting and salmon fishing. There was nothing grim about the Major, though his features had a certain severity, slightly reminiscent of the late Lord Kitchener. He was a reserved and dignified man, much more so than the other Majors. These convivial characters were ostensibly directing the interior economy of the Camp, and as the troops were well fed and looked after they must be given credit for it. The training of recruits was left to sergeant-instructors, most of whom were Regular N.C.O.'s of the best pattern, hard-worked men who were on their legs from morning to night, and strict because they had to be strict. The raw material to be trained was growing steadily worse. Most of those who came in now had joined the Army unwillingly, and there was no reason why they should find military service tolerable. The War had become undisguisedly mechanical and inhuman. What in earlier days had been drafts of volunteers

were now droves of victims. I was just beginning to be aware
of this.

But Clitherland had accessible compensations. One of them
was the Golf Course at Formby. The electric train took only
twenty minutes to get there, and Formby was famous for its
bracing air, comfortable Club House, and superlatively good
war-time food. I went there at least one afternoon a week;
usually I played alone, and often I had the links to myself,
which was no disadvantage, since I have always been considerably addicted to my own company.

Hounds

My main purpose, however, was a day with the hounds. For
this I was readily given leave off Saturday morning duties,
since an officer who wanted to go out hunting was rightly
regarded as an upholder of pre-war regimental traditions. The
Saturday Meets of the Cheshire Hounds were a long way off,
but nothing short of impossibility deterred me, and the working out of my plans was an effective antidote to war-weariness.
It was, in fact, very like achieving the impossible, when I sat in
my hut of an evening, cogitating with luxurious deliberation,
consulting a map and calculating how my hireling could meet
me at such and such a station, measuring the distance from
there to the meet, and so on in the manner known to enthusiastic young sportsmen. On such Saturdays I would get up in
the dark with joyful alacrity. Leaving Liverpool by an early
train, I would eagerly observe the disconsolate beginnings of a
dull December day, encouraging as far as I could the illusion
that I was escaping from everything associated with the uniform which I wore; and eyeing my brown Craxwell field-boots
affectionately.

Under such conditions no day could be a bad one, and
although more than one Saturday's hunting was stopped by
frost, I derived singular consolation from the few hunts I had.
My consolations included a heavy fall over some high timber
which I ought to have had more sense than to tackle, since my
hireling was a moderate though willing performer. Anyhow,
the contrast between Clitherland Camp and the Cheshire

Saturday country was like the difference between War and Peace – especially when – at the end of a good day – I jogged a few miles homeward with the hounds, conversing with the cheery huntsman in my best pre-war style.

Apart from these compensations I had the companionship of David who was now quite the 'old soldier' and as argumentative as ever. In fact, while I pored over my one-inch-to-the-mile map of Cheshire after dinner, he was usually sitting on in the Mess and taking an active part in the wordy warfare of other 'old soldiers', among whom he was now listened to as one having authority. It was something to have been in the Battle of the Somme; but to have been at the Battle of Loos as well made him feel quite a big gun. In our hut, however, we sought fresher subjects than bygone battles and obliterated trenches. I enjoyed talking about English literature, and listened to him as to an oracle which I could, now and then, venture to contradict. Although he was nine years younger than I was, I often found myself reversing our ages, since he knew so much more than I did about almost everything except foxhunting. He made short work of most books which I had hitherto venerated, for David was a person who consumed his enthusiasms quickly, and he once fairly took my breath away by pooh-poohing *Paradise Lost* as 'that moribund academic concoction'. I hadn't realized that it was possible to speak disrespectfully about Milton. Anyhow, John Milton was consigned to perdition, and John Skelton was put forward as 'one of the few really good poets'. But somehow I could never quite accept his supremacy over Milton as an established fact. At that period Samuel Butler was the source of much of David's ingenuity at knocking highly-respected names and notions off their perches.

Anyhow, I was always ready to lose another literary illusion, for many of my friend's quiddities were as nicely rounded, and as evanescent, as the double smoke rings he was so adroit at blowing. He was full of such entertaining little tricks, and I never tired of hearing him imitate the talk of excitable Welshmen. He was fond of music, too; but it was a failure when we went to an orchestral concert in Liverpool. David said that it 'upset him psychologically'. It was no good as music either. No music was really any good except the Northern Folk-Ballad tunes which he was fond of singing at odd moments. 'The Bonny Earl of Murray' was one of his favourites, and he sang it in agreeably melancholy style. But much though I admired these plaintive ditties I could not believe that they abolished Beethoven's Fifth Symphony, which we'd heard at the concert. I realize now that what I ought to have said was 'Oh rats, David!' Instead of which I clumsily tried to explain the merits of various composers other than the inventors of *The Minstrelsy of the Border*, which was exactly what he wanted me to do. Sometimes he made me quite angry. I remember one morning when he was shaving with one hand and reading *Robinson Crusoe* in the other. Crusoe was a real man, he remarked; fox-hunting was the sport of snobs and half-wits. Since it was too early in the day for having one's leg pulled, I answered huffily that I supposed Crusoe was all right, but a lot of people who hunted were jolly good sorts, and even great men in their own way. I tried to think of someone to support my argument, and after a moment exclaimed: 'Anthony Trollope, for instance! He used to hunt a lot, and you can't say he was a half-wit.' 'No, but he was probably a snob!' I nearly lost my temper while refuting the slur on Trollope's character, and David made things worse by saying that I had no idea how funny I was when I reverted to my peace-time self. 'I had an overdose of the hunting dope when I was with the Second Battalion in '15,' he added. 'If I'd been able to gas about Jorrocks and say I'd hunted with the Bedfordshire Hounds all my life, the Colonel and the Adjutant would have behaved quite decently to me.' 'You can't be certain of that,' I replied, 'and anyway, there's no such thing as "the Bedfordshire Hounds". Bedfordshire's mostly the Oakley, and that isn't a first-class country either. You might as well get the names right when you're talking through your hat about things you don't understand.' What did it matter to David whether the Oakley was bordered by the Grafton, Fitzwilliam, and Whaddon Chase – none of which I'd ever hunted with, but I knew they were good countries and I didn't pretend that I wasn't interested in them, and

I strongly objected to them being sneered at by a crank – yes, a fad-ridden crank – like David. 'You're a fad-ridden crank,' I remarked aloud. But as he always took my admonitions for what they were worth, the matter ended amicably, and a minute later I was able to remind him that he was going on parade without a tie.

I have already said that, as a rule, we avoided war-talk. Outwardly our opinions did not noticeably differ, though his sense of 'the regimental tradition' was stronger than mine, and he 'had no use for anti-war idealism'. But each of us had his own attitude toward the War. My attitude (which had not always been easy to sustain) was that I wanted to have fine feelings about it. I wanted the War to be an impressive experience – terrible, but not horrible enough to interfere with my heroic emotions. David, on the other hand, distrusted sublimation and seemed to want the War to be even uglier than it really was. His mind loathed and yet attached itself to rank smells and squalid details. Like his face (which had a twist to it, as though seen in a slightly distorting mirror) his mental war-pictures were a little uncouth and out of focus. Though in some ways more easily shocked than I was, he had, as I once informed him, 'a first-rate nose for anything nasty'. It is only fair to add that this was when he'd been discoursing about the ubiquity of certain establishments in France. His information was all second-hand; but to hear him talk – round-eyed but quite the man of experience – one might have imagined that Amiens, Abbeville, Béthune, and Armentières were mainly illuminated by 'Blue Lamps' and 'Red Lamps', and that for a good young man to go through Havre or Rouen was a sort of Puritan's Progress from this world to the next.

2

Going into Liverpool was, for most of us, the only antidote to the daily tedium of the Depot. Liverpool usually meant the Olympic Hotel. This palatial contrast to the Camp was the chief cause of the overdrafts of Ormand and other young officers. Never having crossed the Atlantic, I did not realize that the Hotel was an American importation, but I know now that the whole thing might have been brought over from New York in the mind of a first-class passenger. Once inside the Olympic, one trod on black and white squares of synthetic rubber, and the warm interior smelt of this pseudo-luxurious flooring. Everything was white and gilt and smooth; it was, so to speak, an air-tight Paradise made of imitation marble. Its loftiness made resonance languid; one of its attractions was a swimming-bath, and the whole place seemed to have the acoustics of a swimming-bath; noise was muffled and diluted to an aqueous undertone, and even the languishing intermezzos of the string band throbbed and dilated as though a degree removed from ordinary audibility. Or so it seemed to the Clitherland subaltern who lounged in an ultra-padded chair eating rich cakes with his tea, after drifting from swimming-bath to hairdresser, buying a few fiction-magazines on his way. Later on the cocktail bar would claim him; and after that he would compensate himself for Clitherland with a dinner that defied digestion.

'Fivers' melted rapidly at the Olympic, and many of them were being melted by people whose share in the national effort was difficult to diagnose. In the dining-room I began to observe that some non-combatants were doing themselves pretty well out of the War. They were people whose faces lacked nobility, as they ordered lobsters and selected colossal cigars. I remember drawing Durley's attention to some such group when he dined with me among the mirrors and mock magnificence. They had concluded their spectacular feed with an ice-cream concoction, and now they were indulging in an afterthought – stout and oysters. I said that I supposed they must be profiteers. For a moment Durley regarded them with unspeculative eyes, but he made no comment; if he found them incredible, it wasn't surprising; both his brothers had been killed in action and his sense of humour had suffered in proportion. I remarked that we weren't doing so badly ourselves and replenished his champagne glass. Durley was on sick leave and had come to

Liverpool for a night so as to see me and one or two others at
the Depot. The War was very much on his mind, but we avoided
discussing it during dinner. Afterwards, when we were sitting
in a quiet corner, he gave me an account of the show at Delville
Wood on September 3rd. Owing to his having been wounded
in the throat, he spoke in a strained whisper. His narrative was
something like this:

'After our first time up there – digging a trench in front of Delville
Wood – we came back to Bonté Redoubt and got there
soon after daylight on the 30th. That day and the next we
were being shelled by long-range guns. About ten o'clock on
the night of the 31st, Kinjack decided to shift camp. That took
us two hours, though it was only 1,500 yards away, but it was
pitch dark and pouring with rain. I'd got into "slacks" and
was just settling down in a bell-tent when we got the order to
move up to Montauban in double quick time. Kinjack went on
ahead. You can imagine the sort of mix-up it was – the men
going as fast as they could, getting strung out and losing touch
in the dark, and the Adjutant galloping up and down cursing
everyone; I never saw him in such a state before – you know
what a quiet chap he usually is. We'd started in such a hurry
that I'd got my puttees on over my "slacks"! It must have been
nearly five miles, but we did it in just over the hour. When we
got there no one could say what all the "wind-up" was about;
we were in reserve all next day and didn't move up to the
Wood till the evening after that. We were to attack from the
right-hand corner of the Wood, with the East Surreys covering
our left and the Manchesters attacking Ginchy on our right.
Our objective was Pint Trench, taking Bitter and Beer and
clearing Ale and Vat, and also Pilsen Lane in which the Brigade
thought there were some big dug-outs. When I showed
the battle-plan to the Sergeant-Major, all he said was "We'll
have a rough house from Ale Alley". But no one had any idea
it was going to be such a schimozzle as it was! . . . Anyhow by
8.30 on the night of September 2nd I got C Company inside
the Wood, with Perrin and his Company just in front of us. A
lot of the trees were knocked to splinters and most of the

undergrowth had gone, so it wasn't difficult to get about. But while we were getting into position in shell-holes and a trench through the Wood there were shells coming from every direction and Véry lights going up all round the Wood, and more than once I had to get down and use my luminous compass before I could say which side was which. Young Fernby and the Battalion bombers were on my right, and I saw more of him than of Perrin during the night; he was quite cheerful; we'd been told it was going to be a decent show. The only trouble we struck that night was when a shell landed among some men in a shell-hole; two of the stretcher-bearers were crying and saying it was bloody murder. *What happened?*

'Next day began grey and cheerless; shells screeching overhead, the earth going up in front of the Wood, and twigs falling on my tin hat. When it got near zero, the earth was going up continuously. Boughs were coming down. You couldn't hear the shells coming – simply felt the earth quake when they arrived. There was some sort of smoke-screen but it only let the Boches know we were coming. No one seems to be able to explain exactly what happened, but the Companies on the left never had a hope. They got enfiladed from Ale Alley, so the Sergeant-Major was right about the "rough house". Edmunds was killed almost at once and his Company and B were knocked to bits as soon as they came out of the Wood. I took C along just behind Perrin and his crowd. We advanced in three rushes. It was nothing but scrambling in and out of shell-holes, with the ground all soft like potting-mould. The broken ground and the slope of the hill saved us a bit from their fire. Bitter Trench was simply like a filled-in ditch where we crossed it. The contact-aeroplane was just over our heads all the time, firing down at the Boches. After the second rush I looked round and saw that a few of the men were hanging back a bit, and no wonder, for a lot of them were only just out from England! I wondered if I ought to go back to them, but the only thing I'd got in my head was a tag from what some instructor had told me when I was a private in the Artists' Rifles before the War. *In an attack always keep going forward!* Except for that, I couldn't think much; the noise was appalling and I've

New fighters

never had such a dry tongue in my life. I knew one thing, that we must keep up with the barrage. We had over 500 yards to go before the first lift and had been specially told we must follow the barrage close up. It was a sort of cinema effect; all noise and no noise. One of my runners was shot through the face from Ale Alley; I remember something like a half-brick flying over my head, and the bullets from the enfilade fire sort of smashing the air in front of my face. I saw a man just ahead topple over slowly, almost gracefully, and thought "poor little chap, that's his last Cup Tie". Anyhow, the two companies were all mixed up by the time we made the third rush, and we suddenly found ourselves looking down into Beer Trench with the Boches kneeling below us. Just on my left, Perrin, on top, and a big Boche, standing in the trench, fired at one another; down went the Boche. Then they cleared off along Vat Alley, and we blundered after them. I saw one of our chaps crumpled up, with a lot of blood on the back of his neck, and I took his rifle and bandolier and went on with Johnson, my runner. The trench had fallen in in a lot of places. They kept turning round and firing back at us. Once, when Johnson was just behind me, he fired (a cool careful shot – both elbows rested) and hit one of them slick in the face; the red jumped out of his face and up went his arms. After that they disappeared. Soon afterwards we were held up by a machine-gun firing dead on the trench where it was badly damaged, and took refuge in a big shell-hole that had broken into it. Johnson went to fetch Lewis guns and bombers. I could see four or five heads bobbing up and down a little way off so I fired at them and never hit one. The rifle I'd got was one of those "wirer's rifles" which hadn't been properly looked after, and very soon nothing happened when I pressed the trigger which had come loose somehow and wouldn't fire the charge. I reloaded and tried again, then threw the thing away and got back into the trench. There was a man kneeling with his rifle sticking up, so I thought I'd use that; but as I was turning to take it another peace-time tag came into my head – *Never deprive a man of his weapon in a post of danger!*

'The next thing I knew was when I came to and found

myself remembering a tremendous blow in the throat and right shoulder, and feeling speechless and paralysed. Men were moving to and fro above me. Then there was a wild yell – "They're coming back!" and I was alone. I thought "I shall be bombed to bits lying here" and just managed to get along to where a Lewis gun was firing. I fell down and Johnson came along and cut my equipment off and tied up my throat. Someone put my pistol in my side pocket, but when Johnson got me on to my legs it was too heavy and pulled me over so he threw it away. I remember him saying, "Make way; let him come," and men saying "Good luck, sir" – pretty decent of them under such conditions! Got along the trench and out at the back somehow – everything very hazy – drifting smoke and shell-holes – down the hill – thinking "I must get back to Mother" – kept falling down and getting up – Johnson always helping. Got to Battalion Headquarters; R.S.M. outside; he took me very gently by the left hand and led me along, looking terribly concerned. Out in the open again at the back of the hill I knew I was safe. Fell down and couldn't get up any more. Johnson disappeared. I felt it was all over with me till I heard his voice saying, "Here he is," and the stretcher-bearers picked me up. . . . When I was at the dressing-station they took a scrap of paper out of my pocket and read it to me. "I saved your life under heavy fire"; signed and dated. The stretcher-bearers do that sometimes, I'm told!'

He laughed huskily, his face lighting up with a gleam of his old humour. . . .

I asked whether the attack had been considered successful. He thought not. The Manchesters had failed, and Ginchy wasn't properly taken till about a week later. 'When I was in hospital in London,' he went on, 'I talked to a son of a gun from the Brigade Staff; he'd been slightly gassed. He told me we'd done all that was expected of us; it was only a holding attack in our sector, so as to stop the Boches from firing down the hill into the backs of our men who were attacking Guillemont. They knew we hadn't a hope of getting Ale Alley.'

He had told it in a simple unemphatic way, illustrating the story with unconscious gestures – taking aim with a rifle, and

MoTTer ot facT

so on. But the nightmare of smoke and sunlight had been in his eyes, with a sense of confusion and calamity of which I could only guess at the reality. He was the shattered survivor of a broken battalion which had 'done all that was expected of it'.

I asked about young Fernby. Durley had been in the same hospital with him at Rouen and had seen him once. 'They were trying to rouse him up a bit, as he didn't seem to recognize anybody. They knew we'd been in the same Battalion, so I was taken into his ward one night. His head was all over shrapnel wounds. I spoke to him and tried to get him to recognize me, but he didn't know who I was; he died a few hours later.'

Silence was the only comment possible; but I saw the red screens round the bed and Durley whispering to Fernby's bandaged head and irrevocable eyes, while the nurse stood by with folded hands.

3

At the beginning of January David got himself passed for General Service abroad. I was completely taken by surprise when he came back and told me. Apparently the doctor asked him whether he wanted some more home service, but a sudden angry pride made him ask to be given G.S. A couple of weeks later he'd had his final leave and I was seeing him off at Liverpool Station.

A glum twenty-one-year-old veteran (unofficially in charge of a batch of young officers going out for the first time) he butted his way along the crowded platform with shoulders hunched, collar turned up to his ears, and hands plunged in pockets. A certain philosophic finality was combined with the fidgety out-of-luck look which was not unusual with him. 'I've reduced my kit to a minimum this time. No revolver. I've worked it out that the chances are about five to one against my ever using it,' he remarked, as he stood shuffling his feet to try and keep them warm. He hadn't explained how he'd worked the chances out, but he was always fond of a formula. Then the train began to move and he climbed awkwardly into his compartment. 'Give my love to old Joe when you get to the First Battalion,' was my final effort at heartiness. He nodded with a crooked smile. Going out for the third time was a rotten business and his face showed it.

'I ought to be going with him,' I thought, knowing that I could have got G.S. at my last Board if I'd had the guts to ask for it. But how could one ask for it when there was a hope of getting a few more days with the Cheshire and the weather was so perishing cold out in France? 'What a queer mixture he is,' I thought, as I wandered absent-mindedly away from the station. Nothing could have been more cheerless than the rumbling cobbled street by the Docks, with dingy warehouses shutting out the dregs of daylight and an ash-coloured sky which foretold some more snow.

I remember going back to the hut that night after Mess. There was snow on the ground, and the shuttered glare and muffled din of the explosive works seemed more than usually grim. Sitting by the stove I began to read a magazine which David had left behind. It was a propagandist weekly containing translations from the Foreign Press. A Copenhagen paper said: 'The sons of Europe are being crucified on the barbed wire because the misguided masses are shouting for it. They do not know what they do, and the statesmen wash their hands. They dare not deliver them from their martyr's death. . . . ' Was this really the truth, I wondered; wild talk like that was new to me. I thought of Dick Tiltwood, and how he used to come into this hut with such shining evidences of youth in his face; and of dark-haired little Fernby who was just such another; and of Lance-Corporal Kendle, and all those others whose violent deaths had saddened my experience. David was now returning to be a candidate for this military martyrdom, and so (I remembered it with a sick assurance) was I.

Lying awake while the stove-light died redly in the corner of the room, I remembered the wine-faced Army Commander with his rows of medal-ribbons, and how young Allgood and I

had marched past him at the Army School last May, with the
sun shining and the band playing. He had taken the salute
from four hundred officers and N.C.O.s of his Army. How
many of them had been killed since then, and how deeply was
he responsible for their deaths? Did he know what he was
doing, or was he merely a successful old cavalryman whose
peace-time popularity had pushed him up on to his present
perch?

It was natural that I should remember Flixécourt. Those
four weeks had kept their hold on my mind, and they now
seemed like the First Act of a play – a light-hearted First Act
which was unwilling to look ahead from its background of
sunlight and the glorying beauty of beech forests. Life at the
Army School, with its superb physical health, had been like a
prelude to some really conclusive sacrifice of high-spirited
youth. Act II had carried me along to the fateful First of July.
Act III had sent me home to think things over. The autumn
attacks had been a sprawling muddle of attrition and inconclu-
siveness. In the early summer the Fourth Army had been ready
to advance with a new impetus. Now it was stuck in the frozen
mud in front of Bapaume, like a derelict tank. And the story
was the same all the way up to Ypres. Bellicose politicians and
journalists were fond of using the word 'crusade'. But the
'chivalry' (which I'd seen in epitome at the Army School) had
been mown down and blown up in July, August, and September, and its remnant had finished the year's 'crusade' in a
morass of torment and frustration. Yet I was haunted by the
memory of those Flixécourt weeks – almost as though I were
remembering a time when I'd been in love. Was it with life that
I'd been in love then? – for the days had seemed saturated with
the fecundity of physical health and fine weather, and it had
been almost as if my own germinant aliveness were interfused
with some sacrificial rite which was to celebrate the harvest.
'Germinating and German-hating,' I thought, recovering my
sense of reality with a feeble joke. After that I fell asleep.

I had an uncomfortable habit of remembering, when I woke up
in the morning, that the War was still going on and waiting for

me to go back to it; but apart from that and the times when my inmost thoughts got the upper hand of me, life at the Camp was comparatively cheerful, and I allowed myself to be carried along by its noisy current of good-humoured life. At the end of each day I found consolation in the fact that I had shortened the winter, for the new year had begun with a spell of perishing cold weather. Our First Battalion, which had been up to its neck in mud in front of Beaumont-Hamel, was now experiencing fifteen degrees of frost while carrying on minor operations connected with straightening the line. Dottrell wrote that they 'weren't thinking beyond the mail and the rum ration', and advised me to stay away until the weather improved. It wasn't difficult to feel like following his advice; but soon afterwards I went into Liverpool for what I knew to be my final Medical Board. It was a dark freezing day, and all the officers in the waiting-room looked as if they wanted to feel their worst for the occasion. A sallow youth confided in me that he'd been out on the razzle the night before and was hoping to get away with another four weeks' home service.

There were two silver-haired Army doctors sitting at a table, poring over blue and white documents. One, with a waxed moustache, eyed me wearily when I came into the office. With a jerk of the head he indicated a chair by the table. 'Feel fit to go out again?' 'Yes; quite well, thank you.' His pen began to move across the blue paper. 'Has been passed fit for General Ser. . . . ' He looked up irritably. 'Don't shake the table!' (I was tapping it with my fingers.) The other Colonel gazed mildly at me over his pince-nez. Waxed moustache grunted and went on writing. Shaking the table wouldn't stop that pen of his!

PART SEVEN

ROUEN IN FEBRUARY

1

Sometime in the second week of February I crossed to Havre on a detestable boat named *Archangel*. As soon as the boat began to move I was aware of a sense of relief. It was no use worrying about the War now; I was in the Machine again, and all responsibility for my future was in the haphazard control of whatever powers manipulated the British Expeditionary Force. Most of us felt like that, I imagine, and the experience was known as 'being for it again'. Apart from that, my only recollection of the crossing is that someone relieved me of my new trench-coat while I was asleep.

At nine o'clock in the evening of the next day I reported myself at the 5th Infantry Base Depot at Rouen. The journey from London had lasted thirty-three hours (a detail which I record for the benefit of those who like slow-motion war-time details). The Base Camp was a couple of miles from the town, on the edge of a pine forest. In the office where I reported I was informed that I'd been posted to our Second Battalion; this gave me something definite to grumble about, for I wanted to go where I was already known, and the prospect of joining a strange battalion made me feel more homeless than ever. The 5th I.B.D. Adjutant advised me to draw some blankets; the storeroom was just round the corner, he said. After groping about in the dark and tripping over tent ropes I was beginning to lose my temper when I opened a door and found myself in a Guard Room. A man, naked to the waist, was kneeling in the middle of the floor, clutching at his chest and weeping uncontrollably. The Guard were standing around with embarrassed looks, and the Sergeant was beside him, patient and unpitying.

While he was leading me to the blanket store I asked him what was wrong. 'Why, sir, the man's been under detention for assaulting the military police, and now 'e's just 'ad news of his brother being killed. Seems to take it to 'eart more than most would. 'Arf crazy, 'e's been, tearing 'is clothes off and cursing the War and the Fritzes. Almost like a shell-shock case, 'e seems. It's his third time out. A Blighty one don't last a man long nowadays, sir.' As I went off into the gloom I could still hear the uncouth howlings.

'Well, well; this is a damned depressing spot to arrive at!' I thought, while I lay awake trying to keep warm and munching a bit of chocolate, in a narrow segment of a canvas shed about four feet high. Beyond the army-blanket which served as a partition, two officers were chattering interminably in rapid Welsh voices. They were comparing their experiences at some squalid pleasure house in Rouen, and their disclosures didn't make the War seem any jollier. It was, in fact, the most disgusting little conversation I'd ever listened to. But what right had I to blame the poor devils for trying to have a good time before they went up to the Line? . . . Nevertheless, the War seemed to be doing its best to make me feel un-heroic.

Next day I found the 5th I.B.D. Mess dispiriting. I knew nobody, and it wasn't a place where people felt inclined to be interested in one another, since none of them were there for more than a few days. They agreed in grumbling about the alcoholic R.C. padre who managed the mess; the food was bad, and four and threepence a day was considered an exorbitant charge. When they weren't on the training ground (known as 'the Bull Ring') officers sat about in the Mess Room playing cards, cursing the cold weather, and talking tediously about the War with an admixture of ineffective cynicism which hadn't existed twelve months before. I watched them crowding round the notice board after a paper had been pinned to it. They were looking to see if their names were on the list of those going up to the Line next day. Those who were on the list laughed harshly and sat down, with simulated unconcern, to read a stale picture paper. On the same notice board were the names of three private soldiers who had been shot for cowardice since the end of January. 'The sentence was duly carried out. . . . ' In the meantime we could just hear the grumbling of the guns and there was the Spring Offensive to look forward to.

I was feeling as if I'd got a touch of fever, and next morning the doctor told me I'd got German measles. So I transferred myself ingloriously to No. 25 Stationary Hospital, which was a compound of tents with a barbed wire fence round it, about 300 yards from the Camp. There were six in the tent already and my arrival wasn't popular. An extra bed had to be brought in, and the four card players huddled against a smoky stove were interrupted by a gust of Arctic wind. There was snow on the ground and the tent was none too warm at the best of times. 'Now, Mr Parkins, I'm afraid you must shift round a bit to make room for the new patient,' said the nurse. While my bed was being lugged into position by an orderly, Mr Parkins made it plain that six had been company in that tent and seven was an inconvenience. One of his opponents told him to stop chewing the rag and deal again. The cards had been blown off the table and Parkins had lost what, he said, was the first decent hand he'd held that morning. But the additional overcrowding soon ceased to be a grievance, and I didn't spoil their well established circle by offering to butt in at bridge, for I was content to read a book and observe my fellow-invalids.

The quietest of them was Strangford, a specimen of adolescent simplicity, lanky and overgrown and credulous. He wore a kilt, but came of good North Irish stock. Though barely nineteen, he had done several months in the trenches. His father kept a pack of harriers in County Down, and his face would light up when I encouraged him to tell me about them. But unless he was talking or had some little job to keep him busy, his brain appeared to cease working altogether. He would sit on the edge of his bed, slowly rubbing his knee which had a bad sore on it; a mop of untidy brown hair hung over his forehead, and his huge clumsy hands and red wrists had outgrown his tunic. After rubbing his knee, he takes a letter from his breast pocket, bending his gawky, unformed face over it; once he smiles secretly, but when he has read it through he is solemn – wondering, perhaps, when he will see his home and the harriers again.

Parkins was an obvious contrast to this modest youth. Pent up in the accidental intimacy of army life, men were usually anxious to exhibit themselves to the best advantage, particularly as regards their civilian antecedents. 'I'll bet he was jolly well-dressed before the war,' was a type of remark frequently made by young platoon commanders. Parkins was about thirty, and often reminded us that he had been to Cambridge; in private life he had been a school-master. Plausible at first, he soon revealed his defects, for the slovenly tedium of that tent brought greed and selfishness to the surface. With his muddy eyes and small dark moustache, he wasn't a man one took to. But he was self-satisfied, and did his best to amuse us with indecent rhymes and anecdotes. He was also fond of using certain stilted expressions, such as 'for the nonce' and 'anent'. 'I've no complaints to make anent this hand,' he would say when playing cards. He posed as a gay dog, chaffing the nurses when they brought in the food, and quoting Omar Khayyám at them – 'a jug of wine, a loaf of bread and thou beside me, singing in the Wilderness' – and referring to the tent as 'this battered Caravanserai whose portals are alternate Night and Day'. Parkins did not conceal his dislike of the Front Line, and was now in hopes of getting a job as Railway Transport Officer. But he was the sort of man who would get killed in some unutterably wretched attack after doing his best to dodge it.

Young Holt was another second-rate character, plump, smooth-faced and spuriously smart. He had escaped from the Infantry into the Balloon Section, and now fancied himself in a leather overcoat with a fur collar – playing at 'being in the Royal Flying Corps'. He felt that R.F.C. officers had a social superiority to the Infantry. Being up in a balloon elevated a man in more ways than one, and he often aired his discrimination in such matters. Speaking of the Artillery, he would say: 'Yes, there's more *tone* in the R.F.A. – much more tone than you find in the Garrison Gunners!' Holt was a harmless easy-going creature, but we got very tired of his incessant repetition of a stale joke which consisted in saying in a loud voice, *I will*

*arise and will go unto my father and will say unto him: Father,
stand-at-ease!*

Then there was White, a sensible Territorial Captain who
had been in charge of Heavy Trench Mortars. Short and thick-
set, with a deep, humorous voice, he talked in a muddled way
about the War – sardonic about English methods, but easily
impressed by notable 'public names' of politicians and generals. He liked discussing Trench Mortar technicalities, and
from the way he spoke about his men I knew that he had
earned their gratitude.

There was another youngish man who had been a clerk in
the Colonial Office and had gone to Egypt as a Yeomanry Sergeant before getting his Infantry commission. He talked to
me, in a cockney accent, about his young wife, and was evidently kindly and reliable, though incapable of understanding
an original idea. Two days after I'd seen the last of him, I
couldn't remember either his face or his name.

The last of my six companions was Patterson, aged nineteen
and fresh from Edinburgh University with a commission in the
Field Artillery. His home was in Perth and he admitted that he
loved porridge, when asking the nurse to try and wangle him a
second helping of it. He talked broad Scots and made simple-
minded war jokes, and then surprised me by quoting Milton
and Keats. Self-reliant with a sort of pleasant truculence, he
was thorough and careful in everything he did. With his crisp
fair hair, grey eyes, and fresh complexion, he was a pattern of
charming youthfulness. If he lived, he would be a shrewd,
kindly man. Did he live, I wonder? . . .

After the first few days I used to slip through the wire fence
and walk in the clean-smelling pine woods. The surf-like sigh-
ing of the lofty colonnades could tranquillize my thoughts after
the boredom of the tent and the chatter of the card players
crouching by the stove. The pine-trees are patiently waiting for
the guns to stop, I thought, and I felt less resentment against
the War than I had done since I left England. . . . One afternoon I followed an alley which led downhill to a big shuttered
house. Blackbirds were scolding among the bushes as I tres-
passed in the untidy garden, and someone was chopping timber

in a brown copse below the house. A dog barked from the stable-yard; hens clucked, and a cow lowed. Such homely sounds were comforting when one was in the exile of army life. I thought of the lengthening spring twilights and the lovely wakening of the year, forgetful of the 'Spring Offensive'. But it was only for a short while, and the bitter reality returned to me as I squeezed myself through the hospital's barbed wire fence. I was losing my belief in the War, and I longed for mental acquiescence – to be like young Patterson, who had come out to fight for his country undoubting, who could still kneel by his bed and say his simple prayers, steadfastly believing that he was in the Field Artillery to make the world a better place. I had believed like that, once upon a time, but now the only prayer which seemed worth uttering was Omar Khayyám's:

> For all the Sin wherewith the face of Man
> Is blackened – Man's forgiveness give – and take.

2

Back at the Infantry Base Depot after my ten days of German measles, I stared at the notice board on nine successive mornings before my own name (typewritten and slightly misspelt Sharston) caused me to saunter away with the correct air of unconcern. At that moment the Medical Officer came in, shaking some snow off his coat. Sturdy, pink-faced and chubby, he looked a typical optimist. He had been two years with a fighting battalion and was now down at the Base for good, with a well-earned D.S.O. He and I got on well together, but his appearance was deceptive, for he was a profound pessimist. He now exclaimed, rather crustily, that he supposed there'd only be one more winter out here, if we were lucky. I'd heard this remark from him before, and the first time had made me feel gloomy, for I had been hoping that the War would be over by next autumn. When the Mess waiter had brought him a whisky I ventured to ask his opinion about the

German withdrawal on the Ancre; for at that time they were retiring to the Hindenburg Line, and sanguine subalterns were rejoicing over this proof that we'd 'got them on the run'. The Doctor assured me that the Germans were 'pulling our legs properly'. The idea seemed to please him; he always looked his brightest when he was announcing that we were certain to lose the War. We were now joined by a Rifle Brigade Major with an Irish brogue, who had been a cavalryman in the South African War. He had got his skull fractured by a bit of shell at the first battle of Ypres, but in spite of this he was a resolute optimist and was delighted to be back in France as second-in-command of a New Army Battalion. England, he said, was no place for an honest man; the sight of all those dirty dogs swindling the Government made him sick. When the Doctor grumbled about the rotten outlook, the Major would say: 'Yes, things couldn't be much worse, but another two or three years ought to see the job finished.' I found him surly and contradictory at first, but he softened when he got to know me, though he wasn't an easy man to discuss anything with, for he simply stated his opinions in a loud voice and only listened to one's replies in a detached one-eared way (which was literally true, since he was stone deaf on one side of his head, and had only got himself passed for active service after a tussle with the War Office). His rough and ready philosophy was refreshing, and he was a wholesome example of human inconsistency. He was a good-hearted man, I felt; but his attitude toward Conscientious Objectors was frankly brutal. He described, with evident relish, his methods of dealing with two of them who had turned up at the Rifle Brigade Depot. One had been a tough nut to crack, for he was a well-educated man, and the authorities were afraid of him. But the Major had got him run in for two years' hard labour. He'd have knocked him about a bit if he'd been allowed to, he said. The other one was some humble inarticulate wretch who refused to march. So the Major had him tied to the back of a wagon and dragged along a road until he was badly cut about. 'After a few hundred yards he cried enough, and afterwards turned out to be quite a decent soldier. Made good, and was killed in the trenches.' He smiled grimly. Discipline had to be enforced by brutality, said the Major; and, as I have already remarked, he wasn't amenable to argument.

I hadn't formed any opinion about Conscientious Objectors, but I couldn't help thinking that they must be braver men than some I'd seen wearing uniforms in safe places and taking salutes from genuine soldiers.

Resolved to make the most of my last day at the Base, I went down to Rouen early in the afternoon without having wasted any time in applying for leave from the Adjutant. A tram took me most of the way; the city looked fine as we crossed the river. There wasn't so very much to be done when I got there, but the first thing was to have a hair-cut. I'd had one a week ago, but this one might have to last me a longish while, for I wasn't keen on Battalion barbers. So I told the man to cut off as much as he could, and while he clipped and snipped I gazed gloomily at myself in the glass, speculating prosaically on the probabilities of my head of hair ever needing another trim up. A captain in the next chair had been through the whole repertoire – hair-cut, shave, shampoo, face-massage, and friction. 'Now I feel a quid better,' he remarked when he got up to go. He was wearing trench boots and was evidently on his way to the Line. I had heard him treating the barber, who spoke English, to a panegyric on the prospects of an Allied success in the Spring. 'We're going to give them the knock all right this journey!' The barber asked him about a long scar which seamed his head. He smiled: 'A souvenir of Devil's Wood.' I wondered how much longer he would retain his enthusiasm for the Western Front. Personally I preferred rambling around Rouen and pretending that I was an ordinary peacetime tourist. In the old quarters of the town one could stroll about without meeting many English soldiers.

Later on I was going to the Hôtel de la Poste for a valedictory bath and dinner. In the meantime I was content to stare at shop-windows and explore side streets. It was a Saturday afternoon and the people were busy marketing. At the end of my wanderings I went into the Cathedral, leaving behind me the bustling Square and the sallow gusty sunset which flared above the roofs. In the Cathedral, perhaps, I could escape from the War for a while, although the Christian Religion had apparently no claim to be regarded as a Benevolent Neutral Power.

It was some Saint's Day, and the nave was crowded with drifting figures, their footfalls echoing in the dusk. Sometimes a chair scrooped when a worshipper moved away. Candles burned in clear clusters, like flickering gold flowers, in the shrines where kneeling women gazed and whispered and moved their hands devoutly. In the pulpit a priest was urging the Lenten significance of 'Jésu', tilting his pallid square face from side to side and gesticulating mechanically. A congregation sat or stood to hear him; among them, at my elbow, a small child stared up at the priest with stupid innocent eyes. That child couldn't understand the sermon any more than it understood the War. It saw a man, high up and alone, clenching his hands and speaking vehemently; it also saw the figures of people called soldiers who belonged to something that made a much bigger noise than the preacher, who now stopped suddenly, and the monotonous chanting began again in front of the altar (sounding, I thought, rather harsh and hopeless).

The preacher, I inferred, had been reminding us that we ought to love one another and be like little children. 'Jésu' had said so, and He had died to save us (but not to save the Germans or the Austrians or any of that lot). It was no good trying to feel uplifted, when such thoughts grimaced at me; but there was a certain consolation in the solemnity of the Cathedral, and I remained there after the service had ended. Gradually, the glory faded from the rose-window above the organ. I looked at all the windows, until their lights were only blurs and patches, and the prophets and martyrs robed in blue and crimson and green were merged in outer darkness.

The Hôtel de la Poste hadn't altogether modernized its interior, but it contained much solid comfort and supplied the richest meals in Rouen. Consequently it was frequented by every British officer employed in the district, and had become a sort of club for those indispensable residents – so much so that strong suggestions had been advanced by senior officers to the effect that the _Poste_ should be put out of bounds for all Infantry subalterns on their way to the Line. The place, they felt, was becoming too crowded, and the deportment of a 'temporary gentleman' enjoying his last decent dinner was apt to be more suitable to a dug-out than a military club.

Leaning back in a wicker chair, I enjoyed the after-effects of a hot bath and wondered what I'd have for dinner. The lift came sliding down from nowhere to stop with a dull bump. A bulky grey-haired Colonel, with green tabs and a Coronation Medal, stepped heavily out, leaning on a stick and glaring around him from under a green and gold cap and aggressive eyebrows. His disapproval focused itself on a group of infantry subalterns whose ungainly legs were cumbered with high trench boots; trench-coats and haversacks were slung untidily across their chairs; to-night, or to-morrow, or 'some old time or other' they'd be crawling up to the War in an over-ventilated reinforcement train, gazing enviously at the Red Cross trains which passed them – going the other way – and disparaging the French landscape, 'so different to good old Blighty'. Compared with 'the troops', who travelled in vans designed for horses and cattle, they were in clover. The Colonel, on the other hand, probably supervised an office full of clerks who made lists of killed, wounded, and reinforcements. I had visited such a place myself in an attempt to get my name transferred to the First Battalion, and had been received with no civility at all. They were all much too busy to rearrange the private affairs of a dissatisfied second-lieutenant, as might have been expected. But the contrast between the Front Line and the Base was an old story, and at any rate the Base Details were at a disadvantage as regards the honour and glory which made the War such an uplifting experience for those in close contact with it. I smiled sardonically at the green and gold Colonel's back view. The lift ascended again, leaving a confused murmur of male voices and a clatter of feet on the polished wood floor. Officers pushed through the swing-doors in twos and threes, paused to buy an English paper from the

concierge, vanished to hang up their overcoats, and straddled
in again, pulling down their tunics and smoothing their hair,
conscious of gaiters, neatly-fitting or otherwise. Young caval-
rymen were numerous, their superior social connections demonstrated by well-cut riding boots and predominantly small
heads. Nice-looking young chaps with nice manners, they
sipped cocktails and stood up respectfully when a Cavalry
Brigadier strode past them. The Cavalry were still waiting for
their chance on the Western Front. . . . Would they ever get it,
I wondered. Personally, I thought it would be a pity if they did,
for I disliked the idea of a lot of good horses being killed and
wounded, and I had always been soft-hearted about horses. By
the time I'd finished my dinner and a bottle of Burgundy, I felt
soft-hearted about almost everything. The large dining-room
was full of London Clubmen dressed as Colonels, Majors, and
Captains with a conscientious objection to physical discomfort. But, after all, somebody had to be at the Base; modern
warfare offered a niche for everyone, and many of them looked
better qualified for a card-table than a military campaign.
They were as much the victims of circumstances as the unfortunate troops in the trenches. Puffing a cigar, I decided that
there was a tolerant view to be taken about almost everybody,
especially after a good dinner at the Hôtel de la Poste.

PART EIGHT

THE SECOND BATTALION

1

Although the War has been described as the greatest event in history, it could be tedious and repetitional for an ordinary Infantry Officer like myself.

From Corbie Station the War had started me on my home journey in a Hospital Train. Rather more than seven months later, at midnight, it again deposited me at Corbie Station after eight hours in an unlit and overcrowded carriage which had no glass in its windows. My valise was on a truck and though I made a scrambling attempt to get it unloaded the train clanked away into the gloom with all my belongings on board. We slept on the floor of the Field Ambulance Hut outside the station; my companions grumbled a good deal, for several of them were out again after being wounded last year, and one of them claimed to have been hit in both lungs. Two cadet-officers were going with me to the Second Battalion, but I had little in common with them except our lost valises, which were returned to us a week later (with one sample of every-thing abstracted by someone at the Army Service Corps Dump). Next morning, after glumly congratulating myself that I'd packed my safety razor in my haversack, I walked to my new unit, which was seven miles away. I was wearing my best friends, a pair of greased marching boots whose supple strength had never failed to keep the water out; how much those boots meant to me can only be understood by persons who have shared my type of experience; I can only say that they never gave me sore feet; and if this sounds irrelevant, I must re-mind the reader that a platoon commander's feet were his fortune.

The Second Battalion of the Flintshire Fusiliers had recently returned from two months in the Cléry sector of the Somme Front, where they had endured some of the severest weather of the War. Battalion records relate that there were no braziers in the trenches, fuel was so scarce that wooden crosses were taken from casual graves, and except for the tepid tea that came up in tins wrapped in straw, food was mostly cold. Major-General Whincop, who commanded the Division, had made himself obnoxiously conspicuous by forbidding the Rum Ration. He was, of course, over anxious to demonstrate his elasticity of mind, but the 'No Rum Division' failed to appreciate their uniqueness in the Expeditionary Force. He also thought that smoking impaired the efficiency of the troops and would have liked to restrict their consumption of cigarettes. General Whincop had likewise demonstrated his independence of mind earlier in the War by forbidding the issue of steel helmets to his Division. His conservative objection (which was based on a belief that this new War Office luxury would weaken the men's fighting spirit – 'make them soft', in fact) was, of course, only a flash in the pan (or brain-pan) and Whincop's reputation as an innovator was mainly kept alive by his veto on the Rum Ration. G.O.C.'s, like platoon commanders, were obliged to devise 'stunts' to show their keenness, and opportunities for originality were infrequent. But since 1918 Generals have received their full share of ridicule and abuse, and it would not surprise me if someone were to start a Society for the Prevention of Cruelty to Great War Generals. If such a Society were formed, I, for one, would gladly contribute my modest half-guinea per annum; for it must be remembered that many an unsuccessful General had previously been the competent Colonel of an Infantry Battalion, thereby earning the gratitude and admiration of his men.

Anyhow, the frost had been intense, and owing to the rationing of coal in England the issue to the Army had been limited and coke-issues had caused many cases of coke-fume poisoning where the men slept in unventilated dug-outs. After this miserable experience (which had ended with a thaw and a hundred cases of trench-feet) the Second Battalion was now resting at Camp 13, about two miles from Morlancourt. The huts of Camp 13 had been erected since last summer; they disfigured what I had formerly known as an inoffensive hollow about half a mile from the reedy windings of the Somme. No one had a good word for the place. The Battalion was in low spirits because the Colonel had been wounded a few weeks before, and he had been so popular that everyone regarded him as irreplaceable. His successor was indulgent and conciliatory, but it seemed that greater aggressiveness would have been preferable. Contrasting him with the rough-tongued efficiency of Kinjack, I began to realize that, in a Commanding Officer, amiability is not enough.

Meanwhile we were in what was called 'Corps Reserve', and Colonel Easby had issued the order 'carry on with platoon training' (a pronouncement which left us free to kill time as best we could). No. 8 Platoon, which was my own compact little command, was not impressive on parade. Of its thirty-four N.C.O.s and men, eight were Lewis gunners and paraded elsewhere. Eight was likewise the number of Private Joneses in my platoon, and my first difficulty was to differentiate between them. The depleted Battalion had been strengthened by a draft from England, and these men were mostly undersized, dull-witted, and barely capable of carrying the heavy weight of their equipment. As an example of their proficiency, I can say that in one case platoon training began with the man being taught how to load his rifle. Afterwards I felt that he would have been less dangerous in his pre-existing ignorance.

It was difficult to know what to do with my bored and apathetic platoon. I wasn't a competent instructor, and my sergeant was conscientious but unenterprising. *Infantry Training*, which was the only manual available, had been written years before trench-warfare 'came into its own' as a factor in world affairs, and the condensed and practical *Handbook for the Training of Platoons* was not issued until nearly twelve months afterwards. One grey afternoon, when we had gone through all our monotonous exercises and the men's eyes were more than usually mindless, I had a bright unmilitary idea and ordered them to play hide-and-seek among some trees. After a self-conscious beginning they livened up and actually enjoyed themselves. When I watched them falling in again with flushed and jolly faces I was aware that a sense of humanity had been restored to them, and realized how intolerable the ordinary exercises were unless the instructor was an expert. Even football matches were impossible, since there was no suitable ground.

The main characteristics of Camp 13 were mud and smoke. Mud was everywhere. All the Company officers lived in one long gloomy draughty hut with an earth floor. Smoke was always drifting in from the braziers of the adjoining kitchen. After dark we sat and shivered in our 'British Warm' coats, reading, playing cards, and writing letters with watering eyes by the feeble glimmer of guttering candles. Orderlies brought in a clutter of tin mugs and plates, and Maconochie stew was consumed in morose discomfort. It was an existence which suffocated all pleasant thoughts; nothing survived except animal cravings for warmth, food, and something to break the monotony of Corps Rest routine.

The only compensation for me was that my body became healthy, in spite of lesser discomforts such as a continuous cold in the head. The landscape was a compensation too, for I liked its heaving grey and brown billows, dotted with corn-stacks, patched and striped by plough and stubble and green crops, and crossed by bridle tracks and lonely wandering roads. Hares and partridges hurried away as I watched them. Along the horizon the guns still boomed and thudded, and bursting shells made tiny puffs of smoke above ridges topped by processions of trees, with here and there the dark line of woods. But from some windy upland I looked down on villages, scattered in the folds of hill and valley like handfuls of pebbles, grey and dull red, and from such things I got what consolation I could.

One Sunday afternoon I walked across to Heilly. I'd been there for a few days with the First Battalion last July, before we marched back to the Line in dust and glare. The water still sang its undertones by the bridge and went twinkling to the bend, passing the garden by the house where the Field Cashier used to hand us our money. I remembered going there with Dick Tiltwood, just a year ago. Ormand was with me this time,

for he had joined the Second Battalion soon after I did. He had
still got his little gramophone, and we reminded ourselves how
Mansfield and Barton used to be for ever 'chipping' him about
it. 'I must say I used to get jolly fed-up with them sometimes;
they overdid it, especially about that record *Lots of Loving*.'
He laughed, rolling his good-humoured eyes round at me under
the strongly marked black eyebrows which indicated that he
had a strong temper when roused. The joke about *Lots of Loving* had consisted in the others pretending that it contained an
unprintable epithet. On one occasion they conspired with the
Adjutant, who asked Ormand to play *Lots of Loving* and then
simulated astonishment at a certain adjective which was indistinct owing to the worn condition of the disc. Whereupon
Ormand explained angrily, 'I ask you, is it bloody likely that
"His Master's Voice" would send out a record with the
word —— in it?'

As we trudged back from Heilly the sun was sinking red
beyond the hazy valleys, a shrewd wind blowing, and plough
teams turning a last furrow along the ridges. We'd had quite a
good afternoon, but Ormand's cheerfulness diminished as we
neared the Camp. He didn't fancy his chance in the Spring
Offensive and he wanted to be back with the 'good old First
Battalion', though he wouldn't find many of the good old faces
when he got there. He spoke gloomily about his longing for an
ordinary civilian career and his hatred of 'this silly stunt which
the blasted Bishops call the Great Adventure'. He had been
on a Court Martial the day before, and though nothing had
been required of him except to make up the quorum of officers trying the case, he had been upset by it. Some poor wretch
had been condemned to be shot for cowardice. The court had
recommended the prisoner to mercy, but the proceedings had
been bad for young Ormand. However, he relieved the situation by exclaiming, 'And to-morrow I've got to have my . . .
anti-typhoid injection!' and I reminded him that he was reducing his overdraft at Cox's by being at the Front. So our walk
ended; we passed the looming aerodrome, and the lines of lor-
ries under the trees along the main road, and the sentry who
stood by a glowing brazier at the crossroads. Down in the

hollow crouched the Camp; a disgusting dinner in the smoky hut and then early to bed, was all it could offer us. 'Summer time' began at midnight, which meant one hour less sleep and absolutely nothing else.

2

Palm Sunday was on April 1st that year. On April 2nd we left Camp 13. No one wanted to see it again, and as we went up hill to the Corbie road the smoke from the incinerators made the place look as if we had set fire to it.

I had a feeling that we were marching away to a better land. Camp 13 had clogged our minds, but the troops were in better spirits to-day and the Battalion seemed to have recovered its consciousness as a unit. The wind was blowing cold enough for snow, but the sun shone and wintry weather couldn't last much longer. Where were we walking to, I wondered; for this was known to be the first stage of a longish migration northwards. Arras, perhaps; rumours of an impending battle there had been active lately. As second-in-command of the Company I went along behind it, rather at my ease. Watching the men as they plodded patiently on under their packs, I felt as if my own identity was becoming merged in the Battalion. We were on the move and the same future awaited all of us (though most of the men had bad boots and mine were quite comfortable).

More light-hearted than I'd been for some time, I contemplated my Company Commander, who was in undisputed occupation of a horse which looked scarcely up to his weight. Captain Leake had begun by being rude to me. I never discovered the reason. But he had been a Special Reserve officer before the War, and he couldn't get certain regimental traditions out of his head. In the good old days, all second-lieutenants had been called 'warts', and for their first six months a senior officer never spoke to them, except on parade. Leake evidently liked the idea, for he was a man who enjoyed standing on his dignity; but such behaviour was inappropriate to active service, and six months at the Front usually sufficed to finish the career of a second-lieutenant. On my second morning at Camp 13 Leake had remarked (for my special benefit) that 'these newly joined warts were getting too big for their boots'. This was incorrect, for I was bemoaning the loss of my valise, and the M.O. had just given me my anti-typhoid injection. Leake also resented the fact that I had served with the First Battalion, which he appeared to regard as a hated rival. He thawed gradually after my first week, and was now verging on cordiality, which I did my best to encourage. The other Company Commanders had been friendly from the first, for I had known them at Clitherland in 1915.

Then there was the Doctor, who was now away on leave but would certainly be back before things became lively. Captain Munro had been with the Second Battalion about eighteen months. The first time I saw him was when he gave me my anti-typhoid injection. I looked at him with interest, for he was already known to me by reputation. 'Hullo, here's Sherston, the man who did stunts with the First Battalion,' he remarked, as I unbuttoned my shirt for the perforation process. He was giving double injections, so as to save us the trouble of feeling unwell twice. 'That'll keep you quiet for forty-eight hours,' he observed; and I retired, with a sickly grin. The M.O. was a famous character in the Battalion, and I was hoping to get to know him better. (At the time of writing I can indeed claim to have achieved my hope. But the Doctor is a man averse to the idea of being applauded in print, and he would regard any reference to his local renown as irrelevant to this narrative.)

Equally popular was Bates, the Quartermaster, who was a burlier prototype of Joe Dottrell, with fewer political prejudices. When, at Camp 13, there had been rumours of a Divisional Race Meeting, Bates had asked me to ride his mare. The Races had been cancelled, but the notion had delighted me for a day or two. This mare could gallop quite well and was the apple of the Quartermaster's eye. It was said that on one occasion, when the Transport was having a rough time, Bates had rigged up a tarpaulin shelter for his mare and slept out in the open himself. I was mentally comparing Bates and Dottrell, to their mutual credit, when we came to the end of our first fifty minutes and the men fell out at the side of the road and slipped their packs off. A gang of red and blue capped German prisoners was at work on the road close by, and their sullen undernourished faces made our own troops look as if they were lucky in some sort of liberty. But whistles blew, pack straps were adjusted, and on we went. By half-past one the Battalion was in its billets in Corbie.

Before dinner Ralph Wilmot came round to our Company Mess to suggest that Leake and myself should join 'a bit of a jolly' which he'd arranged for that evening. Wilmot was a dark, monocled young man, mature for his years. His war experience had begun with despatch riding on a motor-bicycle in 1914. Afterwards he had gone to Gallipoli, where he had survived until the historic Evacuation. He had now done a long spell of service in France, and was a popular character in the Second Battalion. He had the whimsical smile which illuminated a half-melancholy temperament, and could give an amusing twist to the sorriest situation, since he liked to see life as a tragi-comedy and himself as a debonair philosopher, a man with a gay past who had learned to look at the world more in sorrow than in anger. His unobtrusive jests were enunciated with a stammer which somehow increased their effect. With some difficulty he now told us that he had discovered a place where we could 'buy some bubbly and tickle the ivories'. The ivory-tickling would be his own contribution, for he had a passion for playing the piano. So we spent the evening in a sparsely furnished little parlour on the ground-floor of a wine-merchant's house. The wine-merchant's wife, a sallow silent woman, brought in bottle after bottle of 'bubbly' which, whatever its quality, produced conviviality. We drank farewell to civilization with an air of finality, while Wilmot performed on an upright piano, the tone of which was meretriciously agreeable, like the flavour of the champagne. He played, mostly by ear, familiar passages from *Tosca* and *Bohème*, musical comedy extracts, and sentimental ballads. We all became confidential and almost emotional. I felt that at last I was really getting on good terms with Leake; every glass of wine made us dislike one another a little less. Thus the proceedings continued until after midnight, while Wilmot became more and more attached to a certain popular song. We sang the chorus over and over again:

> Moon, moon, see-reen-ly shy-ning,
> Don't go home too soo-oon;
> You've such a charm about you
> That we – can't get – on with-out you.
> Da-da-da, de-dum . . . etc.

The atmosphere of the room had become tropical, for we had all been smoking like chimneys. But Wilmot couldn't tear himself away from that piano, and while he caressed the keys with lingering affection, the wine-merchant's wife received I don't know how many francs and we all wrote our names in her album. From the number of shaky signatures in it I judged that she must have made a handsome profit out of the War.

Out in the white moonlight, Leake and I meandered along the empty street, accompanied by our tipsy shadows. At the door of my billet we shook hands 'sholemnly', and I assured him that he could always rely on me to 'blurry well do my damndest for him'. He vanished heavily, and I spent several minutes prodding at the keyhole of the greengrocer's shop. Once inside the door, my difficulties were almost ended. I remember balancing myself in the dark little shop, which was full of strong-smelling vegetables, and remarking aloud, 'Well, old boy, here you are, and now you gotter get up the stairs.' My room was an unventilated cupboard which reeked of onions; the stairs were steep, but my flea-bag was on the floor and I fell asleep fully dressed. What with the smell of onions and the bad champagne, I awoke feeling like nothing on earth, and to say that Leake was grumpy at breakfast would be to put it mildly. But we were on the march by nine, in cold bright weather, and by the first halt I was feeling surprisingly clear-headed and alert.

We had halted on some high ground above Pont Noyelles: I

can remember the invigorating freshness of the air and the delicate outlines of the landscape towards Amiens, and how I gazed at a line of tall trees by the river beyond which, not two miles away, was the village of Bussy where I'd been last June before the Somme battle began. At such a moment as that the War felt quite a friendly affair and I could assure myself that being in the Infantry was much better than loafing about at home. And at the second halt I was able to observe what a pleasant picture the men made, for some of them were resting in warm sunlight under a crucifix and an old apple-tree. But by midday the march had become tedious; the road was dusty, the sun glared down on us, and I was occupied in preventing exhausted men from falling out. It was difficult to keep some of them in the ranks, and by the time we reached Villers-Bocage (nearly fourteen miles from Corbie) I was pushing two undersized men along in front of me, another one staggered behind hanging on to my belt, and the Company Sergeant-Major was carrying three rifles as well as his own. By two o'clock they were all sitting on dirty straw in a sun-chinked barn, with their boots and socks off. Their feet were the most important part of them, I thought, as I made my sympathetic inspection of sores and blisters. The old soldiers grinned at me philosophically, puffing their Woodbines. It was all in the day's work, and the War was the War. The newly-joined men were different; white and jaded, they stared up at me with stupid trusting eyes. I wished I could make things easier for them, but I could do nothing beyond sending a big batch of excruciating boots to the Battalion boot-menders, knowing that they'd come back roughly botched, if anything were done to them at all. But one Company's blisters were a small event in the procession of sore feet that was passing through Villers-Bocage. The woman in my billet told me in broken English that troops had been going through for fifteen days, never stopping more than one night and always marching towards Doullens and Arras. My only other recollection of Villers-Bocage is the room in which our Company's officers dined and slept. It contained an assortment of stuffed and mouldy birds with outspread wings. There was a stork, a jay, and a sparrow-hawk; also a pair of squirrels. Lying awake on the tiled floor I could watch a seagull suspended by a string from the ceiling; very slowly it revolved in the draughty air; and while it revolved I fell asleep, for the day had been a long one.

Next day's march took us to Beauval, along a monotonous eight-mile stretch of the main road from Amiens to St Pol. Wet snow was falling all the way. We passed into another 'Army area'; the realm of Rawlinson was left behind us and our self-sacrificing exertions were now to be directed by Allenby. Soon after entering the Allenby Area we sighted a group of mounted officers who had stationed themselves under the trees by the roadside. Word was passed back that it was the Corps Commander. Since there were only three Corps Commanders in each Army they were seldom seen, so it was with quite a lively interest that we put ourselves on the alert to eyes-left this one. While we were trudging stolidly nearer to the great man, Colonel Easby detached himself from the head of the column, rode up to the General, and saluted hopefully. The Corps Commander (who was nothing much to look at, for his interesting accumulation of medal-ribbons was concealed by a waterproof coat) ignored our eyes-lefting of him; he was too busy bellowing at poor Colonel Easby, whom he welcomed thus. C.C. 'Are you stuck to that bloody horse?' Col. E. 'No, sir.' (Dismounts hastily and salutes again.) As Leake's Company went by, the General was yelling something about why the hell hadn't the men got the muzzles of their rifles covered (this being one of his 'special ideas'). 'Pity he don't keep his own muzzle covered,' remarked someone in the ranks, thereby voicing a prevalent feeling. The Corps Commander was equally abusive because the 'Cookers' were carrying brooms and other utilitarian objects. Also the Companies were marching with fifty yard intervals between them (by a special order of the late Rawlinson). In Allenby's Army the intervals between Companies had to be considerably less, as our Colonel was now finding out. However, the episode was soon behind us and the 'Cookers' rumbled peacefully on their way, brooms and all, emitting smoke and stewing away at the men's dinners.

Very few of us ever saw the Corps Commander again. It was a comfort to know that Allenby, at any rate, could be rude to him if he wanted to.

We started from Beauval at four o'clock on a sunny afternoon and went another eight miles to a place called Lucheux. . . . There is nothing in all this, the reader will expostulate. But there was a lot in it, for us. We were moving steadily nearer to the Spring Offensive; for those who thought about it the days had an ever intensifying significance. For me, the idea of death made everything seem vivid and valuable. The War could be like that to a man, until it drove him to drink and suffocated his finer apprehensions.

Among the troops I observed a growing and almost eager expectancy; their cheerfulness increased; something was going to happen to them; perhaps they believed that the Arras Battle would end the War. It was the same spirit which had animated the Army before the Battle of the Somme. And now, once again, we could hear along the horizon that blundering doom which bludgeoned armies into material for military histories. 'That way to the Sausage Machine!' some old soldier exclaimed as we passed a signpost marked *Arras, 32 k*. We were entering Doullens with the brightness of the setting sun on our faces. As we came down the hill our second-in-command (a gentle middle-aged country solicitor) was walking beside me, consoling himself with reminiscences of cricket and hunting.

Thus the Battalion slogged on into an ominous Easter, and every man carried his own hazardous hope of survival. Overshadowed by the knowledge of what was ahead of us, I became increasingly convinced that a humble soldier holding up a blistered foot could have greater dignity than a blustering Corps Commander.

That night we were in huts among some wooded hills. I can remember how we had supper out in the moonlight sitting round a brazier with plates of ration stew on our knees. The wind was from the east and we could hear the huge bombardment up at Arras. Brown and leafless, the sombre woods hemmed us in. Soon the beeches would be swaying and quiver-

ing with the lovely miracle of spring. How many of us will
return to that, I wondered, forgetting my hatred of the War in
a memory of all that April had ever meant for me. . . .

On Good Friday morning I woke with sunshine streaming
in at the door and broad Scots being shouted by some Cameronians in the next hut. Someone was practising the bagpipes at
the edge of the wood, and a mule contributed a short solo
from the Transport Lines.

On Saturday afternoon we came to Saulty, which was only ten
miles from Arras and contained copious indications of the
Offensive, in the form of ammunition and food dumps and the
tents of a Casualty Clearing Station. A large Y.M.C.A. canteen gladdened the rank and file, and I sent my servant there to
buy a pack full of Woodbines for an emergency which was a
certainty. Canteens and *estaminets* would be remote fantasies
when we were in the devastated area. Twelve dozen packets of
Woodbines in a pale green cardboard box were all I could
store up for the future consolation of B Company; but they
were better than nothing and the box was no weight for my
servant to carry.

Having seen the men settled into their chilly barns and sheds,
I stuffed myself with coffee and eggs and betook myself to a
tree stump in the peaceful park of a white château close to the
village. Next day we were moving to our concentration area,
so I was in a meditative mood and disposed to ask myself a
few introspective questions. The sun was just above the tree-
tops; a few small deer were grazing; a rook flapped overhead;
and some thrushes and blackbirds were singing in the brown
undergrowth. Nothing was near to remind me of the War;
only the enormous thudding on the horizon and an aeroplane
humming across the clear sky. For some obscure reason I felt
confident and serene. My thoughts assured me that I wouldn't
go back to England to-morrow if I were offered an improbable
choice between that and the battle. Why should I feel elated at
the prospect of the battle, I wondered. It couldn't be only the
coffee and eggs which had caused me to feel so acquiescent.
Last year, before the Somme, I hadn't known what I was in

for. I knew now; and the idea was giving me emotional satisfaction! I had often read those farewell letters from second-
lieutenants to their relatives which the newspapers were so
fond of printing. 'Never has life brought me such an abundance of noble feelings,' and so on. I had always found it difficult to believe that these young men had really felt happy
with death staring them in the face, and I resented any senti-
mentalizing of infantry attacks. But here I was, working myself
up into a similar mental condition, as though going over the
top were a species of religious experience. Was it some suicidal
self-deceiving escape from the limitless malevolence of the
Front Line? . . . Well, whatever it was, it was some compensation for the loss of last year's day dreams about England
(which I could no longer indulge in, owing to an indefinite
hostility to 'people at home who couldn't understand'). I was
beginning to feel rather arrogant toward 'people at home'. But
my mind was in a muddle; the War was too big an event for
one man to stand alone in. All I knew was that I'd lost my faith
in it and there was nothing left to believe in except 'the Battalion spirit'. The Battalion spirit meant living oneself into comfortable companionship with the officers and N.C.O.s around
one; it meant winning the respect, or even the affection, of
platoon and company. But while exploring my way into the
War I had discovered the impermanence of its humanities.
One evening we could be all together in a cosy room in Corbie, with Wilmot playing the piano and Dunning telling me
about the eccentric old ladies who lived in his mother's board-
ing house in Bloomsbury. A single machine-gun or a few shells
might wipe out the whole picture within a week. Last summer
the First Battalion had been part of my life; by the middle of
September it had been almost obliterated. I knew that a soldier
signed away his independence; we were at the front to fight,
not to think. But it became a bit awkward when one couldn't
look even a week ahead. And now there was a steel curtain
down between April and May. On the other side of the curtain, if I was lucky, I should meet the survivors, and we should
begin to build up our little humanities all over again.

That was the bleak truth, and there was only one method of

evading it; to make a little drama out of my own experience –
that was the way out. I must play at being a hero in shining
armour, as I'd done last year; if I didn't, I might crumple up
altogether. (Self-inflicted wounds weren't uncommon on the
Western Front, and brave men had put bullets through their
own heads before now, especially when winter made trench
warfare unendurable.) Having thus decided on death or glory,
I knocked my pipe out and got up from the tree stump with a
sense of having solved my problems. The deer were still grazing peacefully in the park; but the sun was a glint of scarlet
beyond the strip of woodland and the air was turning chilly.
Along the edge of the world that infernal banging was going
on for all it was worth. Three Army Corps were to attack on
Easter Monday.

On a sunny Easter morning we moved another seven miles, to
Basseux, a village which had been quite close to the trenches
before the Germans withdrew to the Hindenburg Line. The
Sausage Machine was now only eight miles away from us, and
the preliminary bombardment was, as someone in the ranks
remarked, 'a fair bloody treat to listen to'. We insisted on
being optimistic. The Tanks were going to put the fear of God
into the Boches, and the Cavalry would get their opportunity
at last. We passed a squadron of Lancers on the road. Oh yes,
they were massing for a break-through. Allenby knew what he
was up to all right. And our Divisional General had told someone that it would be a walk-over for the infantry this time.
    That afternoon I strolled out to inspect our old front-line
trenches. As usual they gave me a queer feeling; it would be
almost accurate to say that they fascinated me. Derelict ditches
as they now were, battalion after battalion had endured inten-
sities of experience in that intensified strip of territory. Night
after night the tea-dixies had been carried up that twisting
communication trench. Night after night sentries had stared
over sodden parapets until the sky reddened and the hostile territory emerged, familiar and yet foreign. Not a very
good sector to hold, I thought, observing how our cramped
trench system had been overlooked by the Germans. That

mile-and-a-bit back to Basseux hadn't been so easy a couple of months ago.

In peace-time the village must have been quite a pretty little place, and even now it wasn't very badly damaged. All our officers were billeted in a dilapidated white château, which I now explored until I was sitting with my feet out of the window of an attic. Down in the courtyard Ormand and Dunning and one or two others were playing cricket with a stump and a wooden ball, using an old brazier as a wicket. Wilmot had found a ramshackle piano from which he was extracting his favourite melodies. Pigeons fluttered around the red tiled roofs and cooed in the warm evening sunshine. Three yellow balloons were visible. Then the little Adjutant bustled across the courtyard with a bunch of papers in his hand. There was no time for relaxation in the orderly room, for after to-day we were under orders to move at the shortest notice. . . . Young Ormand shouted up at me, 'Come down and have a knock at the nets.'

The Battle of Arras began at 5.30 next morning. For two days we hung about the château, listening to the noise (of Military History being manufactured regardless of expense) and waiting for the latest rumours. With forced uneasy gaiety we talked loudly about the successes reported from the Line. 'Our objectives gained at Neuville-Vitasse', 'five thousand prisoners taken', and so on. But every one of us had something in his mind which he couldn't utter, even to his best friend.

Meanwhile the weather was misbehaving itself badly. Snow showers passed by on a bitterly cold wind, and I began an intimate battle in which a chill on the intestines got the better of me. It wasn't so easy to feel like a happy warrior turning his necessities to glorious gain, when doomed to go in company with gastritis, a sore throat, and several festering scratches on each hand. No more clean socks or handkerchiefs either. A big mail came in on Tuesday – the first we'd had for a week – and this kept us quiet for an interval of flimsy consolation. My only letter was from Aunt Evelyn, who apologized as usual for having so little to say. She had been reading *The Life of*

Disraeli – 'such a relief to get away from all these present-day horrors. What a wonderful man he was. Are you still in the Rest Camp? I do hope so.' She added that spring-cleaning had been going on vigorously, with the usual floods of conversation from the maids. . . . This didn't help my gastritis, which was getting beyond a joke. The M.O. wasn't back from leave yet, but one of his orderlies handed me an opium pill of such constipating omnipotence that my intestines were soon stabilized to a condition suitable for open warfare.

In the middle of Wednesday afternoon we were having an eleven-a-side single-brazier cricket match on a flat piece of ground in the château garden. The sun was shining between snow showers, and most of the men were watching from the grassy bank above. One of the Company Sergeant-Majors was playing a lively innings, though the ball was beginning to split badly. Then a whistle blew and the match ended abruptly. Less than an hour later the Battalion marched away from Basseux.

3

A heavy snowstorm set in soon after we started. A snowstorm on April 11th was the sort of thing that one expected in the War and it couldn't be classed as a major misfortune. Nevertheless we could have done without it, since we were marching away from all comfort and safety; greatcoats had been left behind and we had nothing but what we stood up in. As we slogged along narrow winding lanes the snow melted on the shiny waterproof sheets which kept the men uncomfortably warm. We were now in the devastated area; villages had been levelled to heaps of bricks; fruit trees, and even pollard-willows, had been hacked down, and there was still a chance that we might be the victims of a booby trap in the shape of a dynamite charge under a causeway. A signpost pointed to Blairville; but a couple of inches of snow was enough to blot out Blairville. The next village was Ficheux (the men called it 'Fish Hooks' – any joke being better than none in that snowstorm); but Ficheux wasn't there at all; it had vanished from the landscape.

The snow had stopped when, after marching eight miles, we bivouacked in the dregs of daylight by a sunken road near Mercatel, a place which offered no shelter except the humanity of its name. After dark I found my way into a small dug-out occupied by a Trench Mortar Sergeant-Major and two signallers who were working a field telephone. With Shirley (one of our Company officers) I considered myself lucky to be there, crouching by a brazier, while the Sergeant-Major regaled us, in omniscient tones, with rumours about the desperate fighting at Wancourt and Heninel, names which meant nothing to me. I dozed through the night without ever being unaware of the coke fumes from the brazier and the tick-tack of the telephone.

Daylight discovered us blear-eyed and (to abbreviate a contemporary phrase) 'fed up and far from home.' We got through the morning somehow and I issued some of my 'emergency Woodbines'. Rifle-cleaning and inspection was the only occupation possible. Early in the afternoon the Battalion moved on four miles to St Martin-Cojeul. The snow had melted, leaving much mud which rain made worse. St Martin was a demolished village about a mile behind the battle-line. As we entered it I noticed an English soldier lying by the road with a horribly smashed head; soon such sights would be too frequent to attract attention, but this first one was perceptibly unpleasant. At the risk of being thought squeamish or even unsoldierly, I still maintain that an ordinary human being has a right to be momentarily horrified by a mangled body seen on an afternoon walk, although people with sound common sense can always refute me by saying that life is full of gruesome sights and violent catastrophes. But I am no believer in wild denunciations of the War; I am merely describing my own experiences of it; and in 1917 I was only beginning to learn that life, for the majority of the population, is an unlovely struggle against unfair odds, culminating in a cheap funeral. Anyhow, the man with his head bashed in had achieved theoretical glory by dying for his country in the Battle of Arras, and we who marched past him had an excellent chance of following his example.

We took over an old German reserve trench (captured on Easter Monday). Company Headquarters was a sort of rabbit-hole, just wide enough to accommodate Leake, a tiny stove, and myself. Leake occupied himself in enlarging it with a rusty entrenching tool. When dusk was falling I went out to the underground dressing-station to get my festering fingers attended to. I felt an interloper, for the place was crowded with groaning wounded. As I made my way back to our trench a few shells exploded among the ruinous remains of brickwork. All this, I thought, is disgustingly unpleasant, but it doesn't really count as war experience. I knew that if I could get the better of my physical discomforts I should find the War intensely interesting. B Company hadn't arrived at the groaning stage yet; in fact, they were grimly cheerful, though they'd only had one meal that day and the next was to-morrow morning. Leake and I had one small slice of ration bacon between us; I was frizzling my fragment when it fell off the fork and disappeared into the stove. Regardless of my unfortunate fingers I retrieved and ate it with great relish.

The night was cold and sleep impossible, since there was no space to lie down in. Leake, however, had a talent for falling asleep in any position. Chiselling away at the walls by candle-light, I kept myself warm, and in a couple of hours I had scooped out sufficient space for the other two officers. They were a well contrasted couple. Rees was a garrulous and excitable little Welshman; it would be flattery to call him anything except uncouth, and he made no pretensions to being 'a gentleman'. But he was good-natured and moderately efficient. Shirley, on the other hand, had been educated at Winchester and the War had interrupted his first year at Oxford. He was a delicate-featured and fastidious young man, an only child, and heir to a comfortable estate in Flintshire. Rees rather got on our nerves with his table manners, and Shirley deprecated the way he licked his thumb when dealing the cards for their games of nap. But social incompatibilities were now merged in communal discomfort. Both of them were new to the line, so I felt that I ought to look after them, if possible. I noticed that Rees kept his courage up by talking incessantly and making jokes about the battle; while Shirley, true to the traditions of his class, simulated nonchalance, discussing with Leake (also an Oxford man) the comparative merits of Magdalen and Christ Church, or Balliol and New College. But he couldn't get the nonchalance into his eyes. . . . Both Shirley and Rees were killed before the autumn.

From our obsolete trench we looked toward the naked ground which rose to the ridge. Along that ridge ran the Hindenburg Line (a mile and a half away) from which new attacks were now being attempted. There was another attack next morning. Rees was detailed for an ammunition-carrying party, and he returned noisier than ever. It had been his first experience of shell-fire. Narrating his numerous escapes from hostile explosives, he continually invoked the name of the founder of his religion; now that it was all over he enjoyed the retrospective excitement, roaring with laughter while he told us how he and his men had flung themselves on their faces in the mud. Rees never minded making himself look ridiculous, and I began to feel that he was capable of taking care of himself. Shirley raised his eyebrows during the recital, evidently disapproving of such volubility and not at all sure that officers ought to throw themselves flat on their faces when shells burst. Later in the day I took him for a walk up the hill; I wanted to educate him in unpleasant sights. The wind had dropped and the sunset sky was mountainous with calm clouds. We inspected a tank which had got stuck in the mud while crossing a wide trench. We succeeded in finding this ungainly monster interesting. Higher up the hill the open ground was dotted with British dead. It was an unexpectedly tidy scene, since most of them had been killed by machine-gun fire. Stretcher-bearers had been identifying the bodies and had arranged them in happy warrior attitudes, hands crossed and heads pillowed on haversacks. Often the contents of a man's haversack were scattered around him. There were letters lying about; the pathos of those last letters from home was obvious enough. It

was a queer thing, I thought, that I should be taking a young
Oxford man for this conducted tour of a battlefield on a fine
April evening. Here we were, walking about in a sort of visible
fraction of the Roll of Honour, and my pupil was doing his
best to behave as if it were all quite ordinary and part of the
public-school tradition. He was being politely introduced to
the horrors of war, and he made no comment on them. Earlier
in the day an attack on Fontaine-les-Croiselles had fizzled out
in failure. Except for the intermittent chatter of machine-guns,
the country ahead of us was quiet. Then, somewhere beyond
the ridge, a huge explosion sent up a shapeless tower of yellow
vapour. I remarked sagely that a German dump had probably
been blown up. Shirley watched it intently as though the experience would be of use to him during future operations.

At five-thirty next morning our Brigade renewed the attack on
Fontaine-les-Croiselles, but we remained in reserve. Enveloped by the din of the bombardment I leaned my elbows on
the parapet and looked at the ridge. A glowering red sun was
rising; the low undulant hills were grey-blue and deeply shadowed; the landscape was full of gun flashes and drifting smoke.
It was a genuine battle picture, and I was aware of its angry
beauty. Not much more than a mile away, on the further side
of that menacing slope, lines of muttering men were waiting,
strained to an intolerable expectancy, until the whistles blew
and the barrage crept forward, and they stumbled across the
open with the good wishes of General Allenby and the bad
wishes of the machine-guns in the German strong-posts. Perhaps I tried to visualize their grim adventure. In my pocket I
had a copy of a recent *communiqué* (circulated for instructive
purposes) and I may as well quote it now. 'That night three
unsuccessful bombing attacks were made on the Tower at
Wancourt. During the Battalion relief next night the enemy
opened a heavy bombardment on the Tower and its immediate
vicinity, following it up with an attack which succeeded,
mainly owing to the relief being in progress. A local counter-
attack delivered by the incoming battalion failed owing to the
darkness, pouring rain, and lack of knowledge of the ground.

It was then decided that nothing could be done till daylight.'
The lesson to be drawn from this episode was, I think, that
lack of Artillery preparation is a mistake. . . . The Wancourt
Tower was only a couple of miles away on our left, so I felt
vaguely impressed by being so close to events which were, undoubtedly, of historic importance in the annals of the War.
And anyone who has been in the front line can amplify that
communiqué for himself.

4

On Saturday afternoon the order to move up took us by surprise. Two days of stagnation in the cramped little trench had
relaxed expectancy, which now renewed itself in our compact
preparations for departure. As usual on such occasions, the
Company Sergeant-Major was busier than anybody else. I
have probably said so before, but it cannot be too often
repeated that C.S.M.s were the hardest worked men in the
infantry; everything depended on them, and if anyone deserved
a K.C.B. it was a good C.S.M.

At 9 p.m. the Company fell in at the top of the ruined street
of St Martin. Two guides from the outgoing battalion awaited
us. We were to relieve some Northumberland Fusiliers in the
Hindenburg Trench – the companies going up independently.

It was a grey evening, dry and windless. The village of St
Martin was a shattered relic; but even in the devastated area
one could be conscious of the arrival of spring, and as I took
up my position in the rear of the moving column there was
something in the sober twilight which could remind me of April
evenings in England and the Butley cricket field where a few
of us had been having our first knock at the nets. The cricket
season had begun. . . . But the Company had left the shell-pitted
road and was going uphill across open ground. Already the
guides were making the pace too hot for the rear platoon; like
most guides they were inconveniently nimble owing to their
freedom from accoutrement, and insecurely confident that

they knew the way. The muttered message 'pass it along –
steady the pace in front' was accompanied by the usual muffled clinkings and rattlings of arms and equipment. Unwillingly
retarded, the guides led us into the deepening dusk. We hadn't
more than two miles to go, but gradually the guides grew
less authoritative. Several times they stopped to get their
bearings. Leake fussed and fumed and they became more
and more flurried. I began to suspect that our progress was
circular.

At a midnight halt the hill still loomed in front of us; the
guides confessed that they had lost their way, and Leake
decided to sit down and wait for daylight. (There were few
things more uncomfortable in the life of an officer than to be
walking in front of a party of men all of whom knew that he
was leading them in the wrong direction.) With Leake's permission I blundered experimentally into the gloom, fully
expecting to lose both myself and the Company. By a lucky
accident, I soon fell headlong into a sunken road and found
myself among a small party of Sappers who could tell me
where I was. It was a case of 'Please, can you tell me the way
to the Hindenburg Trench?' Congratulating myself on my
cleverness I took one of the Sappers back to poor benighted B
Company, and we were led to our Battalion rendezvous.

The rendezvous took some finding, since wrong map references had been issued by the Brigade Staff; but at last, after
many delays, the Companies filed along to their ordained (and
otherwise anathematized) positions.

We were at the end of a journey which had begun twelve
days before, when we started from Camp 13. Stage by stage,
we had marched to the life-denying region which from far
away had threatened us with the blink and growl of its bombardments. Now we were groping and stumbling along a deep
ditch to the place appointed for us in the zone of inhuman
havoc. There must have been some hazy moonlight, for I
remember the figures of men huddled against the sides of communication trenches; seeing them in some sort of ghastly glimmer (was it, perhaps, the diffused whiteness of a sinking flare
beyond the ridge?) I was doubtful whether they were asleep or

dead, for the attitudes of many were like death, grotesque and distorted. But this is nothing new to write about, you will say; just a weary company, squeezing past dead or drowsing men while it sloshes and stumbles to a front-line trench. Nevertheless that night relief had its significance for me, though in human experience it had been multiplied a millionfold. I, a single human being with my little stock of earthly experience in my head, was entering once again the veritable gloom and disaster of the thing called Armageddon. And I saw it then, as I see it now – a dreadful place, a place of horror and desolation which no imagination could have invented. Also it was a place where a man of strong spirit might know himself utterly powerless against death and destruction, and yet stand up and defy gross darkness and stupefying shell-fire, discovering in himself the invincible resistance of an animal or an insect, and an endurance which he might, in after days, forget or disbelieve.

Anyhow, there I was, leading that little procession of Flintshire Fusiliers many of whom had never seen a front-line trench before. At that juncture they asked no compensation for their efforts except a mug of hot tea. The tea would have been a miracle, and we didn't get it till next morning, but there was some comfort in the fact that it wasn't raining.

It was nearly four o'clock when we found ourselves in the Hindenburg Main Trench. After telling me to post the sentries, Leake disappeared down some stairs to the Tunnel (which will be described later on). The Company we were relieving had already departed, so there was no one to give me any information. At first I didn't even know for certain that we were in the Front Line. The trench was a sort of gully, deep, wide, and unfinished looking. The sentries had to clamber up a bank of loose earth before they could see over the top. Our Company was only about eighty strong and its sector was fully 600 yards. The distance between the sentry-posts made me aware of our inadequacy in that wilderness. I had no right to feel homeless, but I did; and if I had needed to be reminded of my forlorn situation as a living creature I could have done it merely by thinking of a Field Cashier. Fifty franc notes were comfortable things, but they were no earthly use up here, and the words

'Field Cashier' would have epitomized my remoteness from snugness and security, and from all assurance that I should be alive and kicking the week after next. But it would soon be Sunday morning; such ideas weren't wholesome, and there was a certain haggard curiosity attached to the proceedings; combined with the self-dramatizing desperation which enabled a good many of us to worry our way through much worse emergencies than mine.

When I had posted the exhausted sentries, with as much cheeriness as I could muster, I went along to look for the Company on our left. Rather expecting to find one of our own companies, I came round a corner to a place where the trench was unusually wide. There I found myself among a sort of panic party which I was able to identify as a platoon (thirty or forty strong). They were jostling one another in their haste to get through a cavernous doorway, and as I stood astonished one of them breathlessly told me that 'the Germans were coming over'. Two officers were shepherding them downstairs and before I'd had time to think the whole lot had vanished. The Battalion they belonged to was one of those amateur ones which were at such a disadvantage owing to lack of discipline and the absence of trained N.C.O.s. Anyhow, their behaviour seemed to indicate that the Tunnel in the Hindenburg Trench was having a lowering effect on their *morale*.

Out in no-man's-land there was no sign of any German activity. The only remarkable thing was the unbroken silence. I was in a sort of twilight, for there was a moony glimmer in the low-clouded sky; but the unknown territory in front was dark, and I stared out at it like a man looking from the side of a ship. Returning to my own sector I met a runner with a verbal message from Battalion H.Q. B Company's front was to be thoroughly patrolled at once. Realizing the futility of sending any of my few spare men out on patrol (they'd been walking about for seven hours and were dead beat) I lost my temper, quietly and inwardly. Shirley and Rees were nowhere to be seen and it wouldn't have been fair to send them out, inexperienced as they were. So I stumped along to our right-flank post, told them to pass it along that a patrol was going out from right to left, and then started sulkily out for a solitary stroll in no-man's-land. I felt more annoyed with Battalion Headquarters than with the enemy. There was no wire in front of the trench, which was, of course, constructed for people facing the other way. I counted my steps; 200 steps straight ahead; then I began to walk the presumptive 600 steps to the left. But it isn't easy to count your steps in the dark among shell-holes, and after a problematic 400 I lost confidence in my automatic pistol, which I was grasping in my right-hand breeches pocket. Here I am, I thought, alone out in this god-forsaken bit of ground, with quite a good chance of bumping into a Boche strong-post. Apparently there was only one reassuring action which I could perform; so I expressed my opinion of the War by relieving myself (for it must be remembered that there are other reliefs beside Battalion reliefs). I insured my sense of direction by placing my pistol on the ground with its muzzle pointing the way I was going. Feeling less lonely and afraid, I finished my patrol without having met so much as a dead body, and regained the trench exactly opposite our left-hand post, after being huskily challenged by an irresolute sentry, who, as I realized at the time, was the greatest danger I had encountered. It was now just beginning to be more daylight than darkness, and when I stumbled down a shaft to the underground trench I left the sentries shivering under a red and rainy-looking sky.

There were fifty steps down the shaft; the earthy smell of that triumph of Teutonic military engineering was strongly suggestive of appearing in the Roll of Honour and being buried until the Day of Judgment. Dry-mouthed and chilled to the bone, I lay in a wire-netting bunk and listened to the dismal snorings of my companions. Along the Tunnel the air blew deathly cold and seasoned with mephitic odours. In vain I envied the snorers; but I was getting accustomed to lack of sleep, and three hours later I was gulping some peculiar tea with morose enjoyment. Owing to the scarcity of water (which had to be brought up by the Transport who were eight miles back, at Blairville) washing wasn't possible; but I contrived a refreshing shave, utilizing the dregs of my tea.

By ten o'clock I was above ground again, in charge of a fatigue party. We went half-way back to St Martin, to an ammunition dump, whence we carried up boxes of trench mortar bombs. I carried a box myself, as the conditions were vile and it seemed the only method of convincing the men that it had to be done. We were out nearly seven hours; it rained all day and the trenches were a morass of glue-like mud. The unmitigated misery of that carrying party was a typical infantry experience of discomfort without actual danger. Even if the ground had been dry the boxes would have been too heavy for most of the men; but we were lucky in one way; the wet weather was causing the artillery to spend an inactive Sunday. It was a yellow corpse-like day, more like November than April, and the landscape was desolate and treeless. What we were doing was quite unexceptional; millions of soldiers endured the same sort of thing and got badly shelled into the bargain. Nevertheless I can believe that my party, staggering and floundering under its loads, would have made an impressive picture of 'Despair'. The background, too, was appropriate. We were among the débris of the intense bombardment of ten days before, for we were passing along and across the Hindenburg Outpost Trench, with its belt of wire (fifty yards deep in places); here and there these rusty jungles had been flattened by tanks. The Outpost Trench was about 200 yards from the Main Trench, which was now our front line. It had been solidly made, ten feet deep, with timbered fire-steps, splayed sides, and timbered steps at intervals to front and rear and to machine-gun emplacements. Now it was wrecked as though by earthquake and eruption. Concrete strong-posts were smashed and tilted sideways; everywhere the chalky soil was pocked and pitted with huge shell-holes; and wherever we looked the mangled effigies of the dead were our *memento mori*. Shell-twisted and dismembered, the Germans maintained the violent attitudes in which they had died. The British had mostly been killed by bullets or bombs, so they looked more resigned. But I can remember a pair of hands (nationality unknown) which protruded from the soaked ashen soil like the roots of a tree turned upside down; one hand seemed to be pointing at the sky with an accusing gesture. Each time I passed that place the protest of those fingers became more expressive of an appeal to God in defiance of those who made the War. Who made the War? I laughed hysterically as the thought passed through my mud-stained mind. But I only laughed mentally, for my box of Stokes gun ammunition left me no breath to spare for an angry guffaw. And the dead were the dead; this was no time to be pitying them or asking silly questions about their outraged lives. Such sights must be taken for granted, I thought, as I gasped and slithered and stumbled with my disconsolate crew. Floating on the surface of the flooded trench was the mask of a human face which had detached itself from the skull.

5

Plastered with mud and soaked to the skin, the fatigue-party clumped down the steps to the Tunnel. The carrying job was finished; but a stimulating surprise awaited me, for Leake was just back from Battalion H.Q. (somewhere along the Tunnel) and he breezily informed me that I'd been detailed to take command of a hundred bombers in the attack which had been arranged for next morning. 'Twenty-five bombers from each Company; you're to act as reserve for the Cameronians,' he remarked. I stared at him over my mug of reviving but trench-flavoured tea (made with chlorinated water) and asked him to tell me some more. He said: 'Well, they're a bit hazy about it at Headquarters, but the General is frightfully keen on our doing an underground attack along the Tunnel, as well as along the main trench up above. You've got to go and discuss the tactical situation with one of the Company commanders up in the Front Line on our right.' All that I knew about the tactical situation was that if one went along the Tunnel one arrived at a point where a block had been made by blowing it in. On the other side one bumped into the Germans. Above ground there was a barrier and the situation was similar. Bombing along a

Tunnel in the dark. . . . Had the War Office issued a text book
on the subject? . . . I lit my pipe, but failed to enjoy it, probably
because the stewed tea had left such a queer taste in my mouth.

Ruminating on the comfortless responsibility imposed on
me by this enterprise, I waited until nightfall. Then a superbly
cheerful little guide bustled me along a maze of waterlogged
ditches until I found myself in a small dug-out with some
friendly Scotch officers and a couple of flame-wagging candles. The dug-out felt more like old times than the Hindenburg Tunnel, but the officers made me feel incompetent and
uninformed, for they were loquacious about local trench
topography which meant nothing to my newly-arrived mind.
So I puffed out my Military Cross ribbon (the dug-out contained two others), nodded my head knowingly, and took an
acquiescent share in the discussion of the strategic situation.
Details of organization were offered me and I made a few
smudgy notes. The Cams didn't think that there was much
chance of my party being called on to support them, and they
were hoping that the underground attack would be eliminated
from operation orders.

I emerged from the desperation jollity of their little den with
only a blurred notion of what it was all about. The objective
was to clear the trench for 500 yards while other battalions
went over the top on our left to attack Fontaine-les-Croiselles.
But I was, at the best of times, only an opportunist officer;
technical talk in the Army always made me feel mutely ineffi-
cient. And now I was floundering home in the dark to organize
my command, put something plausible on paper, and take it
along to the Adjutant. If only I could consult the Doctor, I
thought; for he was back from leave, though I hadn't seen him
yet. It seemed to me, in my confused and exhausted condition,
that I was at a crisis in my military career; and, as usual, my
main fear was that I should make a fool of myself. The idea of
making a fool of oneself in that murderous mix-up now
appears to me rather a ludicrous one; for I see myself merely as
a blundering flustered little beetle; and if someone happens to
put his foot on a beetle, it is unjust to accuse the unlucky insect
of having made a fool of itself. When I got back to Leake and

Rees and Shirley I felt so lost and perplexed that I went straight on to Battalion H.Q.

The Tunnel was a few inches higher than a tall man walking upright; it was fitted with bunks and recessed rooms; in places it was crowded with men of various units, but there were long intervals of unwholesome-smelling solitude. Prying my way along with an electric torch, I glimpsed an assortment of vague shapes, boxes, tins, fragments of broken furniture and frowsy mattresses. It seemed a long way to Headquarters, and the Tunnel was memorable but not fortifying to a fatigued explorer who hadn't slept for more than an hour at a stretch or taken his clothes off since last Tuesday. Once, when I tripped and recovered myself by grabbing the wall, my tentative patch of brightness revealed somebody half hidden under a blanket. Not a very clever spot to be taking a nap, I thought as I stooped to shake him by the shoulder. He refused to wake up, so I gave him a kick. 'God blast you, where's Battalion Headquarters?' My nerves were on edge; and what right had he to be having a good sleep, when I never seemed to get five minutes' rest? . . . Then my beam settled on the livid face of a dead German whose fingers still clutched the blackened gash on his neck. . . . Stumbling on, I could only mutter to myself that this was really a bit too thick. (That, however, was an exaggeration; there is nothing remarkable about a dead body in a European War, or a squashed beetle in a cellar.) At Headquarters I found the Adjutant alone, worried and preoccupied with clerical work. He had worked in an office, at accountancy, I believe, before the War; and now most of his fighting was done in writing, though he had served his apprenticeship as a brave and indefatigable platoon commander. He told me that the underground attack had been washed out by a providential counter-order from Division, and asked me to send my organization scheme along as soon as possible. 'Right-O!' I replied, and groped my way back again feeling the reverse of my reply. By a stroke of luck I discovered Ralph Wilmot, sitting by himself in a small recessed room – his dark hair smoothly brushed and his countenance pensive but unperturbed. He might conceivably have been twiddling a liqueur glass in a Piccadilly restaurant. Unfortunately he had no liquid refreshment to offer, but his philosophic way of greeting me was a consolation and in him I confided my dilemma. With an understanding air he assumed his monocle, deliberated for a while, snuffed the candle wick, and wrote out an authoritative-looking document headed 'Organization of F.F. Parties'. The gist of it was '15 Bombers (each carrying 5 grenades). 5 Carriers (also act as bayonet men). 1 Full Rank.' There wasn't much in it, he remarked, as he appended 'a little bit of skite about consolidation and defensive flanks'. It certainly looked simple enough when it was done, though I had been at my wits' end about it.

While he was fixing up my future for me I gazed around and thought what a queer refuge I'd found for what might possibly be my final night on earth. Dug-out though it was, the narrow chamber contained a foggy mirror and a clock. The clock wasn't ticking, but its dumb face stared at me, an idiot reminder of real rooms and desirable domesticity. Outside the doorless doorway people were continually passing in both directions with a sound of shuffling feet and mumbling voices. I caught sight of a red-capped Staff Officer, and a party of sappers carrying picks and shovels. The Tunnel was a sort of highway and the night had brought a considerable congestion of traffic. When we'd sent my document along to the Adjutant there was nothing more to be done except sit and wait for operation orders. It was now about ten o'clock.

As evidence of my own soldierly qualities I would like to be able to declare that we eagerly discussed every aspect of the situation as regards next morning's attack. But the truth is that we said nothing at all about it. The thing had to be attempted and there was an end of it (until zero hour). The Brigadier and his Staff (none too bright at map-references) were hoping to satisfy (vicariously) General Whincop (who'd got an unpopular bee in his bonnet about the Rum Ration, and had ordered an impossible raid, two months ago, which had been prevented by a providential thaw and caused numerous deaths in a subsequently sacrificed battalion).

Whincop was hoping to satisfy the Corps Commander, of whom we knew nothing at all, except that he had insulted our Colonel on the Doullens road. The Corps Commander hoped to satisfy the Army Commander, who had as usual informed us that we were 'pursuing a beaten enemy', and who had brought the Cavalry up for a 'break-through'. (It is worth mentioning that the village which was now our Division's objective was still held by the Germans eight months afterwards.) And the Army Commander, I suppose, was in telephonic communication with the Commander-in-Chief, who, with one eye on Marshal Foch, was hoping to satisfy his King and Country. Such being the case, Wilmot and myself were fully justified in leaving the situation to the care of the military caste who were making the most of their Great Opportunity for obtaining medal-ribbons and reputations for leadership; and if I am being caustic and captious about them I can only plead the need for a few minutes' post-war retaliation. Let the Staff write their own books about the Great War, say I. The Infantry were biased against them, and their authentic story will be read with interest.

As for our conversation between ten o'clock and midnight (when my operation orders arrived from the Adjutant) I suppose it was a form of drug, since it was confined to pleasant retrospections of peace. Wilmot was well acquainted with my part of the world and he'd come across many of our local worthies. So we were able to make a little tour of the Kentish Weald and the Sussex border, as though on a couple of mental bicycles. In imagination we cycled along on a fine summer afternoon, passing certain milestones which will always be inseparable from my life history. Outside Squire Maundle's park gate we shared a distinct picture of his angular attitudes while he addressed his golf-ball among the bell-tinklings and baaings of sheep on the sunny slopes above Amblehurst (always followed by a taciturn black retriever). Much has been asserted about the brutalized condition of mind to which soldiers were reduced by life in the Front Line; I do not deny this, but I am inclined to suggest that there was a proportionate

amount of simple-minded sentimentality. As far as I was concerned, no topic could be too homely for the trenches.

Thus, while working parties and machine-gunners filed past
the door with hollow grumbling voices, our private recess in
the Hindenburg Tunnel was precariously infused with evoca-
tions of rural England and we challenged our surroundings
with remembrances of parish names and farm-houses with
friendly faces. A cottage garden was not an easy idea to recover
convincingly. . . . Bees among yellow wall-flowers on a warm
afternoon. The smell of an apple orchard in autumn. . . . Such
details were beyond our evocation. But they were implied
when I mentioned Squire Maundle in his four-wheeled dog-
cart, rumbling along the Dumbridge Road to attend a County
Council Meeting.

'*Secret.* The Bombing Parties of 25 men will rendezvous at
2.30 a.m. to-morrow morning, 16th inst. in shafts near C Coy.
H.Q. The greatest care will be taken that each separate Company Party keeps to one side of the Shaft and that the Dump of
Bombs be in the trench at the head of these shafts, suitably
split. The necessity of keeping absolute silence must be
impressed on all men. These parties (under 2nd Lt. Sherston)
will come under the orders of O.C. Cameronians at ZERO
minus 10. Lt. Dunning and 2 orderlies will act liaison and
report to O.C. Cameronians at ZERO minus 5. While the parties are in the shaft they must keep a free passage way clear for
runners, etc.'

Such was the document which (had I been less fortunate)
would have been my passport to the Stygian shore. In the
meantime, with another two hours to sit through, we carried
on with our world without end conversation. We were, I think,
on the subject of Canterbury Cricket Week when my watch
warned me that I must be moving on. As I got up from the
table on which we'd been leaning our elbows, a blurred version of my face looked at me from the foggy mirror with an
effect of clairvoyance. Hoping that this was an omen of survival, I went along to the rendezvous-shaft and satisfied myself

that the Bombing Parties were sitting on the stairs in a bone-chilling draught, with my two subordinate officers in attendance.

Zero hour was at 3 a.m. and the prefatory uproar was already rumbling overhead. Having tightened my mud-caked puttees and put my tie straight (there was no rule against wearing a tie in an attack) diffidently I entered the Cameronian H.Q. dug-out, which was up against the foot of the stairs. I was among strangers, and Zero minus 10 wasn't a time for conversational amenities, so I sat self-consciously while the drumming din upstairs was doing its utmost to achieve a reassuring climax. Three o'clock arrived. The tick-tacking telephone-orderly in a corner received a message that the attack had started. They were over the barrier now, and bombing up the trench. The Cameronian Colonel and his Adjutant conversed in the constrained undertones of men who expect disagreeable news. The Colonel was a fine-looking man, but his well-disciplined face was haggard with anxiety. Dunning sat in another corner, serious and respectful, with his natural jollity ready to come to the surface whenever it was called for.

At the end of twenty minutes' tension the Colonel exclaimed abruptly, 'Good God, I wish I knew how they're doing!' . . . And then, as if regretting his manifestation of feeling, 'No harm in having a bit of cake, anyhow.' There was a large home-made cake on the table. I was offered a slice, which I munched with embarrassment. I felt that I had no business to be there at all, let alone helping to make a hole in the Colonel's cake, which was a jolly good one. I couldn't believe that these competent officers were counting on me to be of any use to them if I were required to take an active part in the proceedings upstairs. Then the telephone-orderly announced that communication with Captain Macnair's headquarters had broken down; after that the suspense continued monotonously. I had been sitting there about two and a half hours when it became evident that somebody was descending the steps in a hurry. H.Q. must have kept its cooking utensils on the stairs, for the visitor arrived outside the doorway in a clattering cascade of pots and pans. He was a breathless and dishevelled

sergeant, who blurted out an incoherent statement about their
having been driven back after advancing a short distance.
While the Colonel questioned him in a quiet and controlled
voice I rose stiffly to my feet. I don't remember saying anything or receiving any orders; but I felt that the Cameronian
officers were sensitive to the delicacy of my situation. There
was no question of another slice of home-made cake. Their
unuttered comment was, 'Well, old chap, I suppose you're for
it now.'

Leaving them to get what satisfaction they could from the
sergeant's story, I grinned stupidly at Dunning, popped my
helmet on my head, and made for the stairway. It must have
been a relief to be doing something definite at last, for without
pausing to think I started off with the section of twenty-five
who were at the top of the stairs. Sergeant Baldock got them
on the move at once, although they were chilled and drowsy
after sitting there for over three hours. None of them would
have been any the worse for a mouthful of rum at that particular moment. In contrast to the wearisome candlelight of the
lower regions, the outdoor world was bright and breezy; animated also by enough noise to remind me that some sort of
battle was going on. As we bustled along, the flustered little
contingent at my heels revived from its numbness. I had no
idea what I was going to do; our destination was in the brain
of the stooping Cameronian guide who trotted ahead of me.
On the way we picked up a derelict Lewis gun, which I thought
might come in handy though there was no ammunition with
it. At the risk of being accused of 'taking the wrong half of the
conversation' (a favourite phrase of Aunt Evelyn's) I must say
that I felt quite confident. (Looking back on that emergency
from my arm-chair, I find some difficulty in believing that I
was there at all.) For about ten minutes we dodged and stumbled up a narrow winding trench. The sun was shining; large
neutral clouds voyaged willingly with the wind; I felt intensely
alive and rather out of breath. Suddenly we came into the main
trench, and where it was widest we met the Cameronians. I
must have picked up a bomb on the way, for I had one in my
hand when I started my conversation with young Captain

Macnair. Our encounter was more absurd than impressive.
Macnair and his exhausted men were obviously going in the
wrong direction, and I was an incautious newcomer. Consequently I had the advantage of him while he told me that the
Germans were all round them and they'd run out of bombs.
Feeling myself to be, for the moment, an epitome of Flintshire
infallibility, I assumed an air of jaunty unconcern; tossing my
bomb carelessly from left hand to right and back again, I
inquired, 'But where *are* the Germans?' – adding 'I can't see
any of them.' This effrontery had its effect (though for some
reason I find it difficult to describe this scene without disliking
my own behaviour). The Cameronian officers looked around
them and recovered their composure. Resolved to show them
what intrepid reinforcements we were, I assured Macnair that
he needn't worry any more and we'd soon put things straight.
I then led my party past his, halted them, and went up the
trench with Sergeant Baldock – an admirably impassive little
man who never ceased to behave like a perfectly trained and
confidential man-servant. After climbing over some sort of
barricade, we went about fifty yards without meeting anyone.
Observing a good many Mills' bombs lying about in little
heaps, I sent Baldock back to have them collected and carried
further up the trench. Then, with an accelerated heart beat, I
went round the corner by myself. Unexpectedly, a small man
was there, standing with his back to me, stockstill and watchful, a haversack of bombs slung over his left shoulder. I saw
that he was a Cameronian corporal; we did not speak. I also
carried a bag of bombs; we went round the next bay. There my
adventurous ardour experienced a sobering shock. A fair-
haired Scotch private was lying at the side of the trench in a
pool of his own blood. His face was grey and serene, and his
eyes stared emptily at the sky. A few yards further on the body
of a German officer lay crumpled up and still. The wounded
Cameronian made me feel angry, and I slung a couple of
bombs at our invisible enemies, receiving in reply an egg-
bomb, which exploded harmlessly behind me. After that I
went bombing busily along, while the corporal (more artful
and efficient than I was) dodged in and out of the saps –

a precaution which I should have forgotten. Between us we
created quite a demonstration of offensiveness, and in this
manner arrived at our objective without getting more than a
few glimpses of retreating field-grey figures. I had no idea
where our objective was, but the corporal informed me that
we had reached it, and he seemed to know his business. This,
curiously enough, was the first time either of us had spoken
since we met.

The whole affair had been so easy that I felt like pushing
forward until we bumped into something more definite. But
the corporal had a cooler head and he advised discretion. I
told him to remain where he was and started to explore a narrow sap on the left side of the trench. (Not that it matters
whether it was on the left side or the right, but it appears to be
the only detail I can remember; and when all is said and done,
the War was mainly a matter of holes and ditches.) What I
expected to find along that sap, I can't say. Finding nothing, I
stopped to listen. There seemed to be a lull in the noise of the
attack along the line. A few machine-guns tapped, spiteful and
spasmodic. High up in the fresh blue sky an aeroplane droned
and glinted. I thought what a queer state of things it all was,
and then decided to take a peep at the surrounding country.
This was a mistake which ought to have put an end to my ter-
restrial adventures, for no sooner had I popped my silly head
out of the sap than I felt a stupendous blow in the back between
my shoulders. My first notion was that a bomb had hit me
from behind, but what had really happened was that I had
been sniped from in front. Anyhow my foolhardy attitude
toward the Second Battle of the Scarpe had been instanta-
neously altered for the worse. I leant against the side of the sap
and shut my eyes. . . . When I reopened them Sergeant Baldock was beside me, discreet and sympathetic, and to my surprise I discovered that I wasn't dead. He helped me back to the
trench, gently investigated my wound, put a field-dressing on
it, and left me sitting there while he went to bring up some men.

After a short spell of being deflated and sorry for myself,
I began to feel rabidly heroical again, but in a slightly different style, since I was now a wounded hero, with my arm in

a superfluous sling. All my seventy-five men were now on the scene (minus a few who had been knocked out by our own shells, which were dropping short). I can remember myself talking volubly to a laconic Stokes-gun officer, who had appeared from nowhere with his weapon and a couple of assistants. I felt that I must make one more onslaught before I turned my back on the War and my only idea was to collect all available ammunition and then renew the attack while the Stokes-gun officer put up an enthusiastic barrage. It did not occur to me that anything else was happening on Allenby's Army Front except my own little show. My over-strained nerves had wrought me up to such a pitch of excitement that I was ready for any suicidal exploit. This convulsive energy might have been of some immediate value had there been any objective for it. But there was none; and before I had time to inaugurate anything rash and irrelevant Dunning arrived to relieve me. His air of competent unconcern sobered me down, but I was still inflamed with the offensive spirit and my impetuosity was only snuffed out by a written order from the Cameronian Colonel, who forbade any further advance owing to the attack having failed elsewhere. My ferocity fizzled out then, and I realized that I had a raging thirst. As I was starting my return journey (I must have known then that nothing could stop me till I got to England) the M.O. came sauntering up the trench with the detached demeanour of a gentle botanist. 'Trust him to be up there having a look round,' I thought. Within four hours of leaving it I was back in the Tunnel.

Back at Battalion Headquarters in the Tunnel I received from our Colonel and Adjutant generous congratulations on my supposedly dashing display. In the emergency candlelight of that draughty cellar recess I bade them good-bye with voluble assurances that I should be back in a few weeks; but I was so over-strained and excited that my assurances were noises rather than notions. Probably I should have been equally elated without my wound; but if unwounded, I'd have been still up at the Block with the bombing parties. In the meantime, nothing that happened to me could relieve Battalion H.Q. of its burdens. The

Adjutant would go on till he dropped, for he had an inexhaust-
ible sense of duty. I never saw him again; he was killed in the
autumn up at Ypres. . . . I would like to be able to remember
that I smiled grimly and departed reticently. But the 'bombing
show' had increased my self-importance, and my exodus from
the Front Line was a garrulous one. A German bullet had passed
through me leaving a neat hole near my right shoulder-blade
and this patriotic perforation had made a different man of me. I
now looked at the War, which had been a monstrous tyrant,
with liberated eyes. For the time being I had regained my right
to call myself a private individual.

The first stage of my return journey took me to the Advanced
Dressing Station at Henin. My servant went with me, carrying
my haversack. He was a quiet clumsy middle-aged man who
always did his best and never complained. While we picked
our way along the broken ground of Henin Hill I continued
talkative, halting now and again to recover breath and take a
last stare at the blighted slope where yesterday I had stumbled
to and fro with my working party.

The sky was now overcast and the landscape grey and derelict. The activities of the attack had subsided, and we seemed
to be walking in a waste land where dead men had been left
out in the rain after being killed for no apparent purpose. Here
and there, figures could be seen moving towards the Dressing
Station, some of them carrying stretchers.

It was the mid-day stagnation which usually followed an
early morning attack. The Dressing Station was a small underground place crowded with groaning wounded. Two doctors
were doing what they could for men who had paid a heavy
price for their freedom. My egocentricity diminished among
all that agony. I remember listening to an emotional padre
who was painfully aware that he could do nothing except
stand about and feel sympathetic. The consolations of the
Church of England weren't much in demand at an Advance
Dressing Station. I was there myself merely to go through the
formality of being labelled 'walking wounded'. I was told to
go on to a place called 'B. Echelon', which meant another three
miles of muddy walking. Beat to the world, I reached B.

Echelon, and found our Quartermaster in a tent with several officers newly arrived from the Base and one or two back from leave. Stimulated by a few gulps of whisky and water, I renewed my volubility and talked nineteen to the dozen until the kind Quartermaster put me into the mess-cart which carried me to a cross road where I waited for a motor bus. There, after a long wait, I shook hands with my servant, and the handshake seemed to epitomize my good-bye to the Second Battalion. I thanked him for looking after me so well; but one couldn't wish a man luck when he was going back to the Hindenburg Trench. It may be objected that my attitude toward the Western Front was too intimate; but this was a question of two human beings, one of whom was getting out of it comfortably while the other went back to take his chance in the world's worst war. . . . In the bus, wedged among 'walking wounded', I was aware that I had talked quite enough. For an hour and a half we bumped and swayed along ruined roads till we came to the Casualty Clearing Station at Warlencourt. It was seven o'clock and all I got that night was a cup of Bovril and an anti-tetanus injection.

The place was overcrowded with bad cases and I had to wait until after midnight for a bed. I remember sitting in a chair listening to the rain pelting on the roof of the tent and the wailing of a wintry wind. I was too exhausted to sleep; my head had lost control of its thoughts, which continued to re-echo my good-bye garrulities; the injection had made me feel chilly and queer, and my wound began to be painful. But I was able to feel sorry for 'the poor old Battalion' (which was being relieved that night) and to be thankful for my own lucky escape.

What I'd been through was nothing compared with the sort of thing that many soldiers endured over and over again; nevertheless I condoled with myself on having had no end of a bad time.

Next afternoon a train (with 500 men and 35 officers on board) conveyed me to a Base Hospital. My memories of that train are strange and rather terrible, for it carried a cargo of

men in whose minds the horrors they had escaped from were
still vitalized and violent. Many of us still had the caked mud
of the war zone on our boots and clothes, and every bandaged
man was accompanied by his battle experience. Although
many of them talked lightly and even facetiously about it,
there was an aggregation of enormities in the atmosphere of
that train. I overheard some slightly wounded officers who
were excitedly remembering their adventures up at Wancourt,
where they'd been bombed out of a trench in the dark. Their
jargoning voices mingled with the rumble and throb of the
train as it journeyed – so safely and sedately – through the
environing gloom. The Front Line was behind us; but it could
lay its hand on our hearts, though its bludgeoning reality diminished with every mile. It was as if we were pursued by the
Arras Battle which had now become a huge and horrible idea.
We might be boastful or sagely reconstructive about our experience, in accordance with our different characters. But our
minds were still out of breath and our inmost thoughts in disorderly retreat from bellowing darkness and men dying out in
shell-holes under the desolation of returning daylight. We were
the survivors; few among us would ever tell the truth to our
friends and relations in England. We were carrying something
in our heads which belonged to us alone, and to those we had
left behind us in the battle. There were dying men, too, on
board that Red Cross train, men dying for their country in comparative comfort.

We reached our destination after midnight, and the next
day I was able to write in my diary: 'I am still feeling warlike
and quite prepared to go back to the Battalion in a few weeks;
I am told that my wound will be healed in a fortnight. The
doctor here says I am a lucky man as the bullet missed my jug-
ular vein and spine by a fraction of an inch. I know it would be
better for me not to go back to England, where I should probably be landed for at least three months and then have all the
hell of returning again in July or August.' But in spite of my
self-defensive scribble I was in London on Friday evening, and
by no means sorry to be carried through the crowd of patriotic

spectators at Charing Cross Station. My stretcher was popped into an ambulance which took me to a big hospital at Denmark Hill. At Charing Cross a woman handed me a bunch of flowers and a leaflet by the Bishop of London who earnestly advised me to lead a clean life and attend Holy Communion.

PART NINE

HOSPITAL AND CONVALESCENCE

1

The first few days were like lying in a boat. Drifting, drifting, I watched the high sunlit windows or the firelight that flickered and glowed on the ceiling when the ward was falling asleep. Outside the hospital a late spring was invading the home-service world. Trees were misty green and sometimes I could hear a blackbird singing. Even the screech and rumble of electric trams was a friendly sound; trams meant safety; the troops in the trenches thought about trams with affection. With an exquisite sense of languor and release I lifted my hand to touch the narcissi by my bed. They were symbols of an immaculate spirit – creatures whose faces knew nothing of War's demented language.

For a week, perhaps, I could dream that for me the War was over, because I'd got a neat hole through me and the nurse with her spongings forbade me to have a bath. But I soon emerged from my mental immunity; I began to think; and my thoughts warned me that my second time out in France had altered my outlook (if such a confused condition of mind could be called an outlook). I began to feel that it was my privilege to be bitter about my war experiences; and my attitude toward civilians implied that they couldn't understand and that it was no earthly use trying to explain things to them. Visitors were, of course, benevolent and respectful; my wound was adequate evidence that I'd 'been in the thick of it', and I allowed myself to hint at heroism and its attendant horrors. But as might have been expected my behaviour varied with my various visitors; or rather it would have done so had my visitors been more various. My inconsistencies might become tedious if tabulated

collectively, so I will confine myself to the following imaginary
instances.

Some Senior Officer under whom I'd served: Modest, politely
subordinate, strongly imbued with the 'spirit of the Regiment'
and quite ready to go out again. 'Awfully nice of you to come
and see me, sir.' Feeling that I ought to jump out of bed and
salute, and that it would be appropriate and pleasant to introduce him to 'some of my people' (preferably of impeccable social
status). Willingness to discuss active service technicalities and
revive memories of shared front-line experience.

Middle-aged or elderly Male Civilian: Tendency (in response
to sympathetic gratitude for services rendered to King and
Country) to assume haggard facial aspect of one who had 'been
through hell'. Inclination to wish that my wound was a bit worse
than it actually was, and have nurses hovering round with discreet reminders that my strength mustn't be overtaxed. Inability
to reveal anything crudely horrifying to civilian sensibilities.
'Oh yes, I'll be out there again by the autumn.' (Grimly wan
reply to suggestions that I was now honourably qualified for a
home-service job.) Secret antagonism to all uncomplimentary
references to the German Army.

Charming Sister of Brother Officer: Jocular, talkative, debonair, and diffidently heroic. Wishful to be wearing all possible medal-ribbons on pyjama jacket. Able to furnish a bright
account of her brother (if still at the front) and suppressing all
unpalatable facts about the War. 'Jolly decent of you to blow
in and see me.'

Hunting Friend (a few years above Military Service Age):
Deprecatory about sufferings endured at the front. Tersely
desirous of hearing all about last season's sport. 'By Jingo, that
must have been a nailing good gallop!' Jokes about the Germans, as if throwing bombs at them was a tolerable substitute
for fox-hunting. A good deal of guffawing (mitigated by
remembrance that I'd got a bullet hole through my lung). Optimistic anticipations of next season's Opening Meet and an
early termination of hostilities on all fronts.

Nevertheless my supposed reactions to any one of these
hypothetical visitors could only be temporary. When alone with

my fellow patients I was mainly disposed toward self-pitying estrangement from everyone except the troops in the Front Line. (Casualties didn't count as tragic unless dead or badly maimed.)

When Aunt Evelyn came up to London to see me I felt properly touched by her reticent emotion; embitterment against civilians couldn't be applied to her. But after she had gone I resented her gentle assumption that I had done enough and could now accept a safe job. I wasn't going to be messed about like that, I told myself. Yet I knew that the War was unescapable. Sooner or later I should be sent back to the Front Line, which was the only place where I could be any use. A cushy wound wasn't enough to keep me out of it.

I couldn't be free from the War; even this hospital ward was full of it, and every day the oppression increased. Outwardly it was a pleasant place to be lazy in. Morning sunshine slanted through the tall windows, brightening the grey-green walls and the forty beds. Daffodils and tulips made spots of colour under three red-draped lamps which hung from the ceiling. Some officers lay humped in bed, smoking and reading newspapers; others loafed about in dressing-gowns, going to and from the washing room where they scraped the bristles from their contented faces. A raucous gramophone continually ground out popular tunes. In the morning it was rag-time – *Everybody's Doing it* and *At the Fox-Trot Ball*. (*Somewhere a Voice is calling, God send you back to me,* and such-like sentimental songs were reserved for the evening hours.) Before midday no one had enough energy to begin talking war shop, but after that I could always hear scraps of conversation from around the two fireplaces. My eyes were reading one of Lamb's Essays, but my mind was continually distracted by such phrases as 'Barrage lifted at the first objective', 'shelled us with heavy stuff', 'couldn't raise enough decent N.C.O.s', 'first wave got held up by machine-guns', and 'bombed them out of a sap'.

There were no serious cases in the ward, only flesh wounds and sick. These were the lucky ones, already washed clean of squalor and misery and strain. They were lifting their faces to the sunlight, warming their legs by the fire; but there wasn't much to talk about except the War.

In the evenings they played cards at a table opposite my bed; the blinds were drawn, the electric light was on, and a huge fire glowed on walls and ceiling. Glancing irritably up from my book I criticized the faces of the card-players and those who stood watching the game. There was a lean airman in a grey dressing-gown, his narrow whimsical face puffing a cigarette below a turban-like bandage; he'd been brought down by the Germans behind Arras and had spent three days in a bombarded dug-out with Prussians, until our men drove them back and rescued him. The Prussians hadn't treated him badly, he said. His partner was a swarthy Canadian with a low beetling forehead, sneering wideset eyes, fleshy cheeks, and a loose heavy mouth. I couldn't like that man, especially when he was boasting how he 'did in some prisoners'. Along the ward they were still talking about 'counter-attacked from the redoubt', 'permanent rank of captain', 'never drew any allowances for six weeks', 'failed to get through their wire'. . . . I was beginning to feel the need for escape from such reminders. My brain was screwed up tight, and when people came to see me I answered their questions excitedly and said things I hadn't intended to say.

From the munition factory across the road, machinery throbbed and droned and crashed like the treading of giants; the noise got on my nerves. I was being worried by bad dreams. More than once I wasn't sure whether I was awake or asleep; the ward was half shadow and half sinking firelight, and the beds were quiet with huddled sleepers. Shapes of mutilated soldiers came crawling across the floor; the floor seemed to be littered with fragments of mangled flesh. Faces glared upward; hands clutched at neck or belly; a livid grinning face with bristly moustache peered at me above the edge of my bed; his hands clawed at the sheets. Some were like the dummy figures used to deceive snipers; others were alive and looked at me reproachfully, as though envying me the warm safety of life which they'd longed for when they shivered in the gloomy dawn, waiting for the whistles to blow and the bombardment to lift. . . . A young English private in battle equipment pulled himself painfully toward me and fumbled in his tunic for a letter; as he reached forward to give it to me his head lolled sideways and he collapsed; there was a hole in his jaw and the blood spread across his white face like ink spilt on blotting paper. . . .

Violently awake, I saw the ward without its phantoms. The sleepers were snoring and a nurse in grey and scarlet was coming silently along to make up the fire.

2

Although I have stated that after my first few days in hospital I 'began to think', I cannot claim that my thoughts were clear or consistent. I did, however, become definitely critical and inquiring about the War. While feeling that my infantry experience justified this, it did not occur to me that I was by no means fully informed on the subject. In fact I generalized intuitively, and was not unlike a young man who suddenly loses his belief in religion and stands up to tell the Universal Being that He doesn't exist, adding that if He does, He treats the world very unjustly. I shall have more to say later on about my antagonism to the World War; in the meantime it queered my criticisms of it by continually reminding me that the Adjutant had written to tell me that my name had been 'sent in for another decoration'. I could find no fault with this hopeful notion, and when I was allowed out of hospital for the first time my vanity did not forget how nice its tunic would look with one of those (still uncommon) little silver rosettes on the M.C. ribbon, which signified a Bar; or, better still, a red and blue D.S.O.

It was May 2nd and warm weather; no one appeared to be annoyed about the War, so why should I worry? Sitting on the top of a bus, I glanced at the editorial paragraphs of the *Unconservative Weekly*. The omniscience of this ably written journal had become the basis of my provocative views on

world affairs. I agreed with every word in it and was thus comfortably enabled to disagree with the bellicose patriotism of
the *Morning Post*. The only trouble was that an article in the
Unconservative Weekly was for me a sort of divine revelation.
It told me what I'd never known but now needed to believe,
and its ratiocinations and political pronouncements passed
out of my head as quickly as they entered it. While I read I
concurred; but if I'd been asked to restate the arguments I
should have contented myself with saying 'It's what I've always
felt myself, though I couldn't exactly put it into words.'

The Archbishop of Canterbury was easier to deal with.
Smiling sardonically, I imbibed his 'Message to the Nation
about the War and the Gospel'. 'Occasions may arise', he
wrote, 'when exceptional obligations are laid upon us. Such an
emergency having now arisen, the security of the nation's food
supply may largely depend upon the labour which can be
devoted to the land. This being so, we are, I think, following
the guidance given in the Gospel if in such a case we make a
temporary departure from our rule. I have no hesitation in
saying that in the need which these weeks present, men and
women may with a clear conscience do field-work on Sundays.' Remembering the intense bombardment in front of
Arras on Easter Sunday, I wondered whether the Archbishop
had given the sanction of the Gospel for that little bit of Sabbath field-work. Unconscious that he was, presumably, pained
by the War and its barbarities, I glared morosely in the direction of Lambeth Palace and muttered, 'Silly old fossil!' Soon
afterwards I got off the bus at Piccadilly Circus and went into
the restaurant where I had arranged to meet Julian Durley.

With Durley I reverted automatically to my active-service
self. The war which we discussed was restricted to the
doings of the Flintshire Fusiliers. Old So-and-so had been
wounded; poor old Somebody had been killed in the Bulle-
court show; old Somebody Else was still commanding B Company. Old jokes and grotesquely amusing trench incidents were
re-enacted. The Western Front was the same treacherous blundering tragi-comedy which the mentality of the Army had
agreed to regard as something between a crude bit of fun and

an excuse for a good grumble. I suppose that the truth of the matter was that we were remaining loyal to the realities of our war experience, keeping our separate psychological secrets to ourselves, and avoiding what Durley called 'his dangerous tendency to become serious'. His face, however, retained the haunted unhappy look which it had acquired since the Delville Wood attack last autumn, and his speaking voice was still a hoarse whisper.

When I was ordering a bottle of hock we laughed because the waiter told us that the price had been reduced since 1914, as it was now an unpopular wine. The hock had its happy effect, and soon we were agreeing that the Front Line was the only place where one could get away from the War. Durley had been making a forlorn attempt to enter the Flying Corps, and had succeeded in being re-examined medically. The examination had started hopefully, as Durley had confined himself to nods and headshakings in reply to questions. But when conversation became inevitable the doctor had very soon asked angrily, 'Why the hell don't you stop that whispering?' The verdict had been against his fractured thyroid cartilage; though, as Durley remarked, it didn't seem to him to make much difference whether you shouted or whispered when you were up in an aeroplane. 'You'll have to take some sort of office job,' I said. But he replied that he hated the idea, and then illogically advised me to stay in England as long as I could. I asserted that I was going out again as soon as I could get passed for General Service, and called for the bill as though I were thereby settling my destiny conclusively. I emerged from the restaurant without having uttered a single antiwar sentiment.

When Durley had disappeared into his aimless unattached existence, I sat in Hyde Park for an hour before going back to the hospital. What with the sunshine and the effect of the hock, I felt rather drowsy, and the columns of the *Unconservative Weekly* seemed less stimulating than usual.

On the way back to Denmark Hill I diverted my mind by observing the names on shops and business premises. I was rewarded by Pledge (pawnbroker), Money (solicitor), and Stone (builder). There was also an undertaker named Bernard

Shaw. But perhaps the most significant name was Fudge (print-ing works). What use, I thought, were printed words against a war like this? Durley represented the only reality which I could visualize with any conviction. People who told the truth were likely to be imprisoned, and lies were at a premium. . . . All my energy had evaporated and it was a relief to be back in bed. After all, I thought, it's only sixteen days since I left the Sec-ond Battalion, so I've still got a right to feel moderately unwell. How luxurious it felt, to be lying there, after a cup of strong tea, with daylight diminishing, and a vague gratitude for being alive at the end of a fine day in late spring. Anyhow the War had taught me to be thankful for a roof over my head at night. . . .

Lying awake after the lights were out in the ward, it is pos-sible that I also thought about the Second Battalion. Someone (it must have been Dunning) had sent me some details of the show they'd been in on April 23rd. The attack had been at the place where I'd left them. A little ground had been gained and lost, and then the Germans had retreated a few hundred yards. Four officers had been killed and nine wounded. About forty other ranks killed, including several of the best N.C.O.s. It had been an episode typical of uncountable others, some of which now fill their few pages in Regimental Histories. Such stories look straightforward enough in print, twelve years later; but their reality remains hidden; even in the minds of old soldiers the harsh horror mellows and recedes.

Of this particular local attack the Second Battalion Doctor afterwards wrote, 'The occasion was but one of many when a Company or Battalion was sacrificed on a limited objective to a plan of attack ordered by Division or some higher Command with no more knowledge of the ground than might be got from a map of moderate scale.' But for me (as I lay awake and won-dered whether I'd have been killed if I'd been there) April 23rd was a blurred picture of people bombing one another up and down ditches; of a Company stumbling across open ground and getting mown down by machine-guns; of the Doctor out in the dark with his stretcher-bearers, getting in the wounded; and of an exhausted Battalion staggering back to rest-billets to

be congratulated by a genial exculpatory Major-General, who
explained that the attack had been ordered by the Corps Commander. I could visualize the Major-General all right, though
I wasn't aware that he was 'blaming it on the Corps Com
mander'. And I knew for certain that Ralph Wilmot was now
minus one of his arms, so my anti-war bitterness was enabled
to concentrate itself on the fact that he wouldn't be able to
play the piano again. Finally, it can safely be assumed that my
entire human organism felt ultra-thankful to be falling asleep
in an English hospital. Altruism is an episodic and debatable
quality; the instinct for self-preservation always got the last
word when an infantryman was lying awake with his thoughts.

With an apology for my persistent specifyings of chronology, I
must relate that on May 9th I was moved on to a Railway Ter-
minus Hotel which had been commandeered for the accom-
modation of convalescent officers. My longing to get away
from London made me intolerant of the Great Central Hotel,
which was being directed by a mind more military than thera-
peutic. The Commandant was a non-combatant Brigadier-
General, and the convalescents grumbled a good deal about
his methods, although they could usually get leave to go out in
the evenings. Many of them were waiting to be invalided out
of the Army, and the daily routine orders contained incongruous elements. We were required to attend lectures on, among
other things, Trench Warfare. At my first lecture I was astonished to see several officers on crutches, with legs amputated,
and at least one man had lost that necessary faculty for trench
warfare, his eyesight. They appeared to be accepting the
absurd situation stoically; they were allowed to smoke. The
Staff Officer who was drawing diagrams on a black-board was
obviously desirous of imparting information about the lesson
which had been learnt from the Battle of Neuve Chapelle or
some equally obsolete engagement. But I noticed several faces
in the audience which showed signs of tortured nerves, and it
was unlikely that their efficiency was improved by the lecturer
who concluded by reminding us of the paramount importance
of obtaining offensive ascendancy in no-man's-land.

In the afternoon I had an interview with the doctor who was empowered to decide how soon I went to the country. One of the men with whom I shared a room had warned me that this uniformed doctor was a queer customer. 'The blighter seems to take a positive pleasure in tormenting people,' he remarked, adding, 'He'll probably tell you that you'll have to stay here till you're passed fit for duty.' But I had contrived to obtain a letter from the Countess of Somewhere, recommending me for one of the country houses in her Organization; so I felt fairly secure. (At that period of the War people with large houses received convalescent officers as guests.)

The doctor, a youngish man dressed as a temporary Captain, began by behaving quite pleasantly. After he'd examined me and the document which outlined my insignificant medical history, he asked what I proposed to do now. I said that I was hoping to get sent to some place in the country for a few weeks. He replied that I was totally mistaken if I thought any such thing. An expression, which I can only call cruel, overspread his face. 'You'll stay here; and when you leave here, you'll find yourself back at the front in double-quick time. How d'you like that idea?' In order to encourage him, I pretended to be upset by his severity; but he seemed to recognize that I wasn't satisfactory material for his peculiar methods, and I departed without having contested the question of going to the country. I was told afterwards that officers had been known to leave this doctor's room in tears. But it must not be supposed that I regard his behaviour as an example of Army brutality. I prefer to think of him as a man who craved for power over his fellow men. And though his power over the visiting patients was brief and episodic, he must have derived extraordinary (and perhaps sadistic) satisfaction from the spectacle of young officers sobbing and begging not to be sent back to the front.

I never saw the supposedly sadistic doctor again; but I hope that someone gave him a black eye, and that he afterwards satisfied his desire for power over his fellow men in a more public-spirited manner.

Next morning I handed the letter of the Countess to a slightly higher authority, with the result that I only spent three nights in the Great Central Hotel, and late on a fine Saturday afternoon I travelled down to Sussex to stay with Lord and Lady Asterisk.

3

Nutwood Manor was everything that a wounded officer could wish for. From the first I was conscious of a kindly welcome. It was the most perfect house I'd ever stayed in. Also, to put the matter plainly, it was the first time I'd ever stayed with an Earl. 'Gosh! This is a slice of luck,' I thought. A reassuring man-servant conducted me upstairs. My room was called 'The Clematis Room'; I noticed the name on the door. Leaning my elbows on the window-sill, I gazed down at the yew hedges of a formal garden; woods and meadows lay beyond and below, glorious with green and luminous in evening light; far away stood the Sussex Downs, and it did my heart good to see them. Everything in the pretty room was an antithesis to ugliness and discomfort. Beside the bed there was a bowl of white lilac and a Bible. Opening it at random to try my luck, I put my fin-ger on the following verse from the Psalms: 'The words of his mouth were smoother than butter, but war was in his heart.' Rather an odd coincidence, I thought, that the word 'war' should turn up like that; but the Old Testament's full of fight-ing. . . . While I was changing into my best khaki uniform I could hear quiet feet and murmurous voices moving about the house; doors closed discreetly on people about to dress for dinner. Still almost incredulous at my good fortune I went downstairs, to be greeted by a silver-haired and gracious host-ess, and introduced to three other officers, all outwardly healthy and gentlemanly-looking. I was presented to Lord Asterisk, over eighty and crippled with rheumatism, but reso-lutely holding on to a life which had been devoted to useful public service. Respectfully silent, I listened to his urbane elo-quence and felt sufficiently at my ease to do justice to a very good dinner. The port wine went its round; and afterwards in the drawing-room, I watched Lady Asterisk working at some embroidery while one of the officers played Gluck and Handel on the piano. Nothing could have been more tranquil and harmonious than my first evening at Nutwood Manor. Nevertheless I failed to fall asleep in the Clematis Room. Lying awake didn't matter much at first; there was plenty to ruminate about; the view across the Weald at sunset had revived my memories of 'the good old days when I hunted with the Ringwell'. I had escaped from the exasperating boredom of hospital life, and now for a few weeks I could forget about the War. . . . But the War insisted on being remembered, and by 3 a.m. it had become so peremptory that I could almost believe that some of my friends out in France must be waiting to go over the top. One by one, I thought of as many of them as I could remember. . . .

I'd overheard Lady Asterisk talking about spiritualism to one of the officers; evidently she was a strong believer in the 'unseen world'. Perhaps it was this which set me wondering whether, by concentrating my mind on, say, young Ormand (who was still with the Second Battalion), I might be able to receive some reciprocal communication. At three o'clock in the morning a sleepless mind can welcome improbabilities and renounce its daylight scepticism. Neither voice nor vision rewarded my expectancy.

But I was rewarded by an intense memory of men whose courage had shown me the power of the human spirit – that spirit which could withstand the utmost assault. Such men had inspired me to be at my best when things were very bad, and they outweighed all the failures. Against the background of the War and its brutal stupidity those men had stood glorified by the thing which sought to destroy them. . . .

I went to the window and leant out. The gables of the house began to loom distinct against a clear sky. An owl hooted from the woods; cocks were crowing from distant farms; on the mantelpiece a little clock ticked busily. Oppressed by the comfort of my surroundings, I felt an impulse to dress and go out for a walk. But Arras and the Somme were a long way off; I couldn't walk there and didn't want to; but they beckoned me with their bombardments and the reality of the men who endured them. I wanted to be there again for a few hours, because the trenches really were more interesting than Lady Asterisk's rose-garden. Seen from a distance, the War had a sombre and unforgettable fascination for its bondsmen. I would have liked to go and see what was happening, and perhaps take part in some exciting little exploit. I couldn't gainsay certain intense emotional experiences which I'd lived through in France. But I also wanted to be back at Nutwood Manor for breakfast. . . . Returning to my bed I switched on the yellow shaded light. Yes; this was the Clematis Room, and nothing could be less like the dug-out where I'd sat a month ago talking about Sussex with Ralph Wilmot. Through the discurtained window the sky was deep nocturnal blue. I turned out the lamp, and the window became a patch of greyish white, with tree-tops dark and still in the strange quietude before dawn. I heard the cuckoo a long way off. Then a blackbird went scolding along the garden.

I awoke to a cloudless Sabbath morning. After breakfast Lady Asterisk led me into the garden and talked very kindly for a few minutes.

'I am sure you have had a very trying time at the front', she said, 'but you must not allow yourself to be worried by unpleasant memories. We want our soldier-guests to forget the War while they are with us.'

I replied, mumbling, that in such surroundings it wouldn't be easy to worry about anything; and then the old Earl came out on to the terrace, pushing the wheeled apparatus which enabled him to walk.

Often during the next three weeks I was able to forget about the War; often I took refuge in the assuasive human happiness which Nutwood Manor's hospitality offered me. But there were times when my mental mechanism was refractory, and I reverted to my resolution to keep the smoke-drifted battle memories true and intense, unmodified by the comforts of convalescence. I wasn't going to be bluffed back into an easy-going tolerant state of mind, I decided, as I opened a daily

paper one morning and very deliberately read a despatch from
'War Correspondents' Headquarters'.

'I have sat with some of our lads, fighting battles over again,
and discussing battles to be,' wrote some amiable man who
had apparently mistaken the War for a football match between
England and Germany. 'One officer – a mere boy – told me
how he'd run up against eleven Huns in an advanced post. He
killed two with a Mills' bomb ("Grand weapon, the Mills'!"
he laughed, his clear eyes gleaming with excitement), wounded
another with his revolver, and marched the remainder back to
our own lines. . . . ' I opened one of the illustrated weeklies
and soon found an article on 'War Pictures at the Royal Acad-
emy'. After a panegyric about 'Forward the Guns!' (a patriotic
masterpiece by a lady who had been to the Military Tournament in pre-War days) the following sentence occurred: 'I
think I like Mr Blank's "Contalmaison" picture best. He almost
makes one feel that he must have been there. The Nth Division
are going over the second line I expect – the tips of their bayonets give one this impression – and it is a picture which makes
one's pulse beat a lot faster. . . . '

'The tips of their bayonets give one that impression.' . . .
Obviously the woman journalist who wrote those words was
deriving enjoyment from the War, though she may not have
been aware of the fact. I wondered why it was necessary for
the Western Front to be 'attractively advertised' by such intolerable twaddle. What *was* this camouflage War which was
manufactured by the press to aid the imaginations of people
who had never seen the real thing? Many of them probably
said that the papers gave them a sane and vigorous view of the
overwhelming tragedy. 'Naturally', they would remark, 'the
lads from the front are inclined to be a little morbid about it;
one expects that, after all they've been through. Their close
contact with the War has diminished their realization of its
spiritual aspects.' Then they would add something about 'the
healing of Nations'. Such people needed to have their noses
rubbed in a few rank physical facts, such as what a company
of men smelt like after they'd been in action for a week. . . .

The gong rang for luncheon, and Lady Asterisk left off reading a book by Tagore (whose mystical philosophies had hitherto seemed to me nebulous and unsatisfying).

It must not be supposed that I was ungrateful for my good luck. For several days on end I could feel obliviously contented, and in weaker moments there was an absurd hope that the War might be over before next autumn. Rambling among woods and meadows, I could 'take sweet counsel' with the country-side; sitting on a grassy bank and lifting my face to the sun, I could feel an intensity of thankfulness such as I'd never known before the War; listening to the little brook that bubbled out of a copse and across a rushy field, I could discard my personal relationship with the military machine and its ant-like armies. On my way home I would pass old Mr Jukes leaning on his garden gate, or an ancient labourer mending gaps in a hedge. I would stop to gaze at the loveliness of apple-blossom when the sun came out after a shower. And the protective hospitality of Nutwood Manor was almost bewildering when compared with an average twenty-four hours in a front-line trench.

All this was well enough; but there was a limit to my season of sauntering; the future was a main road where I must fall into step and do something to earn my 'pay and allowances'. Lady Asterisk liked to have serious helpful little talks with her officers, and one evening she encouraged me to discuss my immediate horizon. I spoke somewhat emotionally, with self-indulgence in making a fine effect rather than an impartial resolve to face facts. I suggested that I'd been trying to make up my mind about taking a job in England, admitting my longing for life and setting against it the idea of sacrifice and disregard of death. I said that most of my friends were assuring me that there was no necessity for me to go out for the third time. While I talked I saw myself as a noble suffering character whose death in action would be deeply deplored. I saw myself as an afflicted traveller who had entered Lady Asterisk's gates to sit by the fire and rest his weary limbs. I did not complain about the War; it would have been bad form to be bitter about it at Nutwood Manor; my own 'personal problem' was what I was concerned with. . . .

We were alone in the library. She listened to me, her silver hair and handsome face bent slightly forward above a piece of fine embroidery. Outwardly emotionless, she symbolized the patrician privileges for whose preservation I had chucked bombs at Germans and carelessly offered myself as a target for a sniper. When I had blurted out my opinion that life was preferable to the Roll of Honour she put aside her reticence like a rich cloak. 'But death is nothing,' she said. 'Life, after all, is only the beginning. And those who are killed in the War – they help us from up there. They are helping us to win.' I couldn't answer that; this 'other world', of which she was so certain, was something I had forgotten about since I was wounded. Expecting no answer, she went on with a sort of inflexible sympathy (almost 'as if my number was already up', as I would have expressed it), 'It isn't as though you were heir to a great name. No; I can't see any definite reason for your keeping out of danger. But, of course, you can only decide a thing like that for yourself.'

I went up to the Clematis Room feeling caddishly estranged and cynical; wondering whether the Germans 'up there' were doing anything definite to impede the offensive operations of the Allied Powers. But Lady Asterisk wasn't hard-hearted. She only wanted me 'to do the right thing'. . . . I began to wish that I could talk candidly to someone. There was too much well-behaved acquiescence at Nutwood Manor; and whatever the other officers there thought about the War, they kept it to themselves; they had done their bit for the time being and were conventional and correct, as if the eye of their Colonel was upon them.

Social experience at Nutwood was varied by an occasional visitor. One evening I sat next to the new arrival, a fashionable young woman whose husband (as I afterwards ascertained) was campaigning in the Cameroons. Her manner implied that she was ready to take me into her confidence, intellectually;

but my responses were cumbersome and uneasy, for her conversation struck me as containing a good deal of trumped-up
intensity. A fine pair of pearls dangled from her ears, and her
dark blue eyes goggled emptily while she informed me that she
was taking lessons in Italian. She was 'dying to read Dante',
and had already started the Canto about Paolo and Francesca;
adored D'Annunzio, too, and had been reading *his* Paolo and
Francesca (in French). 'Life is so wonderful – so great – and yet
we waste it all in this dreadful War!' she exclaimed. Rather
incongruously, she then regaled me with some typical gossip
from high quarters in the Army. Lunching at the Ritz recently,
she had talked to Colonel Repington, who had told her – I
really forget what, but it was excessively significant, politi-
cally, and showed that there was no need for people to worry
about Allenby's failure to advance very far at Arras. Unsuscep-
tible to her outward attractions, I came to the conclusion that
she wasn't the stamp of woman for whom I was willing to
make the supreme sacrifice. . . .

Lord Asterisk had returned that evening from London,
where he'd attended a dinner at the House of Lords. The dinner had been in honour of General Smuts (for whom I must
parenthetically testify my admiration). This name made me
think of Joe Dottrell, who was fond of relating how, in the
Boer War, he had been with a raiding party which had noctur-
nally surprised and almost captured the Headquarters of General Smuts. I wondered whether the anecdote would interest
Lord Asterisk; but (the ladies having left the table) he was
embarking on his customary after-dinner oratory, while the
young officer guests sipped their port and coffee and occasionally put in a respectful remark. The old fellow was getting very
feeble, I thought, as I watched the wreckage of his fine and
benevolent face. He sat with his chin on his chest; his brow
and nose were still firm and authoritative. Sometimes his voice
became weak and querulous, but he appeared to enjoy rolling
out his deliberate parliamentary periods. Talking about the
War, he surprised me by asserting the futility of waiting for a
definite military decision. Although he had been a Colonial
Governor, he was 'profoundly convinced of the uselessness of

some of our Colonies', which, he said, might just as well be
handed over to the Germans. He turned to the most articulate
officer at the table. 'I declare to you, my dear fellow' (voice
sinking to a mumble), 'I declare to you' (louder), 'have you any
predominating awareness' (pause) 'of – *Sierra Leone*?'

As for Belgium, he invoked the evidence of history to support him in his assertion that its 'redemption' by the Allies was
merely a manifestation of patriotic obliquity. The inhabitants
of Belgium would be just as happy as a German Subject-State.
To the vast majority of them their national autonomy meant
nothing. While I was trying to remember the exact meaning of
the word autonomy, he ended the discussion by remarking,
'But I'm only an old dotard!' and we pretended to laugh, naturally, as if it were quite a good joke. Then he reverted to a
favourite subject of his, viz., the ineffectiveness of ecclesiastical administrative bodies. 'Oh what worlds of dreary (mumble) are hidden by the hats of our episcopal dignitaries! I
declare to you, my dear fellow, that it is my profound conviction that the preponderance of mankind is entirely – yes, most
grievously indifferent to the deliberations of that well-
intentioned but obtuse body of men, the Ecclesiastical Com-
missioners!' Slightly sententious, perhaps; but no one could
doubt that he was a dear old chap who had done his level best
to leave the world in better order than he'd found it.

There were times when I felt perversely indignant at the 'cush-
iness' of my convalescent existence. These reactions were
mostly caused by the few letters which came to me from the
front. One of Joe Dottrell's hastily pencilled notes could make
me unreasonably hostile to the cheerful voices of croquet players and inarticulately unfriendly to the elegant student of Italian when she was putting her pearl necklace out in the sun,
'because pearls do adore the sun so!'

It wasn't easy to feel animosity against the pleasant-mannered
neighbours who dropped in to tea. Nibbling cucumber sandwiches, they conceded full military honours to any officer who
had been wounded. They discussed gardening and joked about

domestic difficulties; they talked about war-work and public affairs; but they appeared to be refusing to recognize the realities which were implied by a letter from an indomitable quartermaster in France. 'The Battalion has been hard at it again and had a rough time, but as usual kept their end up well – much to the joy of the Staff, who have been round here to-day like flies round a jam-pot, congratulating the Colonel and all others concerned. I am sorry to say that the Padre got killed. . . . He was up with the lads in the very front and got sniped in the stomach and died immediately. I haven't much room for his crowd as a rule, but he was the finest parson I've ever known, absolutely indifferent to danger. Young Brock (bombing officer – he said he knew you at Clitherland) was engaging the Boche single-handed when he was badly hit in the arm, side, and leg. They amputated his left leg, but he was too far gone and we buried him to-day. Two other officers killed and three wounded. Poor Sergeant Blaxton was killed. All the best get knocked over. . . . The boys are now trying to get to Amiens to do a bit of courting.' Morosely I regarded the Clematis Room. What earthly use was it, ordering boxes of kippers to be sent to people who were all getting done in, while everyone at home humbugged about with polite platitudes?

. . Birdie Mansfield wrote from Yorkshire; he had been invalided out of the Army. 'I'm fed to the teeth with wandering around in mufti and getting black looks from people who pass remarks to the effect that it's about time I joined up. Meanwhile I exist on my provisional pension (3s. a day). A few days' touring round these munition areas would give you food for thought. The average conversation is about the high cost of beer and the ability to evade military service by bluffing the Tribunals.'

I looked at another letter. It was from my servant (to whom I'd sent a photograph of myself and a small gramophone). 'Thank you very much for the photo, which is like life itself, and the men in the Company say it is just like him. The gramophone is much enjoyed by all. I hope you will pardon my neglect in not packing the ground-sheet with your kit.' What could one do about it? Nothing short of stopping the War could alter the inadequacy of kippers and gramophones or sustain my sense of unity with those to whom I sent them.

On the day before I departed from Nutwood Manor I received another letter from Dottrell. It contained bad news about the Second Battalion. Viewed broadmindedly, the attack had been quite a commonplace fragment of the War. It had been a hopeless failure, and with a single exception all officers in action had become casualties. None of the bodies had been brought in. The First and Second Battalions had been quite near one another, and Dottrell had seen Ormand a day or two before the show. 'He looked pretty depressed, though outwardly as jolly as ever.' Dunning had been the first to leave our trench; had shouted 'Cheerio' and been killed at once. Dottrell thanked me for the box of kippers. . . .

Lady Asterisk happened to be in the room when I opened the letter. With a sense of self-pitying indignation I blurted out my unpleasant information. Her tired eyes showed that the shock had brought the War close to her, but while I was adding a few details her face became self-defensively serene. 'But they are safe and happy now,' she said. I did not doubt her sincerity, and perhaps they *were* happy now. All the same, I was incapable of accepting the deaths of Ormand and Dunning and the others in that spirit. I wasn't a theosophist. Nevertheless I left Nutwood with gratitude for the kindness I had received there. I had now four weeks in which to formulate my plans for the future.

PART TEN

INDEPENDENT
ACTION

1

At daybreak on June 7th the British began the Battle of Messines by exploding nineteen full-sized mines. For me the day was made memorable by the fact that I lunched with the editor of the *Unconservative Weekly* at his club. By the time I entered that imposing edifice our troops had advanced more than two miles on a ten mile front and a great many Germans had been blown sky-high. Tomorrow this news would pervade clubland on a wave of optimism and elderly men would glow with satisfaction.

In the meantime prospects on the Russian Front were none too bright since the Revolution; but a politician called Kerensky ('Waiter, bring me a large glass of light port') appeared to be doing his best for his country and one could only hope that the Russian Army would – humph – stick to its guns and remember its obligations to the Allies and their War Aims.

My luncheon with Mr Markington was the result of a letter impulsively written from Nutwood Manor. The letter contained a brief outline of my War service and a suggestion that he ought to publish something outspoken so as to let people at home know what the War was really like. I offered to provide such details as I knew from personal experience. The style of my letter was stilted, except for a postscript: 'I'm fed up with all the hanky-panky in the daily papers.' His reply was reticent but friendly, and I went to his club feeling that I was a mouthpiece for the troops in the trenches. However, when the opportunity for altruistic eloquence arrived, I discovered, with relief, that none was expected of me. The editor took most of my horrifying information on trust, and I was quite content to listen to his own acrimonious comments on contemporary affairs.

Markington was a sallow spectacled man with earnest uncompromising eyes and a stretched sort of mouth which looked as
if it had ceased to find human follies funny. The panorama of
public affairs had always offered him copious occasions for
dissent; the Boer War had been bad enough, but this one had
provided almost too much provocation for his embitterment. In
spite of all this he wasn't an alarming man to have lunch with;
relaxing into ordinary humanity, he could enjoy broad humour,
and our conversation took an unexpected turn when he encouraged me to tell him a few army anecdotes which might be cen-
sored if I were to print them. I felt quite fond of Markington
when he threw himself back in his chair in a paroxysm of
amusement. Most of his talk, however, dealt with more serious
subjects, and he made me feel that the world was in an even
worse condition than my simple mind had suspected. When I
questioned him about the probable duration of the War he
shrugged his shoulders. The most likely conclusion that he
could foresee was a gradual disintegration and collapse of all
the armies. After the War, he said, conditions in all countries
would be appalling, and Europe would take fifty years to recover. With regard to what I suggested in my letter, he explained
that if he were to print veracious accounts of infantry experience his paper would be suppressed as prejudicial to recruiting.
The censorship officials were always watching for a plausible
excuse for banning it, and they had already prohibited its foreign circulation. 'The soldiers are not allowed to express their
point of view. In war-time the word patriotism means suppres-
sion of truth,' he remarked, eyeing a small chunk of Stilton
cheese on his plate as if it were incapable of agreeing with any
but ultra-Conservative opinions. 'Quite a number of middle-
aged members of this club have been to the front,' he continued. 'After a dinner at G.H.Q. and a motor drive in the direction
of the trenches, they can talk and write in support of the War
with complete confidence in themselves. Five years ago they
were probably saying that modern civilization had made a
European War unthinkable. But their principles are purchas-
able. Once they've been invited to visit G.H.Q. they never look
back. Their own self-importance is all that matters to them.

And any lie is a good lie as long as it stimulates unreasoning hatred of the enemy.'

He listened with gloomy satisfaction to my rather vague remarks about incompetent Staff work. I told him that our Second Battalion had been almost wiped out ten days ago because the Divisional General had ordered an impossible attack on a local objective. The phrase 'local objective' sounded good, and made me feel that I knew a hell of a lot about it. . . .

On our way to the smoking-room we passed a blandly Victorian bust of Richard Cobden, which caused Markington to regret that the man himself wasn't above ground to give the present Government a bit of his mind. Ignorant about Cobden's career, I gazed fixedly at his marble whiskers, nodded gravely, and inwardly resolved to look up a few facts about him. 'If Cobden were alive now,' said Markington, 'the *Morning Post* would be anathematizing him as a white-livered defeatist! You ought to read his speeches on International Arbitration – not a very popular subject in these days!'

I was comfortably impressed by my surroundings, for the club was the Mecca of the Liberal Party. From a corner of the smoking-room I observed various eminent-looking individuals who were sipping coffee and puffing cigars, and I felt that I was practically in the purlieus of public life. Markington pointed out a few Liberal politicians whose names I knew, and one conspicuous group included a couple of novelists whose reputations were so colossal that I could scarcely believe that I was treading the same carpet as they were. I gazed at them with gratitude; apart from their eminence, they had provided me with a great deal of enjoyment, and I would have liked to tell them so. For Markington, however, such celebrities were an everyday occurrence, and he was more interested in my own sensations while on active service. A single specimen of my eloquence will be enough. 'As a matter of fact I'm almost sure that the War doesn't seem nearly such a bloody rotten show when one's out there as it does when one's back in England. You see as soon as one gets across the Channel one sort of feels as if it's no good worrying any more – you know what I mean – like being part of the Machine again, with nothing to be done except take one's chance. After that one can't bother about anything except the Battalion one's with. Of course, there's a hell of a lot of physical discomfort to be put up with, and the unpleasant sights seem to get worse every year; but apart from being shelled and so on, I must say I've often felt extraordinarily happy even in the trenches. Out there it's just one thing after another, and one soon forgets the bad times; it's probably something to do with being in the open air so much and getting such a lot of exercise. . . . It's only when one gets away from it that one begins to realize how stupid and wasteful it all is. What I feel now is that if it's got to go on there ought to be a jolly sound reason for it, and I can't help thinking that the troops are being done in the eye by the people in control.' I qualified these temperate remarks by explaining that I was only telling him how it had affected me personally; I had been comparatively lucky, and could now see the War as it affected infantry soldiers who were having an infinitely worse time than I'd ever had – particularly the privates.

When I inquired whether any peace negotiations were being attempted, Markington said that England had been asked by the new Russian Government, in April, to state definitely her War Aims and to publish the secret treaties made between England and Russia early in the War. We had refused to state our terms or publish the treaties. 'How damned rotten of us!' I exclaimed, and I am afraid that my instinctive reaction was a savage desire to hit (was it Mr Lloyd George?) very hard on the nose. Markington was bitter against the military caste in all countries. He said that all the administrative departments in Whitehall were trying to get the better of one another, which resulted in muddle and waste on an unprecedented scale. He told me that I should find the same sort of things described in Tolstoy's *War and Peace*, adding that if once the common soldier became articulate the War couldn't last a month. Soon afterwards he sighed and said he must be getting back to the office; he had his article to write and the paper went to press that evening. When we parted in Pall Mall he told me to keep in touch with him and not worry about the War more than I could help, and I mumbled something about it having been frightfully interesting to meet him.

As I walked away from Markington my mind was clamorous with confused ideas and phrases. It seemed as if, until to-day, I had been viewing the War through the loop-hole of a trench parapet. Now I felt so much 'in the know' that I wanted to stop strangers in the street and ask them whether they realized that we ought to state our War Aims. People ought to be warned that there was (as I would have expressed it) some dirty work going on behind their backs. I remembered how sceptical old Lord Asterisk had been about the redemption of 'gallant little Belgium' by the Allies. And now Markington had gloomily informed me that our Aims were essentially acquisitive, what we were fighting for was the Mesopotamian Oil Wells. A jolly fine swindle it would have been for me, if I'd been killed in April for an Oil Well. But I soon forgot that I'd been unaware of the existence of the Oil Wells before Markington mentioned them, and I conveniently assimilated them as part of my evidential repertoire.

Readers of my pedestrian tale are perhaps wondering how soon I shall be returning to the temperate influence of Aunt Evelyn. In her latest letter she announced that a Zeppelin had dropped a bomb on an orchard about six miles away; there had also been an explosion at the Powder Mills at Dumbridge, but no one had been hurt. Nevertheless Butley was too buzzing and leisurely a background for my mercurial state of mind; so I stayed in London for another fortnight, and during that period my mental inquietude achieved some sort of climax. In fact I can safely say that my aggregated exasperations came to a head; and, naturally enough, the head was my own. The prime cause of this psychological thunderstorm was my talk with Markington, who was unaware of his ignitionary effect until I called on him in his editorial room on the Monday after our first meeting. Ostensibly I went to ask his advice; in reality, to release the indignant emotions which his editorial utterances had unwittingly brought to the surface of my consciousness. It was a case of direct inspiration; I had, so to speak, received the call, and the editor of the *Unconservative Weekly* seemed the most likely man to put me on the shortest road to martyrdom.

It really felt very fine, and as long as I was alone my feelings carried me along on a torrent of prophetic phrases. But when I was inside Markington's office (he sitting with fingers pressed together and regarding me with alertly mournful curiosity) my internal eloquence dried up and I began abruptly. 'I say, I've been thinking it all over, and I've made up my mind that I ought to do something about it.' He pushed his spectacles up on to his forehead and leant back in his chair. 'You want to do something?' 'About the War, I mean. I just can't sit still and do nothing. You said the other day that you couldn't print anything really outspoken, but I don't see why I shouldn't make some sort of statement – about how we ought to publish our War Aims and all that and the troops not knowing what they're fighting about. It might do quite a lot of good, mightn't it?' He got up and went to the window. A secretarial typewriter tick-tacked in the next room. While he stood with his back to me I could see the tiny traffic creeping to and fro on Charing Cross Bridge and a barge going down the river in the sunshine. My heart was beating violently. I knew that I couldn't turn back now. Those few moments seemed to last a long time; I was conscious of the stream of life going on its way, happy and untroubled, while I had just blurted out something which alienated me from its acceptance of a fine day in the third June of the Great War. Returning to his chair, he said, 'I suppose you've realized what the results of such an action would be, as regards yourself?' I replied that I didn't care two damns what they did to me as long as I got the thing off my chest. He laughed, looking at me with a gleam of his essential kindness. 'As far as I am aware, you'd be the first soldier to take such a step, which would, of course, be welcomed by the extreme pacifists. Your service at the front would differentiate you from the conscientious objectors. But you must on no account make this gesture – a very fine one if you are really in earnest about it – unless you can carry it through effectively. Such an action would require to be carefully thought out, and for the present I advise you to be extremely cautious in what you say and do.' His words caused me an uncomfortable feeling that perhaps I was only making a fool of myself; but this was soon mitigated by a glowing sense of martyrdom. I saw myself 'attired with sudden brightness, like a man inspired', and while Markington continued his counsels of prudence my resolve strengthened toward its ultimate obstinacy. After further reflection he said that the best man for me to consult was Thornton Tyrrell. 'You know him by name, I suppose?' I was compelled to admit that I didn't. Markington handed me *Who's Who* and began to write a letter while I made myself acquainted with the details of Tyrrell's biographical abridgement, which indicated that he was a pretty tough proposition. To put it plainly he was an eminent mathematician, philosopher, and physicist. As a mathematician I'd never advanced much beyond 'six from four you can't, six from fourteen leaves eight'; and I knew no more about the functions of a physicist than a cat in a kitchen. 'What sort of a man is he to meet?' I asked dubiously. Markington licked and closed the envelope of his rapidly written letter. 'Tyrrell is the most uncompromising character I know. An extraordinary brain, of course. But you needn't be alarmed by that; you'll find him perfectly easy to get on with. A talk with him ought to clarify your ideas. I've explained your position quite briefly. But, as I said before, I hope you won't be too impetuous.'

I put the letter in my pocket, thanked him warmly, and went soberly down the stairs and along the quiet sidestreet into the Strand. While I was debating whether I ought to buy and try to read one of Tyrrell's books before going to see him, I almost bumped into a beefy Major-General. It was lunch-time and he was turning in at the Savoy Hotel entrance. Rather grudgingly, I saluted. As I went on my way, I wondered what the War Office would say if it knew what I was up to.

2

Early in the afternoon I left the letter at Tyrrell's address in Bloomsbury. He telegraphed that he could see me in the evening, and punctually at the appointed hour I returned to the

quiet square. My memory is not equal to the effort of recon-
structing my exact sensations, but it can safely be assumed that
I felt excited, important, and rather nervous. I was shown into
an austere-looking room where Tyrrell was sitting with a reading lamp at his elbow. My first impression was that he looked
exactly like a philosopher. He was small, clean-shaven, with
longish grey hair brushed neatly above a fine forehead. He had
a long upper lip, a powerful ironic mouth, and large earnest
eyes. I observed that the book which he put aside was called
The Conquest of Bread by Kropotkin, and I wondered what on
earth it could be about. He put me at my ease by lighting a
large pipe, saying as he did so, 'Well, I gather from Markington's letter that you've been experiencing a change of heart
about the War.' He asked for details of my career in the Army,
and soon I was rambling on in my naturally inconsequent style.
Tyrrell said very little, his object being to size me up. Having
got my mind warmed up, I began to give him a few of my
notions about the larger aspects of the War. But he interrupted
my 'and after what Markington told me the other day, I must
say', with, 'Never mind about what Markington told you. It
amounts to this, doesn't it – that you have ceased to believe
what you are told about the objects for which you supposed
yourself to be fighting?' I replied that it did boil down to something like that, and it seemed to me a bloody shame, the troops
getting killed all the time while people at home humbugged
themselves into believing that everyone in the trenches enjoyed
it. Tyrrell poured me out a second cup of tea and suggested that
I should write out a short personal statement based on my conviction that the War was being unnecessarily prolonged by the
refusal of the Allies to publish their war aims. When I had done
this we could discuss the next step to be taken. 'Naturally I
should help you in every way possible,' he said. 'I have always
regarded all wars as acts of criminal folly, and my hatred of
this one has often made life seem almost unendurable. But
hatred makes one vital, and without it one loses energy. "Keep
vital" is a more important axiom than "love your neighbour".
This act of yours, if you stick to it, will probably land you in
prison. Don't let that discourage you. You will be more alive in

prison than you would be in the trenches.' Mistaking this last remark for a joke, I laughed, rather half-heartedly. 'No; I mean that seriously,' he said. 'By thinking independently and acting fearlessly on your moral convictions you are serving the world better than you would do by marching with the unthinking majority who are suffering and dying at the front because they believe what they have been told to believe. Now that you have lost your faith in what you enlisted for, I am certain that you should go on and let the consequences take care of themselves. Of course your action would be welcomed by people like myself who are violently opposed to the War. We should print and circulate as many copies of your statement as possible. . . . But I hadn't intended to speak as definitely as this. You must decide by your own feeling and not by what anyone else says.' I promised to send him my statement when it was written and walked home with my head full of exalted and disorderly thoughts. I had taken a strong liking for Tyrrell, who probably smiled rather grimly while he was reading a few more pages of Kropotkin's *Conquest of Bread* before going upstairs to his philosophic slumbers.

Although Tyrrell had told me that my statement needn't be more than 200 words long, it took me several days to formulate. At first I felt that I had so much to say that I didn't know where to begin. But after several verbose failures it seemed as though the essence of my manifesto could be stated in a single sentence: 'I say this War ought to stop.' During the struggle to put my unfusilierish opinions into some sort of shape, my confidence often diminished. But there was no relaxation of my inmost resolve, since I was in the throes of a species of conversion which made the prospect of persecution stimulating and almost enjoyable. No; my loss of confidence was in the same category as my diffidence when first confronted by a Vickers Machine-gun and its Instructor. While he reeled off the names of its numerous component parts, I used to despair of ever being able to remember them or understand their workings. 'And unless I know all about the Vickers Gun I'll never get sent out to the front,' I used to think. Now, sitting late at night

in an expensive but dismal bedroom in Jermyn Street, I inter-
nally exclaimed, 'I'll never be able to write out a decent statement and the whole blasted protest will be a washout! Tyrrell
thinks I'm quite brainy, but when he reads this stuff he'll realize what a dud I am.'

What could I do if Tyrrell decided to discourage my candida-
ture for a court martial? Chuck up the whole idea and go out
again and get myself killed as quick as possible? 'Yes,' I thought,
working myself up into a tantrum, 'I'd get killed just to show
them all I don't care a damn.' (I didn't stop to specify the identity of 'them all'; such details could be dispensed with when
one had lost one's temper with the Great War.) But common
sense warned me that getting sent back was a slow business,
and getting killed on purpose an irrelevant gesture for a platoon commander. One couldn't choose one's own conditions
out in France. . . . Tyrrell had talked about 'serving the world
by thinking independently'. I must hang on to that idea and
remember the men for whom I believed myself to be interced-
ing. I tried to think internationally; the poor old Boches must
be hating it just as much as we did; but I couldn't propel my
sympathy as far as the Balkan States, Turks, Italians, and all
the rest of them; and somehow or other the French were just
the French and too busy fighting and selling things to the troops
to need my intervention. So I got back to thinking about 'all the
good chaps who'd been killed with the First and Second Battalions since I left them'. . . . Ormand, dying miserably out in a
shell-hole. . . . I remembered his exact tone of voice when saying that if his children ever asked what he did in the Great War,
his answer would be, 'No bullet ever went quick enough to
catch me;' and how he used to sing 'Rock of ages cleft for me,
let me hide myself in thee,' when we were being badly shelled. I
thought of the typical Flintshire Fusilier at his best, and the
vast anonymity of courage and cheerfulness which he represented as he sat in a front-line trench cleaning his mess-tin.
How could one connect him with the gross profiteer whom
I'd overheard in a railway carriage remarking to an equally
repulsive companion that if the War lasted another eighteen
months he'd be able to retire from business? . . . How could I

co-ordinate such diversion of human behaviour, or believe that heroism was its own reward? Something must be put on paper, however, and I re-scrutinized the rough notes I'd been making: *Fighting men are victims of conspiracy among (a) politicians; (b) military caste; (c) people who are making money out of the War.* Under this I had scribbled, *Also personal effort to dissociate myself from intolerant prejudice and conventional complacence of those willing to watch sacrifices of others while they sit safely at home.* This was followed by an indignant afterthought. *I believe that by taking this action I am helping to destroy the system of deception, etc., which prevents people from facing the truth and demanding some guarantee that the torture of humanity shall not be prolonged unnecessarily through the arrogance and incompetence of . . .* Here it broke off, and I wondered how many c's there were in 'unnecessarily'. *I am not a conscientious objector. I am a soldier who believes he is acting on behalf of soldiers.* How inflated and unconvincing it all looked! If I wasn't careful I should be yelling like some crank on a barrel in Hyde Park. Well, there was nothing for it but to begin all over again. I couldn't ask Tyrrell to give me a few hints. He'd insisted that I must be independent-minded, and had since written to remind me that I must decide my course of action for myself and not be prompted by anything he'd said to me.

Sitting there with my elbows on the table I stared at the dingy red wallpaper in an unseeing effort at mental concentration. If I stared hard enough and straight enough, it seemed, I should see through the wall. Truth would be revealed, and my brain would become articulate. *I am making this statement as an act of wilful defiance of military authority because I believe that the War is being deliberately prolonged by those who have the power to end it.* That would be all right as a kick-off, anyhow. So I continued my superhuman cogitations. Around me was London with its darkened streets; and far away was the War, going on with wave on wave of gunfire, devouring its victims, and unable to blunder forward either to Paris or the Rhine. The air-raids were becoming serious, too. Looking out of the window at the searchlights, I thought how ridiculous it

would be if a bomb dropped on me while I was writing out my
statement.

3

Exactly a week after our first conversation I showed the statement to Tyrrell. He was satisfied with it as a whole and helped
me to clarify a few minor crudities of expression. Nothing
now remained but to wait until my leave had expired and then
hurl the explosive document at the Commanding Officer at
Clitherland (an event which I didn't permit myself to contemplate clearly). For the present the poor man only knew that I'd
applied for an instructorship with a Cadet Battalion at Cambridge. He wrote that he would be sorry to lose me and congratulated me on what he was generous enough to describe
as my splendid work at the front. In the meantime Tyrrell
was considering the question of obtaining publicity for my
protest. He introduced me to some of his colleagues on the
'Stop the War Committee' and the 'No Conscription Fellowship'. Among them was an intellectual conscientious objector
(lately released after a successful hunger-strike). Also a genial
veteran Socialist (recognizable by his red tie and soft grey hat)
who grasped my hand with rugged good wishes. One and all,
they welcomed me to the Anti-War Movement, but I couldn't
quite believe that I had been assimilated. The reason for this
feeling was their antipathy to everyone in uniform. I was still
wearing mine, and somehow I was unable to dislike being a
Flintshire Fusilier. This little psychological dilemma now seems
almost too delicate to be divulged. In their eyes, I suppose,
there was no credit attached to the fact of having been at the
front; but for me it had been a supremely important experience. I am obliged to admit that if these anti-war enthusiasts
hadn't happened to be likeable I might have secretly despised
them. Any man who had been on active service had an unfair
advantage over those who hadn't. And the man who had really

endured the War at its worst was everlastingly differentiated from everyone except his fellow soldiers.

Tyrrell (a great man and to be thought of as 'in a class by himself') took me up to Hampstead one hot afternoon to interview a member of Parliament who was 'interested in my case'. Walking alongside of the philosopher I felt as if we were a pair of conspirators. His austere scientific intellect was far beyond my reach, but he helped me by his sense of humour, which he had contrived, rather grimly, to retain, in spite of the exasperating spectacle of European civilization trying to commit suicide. The M.P. promised to raise the question of my statement in the House of Commons as soon as I had sent it to the Colonel at Clitherland, so I began to feel that I was getting on grandly. But except for the few occasions when I saw Tyrrell, I was existing in a world of my own (in which I tried to keep my courage up to protest-pitch). From the visible world I sought evidence which could aggravate my quarrel with acquiescent patriotism. Evidences of civilian callousness and complacency were plentiful, for the thriftless licence of war-time behaviour was an unavoidable spectacle, especially in the Savoy Hotel Grill Room which I visited more than once in my anxiety to reassure myself of the existence of bloated profiteers and uniformed jacks in office. Watching the guzzlers in the Savoy (and conveniently overlooking the fact that some of them were officers on leave) I nourished my righteous hatred of them, anathematizing their appetites with the intolerance of youth which made me unable to realize that comfort-loving people are obliged to avoid self-knowledge – especially when there is a war on. But I still believe that in 1917 the idle, empty-headed, and frivolous ingredients of Society were having a tolerably good time, while the officious were being made self-important by nicely graded degrees of uniformed or un-uniformed war-emergency authority. For middle-aged persons who faced the War bleakly, life had become unbearable unless they persuaded themselves that the slaughter was worth while. Tyrrell was comprehensively severe on everyone except inflexible pacifists. He said that the people who tried to resolve the discords of the War into what they called 'a higher harmony' were merely enabling themselves to contemplate the massacre of the young men with an easy conscience. 'By Jingo, I suppose you're right!' I exclaimed, wishing that I were able to express my ideas with such comprehensive clarity.

Supervising a platoon of Cadet Officers at Cambridge would have been a snug alternative to 'general service abroad' (provided that I could have bluffed the cadets into believing that I knew something about soldiering). I was going there to be interviewed by the Colonel and clinch my illusory appointment; but I was only doing this because I considered it needful for what I called 'strengthening my position'. I hadn't looked ahead much, but when I did so it was with an eye to safeguarding myself against 'what people would say'.

When I remarked to Tyrrell that 'people couldn't say I did it so as to avoid going back to France if I had been given a job in England', he pulled me up short.

'What people say doesn't matter. Your own belief in what you are doing is the only thing that counts.' Knowing that he was right, I felt abashed; but I couldn't help regretting that my second decoration had failed to materialize. It did not occur to me that a bar to one's Military Cross was a somewhat inadequate accretion to one's qualifications for affirming that the War was being deliberately prolonged by those who had the power to end it. Except for a bullet-hole in my second best tunic, all that I'd got for my little adventure in April consisted of a gilt-edged card on which the Divisional General had inscribed his congratulations and thanks. This document was locally referred to as 'one of Whincop's Bread Cards', and since it couldn't be sewn on to my tunic I did my best to feel that it was better than nothing.

Anyhow, on a glaring hot morning I started to catch a train to Cambridge. I was intending to stay a night there for it would be nice to have a quiet look round and perhaps go up to Grantchester in a canoe. Admittedly, next month was bound to be ghastly; but it was no good worrying about that. . . . Had I enough money on me? Probably not; so I decided to stop and change a cheque at my bank in Old Broad Street. Changing a cheque was always a comforting performance. 'Queer thing, having private means,' I thought. 'They just hand you out the money as if it was a present from the Bank Manager.' It was funny, too, to think that I was still drawing my Army pay. But it was the wrong moment for such humdrum cogitations, for when my taxi stopped in that narrow thoroughfare, Old Broad Street, the people on the pavement were standing still, staring up at the hot white sky. Loud bangings had begun in the near neighbourhood, and it was obvious that an air-raid was in full swing. This event could not be ignored; but I needed money and wished to catch my train, so I decided to disregard it. The crashings continued, and while I was handing my cheque to the cashier a crowd of women clerks came wildly down a winding stairway with vociferations of not unnatural alarm. Despite this commotion the cashier handed me five one-pound notes with the stoical politeness of a man who had made up his mind to go down with the ship. Probably he felt as I did – more indignant than afraid; there seemed no sense in the idea of being blown to bits in one's own bank. I emerged from the building with an air of soldierly unconcern; my taxi-driver, like the cashier, was commendably calm, although another stupendous crash sounded as though very near Old Broad Street (as indeed it was). 'I suppose we may as well go on to the station,' I remarked, adding, 'it seems a bit steep that one can't even cash a cheque in comfort!' The man grinned and drove on. It was impossible to deny that the War was being brought home to me. At Liverpool Street there had occurred what, under normal conditions, would be described as an appalling catastrophe. Bombs had been dropped on the station and one of them had hit the front carriage of the noon express to Cambridge. Horrified travellers were hurrying away. The hands of the clock indicated 11.50; but railway time had been interrupted; for once in its career, the imperative clock was a passive spectator. While I stood wondering what to do, a luggage trolley was trundled past me; on it lay an elderly man, shabbily dressed, and apparently dead. The sight of blood caused me to feel quite queer. This sort of danger seemed to demand a quality of courage dissimilar to front-line fortitude. In a trench one was acclimatized to the notion of being exterminated and there was a sense of organized retaliation. But here one was helpless; an invisible enemy sent destruction spinning down from a fine weather sky; poor old men bought a railway ticket and were trundled away again dead on a barrow; wounded women lay about in the station groaning. And one's train didn't start. . . . Nobody could say for certain when it *would* start, a phlegmatic porter informed me; so I migrated to St Pancras and made the journey to Cambridge in a train which halted goodnaturedly at every station. Gazing at sleepy green landscapes, I found difficulty in connecting them (by the railway line) with the air-raid which (I was afterwards told) had played hell with Paternoster Avenue. 'It wouldn't be such a bad life', I thought, 'if one were a station-master on a branch line in Bedfordshire.' There was something attractive, too, in the idea of being a commercial traveller, creeping about the country and doing business in drowsy market towns and snug cathedral cities.

If only I could wake up and find myself living among the parsons and squires of Trollope's Barsetshire, jogging easily from Christmas to Christmas, and hunting three days a week with the Duke of Omnium's Hounds. . . .

The elms were so leafy and the lanes invited me to such rural remoteness that every time the train slowed up I longed to get out and start on an indefinite walking tour – away into the delusive Sabbath of summer – away from air-raids and inexorable moral responsibilities and the ever-increasing output of munitions.

But here was Cambridge, looking contented enough in the afternoon sunshine, as though the Long Vacation were on. The colleges appeared to have forgotten their copious contributions to the Roll of Honour. The streets were empty, for the Cadets were out on their afternoon parades – probably learning how to take compass-bearings, or pretending to shoot at an enemy who was supposedly advancing from a wood nine hundred yards away. I knew all about that type of training.

'Half-right; haystack; three fingers left of haystack; copse; nine hundred; AT THE COPSE, ten rounds rapid, FIRE!' There wasn't going to be any musketry-exercise instructing for me, however. I was only 'going through the motions' of applying for a job with the Cadet Battalion. The orderly room was on the ground floor of a college. In happier times it had been a library (the books were still there) and the Colonel had been a History Don with a keen interest in the Territorials. Playing the part of respectful young applicant for instructorship in the Arts of War, I found myself doing it so convincingly that the existence of my 'statement' became, for the moment, an improbability. 'Have you any specialist knowledge?' inquired the Colonel. I told him that I'd been Battalion Intelligence Officer for a time (suppressing the fact that I'd voluntarily relinquished that status after three days of inability to supply the necessary eye-wash reports). 'Ah, that's excellent. We find the majority of men very weak in map-reading,' he replied, adding, 'our main object, of course, is to instill first-rate morale. It isn't always easy to impress on these new army men what we mean by the tradition of the pre-War regimental officer. . . . Well, I'm sure you'll do very good work. You'll be joining us in two or three weeks, I think? Good-bye till then.' He shook my hand rather as if I'd won a History Scholarship, and I walked out of the college feeling that it was a poor sort of joke on him. But my absence as an instructor was all to the good as far as he was concerned, and I was inclined to think that I was better at saying the War ought to stop than at teaching cadets how to carry it on. Sitting in King's Chapel I tried to recover my conviction of the nobility of my enterprise and to believe that the pen which wrote my statement had 'dropped from an angel's wing'. I also reminded myself that Cambridge had dismissed Tyrrell from his lectureship because he disbelieved in the War. 'Intolerant old blighters!' I inwardly exclaimed. 'One can't possibly side with people like that. All they care about is keeping up with the other colleges in the casualty lists.' Thus refortified, I went down to the river and hired a canoe.

4

Back at Butley, I had fully a fortnight in which to take life easily before tackling 'wilful defiance of military authority'. I was, of course, compelled to lead a double life, and the longer it lasted the less I liked it. I am unable to say for certain how far I was successful in making Aunt Evelyn believe that my mind was free from anxiety. But I know that it wasn't easy to sustain the evangelistic individuality which I'd worked myself up to in London. Outwardly those last days of June progressed with nostalgic serenity. I say nostalgic, because in my weaker moods I longed for the peace of mind which could have allowed me to enjoy having tea out in the garden on fine afternoons. But it was no use trying to dope my disquiet with Trollope's novels or any of my favourite books. The purgatory I'd let myself in for always came between me and the pages; there was no escape for me now. Walking restlessly about the garden at night I was oppressed by the midsummer silence and found no comfort in the twinkling lights along the Weald. At one end of the garden three poplars tapered against the stars; they seemed like sentries guarding a prisoner. Across the uncut orchard grass, Aunt Evelyn's white beehives glimmered in the moonlight like bones. The hives were empty, for the bees had been wiped out by the Isle of Wight disease. But it was no good moping about the garden. I ought to be indoors improving my mind, I thought, for I had returned to Butley resolved to read for dear life – circumstances having made it imperative that I should accumulate as much solid information as I could. But sedulous study only served to open up the limitless prairies of my ignorance, and my attention was apt to wander away from what I was reading. If I could have been candid with myself I should have confessed that a fortnight was inadequate for the completion of my education as an intellectual pacifist. Reading the last few numbers of Markington's weekly was all very well as a tonic for disagreeing with organized public opinion, but even if I learnt a whole article off by heart I should only have built a little hut on the edge of the prairie. 'I must have all the arguments at my fingers' ends,' I had thought when I left London. The arguments, perhaps, were epitomized in Tyrrell's volume of lectures ('given to me by the author,' as I had written on the flyleaf). Nevertheless those lectures on political philosophy, though clear and vigorous in style, were too advanced for my elementary requirements. They were, I read on the first page, 'inspired by a view of the springs of action which has been suggested by the War. And all of them are informed by the hope of seeing such political institutions established in Europe as shall make men averse from war – a hope which I firmly believe to be realizable, though not without a great and fundamental reconstruction of economic and social life.' From the first I realized that this was a book whose meanings could only be mastered by dint of copious underlining. *What integrates an individual life is a consistent creative purpose or unconscious direction.* I underlined that, and then looked up 'integrate' in the dictionary. Of course, it meant the opposite to *disintegrate*, which was what the optimists of the press said would soon happen to the Central Powers of Europe. Soon afterwards I came to the conclusion that much time would be saved if I underlined the sentences which *didn't* need underlining. The truth was that there were too many ideas in the book. I was forced to admit that nothing in Tyrrell's lectures could be used for backing up my point of view when I was being interrogated by the Colonel at Clitherland. . . . The thought of Clitherland was unspeakably painful. I had a vague hope that I could get myself arrested without going there. It would be so much easier if I could get my case dealt with by strangers.

Aunt Evelyn did her best to brighten the part of my double life which included her, but at meal times I was often morose and monosyllabic. Humanly speaking, it would have been a relief to confide in her. As a practical proposition, however, it was impossible. I couldn't allow my protest to become a domestic controversy, and it was obviously kinder to keep my aunt in the dark about it until she received the inevitable shock. I remember one particular evening when the suspense was growing acute. At dinner Aunt Evelyn, in her efforts to create cheerful conversation, began by asking me to tell her more about Nutwood Manor. It was, she surmised, a very well-arranged house, and the garden must have been almost perfection. 'Did azaleas grow well there?' Undeterred by my gloomily affirmative answer, she urged me to supply further information about the Asterisks and their friends. She had always heard that old Lord Asterisk was such a fine man, and must have had a most interesting life, although, now she came to think of it, he'd been a bit of a Radical and had supported Gladstone's Home Rule Bill. She then interrupted herself by exclaiming: 'Naughty, naughty, naughty!' But this rebuke was aimed at one of the cats who was sharpening his claws on the leather seat of one of the Chippendale chairs. Having thrown my napkin at the cat, I admitted that Lord Asterisk was a dear old chap, though unlikely to live much longer. Aunt Evelyn expressed concern about his infirmity, supplementing it with her perennial 'Don't eat so fast, dear; you're simply bolting it down. You'll ruin your digestion.' She pressed me to have some more chicken, thereby causing me to refuse, although I should have had some more if she'd kept quiet about it. She now tried the topic of my job at Cambridge. What sort of rooms should I live in? Perhaps I should have rooms in one of the colleges which would be very nice for me – much nicer than those horrid huts at Clitherland. Grumpily I agreed that Cambridge was preferable to Clitherland. A bowl of strawberries, perhaps the best ones we'd had that summer, created a diversion. Aunt Evelyn regretted the unavoidable absence of cream, which enabled me to assure her that some of the blighters I'd seen in London restaurants weren't denying themselves much; and I went off into a diatribe against profiteers and officials who gorged at the Ritz and the Savoy while the poorer classes stood for hours in queues outside food shops. Much relieved at being able to agree with me about something, Aunt Evelyn almost overdid her indignant ejaculations, adding that it was a positive scandal – the disgracefully immoral way most of the young women were behaving while doing war-work. This animation subsided when we got up from the table. In the drawing-room she lit the fire 'as the night felt a bit chilly and a fire would make the room more cheerful'. Probably she was hoping to spend a cosy evening with me; but I made a bad beginning, for the lid fell off the coffee-pot and cracked one of the little blue and yellow cups, and when Aunt Evelyn suggested that we might play one of our old games of cribbage or halma, I said I didn't feel like that sort of thing. Somehow I couldn't get myself to behave affectionately toward her, and she had irritated me by making uncomplimentary remarks about Markington's paper, a copy of which was lying on the table. (She said it was written by people who were mad with their own self-importance and she couldn't understand how I could read such a paper.) Picking it up I went grumpily upstairs and spent the next ten minutes trying to teach Popsy the parrot how to say 'Stop the War'. But he only put his head down to be scratched, and afterwards obliged me with his well-known rendering of Aunt Evelyn calling the cats. On her way up to bed she came in (with a glass of milk) and told me that she was sure I wasn't feeling well. Wouldn't it be a good thing if I were to go to the seaside for a few days' golf? But this suggestion only provided me with further evidence that it was no earthly use expecting her to share my views about the War. Games of golf indeed! I glowered at the glass of milk and had half a mind to throw it out of the window. Afterwards I decided that I might as well drink it, and did so.

Late on a sultry afternoon, when returning from a mutinous-minded walk, I stopped to sit in Butley Churchyard. From Butley Hill one looks across a narrow winding valley, and that afternoon the woods and orchards suddenly made me feel almost as fond of them as I'd been when I was in France. While I was resting on a flat-topped old tombstone I recovered something approximate to peace of mind. Gazing at my immediate surroundings, I felt that 'joining the great majority' was a homely – almost a comforting – idea. Here death differed from extinction in modern warfare. I ascertained from the nearest headstone that *Thomas Welfare, of this Parish, had died on October 20th, 1843, aged 72.* 'Respected by all who knew him.' Also Sarah, wife of the above. 'Not changed but *glorified.*' Such facts were resignedly acceptable. They were in harmony with the simple annals of this quiet corner of Kent. One could speculate serenely upon the homespun mortality of such worthies, whose lives had 'taken place' with the orderly and inevitable progression of a Sunday service. They made the past seem pleasantly prosy in contrast with the monstrous emergencies of to-day. And Butley Church, with its big-buttressed square tower, was protectively permanent. One could visualize it there for the last 599 years, measuring out the unambitious local chronology with its bells, while English history unrolled itself along the horizon with coronations and rebellions and stubbornly disputed charters and covenants. Beyond all that, the 'foreign parts' of the world widened incredibly toward regions reported by travellers' tales. And so outward to the windy universe of astronomers and theologians. Looking up at the battlemented tower, I improvised a clear picture of some morning – was it in the seventeenth century? Men in steeple-crowned hats were surveying a rudimentary-looking landscape with anxious faces, for trouble was afoot and there was talk of the King's enemies. But the insurgence always passed by. It had never been more than a rumour for Butley, whether it was Richard of Gloucester or Charles the First who happened to be losing his kingdom. It was difficult to imagine that Butley had contributed many soldiers for the Civil Wars, or even for Marlborough and Wellington, or that the village carpenter of those days had lost both his sons in Flanders. Between the church door and the lych gate the plump yews were catching the rays of evening. Along that path the coffined generations had paced with sober church-going faces. There they had stood in circumspect groups to exchange local gossip and discuss the uncertainly reported events of the outside world. They were a long way off now, I thought – their names undecipherable on tilted headstones or humbly oblivioned beneath green mounds. For the few who could afford a permanent memorial, their remoteness from posterity became less as the names became more legible, until one arrived at those who had watched the old timbered inn by the churchyard being burnt to the ground – was it forty years ago? I remembered Captain Huxtable telling me that the catastrophe was supposed to have been started by the flaring up of a pot of glue which a journeyman joiner had left on a fire while he went to the tap-room for a mug of beer. The burning of the old Bull Inn had been quite a big event for the neighbourhood; but it wouldn't be thought much of in these days; and my mind reverted to the demolished churches along the Western Front, and the sunlit inferno of the first day of the Somme Battle. There wouldn't be much Gray's Elegy atmosphere if Butley were in the Fourth Army area!

Gazing across at the old rifle butts – now a grassy indentation on the hillside half a mile away – I remembered the volunteers whose torchlight march-past had made such a glowing impression on my nursery-window mind, in the good old days before the Boer War. Twenty years ago there had been an almost national significance in the fact of a few Butley men doing target practice on summer evenings.

Meanwhile my meditations had dispelled my heavy-heartedness, and as I went home I recovered something of the exultation I'd felt when first forming my resolution. I knew that no right-minded Butley man could take it upon himself to affirm that a European war was being needlessly prolonged by those who had the power to end it. They would tap their foreheads and sympathetically assume that I'd seen more of the fighting than was good for me. But I felt the desire to suffer, and once again I had a glimpse of something beyond and above my present troubles – as though I could, by cutting myself off from my previous existence, gain some new spiritual freedom and live as I had never lived before.

'They can all go to blazes,' I thought, as I went home by the field path. 'I know I'm right and I'm going to do it,' was the rhythm of my mental monologue. If all that senseless slaughter had got to go on, it shouldn't be through any fault of mine. 'It won't be any fault of mine,' I muttered.

A shaggy farm horse was sitting in the corner of a field with his front legs tucked under him; munching placidly, he watched me climb the stile into the old green lane with its high thorn hedges.

5

Sunshade in one hand and prayer-book in the other, Aunt Evelyn was just starting for morning service at Butley. 'I really must ask Captain Huxtable to tea before you go away. He looked a little hurt when he inquired after you last Sunday,' she remarked. So it was settled that she would ask him to tea when they came out of church. 'I really can't think why you haven't been over to see him,' she added, dropping her gloves and then deciding not to wear them after all, for the weather was hot and since she had given up the pony cart she always walked to church. She put up her pink sunshade and I walked with her to the front gate. The two cats accompanied us, and were even willing to follow her up the road, though they'd been warned over and over again that the road was dangerous. Aunt Evelyn was still inclined to regard all motorists as reckless and obnoxious intruders. The roads were barely safe for human beings, let alone cats, she exclaimed as she hurried away. The church bells could already be heard across the fields, and very peaceful they sounded.

July was now a week old. I had overstayed my leave several days and was waiting until I heard from the Depot. My mental condition was a mixture of procrastination and suspense, but the suspense was beginning to get the upper hand of the procrastination, since it was just possible that the Adjutant at Clitherland was assuming that I'd gone straight to Cambridge.

Next morning the conundrum was solved by a telegram, *Report how situated.* There was nothing for it but to obey the terse instructions, so I composed a letter (brief, courteous, and regretful) to the Colonel, enclosing a typewritten copy of my statement, apologizing for the trouble I was causing him, and promising to return as soon as I heard from him. I also sent a copy to Dottrell, with a letter in which I hoped that my action would not be entirely disapproved of by the First Battalion. Who else was there, I wondered, feeling rather rattled and confused. There was Durley, of course, and Cromlech also – fancy my forgetting him! I could rely on Durley to be sensible and sympathetic; and David was in a convalescent hospital in the Isle of Wight, so there was no likelihood of his exerting himself with efforts to dissuade me. I didn't want anyone to begin interfering on my behalf. At least I hoped that I didn't; though there were weak moments later on when I wished they would. I read my statement through once more (though I could have recited it only too easily) in a desperate effort to calculate its effect on the Colonel. '*I am making this statement as an act of wilful defiance of military authority, because I believe that the War is being deliberately prolonged by those who have the power to end it. I am a soldier, convinced that I am acting on behalf of soldiers. I believe that this War, upon which I entered as a war of defence and liberation, has now become a war of aggression and conquest. I believe that the purposes for which I and my fellow soldiers entered upon this War should have been so clearly stated as to have made it impossible to change them, and that, had this been done, the objects which actuated us would now be attainable by negotiation. I have seen and endured the sufferings of the troops, and I can no longer be a party to prolong these sufferings for ends which I believe to be evil and unjust. I am not protesting against the conduct of the War, but against the political errors and insincerities for which the fighting men are being sacrificed. On behalf of those who are suffering now I make this protest against the deception which is being practised on them; also I believe that I may help to destroy the callous complacency with which the majority of those at home regard the continuance of agonies which they do not share, and which they have not sufficient imagination to realize.*' It certainly sounds a bit pompous, I thought, and God only knows what the Colonel will think of it.

Thus ended a most miserable morning's work. After lunch I walked down the hill to the pillar-box and posted my letters with a feeling of stupefied finality. I then realized that I had a headache and Captain Huxtable was coming to tea. Lying on my bed with the window curtains drawn, I compared the prospect of being in a prison cell with the prosy serenity of this buzzing summer afternoon. I could hear the cooing of the

white pigeons and the soft clatter of their wings as they fluttered down to the little bird-bath on the lawn. My sense of the
life-learned house and garden enveloped me as though all the
summers I had ever known were returning in a single thought.
I had felt the same a year ago, but going back to the War next
day hadn't been as bad as this.

Theoretically, to-day's tea-party would have made excellent
material for a domestic day-dream when I was at the front. I
was safely wounded after doing well enough to be congratulated by Captain Huxtable. The fact that the fighting men
were still being sacrificed needn't affect the contentment of the
tea-party. But everything was blighted by those letters which
were reposing in the local pillar-box, and it was with some difficulty that I pulled myself together when I heard a vigorous
ring of the front-door bell, followed by the firm tread of the
Captain on the polished wood floor of the drawing-room, and
the volubility of Aunt Evelyn's conversational opening alter-
nating with the crisp and cheery baritone of her visitor. Captain Huxtable was an essentially cheerful character ('waggish'
was Aunt Evelyn's favourite word for him) and that afternoon
he was in his most jovial mood. He greeted me with a reference to Mahomet and the Mountain, though I felt more like a
funeral than a mountain, and the little man himself looked by
no means like Mahomet, for he was wearing brown corduroy
breeches and a white linen jacket, and his face was red and
jolly after the exertion of bicycling. His subsequent conversation was, for me, strongly flavoured with unconscious irony.
Ever since I had joined the Flintshire Fusiliers our meetings
always set his mind alight with memories of his 'old corps', as
he called it; I made him, he said, feel half his age. Naturally, he
was enthusiastic about anything connected with the fine record
of the Flintshires in this particular war, and when Aunt Evelyn
said, 'Do show Captain Huxtable the card you got from your
General,' he screwed his monocle into his eye and inspected
the gilt-edged trophy with intense and deliberate satisfaction. I
asked him to keep it as a souvenir of his having got me into the
Regiment – (bitterly aware that I should soon be getting myself
out of it pretty effectively!). After saying that I couldn't have

given him anything which he'd value more highly, he suggested that I might do worse than adopt the Army as a permanent career (forgetting that I was nearly ten years too old for such an idea to be feasible). But no doubt I was glad to be going to the Depot for a few days, so as to have a good crack with some of my old comrades, and when I got to Cambridge I must make myself known to a promising young chap (a grandson of his cousin, Archdeacon Crocket) who was training with the Cadet Battalion. After a digression around this year's fruit crop, conversation turned to the Archbishop of Canterbury's message to the nation about Air Raid Reprisals. In Captain Huxtable's opinion the Church couldn't be too militant, and Aunt Evelyn thoroughly agreed with him. With forced facetiousness I described my own air-raid experience. 'The cashier in the bank was as cool as a cucumber,' I remarked. There were cucumber sandwiches on the table, but the implications of the word 'cashier' were stronger, since for me it was part of the price of martyrdom, while for the Captain it epitomized an outer darkness of dishonour. But the word went past him, innocent of its military meaning, and he referred to the increasing severity of the German air-raids as 'all that one can expect from that gang of ruffians.' But there it was, and we'd got to go through with it; nothing could be worse than a patched-up peace; and Aunt Evelyn 'could see no sign of a change of heart in the German nation'.

The Captain was delighted to see in to-day's *Times* that another of those cranky pacifist meetings had been broken up by some Colonial troops; and he added that he'd like to have the job of dealing with a 'Stop the War' meeting in Butley. To him a conscientious objector was the antithesis of an officer and a gentleman, and no other point of view would have been possible for him. The Army was the framework of his family tradition; his maternal grandfather had been a Scotch baronet with a distinguished military career in India – a fact which was piously embodied in the Memorial Tablet to his mother in Butley Church. As for his father – 'old Captain Huxtable' – (whom I could hazily remember, white-whiskered and formidable) he had been a regular roaring martinet of the gouty old school of retired officers, and his irascibilities were still legendary in our neighbourhood. He used to knock his coachman's hat off and stamp on it. 'The young Captain,' as he was called in former days, had profited by these paroxysms, and where the parent would have bellowed 'God damn and blast it all' at his bailiff, the son permitted himself nothing more sulphurous than 'con-found', and would have thought twice before telling even the most red-hot Socialist to go to the devil.

Walking round the garden after tea – Aunt Evelyn drawing his attention to her delphiniums and he waggishly affirming their inferiority to his own – I wondered whether I had exaggerated the 'callous complacency' of those at home. What could elderly people do except try and make the best of their inability to sit in a trench and be bombarded? How could they be blamed for refusing to recognize any ignoble elements in the War except those which they attributed to our enemies?

Aunt Evelyn's delphinium spires were blue against the distant blue of the Weald and the shadows of the Irish yews were lengthening across the lawn. . . . Out in France the convoys of wounded and gassed were being carried into the Field Hospitals, and up in the Line the slaughter went on because no one knew how to stop it. 'Men are beginning to ask for what they are fighting,' Dottrell had written in his last letter. Could I be blamed for being one of those at home who were also asking that question? Must the War go on in order that colonels might become brigadiers and brigadiers get Divisions, while contractors and manufacturers enriched themselves, and people in high places ate and drank well and bandied official information and organized entertainments for the wounded? Some such questions I may have asked myself, but I was unable to include Captain Huxtable and Aunt Evelyn in the indictment.

6

I had to wait until Thursday before a second Clitherland telegram put me out of my misery. Delivered early in the afternoon and containing only two words, *Report immediately*, it was obviously a telegram which did not need to be read twice. But the new variety of suspense which it created was an improvement on what I'd been enduring, because I could end it for certain by reporting at Clitherland within twenty-four hours. All considerations connected with my protest were now knocked on the head. It no longer mattered whether I was right or whether I was wrong, whether my action was public-spirited or whether it was preposterous. My mind was insensible to everything but the abhorrent fact that I was in for an appalling show, with zero hour fixed for to-morrow when I arrived at the Depot.

In the meantime I must pack my bag and catch the five-something train to town. Automatically I began to pack in my usual vacillating but orderly manner; then I remembered that it would make no difference if I forgot all the things I needed most. By this time to-morrow I shall be under arrest, I thought, gloomily rejecting my automatic pistol, water bottle, and whistle, and rummaging in a drawer for some khaki socks and handkerchiefs. A glimpse of my rather distracted-looking face in the glass warned me that I must pull myself together by to-morrow. I must walk into the Orderly Room neat and self-possessed and normal. Anyhow the parlourmaid had given my tunic buttons and belt a good rub up, and now Aunt Evelyn was rapping on the door to say that tea was ready and the taxi would be here in half an hour. She took my abrupt departure quite as a matter of course, but it was only at the last moment that she remembered to give me the bundle of white pigeons' feathers which she had collected from the lawn, knowing how I always liked some for pipe-cleaners. She also reminded me that I was forgetting to take my golf clubs; but I shouldn't get any time for golf, I said, plumping myself into the taxi, for there wasn't too much time to catch the train.

The five-something train from Baldock Wood was a slow affair; one had to change at Dumbridge and wait forty minutes. I remember this because I have seldom felt more dejected than I did when I walked out of Dumbridge Station and looked over the fence of the County Cricket Ground. The afternoon

was desolately fine and the ground, with its pavilion and enclo-
sures, looked blighted and forsaken. Here, in pre-eminently
happier times, I had played in many a club match and had
attentively watched the varying fortunes of the Kent Eleven;
but now no one had even troubled to wind up the pavilion
clock.

Back in the station I searched the bookstall for something to
distract my thoughts. The result was a small red volume which
is still in my possession. It is called *The Morals of Rousseau*,
and contains, naturally enough, extracts from that celebrated
author. Rousseau was new to me and I cannot claim that his
morals were any help to me on that particular journey or during the ensuing days when I carried him about in my pocket.
But while pacing the station platform I remembered a certain
couplet, and I mention this couplet because, for the next ten
days or so, I couldn't get it out of my head. There was no
apparent relevancy in the quotation (which I afterwards found
to be from Cowper). It merely persisted in saying:

> *I shall not ask Jean Jacques Rousseau*
> *If birds confabulate or no.*

London enveloped my loneliness. I spent what was presumably my last night of liberty in the bustling dreariness of one of
those huge hotels where no one ever seems to be staying more
than a single night. I had hoped for a talk with Tyrrell, but he
was out of town. My situation was, I felt, far too serious for
theatre going – in fact I regarded myself as already more or
less under arrest; I was going to Clitherland under my own
escort, so to speak. So it may be assumed that I spent that evening alone with J. J. Rousseau.

Next morning – but it will suffice if I say that next morning
(although papers announced *Great Russian Success in Gali-
cia*) I had no reason to feel any happier than I had done the
night before. I am beginning to feel that a man can write too
much about his own feelings, even when 'what he felt like' is
the nucleus of his narrative. Nevertheless I cannot avoid a

short summary of my sensations while on the way to Liverpool. I began by shutting my eyes and refusing to think at all;
but this effort didn't last long. I tried looking out of the window; but the sunlit fields only made me long to be a munching
cow. I remembered my first journey to Clitherland in May
1915. I had been nervous then – diffident about my ability to
learn how to be an officer. Getting out to the Front had been
an ambition rather than an obligation, and I had aimed at
nothing more than to become a passably efficient second-
lieutenant. Pleasantly conscious of my new uniform and anxious to do it credit, I had felt (as most of us did in those days)
as if I were beginning a fresh and untarnished existence. Probably I had travelled by this very train. My instant mental tran-
sition from that moment to this (all intervening experience
excluded) caused me a sort of vertigo. Alone in that first-class
compartment, I shut my eyes and asked myself out loud what
this thing was which I was doing; and my mutinous act suddenly seemed outrageous and incredible. For a few minutes I
completely lost my nerve. But the express train was carrying
me along; I couldn't stop it, any more than I could cancel my
statement. And when the train pulled up at Liverpool I was
merely a harassed automaton whose movements were being
manipulated by a type-written manifesto. To put it plainly, I
felt 'like nothing on earth' while I was being bumped and
jolted out to the Camp in a ramshackle taxi.

It was about three o'clock when the taxi passed the gates of
Brotherhood's Explosive Works and drew up outside the officers' quarters at Clitherland. The sky was cloudless and the
lines of huts had an air of ominous inactivity. Nobody seemed
to be about, for at that hour the troops were out on the training
field. A bored sentry was the only witness of my arrival, and for
him there was nothing remarkable in a second-lieutenant telling a taxi-man to dump his luggage down outside the officers'
mess. For me, however, there now seemed something almost
surreptitious about my return. It was as though I'd come skulk-
ing back to see how much damage had been caused by that
egregious projectile, my protest. But the camp was exactly as it
would have been if I'd returned as a dutiful young officer. It

was I who was desolate and distracted; and it would have been
no consolation to me if I could have realized that, in my mind,
the familiar scene was having a momentary and ghastly existence which would never be repeated.

For a few moments I stared wildly at the huts, conscious
(though my brain was blank) that there was some sort of climax in my stupefied recognition of reality. One final wrench,
and all my obedient associations with Clitherland would be
shattered.

It is probable that I put my tie straight and adjusted my belt-
buckle to its central position between the tunic buttons. There
was only one thing to be done after that. I walked into the
Orderly Room, halted in front of a table, and saluted dizzily.

After the glaring sunlight, the room seemed almost dark.
When I raised my eyes it was not the Colonel who was sitting at
the table, but Major Macartney. At another table, ostensibly
busy with Army forms and papers, was the Deputy-Assistant-
Adjutant (a good friend of mine who had lost a leg in Gallipoli). I stood there, incapable of expectation. Then, to my
astonishment, the Major rose, leant across the table, and shook
hands with me.

'How are you, Sherston? I'm glad to see you back again.' His
deep voice had its usual kindly tone, but his manner betrayed
acute embarrassment. No one could have been less glad to see
me back again than he was. But he at once picked up his cap
and asked me to come with him to his room, which was only a
few steps away. Silently we entered the hut, our feet clumping
along the boards of the passage. Speechless and respectful, I
accepted the chair which he offered me. There we were, in the
comfortless little room which had been his local habitation for
the past twenty-seven months. There we were; and the unfortunate Major hadn't a ghost of an idea what to say.

He was a man of great delicacy of feeling. I have seldom
known as fine a gentleman. For him the interview must have
been as agonizing as it was for me. I wanted to make things
easier for him; but what could I say? And what could he do for
me, except, perhaps, offer me a cigar? He did so. I can honestly
say that I have never refused a cigar with anything like so much

regret. To have accepted it would have been a sign of surrender. It would have meant that the Major and myself could have puffed our cigars and debated – with all requisite seriousness, of course – the best way of extricating me from my dilemma. How blissful that would have been! For my indiscretion might positively have been 'laughed off' (as a temporary aberration brought on, perhaps, by an overdose of solitude after coming out of hospital). No such agreeable solution being possible, the Major began by explaining that the Colonel was away on leave. 'He is deeply concerned about you, and fully prepared to overlook the' – here he hesitated – 'the paper which you sent him. He has asked me to urge you most earnestly to – er – dismiss the whole matter from your mind.' Nothing could have been more earnest than the way he looked at me when he stopped speaking. I replied that I was deeply grateful but I couldn't change my mind. In the ensuing silence I felt that I was committing a breach, not so much of discipline as of decorum.

The disappointed Major made a renewed effort. 'But, Sherston, isn't it *possible* for you to reconsider your – er – ultimatum?' This was the first time I'd heard it called an ultimatum, and the locution epitomized the Major's inability to find words to fit the situation. I embarked on a floundering explanation of my mental attitude with regard to the War; but I couldn't make it sound convincing, and at the back of my mind was a misgiving that I must seem to him rather crazy. To be telling the acting-Colonel of my regimental Training Depot that I had come to the conclusion that England ought to make peace with Germany – was this altogether in focus with right-mindedness? No; it was useless to expect him to take me seriously as an ultimatumist. So I gazed fixedly at the floor and said, 'Hadn't you better have me put under arrest at once?' – thereby causing poor Major Macartney additional discomfort. My remark recoiled on me, almost as if I'd uttered something unmentionable. 'I'd rather die than do such a thing!' he exclaimed. He was a reticent man, and that was his way of expressing his feeling about those whom he had watched, month after month, going out to the trenches, as he would have gone himself had he been a younger man.

At this point it was obviously his duty to remonstrate with me severely and to assert his authority. But what fulminations could be effective against one whose only object was to be put under arrest? . . . 'As long as he doesn't really think I'm dotty!' I thought. But he showed no symptom of that, as far as I was aware; and he was a man who made one feel that he trusted one's integrity, however much he might disagree with one's opinions.

No solution having been arrived at for the present, he now suggested – in confidential tones which somehow implied sympathetic understanding of my predicament – that I should go to the Exchange Hotel in Liverpool and there await further instructions. I gladly acquiesced, and we emerged from the hut a little less funereally than we had entered it. My taxi-man was still waiting, for in my bewilderment I had forgotten to pay him. Once more the Major grasped my hand, and if I did not thank him for his kindness it was because my gratitude was too great. So I trundled unexpectedly back to Liverpool; and although, in all likelihood, my troubles were only just starting, an immense load had been lifted from my mind. At the Exchange Hotel (which was quiet and rarely frequented by the Clitherland officers) I thoroughly enjoyed my tea, for I'd eaten nothing since breakfast. After that I lit my pipe and thought how nice it was not to be under arrest. I had got over the worst part of the show, and now there was nothing to be done except stick to my statement and wait for the M.P. to read it out in the House of Commons.

7

For the next three days I hung about the Exchange Hotel in a state of mind which need not be described. I saw no one I knew except a couple of Clitherland subalterns who happened to be dining in the Hotel. They cheerily enquired when I was coming out to the Camp. Evidently they were inquisitive about me, without suspecting anything extraordinary, so I inferred that Orderly Room had been keeping my strange behaviour secret. On Tuesday my one-legged friend, the Deputy-Assistant-Adjutant, came to see me. We managed to avoid mentioning everything connected with my 'present situation', and he regaled me with the gossip of the Camp as though nothing were wrong. But when he was departing he handed me an official document which instructed me to proceed to Crewe next day for a Special Medical Board. A railway warrant was enclosed with it.

Here was a chance of turning aside from the road to court-martialdom, and it would be inaccurate were I to say that I never gave the question two thoughts. Roughly speaking, two thoughts were exactly what I did give to it. One thought urged that I might just as well chuck the whole business and admit that my gesture had been futile. The other one reminded me that this was an inevitable conjuncture in my progress, and that such temptations must be resisted inflexibly. Not that I ever admitted the possibility of my accepting the invitation to Crewe; but I did become conscious that acceptance would be much pleasanter than refusal. Submission being impossible, I called in pride and obstinacy to aid me, throttled my warm feelings toward my well-wishers at Clitherland Camp and burnt my boats by tearing up both railway warrant and Medical Board instructions.

On Wednesday I tried to feel glad that I was cutting the Medical Board, and applied my mind to Palgrave's *Golden Treasury of Songs and Lyrics*. I was learning by heart as many poems as possible, my idea being that they would be a help to me in prison, where, I imagined, no books would be allowed. I suppose I ought to try and get used to giving up tobacco, I thought, but I went on smoking just the same (the alternative being to smoke as many pipes as I could while I'd got the chance).

On Thursday morning I received an encouraging letter from the M.P. who urged me to keep my spirits up and was hoping to raise the question of my statement in the House next week. Early in the afternoon the Colonel called to see me. He found me learning Keats's *Ode to a Nightingale*. 'I cannot see what

flowers are at my feet, Nor what soft. . . . ' What soft was it, I
wondered, re-opening the book. But here was the Colonel,
apparently unincensed, shaking my hand, and sitting down
opposite me, though already looking fussed and perplexed. He
wasn't a lively-minded man at the best of times, and he didn't
pretend to understand the motives which had actuated me. But
with patient common-sense arguments, he did his best to persuade me to stop wanting to stop the War. Fortified by the
M.P.'s letter in my pocket, I managed to remain respectfully
obdurate, while expressing my real regret for the trouble I was
causing him. What appeared to worry him most was the fact
that I'd cut the Medical Board. 'Do you realize, Sherston, that
it had been specially arranged for you and that an R.A.M.C.
Colonel came all the way from London for it?' he ejaculated
ruefully, wiping the perspiration from his forehead. The poor
man – whose existence was dominated by documentary
instructions from 'higher quarters' – had probably been
blamed for my non-appearance; and to disregard such an
order was, to one with his habit of mind, like a reversal of the
order of nature. As the interview dragged itself along, I began
to feel quite optimistic about the progress I was making. The
Colonel's stuttering arguments in support of 'crushing Prussian militarism' were those of a middle-aged civilian; and as
the overworked superintendent of a reinforcement manufac-
tory, he had never had time to ask himself why North Welshmen were being shipped across to France to be gassed,
machine-gunned, and high explosived by Germans. It was
absolutely impossible, he asserted, for the War to end until it
ended – well, until it ended as it ought to end. Did I think it
right that so many men should have been sacrificed for no purpose? 'And surely it stands to reason, Sherston, that you must
be wrong when you set your own opinion against the practically unanimous feeling of the whole British Empire.' There
was no answer I could make to that, so I remained silent, and
waited for the British Empire idea to blow over. In conclusion
he said, 'Well, I've done all I can for you. I told Mersey
Defences that you missed your Board through a misunderstanding of the instructions, but I'm afraid the affair will soon

go beyond my control. I beg you to try and reconsider your refusal by to-morrow, and to let us know at once if you do.'

He looked at me almost irately, and departed without another word. When his bulky figure had vanished I felt that my isolation was perceptibly increasing. All I needed to do was to wait until the affair had got beyond his control. I wished I could have a talk with Tyrrell. But even he wasn't infallible, for in all our discussions about my plan of campaign he had never foreseen that my senior officers would treat me with this kindly tolerance which was so difficult to endure.

During the next two days my mind groped and worried around the same purgatorial limbo so incessantly that the whole business began to seem unreal and distorted. Sometimes the wording of my thoughts became incoherent and even nonsensical. At other times I saw everything with the haggard clarity of insomnia.

So on Saturday afternoon I decided that I really must go and get some fresh air, and I took the electric train to Formby. How much longer would this ghastly show go on, I wondered, as the train pulled up at Clitherland Station. All I wanted now was that the thing should be taken out of my own control, as well as the Colonel's. I didn't care how they treated me as long as I wasn't forced to argue about it any more. At Formby I avoided the Golf Course (remembering, with a gleam of woeful humour, how Aunt Evelyn had urged me to bring my 'golf sticks', as she called them). Wandering along the sand dunes I felt outlawed, bitter, and baited. I wanted something to smash and trample on, and in a paroxysm of exasperation I performed the time-honoured gesture of shaking my clenched fists at the sky. Feeling no better for that, I ripped the M.C. ribbon off my tunic and threw it into the mouth of the Mersey. Weighted with significance though this action was, it would have felt more conclusive had the ribbon been heavier. As it was, the poor little thing fell weakly on to the water and floated away as though aware of its own futility. One of my point-to-point cups would have served my purpose more satisfyingly, and they'd meant much the same to me as my Military Cross.

Watching a big boat which was steaming along the horizon, I realized that protesting against the prolongation of the War was about as much use as shouting at the people on board that ship.

Next morning I was sitting in the hotel smoking-room in a state of stubborn apathy. I had got just about to the end of my tether. Since it was Sunday and my eighth day in Liverpool I might have chosen this moment for reviewing the past week, though I had nothing to congratulate myself on except the fact that I'd survived seven days without hauling down my flag. It is possible that I meditated some desperate counter-attack which might compel the authorities to treat me harshly, but I had no idea how to do it. 'Damn it all, I've half a mind to go to church,' I thought, although as far as I could see there was more real religion to be found in the *Golden Treasury* than in a church which only approved of military-aged men when they were in khaki. Sitting in a sacred edifice wouldn't help me, I decided. And then I was taken completely by surprise; for there was David Cromlech, knobby-faced and gawky as ever, advancing across the room. His arrival brought instantaneous relief, which I expressed by exclaiming: 'Thank God you've come!'

He sat down without saying anything. He, too, was pleased to see me, but retained that air of anxious concern with which his eyes had first encountered mine. As usual he looked as if he'd slept in his uniform. Something had snapped inside me and I felt rather silly and hysterical. 'David, you've got an enormous black smudge on your forehead,' I remarked. Obediently he moistened his handkerchief with his tongue and proceeded to rub the smudge off, tentatively following my instructions as to its whereabouts. During this operation his face was vacant and childish, suggesting an earlier time when his nurse had performed a similar service for him. 'How on earth did you manage to roll up from the Isle of Wight like this?' I inquired. He smiled in a knowing way. Already he was beginning to look less as though he were visiting an invalid; but I'd been so much locked up with my own thoughts lately that for the next few minutes I talked nineteen to the dozen, telling him what a hellish time I'd had, how terribly kind the depot officers had been to me, and so on. 'When I started this anti-war stunt I never dreamt it would be such a long job, getting myself run in for a court martial,' I concluded, laughing with somewhat hollow gaiety.

In the meantime David sat moody and silent, his face twitching nervously and his fingers twiddling one of his tunic buttons. 'Look here, George,' he said, abruptly, scrutinizing the button as though he'd never seen such a thing before, 'I've come to tell you that you've got to drop this anti-war business.' This was a new idea, for I wasn't yet beyond my sense of relief at seeing him. 'But I can't drop it,' I exclaimed. 'Don't you realize that I'm a man with a message? I thought you'd come to see me through the court martial as "prisoner's friend".' We then settled down to an earnest discussion about the 'political errors and insincerities for which the fighting men were being sacrificed'. He did most of the talking, while I disagreed defensively. But even if our conversation could be reported in full, I am afraid that the verdict of posterity would be against us. We agreed that the world had gone mad; but neither of us could see beyond his own experience, and we weren't life-learned enough to share the patient selfless stoicism through which men of maturer age were acquiring anonymous glory. Neither of us had the haziest idea of what the politicians were really up to (though it is possible that the politicians were only feeling their way and trusting in providence and the output of munitions to solve their problems). Nevertheless we argued as though the secret confabulations of Cabinet Ministers in various countries were as clear as daylight to us, and our assumption was that they were all wrong, while we, who had been in the trenches, were far-seeing and infallible. But when I said that the War ought to be stopped and it was my duty to do my little bit to stop it, David replied that the War was bound to go on till one side or the other collapsed, and the Pacifists were only meddling with what they didn't understand. 'At any rate Thornton Tyrrell's a jolly fine man and knows a bloody sight more about everything than you do,' I exclaimed. 'Tyrrell's only a doctrinaire,' replied David, 'though I grant you he's a courageous one.' Before I had time to ask what the hell he knew about doctrinaires, he continued, 'No one except people who've been in the real fighting have any right to interfere about the War; and even they can't get anything done about it. All they can do is to remain loyal to one another. And you know perfectly well that most of the conscientious objectors are nothing but skrimshankers.' I retorted that I knew nothing of the sort, and mentioned a young doctor who'd played Rugby Football for Scotland and was now in prison although he could have been doing hospital work if he'd wanted to. David then announced that he'd been doing a bit of wire-pulling on my behalf and that I should soon find that my Pacifist M.P. wouldn't do me as much good as I expected. This put my back up. David had no right to come butting in about my private affairs. 'If you've really been trying to persuade the authorities not to do anything nasty to me,' I remarked, 'that's about the hopefullest thing I've heard. Go on doing it and exercise your usual tact, and you'll get me two years' hard labour for certain, and with any luck they'll decide to shoot me as a sort of deserter.' He looked so aggrieved at this that I relented and suggested that we'd better have some lunch. But David was always an absent-minded eater, and on this occasion he prodded disapprovingly at his food and then bolted it down as if it were medicine.

A couple of hours later we were wandering aimlessly along the shore at Formby, and still jabbering for all we were worth. I refused to accept his well-meaning assertion that no one at the Front would understand my point of view and that they would only say that I'd got cold feet. 'And even if they do say that,' I argued, 'the main point is that by backing out of my statement I shall be betraying my real convictions and the people who are supporting me. Isn't that worse cowardice than being thought cold-footed by officers who refuse to think about anything except the gentlemanly traditions of the Regiment? I'm not doing it for fun, am I? Can't you understand that this is the most difficult thing I've ever done in my life? I'm not going to be talked out of it just when I'm forcing them to make a martyr of me.' 'They won't make a martyr of you,' he replied. 'How do you know that?' I asked. He said that the Colonel at Clitherland had told him to tell me that if I continued to refuse to be 'medically-boarded' they would shut me up in a lunatic asylum for the rest of the War. Nothing would induce them to court martial me. It had all been arranged with some big bug at the War Office in the last day or two. 'Why didn't you tell me before?' I asked. 'I kept it as a last resort because I was afraid it might upset you,' he replied, tracing a pattern on the sand with his stick. 'I wouldn't believe this from anyone but you. Will you swear on the Bible that you're telling the truth?' He swore on an imaginary Bible that nothing would induce them to court martial me and that I should be treated as insane. 'All right, then, I'll give way.' As soon as the words were out of my mouth I sat down on an old wooden breakwater.

So that was the end of my grand gesture. I ought to have known that the blighters would do me down somehow, I thought, scowling heavily at the sea. It was appropriate that I should behave in a glumly dignified manner, but already I was aware that an enormous load had been lifted from my mind. In the train David was discreetly silent. He got out at Clitherland. 'Then I'll tell Orderly Room they can fix up a Board for you to-morrow,' he remarked, unable to conceal his elation. 'You can tell them anything you bloody well please!' I answered ungratefully. But as soon as I was alone I sat back and closed my eyes with a sense of exquisite relief. I was unaware that David had, probably, saved me from being sent to prison by telling me a very successful lie. No doubt I should have done the same for him if our positions had been reversed.

It was obvious that the less I said to the Medical Board the better. All the necessary explanations of my mental condition were contributed by David, who had been detailed to give evidence on my behalf. He had a long interview with the doctors while I waited in an ante-room. Listening to their muffled mumblings, I felt several years younger than I'd done two days before. I was now an irresponsible person again, absolved from any obligation to intervene in world affairs. In fact the present performance seemed rather ludicrous, and when David emerged, solemn and concerned, to usher me in, I entered the 'Bird Room' assuring myself that I should not ask Jean Jacques Rousseau if birds confabulated or no. The Medical Board consisted of a Colonel, a Major, and a Captain. The Captain was a civilian in uniform, and a professional neurologist. The others were elderly Regular Army doctors, and I am inclined to think that their acquaintance with Army Forms exceeded their knowledge of neurology.

While David fidgeted about the ante-room I was replying respectfully to the stereotyped questions of the Colonel, who seemed slightly suspicious and much mystified by my attitude to the War. Was it on religious grounds that I objected to fighting, he inquired. 'No, sir; not particularly,' I replied. 'Fighting on religious grounds' sounded like some sort of a joke about the Crusades. 'Do you consider yourself qualified to decide when the War should stop?' was his next question. Realizing that he was only trying to make me talk rubbish, I evaded him by admitting that I hadn't thought about my qualifications, which wasn't true. 'But your friend tells us that you were very good at bombing. Don't you still dislike the Germans?' I have forgotten how I answered that conundrum. It didn't matter what I said to him, as long as I behaved politely. While the interrogations continued, I felt that sooner or later I simply must repeat that couplet out loud – 'if birds confabulate or no'. Probably it would be the best thing I could do, for it would prove conclusively and comfortably that I was a harmless lunatic. Once I caught the neurologist's eye, which signalled sympathetic understanding, I thought. Anyhow, the Colonel (having demonstrated his senior rank by asking me an adequate number of questions) willingly allowed the Captain to suggest that they couldn't do better than send me to Slateford Hospital. So it was decided that I was suffering from shell-shock. The Colonel then remarked to the Major that he supposed there was nothing more to be done now. I repeated the couplet under my breath. 'Did you say anything?' asked the

Colonel, frowning slightly. I disclaimed having said anything and was permitted to rejoin David.

When we were walking back to my hotel I overheard myself whistling cheerfully, and commented on the fact. 'Honestly, David, I don't believe I've whistled for about six weeks!' I gazed up at the blue sky, grateful because, at that moment, it seemed as though I had finished with the War.

Next morning I went to Edinburgh. David, who had been detailed to act as my escort, missed the train and arrived at Slateford War Hospital several hours later than I did. And with my arrival at Slateford War Hospital this volume can conveniently be concluded.

AVAILABLE FROM PENGUIN CLASSICS IN THE GEORGE SHERSTON TRILOGY

Introduction by Paul Fussell

Memoirs of a Fox-Hunting Man	*Memoirs of an Infantry Officer*	*Sherston's Progress*
ISBN 978-0-14-310715-6	ISBN 978-0-14-310716-3	ISBN 978-0-14-310717-0

Acclaimed poet, novelist, and highly decorated World War I soldier Siegfried Sassoon captures the brutal realities of war in this trilogy of fictionalized autobiographies. In *Memoirs of a Fox-Hunting Man*, Sassoon recounts his pastoral childhood and his enlistment in the British army through the character of George Sherston. *Memoirs of an Infantry Officer* and *Sherston's Progress* follow Sherston into the trenches, his hospitalization after being wounded, and his ultimate dedication to the antiwar cause.

PENGUIN CLASSICS